BLACK MARKET

HIDE AND SEEK

BY JAMES PATTERSON

JAMES PATTERSON

BLACK MARKET

HIDE AND SEEK

HarperCollins*Publishers*

For Janie, who is Nora.
For Mary Katherine, who is a saint.

*For anyone who's ever dreamed about some small and delicious revenge
against the moneychangers on Wall Street and around the world.*

The characters and events in this book are fictitious.
Any similarity to real persons, living or dead,
is coincidental and not intended by the author.

This omnibus edition published in 1998 by HarperCollins*Publishers*

HarperCollins*Publishers*
77–85 Fulham Palace Road,
Hammersmith, London W6 8JB

A catalogue record for this book
is available from the British Library

ISBN 0 261 67156 1

Printed and bound in Great Britain by
Creative Print and Design (Wales), Ebbw Vale

Acknowledgments

Although *Black Market* is written as fiction, all of what follows could happen, especially the Wall Street financial parts. I would like to thank the people who helped me so much in making the background information interesting and authentic.

Sidney Rutberg – financial editor, Fairchild Publications
James Dowd – Wall Street attorney, formerly of the U.S. Army
Stephen Bowen – former captain, U.S. Marines
Katherine McMahon – New York and Paris backgrounds
Joan Ennis – Irish Tourist Board
Thomas Altman – Sedona, Arizona
Barbara Maddalena – New York, Wall Street area
Mindy Zepp – New York
M. Blackstone – Soho

BROADWAY

25	Broadway	Chase Manhattan Bank
26	Broadway	Aeicor, Inc.
26	Broadway	Fuji Industrial Corp.
61	Broadway	Chemical Fund, Inc.
61	Broadway	Latin Advisors Corp.
65	Broadway	American Bureau of Shipping
65	Broadway	Bank America Securities Service
100	Broadway	Bank of Tokyo
120	Broadway	French American Bank
120	Broadway	Southern Peru Copper
140	Broadway	Paine Webber, Inc.

BROAD STREET

25	Broad St.	American Securities Co.
25	Broad St.	Metals Quality Co.
30	Broad St.	Renault Capital Development Corp.
41	Broad St.	Bank of America International
50	Broad St.	National Aviation Tec
55	Broad St.	Goldman Sachs & Co.
60	Broad St.	Gatz-Oswego Corp.
60	Broad St.	RCA Global Communications
67	Broad St.	All American Cable
67	Broad St.	ITT World Communications

WALL STREET

1	Wall St.	Industrial Bank of Japan
1	Wall St.	Irving Bank Corp.
1	Wall St.	Irving Trust Co.
1	Wall St.	Nation-Wide Securities
16	Wall St.	Bankers Trust Co.
23	Wall St.	Morgan Guaranty
30	Wall St.	Seamans Bank for Savings
40	Wall St.	Atlantic Capital
40	Wall St.	Manufacturers Hanover Trust
44	Wall St.	National Bank of N.A.
45	Wall St.	U.S. Trust Corp.

48	Wall St.	Bank of N.Y.
63	Wall St.	Affiliated Fund
80	Wall St.	Empire Steel Trade

MISC

7	Hanover Square	E.F Hutton
1	Liberty Plaza	Merrill Lynch, Pierce, Fenner & Smith, Inc.

PART ONE

Green Band

The pure products of America go crazy.
— William Carlos Williams

December 4; Early Morning; Vets Cabs and Messengers

1

David Hudson; Wall Street; 0500 Hours

Colonel David Hudson leaned his tall, classically athletic body against the squat, battered trunk of one of New York's Checker-style taxis. At five in the morning, the tawdry yellow cab was double-parked at the base of Wall Street, where it intersects with Water Street and the East River.

Raising one hand to his eye, Hudson loosely curled his fingers to fashion a makeshift telescope. He began to watch morning's earliest light fall on the Wall Street scene.

He carefully studied 40 Wall Street where Manufacturers Hanover Trust had offices. Then, No. 23 Wall, which housed executive suites for Morgan Guaranty. The New York Stock Exchange Building. Trinity Church. Chase Manhattan Plaza. The towering buildings were as impressive and striking as monuments; the feeling of history and stability was a little overwhelming.

Once he had it all vividly in sight, Colonel Hudson squeezed his fingers tightly together. *"Boom,"* he whispered quietly.

The financial capital of the world completely disappeared behind his clenched right fist.

Vets 24; Harry Stemkowsky; Brooklyn; 0530

Seconds before 5:30 on that same morning, Sergeant Harry Stemkowsky, the man designated as Vets 24, sped

11

down the steep, icicle-slick Metropolitan Avenue Hill in the Greenpoint section of Brooklyn. He was riding in a nine-year-old Everest and Jennings wheelchair, from the Queens VA. Right now, he was pretending the chair was a Datsun 280-Z, silver metallic, with a shining T-roof.

"Aahh-eee-ahh!" He let out a banshee screech that pierced the deserted, solemnly quiet morning streets.

His long thin face was buried in the oily collar of a khaki Army fatigue parka replete with peeling sergeant's stripes, and his frizzy blond ponytail blew behind him like ribboning bike streamers. Periodically, he closed his eyes which were tearing badly in the burning cold wind. His tightly pinched face was getting as red as the gleaming Berry Street stoplight he was racing through with absolute abandon.

His forehead was burning, but he *loved* the sensation of unexpected freedom.

He thought he could actually feel streams of blood surge through both his wasted legs again.

Harry Stemkowsky's rattling wheelchair finally came to a halt in front of the all-night Walgreen's Drugs. Under the fatigue jacket and the two bulky sweaters he wore, his heart was hammering wildly. He was so goddamn excited – his whole life was beginning all over again.

Today, Harry Stemkowsky felt he could do just about *anything*.

The drugstore's glass door, which he nudged open, was covered with a montage of cigarette posters. Almost immediately, he was blessed with a draught of welcoming warm air, filled with the smells of greasy bacon and fresh-perked coffee. He smiled and rubbed his hands together in a gesture that was almost gleeful. For the first time in years he was no longer a cripple.

And for the first time in more than a dozen hard years Harry Stemkowsky had a purpose.

He *had* to smile. When he wrapped his mind around the whole deal, the full, unbelievable implications of Green Band, *he just had to smile*.

Right at this moment, Sergeant Harry Stemkowsky,

12

the official messenger for Green Band, was safely at his firebase inside New York City. Now everything could begin.

Inside the fortress that was New York FBI headquarters in Federal Plaza, a tall, silver-haired man, Walter Trentkamp, repeatedly tapped the eraser of his pencil against a faded desk blotter.

Scrawled on the soiled blotter was a single phone number *202-456-1414*. It was a private number for the White House, a direct line to the President of the United States.

Trentkamp's telephone rang at 6:00 exactly.

"All right everybody, please start up audio surveillance now." It was early in the morning, and his voice was harsh. "I'll hold them as long as I possibly can. Is audio surveillance ready? Well, let's go then."

The legendary FBI Eastern Bureau Chief cleared his throat self-consciously. Then he picked up the signaling telephone. The words *Green Band* echoed perilously inside his brain. He'd never known anything like this in his Bureau experience, which was long and varied and not without bizarre encounters.

Gathered in a grim, tight circle around the FBI head were some of the more powerfully connected men and women in New York. Not a person in the group had ever experienced anything like this emergency situation either.

In silence, they listened to Trentkamp answer the expected phone call. "This is the Federal Bureau. . . . Hello?"

There was no answer over the outside line. The tension inside the room was as sharp as the cutting edge of a surgical blade. Even Trentkamp, whose calm in critical police situations was well known, appeared nervous and uncertain.

"I said hello. Is anyone there on the line? *Is anyone out there? . . .* Who is on this line?"

Vets 24; Brooklyn; 0602

Walter Trentkamp's tentative, frustrated voice was being electronically monitored in a battered mahogany phone booth at the rear of the Walgreen's Drugstore in Greenpoint, Brooklyn.

Inside the booth, Sergeant Harry Stemkowsky finger-combed his long unkempt hair as he listened. His heart had gone beyond mere pounding; now it was threatening to detonate inside his chest. There were new and unusual pulses beating all through his body, opening and closing with the sharpness of mechanical claws.

This was the long overdue time of truth. *There would be no more war game rehearsals for the twenty-eight members of Green Band.*

"Hello? This is Trentkamp. New York FBI." The plain black phone receiver cradled between Stemkowsky's shoulder and his jaw seemed to tremble and vibrate on each phrase.

After another interminable minute, Harry Stemkowsky firmly depressed the play button on a Sony 114 portable recorder. He then carefully held the pocket recorder flush against the pay phone's receiver.

Stemkowsky had cued the recorder to the first word of the message – "Good." The "good" stretched to "goood" as the recorder hitched once, then rolled forward with a soft whir.

"Good morning. This is Green Band speaking. Today is December fourth. A Friday. A history-making Friday, we believe."

Over a squawk box the eerie, high-pitched voice brought the unprecedented message the men and women sequestered inside the Manhattan FBI office had been waiting for.

Green Band was beginning.

14

Ryan Klauk from FBI Surveillance made a quick judgment that the prerecorded track had been purposely speeded-up and echoed, to sound even more eerie than the circumstance made it; to be virtually unrecognizable, probably untraceable.

"As we promised, there are vitally important reasons for our past phone calls this week, for all the elaborate preparations we've made, and had you make to date . . .

"Is everyone listening? I can only assume you have company, Mr. Trentkamp. No one in corporate America seems to make a decision alone these days. . . . Listen closely then. Everybody please listen . . .

"The Wall Street financial district, from the East River to Broadway, is scheduled to be firebombed today. A large number of randomly selected targets will be completely destroyed late this afternoon.

"I will repeat. Selected targets in the Wall Street financial district will be destroyed today. Our decision is irrevocable. Our decision is nonnegotiable.

"The firebombing of Wall Street will take place at five minutes past five tonight. It might be an attack by air; it might be a ground attack. Whichever – it will occur at five minutes past five precisely."

"Wait a minute. You can't – " Walter Trentkamp vehemently began to object, then he stopped just as suddenly. He remembered he was attempting to talk back to a recorded message.

"All of Manhattan, everything below Fourteenth Street, must be evacuated," the voice track continued methodically.

"The Target Area Nuclear Survival Plan for New York should be activated right now. Are you listening Mayor Ostrow? Susan Hamilton from the Office of Civil Preparedness?

"The Nuclear Target Plan can save thousands of lives. Please employ it now . . .

"In case any of you require further concrete convincing, this will be provided as well. Such requests have been anticipated.

15

"Our seriousness, our utter commitment to this mission, must not be underestimated. Not at any time during this or any future talk we might decide to have.

"Begin the evacuation of the Wall Street financial district now. Green Band cannot possibly be stopped or deterred. Nothing I've said is negotiable. Our decision is irrevocable."

Harry Stemkowsky abruptly pushed down the stop button. He quickly replaced the telephone receiver. He then rewound the Sony recorder, and stuffed it in the drooping pocket of his Army fatigue jacket.

Done.

He took a deep breath that seemed to grab into the very pit of his stomach. He shivered uncontrollably. Christ, he'd done it. He'd actually goddamn done it!

He'd delivered Green Band's message and he felt terrific. He wanted to scream out inside the drugstore. More than that, he wished he could leap two feet in the air and punch the sky.

No formal demands had been made.

Not a single clue had been offered as to why Green Band was happening.

Harry Stemkowsky's heart was still beating loudly as he numbly maneuvered his wheelchair along an aisle lined with colorful deodorants and toiletries, up toward the gleaming soda fountain counter.

The short order cook, Wally Lipsky, a cheerfully mountainous three-hundred-and-ten-pound man, turned from scraping the grill as Stemkowsky and his wheelchair approached. Lipsky's pink-cheeked face immediately brightened. The semblance of a third and fourth chin appeared out of rolling mounds of neck fat.

"Well, look what Sylvester the Cat musta dragged in offa the street! It's my man Pennsylvania. Whereyabeen keepin' yourself, champ? Long time no see."

Harry Stemkowsky had to smile at the irresistible fat cook, who had a well-deserved reputation as the Greenpoint neighborhood clown. Hell, he was in the mood to smile at almost anything this morning.

16

"Oh he-he-here and there, Wally." Harry Stemkowsky burst into a nervous stutter. "Muh-Manhattan the mo-most part. I been wuh-working up in Manhattan a lot these days."

Stemkowsky tapped his index finger against the tattered cloth tag sewn into the shoulder of his jacket. The patch said VETS CABS AND MESSENGERS. Harry Stemkowsky was one of seven licensed wheelchair cabbies in New York; three of them worked for Vets in Manhattan.

"Gah-gotta good job. *Real* job now, Wah-Wally. . . . Why don't you make us some breakfast?"

"You got it, Pennsylvania. Cabdriver special comin' up. You got it my man, anything you want."

2

Wall Street; New York City; 0630

As early as six-fifteen that morning, an endless stream of sullen-looking men and women carrying bulging, black briefcases had begun to rise out of the steam-blooming subway station at Broadway and Wall Street.

These were the appointed drones of New York's financial district; the straight salary employees who understood abstract accounting principles and fine legal points, but perceived little else about the Street and its black magic. These unfortunates couldn't make the intuitive leap to the larger truth, that on Wall Street millions were made not by accepting a fixed salary, but by taking a ten, or twenty, or fifty percent *vig* on *somebody else's* thousands; on somebody else's hundreds of millions.

By seven-thirty, gum-popping secretaries were slouching off the Red and Tan line buses arriving from Staten Island and Brooklyn. Aside from their habitual gum-chewing, several of the secretaries looked impressively chic, almost elegant that Friday morning.

As the ornate, golden arms on the Trinity Church clock solemnly reached for eight o'clock, every main and side street of the financial district was choked with thick, hypertense pedestrian traffic as well as with buses and honking cabs.

Over nine hundred and fifty thousand people were being melted into less than half a square mile of outrageously expensive real estate; seven solid stone blocks where *billions* were bought and sold every workday: *still the unsurpassed financial capital of the world.*

18

The New York police hadn't known whether or not to try and stop the morning's regular migration. Then it was simply too late – the slim possibility had disintegrated in a frantic series of telephone calls between the Commissioner's office and various powerful precinct chiefs. It had petered out into a nightmare of impossible logistics and mounting panic.

At that moment, a wraithlike black man, Abdul Calvin Mohammud, was very calmly entering the bobbing parade of heads and winter hats on Broad Street, just south of Wall.

As he walked within the spirited crowd, Calvin Mohammud found himself noticing corporate flags waving colorfully from the massive stone buildings. The flags signaled BBH and Company, the National Bank of North America, Manufacturers Hanover, the Seaman's Bank. The flags were like crisp sails driven by strong East River winds.

Calvin Mohammud continued up the steep hill toward Wall Street. He was hardly noticed. But then the messenger caste usually wasn't. They were invisible men, props only.

Today, like every other workday, Calvin Mohammud wore a thigh-length, pale gray clerk's tunic with a frayed arm band that said VETS MESSENGERS. On either side of the capitalized words were fierce Eighty-second Airborne fighting eagles.

But none of that was noticed either.

Calvin Mohammud didn't look like it now, but in Vietnam and Cambodia, he'd been a first-rate, Kit Carson Army scout. He'd won a Distinguished Service Cross, then the Medal of Honor for conspicuous gallantry at the risk of his life. After returning to the U.S. in 1971, Mohammud had been further rewarded by a grateful society with jobs as a porter at Penn Station, a delivery boy for Chick-Teri, a baggage carrier at LaGuardia Airport.

Calvin Mohammud, Vets 11, unslung his heavy messenger's shoulder bag as he reached the graffiti-covered news kiosk at the corner of Broadway and Wall. He tapped out a Kool and lit up behind a plume of yellow flame.

Slouched in a nearby doorway, Vets 11 then casually reached into his shoulder bag and slid out a standard U.S. Army field telephone. Still concealed in the deep cloth bag was a sixteen-inch machine gun pistol, along with half a dozen 40-millimeter antipersonnel grenades.

"Contact." He moved back into the cold building shadows, then whispered into the field telephone. "This is Vets Eleven at the Stock Exchange. I'm at the northeast entrance, off Wall. . . . Everything's very nice and peaceful at position three. . . . No police in sight. No armed resistance anywhere. Almost looks too easy. Over."

Vets 11 took another short drag on his dwindling cigarette. He calmly peered around at the noisy hustle and bustle that was so characteristic of Wall Street on a weekday.

Broad daylight. What an amazing, completely unbelievable scene, just to imagine the apocalyptic firefight that would be coming down here at five o'clock. He finally began to smile, exposing crooked yellow teeth. This was going to be so sweet, so satisfying and right.

At 0830, Calvin Mohammud carefully wound a tattered strip of cloth around a polished brass door handle at the back entrance of the all-powerful New York Stock Exchange – *a proud, beautiful green band.*

Pier 33–34; 0920

Green Band started savagely and suddenly, as if meteors had hurtled themselves with malevolent intensity against New York City. It blew out two-storey-tall windows, and shattered asphalt roofs, and shook whole streets in the vicinity of Pier 33–34 on Twelfth Avenue between 12th and 15th streets. It all came in an enormous white flash of painful blinding light.

At approximately 9:20 that morning, Pier 33–34 – which

20

had once hosted such regal ships as the *Queen Elizabeth* and the *QE II* – was a sudden fiery cauldron, a crucible of flame that raked the air and spread with such rapid intensity that even the Hudson River seemed to be spurting colossal columns of flames, some at least four hundred feet high.

Dense hydrocarbon clouds of smoke bloomed over Twelfth Avenue like huge black umbrellas being thrown open. Six-foot-long shards of glass, unguided missiles of molten steel, were flying upward, launching themselves in eerie, tumbling slow motion. And as the river winds suddenly shifted there were otherworldly glimpses of the glowing, red-hot metal skeleton that was the pier itself.

The blistering fireball had erupted and spread in less than sixty seconds' time.

It was precisely as the Green Band warning had said it would be: an unspeakable sound and light show, a ghostly demonstration of promised horrors and terrors to come . . .

The dock for the *Mauretania*, for the *Aquitania*, the *Ile de France*, had been effectively vaporized by the powerful explosions, by the sudden, graphic flash fires.

Inside a police surveillance helicopter quivering and bumping on serrated upcurrents of hot smoke, New York Mayor Arnold Ostrow and Police Commissioner Michael Kane were shocked beyond words. They both understood that one of New York's worst, recurring nightmares was finally coming true.

This time, one of the thousands of routinely horrifying threats to New York was absolutely real. Radio listeners and TV viewers all over New York would soon hear the unprecedented message:

"This is *not a test* of the Emergency Broadcast System."

The New York Stock Exchange; 1035

At 10:35 on the morning of December 4, more than seven thousand dedicated capitalists – DOT system clerks, youthful pages with their jaunty epaulets and floppy Connecticut Yankee haircuts, grimly determined stock-brokers, bond analysts, bright-green-jacketed supervisors – were busily, if somewhat nonchalantly, promenading through the three jam-packed main rooms of the New York Stock Exchange.

The twelve elevated ticker-tape TV monitors in the busy room were spewing stock symbols and trades comprehensible only to the trained eyes of Exchange professionals. The day's volume, if it was only an average Friday, would easily exceed a hundred fifty million shares.

No doubt the original forebears, the first Bears and Bulls, had been ferocious negotiators and boardroom masters. Their descendants, however, their mostly thin-blooded *heirs*, were not particularly adroit at money-changing.

The heirs were a strikingly homogenous group; for the most part smug and vainglorious bean-counters; they all *looked* blood-related.

The heirs tended toward either red-faced babyfat, or an almost tubercular gauntness.

The heirs' pale blue eyes were forever distant, looking like splintered marbles glued together again.

Moreover, *the heirs* were helplessly standing by while American business was losing "World War III," as the most recent fight over the world's economy had sometimes been called. They were quietly, though quite rapidly, surrendering world economic leadership to the Japanese, the Germans, and the Arab World.

At 10:57 on Friday morning, "the Bell" – which had once actually been a brass fire bell struck by a rubber mallet, and which still signaled the official beginning of trading at 10:00 sharp, the end of trading at 4:00 – went off inside the New York Stock Exchange. "The Bell" sounded with all the shock value of a firework popping in a cathedral.

Absolute silence followed. *Shocked* silence.

Then came uncontrollable buzzing; frantic rumor-trading. Almost three minutes of unprecedented confusion and chaos on the Stock Exchange floor.

Finally, there was the deep and resonant voice of the Stock Exchange Manager blaring over the antiquated p.a. system.

"Gentlemen . . . ladies . . . the New York Stock Exchange is officially closed. . . . *Please leave the Stock Exchange floor. Please leave the trading floor immediately.* This is not a bomb scare. This is an actual emergency! This is a serious police emergency!"

The Pinnacle Club; Manhattan; 1600

Outside the heavy stone and steel entranceway to the Mobil Building on East 42nd Street, a series of personal stretch limousines – Mercedes, Lincolns, Rolls-Royces – were arriving and departing with dramatic haste.

Important-looking men, and a few women, most of them in dark overcoats, hurriedly disembarked from the limousines and entered the building's familiar Deco lobby. Upstairs on the forty-second floor, other CEOs and presidents of the major Wall Street banks and brokerage houses were already gathered inside the exclusive Pinnacle Club.

The emergency meeting had commandeered the luxurious main dining room of the private club, which was glowing with crisp white linen, shining silver and crystal set up and never used for lunch.

Several of the dark-suited executives stood dazed and disoriented before floor-to-ceiling nonglare windows, which faced downtown. None of them had ever experienced anything remotely like this, nor had they ever expected to.

The view was a spectacular, if chilling one, down uneven canyons to lower Manhattan, all the way to the pencil pocket of skyscrapers which was the financial center itself. About halfway, at 14th Street, there were massive police barricades. Police department buses, EMS ambulances, and a parade-like crowd could be seen waiting, watching Wall Street as if they were studying some puzzling work of art in a Midtown museum.

None of this was possible; it was sheer madness. Every rational mind in the executive dining room had already reached this conclusion privately.

"They haven't even bothered to reestablish contact with us. Not since six this morning," said the Secretary of the Treasury, Walter O'Brien. "What the hell are they up to?"

Standing stiffly among four or five prominent Wall Street executives, George Firth, the Attorney General of the United States, was quietly relighting his pipe. He appeared surprisingly casual and controlled, except that he'd given up smoking more than three years before.

"They certainly were *damned* clear when it came to stating their deadline. Five minutes past five. Five minutes past or *what?* What do the bastards want from us?" The Attorney General's pipe went out in his hand and he relit it with a look of exasperation. The closest observers noticed tiny nervous tremors running the length of his fingers.

Madness.

What they'd experienced for a decade in terrorist-plagued Europe. But never before in the United States.

A somber businessman named Jerrold Gottlieb from Lehman Brothers held up his wristwatch. "Well, gentlemen, it's one minute past five . . ." He looked as if he were about to add something, but whatever it was, he left it unsaid.

But that was the unlikely place they had all entered now. An unfamiliar territory where things couldn't be properly articulated: the uncharted territory of the unspeakable.

"They've been extremely punctual up to now. Almost obsessive about getting details and schedules perfect. They'll call. I wouldn't worry, they'll call."

The speaker was the Vice-president of the United

States, who'd been rushed from the U.N. to the nearby Mobil Building. Thomas More Elliot was a stern man with the look of an Ivy League scholar. He was a Brahmin who was out of touch with the complexities of contemporary America, his harshest critics carped. He'd spent the better part of his public career inside the State Department – traveling extensively in Europe during the turbulent sixties, then in South America through the seventies. And now this.

For the next hundred and eighty seconds, there was almost uninterrupted silence in the Pinnacle Club dining room.

This tingling silence was all the more frightening because there were so may highly articulate men crowded into the room – the senior American business executives, used to having their own way, used to being listened to, and obeyed, almost without question. Now their voices were stilled, virtually powerless. They weren't used to the frustration and tension that this terrifying mystery had thrust into their lives. And their power, normally awesome, had distilled itself into a sequence of small, distinct, noises:

The scratchy rasp of a throat being cleared.

Ice cracking in a glass with an almost glacial effect.

The tapping of fingers on the bowl of a dead pipe.

Madness. The thought seemed to echo in the room.

The most fearsome urban terrorism had finally struck deep inside the United States, stabbing right to the heart of America's economic power.

There were anxious, repeated glances at the glinting faces of Rolex, Cartier, and Piaget wristwatches.

What did Green Band want?

Where were the final demands? What was the no-doubt outragious ransom for Wall Street to be?

Edward Palin, the seventy-seven-year-old Chief Executive of one of the largest investment firms, had to slowly back away from the darkly reflective picture windows. A few of the others embarrassedly watched as he sat down in a Harvard chair pulled up beside one of the dining

25

tables and, in a gesture that was almost poignant, put his head between his gray pinstriped knees. He felt faint; it was too much to watch. *Were they about to lose everything now?*

There were less than twenty seconds left to the expiration of the Green Band deadline.

"Please call. Call, you bastards," the Vice-president muttered.

What seemed like thousands of emergency sirens were screaming, a peculiar high-low wail, all over New York. It was the first time the emergency warning system had been seriously in use since 1963 and the nuclear war scares.

Finally, it was five minutes past five.

The sudden, terrifying realization struck every person in the Pinnacle Club's dining room – they weren't going to call again!

They weren't going to negotiate at all.

Without any further warning, Green Band was going to strike.

President Justin Kearney; Washington, D.C.; 1705

"A fast recap for you," said Lisa Pelham, who was the President's Chief of Staff, an efficient, well-organized woman who'd been trained at Harvard and spoke in the clipped manner of one whose mind was used to making succinct outlines from mountains of information.

"By 12:00 noon, all trading had been halted on the New York and all regional exchanges in the U.S. There is no trading in London, Paris, Geneva, Bonn. The key New York business people are meeting right now at the Pinnacle Club inside the Mobil Building.

"All the important securities and commodities exchanges have ceased trading around the world. The unanswered question is the same everywhere. What's the nature of the demands we are *secretly negotiating?"*

26

Lisa Pelham paused and stroked a strand of hair away from her oval face. "Everyone believes we're negotiating with somebody, sir."

"And we are definitely not?" President Justin Kearney's expression was one of extreme doubt and suspicion. He had discovered the awkward fact during his term of office that one branch of government all too frequently didn't know what another was doing.

"Which we are not, Mr. President. Both the CIA and FBI have assured us of that. Sir, Green Band has still made *no* demands."

President Justin Kearney had been rushed, under intensified Secret Service guard, to a windowless, lead-shielded room buried deep inside the White House. There, in the White House Communications Center, several of the most important political leaders in the United States were standing around the President in a manner that suggested they intended to protect him from whatever forces were presently at work inside the country.

From the White House Communications Center, the President had been put into audio and visual contact with the Pinnacle Club in New York City.

The FBI Chief, Walter Trentkamp, stepped forward to appear on the monitor screen from New York. Trentkamp had short, silver-gray hair; time and his job had also added a tough, weathered policeman's look and a harassed attitude to match.

"There's been no further contact from Green Band, other than the firebombing of Pier 33–34, which is the demonstration they promised us, Mr. President. It's the kind of guerrilla warfare we've seen in Belfast, Beirut, Tel Aviv. *Never* before in the United States . . .

"We're all waiting, Mr. President," Trentkamp went on. "It's five zero six and about forty seconds. We're clearly *past* their stated deadline."

"Have any of the terrorist groups come forward and claimed responsibility?"

"They have. We're checking into them. So far none has

27

shown any knowledge of the content of the warning phone call this morning."

5:06 became 5:07. The time was leaden.

5:07 became 5:08. A minute had never seemed so long. It was 5:09 . . . 5:10 and slowly, slowly counting.

The Director of the CIA moved before the lights and cameras in the White House emergency room. Philip Berger was a small, irascible man, highly unpopular in Washington, chiefly skilled at keeping the major American intelligence agencies competitive among themselves. "Is there *any* activity you can make out on Wall Street? Any people down there? Any moving vehicles? Small plane activity?"

"Nothing, Phil. Apart from the police, the fire department vehicles on the periphery of the area, it could be a peaceful Sunday morning."

"They're goddamn bluffing," someone said in Washington.

"Or," President Kearney said, "they're playing an enormous game of fucking nerves."

No one agreed, or disagreed, with the President.

No one said anything now.

Speech had been replaced by the terrifying anxiety and uncertainty of waiting.

Just waiting.

5:15 . . .

5:18 . . .

5:20 . . .

5:24 . . .

5:30 . . .

Waiting for what, though?

Vets 1, Colonel David Hudson; 1820

At 6:20 P.M., Colonel David Hudson was doing the single thing that still mattered – *that mattered more than anything else in his life.*

David Hudson was on patrol. He was back in major

28

combat; he was leading a quality-at-every-position platoon into the field again – only the field was now an American city.

Hudson was one of those men who looked vaguely familiar to people, only they couldn't say precisely why. His wheat-blond hair was cut in a short crew, which was suddenly back in vogue again. He was handsome; his looks were very American. He had the kind of strong, almost noble face that photographs extremely well, and a seemingly unconscious air of self-confidence, a consistently reassuring look that emphatically said, *"Yes, I can do that – whatever it is."*

There was only one thing wrong, which a lot of people didn't notice right away – David Hudson had lost his left arm in the Viet Nam War.

His Checker cab marked VETS CABS AND MESSENGERS rolled cautiously forward, reconnoitering past the bright green pumps at the Hess gas station on Eleventh Avenue and 45th Street. This was one of those times when David Hudson could see himself, as if in an eerie dream, when he could objectively watch himself from somewhere outside the scene. He knew this uncomfortable, distorted feeling extremely well from combat duty.

He'd felt it like a second skin since he'd stepped off a crowded USMC transport, and watched himself encounter the ' one-hundred-seven-degree heat, the gagging, decaying, sweet-shit smell of the cities of Southeast Asia. He'd known this awful sensation of detachment, of distance from himself, ever since he'd come to the realization that he could actually die at any given beat of his heart . . .

Now he felt it again, this time in the sharp wintry wind blowing through the snowy gray streets of New York City.

Colonel David Hudson was purposely allowing the Green Band mission to wind out just a little longer; one highly important notch tighter. It was all moving according to the elaborate final plan.

Every second had been rigidly accounted for. More

than anything else, David Hudson's mind appreciated the subtleties of precision; Hudson appreciated detail and the fine-tuning involved in getting everything absolutely right.

He was back in full combat again.

This strange, strange passion was alive again inside David Hudson.

He finally released the hand microphone from the PRC transmitter built into the Vets cab's dash.

"Contact. Come in Vets Five." Colonel David Hudson spoke in the firm, charismatic tones which had characterized his commands through the latter war years in Southeast Asia. It was a voice that had always elicited loyalty and obedience in the men whose lives he controlled.

"This is Vets One. . . . Come in Vets Five. Over."

A reply immediately crackled back through heavy static over the PRC transmitter-receiver. "Hello, sir. How are you, sir? This is Vets Five. Over."

"Vets Five. Green Band is now affirmative. I will repeat – Green Band is now affirmative. . . . *Blow it all up.* . . . And God help us all."

December 4; the Evening; Archer Carroll

3

Crusader Rabbit

"Yougotaquarter, sir? Please! It's real cold out here, sir. You got two bits? . . . Awhh, thank you. Thanks a lot, sir. You just saved my life."

Around 7:30 that evening, on Brooklyn's Atlantic Avenue, a familiar bag man called Crusader Rabbit was expertly soliciting loose change and cigarettes. The bag man begged while he sat huddled like trash against the crumbling red brick facade of the Atlantic House Yemen and Middle East Restaurant. The money came to him as if he were a magnet made of soiled rags.

After a successful hit, forty-eight cents from a trendy-looking Brooklyn Heights teacher-type and his date, the street bum allowed himself a short pull on a dwindling half pint of Four Roses.

Drinking while begging change was counterproductive, he knew, but sometimes necessary against the raw cold wintertime. Besides, it was his image . . .

The deep, slack cough that followed the sip of whiskey sounded convincingly tubercular. The bag man's lips were bloated and pale. They were corpse white and cracked, and they looked as if they'd bled recently.

For this year's winter wardrobe, he'd carefully selected a sleeveless navy parka over several layers of assorted, colored lumberman's shirts. He'd picked out open-toed high top black sneakers, basketball player snow bird socks, and painter's pants that were now thickly caked with mud, vomit and spit.

The tourists, at least, seemed to love him. Sometimes, they snapped his picture to bring home as an example of New York City's famed squalor and heartlessness. He enjoyed posing: asking them for a buck or whatever the traffic would bear. He'd hold his two puffy shopping bags, and smile extra pathetically for the camera. *Pay the cashier, sport.*

Now, through gummy, half-closed eyes, Crusader Rabbit stealthily watched the usual early evening promenade along Atlantic Avenue's Middle Eastern restaurant row.

It was a constant, day-in day-out noisy bazaar here: transplanted ragheaded Arabs, college assholes, Brooklyn professionals who came to eat ethnic. In the distance, there was always the *clickety-clack* of the El.

A troupe of McDonalds counter kids was passing by Crusader Rabbit, walking home from work. Two chunky black girls; a skinny mulatto boy around eighteen, nineteen.

"Hey, McDonalds. Whopper beat the Big Mac. Real tough break. Gotta quarter? Something for some Mccoffee?" Crusader coughed and wheezed at the passing trio of teens.

The McDonalds kids looked offended; then they all laughed together in a high-pitched chorus. "Who asked you, Aqualung? You old geek sheet-head. Kick your ass."

The kids continued merrily on. Rude little bastards when Ronald McDonald wasn't watching over their act.

If any of the various passersby had looked closer, they might have noticed certain visual inconsistencies about the bag man called Crusader Rabbit. For one thing, he had impressive muscle tone for a sedentary street bum. His shoulders were unusually broad, his legs and arms were as thick as tree limbs.

Even more unusual were his eyes, which were almost always intently focused. They scanned the teeming avenue over and over again, relentlessly watching all the street action, everything that happened.

There was also the small matter of the quality of the dirt and dust thickly caked on his ankles, on his exposed toes. It was all a little too perfect. It was almost as if it might actually be black Kiwi shoe polish -- *shoe polish carefully applied to look like dirt.*

The conclusion was obvious after a careful and close look at the street bum. Crusader Rabbit was some kind of undercover New York cop. He had to be some kind of cop on a stakeout . . .

Which Crusader Rabbit truly was.

His real name was Arch Carroll and he was presently the chief terrorist deterrent inside the United States. He *was* on a stakeout, a five-week one, with no end anywhere in sight.

Meanwhile, across the busy Brooklyn street, inside the Sinbad Star Restaurant, two Iraqi men in their early thirties were sampling what they believed to be the finest Middle Eastern cooking available in New York City. They were the objects of Arch Carroll's long and painful stakeout.

The Iraqi men had purposely chosen a rear alcove of the small, cozy restaurant, where they noisily slurped thick carob bean soup. They gobbled up mint-flecked tabbouli, and cream-colored humus. They eagerly munched greasy mixtures of raisins, pine nuts, lamb, Moroccan olives, their favorite things to eat in the world.

As they savored the delectable food, Wadih and Anton Rashid were also enjoying immensely their *official* American immunity from criminal prosecution and harassment, something guaranteed to them by the FBI. On the strictest orders from Washington, the two brothers, admitted Third World terrorists, were to be treated like foreign diplomats on U.N. duty in New York. In return, three U.S. Marines, convicted "spies," were soon to be released from a Lebanese jail.

New York and Federal police authorities were permitted to act against the Rashid brothers only if the Black September killers actually moved to endanger property or life in the U.S. These, of course, were two of

33

their favorite avocations in past residences: Tel Aviv, Jerusalem, Paris, Beirut, and most recently London, where they had cold-bloodedly murdered three young women, college-age daughters of Lebanese politicians, in a Chelsea sweet shop.

Arch Carroll

Back out on Atlantic Avenue, Arch Carroll shivered unhappily in the probing icy-cold fingers of the rising night wind.

At times like these, Carroll sometimes wondered why it was that a reasonably intelligent thirty-five-year-old man, someone with decent enough prospects, someone with a law degree, could regularly be working sixty- to seventy-hour weeks, invariably eating stone-cold pizza and Pepsi-Cola for dinner, was sitting outside a Middle Eastern restaurant on a Friday night stakeout?

Was it perhaps because his father and two uncles had been pavement-pounding city cops?

Was it because his Mickey Finn grandfather had been a rough and tumble example of New York's finest?

Or did it have to do with incomprehensible things he'd seen a decade and a half ago in Viet Nam?

Maybe he just wasn't a reasonable, intelligent man, as he'd somehow always presumed? Maybe, if you got right down to it, there was some kind of obvious short-circuit in the wires of the old brain, some form of synaptic fuck-up. *After all, would a really bright guy with all his marbles in hand be standing here freezing his dick off like this?*

As Arch Carroll pondered the tangible mistakes of his life, he noticed that his full attention had begun to wander. For several minutes at a clip, he'd stare at his sadly wiggling toes, at the equally fascinating burning ember of his cigarette, at almost anything mildly distracting.

Five-week-long stakeouts weren't exactly recommended for their entertainment value. That was exactly how long he'd been watching Anton and Wadih Rashid,

34

ever since the State Department had let them come into New York for their sabbatical.

Now Carroll's attention had suddenly snapped back . . .

"What the . . ." he mumbled out loud as he stared down the congested street. *Is that who it looks like? . . . Can't be . . . I think it is . . . but it can't be.*

Carroll had suddenly noticed a skinny, frazzle-haired man coming directly his way from the Frente Unido Bar and Data Indonesia. The man was scurrying up Atlantic Avenue, periodically looking back over his right shoulder. At a distance, he looked like a baggy coat walking on a stick.

Carroll slowly pushed himself up out of his half-frozen lounging position against the restaurant wall.

He squinted his eyes tight for a better look at the figure approaching from down the street.

He just couldn't believe it!

He *stared* down the street, his eyes smarting from the bite of the wind. He had to make sure.

Jesus. *He was sure.*

The fast-walking man had a huge puffy burr of bushy, very wiry black hair. The greasy hair was combed straight back; it hung like a limp sack over the collar of his black cloth jacket. The man's clothes were soberly black; if he hadn't known better, Carroll would have taken him for a minister of some obscure religious sect.

Carroll knew the man by two names: one was Hussein Moussa; the other was the *Lebanese Butcher*. A decade before, Moussa had been recruited by the Russians; he'd been efficiently trained at their famed Third World school in Tripoli. During the late seventies, he'd worked in the European network under the guidance of the supreme terrorist himself, Juan Carlos.

Since then Moussa had been busily free-lancing terror and sophisticated murder techniques all over the world: in Paris, Rome, Zaire, New York, in Lebanon for Colonel Qadaffi. Recently, he'd worked for François Monserrat, who had taken over not only Juan Carlos's European terrorist cell, but South America, and now the United States as well.

35

Hussein Moussa halted in front of the Sinbad Star restaurant. Like a very careful driver at a tricky intersection, he looked both ways. Twice more he looked up and down Atlantic Avenue. He even noticed the bag man camped out across the traffic-busy street.

Apparently he saw nothing to fear, nothing of real concern or interest. He finally disappeared behind the gaudy red door of the Sinbad Star.

Arch Carroll sat up rigidly straight against the crumbling brick wall of the Syrian restaurant.

He groped inside his jacket and produced a stubby third of a Camel cigarette. He lit up and inhaled the gruff, North Carolina dirt farm tobacco.

What an unexpected little Christmas present. What a just reward for endless winter nights trailing the Rashids. *The Lebanese Butcher on a silver platter*. His bosses in State had said not to touch the Rashids without extremely strong physical evidence. But they'd issued no such orders for the Lebanese Butcher.

What was Hussein Moussa doing in New York, anyway? Carroll's mind was reeling. Why was Moussa here with the Rashids?

The firebombing of Pier 33 – 34 went through his mind quickly. He had picked up strands of information from gossip he'd heard all day long on the street – somebody had taken it into his head to blow a dock and the surrounding West Side area, it seemed, and for a moment Carroll pondered a possible connection between Hussein Moussa and the events on the Hudson River.

He'd heard nothing definitive, though. Gossip, whispers, street rumors, nothing more substantial. Somebody had finally said it was some kind of natural gas explosion. Another street-rumor had offered the opinion that the city of New York was now being held for ransom. Mainly, the speculations he'd heard were vague. Until he knew more he couldn't begin to link the Lebanese Butcher to the West Side firebombing.

Arch Carroll had been ramrodding the Anti-Terrorist Division of the DIA for almost four years now. In that

36

span of time only a few of the mass murderers he'd learned about had gotten to him emotionally and caused him to lose his usual policeman's objectivity. Hussein Moussa was one of those few.

The Lebanese Butcher liked to torture. The Butcher apparently liked to kill. The Butcher actually enjoyed maiming innocent civilians . . .

So Carroll didn't particularly want Moussa dead, as he studied the Sinbad Star Restaurant. Carroll wanted the Butcher locked away in a maximum security cage for the rest of his natural life. Give the animal *lots* of time to *think* about what he'd done, *if he did think.*

From underneath newspapers and rags inside one of his shopping bags, Carroll began to slide out a heavy black metal object. Very carefully, peering down close, he checked the firing chamber of a Browning automatic. He quickly fed in eight shells with an autoloader.

A stooped, ancient Hasid was passing by on the sidewalk. He stared incredulously at the street bum loading up a Browning handgun. His watery gray eyes almost fell out of his sagging face. The old man kept slowly walking away, looking back constantly as he moved. Then he cantered a little faster. New York street bums with guns now! The city was beyond all prayers, all possible hope.

Arch Carroll finally pushed himself up off the cold, gritty sidewalk with both hands. He felt stiff as ice all over. One globe of his rear end was completely numb.

He was getting too old for extended street-duty. He had to remember that in the future: it might be a very important fact for staying alive and intact one of these days.

The Sinbad Star

Carroll finally began to weave forward through the thick, fuzzy night traffic. He only half heard the bleating car horns and angry curses directed at him.

He was drifting in and out of reality now; there was a little nausea involved here, too. The same thing, the same absolutely identical feeling came to him every time: just the idea of possibly killing another person, just the notion was so foreign and absurd to something inside him. It left a bitter, sulphuric taste at the back of his throat.

A middle-aged couple was leaving the Sinbad, the fat wife pulling her red overcoat tight around bursting hips.

She stared at Crusader Rabbit and the look said, *You don't belong inside there, Mister. You know you don't belong in there.*

Carroll pulled open the ornate red door the departing couple had let slam in his face.

Hot, garlicky air escaped as he started inside. A muffled *snick* of the Browning under his coat. A deep silent breath. Okay, hotshot.

The tiny restaurant was infinitely more crowded than it had looked from the outside. Arch Carroll cursed and felt his stomach drop. Every available dining table was filled to overflowing. *Every one.*

Six or seven more people, a group of boisterously laughing friends, were waiting in the front to be seated. Carroll pushed past them. Waiters wearing black half-jackets hurried in and out of the swinging kitchen doors in the rear.

Carroll's eyes slowly drifted along the back of the crowded dining room. Only his eyes moved. His head was absolutely still.

Hussein Moussa had already seen him. Even in the packed, bustling restaurant, the terrorist had noticed his entrance. The Lebanese Butcher had been instinctively watching every person who came in from Atlantic Avenue.

So had the restaurant's owner. An enormous, two-hundred-and-fifty-pound man, he charged forward now, an enraged bull guarding his herd at mealtime.

"Get out of here! You get out, bum! Go now!" the owner screamed. The diners were suddenly silent.

Carroll tried to look desperately lost, dizzily confused,

as surprised as everyone else that he was inside the small neighborhood restaurant.

He stumbled over his own flopping black sneakers.

He weaved sideways toward the left, before moving suddenly toward the right rear corner of the dining room.

He hoped to God he looked cockeyed drunk and absolutely helpless. Maybe even a little funny right now. Everybody should start laughing. If he did this exactly right, he'd have Hussein Moussa and the Rashids without firing a shot.

Carroll groped down his body with both hands, graphically scratching between his legs. A middle-aged woman turned away with obvious disgust.

"Bayt-room?" Carroll convincingly slobbered, rolled his eyes back into his forehead. "Gotta go to the bayt-room!"

A young bearded man and his girlfriend started laughing at a front table. Bathroom humor got the youth crowd every time. This was the success lesson of modern Broadway and 1980s Hollywood.

Hussein Moussa had stopped eating. His teeth finally showed – a serrated blade of shining yellow. It was the smile of an animal, a brutal scavenger. He apparently thought this scene was pretty funny, too.

"*Gotta go to the bayt-room!*" Carroll continued a little louder, sounding, he thought, like a drunken Jerry Lewis. But, Jesus, you had to be a decent actor in this line of street work.

"Mohamud! Tarek! Get bum out! Get bum out now!" The owner was hysterically screeching at his waiters. Pandemonium had completely overtaken the Sinbad Star.

Suddenly, fluidly, expertly, Arch Carroll wheeled hard to his extreme left.

The Browning automatic flew out of the ratty and cumbersome parka. It was completely out of place in the family restaurant: a gun as ugly and menacing as unexpected death. Women and children began screaming at the top of their voices.

"Freeze! Don't move! *Freeze God damn you!"*

At the same time, one of the Lebanese waiters hit Carroll hard from his blind side, spinning him in a fast half circle to the right.

He had ruined the drop Carroll had on the three terrorists; he had turned everything into a complete, instantaneous disaster.

Moussa and the Rashids were already scattering, rolling sideways off the red vinyl dining chairs. Anton Rashid yanked out a silver automatic from under his brown leather car coat.

Movies sometimes show particularly violent scenes in very flowing slow motion. It wasn't like that at all, Carroll knew. It was a jumpy collage of loud, shocking still photos. The disconnected photos clicked at him now in random order. They stopped. They started. They stopped. They started again. It was as if someone with the palsy were operating a slide projector.

"Everybody hit the floor!" Carroll screamed. At the same instant, he fired the Browning.

He didn't watch the results. The first bullet brutally uncorked the right side of Anton Rashid's throat, spilling his blood like wine from a broken jug.

Hussein Moussa's gun flashed; it roared as Carroll dove across the backs of a couple already lying on the floor.

Seconds later, Carroll peered back over the table. His eyes and forehead were exposed for an instant. He fired off three more quick shots.

Two of the bullets drove stocky Wadih Rashid hard against a hollow partition wall, decorated with black skillets. Twin rat holes opened in the terrorist's chest. The heavy skillets clattered noisily to the tile floor.

"Moussa! Hussein Moussa! You can't get out! You can't get past me." Carroll began to scream, to negotiate with the final man.

There was no answer.

Somewhere in the front of the restaurant, an old woman was wailing like an Arab imam. Several people were crying loudly. Outside, distant police and ambulance sirens screamed through the night.

"Give up now, and you live. . . . Otherwise, I'll kill you. No matter what, Moussa. I swear it!"

Carroll had to chance another fast look. He was gasping for a breath. *One, two, three.* He raised his head.

He saw nothing of the Lebanese Butcher this time. Moussa was down under the tables as well, hiding and crawling, looking for some advantage. He was moving either toward the front door or the kitchen. Which one was it?

Carroll guessed it would be the kitchen. Pure unadulterated guess work. Sometimes it was the only way.

He began to scramble toward the kitchen.

"I have antipersonnel grenades!" The Butcher suddenly let out a piercing, high scream. "Everybody dies in here! *Everybody dies* in this restaurant! Everybody dies with me! Women, children, I don't care."

Carroll stopped moving suddenly; he almost didn't breathe. Straight ahead, he stared at a badly shaking, very frightened woman curled like a snail on the floor. She looked about thirty years old. She didn't want to die in the middle of her big night out with her husband. He didn't want her to, either.

Carroll peeked above the dining tables again. A gunshot rang out to his immediate left. A salt shaker disintegrated in his eyes.

Moussa was in the far right corner!

The question now was whether he did have grenades. It could be a bluff, but the worst was always possible with somebody like the Lebanese Butcher. He had been known to bring a machine gun pistol to a child's birthday party.

Carroll had to make an instant decision, and he had to make it for everybody trapped in the restaurant now.

The people sprawled on the floor were inching toward panic; they were close to rising en masse and bolting for the door. This would be perfect for Hussein Moussa. In the inevitable confusion, Carroll wouldn't run the

41

risk of shooting. Moussa would have his best chance of escape.

Food was spattered everywhere on the dining room floor. Carroll finally reached for a platter holding the relics of an unfinished meal of pungent lamb and rice. With a sudden wrist snap, he hurled the dripping plate hard against the kitchen door.

At the same time he shifted upright into a professional shooting crouch – a two-handed pistol grip with both arms rigid. He was ready. He was as confident as he could be right now.

Moussa came up again, shooting. The Butcher fired twice at the slapping noise against the kitchen door. *Moussa had a grenade in his left hand! Son of a bitch!*

Arch Carroll squeezed the trigger.

Moussa looked incredibly surprised.

The far right of Hussein Moussa's forehead gushed blood. He slid down against a table still covered with mounds of food and tableware. His back dragged the cloth, plates, wine and water glasses. He spat out a throaty curse across the room.

Then the terrorist's gun rose again.

Carroll shot Hussein Moussa a second time, the bullet exploding his right cheek. The Lebanese Butcher fell heavily forward onto the back of a fat diner lying on the floor.

Carroll shot Moussa again, as the man trapped underneath wiggled like a beached fish and screamed. The top of the terrorist's head flapped off like loose skin.

There was an eerie, terrible silence inside the Sinbad Star. A second or two passed like that. Then loud crying started. There were angry shouts and relieved hugging all over the restaurant.

His gun thrust stiffly forward, Arch Carroll moved awkwardly across the chaotic room. He was still in a police school crouch. It was as if he were locked into that position. Both his hands were trembling; so were his legs.

He carefully examined the Rashid brothers. Wadih and

Anton were still alive. He looked at Moussa. The Butcher was dead, and the world was instantly a better place in which to live.

"Please call me an ambulance," Carroll spoke softly to the astonished restaurant owner. "I'm sorry. I'm very sorry this had to happen in your establishment. These men are terrorists. Professional killers."

The Sinbad Star restaurant owner continued to stare with disbelief at Carroll. His black eyes were small, shiny beads stuck in his broad forehead and they pierced to the rear of Arch Carroll's skull.

"And what are you? What are *you*, please tell me, mister?"

4

Wall Street

Green Band struck the Wall Street financial district at
6:34 P.M. on December 4.

There had been no demands, no further warning or
attempt at justification of any kind. There was no reason
given why the massive attack came an hour and twenty-
nine minutes past the deadline. When it happened, it
happened with a shattering inevitability, with the
searing force of fissures opening under the tremendous pressure of flame, almost as if the earth had
cracked to let loose a part of its molten core. One small,
essential corner of New York seemed for a moment
to tilt on its axis, like something spinning out of
balance. And the black Manhattan sky, which had been
settling down in wintry sullenness, came abruptly alive
with flares of chaotic light, much like a battlefield at
night.

Under towering, half-mile-high plumes of roiling black
smoke, trapped beneath tons of cinder and fluttering,
wet ash, the canyons of Wall Street suddenly blazed with
fierce individual fires.

The blossoming fires, which rose like malevolent
flowers, raged completely out of control on Wall and
Broad streets, on Pine, South William, and Exchange
Place. The scene of sudden random destruction was
impossible to fully comprehend. It reminded some news
observers of Beirut; others thought back to banished
memories of Berlin, London during the second war,
North and South Viet Nam.

Shrill, deafening choruses of police and hospital

emergency sirens screamed like hellish birds streaming through the glowing darkness. The streets were thick with every variety of uniformed police, NYU hospital medics, forensic vans, detectives' and commanders' vehicles. Army, network news and New York Police helicopters chattered overhead, barely avoiding tragic collisions among themselves.

A well-known and respected eyewitness TV reporter stood without hat or coat on what had recently been the stately corner of Wall and Broadway, right under Trinity Church spires. He spoke solemnly into a gaping ABC videotape camera lens. Genuine awe was softening his usually thespian voice and his eyes were lit by reflections of flame.

"Thus far this is our definite information, and more is coming in all the time. . . . The following sites in the Wall Street area were either partially or completely destroyed tonight: *the Federal Reserve Bank of New York*, where over one hundred billion dollars in foreign-owned gold bullion is stored . . . *Salomon Brothers*, who are the country's largest traders in government securities . . . *Merrill-Lynch* at One Liberty Plaza . . . *The Depository Trust Company*, which handles debits and credits for brokerages via computer . . . *Lehman Brothers*, an old-line investment house. . . .

"Also reportedly struck during the siege of unexplained bombings: safe deposit and storage vaults at Chase and the U.S. Trust Company; the New York offices of NASDAQ, Inc., the venerable New York Stock Exchange Building; Number Three Hanover Square, which is where Manufacturers Hanover and European-American Bank were located.

"The full extent of this awesome damage, the complete toll, will not be known tonight. Probably not for days from the look of this incredible chaos. First estimates of the actual number of explosions range from a dozen, to as many as forty separate blasts. . . . It is an *awful, awful* scene here in what remains of the once-proud and lofty financial district of New York."

The Federal Reserve Bank

Green Band had struck like an invisible army.

Two justifiably nervous New York City TAC patrolmen, Alry Simmons and Robert Havens, were carefully threading a path through the smoldering ruins of the Federal Reserve Bank located on Maiden Lane. The two men were attached at their belts to five-hundred-yard-long safety lines snaking back toward the street.

The patrolmen were now deep inside what had once been the Fed's massive and richly ornamental public lobby. Indeed, the gray and blue limestone, the sandstone bricks of the Federal Reserve had always impressed visitors with a sense of their durability and authority. The fortlike appearance, the stout iron bars on every window, had reinforced the image of self-importance and impregnability. The image had obviously been a sham.

The destruction which officers Simmons and Havens found downstairs in the Coin Section was difficult to comprehend and even more difficult to assess. Mountainous coin-weighing machines had been blown apart like a child's toys. Fifty-pound coin bags were strewn open everywhere.

The marble floor was easily three feet deep in quarters, dimes, nickels. Building support columns had been knocked down everywhere on the basement floor. The entire structure seemed to be trembling.

In the deepest basement of the Federal Reserve Bank was the largest single accumulation of gold stored anywhere in the world. It all belonged to foreign governments. The Fed both guarded the gold and kept track of who owned what. In an ordinary change of ownership, the Fed merely moved gold from one country's bin into another's. The gold was transported on ordinary metal carts, like books in a library. The security system in the deep basement was so highly elaborate that even the Reserve Bank's president had to be accompanied when he ventured into the gold storage area.

Now patrolmen Havens and Simmons were alone in the cavernous basement. Suddenly gold was everywhere around them. Rivers of shining gold ran through the dust and rubble. Gold bars, more than they could possibly count, surrounded them. There was well over *a hundred billion dollars* at the day's market price of $386 an ounce, all within their reach.

Patrolman Robert Havens was hyperventilating, taking enormously deep breaths that were almost yawns. His broad, flat face held almost no expression and hadn't since he and Simmons had entered the Fed building.

Both emergency policemen stopped inching forward suddenly. Robert Havens unconsciously let out a sharp gasp. "Christ Jesus! What the hell is *this?*"

An armed Security Guard was sitting in a caned wooden chair directly blocking their path from the gold section into the Fed's main garage. The cane chair still smoldered.

The guard was staring directly into Robert Havens' eyes.

Neither man spoke.

The Federal Reserve Bank guard couldn't; he was beyond words. The man was horribly burned, charred a blistering charcoal black. The sight was so upsetting that the two policemen missed the most important clue at first . . .

Wrapped around the bank guard's right arm was a shiny bright green band.

Archer Carroll

As Archer Carroll carefully maneuvered his battered station wagon along the Major Deegan Expressway, the words of the Atlantic Avenue restaurant owner came back to him with the persistence of an unanswerable philosophical question . . . *And what are you? . . . What are you, please tell me, mister?*

He glanced at his tired face in the rearview mirror.

Yeah, what are you, Arch? The Rashids and Hussein Moussa are bad people, but you're some kind of okay national hero, right?

He was drained, completely numb from the night's terrible carnage. He wanted everything to be quiet and still inside his throbbing head now.

And what are you, mister?

"Nothing worth a shit," he finally answered in the general direction of the station wagon's fogged windshield. He felt as if he were traveling inside a sealed capsule. The world he could see beyond the grimy car windows had retreated one step further away from him.

He turned on the car radio, looking for a diversion from his mood.

Almost immediately he heard the news about Wall Street, delivered by a voice edged in the hushed hysteria so favored by newscasters when they describe events of national importance. Carroll increased the volume and stared at the tiny light emitted by the radio, as if he suspected there was something wrong with the instrument.

He concentrated on the newscaster's tensely delivered reportage. Then there were a couple of man-on-the-street interviews recorded against a brassy background of screaming sirens. It was impossible to mistake the shocked tones of the people who spoke.

Carroll tightened both of his hands on the car steering wheel. His mind was crowded with realistic images of urban guerrilla destruction. He understood that Wall Street was a perfect target for any determined terrorist group – but he couldn't make the necessary jump from his thoughts to the horrible reality of what had just happened.

He didn't want to think about it. He was almost home and he didn't need to drag the world inside the last sanctuary left to him. Not tonight, anyway.

Moments later, Carroll swung his stiff, aching body inside the familiar, musty front hallway of his house in the Riverdale section of the Bronx. Automatically, he hung his coat up on the hook under an ancient totem –

the snoopy-eyed Sacred Heart of Jesus. *Turn out the night light. Home from the wars at last*, he thought.

As he slumped into the living room, Carroll sighed out loud.

"Oh *poor* Arch. It's almost eleven-thirty."

"Sorry. Didn't see you there, Mary K."

Mary Katherine Carroll was sitting neatly curled up on one corner of the couch. The room was only dimly illuminated by an amber light from the dining parlor.

"You look like a skuzzy Bowery bag man. Is that *blood* on your sleeve? *Are you all right?*" She stood up suddenly.

Carroll looked down at his torn, dingy shirt sleeve. He turned it into the dining parlor light. It was blood all right. Dark, dried blood, but not his own.

"I'm fine. The blood isn't mine. At least I don't think it is."

Mary Katherine frowned deeply as she came forward to examine her brother's arm. "The bad guys get banged up too?"

Arch Carroll finally smiled at his twenty-four-year-old "baby" sister. Mary Katherine, who was the keeper of his house, the substitute mother for his four children, the uncomplaining cook and chief bottle washer, all for a two-hundred-dollar-a-month stipend, *"a scholarship."* It was all he could possibly afford to pay her right now.

"I had to kill one of them. He won't be bothering people with his plastique bombs anymore. . . . The kids all asleep?"

The kids, in order of arrival, were Mary III, Clancy, Mickey Kevin and Elizabeth.

All four of them were far too Irish-American cute for their own good: outrageously tow-headed and blue-eyed, with infectious smiles and quick, almost adult wits. Mary Katherine had been their house mother for nearly three years now. Ever since Arch's wife Nora had died on *December 14, 1982.*

After Nora's funeral, after just one desolate night at their old New York apartment, the six of them had moved into the Carroll family homestead in Riverdale. The old house had been closed and boarded-up since the deaths of Carroll's mother and father back in '80 and '81.

Mary Katherine had immediately redecorated. She even set up a huge, light-filled painting studio for herself in the attic. The kids were out of New York City proper, at least. They suddenly had acres of fresh air and space in which to ramble around. There were definite advantages to being up in Riverdale. They had almost everything they needed up here. . . . Everything but a mother.

Carroll had held onto their old rent-controlled apartment on Riverside Drive. Sometimes he even stayed there when he had to work weekends in New York. It wasn't ideal, but it could have been a lot worse. Especially without Mary K.

"I have several important messages for you," Mary Katherine announced brightly.

"Mickey says, if I might paraphrase, that you work too hard and don't make enough skoots. Clancy says, if you don't play catch with him this weekend (and not video game baseball), you're a dead man. That's a *direct* quote. Let's see . . . oh, yes, I almost forgot. Lizzie has decided to become a prima ballerina. Lessons for the spring semester at the Joliere school start at three hundred per, Dad."

"That all?"

"Mairzy Doats left you a humongous kiss, and a hug of equal magnitude and intensity."

"Uncomplicated young woman. Shame she can't stay six years old forever."

"Arch?" Mary Katherine suddenly looked concerned. "Did you hear about this Wall Street thing? The bombing?"

Carroll nodded wearily. He wanted to box Wall Street off in a dark, private corner until he was ready to deal with it. It would still be there in the morning, you could bet on that. He massaged his eyelids, heavy with fatigue. His mind was crowded, all at once, with unwelcome pictures – the Lebanese Butcher, the face of the Atlantic Avenue restaurant owner, fire trucks and EMS ambulances flashing all over Wall Street . . .

50

Carroll finally bent and loosened his flopping high-top sneaks. He peeled off a discolored, satin Tollantine High School jacket. His fatigue had suddenly yielded to a kind of peaceful, ethereal, waking slumber.

In the large bathroom on the second floor, he turned on the tub full blast. Curling hot steam rose toward the ceiling from the chipped and scratched white porcelain. He took off the rest of his squalid street bum ensemble. Finally, he rolled a fluffy bath towel around his waist.

Quick mirror check. Okay. He was still around six-two, solid, durable and sturdy. Pleasant face, even if it was a little pug ordinary, like some friendly mutt people generally take in out of the rain. Generally.

While the hot water ran, Carroll stiffly padded back downstairs to the kitchen and popped the top of a cold Schlitz. Mary Katherine had bought the Schlitz as a "change of pace." Actually, she was trying to stop him from drinking so much.

Carroll took three chilled cans and headed back to the pleasantly steamed bathroom. Stripping off the soft bath towel, he slowly, luxuriously entered the hot, sweet-smelling tub.

As he sipped the cold beer, he began to relax. Carroll used a bath the way some people used psychiatric therapy – to get back in touch, to sort it all out. Among other things, hot water and soap was the only therapy he could afford.

Carroll began to think about Nora almost immediately. *Damn.* Always at night when he got home from work. . . . Their time. The emptiness he felt right then was unbearable. It beat against him with the consistency of a pulse. He was filled with a terrible, hollow longing.

He let his eyes gently close and he could *see* her face. *Oh, Nora, sweet Nora. How could you leave me like this? How could you leave me alone, with all these kids, fighting against this crazy, crazy world out there?*

She had been the best person Carroll had ever met. It was as simple, and no more profound, than that. The two of them had made a perfect fit. Nora had been warm, and thoughtful and funny. That they had found each other convinced Carroll such a thing as fate might indeed exist. It wasn't all randomness and whim and unseeing chance.

Strange, the ways of life and death.

Growing up, all through high school in New York, at College (South Bend, Notre Dame), Carroll had been secretly afraid he'd never find anybody to love him. It was a curious fear, and sometimes he'd imagine that just as some people were born with a talent for art or music, he'd been given a gift of solitude.

Then Nora found him and that was absolute magic. She'd discovered Carroll the second day of law school at Michigan State. Right away, from their very first date, Carroll simply *knew* he could never love anybody else; that he would never need to. He'd never been more comfortable around another person in his life. Nothing even close to the feeling he had for Nora had existed before.

Only now Nora was gone. Nearly three years back in the cancer ward of New York Hospital. *Merry Christmas, Carroll family. Your friend, God* . . .

"I'm just a kid, Arch," Nora had whispered to him once, after she found out she was dying for certain. She'd been thirty-one then, a year younger than he.

Carroll slowly sipped his can of watery beer. An old country song played through his head . . . *"the beer that made Milwaukee famous, made a loser out of me."* Ever since she'd died, he understood he'd been trying to commit slow, sure suicide. He'd been drinking too much; eating most of the wrong things; taking stupid chances on the job . . .

It wasn't as if he didn't understand the problem, because he did. He just couldn't seem to do a damn thing to stop his steep downhill slide. He was like some daredevil skier determined to destroy himself on the most treacherous, glacial slopes. He didn't seem to care enough anymore . . .

Arch Carroll, supposed tough-guy cop, well-quoted cynic around town – there he sat in the tub with one of his kids' rubber toys floating next to him. All four of the kids delighted and astonished Carroll. So why was he screwing up so badly lately?

He was tempted to wake them up now. Maybe go sleigh riding at midnight on the back lawn. Play catch with Mickey Kevin. Teach Lizzie how to do a plié and become a hot-shit little ballerina.

Arch Carroll's ears suddenly tuned in sharply. . . . *Something odd. . . . What was it?*

In another part of the house, he heard voices. Then, a door slammed.

There were steps in the hallway. The floorboards creaked loudly.

The kids were up! Exactly what he needed, Carroll thought, and he began to smile broadly.

There was a light tap on the bathroom door. That had to be Lizzie or Mickey trying to be cute. Soon to be followed by Dolby stereo kid screams and uncontrollable belly laughs.

"*Entrez.* Come right in you little assholes," he called.

The bathroom door opened slowly, and Carroll cupped his hands, ready to splash a tidal wave of water.

He managed to control his impulse just in time.

The man framed in the bathroom door was wearing a black London Fog raincoat, wire-rimmed eyeglasses, a white button-down shirt and striped rep tie. Carroll had never seen him before. "Er. Excuse me, sir," the man said.

"Uh? Can I help you with anything?" Carroll asked.

The intruder looked like a banker, maybe an account executive at a brokerage firm. Carroll started to turn bright red. The blush immediately swept up to his forehead. He couldn't think of anything smart or funny to say, especially when he was still holding a rubber duck in his hand.

The man in the doorway spoke with Ivy League formality, not seeming to notice the duck at all. Nothing even close to a smile crossed his pale, thin lips.

"Sorry to bother you, to trouble you like this at home. I need you to get dressed and come with me, Mr. Carroll. The President wants to see you tonight."

5

Washington, D.C.; The White House

As early as the hot and steamy summer of 1961, John Kennedy had confided to close advisors that the stressful work of the presidency had already aged him ten years. He said it would do the same to anyone who wanted, or needed, the job of chief executive in the most powerful free country in the world.

As he hurried down the plush, half-darkened corridors on the second floor of the White House, Justin Kearney, the forty-first President of the United States, was realizing the same inescapable truth that Kennedy had put into words. He had begun recently to question the motives that had driven him to gain his present residence at 1600 Pennsylvania Avenue. Indeed, he had begun to question the intrinsic value of the office *itself*: he had become acutely aware of the limitations of his power, and this disillusioned him greatly.

Justin Kearney was only forty-two years of age; by one month, he was the youngest American President ever elected and the first Viet Nam War veteran to reach the White House.

At one-fifty on Saturday morning, President Kearney took what he hoped would be a calming breath, then he entered the National Security Council conference room. Those already gathered there rose respectfully, Archer Carroll among them.

Carroll watched the President of the United States take his customary place at the head of the heavy oak conference table. He'd never seen Kearney so nervous, so clearly uncomfortable, during any of his three previous visits to the White House.

54

"First of all, I truly thank all of you for getting here on such very short notice." The President sloughed off his wrinkled navy blue suit coat.

"I think everyone knows everyone else. One, maybe two exceptions . . . down there, sitting between Bill Whittier and Morton Atwater, is Caitlin Dillon. Caitlin is the Chief Enforcement Officer for the SEC. She just might be the toughest enforcer since James Landis himself . . .

"Down at the far right corner, gentleman in the tan corduroy sport coat, is Arch Carroll. Mr. Carroll is the head of the DIA's antiterrorist division. This is the same group that was created following Munich and Lod." The President licked his lips nervously, then he gazed around the assembly.

Commissioner Michael Kane from the New York Police Department was asked to report first.

"Right now, we have men down inside the rubble of all the buildings that were hit. We have explosive-arson squads underground. They've already reported that Number 30 Wall as well as the Fed are badly damaged and extremely dangerous. Either building could conceivably collapse tonight.

"Based solely on a raw visual impression of the explosions, gentlemen, the people who did this are at the highest levels of their trade. The plan was, frankly, brilliantly executed. It was all carefully, *obsessively* worked out in advance."

Claude Williams of the Army Engineers was called to speak next. "There's a disturbing attention to detail in every area – that's what is particularly frightening about this. The river pier, the initial setup with the FBI, the elaborate study of Wall Street itself. I've never seen anything like this, and I'll tell you, I'm not standing here exaggerating for effect. It's as if a well-organized Army hit Wall Street. It's as if a war's been started down there."

Walter Trentkamp from the FBI was asked to go next. Trentkamp had been an old and dear friend of Arch Carroll's father. He'd even helped talk the younger

Carroll into his first police job. Arch Carroll leaned forward to listen to Walter's report.

"I agree with Mike Kane," Trentkamp said in a gravelly, imposing voice. "Everything has the veneer of an expert paramilitary operation. The explosives on Wall Street were placed for maximum damage. Our ordnance boys actually seem to admire the bastards. The whole operation was brilliantly organized, very thoughtfully devised. I haven't seen anything like it either. The closest would be Munich."

"The plan must have taken months, *maybe years* to develop and execute with this high a level of success. PLO? IRA? Red Brigade? I assume we'll know more on that score before too long. They *have* to contact us eventually. They must want something. Nobody goes to this extreme without having some kind of demand in mind." Trentkamp shrugged and looked around at the equally puzzled, solemn faces in the room. "In other words, gentlemen, I've got nothing right now."

Each of those present was called upon to give a report, from the Secretary of Defense to the SEC Representative Caitlin Dillon. They all spoke briefly. Although Caitlin Dillon didn't have a great deal to add, she spoke with the kind of remarkable fluency where you could *see* the semicolons in her speech. Arch Carroll found it challenging to take his eyes away from her face. Only when Caitlin Dillon fell into silence did he glance elsewhere.

"Arch? Are you with us?"

Arch Carroll gave the room a smile of vague embarrassment as he rose to address the group. All the important, mostly recognizable faces now swung his way, like one darkly impassive face.

Carroll was characteristically rumpled. His long brown hair and street clothes brought to mind underground witnesses and policemen called in drug-related grand jury trials. His face was strong. His brown eyes were bright and alert, even though he was exhausted. He'd thought about wearing his one good Barney's Warehouse sale suit, but then he had changed his mind. What was it Thoreau had advised? "Beware all enterprises that require new clothes." Something like that.

Several of the principals attending the emergency session knew Carroll by reputation at least. As a modern-day policeman, Carroll was thought to be appropriately unorthodox, and extremely effective. The team he supervised was credited with helping to make the world's terrorists think twice about their raiding forays into the United States.

Arch Carroll had also occasionally been characterized as a trouble maker; too much of a perfectionist for the Washington politicians to handle, too Off-Broadway theatrical at times. Moreover, he was increasingly becoming known as an Irish drunk. It was a reputation that might not have hurt him too much in the old days of New York police work, but it wasn't doing him any good in these more rarefied circles.

"I'll try to be brief," Carroll began softly. "For starters, I don't think we can make the assumption yet that this *is* an established or known terrorist group.

"*If it is*, then it probably means one of two groups. . . . The Soviets through the GRU – which could include François Monserrat and his network. Or a second possibility – a *free-lance* group, probably sent out of the Middle East. Financed there, anyway.

"I don't believe anyone else has the organization and discipline, the technical know-how or money to manage something this complex." Carroll's intense brown eyes roamed the room. Why did his own remarks sound so hollow? "You can cross out just about everyone else as suspects." Carroll sat down.

Walter Trentkamp raised an index finger and spoke again. "For everyone's general information, we've set up an investigative unit down on Wall Street. The unit is inside the Stock Exchange Building, which suffered limited damage during the raid. Somebody from the New York P.D. already released Number 13 Wall to the press. So that's what we'll call headquarters.

"There's no such address, actually. The Stock Exchange

is on Wall, but the actual address is Broad Street. *That* may be significant. See, we've made our first mistake, and we haven't even started the investigation."

Most everyone laughed inside the White House conference room, but the important irony was lost on none of them. There would be more mistakes; a lot more serious mistakes before anything was resolved. No. 13 was surely an omen of things to come.

President Justin Kearney stood once again at his end of the massive conference table. His face registered the day's extreme stress. He was no longer the good-looking energetic young Senator who'd successfully hit the national campaign trail two years before. Now he seemed cruelly drained.

Justin Kearney said, "I need to clear the air about something else. Something that must never go beyond this room." The President paused, looked up and down the rows of his closest advisors. Then he went on.

"For several weeks now, the White House, Vice-president Elliot and myself, have been receiving reliable intelligence leaks, steady information about a dramatic counterinsurgent plot. Possibly a scenario involving the elusive François Monserrat."

The President paused again, deliberately pacing himself. Arch Carroll turned the name Monserrat over in his mind. "Elusive" didn't quite do Monserrat proper justice. There were times, indeed, when Carroll had seriously doubted the man's existence, times when he considered Monserrat as the *nom-de-guerre* of *several* different individuals acting in collaboration. He was in France one day, Libya the next. He might be reported in Mexico even as somebody else claimed to have seen him at the same time stepping aboard an unmarked plane in Prague.

President Kearney continued. "Our intelligence people have learned that Middle Eastern and South American oil-producing countries have been seriously considering a run on the New York Stock Market.

"This action was to be 'just' retribution for what they

58

considered broken promises, even outright fraud, practiced by U.S. banks and the New York brokerage houses.

"At the very least, the oil cartel hoped to initiate a short-term panic, which they alone would be in a position to take advantage of. *Is this rumored scenario related to tonight?* At this moment, I don't know . . .

"I have serious fears, though, that we're at the beginning of a grave international economic crisis. Gentlemen, it would not be an exaggeration to postulate, to prepare ourselves for the possibility, that the Western economy could effectively collapse on Monday, when the Market will conceivably reopen."

President Kearney's intensely blue eyes continued to make contact around the crisis table.

"We must find out *who* initiated the attack on Wall Street last night. We have to find out how they did it. We have to find out *why*. . . . What is the meaning of this insane, unthinkable thing?"

Walter Trentkamp

Arch Carroll's head was buzzing and his eyes stinging as he filed out of the White House conference room at 2:55 A.M. The other important participants were mostly subdued and silent; they looked either somberly reflective, exhausted, or both.

Carroll had already started down a flight of creaking, thickly carpeted south White House stairs, when a hand rested lightly on his shoulder, startling him.

Arch Carroll twisted around to see Walter Trentkamp, impressive as ever at three in the morning.

"Trying to run out on me?" Trentkamp shook his head in the fashion of a father about to chastise his son in the friendliest terms possible. "How have you been? I haven't seen you in a while. Have a minute to talk?"

"Hello, Walter. Sure we can talk. How about going outside? It might clear both our heads a little."

59

Moments later, Carroll and one of his earliest mentors were walking side by side through the early morning mist shrouding Pennsylvania Avenue. The sky was a heavy gray slab covering the capital city like the roof on a drab mausoleum. In the distance, the Washington Monument looked to Carroll like the sword in the stone.

"I haven't seen enough of your homely face lately. Probably not since you and the kids moved back to the old homestead."

"We miss you, too. It was kind of odd, going back there at first. Now it's good, absolutely the right choice. The kids call it their 'country house.' They think they live on a Nebraska farm now. Riverdale, right?" Carroll grinned in spite of the hour.

"Wonderful kids. Your sister Mary Katherine's a gem, too." Trentkamp hesitated a moment. Carroll thought this was a little like talking to his rabbi on a police force. "How are *you* doing? *You're* the one who concerns me."

"Holding up pretty well. I'm all right. I'm actually doing fine." Carroll shrugged.

Walter Trentkamp shook his closely cropped silver-gray curls. His eyes held a sudden, knowing look, and Carroll felt uncomfortably tense. The cop part of Walter had a knack of wheedling his way inside you, so that you were left feeling transparent and obvious, like thin paper held up to a bright light.

"I don't think so, Archer. I don't think you're doing fine at all."

"No? Well I'm sorry. I *thought* I was all right." Carroll felt his lower back clutch and stiffen.

"You're not so fine. You're not even in the general ballpark of being fine. The late-night drinking bouts have become legend. Risks you're taking with your life. Other cops talk too much about you."

It was the wrong hour for this kind of talk, even from the man he'd grown up calling "Uncle Walter." Carroll bristled. "That all, Father Confessor? That all you wanted to see me about?"

60

Walter Trentkamp abruptly stopped walking. He laid a hand on Carroll's shoulder and lightly squeezed it. "I *wanted* to talk to the son of an old friend of mine. I wanted to help if I could."

Arch Carroll turned his bleary eyes away from those of the FBI director. His face began to redden. "I'm sorry; I guess it *has* been a long day."

"It's been a long day. Been a long couple of years for you since Nora. You're close to being broken out of your unit in the DIA. They like the results, but not your working style. There's talk about replacing you. Matty Reardon's one name I've heard."

Arch Carroll felt his stomach suddenly dropping. He'd known this – somewhere in the back of his mind *he'd known this was coming.*

"Reardon'd be a good choice. He's a good company man. Good man, period."

"Arch, please cut the crap. You're playing games with someone who's known you thirty-five years. *Nobody* can replace you at DIA."

Carroll frowned, and he began to cough in the manner of Crusader Rabbit. He felt like a real shit. "Awhh, hell, I'm sorry Walter. I know what you're trying to do."

"People *understand* what you've been through. I understand; please believe that, Archer. Everybody wants to help . . . I *asked* for you on this one. *I had to ask.*"

Carroll shrugged his broad, sloping shoulders, but inside he was hurt. He hadn't known his reputation had slipped so badly, maybe even in Walter Trentkamp's eyes.

"I don't know what to say. I really don't. Not even a typical Bronx Irish wisecrack. Nothing."

"Talk to me on this one. Let me know what you find out. Just talk to me, okay? . . . Don't go it alone. Will you promise me that?" Trentkamp finally spoke again, a voice of reason and understanding.

"Promise." Carroll nodded slowly.

Walter Trentkamp turned up the collar of his overcoat against the early morning mist. Both he and Carroll were over six feet tall. They looked like father and son that morning in Washington.

"Good," Trentkamp finally said. "It's real good to have you. We'll need you on this nasty son of a bitch. We'll need you at your best, Archer."

Saturday; December 5;
Colonel David Hudson

6

Vets 1; Colonel David Hudson

At six o'clock Saturday morning, December 5, a bleak
Lexington Avenue subway train, its surface covered with
scars of graffiti, lackadaisically rocked and rattled north
toward the Pelham Bay station. The New York subways
were generally a bad joke. This particular train wasn't so
much public transportation as public disgrace.

Colonel David Hudson sat in an inconspicuous huddle
on an uncomfortable metal train seat. As always, he was
wearing clothes no one would look at twice. Uninterest-
ing clothes that created a street camouflage of drab gray
and lifeless, boring brown. He realized it wasn't an
altogether successful disguise because people had
looked at him anyway. Their probing eyes invariably
discovered the missing arm, the empty flap of his coat.

A series of hot and cold flashes coursed through his
body as the train dutifully hurled itself north. He was
drifting in and out of the present, remembering, trying to
accurately replicate long hours spent at a Viet Nam
firebase perimeter listening post. . . . Every one of his
senses had been at its sharpest back then. *Head cocked*:
listening, watching, trusting no one but himself. . . . He
needed exactly the same kind of brilliant clarity right
now, the same kind of absolute self-reliance – which was
probably the greatest high he'd known in his lifetime.

From 14th Street, where he'd boarded the inhospitable

subway train, up past 34th, 42nd, 59th Street, Hudson objectively contemplated the first days of his capture in Viet Nam. An old Doors song, "Moonlight Ride," drifted through his mind. A period piece.

He was vividly remembering the La Hoc Noh prison now . . .

Above all else, Colonel David Hudson was remembering the one known as the Lizard Man . . .

La Hoc Noh Prison; July, 1971

Captain David Hudson, his nervous system a mass of fire, felt each bruising, jarring bump, even the smallest stones underfoot, as four prison guards half carried, half dragged him toward the central thatch-roofed hut at the La Hoc Noh compound.

Through the flat white glare of the Asian sun, which resembled a bleached penny, he squinted at the pathetic hootch, with its tattered North Vietnamese flag and sagging bamboo walls.

The command post.

What an incredible, existential joke this all was. What a cruel joke all of life had recently become.

Well-muscled once, clean-cut and always so perfectly erect, so proper, the young U.S. Army officer was pitiful to behold now. His skin was uniformly wrinkled and sallow, almost yellow; his blond hair looked like it had been pulled out in great, diseased clumps.

He understood and accepted the fact that he was dying. He weighed less than a hundred and fifteen pounds; he'd had the dreaded yellow shits literally for months without end. He'd gone beyond mere exhaustion; he lived in a shifting, hallucinatory world where he doubted even his own sensations and ordinary perceptions.

All Captain Hudson possessed now was his dignity. He refused to give that up, too.

He would die with at least some essential part of

himself intact; that secret place deep inside that nobody could torture out of him.

The SNR officer, the one they had called Lizard Man, was waiting expressly for him inside the dread command hootch. The North Vietnamese leader sat in awful silence, crouched like some feral animal behind a low, lopsided table.

He almost seemed to be posing for a photo beneath a twirling bamboo fan that barely stirred the hundred-and-five-degree air.

North Vietnamese cooking smells – green chili, garlic, lichee and durians, spoiled river prawns – made David Hudson suddenly gag. He clutched violently to his mouth. He felt himself begin to faint. *But he wouldn't allow that. No! Honor and dignity! That was everything. Honor and dignity kept him alive.*

He stopped on his own mental command, drawing on the scant resources, the human spirit that remained inside of him.

The North Vietnamese guards held him up. He collapsed, a weightless puppet in their tangle of bony arms.

A guard punched David Hudson's jaw with a hard bare fist. Hot blood filled his mouth. He gagged repeatedly on the metallic taste. *Honor and dignity. Somehow.*

"*You Cap-tan, ah Hud-sun!*" the senior officer suddenly screeched, cawing like a heat-crazed jungle bird.

He peered down onto the wrinkled note pad he always carried. His fingers struck hard into the page to emphasize certain words.

"Ho-Ho. Twen-six yea-ah old. Veet Nam, Lah-ose since nineteen-six-nine. Yow spy six yeah. Ho-Ho. You 'ssain! 'ssassin! Convic to *die*, Cap-tan."

The prison camp guards let Captain David Hudson fall toward the dirt floor, which was littered with gaping fish heads and rice.

Hudson's fragile mind was reeling, crashing, quite literally exploding with sharp-pointed lights. His own private light show, his own palace of pain, he thought.

He'd understood only a very few of the Lizard Man's

fractured English words. *"Viet Nam . . . spy . . . assassin . . . convicted to die."*

On the low table sagging between him and the North Vietnamese officer, there was a teakwood game board.

Captain David Hudson's eyes absently ran over the highly polished board surface. Games? *Why did they all love games?*

The Lizard Man snorted obscenely. A distorted smile appeared suddenly across his lower face. His jaw moved slowly, seemingly unattached to the rest of his skull. David Hudson imagined he could see, just behind the loose lips, a flicking, reptilian tongue in the man's mouth. He shook his head, trying vainly to find a clearing, a little area of reality within his wildly confused thoughts.

"Yow play game? Yow play game me, Hud-sun?"

David Hudson's eyes were riveted to the low-slung game table, trying to gain focus. *Play a game with Lizard Man?*

The board appeared to be real teak. It was precious wood, exotic and beautiful, incongruous in this sodden armpit of a place.

Even more striking were the hundreds of polished black and white stones, exquisite game playing pieces. They were circular in shape, convex on each side.

For a nearly lucid moment, David Hudson remembered a marble collection. Something magical and forgotten from his youth in Kansas. Father's farm. Collecting solids and cat's-eyes. Had he actually been a boy in this same lifetime? He honestly couldn't seem to remember. *Die with dignity! Dignity!*

"Play game for your life? Ho?" the Lizard Man asked.

The game board was divided into vertical and horizontal lines creating hundreds of intersections. There were 180 white stones, 181 black.

Beside the pile of black stones, the Lizard Man's hand rested on a bulky Moison-Nazant military revolver. One of his long yellowed fingers relentlessly tapped the table.

"Yow play. Play game me! Loser die!"

Captain David Hudson continued to stare hard at the game board, at the beautifully gleaming teak table. *Focus, he thought. Concentrate. Die with dignity.*

He only vaguely understood what was happening. What did this man want from him now? It was some kind of obscene joke, Hudson knew. One more way the Lizard Man had of torturing him.

The black and white stones seemed to be moving by themselves. Spinning, crawling like insects in his badly blurred, tunneling vision.

Finally, Hudson spoke up. His voice was surprisingly strong, angry, even defiant when he finally found it.

"I have never lost at the game of Go," Captain David Hudson said. "You play, asshole!" *Dignity!*

The New York subway noisily braked at a Midtown station stop. The soiled platform was bathed in eerie blue.

A few passengers on the sleepy, early morning train were absently staring at David Hudson. Even at a casual glance, he seemed like someone quietly in control of his environment. Beneath the drab street clothes, there was about him a sense of purpose. He was a man accustomed to taking command.

Hudson stared back at the other passengers. He peered into their hollow, pathetic eyes, until most glanced away. The majority of American people were devoid of any real basic integrity, any sense of themselves. Civilians tended to disappoint David Hudson again and again. Maybe it was because he expected too much from them – he had to remind himself constantly that he couldn't apply his own high standards to others.

More listless passengers struggled onto the subway train at the East 86th Street stop. There were mostly older whites, time-bent men and women, small merchants, ciphers who managed or owned the rip-off clothing stores, the rip-off food markets, in Harlem and the East Bronx.

One of the men boarding at 86th, however, was completely different from the rest.

He appeared to be in his mid-thirties. His striking black hair was brushed straight back. He wore a tan cashmere overcoat with a paisley scarf, pressed navy dress slacks, super-Wasp duck boots. The impression he gave was of someone boarding a subway for the first time in his life and finding something amusing in the phenomenon of a slum on wheels.

He sat beside David Hudson and immediately snapped open Saturday's *New York Times*, idly coughing into his fist. As the subway rumbled forward, he crisply folded the newspaper into quarters.

"You made the front page. Congratulations." Laurence Hadford finally offered a guarded, casual whisper.

His voice was exquisitely controlled and as smooth as his expensive silk scarf. "I watched the intriguing spectacle on the six o'clock, the seven o'clock, the ten and eleven o'clock news shows. You've succeeded in totally baffling them."

"We've done reasonably well so far." Hudson nodded in agreement. "The difficult steps are still ahead, though. The true tests of the plan's legs, Lieutenant."

"You brought me a present, I hope? Christmas present?" As Laurence Hadford slid closer to Hudson on the gray-metal subway bench, Hudson could smell the man's citric cologne.

"Yes. Exactly as we agreed the last time."

David Hudson turned his head sideways for the first time. He stared into the pale blue eyes and persistently mocking half smile of Laurence Hadford. He didn't like what he saw. Never had. Not now and not back in Viet Nam either, when Hadford had been a smug young officer.

Laurence Hadford was impassively cool. He showed nothing of his inner emotions. The well-shaved face might have been a door closed on private rooms. Hudson had a sudden impression of icy places locked away inside the man. Hadford was already a partner at one of the larger Wall Street investment firms and was said to be climbing to even higher rungs on the corporate ladder.

Reaching deep inside his coat, Hudson handed over a thick, over-stuffed manila business envelope. The package bore no external marking, nothing to identify it in case there was any problem, an unlikely slip-up on board the subway.

The envelope disappeared inside the rich softness of cashmere.

"There's one small hitch. A tiny problem has come up. The amount here isn't enough." Hadford smiled so easily. "Not considering what's happened. What you've gone and done now. You've made this a very dangerous business arrangement for me. If you'd told me what you actually planned to do—"

"You wouldn't have helped us then. You would have had too many doubts. You would have been scared shitless."

"My friend, I *am* scared shitless."

The subway train buckled slightly, but only seemed to slow minimally as it charged into the 110th Street station.

Angry graffiti was scrawled on all the walls. It shouted at anyone who cared to look up from their early bird editions of the *Daily News*. Most didn't look up.

"We agreed on a figure before you did any work for us on Wall Street. Your fee, half a million dollars, has now been paid in full." Hudson felt a familiar alarm sounding inside him. His control was slipping away. "Any information you've supplied us, any personal risks you took, were infinitesimal considering your enormous financial gain."

Hadford's perfectly capped white teeth gritted very slightly. "*Please.* Don't tell me how well I've been paid. I know what you're all about now. You've got so much money, you couldn't *possibly* know what to do with it. Another half million is virtually meaningless. What's another million for that matter? Don't be so uptight."

Colonel David Hudson finally managed to smile. "You know, perhaps you're right. Under the circumstances –

what *is* another half million? . . . Especially if you're willing to do a little more investigation for us. We still need your help on Wall Street."

"I suppose for the right price I could be convinced, Colonel."

The next station David Hudson particularly noticed was 157th Street. Between 110th and there, he and Laurence Hadford talked of the next steps to be taken on Wall Street; the kinds of additional information needed for Green Band.

Stenciled numbers announced the train stop on mottled, pale blue standposts. A sullen black face slowly slipped past the spray-painted train windows. The brakes screeched, then let out a loud, gaseous *whump*.

The last few passengers besides Hadford and Hudson exited at the 157th Street stop. The black face didn't get on board. The subway doors slammed tightly shut. They were completely alone. David Hudson felt himself tense. The blood coursed rapidly through his veins. All his senses were suddenly alert, and his perceptions had an astonishing clarity. Everything around him on the train stood out as if illuminated by a harsh arc light.

"I'm sorry, Hadford."

"Excuse . . . *Oh God no!*"

As the train loudly rumbled out of the station, the flashing knife appeared from nowhere. What made David Hudson's parlor trick so completely unexpected was that the blade was so very long, six inches at least, the handle perhaps another four.

The surgically sharp blade jabbed hard and disappeared into Hadford's underbelly, just below the wall of his rib cage.

It shredded the cashmere coat, tearing fibrous material and parting soft flesh and clenched muscle with virtually no effort. Almost instantly, the long blade reappeared dripping red.

As Laurence Hadford was sliding face up off the subway bench, Colonel Hudson relieved him of the weighty envelope. Hadford's rolling eyes were suddenly staring sightlessly at the ceiling. His body underwent a series of wracking convulsions, then went completely limp. He died somewhere between the 157th and 168th Street stations.

Colonel David Hudson quietly slipped off at the next stop. He was shaking now. His mind was filled with tiny white explosions, with dark flowing streaks much like Hadford's blood. It was the first time in his career that David Hudson had ever harmed a fellow officer.

But Hadford's greed had represented a weakness in the Green Band plan. And when you encountered greed, Hudson instinctively understood, you ran into the likelihood, somewhere down the line, of betrayal. He could take no chances now, because there was no margin for error or for human weakness later.

Once he was out on Broadway, David Hudson struggled onto a city bus headed south. The Lizard Man screeched at him like a jungle monkey as the bus lurched forward. The Lizard Man screamed so loudly, David Hudson had to grit his teeth. The Lizard Man laughed and laughed as David Hudson escaped into the awakening daytime city. *Dignity! Revenge!*

Vintage

A little more than an hour later, his composure intact once again, David Hudson climbed off the grunting and growling bus at the last stop – Columbus Circle and the New York Coliseum. Bundled inside his plain brown greatcoat, he waded further south. He was almost sure that people were staring and that worried him.

Anonymity, he thought. He needed the cover of beautiful anonymity. He craved it. Especially now, he had to hold onto his New York cabdriver image. He had to be consistent. He also had to keep firmly in mind that he had been one of the very best Special Forces commanders in the world.

He reached the Washington-Jefferson Hotel, where he

had a room at the far end of a depressingly drab second floor hallway. He'd had this particular room for almost five weeks, and that was pushing his luck perhaps. But the northern Times Square district was so perfectly anonymous, uncaring, and so convenient for the specialized work he still had to do. He specifically hadn't wanted a place too close to either the Vets garage or the Wall Street financial district.

Hudson sat on the edge of his hotel room bed for a moment. His thoughts turned idly back to Laurence Hadford, but he knew he couldn't allow himself to dwell on the death of the man. He stared at the nearby telephone. Finally he decided to forget Laurence Hadford and reward himself for Friday night's success. Some well-deserved, maybe even spectacular R&R was in order. His only vice, really – David Hudson's only remaining human connection, he sometimes thought.

He picked up the telephone, and dialed a familiar local number in Manhattan.

"Hello, this is Vintage." The connection was terrible. He could barely hear the words over the static.

"Yes. This is David . . . I've used Vintage Service before. My number is 323." Hudson spoke in his usual soft but firm voice. "I can tell you exactly the kind of escort I'm looking for. She's between five foot six and five foot ten. I'd like her between the ages of nineteen and twenty-six. I'll be paying cash."

Colonel Hudson waited, then he received a time, and a name for his "date." He spoke into the telephone again. "In thirty minutes at 343 West Fifty-first. Thank you very much. I'll be expecting . . . Billie."

It was just past eleven o'clock when Billie Bogan, her eyes raised to a winking neon hotel sign, stepped from a Checker cab on West 51st Street.

The Washington-Jefferson? Now here was an odd one.

It certainly didn't look like the kind of place where Vintage clients usually stayed. Not the kind of successful men who could afford a hundred fifty dollars and up for an hour with some of the most exquisitely beautiful *escorts* in New York.

Billie finally shrugged and entered the paint-peeling hotel lobby. She had been told the client would be paying cash.

As she walked down the dimly lit second floor hallway she shut off her Vintage beeper. It would be unbelievably tacky to get an electronic message while she was in the middle of a session with a client.

The Washington-Jefferson, though? She shivered involuntarily.

Billie tapped on the hotel room door. The shadowy door swung open almost immediately – and she found herself unexpectedly surprised. He was unusually good-looking, actually. His smile was open and pleasant. He was quite tall, slender, and . . . *uh-oh*.

She saw the not-unexpected problem suddenly. The unfortunate catch! He had only one arm. The left sleeve of his mufti shirt flopped open . . .

Billie couldn't feel too sorry for the man framed in the hotel doorway, though. There was nothing about him that inspired pity, quite the opposite. He was certainly attractive, and his disability didn't seem to trouble him because he was not at all self-conscious as he gazed at her. He had the kind of face she somehow associated with the outdoors. Probably, he was one of those self-reliant types who loved camping and who knew the right knots to tie and the best place to pitch a tent.

"Hi. I'm Billie. How are you today?" She smiled courteously. "You're David?"

Colonel David Hudson stared at her for a few seconds before answering.

She was one of the best-looking prostitutes he'd ever seen. Her hair was an unbelievably rich, ash blond with thick bouncy curls. She was long-legged and thin in the manner cultivated by high-fashion models, but without the glossy emaciation Hudson didn't care for. Her breasts were firm under a pricey silk blouse. She wore a flattering straight skirt, dark stockings, and polished

73

high heels. Her face managed to combine an exotic loveliness with an innocent quality that excited Hudson.

"I'm sorry," he finally managed with another smile. "I was staring, wasn't I? Come in. You're very pretty. Very beautiful. I didn't expect so beautiful a girl."

Billie smiled – as if she'd never heard any of this before. The hint of a blush rose along her high, elegant cheekbones. The sudden color sloped down her neck to the deep hollow of her throat.

"I'm sorry. I wasn't paying attention. It was Billie what? Your last name?"

"Just Billie," she smiled again. All of her gestures were very natural.

For the first time he noticed her accent. She was British. Maybe even upper class from the clipped sound of her phrases.

Hudson gestured around his Spartan hotel room. "I know, it isn't exactly the Plaza. Not just yet . . . you see, I'm writing a play. I hope this qualifies as an artist's garret?"

For some unimagined reason, Billie found herself slowly relaxing with this one. He was actually easy to be with, and he sounded halfway intelligent. The bit about writing a play, whether it was true or not, had come out naturally enough.

Billie sat down tentatively, almost demurely, on the edge of the unmade day bed. As if she were a real date. . . . As if she were a real date, and they hadn't discussed exactly why she'd come up to his room.

Staring at her face, Hudson thought she was twenty-five at the most. She was extremely elegant, even for Vintage.

"I like the theater a great deal. When I first came to New York to live, every single Wednesday I went to a Broadway matinee," she said. "I'd get these half-priced tickets at Times Square. Sometimes at hotel desks. I saw *Death of a Salesman* with Dustin Hoffman, *Torch Song*, *Cats*, *Glengarry*. Everything I could get into."

Very nonchalantly, as she talked about the Broadway

74

theater, she unfastened the top button of her silk blouse, then the next.

"Sit down by me?" A very innocent-sounding question.

Hudson did, and she lightly kissed his cheek. Her perfume was hypnotic, an expensive scent that captivated him. It drifted luxuriously up into his face.

"You said I was beautiful. I'd like to repay the compliment – you're very handsome. I hope you write a good play."

Still innocently, Billie lightly slid her hands inside his sirt. She unbuttoned the middle two buttons. The hair on his chest was downy soft, and his body was muscled and hard.

Her touch was light and warm. Suddenly something extraordinary happened. Something most unusual: Hudson began to feel.

A severe warning went off deep inside. He ignored it. But *something was wrong*.

Yet she was so natural and relaxed.

The lightest touch of fingers.

She was tenderly massaging him as she undressed.

The silk blouse delicately *shushed* off. Then the straight black skirt.

She stood over him – sheer dark stockings, garters, and high heels only.

There was a glistening droplet on her golden patch of hair.

He felt as if he were sinking right through the mattress.

The inner warning sounded again. He ignored it again.

He stopped and watched her breathe – so unexpectedly beautiful – and she smiled when she realized what he was doing.

"You *are* beautiful."

"*You're* beautiful."

Her breasts were swelling in anticipation. Hudson gently touched them, exploring their perfect roundness, exploring each light pink aureole.

She slid on top of him, and her blond hair glowed in

the light from the overhead lamp. She rocked back and forth on top of him, a peaceful, swaying motion. Everything seemed so natural. The warning signals quieted, like a siren fading in the distance.

He was breathing faster and faster.

Her eyes shut, then opened, seemed to smile, shut again.

Faster and faster, faster and faster. He thought of dance rhythms.

He played with her as she gently rocked on top of him like a cresting sea wave. He lightly manipulated her with his hand as she moved to her own rhythm.

Then her whole body stiffened and she began to fall foward against his chest. She arched dramatically backward, and jerked forward again. It was as if currents of electricity were passing through her long, slender body.

He was almost certain . . .

She was coming, her whole body shuddering.

This expensive escort from Vintage.

This beautiful prostitute was having an orgasm with him.

Billie. Just Billie.

Warning signals were going off like a hundred piercing police sirens in his head. Colonel David Hudson listened this time. He didn't come. He never did.

7

Carroll

Arch Carroll was flying on People Express to Miami that morning. It wasn't the most enjoyable experience he'd ever had. People Express happened to be the day's first scheduled Florida flight out of Washington. The light through the jet's tiny windows was dark and ominous for most of the trip, which had begun at the highly uncivilized hour of 4:45 A.M.

The airline service crew was young and inexperienced. They giggled inanely during the seat belt and air bag pep talk. They sold cellophane-wrapped danishes in the aisle for a dollar. Was this the hotshot outfit that had TWA and American shaking in their cockpits?

Carroll shut his eyes. He tried to make everything about the morning, especially about the night before, Black Friday, vanish, vanish far, far away. But nothing went away.

This scenario of terror was more like the state of siege people had learned to live with in the political capitals of Western Europe, all through the teeming urban ghettos of South America – but never inside America until now.

Until now.

The back of Arch Carroll's eyelids became a crisp, white screen for a thousand flashing images of Wall Street ablaze; the frightened faces of ordinary people running amok through the New York streets; the way President Justin Kearney had looked at the White House. Why did he keep returning to that same disturbing image of the President? Christ, he had more than enough to occupy himself right now.

Like this sudden trip to Miami . . .

The first possible break in the Green Band mystery had come quickly. Almost too quickly, Carroll thought cautiously. He'd spotted the clue himself on the FBI sheets for the night before. Immediately, he was on the first flight to Florida to check it out.

He opened his eyes and stared the length of the aisle at two stewardesses talking in conspiratorial whispers. Then, about halfway through the two-hour-and-forty-minute flight, he got up wearily and trudged to the airplane bathroom.

Everyone on the early bird flight looked thoroughly depressed and groggy, as if they'd risen way too early and their constitutions hadn't had time to quite catch up. Several business people had early edition newspapers with stark Wall Street bombing headlines. The intense black letters burned Carroll's mind as he moved up the aisle. Beyond the simplistic language of the headlines, he could sense something else – something that reverberated beyond Wall Street, a far-off thunder that threatened a way of life: nothing less than the free-enterprise systems of the Western world.

Inside the small bathroom, he cupped water in his hands and splashed it over his eyes. He took a tiny red plastic case out of his pants pocket.

When Nora had been sick, she'd used this container to hold her day's supply of Valium and Dilantin, and a few other prescriptions to help control seizures. Carroll slugged down a small yellow pill, a light upper to keep him alive. He would have preferred a drink. An eye-opener Irish whiskey. Double Bloody Mary. But he'd promised Walter Trentkamp.

Carroll continued to stare at himself in the clouded airplane mirror. He thought some more about Green Band, as he examined the puffed, purplish bruises sagging under each eye. He rifled through his mind as if he were sifting a library's massive card index system. When it came to terrorists and their various specialties, Carroll had a long, reliable memory. During his first year with the DIA, all he'd done was to catalogue terrorist activities. He'd learned his early lessons well. In *some* ways, he was an incredibly *orthodox* and thorough policeman.

The hard evidence so far suggested . . . what? Maybe Soviet-inspired GRU activity? *Why*, though? Qadaffi? A very long shot there. The Wall Street plan showed far too much patience for the usual Third World types, especially Middle Eastern hitmen . . .

Cubans? No. Provos? Not likely. Crazed American revolutionaries? Doubtful. Who then? Most of all – *why?*

And how did the latest sketchy report from the Palm Beach Police Department fit? . . . *A South Florida drug dealer had been talking about the Wall Street attack the day before it happened?* The local hood had even dropped the unannounced code name – *Green Band!*

How would a South Florida drug dealer by the name of Diego Alvarez know anything about Green Band? What possible connection could there be?

Like everything so far, it didn't make much sense yet. It didn't seem to lead anywhere Arch Carroll particularly wanted to go. Certainly, he didn't want to be in southern Florida at this ungodly hour of the morning.

He rubbed his eyes, splashed more cold water on his face and looked back at his reflection. Death warmed over, he thought. It was like one of the photographs on wanted posters inside Post Office buildings, the kind that seem always to have been taken in dim lighting.

Carroll turned away from the mirror. It would soon be time to come down in the fantasy land of orange juice, Disneyland, multimillionaire dope dealers, and hopefully Green Band.

Diego Alvarez

The local FBI Chief, Clark Sommers, accompanied by an assistant, was there to meet Carroll at the makeshift People Express arrival gate. As usual, Miami International

Airport was experiencing an electrical brownout. "Mr Carroll, I'm Clark Sommers of the Bureau. This is my associate, Mr. Lewis Sitts."

Carroll nodded. His head ached from the flight and the effects of the upper he'd swallowed, which was just kicking in now, buzzing through his bloodstream.

"Walk and talk?" Sommers suggested. "We've got an awful lot of ground to cover this morning."

"Yeah, sure. Tell me something, though. Every time I come through this airport the lights are half out. Am I just imagining that?"

"I know what you mean. It can seem that way. Dope dealers claim the bright lights hurt their eyes." Clark Sommers flashed a very low key, cynical smile. He was *definitely* FBI all the way. He was a neat, buttoned-down man, with the body of somebody who might have lifted weights years ago and who still occasionally hit the bench.

Sommers' assistant, Mr. Sitts, was wearing a lightweight blue sweater, tan golfing slacks and a matching Banlon shirt. The only thing missing were some espadrilles. Probably getting a promotional fee from Jantzen, Carroll thought. He tried to picture himself as a successful Florida police officer, but he couldn't make the right visual or emotional connection.

As they walked down the corridor, Carroll glanced at the cheery posters depicting surf and sun. They seemed to assault him personally. The sea was a shade too blue, the sun a touch too garish, the people having fun in the photographs a little too all-American beautiful for Carroll's taste. He yearned for New York, where at least there was a sense of reality to the gray, wintry half-tones of the familiar streets.

Sommers, fidgeting with a pair of sunglasses, spoke in a quietly assured voice.

"Mr. Carroll, one thing you probably should understand about this territory down here. For reasons of morale, in order to keep my men fully efficient and organized, this bust has to be mine. I have to make the key calls. These are my men after all. You can understand that, I hope?"

Carroll didn't break stride. His face showed nothing. Almost all policemen were fiercely, irrationally territorial – something he knew from personal experience.

"Sure thing," he nodded. "This is your bust. All I want to do is talk to our drug dealer friend afterward. Ask him how he likes the nice Florida weather."

The South Ocean Boulevard neighborhood was pretty much 1930s Spanish and Mediterranean in style: it was a six-block cluster of pastel blue and pink million-dollar estates. Carroll had the impression of everyone and everything lying dormant around him. People still sleeping peacefully at twenty past eight, flagstone patios sleeping, red clay courts sleeping at the Bath and Tennis Club, putting-green lawns and candy-striped cabanas and swimming pools – all sleeping, as if everything had been placed under a pleasant narcoleptic spell.

Clark Sommers spoke in a steady drone as they rode alongside the glittering, bluish-green ocean. "Real estate dealings on South Ocean here aren't exactly handled by Century Twenty-One. Most sales are actually arranged by Sotheby's, the big antique outfit. Owners in Palm Beach, they think of their homes as valuable works of art. Maybe you can see why?"

"Reminds me of my neighborhood in New York," Carroll said.

Agent Sitts suddenly spoke up from the back seat. His long, well-tanned arm pointed between Carroll and Sommers. "That's our people up ahead there, Clark."

Gathered together at one of the quiet, perfect palm tree and sea grape intersections were six nondescript blue and green sedans.

The cars were parked in clear sight. Several of the FBI men were checking pump-action shotguns and Magnums right out on the street.

"There goes the neighborhood," Carroll muttered. "I hope Sotheby's not showing any houses real early this morning."

"Don't be fooled by the suburban ambiance," Clark Sommers spoke up. "The Mizeners, the real big shots, they don't live around here. This is Palm's ghetto. Drug dealers and South American pimps. These people here are rich, but they're all street scum."

Arch Carroll shrugged and began to check his own gun. He was wondering more than ever how a Florida hood would know about Green Band the day before it happened. Could that mean a connection with South American terrorists? Which ones? The Cubans? If the Cubans *were* involved, he could already foresee some impenetrable network of clues that could lead all the way back to Fidel himself, which wasn't a prospect he liked to consider. Castro had always somehow managed to stay aloof from conspiracies at least the ones that involved his name.

Sommers suddenly snatched up the car's microphone. "All units! We will proceed with extreme caution up South Ocean now. Watch yourselves. These people are probably heavily armed."

The seven-vehicle caravan began to drift slowly up South Ocean Boulevard. Carroll glanced out at the peaceful neighborhood. Every house was set back from the street, isolated by closely cropped, bright green lawns that looked as if they'd been spray-painted on by gangs of meticulous handymen.

A Miami *Herald* paperboy rode by in the opposite direction, mounted on a chugging mo-ped the same impossible blue color as the sky. He braked to a stop, scratched his crewcut and stared.

One of the FBI men frantically signaled for him to keep going.

"That's it. Number 640," Sommers finally spoke up again. "That's where our friend Diego Alvarez lives."

Carroll tucked the loaded Magnum back into his shoulder holster. His stomach was rocking and rolling

82

and the speed was lighting fires throughout his nervous system.

The FBI cars turned single file down an impressive side street off South Palm. They parked one after the other in front of two adjacent Spanish-style estates.

Car doors clicked open and shut very quietly.

Carroll slipped into step with a dozen or so gray-suited FBI agents. They trotted back toward the Alvarez place.

"Remember what I said back at the airport, Mr. Carroll. I give all the orders, okay? I hope the capture of this guy's going to help you get what you want, but don't forget who's running the show, okay?"

"I remember."

Handguns and shotguns caught the hard, bright glint of the early morning Florida sun. Carroll listened to bolt-action apparatus slamming into ready. The FBI agents looked like young professional athletes, as they fanned out in the manner of a dance team.

Combat was *full* of visual paradox.

Carroll could see peaceful gulls rising from the sea, lazily sliding west to check the early morning sunrise party at the Alvarez house. Being a seagull seemed like a pretty good idea right now, but he had never been much for vocational planning.

The ocean wind was pleasantly warm. It carried a curious scent of salty fish and orange blossoms. The sun was already intense, too blinding to look at without a hand shade.

"Elegant house Diego has for himself. Run about two, two point five million with Sotheby. When I give the signal we're going to put men in every wing of the villa. We'll shoot anything that moves to threaten any of our lives."

Arch Carroll remained silent. These were Sommers' men. This was Sommers' little planet where he reigned supreme. Carroll looked at the FBI man for a moment then finally took his handgun out again. He pointed the massive black barrel upward, a safety precaution where people were concerned, though not seagulls.

Just then, as Carroll knelt in a sniper-shooter's crouch,

the heavy wood door of the Alvarez house came flying, crashing open. The door banged hard against the pink stucco front wall.

"What the fuck?" Clark Sommers whispered out loud.

First a blowzy white-haired woman in a tattered Maranca shirt stumbled outside. Then came a dark, well-built man bare chested in white trousers. All across the front lawn automatics and revolvers clicked off their safeties.

Then Diego Alvarez suddenly began to scream at the FBI men. "You motherfuckers! I shoot this old lady, man. She jus' innocent old lady. My fucking cook, man. Put down all those motherfucker guns!"

Sommers was suddenly quiet. His beach-hero tan seemed to be fading fast. The surprised expression on his face was that of a man who sees his private domain slipping out from under his control.

Carroll glared in the direction of the South Florida drug dealer. The dark eyes of the man were frantic, desperate. There were flecks of saliva at the corners of his mouth. Then he turned to Sommers and said, "We have to take him. No matter what, we have to take him. You understand that?"

Sommers continued to be deadly quiet. He didn't even look over at Carroll.

"We *have* to take Alvarez. There are no other options."

Sommers barely glanced at Carroll. His look still said, *You're a New York City cop, this is my backyard, we do things my way down here.* Carroll had a vision of Alvarez escaping, and it was an exasperating vision. That was a possibility he had to prevent. Sommers didn't know what was involved here. So far as the FBI was concerned, this was a dope bust, nothing more.

Diego Alvarez was awkwardly pulling the enormously fat cook toward a red Cadillac parked outside the garage. The drug dealer had on white flare-bottom trousers. He was almost black in skin tone, as well-muscled as a pro fighter. The cook's eyes were as wide and round as two coffee saucers.

Carroll tried to sort through the surprise and sudden, chaotic confusion of the moment. If he controlled his breathing, he could usually concentrate better, which was something he'd learned during his combat days in Southeast Asia.

He had an idea – one possible solution that came to mind.

Actually he'd seen a New York detective demonstrate this particular approach during a robbery in progress in Manhattan's Greenwich Village.

Carroll waited for Alvarez to eye-check the FBI agents on the far left. As he did so, Carroll smoothly slid behind a flower-decked wall which concealed him from the drug dealer. He waited a few seconds to see if he was missed, then continued hustling down behind the flowered wall, back through the side yard between Alvarez's and the house next door. Sparkling clean garbage cans stood in a neat silver row.

A green watering hose snaked up the walkway to a swimming pool with a floating rubber horse which looked ludicrous to Carroll as he started to run. He stopped when he was back out on the street where the FBI team had parked their cars.

A very disturbing thought entered his mind as he climbed into Sommers' Grand Prix.

He never would have done this if Nora was still alive. . . . Never in a thousand years would he have tried this stunt.

Even as he had the thought, which cut deeply, Arch Carroll eased the FBI sedan to the corner, where he made a sweeping right turn, then a quick left onto South Ocean.

A block ahead, he saw Diego Alvarez backing into the Cadillac. He was still holding the white-haired cook against his bare chest. He was screaming wildly at the FBI men, his words lost now in the sea breeze.

Carroll kicked down hard on the accelerator. The sedan's engine twitched from first into third gear. The car licked forward with a screech from the expensive radial tires put on for precisely this kind of breakneck situation.

Suddenly, Carroll's back arched, and his lungs sucked in a deep burst of air.

Don't think about this. Get it over with now.

His gun lay on the car seat right beside him.

The speedometer read thirty, forty, fifty.

Then the front wheels struck the concrete curb loudly with a jolting crunch. The car's front end leaped at least three feet in the air.

All four wheels were off the ground, and the vehicle moved in slow motion because *slow* is the speed at which a car flies.

Carroll double-pumped the sedan's brakes at the last possible moment.

"What the hell—" An FBI man yelled and dove to one side of the lawn.

"Holy shit!" He heard another high-pitched policeman's shout.

Diego Alvarez fired three wildly aimed shots at the careening Pontiac and at Carroll himself inside the car. The sedan's windshield shattered, spitting glass fragments into Carroll's face.

The car was back on all four wheels again, bouncing over the lawn, and over a red tiled walkway. Suddenly it was skidding helplessly on the turf.

Carroll's foot stomped down full force against the gas pedal again. At the last possible instant before contact, he tucked his head down. He held the steering wheel in a vice grip, held on as tight as his arms and hands possibly could.

The bounding FBI car crashed broadside into Diego Alvarez's cherry-red Cadillac. The convertible crumpled. It slid sideways like a hockey puck floating on ice and smashed into the side of the garage.

Half a dozen FBI officers were instantly sprinting across the front lawn. They got there before the two interlocking cars had actually stopped moving.

Revolvers, riot shotguns, M-16 rifles were thrust inside the Cadillac's open front windows.

"Don't move, Alvarez. Don't move an inch," an FBI man screamed. "I said *don't move!*"

Carroll grunted, then he pushed himself painfully out

of the wrecked Pontiac. He roared out Diego Alvarez's name at the top of his voice, surprised by his own intensity. He was still yelling when he grabbed the shirtless drug dealer out of the hands of the FBI agents. The FBI agents stared at him with astonishment.

"Arch Carroll, State Department Special Terrorist Force! You have *no rights!* You hear me? . . . How did you know about Green Band? Who talked to you? You look at me!"

Diego Alvarez said, "Fuck you!" He then spat into Carroll's face.

Carroll shuffled a little to his left, then hit the drug dealer with a sharp-looking right hand delivered to the mouth. Alvarez fell to the ground, already out cold.

"Yeah, fuck you, too!" said the former Bronx street-kid still lurking somewhere inside Carroll. He wiped the dope dealer's saliva from his cheek.

Clark Sommers' mouth fell open, creating a surprised *O* at the center of his suntanned face. A few other Florida FBI studs just shook their heads.

At the FBI office on Collins Avenue in Miami, Diego Alvarez was taken inside a small interrogation room where he told Carroll everything he knew.

"I don't know *who* they are, honest, man. Somebody jus' want you down here to Florida," he said with almost believable sincerity. Because he had been busted with three hundred and fifty thousand dollars' worth of cocaine, and because his prospects of freedom looked grim, he didn't have much to gain by lying. Carroll studied the man as he spoke.

"I swear it. I don't know nothin' more, man. But I got a feelin' somebody playin' some kind of games with you. They set me up, my big mouth. But somebody playin' wit' *you*. . . . Somebody jus' want you come here 'stead of someplace else. They playin' wit' *you*, man. They playin' wit' you real good."

Carroll suddenly wanted to put his head down on the interrogation table in front of him. He'd been used, and he had no idea why. All he knew was that whoever was doing it was extremely smart. They were telling him: *See, we can manipulate you – any which way we like.*

Carroll eventually wandered outside the Miami FBI building and leaned heavily against the warm-baked white stucco wall.

He tried to let the Florida sun soothe his weary brain. He thought that Miami might be a better climate for playing Crusader Rabbit than New York.

He was relatively certain about a couple of disturbing things. . . . The Green Band group, whoever they were, *knew* who he was, and that he would be assigned to the investigation. *How* did they know? What should that tell him about who they might be? . . . They seemed to want him to know how superior, how well organized they were. They wanted him to be a little in awe – and frankly, right now anyway, *he was*.

How did they *know* he'd be assigned to the investigation? Who was trying to send him a cryptic message? Why?

On the plane home – Eastern, the wings of man – Arch Carroll had two beers, then two Irish whiskeys. He could have gone for another two Irish, but he'd promised his rabbi Walter Trentkamp – promised Uncle Walter *something* he couldn't quite remember. Finally, he slept the rest of the way home to New York.

He had a real nice dream on the flight, too. Carroll dreamed that he quit his job with the DIA's antiterrorist division. He and the kids and Nora went to live on the nicest, sugar-white beach in Florida.

In the dream, they all lived happily ever after.

Sunday; December 6;
Green Band Interrogations

8

Caitlin Dillon

Before break of dawn on Sunday morning, Caitlin Dillon waded through a becalmed river of ice and slush that rose four inches above her ankles. Once she successfully emerged on half-deserted Fifth Avenue, the Director of Enforcement for the SEC's Division of Trading and Exchange hailed a yellow cab which reluctantly ferried her down to the 14th Street Police and National Guard Barricades. From 14th Street, Caitlin was transferred by a snazzy police blue and white down into the smoldering chaos and confusion of the financial district itself.

The thirty-block ride went by amazingly fast. There were no working traffic lights below 14th Street. There was almost no other traffic on any of the downtown streets.

The sergeant driving the police car was as good looking as a young actor in a Hollywood cop show. He had long blue-black hair curling over his uniform collar. His name was Signarelli. As she silently rode in the back seat, Caitlin figured he definitely watched "Hill Street Blues."

"Never seen *everything* this bad." The police sergeant revealed a nasal Brooklyn accent when he spoke. His eyes kept darting in and out of the rearview mirror.

"Can't even call in to your normal communications desk. Nerve center they set up is always busy, too. Nobody knows what the Army's doing. What the FBI guys are doing either. It's completely nuts!"

"How would you handle it?" There was nothing patronizing in the question. Caitlin was always curious about the rank and file. That was one reason she made a good boss at the SEC. A second reason was that she was smart, so knowledgeable about Wall Street and the workings of business that most of her associates legitimately held her in awe. "If this was your show, what would you do now, Sergeant?"

"Well . . . I'd hit every terrorist hangout we know about in the city. We know about a hell of a lot of them, too. I'd blow into their little maggot nests. Arrest everybody in sight. That way, we'd sure as hell get some information."

"Sergeant, I believe that's what teams of detectives have been doing all night. Over sixty separate squads of NYPD detectives. But the maggots are just not cooperating on this one."

Caitlin arched her eyebrow, then smiled gently at the cop. Predictably, he asked her for a date next, and just as predictably Caitlin flatly turned him down.

With police and Army helicopters constantly whirring overhead, Caitlin Dillon stood still and numb on the northwest corner of Broadway and Wall. She allowed her eyes to roam across the most chilling surreal scene she hoped to view in her lifetime.

What appeared to be billions of tons of granite block, of gray stone, shattered glass, concrete and mortar had crashed down onto Wall Street and Broad Street and Pell, and all the narrow, interconnecting alleyways. According to the latest Army Intelligence estimate, as many as sixty separate *plastique* bombs had detonated at 6:34 Friday evening. The police theory was that the bombs had been exploded by sophisticated radio signals. The signals could have been transmitted from as far away as ten to twelve miles.

Caitlin craned her neck to gaze up at nearby No. 6 Wall Street. She winced as she observed the sheared, swinging clumps of wiring: thick elevator cables dangling between the highest floors of the office building. Here and there, patches of sky shone through great yawning holes in the building's walls. The overall effect reminded her of a doll house disemboweled, utterly destroyed by a child in a temper tantrum.

She stood all alone, shivering and cold on the stone portal of the New York Stock Exchange. She couldn't stop herself from impassively staring at the abysmal destruction, the incomprehensible damage on Wall Street. More than anything, she wanted to be sick.

She saw an oil painting, a Yankee sailing clipper hanging absurdly in a distant office with two of the room's walls blown away. In the foyer of an adjacent building, an overturned copier had apparently collapsed through several floors before striking the unyielding marble in the lobby. She could see the shattered screens of computer terminals and the melted remains of keyboards that reminded her of some nightmare art form. All over the littered, desolate street, police and hospital emergency vehicles were flashing bright red and blue distress signals.

Caitlin Dillon could feel a cold, dead-weight pushing down on her. Her body was numb. Her ears buzzed softly, as if there had been a sudden drop in air pressure.

She couldn't stop a disturbing feeling of nausea, of sudden weakness in both her legs. She understood what many of the others still didn't – *that an entire way of life had quite possibly been destroyed, here, on Friday night.*

Inside No. 13, Caitlin was confronted immediately by noisy squads of secretaries typing frantically in the marble and stone entryway corridors. Stock Exchange clerks milled around with a kind of busy uselessness, carrying clipboards with a hollow show of self-importance, carting files from one office to another.

Caitlin took in the command post scene and then, as she stepped nimbly around broken glass and debris that had been shaken loose from the ceiling, she was surrounded by heavily armed policemen who demanded to see her identification.

She smiled at herself as she showed her ID. *No one knew who she was*; not a single one of them recognized her here in the Stock Exchange foyer.

How very typical that was. Damn it, how typical.

For the past three years, the SEC's Director of Enforcement had been a most unlikely Wall Street figure: Caitlin Dillon was clearly a major force, yet a person of supreme mystery to almost everybody around her.

Women in general had only been permitted on the floor of the Stock Exchange since 1967. Nevertheless, the idea hadn't particularly caught on. A prominent sign in the visitor's gallery of the Exchange still read:

WOMEN MAKE POOR SPECULATORS. WHEN THROWN UPON THEIR OWN RESOURCES, THEY ARE COMPARATIVELY HELPLESS. EXCELLING IN CERTAIN LINES, THEY ARE FORCED TO TAKE BACKSEATS IN SPECULATION. WITHOUT THE ASSISTANCE OF A MAN, A WOMAN ON WALL STREET IS LIKE A SHIP WITHOUT A RUDDER.

Caitlin Dillon had actually inherited her job because of her predecessor's bad luck in the shape of a sudden, fatal coronary. Caitlin knew that insiders had predicted she wouldn't last two months. They compared the fateful situation with a politician's wife taking over for an unexpectedly invalid husband. Caitlin was called by some "the interim enforcer."

For that reason, and some strong personal ones from her past, she had decided that – for however long she might last in the job – she was going to become the sternest, hardest SEC Enforcement Officer since Professor James Landis had been doing the hiring himself. What did she possibly have to lose?

She was, therefore, stubbornly serious. Some said Caitlin Dillon was unnecessarily obsessed with white-collar criminal investigations, with skillfully prosecuting malfeasance by senior officers of major American Corporations.

"I'll tell you something off the record," Caitlin had once

said to a dear friend, Meg O'Brian, the financial editor of *Newsweek*. "The ten most wanted men in America are all working on Wall Street."

As the "interim" Enforcement Officer at the SEC, Caitlin Dillon made a lot of news very fast. The mystery of Caitlin Dillon – how she had surfaced virtually from nowhere – grew each week she held onto the important job. The powerbrokers on the Street still wanted to replace her, but suddenly they found they couldn't do so very easily. Caitlin was simply too good at what she did. She'd become too visible. She was almost instantly a strong symbol for the disenfranchised in America's financial system.

At seven forty-five that morning, Caitlin finally reached her office inside No. 13 Wall. It was respectably large, even elegant.

She removed her coat and, as she started to sit down, took a deep breath.

On her desk lay a damage report prepared for her the previous night. As her eyes quickly scanned the page, she felt a deepening despair at the sheer amount of destruction done.

The Federal Reserve Bank.
Salomon Brothers.
Bankers Trust.
Affiliated Fund.
Merrill-Lynch.
U.S. Trust Corporation.
The Depository Trust Company.

The list went on to detail fourteen downtown New York buildings that had been partially or completely destroyed.

She closed her eyes, placing the palm of her hand flat against the surface of the report. *Fourteen different buildings in the Wall Street financial district – the whole thing was beyond her, out of control by any measure.*

She opened her eyes.

It was the start of the second day of her formal investigation of Green Band, and she knew no more than she'd known before. This disturbing state of ignorance settled inside her head like a spreading black cloud. It was going to be a long, long Sunday.

Carroll

Arch Carroll strode briskly from a comfortable State Department limousine toward the ominous gray stone entranceway to No. 13 Wall. At least Green Band had left this building mostly intact – a fact that caused him to wonder. If a terrorist cell was going to strike out hard at U.S. capitalism, why wouldn't they destroy the Stock Exchange?

Carroll had on a knee-length, black leather topcoat which Nora had given him the Christmas before her death. At the time she'd joked that it made him look like a tough guy hero in an action movie. The coat was now one of his few personal treasures; that it was a little too tight under the arms didn't matter. There was no way he'd have it altered. He wanted it exactly as it was when Nora had given it to him.

Carroll was smoking a crumpled cigarette. Sometimes on the weekends he wore the coat and smoked crumpled cigarettes when he took Mickey Kevin and Clancy to New York Knick or Ranger games. It made both kids laugh hysterically. They told him he was trying to look like Clint Eastwood in the movies. He wasn't, he knew. Clint Eastwood was trying to look like him: like some nihilistic, tough-guy city cop.

Hurrying down the long, echoing corridors, Carroll pulled his way out of the leather coat. For a few long strides, he left it cape-like over his shoulders. Then he folded it over one arm, in the hope that he'd look a little more civilized. There were a lot of very straight business people in the hallowed halls of No. 13 Wall Street.

Carroll pushed open leather-covered doors into a formal meeting room thick with perspiration and stale tobacco smoke. The room where the New York Stock

Exchange professional staff usually met was the size of a large theater.

The scheduled meeting was already in progress. He was late. He was also weary from his flight, and his nerves – kept moderately alert by an infusion of amphetamine – were beginning to complain. He glanced at his watch. There was another long day ahead of him.

Carroll quickly glanced around the shadowy room. It was filled with New York City police and U.S. Army personnel, with corporate lawyers and investigators from the major banks and brokerage houses on Wall Street. The only seats left were way in front.

Groaning under his breath, Carroll crouched low and made his move toward the front row. He clumsily climbed over gray and blue pinstriped legs, and over someone's abundant lap. It felt like everybody in the room was staring at him – which was probably true enough.

The speaker was saying, "Let me tell you how to make a hell of a lot of money on Wall Street. All you have to do is steal a little from the rich, steal a little from the middle rich, steal a lot from the lower rich . . ."

Nervous laughter cascaded around the vast meeting room. It was a muted, mirthless outbreak that sounded more like a release of fears than anything else.

The speaker went on, "The Wall Street security system simply *doesn't* work. As you all know, the computer setup here is one of the most antiquated in all of the business world. That's why this disaster *could* happen."

Carroll finally sat down, sliding lower and lower until only his head peeked above the theater's gray velvet seat back. His knees were actually pressed against the wooden stage in front.

"The computer system on Wall Street is a complete disgrace . . ."

Carroll's eyes finally rose and took in the meeting's speaker. *Jesus.* He was completely taken aback by the sight of Caitlin Dillon on the podium. Her hair was bobbed at the shoulders, a sleek chestnut-brown color.

Long legs, slender waist. Tall – maybe five foot eight. She looked, if anything, even more intriguing than she'd seemed that first night in Washington.

She was staring down at the first row now. Her brown eyes were very calm, measuring everything they saw. Yes, she was staring directly down at Carroll himself.

"Are you expecting trouble during my briefing, Mr. Carroll?" Her eyes had fastened onto his Magnum, his beat-up leather shoulder holster. He was suddenly embarrassed by her question and the way his name had sounded through her microphone. Those pale red lips seemed to be lightly mocking him.

Carroll didn't know what to say. He shrugged and tried to sink a little deeper into his seat. Why didn't he have one of his usual wisecracks to throw back at her?

Caitlin Dillon smoothly switched her attention back to the audience of senior police officers and heavy-duty Wall Street businessmen. She resumed her briefing at exactly the point where she had interrupted herself, without missing a beat.

"In the past decade," she said, and her next chart efficiently appeared on the screen at her back, "foreign investment in the United States has skyrocketed. Billions of francs, yen, pesos, deutschmarks have flowed into our economy to the sum of eighty-five billion dollars. The Midland Bank of England, for instance, took full control of the Crocker National Bank of California. Nippon Kokan purchased half of the National Steel Corporation. The list goes on and on.

"At this rate, I'm sorry to say, the Japanese, the Arabs, the Germans will very soon control our financial destiny." As Caitlin Dillon recited exhaustive facts and numbers which defined the present situation in the financial community, Carroll listened attentively.

He also watched attentively. Nothing could have drawn his eyes away from her, short of a second Wall Street bombing raid . . .

There was a disarming twinkle in her eyes, an unexpected hint of sweetness in her smile. Was it really

96

sweetness though? *Coyness*? How could she hold down the job she had if she was shy and retiring and sweet? Sweet was not in the Wall Street lexicon.

She was chic – even in a conservative, salt and pepper tweed business suit. She looked stylish, and somehow just *right*.

Most of all, though, she looked *untouchable*.

That was the single word, the most precise idea floating through Carroll's head, that seemed to sum up Caitlin Dillon best.

Untouchable.

In Carroll's experience, neither he nor anybody he knew ever actually got to meet the spectacular-looking women you all too frequently saw in Midtown New York, in Washington, in Paris. Who the hell *did* get to know them? . . . Was there a matching species of *untouchable* men, who Carroll never bothered to notice? . . . What sort of man woke up with this Caitlin Dillon woman next to him? Some super-wealthy Wall Street lion? One of those buccaneers of the stock arbitrage game? Yes, he'd bet anything that was the case.

His attention drifted back to her speech, which was a succinct description of the Green Band emergency, of the current state of Wall Street's insufficient computer records, and the stoppage of all international transfers of funds. She had some sobering and scary material up there on the podium.

"Surprisingly, there's still been no further contact by the terrorist group. *Whatever* kind of group they are. . . . As you may know, *no* actual *demands* were made. No ultimatums. Absolutely no reason has been given so far for what happened on Friday.

"There'll be another meeting after this, for my people and for the analysts. We have to get something going with the computers before the Market opens on Monday. If not. . . . I would expect major unpleasantness."

The meeting room was suddenly still. The scraping of feet, all paper shuffling stopped.

"Are we talking about a Stock Market panic? Some

kind of crash? What sort of *major unpleasantness?*" someone called out.

Caitlin paused before she spoke again. It was obvious
to Carroll that she was choosing her next words with
extreme care and diplomacy.

"I think we all have to recognize . . . that there *is a
possibility*, even a likelihood of some form of Market panic
on Monday morning."

"What constitutes a panic in your mind? Give us a
for-instance." A senior Wall Street man spoke.

"The Market *could* lose several hundred points very
quickly. In a matter of hours. That's *if* they decide to open
on Monday. In Tokyo, London, Geneva, the subject's
still under discussion."

"Several hundred points!" Quite a few of the brokers
groaned. Carroll watched them envisage their comfortable lives eroding. The stretch Mercedes, the Westchester
estates, the fashionable clothes – everything gone. It's so
fucking fragile, he thought.

"Are we talking about a potential Black Friday situation? Are you saying there could actually be a Stock
Market crash?" A voice rose from the back of the
auditorium.

Caitlin frowned. She recognized the speaker, a stiff,
stuffy bean counter from one of the larger Midtown New
York banks.

"I'm not saying anything like that yet. As I suggested
before, if we had a more modern system of computers
down here, if Wall Street had joined the rest of the
twentieth century – we'd know a lot more. Tomorrow is
Monday. We'll all see what happens then. We should be
prepared. That's what I'm suggesting – preparedness. *For
a change.*"

With that, Caitlin Dillon abruptly stepped down off the
auditorium stage. As Carroll watched her walk alone to
the back doors of the room, he became conscious of
another figure approaching him from the side.

He turned in his seat and saw Captain Francis Nicolo
from the New York City Bomb Squad, a cop who liked to

think he was something of a dandy in his three-piece pin-striped suits and sleek, waxed moustache.

"A moment, Arch," Nicolo said, and gestured rather mysteriously for Carroll to follow.

They hurried out of the room and along various dimly lit Stock Exchange corridors, Carroll trailing behind. Nicolo opened the door to a small inner office tucked directly behind the Trading Floor. He closed it with a secretive gesture when Carroll was inside.

"What's happening?" Carroll asked, both curious and slightly amused. "Talk to me, Francis."

"Check this," Nicolo said. He pointed to a plain cardboard box propped on the desk. "Open it. Go ahead."

"What is it?" Carroll hesitantly stepped toward the desk. He laid the tips of his fingers lightly against the box lid.

"Open it. Won't bite your widgit off."

Carroll removed the lid. "Where the hell did this come from?" he asked. "Christ, Frank."

"Janitor found it behind a cistern in one of the men's rooms," Nicolo answered. "Scared the living piss out of the poor guy."

Carroll stared at the device, at the length of shiny green ribbon that was wound elaborately around it. *Green Band*.

"It's harmless," Nicolo said. "It was never meant to go off, Arch."

Arch Carroll continued to stare at the makings of a professional terrorist's bomb. *It was never meant to go off,* he thought. *Another warning?*

"They could have totaled this place," Carroll said with a sick feeling.

Nicolo made a clucking sound with his tongue and the roof of his mouth. "Easily," he said. "Plastique, like all the others. Whoever did it knew what the hell he was up to, Arch."

Carroll wandered over to the office window and peered down into the street, where he saw New York cops standing all over the place, where he saw the incomprehensible war zone.

99

9

Vets 24

Using a single outside tine of his fork, Sergeant Harry
Stemkowsky surgically punctured each of the three
sunny-side-up eggs staring up from his breakfast platter
that Sunday morning. He lathered on a thick wave of
ketchup, then buttered and spread strawberry preserves
on a row of four, hot-toasted Bialy halves. He was ready
to rock and roll.

The superb, greasy spoon meal was his usual, corn-
beef hash, eggs and Bialy breakfast. The place was the
Dream Doughnut and Coffee on 23rd Street and Tenth
Avenue. The meal arrived at the table approximately
three hours into his dayshift driving for Vets. Stemkowsky
had been looking forward to the food all through his first
dreary hours on the road.

Harry Stemkowsky almost always went through the
same exact thought process while he was devouring
breakfast at the Dream . . .

It was so unbelievably good to be out of that piss and
shitting hole Erie VA Hospital. It was just so goddamn
tremendous to be alive again.

He had a valid reason to keep going now, to get really
psyched about his life . . .

*And it was all thanks to Colonel David Hudson. Who
happened to be the best soldier, the best friend, one of the best
men Stemkowsky had ever met. Colonel Hudson had given all
the Vets another chance. He'd given them the Green Band
Mission to get even.*

Later that same morning, as he slalomed through the deep slush of Jane Street in the West Village, Colonel David Hudson thought he might be seeing apparitions. He finally leaned his head out of the half-rolled Vets taxi window. His green eyes sparkled intensely against the street's murky gray.

He shouted ahead into the cold driving rain, the dripping winds ripping and grabbing at his face. "You're going to *rust* out there, Sergeant. Get your pitiful ass inside."

Harry Stemkowsky was solidly perched outside in his familiar, battered aluminum wheelchair. He was huddled zombielike against the drowning rain, right in front of the Vets garage entrance.

It was an incredibly moving sight, probably more sad than weird, Hudson thought. A true retrospective on what was ultimately accomplished in Viet Nam. There was Harry Stemkowsky, as poignant as any journalist's picture taken of the wounded in the Southeast Asia combat zone. Hudson could feel a tightening of his jaw muscles, and the beginnings of an old rage. He fought against it successfully. This wasn't the time to allow himself the luxury of personal feelings. This wasn't the time to wallow in old, pointless anger.

Stemkowsky was grinning broadly by the time David Hudson finally jogged to the weathered door of the Vets garage. "You're section eight for life, Sergeant. You're out of your mind," Hudson said firmly. "No explanations accepted."

Actually though, Hudson was beginning to smile. He knew why Stemkowsky was waiting outside, knew all of the Vets' Sad Sack stories by heart now. He was betting everything on knowing the Vets at least as well as he knew their military histories.

"I-I wha-wanted to be ri-right he-here. When, when you got in. That-that-that's all it was, Cah-Cah-Colonel."

Hudson's voice softened. "Yeah, I know, I know. It's

real good to see you again, Sergeant. You're still an asshole, though."

With an audible sigh, Colonel David Hudson suddenly bent low. He then easily scooped up the hundred-and-thirty-seven-pound bundle of Harry Stemkowsky with his powerful good arm.

Since the spring offensive of 1971, Stemkowsky had been a helpless cripple. Harry Stemkowsky had also been a violent, totally incurable stutterer ever since he'd been splattered with seventeen rounds from a Soviet SKS automatic rifle. A pitiful wreck, right up until a few months ago, anyway.

As he pushed his way to the top of the cramped, mildewed stairway inside Vets, Hudson decided not to think about Viet Nam anymore. This was supposed to be an R&R party. Green Band was a rousing operational success so far. George Thorogood's "Bad to the Bone" blared loudly from the room above. Good tune. Good choice.

"It's the Colonel himself!"

As he stalked inside a large, drab yellow room on the second floor, David Hudson heard shrill hollers and shouts all around him. For a moment he was embarrassed by the clamor. Then he thought about the fact that he'd given these twenty-six veterans another lease on their lives, a purpose that transcended the bitterness they had brought back from Viet Nam.

"The Colonel's here! Colonel Hudson's here. Hide the girls."

"Well, shit. Hide the good Johnny Walker booze, too. . . . Just kidding, sir."

"How the hell are you, Bonanno? Hale? Skully?"

"Sir . . . we goddamn did it, didn't we!"

"Yes, we did. So far, anyway."

"Sir! It's great to see you. Went just like you said it would."

"Yeah. The easy part did."

The twenty-six men continued to cheer. Hudson shielded his eyes as he stared around at the dingy room

102

where they'd been plotting together for almost a year and a half. He scanned the rows of familiar faces, the scraggly, homecut beards, the unfashionably long hairstyles, the drab green khaki jackets of the Vets. He was home. He was home and he was obviously welcome. He could feel the vibrations of unadulterated warmth that these men felt toward him. And for one brief moment Colonel David Hudson almost lost control: there was a tightening at the back of his throat, a feeling of moisture behind his eyes.

David Hudson finally offered a wry conspiratorial smile. "It's good to see you all again. Carry on with your party. That's *an order.*"

Hudson ambled on, gripping hands, greeting the rest of the Vets group: Jimmy Cassio, Harold Freedman, Mahoney, Keresty, McMahon, Martinez – all men who hadn't been able to fit back into American society after the South Asian war, all men he'd recruited for Green Band during the past sixteen months.

As he walked, Hudson thought deeply about his men; his final combat command; the final mission.

The twenty-six Vets were antisocial, chronically unemployable; they were dramatic losers by the standard American measurements of success and accomplishments. At least half of them still suffered some form of PTSD, the Post Traumatic Stress Syndrome so common among war veterans, an illness which had startlingly tripled after Viet Nam. PTSD involved constantly re-experiencing combat trauma in an endless series of flashbacks, nightmares, extremely intrusive memories. Among other things, PTSD seemed to cause emotional numbing, a kind of paranoid-schizzy withdrawal from the external environment, sometimes compounded with the guilt of having survived.

David Hudson knew all this from personal experience: he still suffered from PTSD himself. He suffered more pain than anyone would ever be permitted to know.

The twenty-six men packed into the cabdrivers' locker room had performed spectacularly in Viet Nam and

Cambodia. Every one of them had served under Hudson at one time or another. Each man was a highly trained technical specialist; each had a totally unique skill, which no one other than Hudson seemed to want or need in civilian society.

Steve "the Horse" Glickman and Pauly "Mr. Blue" Melindez were the finest rifleman-sniper team Hudson had ever commanded in the field.

Michael Demunn and Rich Scully were experts at ordnance, at assembling and creating complex plastique explosives in particular.

Manning Rubin could have been making a thousand a week for either Ford or GM. *If* his skill at fixing automobiles had been matched by patience, just a little ability to handle suburban bullshit . . .

Davey Hale had an encyclopedic knowledge of just about everything, including the Wall Street Stock Market.

Campbell, Bowen, Kamerer and Generalli were high-caliber professional soldiers and mercenaries. Since Viet Nam they'd soldiered for pay in Angola, in San Salvador, even in the streets of Miami. The combat group was particularly lethal at close quarter, hand-to-hand urban street fighting. That single fact would be their key advantage entering the second stage of the Green Band mission.

"All right gentlemen. We have to do some homework now," Hudson finally spoke. "This is the last time we'll have the chance to review these details and any of our final operating schedules. If this sounds like a formal military briefing, that's because *it damn well is*."

David Hudson paused methodically and looked around at the circle of assembled faces. Each was turned toward him with intense concentration. There was a bond in this intimate war room, he knew, that went beyond Green Band. It was a bond of blood and hopefulness, forged out of a shared, tragic history.

"Personal anecdote, gentlemen. . . . At the highly thought of JFK School at Fort Bragg, they repeatedly told us that 'genius is in the details.' When the truth of that finally sunk in, it held like nothing I've ever learned before or since . . .

"So I want to go over the final details one last time. Maybe two last times with all of you. Details, gentlemen . . .

"If we master the details, we win. If the details master us, we lose. *Just like in Nam.*"

Vets One had purposely modeled his presentation after the concise and always very technical Special Forces field briefings. He wanted these men to vividly remember Viet Nam now. He wanted them to remember precisely how they'd acted: with daring and courage, with dedication to the United States, with honor at all times.

Hudson could feel his own body pulsing and tingling lightly. He spoke to the men without using any written notes – everything was committed to memory.

His personal grasp of minutiae and military theory was riveting that afternoon in early December. For nearly two and a half hours, Colonel David Hudson painstakingly reviewed every foreseeable scenario, every likely and even unlikely change that might occur up to and including the end of the Green Band mission. He used combat-proven memory aids: reconnaissance topographical maps, mnemonics for memorizing; Army-style organizational charts.

A deep gravelled voice finally sounded from the shadowy rear of the Vets locker room.

One of the combat mercenaries, a Southern black named Clint Hurdle, had taken the floor. "Why you so sure there won't be no attacks of conscience? This going to heat up now, Colonel. Who says nobody going to fuck up and run?"

There was a startled hush around the small room.

Hudson seemed to consider the question extremely carefully before answering. He had in fact posed almost the same question hundreds of times in his own head. He always assumed the worst, then created a number of

105

alternative ways to effectively deal with, and avoid, disaster.

"*Nobody*, not a single one of you men, broke during combat. . . . Not even in a war none of you wanted or believed in. . . . *Nobody broke in POW camps! Not one of you!* . . . None of you will break now, either. I'm fully prepared to bet everything we've worked for on that."

There was an uncomfortable silence after the difficult question and emotional answer. David Hudson's intense green eyes slowly surveyed the Vets dressing room one more time.

He wanted them to feel in their guts that he was sure about everything he'd just said. The way he *was* sure. Even though it might not look it, every man in the room had been carefully handpicked from hundreds of possible vets. Every soldier in the room was special.

"If any one of you wants to leave, though, this is the time. . . . *Right now*, gentlemen. This afternoon. . . . Anybody? . . . Anybody who wants to leave us? . . ."

One Vet slowly started to clap. Then the rest of them.

Finally, all twenty-six men were solemnly clapping their hands. Whatever was going to happen, they were together in it now.

Colonel Hudson slowly nodded: the cocksure military commander once again took control.

"I've saved the foreign travel assignments, the specific assignments until last.

"I'm not going to entertain any discussion, any disagreement at all over these assignments. The operational environment is already confused. *We* will not be confused. That's another reason we're going to win *this war*."

Colonel David Hudson walked to a long wooden table from which he began to pass out thick, official-looking portfolios. Each one had a white tag carefully pasted onto the front.

Inside the envelopes were counterfeit U.S. passports and visas, first-class airplane tickets, extremely generous expense monies; copies of elaborate topographical maps from the briefing. *The genius was all in the details.*

"Cassio will go to Zurich," Hudson began to announce.

"Stemkowsky and Cohen have Israel and Iran . . .

"Skully will go to Paris. Harold Freedman to London, then on to Toronto. Jimmy Holm to Tokyo. Vic Fahey to Belfast. The rest of us stay put right here in New York."

A schoolboy's groan went up. Hudson silenced it instantly with a short, chopping hand motion.

"Gentlemen. I'll say this one time only, so you have to remember it. . . . While you're in Europe, in Asia, in South America, it is absolutely *essential* that you act, that you groom and dress yourselves in the *particular style* we've laid out for you. Remember the catch phrase: *nothing succeeds like excess* . . .

"All your air travel arrangements are first class. All your clothing and restaurant expense money is meant to be *spent*. Spend that money. Throw it around. Be more extravagant than you've ever been in your lives. Have fun, if you *can* under the circumstances. That's an order!"

Hudson eased up. "For the next few days, you have to be self-assured, successful American business types. You have to be like the people we've been studying on Wall Street for the past year. *Think* like a Wall Street man, *look* like one, *act* like a high-powered Wall Street executive.

"At 0430, you'll be given self-respecting corporate haircuts, shaves, and – believe it or not – manicures.

"Your wardrobes have been carefully selected for you, too. They're Brooks Brothers and Paul Stuart – your favorite shops, gentlemen. Your shirts and ties are Turnbull and Asser. Your billfolds are from Dunhill. They contain credit cards and plenty of cash in the appropriate denominations you'll need in your respective countries."

Colonel David Hudson paused. His eyes slowly roamed across the room.

"I think that's all I have to say. . . . Except one important thing . . . I wish you all the very best luck possible. I wish you the best, in the future after this mission. . . . *I believe in you. Believe in yourselves."*

Colonel David Hudson briefly shut his eyes, then slowly opened them again. It was impossible to tell what he was thinking. His face gave nothing away. No emotion. No expectation. No anxiety. It might have been a blank mask, as he stared at the handful of men gathered in the dressing room.

He raised his arm and, in a gesture that was almost religious, he said, *"Let us now embark on our rendezvous with destiny."*

10

No. 13 Wall

It was three o'clock on Sunday afternoon when Arch Carroll kicked both weathered Timberland work boots up on his desk inside No. 13. He yawned until his jaw cracked; it felt as if it had just been dislocated.

He'd already finished four absolutely draining and futile interrogations. He'd been lied to by the very best – the most dangerous *provocateurs* and terrorists from all around New York.

Carroll had purposely chosen a cramped office for himself, tucked away at the back of the Wall Street building. His small but hearty DIA group, a half-dozen unorthodox police renegades, two efficient and extremely resilient secretaries, surrounded the uninspiring office in a satellite of Wall Street-style cubicles.

Paint peeled from the walls of Carroll's office like diseased skin; the windowpane had been shattered courtesy of Green Band. He'd tacked a square of brown paper to the hole but rain soaked through anyway. It was a depressing working space for a depressing task. Even the light that managed to fall inside was oppressive, mangy brown, dim and hopeless.

The first four suspects Carroll had interviewed were known terrorists who lived in the New York City area: two FALN, a PLO, an IRA fund-raiser. Unfortunately, the four were no more knowledgeable about the Wall Street mystery than Carroll was himself. There was *nothing circulating on the street*. Each of them convincingly swore to that after exhaustively long sessions.

Carroll wondered how it could be possible. *Somebody*

had to know something about Green Band. You couldn't calmly blow away half of Wall Street and keep it a state secret for over forty hours.

The scarred and rusted wooden door into his office opened again. Carroll watched the door over the smoking cardboard lid of his coffee container.

Mike Caruso, who worked for Carroll at the DIA, finally peeked inside. Caruso was a small, skinny, ex-office cop, with a black fifties pompadour pushed up high over his forehead. He habitually wore wretched Hawaiian shirts outside his baggy pants, attempting to create a splash of colorful identity in the usually drab police world. Carroll liked him immensely for his dedicated lack of style.

"We got Isabella Marqueza up next. She's already screaming for her fancy Park Avenue lawyer. I mean the lady is fucking *screaming* out there."

"That sounds promising. Somebody's upset at least. Why don't you bring her right in?"

Moments later the Brazilian woman appeared like a sudden tropical windstorm inside the office. "You can't do this to me! I'm a citizen of Brazil!"

"Excuse me. You must be mistaking me for somebody who gives a shit. Why don't you please sit down." Carroll spoke without getting up from his cluttered work desk.

"Why? Who do you think you are?"

"I said, sit down, Marqueza. I ask the questions here, not you."

Arch Carroll leaned back in his chair and studied Isabella Marqueza. The Brazilian woman had shoulder-length, gleaming black hair. Her lips were full and painted very red. There was an arrogant tilt to her chin. Her hair, her clothes, even her skin seemed expensive and cosmopolitan. She had on tight gray velvet riding pants, a silk shirt, cowboy boots, a half-length fur jacket. Terrorist chic, Carroll thought.

"You dress like a very wealthy Che Guevara." Carroll finally smiled.

110

"I don't appreciate your attempt of humor, senhor."

"No, well, join the crowd." Arch Carroll's smile now broadened. "I don't appreciate your attempts at mass murder."

Carroll already knew this striking woman by reputation at least. Isabella Marqueza was an internationally renowned journalist and news-magazine photographer. She was the daughter of a wealthy man who owned tire factories in Sao Paulo, Brazil. Though it apparently couldn't be legally proved, Isabella Marqueza had sanctioned at least four American deaths in the past twelve months.

She was responsible, Carroll knew, for the disappearance, then the cold-blooded, heartless murders of a Shell Oil executive and his family. The American businessman, his wife, their two small girls had vanished that past June in Rio. Their pitiful, mutilated bodies had been found in a sewer ditch inside the *favelos*. Isabella Marqueza reportedly worked for the GRU through François Monserrat. According to rumors, Isabella had also been Monserrat's lover. A classic spider woman.

She tossed Carroll the coldest, most indignant look he could imagine. Her dark, sullen eyes smoldered as she stared him down in practiced silence.

Arch Carroll wearily shook his head. He set aside the steaming coffee container. The impression he got from Isabella was that of a tempest about to unleash its force. He watched as she leaned forward and thumped her hands on the desk: the fiery light, the gleam in her dark eyes was really something.

"*I want to see my lawyer!* Right now! I want my lawyer! You get my lawyer. Now, senhor!"

"Nobody even knows you're here." Carroll spoke in a purposely soft, polite voice. Whatever she did, however she acted – he would do the exact opposite, he'd decided. Step one of his interrogation technique.

He said nothing further for the first uncomfortable moments. He'd learned his interrogation technique from the very best – Walter Trentkamp.

111

Carroll knew that two of his DIA agents had illegally intercepted Isabella Marqueza as she walked down East 70th Street after leaving her Midtown apartment that morning. She'd screamed out, struggled and fought as they grabbed her off the streets. "Murder! Somebody please help me!"

Half a dozen East Side New Yorkers, with the anesthetized look of people observing a distant event which interests but doesn't particularly involve them, had watched the terrifying scene. One of them had finally yelled as Isabella Marqueza was dragged, fighting and sobbing, into a waiting station wagon. The rest did nothing at all to help.

"You people kidnap me off the streets," Isabella Marqueza angrily complained. Her red mouth pouted, another part of her routine interrogation act.

"Let me confess to you. Let me be honest, and kind of frank," Carroll said, still going gently. "In the last few years, I've had to kidnap a few people like yourself. Call it the new justice. Call it anything you like. Kidnapping's lost most of its glitter for me."

The louder Isabella Marqueza got, the softer Carroll's speaking voice became. "I kind of like the idea of being a kidnapper. I kidnap terrorists. It's got a nice ring to it, you know. Don't you think?"

"I demand to see my lawyer! Goddam you! My lawyer is Daniel Curzon. You know that name?"

Arch Carroll nodded and shrugged. He knew Daniel Curzon. Curzon worked for both the PLO and Castro's Cubans in New York.

"Daniel Curzon's a piece of sorry shit. I don't want to hear Curzon's name again. I'm serious about that."

Carroll's eyes now fell to a manila package, a plain-looking folder wrapped in brown string on his littered desk. Inside was his moral justification to do whatever he needed to do right now.

Inside the tan envelope were a dozen or so black-and-white and 35-millimeter color photographs of the Jason Miller family, formerly of Rio: the murdered family of the

112

Shell Oil executive. There were also grainy photographs of an American couple who had disappeared in Jamaica, pictures of a Unilever accountant from Colombia, a man named Jordon who had disappeared last spring. Isabella Marqueza was suspected of murdering all eight Americans.

Carroll continued softly. "Anyway, my name's Arch Carroll. Born right here in New York City. Local boy makes good. . . . Son of a cop who was the son of a cop. Not a lot of imagination at work in our family, I'll admit. Just your basic poor working slobs."

Carroll paused briefly. He lit up a leftover cigarette stub, Crusader Rabbit style. "My job is to locate terrorists who threaten the security of the United States. Then, if they're not too strongly politically connected, *protected*, I try my best to put a stop to them . . .

"Put it another way, you *could* say I'm a terrorist for the United States. I play by the same rules you do. . . . *No rules*. So stop talking about Park Avenue lawyers, please. Lawyers are for nice, civilized people who play by the rules. Not for us."

Carroll slowly untied the string bow on the manila envelope. Then he slid out the handful of photographs inside.

He casually passed them over to Isabella Marqueza. The pictures were the most obscene pornography he thought he'd ever seen. Still, he remained calm.

"Jason Miller's body. Jason Miller was an engineer for Shell Oil. He was also a financial investigator for the State Department, as you and your people in Sao Paulo know. A fairly nice man, I understand. . . . Information-gatherer for State, I'll admit. Basically harmless, though. Another poor working slob."

Carroll made soft clicking noises with his tongue. His eyes briefly met those of Isabella Marqueza.

She was quiet suddenly. His putting-green voice was throwing her off slightly. She obviously hadn't expected to encounter the deck of photographs, either.

"Miller's wife Judy there. Alive in this photo. Kind of a

113

nice Midwestern smile. . . . Two little girls. Their bodies, that is. I have two little girls myself. Two girls, two boys. How could anybody kill little kids, huh?"

Carroll smiled again. He cleared his throat. He needed a beer – a beer and a stiff shot of Irish would go down real good right now. He studied Isabella Marqueza a moment. There was an urge inside him to get up and just go around the desk and whack her. Instead, he kept speaking very gently.

"In July of last year, you ordered and then participated in the premeditated murders, the political assassination of all four Millers."

Isabella Marqueza instantly shot up from her seat in the interrogation room. She began to yell at Carroll again.

"I did nothing of this sort! You prove what you say! No! I did not kill anybody. Never. I don't kill children!"

"Bullshit. That's the end of our friendly discussion. Who the fuck do you think you're kidding?"

With that Arch Carroll slapped the wrinkled manila portfolio shut, he jammed it back in his lopsided desk drawer. He looked up at Isabella Marqueza again.

"*Nobody* knows you're here! Do you have that memorized? Nobody's going to know what happened to you after today. That's the truth. Just like the Miller family down in Brazil."

"You're full of shit, Carroll—"

"Yeah? Try me. Push me a little and find out for sure."

"My lawyer, I want to see my lawyer—"

"Never heard of him—"

"I told you his name, Curzon—"

"Did you? I don't remember—"

Isabella Marqueza sighed. She stared at Carroll in silence. Her expression was one of exquisitely cold hatred. She folded her arms, then sat down again. She crossed and uncrossed her long legs and lit a cigarette.

"Why are you doing this to me? You're crazy."

This was a little better, Carroll thought. He could sense she was melting a little, cracking at the edges.

"Tell me about Jack Jordan down in Colombia.

114

American business accountant. Machine-gunned to death in his driveway. His wife got to watch."

"I never heard of him."

Carroll clucked his tongue and slowly shook his head back and forth. He seemed genuinely disappointed. Sitting behind the bare, bleak office desk, he looked like someone whose best friend had just inexplicably lied to him.

"Isabella. Isabella." He gave an exaggerated sigh. "I don't think you get the total picture. I don't think you really understand." He stood up, stretched his arms, fought back a yawn. "You see, *you no longer exist*. You *died* suddenly this morning. Taxi accident on East Seventieth Street. Nobody bothered to tell you?"

Carroll was feeling dangerously overloaded now. He didn't want to finish this brutal interrogation. He walked out of the questioning room without saying another word.

He'd done his best, he thought as he idly patrolled the long, blurry hallway outside, passing busy secretaries who were tapping away at purring typewriters.

He walked with his head down, talking to no one. Blood pounded furiously in his forehead. He was drained and bleached and his throat was dry. The vision of a cold beer and a shot had rooted itself firmly in his mind, and the image was roaring for attention.

He paused at a water fountain, pressed the button and cold water splashed across his face. It was better than nothing. He wiped his puckered lips with the back of his hand, then leaned against the wall. Isabella Marqueza. Green Band. A green ribbon tied neatly, *almost cheerfully*, around a plastique bomb in a cardboard box.

Questions. Too many disconnected questions. He didn't have any answers at all. He doubted whether Walter Trentkamp himself could have cracked through to Isabella Marqueza.

He pushed himself away from the wall and continued to walk in a slight daze.

Ordinarily, Carroll might have felt badly about the

115

harshness of the Marqueza interrogation. Except he kept seeing the creased snapshot faces of the two little Miller girls – senselessly murdered. Those two innocent babies helped put Isabella Marqueza in perspective for him. Beautiful Isabella was a worthless piece of shit.

He finally trudged back to his office where Isabella Marqueza was waiting.

She looked like a sadly wilting flower. He'd read in her files that she'd joined a GRU terrorist cell in 1978, after which she'd worked for François Monserrat in South America, then in Montreal and Paris, finally here in New York. Her supposed weakness was that she had little tolerance for discomfort and physical pain. She'd never had to suffer any in her life. Carroll momentarily considered that, then he moved in for the kill.

An hour and a half later, Carroll and Isabella Marqueza were finally beginning to communicate. Carroll sipped the day's hundredth coffee. His stomach had begun to scream at him for unnecessary abuse.

"You *were* François Monserrat's mistress here in New York. Come on. *We already know about that.* Two summers ago. Right here in Nueva York."

Isabella Marqueza sat with her head hanging. She wouldn't look up at Carroll for long stretches of time. Dark sweat stains had spread under her arms. Her right leg kept nervously tapping the floor, but she didn't seem aware of it. She looked almost physically ill.

"Who the *hell* is Monserrat?" Carroll kept up his staccato attack. Stage three of his interrogation.

"How does Monserrat get his information? How does he get information that no one outside the U.S. government could possibly get? *Who is he?*"

Carroll could hear his own loud voice as if it were a foreign sound in an echo chamber. "Listen. . . . Listen to me very carefully. . . . If you talk to me right now, if you tell me about François Monserrat – *just his part in the bombings on Wall Street.* . . . If you do that much, I can let you leave here, I promise you. No one will know you

116

were here. Just tell me about the Wall Street bombings. Nothing more than that. Nothing else. . . . What does François Monserrat know about the fire bombings? . . ."

It took thirty minutes more of cajoling, threatening, screaming at Marqueza, thirty grueling minutes in which Carroll's voice turned hoarse and his face red, thirty minutes during which his shirt stuck to his sweaty body, before Isabella Marqueza finally stood up and shouted at him.

"Monserrat had nothing to do with it! He doesn't understand it either. . . . Nobody understands what the bombings are all about. He's looking for Green Band too! *Monserrat is looking for them too!"*

"How do you *know* that, Isabella? How do you *know* what Monserrat is doing? You must have seen him!"

The woman clapped the palm of one hand across her hollow, darkened eyes. "I *haven't* seen him. I *don't* see him. Not ever."

"Then how do you know?"

"There are telephone messages. There are sometimes whispers in private places. *Nobody* sees Monserrat."

"Where is he, Isabella? Is he here in New York? Where the hell is he?"

The South American woman stubbornly shook her head. "I don't know that either."

"What does Monserrat look like these days?"

"How should I know that? How should I know anything like that? He changes. Monserrat is always changing. Sometimes dark hair, a moustache. Sometimes gray hair. Dark glasses. Sometimes a beard." She paused. "Monserrat doesn't have a face."

Now, conscious of having said too much, Isabella Marqueza had begun to sob loudly. Carroll sat back and finally let his head rest against the grimy office wall. She didn't know anything more; he was almost certain he'd gone as far into her as he could possibly go.

Nobody knew anything concrete about Green Band.
Only that wasn't possible.
Somebody had to know what the hell Green Band wanted.

117

Who, though?

Carroll looked up at the interrogation room ceiling before he shut his sore and heavy eyes.

Caitlin Dillon

Faded, yellowing newspapers, at least a dozen different ones dated October 25, 1929, were haphazardly spread across a heavy oak library-style work table. The thirty- and forty-point headlines seemed as jarring now as they must have been fifty-odd years before.

WORST STOCK CRASH EVER; 12,894,650-SHARE DAY SWAMPS MARKET; LEADERS CONFER, FIND CONDITIONS SOUND.

WALLS STREET PANIC! RECORD SELLING OF STOCKS! HEAVY FALL IN PRICES!

STOCK PRICES SLUMP $14,000,000,000 IN NATION-WIDE STAMPEDE TO UNLOAD; BANKERS TO SUPPORT MARKET TODAY.

PRICES OF STOCKS CRASH IN HEAVY LIQUIDATION, TOTAL DROP OF BILLIONS.

TWO MILLION SIX HUNDRED THOUSAND SHARES SOLD IN THE FINAL HOUR IN RECORD DECLINE!

MANY INDIVIDUAL ACCOUNTS WIPED OUT COMPLETELY!

WHEAT SMASHED! CHICAGO PIT IN TURMOIL.

HOOVER PROMISES BUSINESS OF THE COUNTRY IS STILL SOUND AND PROSPEROUS!

Caitlin Dillon finally stood up from the work table and its musty newspaper clippings. She stretched her arms high over her head and sighed. She was on the fifth floor of No. 13 Wall, with Anton Birnbaum from the New York Stock Exchange Steering Committee.

Anton Birnbaum was one of America's true financial geniuses, a wizard. If anyone understood that precarious castle of cards called Wall Street, it was Birnbaum. He had started, Caitlin knew, as an insignificant office boy at the age of eleven. Then he'd worked his way up through the market hierarchy to control his own huge investment house. Caitlin respected him more than any other man in the money business. Even at eighty-three his mind remained as sharp as a blade, and a mischievous light still burned in his eyes. She knew that now and then, Anton Birnbaum looked over her appraisingly, delighted to be in the company of a young, attractive, and undeniably sharp-witted woman.

Once, there had even been a bizarre rumor on Wall Street that Birnbaum might be having a final fling with Caitlin Dillon. The relentless, often ridiculous gossip on the male-dominated Street was perhaps the most difficult business reality for any woman to face, or stomach. If a woman broker or lawyer was seen having drinks or dinner with a man, it was assumed they were having a romance. Early on, Caitlin had realized that the sleazy, degrading practice was some men's way of reducing the threat women posed to their power base on Wall Street.

Actually, Caitlin had met Anton Birnbaum years before while she was still at Wharton. Her thesis advisor had invited the Financier for a guest lecture during her final year. After one of his characteristically iconoclastic talks, Birnbaum had consented to private sessions with a few of the business school's brightest students. One of them turned out to be Caitlin Dillon, about whom Birnbaum later told her advisor: "She is extremely intense, and quite brilliant. Her only flaw is that she is beautiful. I mean that quite seriously. It will be a problem for her on Wall Street. It will be a serious handicap."

When Caitlin Dillon graduated from Wharton, Anton Birnbaum nevertheless hired her as an assistant at his brokerage firm. Within a year, Caitlin was one of his personal assistants. Unlike many of the people he hired, Caitlin would disagree with the great Financier when she felt he was off base. Early in 1978, she correctly called the market *bottom*; then the *top* right before the bloody October massacre. Anton Birnbaum began to listen even more closely to his young, and still very intense, assistant after that.

During that period Caitlin also began to make the Wall

Street and Washington connections she needed for the future. Her first job with Anton Birnbaum provided an education she couldn't have paid to receive. Caitlin found the Financier totally impossible to work for, but somehow she worked for him, which proved to Birnbaum that she was as outstanding as he had initially thought she was.

"Anton, *who* would *benefit* from a Stock Market crash right now? Let's make ourselves a complete list, a physical list, as some kind of starting place."

"All right, let's explore that avenue, then. People who would *benefit* from a Market crash?" Anton Birnbaum took a legal pad and pencil in hand. "A multinational that has a huge discrepancy to hide?"

"That's one. Or the Soviets. They'd possibly benefit – in terms of world prestige, anyway . . ."

"Then perhaps one of the Third World madmen? I believe Qadaffi is psychologically capable of something like this. Perhaps capable of getting the necessary financing, as well."

Caitlin looked at her watch, a functional, ten-year-old Bulova, a gift from her father one Christmas back home in Ohio. "I don't know *what* to try next. What are they waiting for? What in God's name happens when the Market opens on Monday?"

Anton Birnbaum took off his horn-rimmed eyeglasses. He rubbed the bridge of his bulbous nose, which was reddened and deeply indented. "Will the Market even open, Caitlin? The French want it to. They're insisting *they* will open in Paris. I don't know, though. Perhaps it's one of their typical bluffs."

"Which means the Arabs want their French Banks open. Some toady in Paris either wants to take advantage of this awful situation – or they hope to get some of their money out, *before* there's a complete panic."

Anton Birnbaum replaced his glasses. He gazed at Caitlin for a moment. Then he gave one of his characteristic shrugs, a huffy gesture of the shoulders that was barely perceptible. "President Kearney is at least talking with the French. They've never appreciated him tremendously, though. We haven't been able to placate them since Kissinger."

"What about London? What about Geneva? How about right here in New York, Anton?"

"They're all watching France, I'm afraid. France is threatening to open their market, business as usual on Monday. The French, my dear, are being carefully, carefully orchestrated. But by whom? And for what possible reason? What is coming next?" Birnbaum placed his fingertips together, making a small cathedral of his ancient hands. He narrowed his eyes and looked thoughtfully at Caitlin.

Both Caitlin and the old man were quiet for several moments. Over the years they had become comfortable with long periods of silent thought when they were examining a problem together. Caitlin watched as the Financier took out a cigar, his only remaining vice, and stroked and lit it methodically.

Within moments, the room was filled with a soft blue fog. Birnbaum studied the glowing tip of the cigar, then set it down in a well-worn brass ashtray.

"I'll tell you something, my dear. In all my years on the Street, I have never felt this apprehensive. Not even in October of 1929."

François Monserrat

Bendel's on 57th had been open all day Sunday for the usual neurotic rush of Christmas shopping. Store sales were dramatically down, however, affected by the Wall Street panic and the financial uncertainty reigning not only in New York but across the United States.

François Monserrat entered the very chic and expensive department store at a little past 6:30 that evening. Another snowstorm was darkly threatening outside. Winter skies had descended like a heavy curtain over the entire East Coast.

121

Monserrat was wearing thick wire-rimmed glasses and an unmemorable gray tweed overcoat. He also wore a matching hat and black gloves, all of which created a monochromatic impression. The wire-rimmed glasses magnified his eyes for observers, but didn't distort his view of the world. He'd had them especially made by a lens grinder on the Rue des Postes in Bizerte, a city north of Tunis.

Monserrat quietly marveled as he got off a crowded elevator onto one of the upper floors. There was nowhere else, no city he knew of, in which one consistently saw quite so many provocative and stunning women. Even the store's perfume demonstrators were dreamily sensual and exotic. A stylishly anorexic black girl approached and asked if he'd like to experience the *new* Opium.

"I've already experienced it. In Thailand, my dear," François Monserrat answered with a shy smile and an effete wave of the hand.

The demonstrator simply smiled back, slinking off to politely, but seductively, try the next customer.

A thick gallery of shoppers hugging glittering shopping bags from other famous department stores moved slowly before Monserrat's wandering eyes. "Winter Wonderland" played gaily from a hidden stereo system.

It was taxing and exceedingly difficult to move forward in certain directions, more like visiting a New York disco than a store at Christmas time.

François Monserrat cautiously moved toward the rear of the store. With some amusement, he wondered how Juan Carlos would have reacted to the blatant outrage of capitalism that was Henri Bendel's. . . . In 1979 – because his flagrant need for publicity had finally rendered him ineffective – Ilych Sanchez, "Juan Carlos," had been quietly retired by the Soviet GRU. Carlos had, in fact, been brought to live in the one capital city where he was reasonably safe from political assassination – Moscow itself.

That same year, François Monserrat expanded his tightfisted control of North and South America to include

Western Europe. Carlos's protégés, Wadi Haddad and George Habbash, reluctantly came under Monserrat's widening sphere. A completely new philosophy for Soviet terror had begun: *strategic and controlled terror; terror more often than not programmed by Moscow's sophisticated computers.*

By its very nature, the world of the terrorist was a foggy, vaporous place and information had a tendency to be either sketchy or hyperbolic. The sinewy avenues of communication and news were vague at times, at other times overloaded with rumor and innuendo. Given these conditions, it wasn't long before all manner of terrorist acts were being attributed to Monserrat and his people. The murder of Anwar Sadat, the attempted assassination of Pope John Paul II, the Provo bombings in central London . . .

As he strolled through the store, Monserrat reflected on his reputation with a measure of pride. What did it matter if he'd been responsible for this act or that one – when his only real goal, his sole driving force, was the total disruption and eventual fall of the West? A dead Egyptian President. A wounded Pope. A few Irish bombs. These amounted to nothing more than grains of sand on a beach. What François Monserrat was interested in changing was the direction of the tide itself . . .

The bubbling crowd inside Bendel's ebbed and flowed. The predominantly female shoppers milled anxiously in all directions around François Monserrat.

He finally saw the woman he'd followed. She was sifting through a long rack of cocktail dresses, always thinking of her appearance, always defining her existence through her beautiful reflection.

Monserrat concealed himself behind a display case of sweaters, and continued to watch. He felt a certain coldness in the center of his head, as if his brain had become a solid fist of ice. It was a feeling he knew in certain situations. Where other men would experience the uncontrollable rush of adrenaline, Monserrat experienced what he thought of as the Chill. It was almost as if he'd been born with a chemical imbalance.

Every man who passed checked Isabella Marqueza out carefully. So did several of the chic, well-dressed women shoppers.

Her fur jacket was left casually open. As she turned, swiveled left or right, a tantalizing glimpse of her breasts floated deliciously into the breech. Of all the very striking women in the department store, Isabella was the most desirable, the most visually dramatic by Monserrat's personal standards.

Now he observed Isabella slink off toward a changing room. He put his hands in the pockets of his overcoat, caught a reflection of himself in a mirror as he moved, then he paused outside the changing room door.

He walked past the closed door, studied the throngs around him pursuing Christmas gifts with forced gaity, and then he darted back the way he had come.

Pretending to examine a silk shirt, like a wealthy East Side husband picking out a stocking-stuffer, he listened outside the changing room. Coming closer, he could hear the whisper of clothing as it peeled away from Isabella's skin.

In one swift move, he stepped inside the tiny room and Isabella Marqueza swung around in astonishment.

Why did she always look so utterly beautiful? Warmth that might have been desire flowed within him. He took his hands from his coat. She was wearing only panties, tight and sheer and black. The cocktail dress she intended to try on hung limply in one hand.

He thought she would have looked very exciting in it.

"François! What are you doing here?"

"I had to see you," he whispered. "I heard you had a little trouble. You must tell me everything."

Isabella Marqueza frowned. "They let me go. What were they going to hold me for, anyhow? They had nothing but a stupid bluff, François." She smiled, but the expression couldn't conceal a look of worry.

He pressed one gloved hand lightly against her breasts.

He could smell Bal à Versailles. Her favorite perfume. His as well. Inwardly, inaudibly, he sighed.

"Are you being followed, Isabella?"

"I don't think so."

"Are you sure?" Monserrat asked.

"As sure as I can be. Why?" A troubled look clouded her dark eyes again. He could see her wince. From beyond the door of the changing room the Christmas Muzak was relentlessly bland, as if the original notes had been squeezed through a strainer, their essence and meaning left behind.

"Good. Good," he whispered soothingly.

Isabella's mouth fell open and she suddenly stepped back against the wall. There was really no place to go in the tiny dressing room. "François, don't you believe me? I told them nothing. Absolutely nothing."

"Then why did they let you go my love? I need an explanation."

"François, don't you know me any better than that? Don't you? Please . . ."

I know you only too well, François Monserrat thought and stepped forward.

The tiny handgun made an inconsequential, guttural spit. Isabella Marqueza moaned softly, then she seemed to faint, collapsing toward the shiny, black-and-white checkered tiles.

Monserrat was already out of the changing room and walking quickly, inconspicuously, toward the nearest exit.

She'd talked. She'd told them too much. She had admitted knowing him, and that was enough.

She'd been broken during the interrogation, skillfully, in a way she might not even have truly recognized. Monserrat had heard the news not ten minutes after Carroll finished with her.

He burst into the cold wind raking West 57th Street. He turned a corner, to all intents and purposes a drab, ordinary man, losing himself in the crowds that hunted the spirit of Christmas with red-faced eagerness.

Monday; December 7;
Carroll and Caitlin Dillon

11

The Stock Market: Monday

Shining white cabin cruisers and myriad other expensive ships had begun to haunt the perimeter of lower Manhattan. More than one inflatable rubber boat was tied to the railing of the seawall at the Battery Park City Esplanade. In fact, there were a considerable number of individuals willing to use the most unorthodox means to return to their Wall Street offices, whether or not such a return was authorized.

Anton Birnbaum appeared live on the "Today Show." The face of the Financier was highly familiar, though few could have matched it with an equally familiar name they'd come upon scores of times in newspapers and magazines.

"Neither the American nor the New York Stock Exchange will sell a single share this Monday. NASDAQ, the over-the-counter market automated quotation system, will be down, as well. The commodities exchange in New York will not open, nor will the metals exchange. This is complete madness," he told the early morning viewers.

It got worse:

The regular Monday auction of the United States Treasury bills wouldn't take place.

Among the chipped and pocked tombstones of Trinity Church cemetery, no drug dealers would palm out their usual glassine envelopes of cocaine.

No messengers would trudge the streets with even more valuable envelopes: filled with securities, with valuable stock certificates, multimillion-dollar checks, legal documents.

None of the all-male luncheon clubs would serve up their bland, overcivilized fare at Monday noon.

All the usual activities of the Wall Street community would be stillborn. It was as if the modern money world had not yet been invented.

Either that, or it had been completely destroyed.

Carroll

"I want you to have lunch with me, Mr. Carroll," Caitlin Dillon had said over the telephone. "Is twelve-fifteen today possible? It's important."

It was a call that took Carroll completely by surprise. He'd been going through his elaborate back files – sifting through the various terrorist organizations in his search for some clue to Green Band – when the call came. The idea of a civilized lunch with a beautiful woman was the last thing on his mind.

"I want you to meet somebody," Caitlin had told him.

"Who?"

"A man called Freddie Hotchkiss. He's important on Wall Street."

She had a rich telephone voice. Music in a tuneless world, Carroll thought, little symphonies coming out of the impersonal Bell system. He'd put his feet up on the desk and tilted his head back against the wall. With his eyes shut, he tried to bring Caitlin Dillon's face firmly into his mind. *Untouchable,* he remembered.

"Freddie Hotchkiss is connected with a man called Michel Chevron," Caitlin said.

"The name rings a bell," Carroll said and tried to place it. "Several bells."

"The information I have is that Chevron's a wheel in the stolen securities market and – this is what should

127

really interest you, Mr. Carroll – there are rumors of a link with François Monserrat."

"Monserrat?" Carroll had suddenly opened his eyes. "So why can't we go direct to Chevron? Why go through this Hotchkiss?"

"Do I detect impatience?"

"When it comes to Monserrat, I'm impatient."

Carroll could hear Caitlin exchange quick words with somebody, and then she said, "The point is that we can't get a direct connection to Michel Chevron unless – and this is a big unless – Hotchkiss is prepared to confirm some of our information. Chevron is a French citizen. Unless we get some hard data on him, we'll never get the cooperation of the French police." Caitlin paused. It made sense, Carroll was thinking. "What I'm saying is that you may have to lean on Freddie Hotchkiss a little. Isn't that the expression the police use?"

"Something like that," Carroll said, hearing himself laugh as if there were some intimate conspiracy between them. "I guess I'll see you for lunch."

Now Carroll loosened his favorite crimson and blue school tie before he took the first inviting sip of John Smith's Pale Ale in the dining room of Christ Cella on East 46th Street. He found ties uncomfortable, which was one of the reasons he rarely wore them. Actually, he thought neckties pretty much without a purpose, unless you impulsively wanted to hang yourself, or get inside some overpriced New York steakhouse.

Christ Cella required a dress jacket and respectable tie. Otherwise, it was comfortable enough, a restaurant with something of the atmosphere of a men's club. Actually, it felt damned good to be sitting here with Caitlin Dillon.

Christ Cella's steaks were sixteen ounces at a minimum, choice prime, and aged properly. The lobsters started at two pounds. The waiters were immaculate and subservient, city cool to a fault. For the moment, Carroll was enjoying the hell out of himself. For this moment only, Green Band had receded from his mind. Wall Street might have been on another planet.

"One of the first things I learned in New York is that you *have* to make 'the steak house' a ritual if you're going to survive on Wall Street." Caitlin smiled across the fading white linen of the table cloth. She'd already told Carroll that she was originally from Lima, Ohio, and he could almost believe it, listening to her unusual perspective on New York City living.

"Even to survive in the SEC, you have to know the conventions. Especially if you're a young 'gal,' as a particular brokerage house CEO once called me. 'I'd like you to meet the new young gal from SEC.'"

Caitlin said the last phrase with such casual, twinkling malice, it almost sounded nice.

Carroll started to laugh. Then they both laughed.

Heads turned at other tables, staid faces looked around. *Was somebody daring to have fun here? Who?*

Carroll and Caitlin were waiting for the arrival of Duncan "Freddie" Hotchkiss, who was fashionably late, despite the fact that Caitlin had specifically asked him to be on time.

A shrimp cocktail eventually found its way to Carroll's place. The fish was perfect and overpriced by at least three hundred percent.

Carroll asked Caitlin about Wall Street – what was it like from her vantage point at the SEC? In answer, Caitlin began regaling him with a few of her favorite horror stories about the Street. She happened to have a treasury of absolutely true, mind-bending stories which circulated in the inner sanctums, but were usually not shared with outsiders. . . . For reasons Carroll soon began to fully understand.

"Embezzlement has never been easier on Wall Street," Caitlin said. Her brown eyes sparkled with dark humor. Carroll momentarily thought how easy it would be to fall over the imaginary edge, to drown in those eyes – a very pleasant end, indeed.

'The computer makes 'cooking the books' an exciting

challenge to anyone modestly gifted in the area. Of course, the potential thief has to know the program code, and have access to the data bank. In short, he or she must be in a position of absolute trust.

"One young economist we prosecuted worked at the Federal Reserve Bank of New York. At twenty-seven, he went off and bought a summer house in the Hamptons, then a new Mercedes convertible *and* a Porsche, then a sable coat for his dear mom. Along the way, he managed to get in debt close to three quarters of a million dollars."

"He's still working for the government?" Carroll finished the second shrimp. "In your story, I mean?"

"He *quits* Treasury right about this time – for a much better paying job. Only he takes with him *the security access codes*, which allow him to find out enough to buy or sell on the credit and stock markets. A very, very profitable bit of knowledge. He's got the ultimate on insider's trading information. . . . You know how it fell through? His mother called the SEC. She was worried that he was spending all this money without any job she could see. His mother turned him in because he gave her a sable fur.

"There was an outfit called OPM Financial Services – that stood for other people's money, I swear to God. Michael Weiss and Anthony Caputo opened their company over a Manhattan candy store in the seventies. Along their merry way, Michael and Anthony managed to defraud Manufacturers Hanover Leasing, Crocker National Bank, and Lehman Brothers for about a hundred and eighty million. Don't ever feel bad if you lose a little money on the market. You're in very good company."

"I'm real lucky in that respect – I don't have any money to lose. Why is it allowed to happen? What about the SEC?"

Carroll was already beginning to feel slightly incensed, though he'd never personally lost a dime on Wall Street. Stocks and bonds and securities had always seemed Olympian things to him, arcane matters in which other classes of people dabbled.

"It's fairly simple, really. As I said in the beginning, these kinds of stories are rarely told outside of Wall Street."

"I'm honored."

"You should be. . . . The Wall Street banks, the brokerage houses, investment bankers, even the computer companies – they know that the success of their marketplace depends on confidence and trust. If they prosecuted all the embezzlers, if they ever admitted how easy it was, how many stock certificates are actually stolen each year, they'd *all* be out of business. They'd have about the same reputation as used car salesmen – which some of them *ought* to have. . . . The point is, Wall Street is more afraid of bad publicity than of the actual thefts."

Suddenly, Caitlin was silent.

"Caitlin, will you forgive me? I'm so very sorry."

Freddie Hotchkiss had finally arrived. It was one o'clock. He was forty-five minutes late for their business lunch.

Carroll looked up and saw a sparsely blond-haired man with a ridiculously innocent grin on his face. He had the palest, watery-blue eyes, bleached of almost all color, and a face as round and expressionless as a pie tin. He would have looked eight years old, if it hadn't been for the lines on his face.

What did they do down on Wall Street? Carroll wondered. Were there genetic laboratories dedicated to the preservation of the pure-blooded, uncontaminated WASP strain? All of them turning out plump little Freddie Hotchkisses?

Caitlin had told Carroll that Hotchkiss was becoming legendary on Wall Street. He was a very hot partner at his firm, a frequent emissary to both the West Coast and Europe – where he had extensive dealings with key European bankers as well as movie moguls.

"Truly sorry about the time." Hotchkiss looked anything *but* sorry. "I completely lost track. Roughing it out of the pied à terre on Park since the trouble on Friday.

131

Kim and the kids are staying down in Boca Raton, her mom and dad's place. Ah, what exquisite timing you have, sir."

A Christ Cella waiter had spotted Hotchkiss arriving and had scurried to the table for the all-important drink order. Carroll stared at Hotchkiss. This was a type he wasn't comfortable with and didn't particularly like. Poor bastard had to rough it on Park Avenue. Carroll thought his heart would break.

"I'd like a Kir. Anyone for seconds?" Hotchkiss asked.

"I'll have another John Smith." Carroll was *trying* to be good: no hard liquor, no neat shots of Irish. He was also trying not to say something impulsive, something that might lose him the advantage of surprise with Freddie Hotchkiss. It might be fun, he decided, to *lean* on this character.

"No, thank you, nothing for me," Caitlin said. "Freddie, this is Arch Carroll. Mr. Carroll is the head of the United States Antiterrorist Division. Out of the DIA."

Freddie Hotchkiss beamed enthusiastically. "Oh, yes, I've read *volumes* about you specialized police folks. The sooner someone can bring a little order and reason to this whole unfortunate affair, the better, I say. I heard yesterday, or maybe I read it somewhere, that there is a Libyan hit team right here in New York. Actually *residing* in Manhattan."

"I doubt it's the Libyans we're looking for," Carroll casually remarked. His darker eyes held Hotchkiss's pale blue ones for an extra beat as he sipped his John Smith. He was going to attack.

He leaned forward, softly nudging a finger into Freddie's pale blue shirt, seeing a faint expression of surprise float across the man's puffy face. It amazed Carroll that such a face was capable of expression.

"I'd like to cut out the chitchat bullshit, okay? You're an hour late, and we're pressed for time. I have absolutely no personal interest in you, Freddie, you understand that? I don't think I like you, but that doesn't matter. I'm only interested in a man named Michel Chevron."

132

"He's not one for small talk, Freddie." Caitlin Dillon smiled and nursed her drink. She threw a quick glance at Carroll, and he thought it was the most intimate thing he'd experienced in years.

Freddie Hotchkiss, meanwhile, seemed to have stopped breathing. He looked down at Carroll's finger sticking in the center of his chest. "I'm not sure . . . I don't think I understand. I mean, I've heard of Michel Chevron, of course."

"Of course you have," Carroll said.

"Tall, austere-looking French gentleman," Caitlin intervened. "Plush Louis Quatorze offices on rue de Faubourg in Paris. Very affluent digs in the heart of Beverly Hills."

Caitlin flipped open a leatherbound notebook on the dining table.

"Let me see if I can jog your memory. Mm, oh yes . . . on February nineteenth of last year, you visited Michel Chevron's Beverly Hills office. You stayed for approximately two hours. On March third, you visited the L.A. offices again. Also on July ninth, July eleventh, July twelfth. In October, you visited Chevron's Paris office. You had dinner with Chevron that night at Laserre. Remember? Can you place him yet?"

Freddie Hotchkiss had begun slowly clasping and unclasping his plump, hairless hands. The watery eyes were even more watery.

"We've known for over two years that Michel Chevron is the largest stolen securities and bond dealer in Europe and the Middle East. We also know he has a personal relationship with François Monserrat," Caitlin continued.

"We know a great deal about your own security trading abilities, as well. Right now, we need to know exactly *who* else Chevron deals with, and we need a rough idea of the nature of these deals, a general feel for the Euro-Asian black market. That's why I thought we all should have lunch." She smiled.

Right then Freddie Hotchkiss found the strength inside himself to frown derisively. He began to snap back, to rally strongly.

133

"Really. You don't expect me to talk about private *and* absolutely legal business dealings here in this restaurant? You had better have *all* your subpoenas and your Justice Department lawyers ready, if you believe that will happen. I can assure you, it won't be *done* over lunch. . . . Good afternoon, Caitlin, Mr., uh, Carroll."

Arch Carroll suddenly sat up very straight at the dining table. He leaned all the way forward and did the oddest, most unexpected thing.

Carroll placed his forefinger behind his thumb and then flicked it three times very hard against Freddie Hotchkiss's starched white shirt collar.

Thwack.

Thwack.

Thwack.

"Just sit tight now, okay? Just put your nice soft ass back down on the chair, Freddie. Try to relax. Okay?"

Hotchkiss was so astonished, he obeyed.

In a soft voice, which to Carroll's ears sounded mildly seductive, Caitlin said, "February twenty-first – you deposited one hundred and twenty-six thousand dollars in Geneva, Switzerland. February twenty-sixth – you deposited another one hundred and fourteen thousand. April seventeenth – you deposited . . . is this a typo? . . . four hundred and sixty-two thousand? April twenty-fourth – another thirty-one thousand. . . . Small potatoes, that one . . ."

"What Caitlin has been politely trying to point out to you, Freddie, is that you are a second-rate thief!" Carroll leaned back and smiled at Hotchkiss, who now sat as expressionless as a ventriloquist's dummy.

Carroll raised his voice above the restaurant's usual buzz. "Poor Kim, the kiddos wintering down in Boca Raton. They have no idea, I'll bet. Tennis pals at the club. The boys at the yacht club. They don't know either. . . . *You ought to be in jail.* You shouldn't be allowed to eat here, you're such a sad piece of shit."

Other diners in the expensive Midtown restaurant were beginning to place their knives and forks on their plates. In a state that resembled a communal hypnotic trance, they stared across the upstairs room.

Carroll finally lowered his voice. He pointed toward a corner table where two men in dull gray suits were seated.

"Those two guys? See them? They can't even afford to eat the nibbles here. See, they're sharing a three-dollar ginger ale. That's the FBI for you. . . . Anyway, they're either going to arrest you, right here and now . . . *or*, Fred, you're going to tell us a long, very convincing story about Michel Chevron. It's absolutely your move. And yes, it's going to happen *right here* in the restaurant.

"*Then*, in that second case I mentioned, you get to go home absolutely scot free to the pied à terre on Park Avenue. No problems, 'cause then you're my main man, see."

Arch Carroll dramatically crossed his two fingers. "We're tight, like that. Except, of course, you're the finger on the bottom."

Freddie Hotchkiss slumped forward pathetically at the restaurant table. He hesitated, then he slowly began to tell yet another Wall Street horror story.

This one was about Monsieur Michel Chevron. It was a truly fascinating story of the most exclusive rat pack of thieves in the world. All of them very respected bankers, high-priced lawyers, successful stockbrokers. Every single one of them was in a position of absolute public trust.

Was this Green Band? Arch Carroll couldn't help wondering.

Was Green Band a powerful international cartel of the richest investment bankers and businessmen in the world? What would be their motivation?

Carroll finally signaled to the two FBI guys patiently waiting at the corner table.

"You can arrest this guy now. . . . Oh, and Freddie? I told a white lie about letting you go scot free. . . . Have your lawyer call my lawyer in the morning. *Ciao*."

Mike Caruso was outside the restaurant when Arch Carroll finally appeared. Carroll's lieutenant was wearing a

135

garish beach shirt beneath his overcoat, a devotee of summer who never embraced the winter season.

He gestured Carroll to step aside from Caitlin. Both policemen huddled together at the far edge of the sidewalk.

"I just got a report on our friend Isabella Marqueza," Caruso said. "Somebody murdered her in Bendel's. She was shot four times."

Carroll glanced at Caitlin, who was standing several feet away, waiting for him. A lovely vision in a dull gray, wintry city. He tried to imagine Isabella Marqueza dead.

"Shot at point-blank range," Caruso said in the offhand manner of someone immunized against murders. "It freaked out all the Christmas shoppers."

"Yeah, I'm sure it would." Carroll was silent a second. "Somebody thought she talked too much. Somebody was keeping close tabs on her."

Caruso nodded. "Somebody who knew all her movements, Arch. Or *yours*."

A ragged wind blew down East 46th Street, dragging around discarded newspapers. Carroll plunged his hands inside the pockets of his coat and stared at the cold grim city surrounding him. He liked this investigation less and less.

He finally pointed back at the doorway of Christ Cella. "Nice place to eat, Mickey. Next time you want to blow a couple of hundred on lunch."

Caruso nodded. He tucked in a flap of his flowered shirt. "I already had a Sabrett's."

Tuesday; December 8;
Vets Cabs and Messengers

12

Stock Market; Tuesday

The following morning, 83-year-old Anton Birnbaum, appearing on a special edition of the PBS show "Wall Street Week," explained why the destruction of Manhattan's financial district did not exactly signal the end of the civilized world.

"The *major* American market was indeed knocked out this past Friday. *More* markets exist out there, however – *believe it or not* – and they may just possibly become the beneficiaries of this disaster. . . . These markets are the Midwestern, the Pacific, and the Philadelphia exchanges. They handle local issues as well as certain board listings. If Joe Investor has to sell fifty shares of AT and T to meet the balloon payment on his mortgage, his local broker may well be able to make a deal for him outside of New York. Of course, he may not find a buyer at a price even close to what he's asking.

"Obviously," Birnbaum went on, "Chicago is where the significant action is this week. Between the Midwest Exchange, and the two premier commodity exchanges, there are still plenty of opportunities for everyone to lose a lot of money."

Even as he gave this purposely calming and reassuring speech, Anton Birnbaum knew that the existing situation was more tragic than he dared admit. Like almost everyone intimately connected with the Market, Birnbaum fully expected a crash.

In a way, somewhere deep in the inner recesses of his mind, he almost welcomed the purification rite, so very long overdue. As of Tuesday morning, the venerable Financier had no idea how large a part he would play in Green Band himself.

13

Carroll

Paris. . . . A powerful man named Michel Chevron . . . Green Band. . . .

The idea of the magnificent city filled Carroll with something akin to dread. Even as he sat inside a dark blue State Department limousine, sailing like a proud ship across the rue Saint Honoré, Carroll didn't want to look out at the streets. He didn't want to acknowledge that he was truly back in the splendid French capital.

The street sounds he heard pressing against the limousine were like the rattling of old bones. For Carroll, this Paris was a city of sharply painful memories. This Paris was Nora and himself in another age and time. This Paris was a fading decal on which were imprinted the spectral shapes of two young, carefree honeymooners, who wandered all the boulevards holding hands, who stopped to kiss impulsively every so often, who couldn't keep from constantly touching each other even in the most casual ways.

Carroll stared at the two American flags that flapped regally on either bumper of the luxury car.

Make believe you're someplace else, he told himself.

Christ, though, the memories kept coming back like a forceful tide. Nora sipping café au lait on the crowded boulevard St. Germain. Nora smiling and laughing as they made all the tourist stops – the Eiffel Tower, Montparnasse, the banks of the Seine, le Quartier Etudiant.

Carroll felt something grab tight around his heart. It was a sense of the injustice that had ended Nora's life, and it uncomfortably crowded him now.

Near the Sorbonne, a crouching man with a reptilian face made as if to hurl a spoiled grapefruit at the smooth, cruising symbol of American wealth and power.

Seated in the gray velvet rear salon of the car, Carroll flinched at the sight of the man. But when the prospect of the grapefruit assault had passed, he relaxed a little and tried to shake his head free of the fog of overseas jet lag and confused time zones. He opened his bulky Green Band file and looked over scribbled notes because he knew work would be a salvation from the memories of this town. If he dug into his material on Green Band, he could make himself a foxhole safe from the scenes that passed outside the windows of the car.

How could Green Band have isolated itself so well from the terrorist underground? How could there be no rumor, no concrete leads anywhere out on the street? And what was the ultimate reason for the New York financial district bombings?

Something else occurred to Carroll now: *What if he was still looking in all the wrong places?*

"Société Générale Bank, monsieur. *Vous êtes ici.* You have arrived safely, comfortably I hope. . . . This is *le Quartier de la Bourse.*"

Arch Carroll climbed out of the official American limousine and slowly walked inside Société Générale.

The bank building itself, the cavernous lobby, the hand-operated elevators, were all carved stone and exquisitely gilded. Everything was regal and impressive, the kind of background against which American tourists would take pictures of their European tours to later paste in scrapbooks.

The prestigious French financial institution reminded Carroll quite powerfully of another era. Compared with Wall Street, it was visually softer and more civilized to behold. It was as if money were not the major game being played here. The aim was something less vulgar, something even spiritual, perhaps. In actuality *le Quartier de la Bourse* occupied the former site of a Dominican convent. On this same site another God had achieved divinity. No matter the history of the place, no matter the artistic

140

appeal, it was the same religion you found on Wall Street. Gentility and manners, these were only illusions. It was the same old God.

Michel Chevron, Carroll thought, remembering why he was there. Chevron and the massive, secretive European black market.

The question was whether Chevron really fit into the frustrating Green Band puzzle, and whether there was a bridge, even a frail one, linking Chevron with François Monserrat.

The French bank executive's personal assistant was a thin, sickly man of perhaps twenty-eight. He had white-blond hair, closely cropped, almost suggestive of punk in style.

He sat stiffly behind an antique desk, which in New York would have seemed inappropriate for anyone except a chief executive. He wore a double-breasted pin-striped suit, a funereal, mauve four-in-hand tie.

Carroll tried to imagine applying for a loan from this chilly character, something for home repair, maybe, a room extension, an underground sprinkler system. He could see the bank assistant sniffling over the application papers with an expression of mild disgust. He knew this particular assistant would turn him down flat, possibly even laugh.

"My name is Archer Carroll. I'm here from New York to see Monsieur Chevron. I spoke to someone yesterday on the telephone."

"Yes, to me." The bank assistant addressed him as a country gentleman would address a stablehand on the subject of a gelding's health. "Director Chevron has provided fifteen minutes . . . *at eleven forty-five.*"

Observing the bank assistant's manner and tone, Carroll had the impression that only a very few words could have been substituted for *"Director Chevron"* in the opening sentence – words like de Gaulle, or Napoleon. Maybe even the Lord God Almighty.

"Director has an important lunch at twelve. You will please wait. The sofa for waiting is there, Monsieur Carroll."

Arch Carroll nodded his head very slowly. Reluctantly, he wandered over to a tight nest of Art Deco couches.

He sat down and clenched his hands together. He was trying to fight back anger now, seething anger. On the telephone, he and the bank assistant had set up a meeting firmly for eleven o'clock. He was right on time, and he'd traveled several thousand miles to be here.

Michel Chevron was right behind those heavy oak doors, Carroll kept thinking.

Chevron was probably laughing up his well-tailored sleeve at the ugly American outside in reception . . .

He steadily drummed his fingers on his knee. His right loafer tapped against the elegant marble floor.

At fifteen minutes to twelve, the bank assistant finally set down his slender silver fountain pen. He looked up from a thick sheaf of paperwork. He smacked his purplish lips before he spoke.

"You may see Director Chevron now. Will you please follow me?"

A moment or so later, Director Michel Chevron, an unexpectedly small man with an equine face and shock of ink-black hair that stood up on his head like a fuzzy yarmulke, said, "Mr. Carroll, so good of you to come to Paris," almost as if this transatlantic journey was something Carroll did every other day of the week.

Carroll was led into an intimidating, Old World chief executive's office. Tall, glass-enclosed bookcases filled with antiquarian books crowded one paneled wall. Along the other, there were crimson-draped casement windows looking out onto a narrow gray stone terrace. The ceiling was at least twelve feet high, beautifully sculpted, ornamented with grinning bronze cherubs. A glass chandelier hung down like the world's heaviest key chain.

Michel Chevron remained standing behind his massive desk. He was obviously impressed with himself, his position and all the trappings of success that surrounded him in his office. A pleasantly regal Fragonard hung directly behind the bank executive.

The Frenchman began to speak rapid, excellent English

142

as soon as his assistant left the room. His tone remained cool and superior, and Carroll felt inferior all over again.

"There is a slight problem, Monsieur Carroll. A regrettable circumstance, beyond anyone's control. I'm very sorry, but I have an important engagement at Tailleuent. The restaurant, monsieur? The rest of my afternoon is equally bad . . . I can spare these few moments with you only."

Arch Carroll could suddenly feel *a very cold place* in his stomach. He knew the sensation well and he tried to ignore it, but a familiar fuse was burning. When the spark reached close to his private emotional arsenal, there was very little he could do to stop the explosion.

"All right, then just shut the hell up now," Carroll suddenly raised his hand, palm out. "I don't have time to be civil anymore. You kept me waiting through my polite and civil period."

The French bank executive broke into a disdainful smile.

"Monsieur, you don't seem to understand whose country you're in now. This is not America, I'm afraid. You have no authority whatsoever here. I freely consented to see you, in the spirit of international cooperation only."

Carroll immediately reached into his sports coat pocket and sent a light tan envelope spinning across Chevron's handsome desk.

"Here's your spirit of international cooperation. It's a signed police warrant. A *French* police warrant for your arrest. It was signed by Commissionnaire Blanche of the Sûreté. I met with the Commissionnaire before I came here. The formal charges include extortion, bribery of public officials, fraud. I'm honored to be the one to deliver the good news to you."

Arch Carroll couldn't help smiling. His only regret was that Chevron's huffy assistant couldn't have been there.

Michel Chevron sat down heavily in his chair.

He covered his face, drained of its color now, with his long, elegantly manicured fingers. His aquiline features appeared to have imploded so that the face seemed squat, crinkled like a concertina that has had air thrust out of it. Carroll loved the look a lot.

"All right, Mr. Carroll. You've made your point, I suppose. Why exactly have you come here? What information is it that you wish to extract from me?"

Carroll eased himself down into a chair across from Michel Chevron. The Frenchman's voice was still cool and controlled even if Chevron's features had undergone an unflattering transformation.

"For starters, I'd like to know about the European and Middle Eastern black markets. I need specific names, places, specific dates. *How* the black market is structured, the principals involved. And I want to hear all about *François Monserrat*."

Chevron hoarsely cleared his throat. "You have no idea what you're saying, what you're asking of me. You have no idea the predicament you're placing me in. We are speaking of billions of dollars. We are speaking of participants of a less than savory nature. . . .The French Corso . . . the Italian Cosa Nostra."

Chevron seemed to wipe imaginery crumbs from his fingertips now. He sat back in his chair and Carroll could see tiny stars of perspiration glistening on his forehead. Even the impressive black hair seemed to have lost its color. Carroll felt relaxed and confident for the first time since he'd arrived in Paris.

"I'm listening," he said. "Keep going. I love stories about the Cosa Nostra."

But Michel Chevron had already spoken the last words of his life. Just then the oak doors into the executive suite splintered and crashed suddenly.

For one frightening, incomprehensible moment Carroll imagined that what had happened on Wall Street was repeating itself in Paris, as he jumped from his chair and turned to face the shattered door.

Three heavily armed men in trench coats had appeared from the direction of the bank director's reception area. Each had a machine-gun pistol drawn. In the narrow corridor behind them stood Michel Chevron's blond assistant, armed with a small black Beretta himself.

Carroll didn't hesitate. His lingering jet lag was gone abruptly. He was already diving across the floor. Glass and expensive wood was suddenly splintering, shattering everywhere around him. Automatic machine-gun explosions slashed through the previously secure and elegant office suite. Carroll's heart felt like it had been caught by a wire garotte.

Out of the corner of his eye, Carroll watched Michel Chevron.

The French banker suddenly twisted and turned horribly, eerily, in the air. He was nailed against the wooden wall by a terrifying machine-gun volley.

His body arched spastically, then spun away slowly toward the floor. His blue suit was instantly blood-soaked. Particles of bone and flesh floated through ghostly spirals of gunsmoke in the office suite.

The professional assailants switched their attention to Carroll. Hollow-head slugs thudded like hammer blows into the oak-paneled walls all around him.

His heart pounding, Carroll lunged forward beyond the heavy drapes, which fanned the air as bullets ripped through the fabric. He smacked himself against the glass door to the terrace and was surrounded all at once by splinters of glass, by snapped pieces of the wooden frame that twisted out of the glass like limbs awkwardly broken . . .

Sharp needles pierced his neck, his hands. Violent, numbing cold clawed at his face.

He scrambled to his feet, the glass slivers slicing deeper with every movement.

The outside terrace was a long, narrow stone catwalk, sixteen stories above the Paris street. The walkway seemed to stretch around the entire length of the floor.

Feet pounding the ancient stone, Carroll ran toward the nearest corner of the building.

He could hear deafening gunshots, followed by screams of incredulous terror and agony inside the French bank offices. Machine gun pistols coughed and fired repeatedly, insanely.

French terrorists? The Brigade? François Monserrat? What was happening now?

Who had known he was going to be here?

Bullets suddenly whistled past Carroll's face, nicking the brooding stone body of a crouching gargoyle.

Behind him and to the left, Carroll registered the direction of the gunfire and quickly glanced back over his shoulder.

Two of the assassins were closing fast. Their leather trenchcoats flapping, they were the kind of European thugs he thought only existed in French movies. Furiously, Carroll raised his own gun. He fired, hearing the slightly unreal, muted spit of the silencer in his ears.

The running man in front grabbed at his upper chest, then stumbled and fell over the stone wall. He continued on down, somersaulting sixteen stories to the street.

"Oh, goddamnit!" Carroll suddenly clutched his own shoulder. Blood spread instantly where he'd been shot. He felt his brain freeze over as the shock descended.

The thick cords of his neck bulged with the concentrated fear of the last few seconds, possibly the final seconds of his life. He felt as sick as he had ever felt. He temporarily lost his breath as he stumbled forward around the next carved stone corner of the French bank building.

He moved now, no longer fully aware of himself. He wasn't connected with events taking place. It was all a bad dream, a very bad nightmare.

Then he started to sprint down another clear stretch of stone terrace. The walkway ended abruptly at a gray brick wall topped by severe iron fencing.

He was dizzy. He could taste warm, metallic blood in his mouth. Piercing chest pains came with each breath. The wounded arm ached with a deep, searing pain he'd never felt before.

To die here in Paris suddenly seemed ironic and appropriate.

To die here surrounded by memories of Nora.

He watched the sky slip away from him. The wintry sun was a hard uncaring disc.

Carroll used his good arm on the restraining wall and vaulted over the side. He saw a spinning flash of cars sixteen floors below. And cold concrete, gray as an undertaker's face . . .

As he safely landed on the terrace six feet below, he struck the wounded shoulder hard against a slab of granite. The pain that exploded into his brain was a savage, biting agony. Blinded by it, he forced himself to reel forward toward a casement door which opened as he leaned into it.

He was bleeding badly now. He stopped running. A package-crowded stockroom lay before him.

Carroll crouched on trembling legs, and waited inside. Emery Airborne mail was stacked all around. There was no possible place to hide if they came through. If they found him now.

His thoughts were shattered. His mind was blurred, almost useless. Nothing was left inside his throbbing chest but rage. Splinters of glass still ached in his forehead, both his cheeks, the back of his neck. He felt dizzy and sick.

Gunshot explosions and horrible screams continued to echo through the Société Générale office building. Then warbling French police sirens shrieked and throbbed outside. They filled the air with the sudden news of terrifying disaster. Carroll finally took off his shirt and wrapped it tightly around his bleeding arm.

Michel Chevron would be telling nothing about the powerful black market in Europe and the Middle East now. Nothing about what Green Band might be.

Who was behind this horrifying noonday massacre? What could the French banker Michel Chevron have possibly known?

Carroll could no longer stand.

He slumped against a plaster wall, his head drawn down between his knees.

What could Chevron have possibly known?
What could be worth this terrifying massacre?
What in the name of God could justify this?

14

The Vets

It was a completely magical moment, one that Sergeant Harry Stemkowsky knew he would never be able to forget. It was like a fantastic movie scene he'd been dreaming about for as long as he could remember.

As dawn edged through soiled, slate gray skies, Stemkowsky rolled his wheelchair down the concrete ramp he'd built to get in and out of his house in Jackson Heights, Queens. His wife Mary, a former nurse, who was ten years older than Harry, sauntered close beside him.

"This is it, sweetheart," she said in a whisper.

"This is definitely it," Harry said brightly.

Mary Stemkowsky carefully set Harry's two new Dunhill travel bags down. She glanced at her husband. She couldn't believe how impressive and businesslike he looked in his dark pin-striped suit. His salt-and-pepper hair and beard were neatly trimmed and shaped. He held a soft leather attaché case that looked like it cost big money, impossible money.

"Excited, Harry? I'll bet you are." Mary Stemkowsky couldn't control a shy, softly blossoming grin as she spoke. She believed that Harry was truly a saint. You could ask any of his friends at the Vets Cab Company, any of the physical therapists who worked with him at the VA, where she and Harry had originally met.

Mary Stemkowsky didn't know how he'd done it, but Harry seemed to completely accept what had happened to him more than a decade before in Viet Nam. He almost never complained about the wounds or the constant

148

pain. In fact, Harry seemed to live his life for other people, for their happiness, especially her own.

"Tell the truth, I'm a li-li-little scared. Nuh-nuh-nice scared." Harry tried to smile, but he looked pale around the gills, she thought.

Mary immediately bent and kissed him on both cheeks, then on his slightly bloated lips. It was strange the way she loved him so much. What with his infirmities, his physical limitations. But she did. She truly loved Harry more than she loved the rest of the world combined.

"Sa-sorry *you* can't go, Muh-Mary."

"Oh, I'll go next time, I guess. Sure, sure. You better believe I will." Mary suddenly laughed and her broad horsey smile was close to radiant. "You look like the president of a bank or something. President of Chase Manhattan Bank. You do, Harry. I'm so proud of you."

She stooped and kissed him again. She didn't want him to ruin one minute, not a single heartbeat of his European trip because she couldn't go with him this time.

"Oh, here he comes! Here Mitchell comes now." She suddenly pointed up along the row of dull, virtually faceless tract houses.

A yellow cab had turned onto their street. Mary could make out Mitchell Cohen at the wheel, wearing his usual, flap-eared Russian fur hat.

She knew that Mitchell and Harry had been working on their business scheme for almost two years. All they would tell her and Neva Cohen was that it had to do with arbitrage – which Mary loosely understood as trading currencies from country to country, making money on discrepancies in the exchange rates – and that this arbitrage scheme was their ticket out of hacking cabs for the rest of their lives.

"He takes two Dilantins before bedtime," Mary said as she and Mitchell Cohen helped load Harry into the Vets cab.

Harry absolutely cracked up at that remark. He loved

the way Mary continually worried about him, worried about dumb things, like the Dilantin which he took regularly every night and three times during the day.

"You have a wonderful trip over to Europe, Harry. Don't work *too* hard. Miss me a little."

"Awhh cah-cah-mon. I muh-muh-miss you already," Harry Stemkowsky muttered, and he sincerely meant it.

He'd never really been able to understand why Mary had decided to live with a cripple in the first place. He was just happy that she had. Now he was going to do something for her, something that both of them deserved. Harry Stemkowsky was going to become an instant winner in life. And fuck everybody who didn't believe in Harry Stemkowsky.

Tears suddenly welled in his red-rimmed eyes. They continued to roll down both his cheeks as the Vets cab slowly bumped up the deserted early morning Queens street. He had desperately wanted to take Mary along – it just wasn't possible. Among other complications, he wasn't going to Geneva, Switzerland, as he'd told her. He and Mitchell Cohen were flying to Tel Aviv, then to Teheran. . . .

They were going to be in considerable danger for the next thirty-six hours. Danger they hadn't seen since Southeast Asia. . . . But there was another side to the trip too. There was a whole other perspective both men couldn't help considering . . .

Harry Stemkowsky and Mitchell Cohen were feeling alive for the first time in almost fifteen years.

The Green Band mission, however it finally turned out, had brought them back to life.

While Stemkowsky and Cohen drove to Kennedy Airport, another of the chosen couriers, Vets 7, was already on board Pan Am flight 311, winging its way toward Japan.

Jimmy Holm was entertaining a first-class stewardess, skillfully recounting the true stories of how he had survived three years in a North Vietnamese prison; then two more years in a Bakersville, California, VA hospital. Bakersville, he said, had been much, much worse.

"And now, here I am. This high and mightly clipper class life-style. Europe, the Far East." Holm smiled and drained his glass of Moët & Chandon. "God bless America. With all the ugly warts we hear so much about, God bless our country. Isn't this the greatest?"

At approximately the same hour, Vets 15, Pauly Melindez, and Vets 9, Steve Glickman, were enjoying similar first-class treatment on another Pan Am flight scheduled for Bangkok's Don Muang Airport. Both Melindez and Glickman had most recently worked as private rent-a-cops in Orlando, Florida. Today, December 9, they were personally in control of something over *sixteen million dollars* . . .

"Samples."

Vets 5, Harold Freedman, had already arrived in London. Vets 12, Jimmy Cassio, was in Zurich. Vets 8, Gary Barr, was settled in Rome – where he was sitting on a classically beautiful stone terrazzo which overlooked the dazzling Tiber.

Barr had most recently been a comedy nightclub bouncer for over four years on Sunset Drive in L.A. Now he was thinking that this had to be a dream. Vets 8 finally closed his eyes. He blinked them open again . . . *and Rome along the Tiber was still there.*

So was the twenty-two million for his upcoming negotiations.

More "samples."

Vets 3

In the West Village section of New York, Vets 3 wasn't flying, or even living very first class. Nick Tricosas had no four-hundred-dollar Brooks Brothers suit. He had no leather Dunhill wallet full of fancy credit cards. Vets 3 was wearing a cut-off USMC T-shirt, a greaser's head bandana, and faded khaki-drab fatigue trousers.

He was play-acting that he was in Nam again. In a weird way, he figured that he was. Green Band was the unofficial end of Viet Nam, wasn't it? It was something close to that.

Tricosas stared around the cramped radio room and felt a rush of claustrophobia tighten his chest. The broom closet was tucked up on the third floor of the Vets garage. The only furniture was a gray metal card table and matching folding chair, the PRC transmitter-receiver, a *First Blood* movie poster taped to the greasy walls.

"Contact. This is Vets Three." Tricosas's index finger finally clicked on the PRC again.

"All right all you brave veterans of foreign wars. You purple heart and medal of honor winners. . . . Who can handle a pickup at Park Ave and Thirty-ninth Street? . . . A Ms. Austin and her day nurse Nazreen . . . Ms. Austin is a very sweet lady with a fold-it-up wheelchair. Fits very nice-like in the trunk of a Checker. She'll be going to Lenox Hill Hospital for her weekly chemotherapy. Over."

"Over. This is Vets Twenty-two. I'm at Mad Ave and five-two. I'll pick up and take Ms. Austin. I know the old chick. Be there in approximately five minutes. Over."

"Thank you kindly, Vets Twenty-two. . . . Okay, here's another hot one. I have a corporate account at Twenty-five Central Park West. Account T-21. Mr. Sidney Solovey is headed for the Yale Club at fifty Vanderbilt. Mr. Solovey used to work for Salomon Brothers. Before somebody blew the living shit out of Wall Street, that is. Over."

"Over. Vets Nineteen. I'm CPS and Sixth. I'll take Mr. Solovey to Yale. Listen, Trichinosis, who you like, Knicks and the Philly Sixers? Knicks laying two and a half *at home*. Over."

"Contact. Bet your life on the powerful shoulders of young Mr. Moses Malone. Knicks are point three nine one lifetime against the Sixers and the spread. Over and out."

Nick Tricosas stood up. He stretched another three inches into his body, and rubbed the small of his back. He needed a break from the taxi dispatcher radio clatter, the constant radio-man duty since five that morning.

152

Tricosas lit up a cigar, gently rolling it between his thumb and index finger.

Then he wandered down the winding back stairs of the Vets building, trailing clouds of expensive smoke. He climbed down another twisting flight of stairs to the main garage itself.

The basement floor was thick with collected filth and debris. It was a typically rat-infested New York cellar. There was a second dispatcher's office flanked by cabbie waiting benches. Off to the left were rusted candy and soda machines, and an unpainted gray metal door.

Tricosas squinted and started down the serpentine, dungeon-type hallway. He sighed out loud. Colonel Hudson had said nobody was to go inside the locked basement room *under any circumstances*.

Tricosas produced a key anyway. He turned it into the stout Chubb mortise lock, and heard the releasing click-click-click. He pushed forward the creaking door.

Then he finally peeked inside Colonel Hudson's forbidden holy of holies . . .

Nick Tricosas couldn't help smiling, almost laughing out loud. His breath got completely sucked away. His deep brown eyes might have doubled in size. His head tensed and felt like it might actually explode, blow off his shoulders. Right back up three flights of stairs to the claustrophobic radio dispatcher room.

Nick Tricosas had never actually seen four and a half billion dollars before! What he was looking at, staring at with what he knew must be a dumbfounded expression, just didn't *seem possible*.

Four and a half billion. That was correct, Nicko.

Billion!

David Hudson

Colonel David Hudson did a highly unusual thing: he hesitated for once before acting. He reconsidered one final time as he waited in the phone booth at the southeast corner of 54th Street and Sixth Avenue and stared at the condensation on the glass panes. He understood that he was taking an unnecessary chance here, asking for the same girl again.

He lightly tapped a quarter against the black metal box, then finally let it drop.

Ding. Ding. Connection made.

Yes, he wanted to see Billie again.

He wanted to see her very much.

Less than an hour later, she glided into the buzzing, and crowded O'Neal's on West 57th and Sixth. Hudson watched her from a stool at the bar. His head began to swim almost instantly.

Yes, he wanted to see her again.

Billie. . . . Just Billie.

She had on a long, specked-charcoal coat, and black leather boots to her thighs. A soft, pearl-gray beret was carefully placed on the side of her flowing blond hair. She stood out in the tide of young and middle-aged business-women crowding into the popular bistro.

She smiled when she finally saw him and smoothly moved his way.

"I see you're coming up in the world. Finished and sold your play already, have you?"

"That's a possibility. Or maybe I robbed a bank so I could afford to see you again." His smile was quiet, genuine.

Billie bowed her head slightly at the mention of payment for their time spent together. The unusual blush he'd seen at the hotel once again streaked her forehead and cheeks. He had the feeling she hadn't been in the business very long – though perhaps that was what he *wanted* to feel. Perhaps it was her best skill as an escort – to seem so innocent, such an ingenue.

"They set an hour for your appointment. Should we go some place? An hour isn't that long."

"I'd like to have a drink here with you. We have time. One drink."

Hudson signaled for the bartender, who came immediately in his crisp white shirt and black bow tie, like a man

154

answering a very urgent summons. Hudson seemed to have a way of getting whatever he wanted, Billie had already noticed. He was *very much* in command for the Washington-Jefferson Hotel type.

She ordered the house white, finally smiling, shaking her head at Hudson – as if he was a little hopeless, bewildering certainly.

A hundred and fifty dollars an hour, plus the O'Neal's bar tab, seemed extremely steep for the honor of tipping a drink with an attractive call girl. He certainly didn't look as if he could afford it – but she knew enough not to put a lot of faith in appearances and superficial impressions.

"You don't have to pay. I'll say you didn't show." She said it, then seemed instantly flustered and embarrassed again.

Now Hudson was quite certain she hadn't been doing this kind of work very long. Sometimes it happened to young actresses, to up-and-coming New York models.

"I like you. I don't think I understand you, but I like you," she said.

They looked into one another's eyes, and it was as if they were all alone in the hectic, buzzing bar room. Hudson could feel a strong desire for her growing again. In his mind, he saw her rose-tipped breasts. He remembered her fast breathing as she came.

He leaned forward and kissed her cheek – he kissed her as gently as he'd ever kissed anyone. He had the desire to get close, to try and open up a little with her. At the same time, he felt a soldier's warning, instinct powerfully holding him back from a mistake here.

"Tell me something about yourself. Just *one* small thing. . . . It doesn't have to be anything important."

She smiled again, actually seeming to be enjoying herself. The missing arm, the way he carried himself, made him quite dashing.

"All right. Sometimes I'm too impulsive. I shouldn't be offering you what's commonly called a freebie. I could be fired from Vintage. Now tell me something about yourself."

"I don't even have enough money to pay this bar tab," Hudson said and laughed.

Billie Bogan started to laugh. "You really don't?"

"Really. Now tell me one *true* fact. Anything, just something true."

She hesitated, then shrugged. "I have two older sisters back in Birmingham. Back in England."

"They're both married. Successfully married. And your mother won't let you forget it," Hudson said with a smile.

"No. They're both married all right. Right on the button there. That's what you do if you're a sensible girl in Birmingham. But neither marriage is successful. And, yes, my mother won't let me forget I'm still single. Are you honestly writing a play in that awful West Side hotel? Your so-called garret?"

Hudson continued to smile. "I have one particular story I have to get out about Viet Nam. It's a factual story about what happened over there. Once that story is told, I think I can go on with the rest of my life. Not until then, though."

He sipped his beer, cautiously watching her almond brown eyes, her lips slightly wet with wine. He found himself wondering what was going on inside *her* head right now.

She laughed out loud, but nicely. "I'm completely losing it! I *don't believe* what I'm doing right now. I really don't believe this."

"Having a drink of white wine? At midday? Not that unusual in New York."

"I think I have to go. I really should go. I have to call and tell them you didn't keep your appointment."

"That's a problem. If you did that, they wouldn't let me see you again. I'd get a bad reputation as somebody completely unreliable. And we wouldn't want that, would we?"

"No, I guess we wouldn't. But I *really* have to go."

"Well, that's not acceptable to me. No. Just hold on a minute."

Hudson reached inside his weatherbeaten, drab brown overcoat. He placed three fifty-dollar bills on the bar.

"Billie what? Tell me your last name at least."

"You can't afford this. Please, David. It really isn't a good idea."

"Billie what? I thought you liked me?"

She looked as if she'd been slapped, as if someone in her lower-middle-class English family had caught her at this escort work in New York. She hesitated, then finally spoke up again.

"It's Billie Bogan. Like the poet, Louise Bogan . . . 'Now that I have your face by heart, I look' . . ."

"You *look* extremely beautiful to me. Let's get out of here now."

David Hudson hadn't felt this way in fifteen years. It was inconvenient and the timing was terrible – but there it was.

Feeling – where there had been none for so many years. *Intense* feeling. And warning signals that were going off everywhere, all at once.

Wednesday; December 9;
Margarita Kupchuck – the Russians

15

President Kearney

The morning of December 9 was a gloomy day in Washington where even the stark, bare trees seemed to be gasping for light and life. A second emergency meeting was held at the White House for members of the National Security Council and other officials associated with the Green Band inquiries.

As he waited patiently for the President to arrive, Arch Carroll was thinking about pain.

It was hard for him not to. His right arm, which was cradled in bandages and a temporary sling, would flare up every now and again. He'd flinch and curse before he had time to remind himself he was lucky just to be alive. Despite the codeine number 4 he'd swallowed since Paris, his nerve endings felt as if they were being gnawed on.

Lucky to be alive, Carroll thought again. There were four less orphans in the world that way.

A morbid little syllogism clicked in his head.

A cat has nine lives.

I am not a cat.

Therefore I don't have nine lives.

So how many lives do I have? How many more chances if I keep playing the game this hard?

President Kearney finally entered the room and everyone stood up.

The President of the United States was dressed casually. He had chosen a navy Lacoste shirt and slightly wrinkled, knock-around khakis. He looked like a kind of regular guy, Arch Carroll thought to himself. You could imagine him, in better times and another season, pottering around the backyard barbecue, poking the center of a sirloin for readiness. Carroll remembered that Kearney had two young boys: maybe he played ball with them. But there wouldn't be much leisure for that these days. President Kearney had taken the brunt of press criticism over Wall Street, a case of the press creating a convenient scapegoat for the public. Suddenly, in the space of a mere couple of days, his political moon had severely waned, shedding almost all its former brightness.

The participants inside the White House conference room avoided formal handshakes this time. They'd all brought bulging leather briefcases and portfolios for the early morning meeting: the artifacts, the physical proof of the past four days of relentless investigations were there to be reviewed and acted upon.

Judging from the impressive *look* of the paperwork, someone had to have discovered something about Green Band, Carroll thought as the meeting began.

He looked across the room at Caitlin Dillon, who smiled back at him. She too had an overstuffed briefcase. Today, she looked businesslike and efficient in a tailored navy-blue suit, plus an unadorned white shirt. She wore a navy necktie in the form of a large bow. For some reason, Carroll found all this severity of style attractive.

"Good morning to all of you – although I don't know what might be *especially* good about it. To be perfectly blunt, I'm even more concerned than I was on Friday night."

President Kearney certainly did nothing to relieve the strain as he delivered his opening remarks. He remained standing stiffly at the head of the long wooden table.

"Every reliable projection we have says that a Stock Market panic, a full-scale crash, may soon be on us. . . . Some of the more manipulative bastards around the

159

world have actually figured how to make this tragedy work to their advantage . . .

"I will tell all of you this in strict confidence – the Western economy cannot survive a major crash at this time. Even a minor Market crash would be catastrophic."

The President had raised his voice and there was the palest flash of his old campaign style, the inspirational voice, the characteristic firmness of the jaw – but then, as suddenly as the echo had come, it vanished. Justin Kearney looked like a man whose spirit has sagged entirely.

The President once again solicited information, new data around the table. Each advisor gave a succinct report on any findings relating to Green Band.

When his turn arrived, Carroll inched his chair closer to the conference table. He tried to make everything very still inside his head. He remained hazy after Paris. His body was still numb and cold following the shooting. And his arm was throbbing again, a palpable pain.

"My news isn't good either," Carroll began. "We have some concrete facts, some statistics, but not a lot that's worthwhile. The raw information about the bombings is complete, anyway. Five packages of plastique were required per building. They could have leveled lower Manhattan if they'd wanted to. *They didn't want to* . . .

"They wanted to do exactly what they did. New York was a controlled, a tightly disciplined *demonstration*. My team has spent forty-eight hours going through every terrorist contact that exists. There are *no connections* to this group.

"There *was* a somewhat unclear, but promising connection with the European black market," Carroll continued, flipping a page on his notepad. *Somewhat unclear*, he thought. Maybe it would have been promising if Michel Chevron had survived, if some ID had been found on the man he'd shot in Paris. There were too many ifs and maybes, twice as many as the usual police case. One thing was certain, you couldn't build an arrest around conditionals.

"Unfortunately, so many Wall Street computers and brokerage house records were destroyed, we have no way to determine the true Stock Market picture. We don't know if securities were taken, or if there's been a computer scam."

The Vice-president, Thomas More Elliot, broke in on Carroll. Of all the men seated in the room, the stern New Englander seemed the sharpest, the most in control of himself. That morning, at least, Vice-president Elliot looked more like the group's leader than the President.

"You're saying we still have *no idea* who it is we're dealing with?"

Carroll frowned and shook his head. "There haven't been any further demands. No bargaining. No contact whatsoever. They seem to have invented a completely new and terrifying game. It's a game where *we don't even get to know what game we're playing!* They move – then we have to try to react."

"Comments?" Vice-president Elliot asked, his tone clearly acerbic. "On Mr. Carroll's contributions?"

The blank faces staring at Carroll certainly weren't encouraging or supportive. The heads of the enforcement agencies were especially cool and distant. The Cabinet members were mostly business-management types who didn't understand the problems of police work in the field. They were indifferent to the trials and demands of a start-from-scratch street investigation.

The Senate majority leader finally spoke. Marshall Turner's familiar voice was Southern and boomed like an echo in a West Virginia cavern. "Mr. President, I'm afraid this simply will not do. All of what I'm hearing is unsatisfactory. Late last week, we came *that* close to a full economic collapse in this country."

"That's what we're told, Marshall."

"Now you tell us we're still in serious danger, maybe even worse danger. A second Black Friday is being discussed. I feel it's our responsibility to make certain we have our best investigative apparatus in place. Now, as I understand it, the Federal Bureau and the CIA are both being underutilized in the current manhunt for terror-ists."

The tone in the Senator's voice was offensive to Carroll. He stared at the political leader, who had the kind of swollen pink face you might encounter in the sawdust-filled back room of a country store.

Phil Berger, the Director of the CIA, stepped into the uncomfortable silence. He was a small, lean man whose head, starkly bald and shining under the lights in the room, came to a domed point. He reminded Carroll of a hard-boiled egg sitting in an eggcup.

Berger spoke, "The FBI and the CIA are working twenty-four-hour shifts. There's no question of under-utilization." The CIA Director turned his eyes toward Archer Carroll. "And I'm sure Mr. Carroll is giving it his very best, even if he hasn't managed to come up with anything."

"All right. Let's not fight among ourselves." President Kearney abruptly rose at the conference table.

Justin Kearney looked at Carroll and said, "I made a hard decision late yesterday. I would have called you, but you weren't in New York, Archer."

"Right. I was in Paris getting shot at."

The President ignored Carroll's remark. "Effective immediately, I'm ordering the following changes. I want you to continue to run the part of the operation that deals directly with known terrorist groups. But I want Phil Berger to supervise *the overall investigation of Green Band*, including the investigation of terrorists inside the U.S. You're to report directly to Phil Berger. You're also to give the CIA a complete record of your personal contacts, all your files."

Carroll stared incredulously at President Kearney. He was almost certain it wasn't legal for him to give his record files to the CIA. He also had the feeling he'd just been floated down the Potomac on a leaky raft. Thanks for all your past help, but your team's working methods leave something to be desired.

He turned his face away from the President who

seemed, in his Olympian wisdom, to have reached this decision single-handedly. That fact troubled and perplexed Carroll. But there was something else, one thing that disturbed him even more.

It was the general boardroom coldness, the sterile, Big Business atmosphere that was growing up everywhere in the government. It was all this super-secrecy, the super-deceit — usually under misleading cover of "security" and "need to know." *They* made the command decision, and they no longer felt they had to explain themselves to anybody.

"I guess I understand, Mr. President, and I'm afraid I have to quit under those circumstances. With all respect, I resign, sir. I'm out of this."

Arch Carroll got up and walked out of the conference room, out of the White House entirely. It was over for him. Washington was a bureaucratic company town, and he just didn't want to work for the company anymore.

Approximately an hour later, Arch Carroll sat inside an Eastern shuttle jet destined for New York. Outside, an electrical storm whipped the sky.

From his window he could see dramatic black clouds rushing as if headlong toward disaster. He stared at the gathering storm and he felt overwhelmed by a curious loneliness.

It was at times like these when he missed Nora most. Nobody he'd met before or since was as good at making him feel whole; nobody else seemed able to make him laugh at himself. And that was the real trick, being able to laugh when you needed to — and right now, Arch Carroll needed to laugh at something.

He felt Caitlin Dillon's hand on his arm. Turning, he gave her a weary half smile. She was trying her hardest to be sympathetic, to be kind.

"You must *know* it isn't your fault. Everybody's frustrated, Arch. Green Band didn't just do a number on Wall Street, it created an atmosphere of panic. Our President, who is turning out to be even less decisive

163

than I imagined he'd be, made a panicky decision. That's all."

She patted his arm and he felt like a kid with a scarred, bloody knee. This warm, almost maternal streak in Caitlin surprised him.

"It isn't your fault. You've got to keep that in mind. Washington is loaded with scared men making inadequate decisions." She paused before asking, "What will you do? Go into legal practice? Draw up wills? Deeds of trust? Maybe something like corporate law?"

Carroll drifted back from somewhere distant inside his mind. Her light sarcasm didn't escape him. He even welcomed it. *Law*, he thought. The reason he'd never used his degree was because he couldn't stomach the idea of law tomes, of hunting down precedents in the dust of unreadable books, and having to fraternize with other lawyers. They were a breed that depressed the hell out of him.

He was quiet for a time. Then he said, "Can you honestly imagine me reporting to that CIA clown Phil Berger?"

Caitlin shook her head. A puff of smoke surrounded her face a moment and she blinked. "He's an *egghead* in more than one sense of the word. The man must have been hatched."

Carroll suddenly laughed. The storm rocked the plane a moment. "When I was a kid, my mother used to give us hard-boiled eggs for breakfast. Some tradition from the old country. All of us kids would beat the tops open with our spoons. That's what I should have had back there in the White House. A goddam big spoon to beat on Phil Berger's head."

Carroll turned his head toward Caitlin Dillon. She was laughing now. It was a musical kind of laugh, like some quirky tune you couldn't forget, one that ran through your mind in a tantalizing way but you couldn't put a name to it.

Carroll finally shook with laughter. "You surprise me. You really surprise me."

164

"Why is that?"

"You look so damn straight and businesslike, but you've got this weird sense of humor underneath all that—"

"Weird for a Wall Street business type, I guess. For a dyed-in-the-wool Midwesterner. A Presbyterian."

Arch Carroll laughed some more, and it felt pretty good. Tension knots in his neck were finally loosening up. "Yeah. Of course. For a country hick from Ohio."

"My father taught me that you need a good sense of humor to survive Wall Street. He survived it, though just barely."

Caitlin gazed at Carroll, saying nothing more. She had stopped laughing and her expression was serious; her eyes searched his face. She looked as if maybe a small important gear had just shifted inside her mind.

Carroll watched her, conscious of something happening in his own body, the slightly unsettling motions of desire. For a moment, he had the uncomfortable feeling that he was betraying Nora, betraying a sacred memory –

Christ, it had been a long time since his body had reacted like this; he was suddenly aware of how deprived he was, how hungry he'd become. He raised one hand, his fingers trembling slightly, and he placed the palm against the side of Caitlin's face.

Gently, tenderly, he kissed her.

And then the moment was over as suddenly as if it had never happened.

Caitlin Dillon was looking from the window at the theatrical cloud display and talking about how soon they'd be back in New York – and what Arch Carroll wondered was whether he'd really kissed this woman. Or if it had been nothing more than a passing hallucination.

No. 13 Wall

When Carroll arrived back at No. 13 Wall, all that remained was for him to clear out his desk and leave the world of pointless stakeouts and twenty-hour work days. It was easy and mostly painless, he thought. Something he probably should have done a long time ago. He'd had enough cops and robbers for one lifetime.

He was interrupted by a knock on his door. When he turned, Walter Trentkamp was standing there. The FBI man walked slowly across the room. He leaned against the cluttered desk and sighed loudly.

"I'd quit too if I had an office like this." Trentkamp frowned. He stared around the room. "I mean, I've seen bleak before."

"What can I do for you, Walter?"

"You can reconsider the decision you made in Washington."

"Did somebody send you up here? Did they tell you to go talk some sense into Carroll?"

Trentkamp pursed his lips. He shook his head. "What'll you do now, anyhow?"

"Law," Carroll lied. It was something to say.

"You're too old already. Law's a young man's game."

Carroll sighed. Quit, Walter. *Quit it right now.*

Trentkamp continued to frown. "Nobody knows terrorists the way you do. If you leave, lives will be lost. And *you know it.* So what if your goddam pride is a little wounded right now?"

Carroll sat down hard behind his desk. He hated Walter Trentkamp just then. He hated the idea that another person could see through him so easily. Walter was so goddam smart. There was an impressive superiority that peeked through his policeman's facade every now and then. "You're a manipulative sonofabitch."

"Do you think I got where I am without some small understanding of human foibles?" Trentkamp asked. He held his hand out to be shaken. "You're a cop. It's in your blood. Every day you remind me a little more of your father. He was a stubborn bastard, too."

Carroll hesitated. With his own hand in mid-air, halfway toward Walter Trentkamp, he hesitated. It was one of those moments when his private world seemed to

166

spin on its own axis. He could choose – right now he had a choice.

He shrugged and shook Trentkamp's hand.

"Welcome back on board, Archer."

On board what? Carroll wondered. "One thing I want you to know. When Green Band is settled, I quit."

"Sure," Trentkamp said. "That's understood. Just keep in touch until Green Band *is* settled."

"I want to be a free man, Walter."

"Don't we all?" Walter Trentkamp asked, and finally smiled. "You're so fucking cute when you pout."

16

Caitlin Dillon

On the second floor of No. 13 Wall, meanwhile, Caitlin
Dillon sat in dark silhouette on a high wooden stool.
Most of the overhead lights in the room known as the
Crisis Room had been dimmed. She listened to the
soothing electronic whirr of half a dozen IBM and
Hewlett-Packard computers, complex machines she was
entirely comfortable around.

It had been Caitlin's original idea to collect and
evaluate all the available newspaper information and
police intelligence flowing in over the word processor
consoles. The news arrived in sudden, urgent bursts,
streams of tiny green letters that came from both the
financial sectors and police agencies all around the
world. As she sat there, her eyes hurting from the glare of
the screens, she pondered two things.

One was the scary and real possibility of a total
financial collapse around the world.

The other was the intricate, the almost hopeless puzzle
of her own private life.

Caitlin was aware that she had lived her thirty-four
years subject to two strong and contrary urges, two
radically different pulls on her energies and emotions.
Part of her wanted to be a traditional woman: feminine,
desirable, the kind of woman who loved to dress in
expensive things from Saks, or Bergdorf Goodman, or
Chloe and Chanel in Paris.

The other separate and equal part was independent,
highly competitive and ambitious, possessed of an
unusually fierce will.

Many years before, Caitlin's father, who was a deeply principled and intelligent investment banker in the Midwest, had tried to stand up to the large Wall Street clique of firms. He had lost his battle, lost an unfair fight, and been thrown into bankruptcy. Year after year, Caitlin had listened as he bitterly lectured against the injustice, the unfairness, and sometimes the utter stupidity built into the American financial system. In the same way that some children grow up wanting to be crusading lawyers, Caitlin had decided that she wanted to help reform the financial system. She had finally come East as a kind of avenging angel. She was both fascinated and repelled by the self-contained world of Big Business, and by Wall Street in particular. In her heart of hearts, Caitlin wanted the financial system to work properly, and she was fierce, almost obsessed with the application of her moral position as the SEC Enforcer . . .

It was likewise the independent, nontraditional part of Caitlin that enjoyed other mild eccentricities – like wandering the streets of New York in tight-fitting Italian jeans, crumpled oversized T-shirts, leather boots that came almost to her butt.

She might happily devote a particular Sunday afternoon to some exotic Italian recipe from Marcella Hazan – but she could easily go weeks abhorring the idea of doing any cooking at all, avoiding all housework in her East Side apartment. She was proud of earning almost six figures a year at the SEC, but sometimes she desperately wanted to throw it all over and have a baby. Sometimes, she was physically afraid she might never have a child. She *ached* with the idea, the way one aches from a real loss. And she had no idea, absolutely none, whether these opposing impulses could ever peacefully coexist.

She had been thinking along these lines ever since that surprising kiss on the Washington-to-New York airplane. It had been quick, casual, and yet she had the instinctive feeling she wanted to go beyond that first kiss with Carroll. The question was: Where?

What was she thinking, anyhow?

She hardly knew Carroll. His kiss had been the kiss of a stranger. She wasn't even sure if it had meant anything to him, or whether it had been something thrown up by the peculiar circumstances of the flight, his way of relieving tension, and disappointment, and more than a little justified anger.

I don't really know the first thing about him, she thought.

A shuffling noise made her turn and she saw Carroll in the computer room doorway. She was embarrassed, as if she suspected he'd been standing there, reading her thoughts.

He had his arm in a fresh white sling and he looked pale. She smiled. She'd already heard about the success of Walter Trentkamp's personal appeal and she was relieved – decisions made under duress were almost always the wrong ones, she knew. Carroll's impetuousness was part of his charm: but one day, she thought, one day he might run into the kind of serious trouble he couldn't extricate himself from.

"I had Michel Chevron all ready to talk about the European black market," he said.

"Don't keep blaming yourself."

"Somebody knows all our moves. Christ, who knows what Michel Chevron could have told me?" Carroll shifted the weight of his body from one foot to the other. She was reminded of a restless, fairly agile prizefighter warming up.

"How's the arm?" she asked. "Hurt?"

"Only when I think about Paris."

"Then don't think." She slid down from the wooden stool. She wanted to go across the room and somehow ease his discomfort, his embarrassment. She didn't. "I'm glad . . ." she said instead.

"Glad?"

She stared at him. Carroll had a vulnerable quality that inspired her to strange sympathies and concerns, but also anxieties she couldn't quite articulate right now. He had a lost boy quality, maybe that was it.

"Glad you didn't get yourself killed," she said and finally smiled. Her eyes widened and were remarkably stunning.

There was a breathless silence in the room.

She finally turned back to one of the computer screens, studying the mass of crawling green letters. The spell between them was broken again.

"Another Baader-Meinhof member was shot and killed in Munich." Caitlin looked up from the display screen message. She watched him, wondering again what the kiss on the airplane had meant.

Carroll merely nodded. "The West Germans are using Green Band as an excuse to solve their local terrorism problems. The BND is very pragmatic. They're probably the toughest police force in Western Europe."

Caitlin perched herself atop the high wooden stool again. She loosely hugged both her legs at the knees. Another message started to blip over the nearest computer. Caitlin turned and watched the computer screen closely.

Her mind had suddenly frozen.

"Look at this, Arch."

MOSCOW. THE KGB HAS INTERCEPTED PYOTR ANDRONOV. IMPORTANT UNDERWORLD BLACK MARKET SPECIALIST. ANDRONOV HOLDING U.S. SECURITIES, PRESUMED STOLEN. ANDRONOV LINKS STOLEN BONDS TO GREEN BAND. AMOUNT: ONE MILLION, TWO HUNDRED FIFTY THOUSAND DOLLARS. REFERRED TO AS "SAMPLES."

Moments later, another equally curious item began to appear on the computer display screen.

The second entry was from the Swiss in Geneva.

INTERPOL. RELIABLE LOCAL INFORMER HAS REPORTED "FLOODING" OF GENEVA MARKET WITH STOLEN BOND OFFERS. SELLER LOOKING FOR "SERIOUS BUYER." AMOUNT SUGGESTED AS HIGH AS FIVE TO TEN MILLION AMERICAN DOLLARS. SOURCE VERY RELIABLE.

171

"I think this might be the moment of truth." Carroll stared and gnawed at his bottom lip.

"*Something's* definitely happening. But why is it happening all at once like this?"

For the next hour and a half, during which the various screens virtually exploded with new information, as many as a dozen U.S. Army and police officials rushed down to look at the messages inside the Crisis Room. News was being transmitted from all over the world now, all at once.

As bad as it seemed, there was relief that *something* was happening. Was Green Band finally moving?

ZURICH. PREVALENT RUMORS HERE TONIGHT OF STOLEN U.S. SECURITIES AVAILABLE. VERY LARGE AMOUNTS. HIGH SEVEN-FIGURE THEFT INDICATED BY SOURCES.

LONDON, SCOTLAND YARD. DURING ROUTINE SEARCH IN KENSINGTON, AMERICAN STOCK CERTIFICATES FOUND. SERIAL NUMBERS TO FOLLOW. SUSPECT NOT IN FLAT WITH CACHE. SUSPECT IS JOHN HALL-FRAZIER, A KNOWN FENCE IN EUROPE BOND MARKET. SUSPECT KNOWN TO MICHEL CHEVRON.

BEIRUT. AHMED JARREL ARRESTED THIS EVENING HERE. TRADED THE FOLLOWING INFORMATION . . . JARREL HAD BEEN ATTEMPTING TO SELL U.S. SECURITIES IN BEIRUT. ASKING PRICE THIRTY FIVE CENTS ON A DOLLAR VALUE. VERY HIGH QUALITY BONDS. SOME BLANK CHEQUES ALSO. JARREL CLAIMS AMOUNT AVAILABLE UP TO ONE HUNDRED MILLION AMERICAN!

Half an hour later, using an ordinary hand calculator, Caitlin added up the amounts indicated on the display screens so far. She gasped as she arrived at the final sum.

It came to just under a hundred million U.S. dollars.
"Samples."

Next, she made a quick printout of the Fortune 500, America's largest individual corporations, to check against the stolen securities reported thus far.

Nearly all the thefts were in the top 100 companies.
Those reported to date created an unusual, elite universe. Was there a clue or potential lead in that?

Rank in Fortune 500	Company	Stockholder Equity
1	Exxon (New York)	$ 29,443,095,000
2	General Motors (Detroit)	20,766,600,000
3	Mobil (New York)	13,952,000,000
5	International Business Machines (Armonk, N.Y.)	23,219,000,000
6	Texaco (Harrison, N.Y.)	14,726,000,000
8	Standard Oil (Indiana) (Chicago)	12,440,000,000
9	Standard Oil of California (San Fransisco)	14,106,000,000
10	General Electric (Fairfield, Conn.)	11,270,000,000
15	U.S. Steel (Pittsburgh)	11,270,000,000
17	Sun (Radnor, Pa.)	5,355,000,000
20	ITT (New York)	6,106,084,000
26	AT&T Technologies (New York)	4,621,300,000
28	Dow Chemical (Midland, Mich.)	5,047,000,000
34	Westinghouse Electric (Pittsburgh)	3,410,300,000
39	Amerada Hess (New York)	2,525,663,000
42	McDonnell-Douglas (St. Louis)	2,067,900,000
43	Rockwell International (Pittsburgh)	2,367,300,000
45	Ashland Oil (Russell, Ky.)	1,084,824,000
50	Lockheed (Burbank, Calif.)	826,200,000
52	Monsanto (St. Louis)	3,667,000,000
55	Anheuser-Busch (St. Louis)	1,766,500,000
67	Gulf & Western Industries (New York)	1,893,924,000
69	Bethlehem Steel (Bethlehem, Pa.)	1,313,100,000
77	Texas Instruments (Dallas)	1,202,700,000
84	Digital Equipment (Maynard, Mass.)	3,541,282,000
89	Diamond Shamrock (Dallas)	2,743,327,000
92	Deere (Moline, Ill.)	2,275,967,000
97	North American Philips (New York)	883,874,000

By 9:15, the Crisis Room at No. 13 Wall was filled with officials from the White House and the Pentagon who scrutinized the computer screens like gamblers nervously watching the outcome of their bets. The Secretary of the Treasury and the Vice-president were both present. Phil Berger of the CIA had been flown in by special Air Force helicopter from Washington.

At eleven o'clock, urgent reports were still chattering in over the computer terminals. The President had been kept informed; another National Security conference had already been called for late that night.

This time, however, neither Arch Carroll nor Caitlin Dillon was invited to travel down to Washington.

"What did *I* do?" Caitlin angrily complained to Carroll when she found out.

"You've got the wrong friends," Carroll said. "You're traveling in some bad company."

"You?" she asked.

"Yeah. Me."

17

Zavidavo, Russia

At four-thirty that morning, three sets of yellow headlights lanced a dense gray wall of fog. The lights stopped suddenly, making circles on a twelve-foot-high electrified gate which dripped snow and ice.

The oppressive gate was meant to help protect the Russian version of Camp David, a heavily fortified hunting lodge called Zavidavo.

"Prajol!" Two militiamen from the Internal Security Division immediately waddled out into the bracing cold. They were carrying machine guns and dressed in bulky coats. It was their job to carefully check the identification of all visitors.

In a matter of seconds, with highly unusual dispatch, a Cheka and two hand-tooled Zil limousines were cleared to proceed up the icy lanes winding to the main hunting lodge.

The automobiles, side-blinds drawn, carried *six* of the most important decision makers in Soviet Russia. The military guards hurried back into their gatehouse and immediately called for emergency security for the woodland resort compound.

Both men had been rudely shocked and surprised by the identity of the six people they had just seen at the front gate. They exchanged looks and muttered quietly to each other, their breath hanging like thick clouds of smoke on the chill air. All at once, the peaceful atmosphere of the compound had changed; the guards were nervous and alarmed.

Inside the main dacha, meanwhile, Major General

175

Radomir Raskov of the GRU Secret Police was feeling apprehensive as well; but he was also heady with excitement and heightened expectation. Raskov had commissioned an elegant country breakfast to be served in a sun parlor, which was heated by a blazing log fire. Everything was ready.

Right after breakfast, General Raskov would drop his private bombshell on the six visiting leaders.

At a little past five A.M., the Politburo steering group sat down to steaming platters heaped with duck eggs, country sausage and freshly caught fish.

The breakfast table group included Yori Ilich Belov, the Russian Premier; a Cossack, Red Army General named Yuri Sergeivitch Iranov; the First Secretary of the Communist Party; General Vasily Kalin; the heads of both the KGB and GRU.

General Radomir Raskov spoke informally over the clacking noise of forks and knives. His smile, which was usually a small tight fist of teeth, was surprisingly warm and inviting. "In addition to the main business of our meeting, I am delighted to report the wood pheasant are back on the north ridge."

Premier Yori Belov clapped his huge hamlike hands. A stiffly formal man wearing thick bifocals, he raised his dark, fuzzy eyebrows and smiled for the first time since he'd arrived. Premier Belov was an obsessive hunter and fisherman. One of the things he liked best about General Raskov was that Raskov was a dedicated and intelligent student of human nature – a classic and unabashed manipulator – something he undoubtedly fine-tuned during his frequent stays in America.

General Raskov continued in a more serious, sober tone. "On December sixth, as you all know, I spoke with our friend and comrade François Monserrat about the dangerous and now potentially uncontrollable economic situation developing in the United States . . .

"At that time, he informed me he had been contacted by persons claiming responsibility for the unprecedented Wall Street attack. . . . During the past two days,

176

Monserrat's representatives have actually met with representatives from the so-called Green Band faction. In London . . ."

Premier Belov turned sharply to Yuri Demurin, director of the KGB. "Comrade Director, has *your* department been successful in discovering anything further about the *provocateur* group? How, for example, were they able to originally contact François Monserrat?"

"We have been working very closely with General Raskov of course," General Demurin lied with unctuous sincerity. He was a sallow man with a face across which ran a network of veins. "Unfortunately, at this time, we have been able to come up with nothing definitive about the precise make-up of the terrorist cell."

General Radomir Raskov clapped his hands harshly, ostensibly for a servant.

Demurin was his only real rival in the highly competitive Soviet police world. Demurin was also a capital shit, a petty bureaucratic turd without a single redeeming characteristic. Whenever he was in a staff meeting with Demurin, General Raskov's blood automatically boiled; his eyes bulged out of the broad slab that was his forehead.

A busty blond maid appeared, hovering nervously like a moth. The peasant maid's name was Margarita Kupchuck, and she had served at Zavidavo since the early 1970s. Margarita Kupchuck's quiet, earthy humor had made her a personal favorite with all the important Soviet government members.

"We're ready for more coffee and tea, my dear Margarita. Some preserves or fruit would be nice, as well. Would anyone prefer a stronger libation? To thicken the blood against the cold of this miserable morning?"

Premier Belov smiled once again. He had placed a navy blue packet of Austrian cigarettes in front of himself. "Yes, Margarita, please bring us a bottle of spirits. Some Georgian white lightning would be appropriate. In case some of our engines don't start so easily in this arctic cold."

Belov laughed now and his various chins shook, giving

everyone the impression that his face was about to slip through layers of his neck and vanish into his body.

General Raskov smiled. It was always politic to smile, at least, whenever Premier Belov took it upon himself to laugh. "We now believe we know the reason for the bombings in America," he said, *finally dropping his bombshell on the group.*

General Raskov silently gazed around the handsome and rustic breakfast parlor. The important men sitting at the table had stopped lighting cigars, stopped taking sips of Russian coffee.

"This Green Band group has made a somewhat frightening proposal to us. Through François Monserrat's terrorist cell, actually. The offer was made last evening. In London. . . . *This* is why I've called all of you here so early in the morning."

General Raskov lightly drummed his fingers on the dining table as he spoke the next words. "Comrades, the Green Band group has requested a payment. A total of *one hundred twenty million dollars in gold bullion.* This sum is in exchange for securities and bonds *stolen* during the December fourth bombings on Wall Street.

"The securities were apparently removed during the seven-hour evacuation itself. How this *incredible robbery* actually took place, I do not know. . . . Comrades, the *net* worth of the stolen goods offered to us . . . is in excess of two billion dollars!"

The men, the elite who ruled Soviet Russia, were uniformly silent; they were obviously reeling at the massive numbers they had just heard.

There was no way anyone could have been effectively prepared for such an announcement.

At first, no word at all from Green Band. And now *this.* Two billion dollars to be ransomed.

"They plan to sell to buyers other than ourselves as well. The total amount would seem to be enough to cripple the Western economic system." General Raskov went on. "This could easily mean a *cataclysmic panic* for the American Stock Market.

"An opportunity for control such as this has rarely before presented itself to the leadership of the Soviet Union. Either way, we must act now. We must act quickly, or they will withdraw their offer."

General Raskov stopped speaking. His very round, widely spaced eyes slowly circled the dining table, pausing at each perplexed face. He nodded with satisfaction; he had everyone's full attention, and more.

At 5:30 A.M., the highest-ranking Soviet leaders began heatedly to discuss the issues, the unbelievable decisions suddenly at hand.

Margarita Kupchuck

Less than ten miles away from Zavidavo, a Russian delivery truck marked *flour* fishtailed, then moderately regained control. It was barreling down a narrow country road which seemed little more than an ice-slicked toboggan track.

The truck finally plowed to a stop in front of a dilapidated cottage in the country village of Staritsa. The Russian driver leaped out and ran crunching through bright new snow up to his knees.

The cottage door opened, and a woman's arm, in a drab gray bathrobe, took an envelope.

The driver then high-stepped back to his truck, and hurriedly drove away into the snow.

From the village of Staritsa, the contents of the envelope were relayed in telephone code to a young woman working at the GUM Department Store in Moscow.

The GUM clerk used a special telephone, and another complex code, to make an urgent transatlantic call to the United States, specifically to the city of Langley, Virginia.

The original message had been sent by Margarita Kupchuck, the peasant housekeeper at Zavidavo. For nearly eleven years Margarita had been one of the most important operatives of the Central Intelligence Agency working inside Russia.

The message provided the American team with their first substantial break in the Green Band investigation.

It consisted of just sixteen words:

Ritz Hotel, London. Thursday morning. Two billion dollars, stolen securities to be finally exchanged . . . Green Band.

18

Carroll

It was probably a dream, and a very bad one.

He was standing in an unfamiliar room whose walls met the ceiling at angles that would have been impossible in anything other than dream geometry. There was a door halfway open and a pale light, the color of pearl, created a slat of dull color.

A shadow moved into the pearl-colored light and stood there just beyond the door. He knew, without even having to look, that the figure was Nora. He wanted to move forward, to step out of the room, he wanted to see Nora and hold her but something held him in place, something kept him rooted to the floor. He cried her name aloud.

And then—

A bell was ringing. And he imagined it rang in Nora's hand.

Disturbed, sweating, Arch Carroll sat upright. He rubbed his eyes, swung his legs over the side of the rumpled covers on his bed.

And then he realized that the bell was real. Someone was ringing the doorbell and this was the sound his dream had absorbed. He wandered from the bedroom. He squinted into the spyhole of the Manhattan apartment he'd once shared with Nora.

"Who is it?"

He could see nothing except swirling blackness where the hallway had definitely been last night.

Years before, he'd lucked into the West Side apartment, a sprawling three bedroom with river views. The apartment was still rent-controlled at two hundred and seventy-nine dollars a month, an impossible bargain. After Nora died, Carroll had decided to hold on to the place and use it nights when he worked late in the city.

"Who is it? Who's out there?" *Doorbell goddamn ring itself or was he still dreaming?*

Whoever was out in the apartment house hallway didn't seem to want to answer.

Carroll reached back for his Magnum.

Arch Carroll finally unlocked the Segal, but he left the heavy link-chain secure. He swung the front door open about four inches and the chain snapped against the sturdy wooden jamb.

Caitlin Dillon was peering in at him through the doorway crack. She looked frightened. Her eyes were hollow and dark.

"I couldn't sleep. I'm sorry if I disturbed you."

"What time is it?"

"I'm embarrassed to say it's before six. It's about twenty to six."

"In the morning?"

"Arch, please laugh at this or something. Oh, God. I'm going." She suddenly turned away up the hallway.

"Hold it. Wait a minute. Hey, *stop walking.*"

She half turned at the elevator. Her hair was wildly wind-blown and her cheeks were flushed, like she'd been riding horses in Central Park.

"Come on in. . . . Please come in and talk. Please?"

Inside his apartment, Carroll whisked clean the kitchen table, and he made coffee. Caitlin sat down and twisted her long fingers together nervously. She opened a box of cigarettes and lit one. When she spoke her voice was husky, slightly unfamiliar.

"I've been chain-smoking for hours, which is uncharacteristic of me. I couldn't sleep, I couldn't stop pacing around, either. All that information about the stolen securities kept spinning through my head, Arch . . ."

Carroll shook the last remnants of the bad dream from his mind, jerking himself into the present. "Green

Band's moving at last. Only I can't figure out the direction they're taking."

"That's one thing that bothers me," Caitlin said. "And then I start to wonder how much has been stolen and how far this whole incredible thing goes. I calculated an amount in the region of a hundred million, but God knows how much more has actually disappeared."

She sighed, crushing her cigarette impatiently. "Also, I'm still really ticked off at not being invited to that meeting in Washington. Do they honestly think I've got nothing to contribute? *None* of them understands the financial world. They really don't."

Carroll had never seen her in quite this frame of mind. It was like watching her from a whole new set of angles – she was angry, she was worried, and she seemed temporarily confused. Her usual business world professionalism couldn't help her now; she was reduced to asking wild questions which neither of them could answer. Suddenly, Caitlin Dillon wasn't quite so untouchable. If he was the son of two generations of New York cops, she was a ruined banker's daughter, and equally serious about her obligations to her past.

Around seven-fifteen they made Sara Lee danishes, the only moderately edible items in Carroll's kitchen.

"When I was thirteen or so I actually won a bakeoff. This was at an Ohio country fair," Caitlin admitted as she pulled the steaming danishes out of the oven. She kind of looked the part at the stove, too – pure Lima, Ohio.

They moved out to a windowed nook which overlooked the river and the New Jersey Palisades. One whole wall of the room was covered with thirty-five millimeter pictures of the kids. A single, fading picture was of Carroll as an Army sergeant in Viet Nam. He'd taken down the last pictures of Nora only a few months before.

"Mmmfff. Tremendous." He licked sticky crumbs off his index and middle fingers.

Caitlin's light brown eyes rolled back into her forehead. "I'm not impressed with your kitchen supplies,

183

Arch. Your cupboard's stocked with four bottles of beer, a half jar of Skippy peanut butter. Haven't you heard – the contemporary man in New York is a gourmet cook."

Maybe *her* boyfriends were, Carroll thought to himself. None of the "contemporary men" Carroll knew could cook anything much more complicated than Campbell's tomato soup.

"What can I tell you, I'm basically an ascetic. Skippy peanut butter happens to be cholesterol free."

A different kind of look crossed Caitlin's face right about then. A private joke smile? Carroll wasn't sure he'd read it correctly. Was she laughing at him now?

Then a quick reassuring smile came that was warm and even more comfortable.

"I think we're going to need at least an hour," she said somewhat mysteriously. "Uninterrupted time. Phone-off-the-hook seclusion and quiet. You didn't have any big plans for the middle-early morning I hope?"

"Just sleep."

"Boring. Also not very ascetic."

Carroll helplessly shrugged his broad shoulders; his eyes burned with curiosity. "I'm a boring person. Daddy, sometimes *mom* of four; straight job with the government; occasional terrorist contact."

There was a dense silence as he and Caitlin finally walked out of the windowed den. They cleared their throats almost at the same moment. Caitlin reached for him, and then they were lightly, just barely holding hands.

Arch Carroll was suddenly very aware of her perfume, the *shh-shh* of her jeans, the soft silhouette of her profile . . .

"This is one of the more impressive New York apartments I've been in. I really didn't expect this. All the hominess, the charm."

"What did you expect: hunting rifles on the wall? . . . Actually, I sew. I can knit. I do iron-on patches for four little kids."

Caitlin had to smile at Carroll again.

It was the first time he'd seen this particular smile.

Irony, but also nice warmth were glowing in her eyes at the same time. He felt like they'd crossed some invisible barrier, made some slightly more solid connection. He wasn't sure what it was, though.

They started to kiss and touch each other lightly in the narrow hallway. They kissed chastely, gently at first. Then the kiss became harder, with urgency and surprising strength on Caitlin's part.

They kissed all the way to the front bedroom where amber morning light was flooding the room. Huge, curtainless windows faced onto the Hudson, which was a flat, slate-blue lake that morning.

"Caitlin? . . . Is this really wise?"

"It *is* really wise. It doesn't mean the end of the world, you know. It's just one morning. I promise not to get hurt. If *you* do."

She put a gentle finger to Carroll's lips. Soften the blow of her last statement. She then lightly kissed the back of her own finger.

"I have one small favor. Don't think about anything for ten minutes or so. No Ohio jokes either. Okay?"

Carroll nodded. She was smart about this kind of thing, too. A little scary smart. She'd been here before . . . *I won't get hurt; don't you get hurt.*

"All right. Whatever you say can be the official rules."

For a moment, they sat together, hugging on the low-slung, quilt-covered double bed. Then they very slowly began to undress. A shivery draft slithered in from the casement windows; the cold air seemed to blow right through the tall black window panes.

Carroll was completely, physically and spiritually entranced. Also frightened. *He hadn't been with anybody for over three years. There hadn't been anything like this for so very long.* He felt a little guilty, automatically comparing Caitlin with Nora, though he didn't want to.

Caitlin's hands had the lightest imaginable touch. Extraordinary control and gentleness as she tugged off his trousers. He felt everything beginning to relax inside.

185

Her fingers were like elegant feathers over his upper back. Tickling. Dusting his neck.

Then Caitlin's palms. Rotating in easy circles. Into his temple. Gently pulling on the curls of his dark hair.

Carroll was inspired to remember that he was ticklish down both sides of his stomach. He had been since he was a little kid, getting baths from his mother up in the West Bronx. The son of a cop, who'd been the son of a cop. Ultimately, he'd been unable to escape from his background. Some days he wondered why he'd ever tried so hard.

More feathery fingers. Teasing Carroll up and down the sides of his legs . . .

Onto the callused balls of his feet, his bony toes, his soles . . .

Then everything was moving slightly faster; up another whole notch in tempo.

His body suddenly, involuntarily spasmed. *Jesus Christ*.

Caitlin was doing some completely unexpected things to him.

She blew softly on the insides of her hands. She cupped warm fingers over his eyelids, then over his ears.

She spoke in a voice that was nearly as gentle and sensual as her touch. "This is called a thrill massage. Believe it or not, it was the fad at little Oberlin College."

"Yeah? You're very good at it. At this. You're wonderful in fact."

"Awh gee blush. . . . Wild youth in long forgotten Midwestern corn fields."

He was beginning to like her.

Maybe an awful lot.

He didn't know if he should, if this truly *was* wise.

She lightly brushed his legs again. . . . His upper back again. . . . Neck, scrotum.

Only much faster, even lighter now. Turning him into jelly, no container.

There was no real impression of fingers, he was noticing.

Quite amazing.

186

More like the softest combs of air.

How had she gotten this good? . . . A little unbelievable in a way . . . being who she was. . . . Who was she, really?

Her lovely face came down very close then. "Smile for the camera, Arch." Faint smiling whisper from Caitlin. "My heart is pure, but my mind is occasionally kinky."

At some time, somewhere in all of the light touching, brushing, tickling, Caitlin had táken her jeans and blouse off. She still wore pink underpants, wool knee socks. Her breasts had the loveliest, delicate, shell-pink nipples. They were hard now; totally aroused. She touched one erect nipple, then the other to the head of Carroll's penis.

She was a classic feminine masterpiece, Carroll couldn't help thinking, completely filling his eyes. She was so elegant to look at; to drink in like the finest wine.

Carroll remembered what she'd said before in the sun parlor. It made him smile a little now, almost laugh out loud. *We're going to need at least an hour.*

There was no longer such a thing as time; no Green Band urgencies existed right now. Carroll had the comfortable, wonderful idea that he trusted Caitlin Dillon. . . . He almost completely trusted her. How could he so easily trust Caitlin already? . . .

"Tell me all about yourself. Whatever comes out. No editing, okay, Carroll?"

To the continuing rhythm of her fingers; to the slight crooning of bed springs; to dancing morning sunbeams, Carroll spoke the truth, as he knew it:

"Whole life story. About thirty seconds. . . . As a little kid I always wanted to play for the Yankees, maybe, *maybe* for the football Giants. I settled for the Golden Gloves – Arch 'White Lightning' Carroll. Son of a New York cop. Very good, honest, *poor* cop. Typical Irish-Catholic family from the West Bronx. That's my youth. Notre Dame on scholarship. . . . Law School at Michigan State, then drafted. I didn't try to dodge it for some crazy reason.

"Four great, absolutely terrific kids. Kind of a perfect marriage until Nora passed away. That's middle-American

187

for *she died* . . . I'm, I think I'm a very different person when I'm with my kids. Childlike and free. Maybe a little retarded . . . um . . . boy . . . that's very nice. Yes, right there. Ohio, huh?"

"What else? You were telling me your life story. *Reader's Digest* condensed version."

"Oh, yeah . . . I have this recurring problem. *Big* problem . . . with *Them*."

"Who's them?"

Arch Carroll suddenly felt a sharp twist of tension. *Not now. He made it go away.*

"Just *them*. . . . Ones who make all the most important decisions. . . . Ones who rob people, without caring one way or the other. On Wall Street, down in Washington. Ones who trade terrorist murderers – for innocent, kidnapped business people. The ones who kill people of brain cancer. The bad guys. As opposed to . . . *us*."

Caitlin gently kissed Arch Carroll's curly brown hair; she kissed his puffed cauliflower ear. She finally found his mouth, which tasted very nice, she thought. Fresh and clean and sweet.

"I don't like *them* either. I think I like you. I think I like *us*. Please like me a little."

"All I can do is try, Caitlin. You're beautiful. You're witty. You seem to be nice as hell. I'll *try* to like you."

Somewhere else that morning . . .

"Now me. Your turn to . . ."

"This an' that, the next thing."

"Really softly, Arch . . . with you that name's more like a verb. To arch. Anybody ever call you Archie?"

"Not more than once."

"Tough guy," she purred.

"Grr. I'm a street cop."

Carroll slowly rose onto his hands, then his knees. He was very hard, almost painfully hard.

At his first touch, Caitlin tightened her stomach. Then she slowly let herself relax. She tightened the abdominal muscles in her long flat stomach then let herself relax again.

Her breathing was magnificently controlled, holding

188

effortlessly for several seconds. Her pulse was slow, a long-distance runner's . . .

Where did she learn all this stuff? Not in Ohio; not at Oberlin College.

Her eyes softly closed. Such smiling eyes. She was unbelievably easy to be with.

Arch Carroll's pulse was thumping so damn hard. He'd never in his life held off orgasm this long, never felt excited in quite this way. His head grew light.

"Please wait. Okay?" Caitlin softly whispered to him. Her body spasmed lightly.

"Trying . . ."

"Just . . . wait . . . please . . . Arch?"

Carroll's brain was screeching, burning up. His body was a million raw exposed nerves – as he floated down, floated down, floated down. Finally – he went inside Caitlin, both of them hyperventilating.

Her eyes slowly, very slowly, shut.

Her mouth opened. Wider and wider, an unbelievably soft, delicately pink mouth.

Her face was generous, so surprisingly sweet in passion. She actually seemed to be smiling all the time . . .

Then Caitlin's eyes flipped open – looked at him – and she made him feel so good. Wanted again. So necessary to somebody.

"Hi there, Arch. Nice to have you here."

"Hi yourself. Nice to be had."

They moved faster together. Her dark hair slowly danced backward and forward. Her thick curls spread across the pillow, brushed, flowed majestically across his face – hid her eyes.

Carroll arched dramatically and nearly fell over backwards. Impossible, acrobatic positions.

He spasmed, shuddered, called out her name so loudly it embarrassed him into a blush.

"Caitlin."

It was a new way of saying . . . *trust.*

Completely new feelings were coming so fast. . . . Old familiar feelings were returning.

Again . . . "Caitlin."

"Oh, Arch. Sweet, dear Arch."

He felt as if she knew him – instantly saw through his defenses, his poses. . . . Finally, somebody . . . Jesus.

When it was over, when it was finally, finally over, neither of them could move at all. . . . Nothing anywhere in the universe could possibly move. Not ever again.

Carroll and Caitlin slept in each other's arms. Carroll was able to sleep deeply for the first time in days. There was a dream and it wasn't a bad one this time at all, it wasn't a dream haunted by past losses and old wounds. This time, he and Caitlin went to a quaint, French seaside village together. They walked hand in hand on a deserted, rock-strewn beach. They met his four kids along the way. The kids had been playing and swimming . . .

A soft ringing came into his ears.

He was suddenly looking all around the beach for the origin of the sound. Caitlin and the kids were searching as well.

Telephone.

Carroll flung out his right arm across a tangle of quilt and bedsheets. The arm was uselessly numb, all pins and prickly needles. He groped for the unseen phone receiver, finally picked it up.

"Yes. Who is it?"

It was Phil Berger of the CIA, who said he had something that might interest Carroll.

The CIA man's voice was characteristically cold. It was obvious he didn't care to pass information along to Carroll but at the same time realized he was under an obligation to do so. The investigation of Green Band was still a team effort, right?

The call was about Margarita Kupchuck's coded letter from Zavidavo.

The call was about the Russians.

About an upcoming meeting in London.

About two billion dollars. At least that much.

About Green Band happening again.

190

"How soon can you leave, Carroll?"

"I'm on my way."

Carroll put the receiver back in place and turned to look at Caitlin, who was watching him through half-open eyes, her look one of pleased satisfaction – as if she'd solved at least one of the puzzles in her life.

"Four minutes?" she smiled outrageously. "Uninterrupted time? Phone-off-the-hook seclusion and quiet?"

Thursday–Saturday;
December 10–12; Europe

19

Chief Customs Officer Thomas O'Neil

Thomas X. O'Neil, Chief of U.S. Customs at Shannon
Airport, Ireland, habitually walked with most of his body
weight ponderously thrown back on his boot heels. As
he walked, his toes splayed out as if he were wearing
ill-fitting bedroom slippers. His size forty-seven waist
protruded obscenely, as did his customary, nine-incher
Cuban cigar. Chief O'Neil looked like an unflattering
caricature of Churchill and he couldn't have cared less.
He had a public image and he enjoyed it. He didn't give a
good goddamn what anyone thought to the contrary.

At twelve noon, O'Neil casually waddled across the
frozen gray tarmac toward North Building Three at the
Irish airfield located outside of Dublin.

As he walked, O'Neil could smell fresh peat settling in
the air. Nothing quite like the blessed aroma, he was
thinking. At the same moment, he looked up and saw a
majestic 727 just gliding in through a blowing fog from
America. Seven years before, he'd come over from New
York himself. He never ever planned to return to that
syphilitic rat's asshole, either. He had even tried to alter
his accent and speech patterns so that he'd sound Irish: it
was a ludicrous attempt and he came off sounding like a
ham in some third-rate touring company doing George
Bernard Shaw.

Inside Building Three there were literally hundreds of
various-sized wooden crates, marked with the usual,

faded corporate logos. A carrot-haired Irish inspector stood with a red marker and clipboard beside a bare wooden desk, right at the center of the cluttered warehouse room.

"This the lot of it, Liam?" Chief O'Neil asked the inspector. "This Pan Am Three Ten from this morning?"

"Aye, sir. These particular boxes're from the Catholic Charities in New York. Clothes and such for sendin' up north. Givin' us all their old Calvin Kleins, their Jordache jeans, so they are. Look very smart and chic on the Provos, I'll bet."

Chief Inspector O'Neil grinned broadly and nodded. He was trailing grand clouds of smoke all around the freight inspection shack. He both chewed and puffed his Cubans, to get his full money's worth.

Thomas O'Neil had been born and raised in New York's Yorkville section; he'd worked as an inspector at Kennedy International, nearly nine years before his fortuitous transfer as Head of the U.S. service at Shannon.

Before that, O'Neil had been a master sergeant in general supply over in Viet Nam. Over in Nam, he'd managed to look like a junior Patton, instead of Churchill.

He was also Vets 28.

"Looks fine and dandy to me, lad. Let the hearty boys load it up for the trip north. Spiffy new clothes for women and wee children. A very good cause."

Chief Inspector O'Neil laughed for no apparent reason. He was in a chipper mood in general that afternoon.

And why not? Had he not just succeeded in getting one billion four worth of freshly stolen stock certificates and securities into Western Europe? Had he not just become an instant multimillionaire himself?

London

4:00 A.M.

Why were there suddenly so many 4:00 A.M.'s crowding into his life? Arch Carroll wondered. For a foggy moment he was disoriented: he felt like a man on a treadmill sent spinning off into space, where time zones collapsed, where clocks had no meaning.

This, he remembered, was the heart of London.

But that didn't matter because 4:00 A.M.'s were mostly alike. A bleached-out, dour hour of the day when cities slept and only cops and criminals wandered around, following some curious ancient chronology all their own.

Everything always started as the same intense four-bell-alarm emergency, but nothing ever happened after you broke every imaginable speed and safety law getting to the supposed crime scene. Not right away, anyway . . .

First you waited.

Almost always you waited.

And waited.

You drank drums of bitter black coffee; you smoked countless stale cigarettes; you paid your full dues every single time on a police case.

His fingers gently massaged his warm, throbbing temple. He felt weirdly numb as he watched Caitlin, who catnapped across the room in the stuffy Ritz Hotel. For the past few hours, Caitlin had been drifting in and out of a restless sleep. Her pale lips parted slightly as she swallowed. The scooped hollow in her throat made her look particularly sweet and vulnerable. Her long legs were neatly curled under her like they had a folding pin inside.

They'd been on emergency alert for twenty straight hours now. They were one of several police/financial teams which had been rushed to London following Margarita Kupchuck's warning transmission from inside Russia.

It was exactly like the unpleasantly tense and chaotic Wall Street deadline on December 4.

Nothing had happened when it was supposed to happen.

No Russians with an extraordinary $120 million payment.

No Green Band with their enormous pilfered hoard of stocks and bonds.

194

First, you wait.

"How in hell did they manage to make contact with François Monserrat? Monserrat is completely unknown. Virtually without a face. Damned fellow's an enigma to every intelligence agency I know of in the world."

A Chief Inspector from Britain's MI6, the secret intelligence service, sat in a leather club chair positioned opposite Carroll in the London hotel suite. Patrick Frazier was a tall man with thinning pale blond hair and a pencil-thin moustache. He wore his clothes in the rumpled manner favored by Oxford dons and he spoke in a cultivated drawl, every word deliberately shaped as if each were a lozenge he had to suck before he spat it out. Frazier, however, was one of Britain's resident experts on urban terrorism.

Physical pain was coursing through Arch Carroll's body as he listened. *Yes, you paid your dues every single time with police work.*

Too much bitter-tasting coffee and unrelieved tension; not enough sleep. Too much being lost and confused without any recognizable point of reference. And the arm still ached like hell even though he'd discarded the sling in favor of a bulky bandage.

Hours later, the hotel room telephone rang and Patrick Frazier eagerly snatched it up. "Ah, Harris. How are you, old man? Oh, we're holding up. I suppose we are. It's for you, Carroll. Scotland Yard."

Perry Harris on the other end was speaking very loudly as Arch Carroll took over the line. Harris was from the Yard's Serious Crime Squad. Carroll had worked with Perry Harris twice before in Europe and Carroll respected the man, who was thorough and honest and who spoke to criminals in a voice that effectively bludgeoned them. A hard man of the fast-disappearing old school.

"Carroll, listen to what we've just found. You're not going to believe it, I'll wager. *There's been an incredible turn.* The IRA . . . the IRA has just contacted us. . . . They want a meeting set up with *you* in Belfast. *You* specifically. They're in the game now, too. The Russians seem to be out."

"In what way? How are the Provos involved, Perry?"

Blood was suddenly distressingly pounding in Carroll's forehead. Green Band came at you extremely hard, then they pulled away just as fast. They came at you – then they disappeared again. The second you dropped your guard, *bang*, right between the eyes. They were like fast-card experts. Carroll was assailed by the same exasperating thought as before – they're still playing games. He sighed wearily.

Come to Florida, Mr. Carroll. A clue there? Florida?

Go see Michel Chevron. A key somewhere in Europe? And now the Provos.

"They've come into some securities, some U.S. bonds. Over a billion American dollars' worth according to the boyos. . . . They listed names and serial numbers for us to check in New York. *They check.*"

"Hold on, wait a minute," Arch Carroll was sitting rigidly upright in his hotel chair now.

"*The IRA has taken over all the stolen securities?*"

"I don't know. They're definitely in possession of *some* stolen goods."

"But how?"

"Who knows. They must have met with Green Band, maybe with François Monserrat's people. They're telling us as little as possible, of course."

"Son of a *bitch*." They'd come so far; they'd seemed so close to some kind of break in the Green Band puzzle. "All right, all right. We'll be back in touch as soon as we sort out some things here. Thanks for calling. We'll be back to you, Perry."

Carroll slammed down the phone receiver. He glared across the London hotel room at Chief Inspector Frazier, at Caitlin, whose eyes were suddenly wide open and alert.

"*Somehow* the IRA has made a move into this thing. More chaos orchestrated by Green Band. . . . It seems the Provos want to talk about selling some securities back to us. *Over a billion* American dollars' worth. They know we're in London. How could they know?"

196

The question stuck in Carroll's brain like a shriek.

And since he couldn't answer it, since he hadn't been able to answer it so far, what was the point in asking it now? Something was deflating inside him.

He wanted to sleep.

How could they know everything ahead of time? Who was telling them?

Monserrat

The man called François Monserrat, who was wearing a black nylon anorak and a dark beret, and who now walked with a pronounced limp, moved down the Portobello Road in the west of London.

He passed through the open market for which this street was famous; now and then he would pause at this stall or that and examine an antique. There were some very fine pieces to be had here. There were also some obvious fakes.

You needed a good eye, a practiced eye, to tell the real article from the false, he thought. In the palm of his hand he turned over a jade piece in the shape of a small lynx. He curled his fingers around it, squeezing hard. . . . He was not a man who gave way to his emotions easily. In fact, he came at them in a circumspect way, circling as if they were live packets of plastique. At any given moment, an emotion could all too easily explode.

Like right now.

The sensation coursing through Monserrat was one of cold anger. If the jade lynx had been fur and bone, the life would have been squeezed out of it. He was angry because he didn't like clever games, *when they were played by the other side's rules.*

Green Band, for instance, had become a threat.

They created their own rules, their own games.

They said one thing. They did another.

They suggested important meetings that never took place.

197

They were like air. They were very much wisps and phantoms. Monserrat's admiration was grudging.

He set the jade lynx down and he closed his eyes. He had a trick to guard against emotion. He would retreat into a dark, cool place in the deepest part of his mind: a monastery of silence. In this sanctuary he almost always had control. Nothing slipped away from him here.

This time, though, his little trick of mind failed. He opened his eyes and the bustling market assaulted his senses.

Green Band was somewhere close by. What did they really want?

Perhaps very soon, he would know all about Green Band.

Belfast

They had to wait one final time. They had to wait at the tiny, rigidly fastidious Regent Hotel in Belfast.

Arch Carroll tried to accept the unpleasant, helpless feeling that they had absolutely no control over anything that was happening. The Green Band strategy – whatever it was – seemed to be working flawlessly.

Well-coordinated economic terror.

Massive psychological disorientation, designed to create escalating chaos and even more worldwide terror.

Patrick Frazier kept up a cheery pep talk under the unusually trying circumstances. The British Special Branch man was almost tirelessly gung-ho, yet at the same time, understated.

"When we do meet with them," Frazier slid off his wire glasses and briskly rubbed his eyes, "you'll be outfitted with an internal transmitter. Absolute state of the art. Designed for the military. Armalite Corporation. You swallow the damn thing."

Carroll politely shook his head. "No comment on that one." Ah, police work. Sometimes he wondered what he'd *thought* it was going to be like – long, long ago when he'd first decided on what he now sometimes called the *wrong side of the law*.

"If we ever do meet up with them, Caitlin of course must verify that the securities are genuine," Frazier said.

"If we ever meet up with them."

Six more hours droned by in the most painfully slow waltz-time. The only perceptible change was the morning sliding into afternoon outside, the day turning to the steel-blue shades of the Northern Irish cityscape.

A red-haired serving girl, no more than sixteen or seventeen, finally brought in steaming tea and hot Irish soda bread. Carroll, Frazier, and Caitlin ate nervously, out of boredom more than anything.

Carroll remembered to check in with Walter Trentkamp's office in New York. He left a message for Walter, *"Naught, zero, bupkis, zip, goose egg . . . as in wild goose egg chase."*

Ten hours passed inside the Regent Hotel suite.

It was exactly like what had happened the night of December 4 in New York, when the final deadline for the bombings had gone past, and the clock hands had begun to move with intolerable slowness. Why, though? How were they supposed to invesitgate a chimera or a mirage?

From the fourth-floor window of the hotel suite, Carroll saw an antiquated bicycle bumping over the cobblestoned street outside. It was ridden by a man of about seventy, whose thin frame didn't look like it could survive the shuddering motions of the bike. Carroll leaned closer to the dormer window. His brain felt like something shapeless lying in a basin of tepid water.

The rider parked his bike almost directly below the Regent Hotel window.

"Could this be our contact?" Carroll asked in a hoarse voice.

Patrick Frazier moved into the window and studied the old man. "Doesn't look the terrorist type. That's a good sign. They never do in Belfast."

The rider hobbled inside the hotel entrance, then disappeared completely from Carroll's sight.

"He's inside now."

"Then we wait and see," Patrick Frazier said, muttering to himself.

Carroll sighed. The tension buzzing inside him was familiar now. He looked toward Caitlin, who smiled bravely at him. How did she always stay so calm? The journey, the tension, the awful waiting. The sense, all around them, of imminent danger. Belfast, after all, was a fully declared war zone – a tragic city where innocent people died on a daily basis, pursuing confusing beliefs that had their roots in a conflict begun hundreds of years before.

Less than ninety seconds after he went inside the Regent, the old man came marching out again. He rigidly climbed back on his bike. Almost immediately there came a solid rap on the hardwood door of the hotel suite.

Caitlin rose up and opened the door with a sharp pull.

"An old man just delivered this message," a young British detective entered and crisply reported. He walked forward to his commander, passing both Caitlin and Carroll without so much as a nod.

Patrick Frazier immediately ripped the envelope open and read it without any discernible expression. Frazier's red-rimmed eyes finally peeked over the wrinkled note page at Carroll. He seemed nervous and concerned suddenly.

He read the words of the message aloud for both Carroll and Caitlin:

"There's no salutation or date. . . . It reads as follows: 'You are to send your representative with the proof of transfer of funds. Your representative is to be at Fox Cross Station, six miles northwest outside of Belfast. That's the railroad. Be there at 0545 hours. The precious securities will be safely waiting nearby. . . . The messenger is to be Caitlin Dillon. *No one else is acceptable to us*. There will be no further contact.'"

20

Caitlin Dillon

At 5:30, the morning air was misty in suburban Belfast.

It was the kind of day in which objects have no hard definition. The railway platform at Fox Cross was silent. All the trees were stripped and bare and looked arthritic in the wintry absence of clear light. Up beyond the mist the sky was dark gray, and the cloud cover low.

Caitlin shivered slightly and folded both arms around her rising and falling chest. She could definitely hear the drumming of her own heart. She wasn't going to let herself be frightened, though. She vowed not to act the way a woman would be expected to act under the difficult circumstances. She wouldn't give in to the sense of hysteria she could feel around the edges of her nerves.

Caitlin sucked in a raw, cold breath. She shifted impatiently from one boot to the other.

No one was visible yet, not anywhere up and down the weathered railway platform.

Was it all going to be over after this?

Who was Green Band finally going to turn out to be?. . . .

What possible part did the North Irish play? And what could have happened between the Russians and Green Band back in London?

A black leather briefcase hung down from her wrist. Inside were codes to release the enormous sums now on deposit at a Swiss bank, which were to be paid outright this morning. The ransom of the century was to take place here at little Fox Cross Station. Historic Fox Cross Station outside Belfast, Ireland.

Caitlin imagined she looked like a successful business-woman with the fine, black leather briefcase. Some regular commuter heading into downtown Belfast. Another day at the bloody office. She thought she was playing the part fairly well – on the outside, at least.

She glanced at her watch and saw it was a few seconds before five forty-five. The time they'd indicated for the exchange had come. Caitlin cautioned herself that they were not necessarily punctual.

What would their lack of punctuality mean right now? What would it mean in terms of any emergency police action planned for the Fox Cross railroad plat-form?

Caitlin's body tensed. Every muscle, every fiber inside her involuntarily tightened.

A faded blue panel truck had appeared, and was approaching the deserted station from a thick row of pine trees to the north.

The slow-moving truck steadily got larger and larger. Caitlin saw that there were three passengers, all of them men.

Then the blue panel truck passed Caitlin by. A gust of frozen wind swept back her hair, and Caitlin let out what must have been the deepest sigh of her lifetime.

Carroll and the British detectives were close by, a thought she found more than a little comforting. They were less than a mile away, according to the plan. Still, there was nothing they could do if trouble suddenly bloomed – if someone panicked, if someone made a simple, foolish mistake now. *Was Green Band nothing more than an outrageous robbery?*

A car, a nondescript sedan approached moments after the panel truck.

Caitlin tried to observe everything about the car as it rolled forward over the parking lot gravel. Very possibly it was just a passenger drop-off for the first scheduled train at 6:04.

It was a late model Ford, grayish-green, with a slightly smashed-in front grill. There was a tiny chip in the

202

windshield. Four passengers inside – two in front, two in the back.

Irish working men? Thick, heavy-set types anyway. Maybe farm workers?

But the second car passed her by, too.

Caitlin was both tremendously relieved and dis-appointed. She was confused, trying desperately to keep her wits and remnants of her concentration.

Then the car stopped suddenly. The tires screeched in reverse. Two burly men in back jumped out; both were wearing black cloth masks, both carried machine gun pistols.

They ran to Caitlin at full speed, workshoes splatting hard against the concrete.

"You're Caitlin Dillon, missus?" one of the masked men asked. He thrust forward his menacing gun muzzle.

"I am." Caitlin's legs had begun to slightly buckle; her knees were suddenly on hinges.

"You were born in Old Lyme, Connecticutt?"

"I was born in Lima, Ohio."

"Birth date – January 23, 1950?"

"1953. Thanks a lot."

The masked IRA terrorist laughed at Caitlin's automa-tic response. He apparently appreciated a modicum of coolness and humor.

"All right then, dearie, we're going to put one of these hangman masks on you. No eyeholes for lookin' out. Nothing to be afraid of, though."

"I'm not afraid of you."

The other man, the silent partner, looped a black hood over her hair, then pulled it down tight over Caitlin's face. He was careful not to bump or touch any other parts of her body. How very Irish Catholic, Caitlin couldn't help thinking. They'd put a bullet into her without blinking, she knew that. But no impure thoughts, no accidental touching of a female breast.

"We're going to lead you back to the car now. Nice and easy. . . . Easy does it . . .

"All right, step up, step inside. Now down in the back. On the car floor here. There we go, all comfy."

Caitlin was feeling numb everywhere; her body seemed no longer to belong to her. She found herself saying, "Thank you. I'm fine right here."

"Your mum's name is Margaret?" Cleverly timed.

"My mother's name is Anna. Her maiden name is Reardon."

"No tracking device anywhere on your person?"

"No."

Caitlin had answered a little too quickly, she thought. Her skin went deathly cold. Suddenly she couldn't breathe at all.

There was no apparent reaction, nothing she could perceive as wrong from the Irish men. They seemed to believe her, not even to question what she'd said about the tracking device.

"I have to check you all the same. Pat you down. All right, here goes."

Clumsy, male hands (Mechanic? Some kind of working man?) groped all over her body. Caitlin stiffly tensed her stockinged legs as the man's hand wedged up between. The intruding hand felt very harsh and rude. The worst part so far. Probably not the worst she was going to experience today though.

"If you have a transmitter, we have orders to kill you. . . . *If you don't tell us right now.* Don't lie about this, dearie. Don't lie, missy. I'm quite serious. Do you? Do you have any tracking device? We'll check you thoroughly, as soon as we're out of here. Please tell me the truth."

"I have no tracking device on me." *Inside me. Could they really find that?*

There was no more talking after that. The horrible body search ended abruptly.

Caitlin's ears stayed plugged, as if she were trapped in a vacuum. Her heart lodged very high up in her throat. The car's engine coughed and came alive.

Someone suddenly wiped her face with a dripping-wet hand cloth.

Jesus. The fumes were everywhere. The fumes wouldn't let her breathe.

"No, I—"

Chloroform!

Carroll

"Oh, bugger it. Look at this hopeless mess," Patrick Frazier testily exclaimed.

Torrents of water jackhammered the black Bentley that Carroll and Inspector Patrick Frazier were riding in. Rain blasted the steamy windshields, hitting with the solid force of a firehose.

It had begun to spit rain at five minutes to six. Then suddenly it was coming down heavily, piercing the mist, making it near impossible to see the road ahead.

"They're on the Falls Road now. That's in the rough and tumble part of Belfast," Frazier said. "The Provisional Irish Republican Army *owns* it. . . . It's your basic urban ghetto where they regularly ambush our soldiers. Hit and run snipers in there, mostly. Urban guerrilla warfare at its best."

Both Carroll and Frazier were hunched forward in the front seat of the Bentley. The transmitter-beeper tracking Caitlin was coming over frighteningly loud and clear. It sounded a little like a sequence of radar blips, all originating somewhere deep in Caitlin's stomach.

Carroll couldn't help thinking of a heart-monitoring device in an intensive care unit, something that registered one's hold on life. Poor Caitlin. But he couldn't have done anything to stop her from going – he couldn't have offered himself as a substitute messenger, the instructions had been specific and final.

The monitoring *blip blip blip* was becoming louder now, and more stubbornly insistent.

The car with Caitlin inside was apparently slowing down. Maybe it was temporarily stopped at a street light? In heavy traffic? What now?

"Range closing fast, sir," reported the driver.

"Hang it. They're at the home base," Patrick Frazier sharply pronounced. His driver immediately stepped down on the gas. The Bentley leaned forward with a thrusting surge of power.

"Either that, or they're switching transportation," Carroll had another thought.

Carroll's mind cocooned tightly around the thought of Caitlin in serious danger. He was both angry and afraid.

"Let's get in closer to her. Come on! Come on, let's move it now!" Carroll snapped at the British Special Service driver.

Home Base Belfast

Less than two miles away, the black cloth hood was raised up over Caitlin's head; she reeled away as acrid smelling salts were briskly passed under her nose. Her watering eyes rolled backward.

"Unhh?"

Focus. There were dull-edged silhouettes rather than faces clustered all around her. Three of them.

Behind the looming shapes stood excessively bright lamps. Behind the lamps were still more shadowy, unidentifiable figures. Green Band?

She couldn't see who the others were. . . . Not yet anyway.

"Welcome back among the living. You're a brave one to accept our invitation. Probably a little scared right now. That's natural enough."

Caitlin still couldn't see them very well, even the men standing closest to her.

"You *do* have authority to transfer the agreed-upon sum of money? You have the necessary bank codes, Ms. Dillon?"

Caitlin nodded. Her neck was stiff, her throat dry and itchy.

When she spoke her voice sounded hollow and lifeless to her, her words clumsily formed, as if she were being spoken through by a ventriloquist.

"Would you mind showing me . . . some of the stolen securities. I need some reassurance, as well. I need to see what we're getting in the exchange."

"You'll be able to estimate the true value by yourself, aye? And you can tell counterfeit from the genuine article? You've that finely trained an eye?"

"*Touch* is more important than the eye," Caitlin calmly said, hiding any anger she felt. "I can tell a great deal by touching the securities. Enough to release the money in Geneva. Please? May I examine the goods?"

They finally brought the "sample" stolen stock certificates and bonds to Caitlin. She used most of her will to hold in a tiny gasp of amazement.

The *look* of the securities was certainly authentic. She quickly read off the top names: IBM, General Motors, AT&T, Digital, Monsanto.

She played with the outrageous numbers in her mind. It was several thousand times the amount of the *great* train robbery. And who knew how much of the *total* stolen amount this was? What was coming still?

"You can *touch* the documents all you like, darling. They're real though. We wouldn't bring you all the way here for nothing. Just to chat, and admire your fine all-American boobies."

The black Bentley sedan Carroll rode in barely slowed as it squeezed around a crumbling white brick wall in the inner city. The wall was blackened in places from petrol bombs. The car's radial tires screeched above bustling city noises.

Suddenly a flatbed truck was in the same narrow, twisting lane as the Bentley. The truck's engine roared and its horn blared loudly.

A blast of gunfire erupted from the cab of the onrushing truck. Spits of gunfire came from the flat tenement rooftops to the right of the threadneedle roadway.

"Ambush!" Inspector Patrick Frazier grunted.

Almost instantly, he slumped back hard against the

car's passenger door. A jagged black hole appeared at the very center of his forehead.

Carroll pushed open the door quickly and followed the driver of the Bentley out. Then he lay pressed tightly against the side of the car. He looked up, staring at Patrick Frazier's wound through the open Bentley doorway. The British MI6 Inspector was dead, his eyes registering a kind of final, glassy surprise.

Carroll angrily swung his gun barrel out in the direction of the flatbed truck. Without any accompanying sound, the weapon opened rapid fire. Gaping bullet holes appeared everywhere on the truck's already mottled surface.

One of the Irish gunsels, astonished because there had been *no gun sound*, blew back away from the faded red hood of the truck. Blood spurted from his black-bearded face and throat. And then the body was rolling and rolling across the road like that of a man trapped in a barrel.

Carroll's machine gun pistol had been developed and perfected by the Israeli Army in 1981. It fired automatically, up to two hundred and fifty rounds in six seconds. The bullets were attracted by body heat. *Silent death*, the Israelis and their enemies called it.

A stout, red-headed man's forehead was angrily stitched straight across with bullet holes. The man performed a brief two-step then spun off a house's steep-shingled roof. He plummeted onto the street with a hollow crunching sound.

Carroll was aware of movement on either side of him.

Crowds, mostly women and children, were streaming out of crumbling, low-slung tenement buildings. They mobbed forward instead of hiding away in the safer shadows. They had deep-red faces – anger coming from the heart.

The two remaining gunmen from the truck immediately dodged back among the women in their plaid bathrobes and tattered men's jackets. They crouched among the dirty faced children, many of whom were still in their pajamas, dragged out of the innocence of sleep and made to confront still another horror in their young, sad lives.

Carroll clicked the machine gun off automatic, so it wouldn't fire into the covering crowds.

"British spies!" The Irish people had suddenly begun to jeer, protecting their revolutionary soldiers, some of whom were immediate family members, some less close relatives and friends.

"Damn British spies! Damn you British!"

"Ga home, damn Brits!"

Carroll cautiously ran forward anyway. He threw himself directly into the fierce, snarling faces, the threatening, murderous shouts. His machine gun jutted out, the ugly black snout just menacing enough to keep them off him for the moment. *Who was the real terrorist here?* his mind rambled.

"Big man with yer gun," someone taunted.

"Fookin' coward with your machine gun. Dirty Brit turd! Filthy Brit bastard!"

Carroll almost didn't hear the angry shouts. He had one thought only – follow the beeper, follow the continuing radar blips. Find out where Caitlin is right now.

Caitlin covered her head with both arms. She was trying desperately to squirm and struggle away from the IRA men. The air in the tenement room was like liquid mold, impossible for her to breathe.

"You filthy whore, you! Whore! You filthy swine!" The head man screeched at the top of his voice, he screamed inches from Caitlin's face. A contact radio was crackling nearby, blaring the latest street reports into the IRA hideout.

"It's a trap! Infuckingsane. She's carryin' some kind of signal, Dermot! Police cars, damn Brit soldiers are swarming the street out there. Soldiers're everywhere!"

It was the most horrifying moment Caitlin could have ever imagined. She knew what they were going to do to her. She knew instinctively she was going to be shot, murdered in seconds. She wondered when that moment of resigned calm would come, that transcendental moment you were supposed to experience when you understood you were facing death.

The IRA group leader continued to scream; his black masked face was up terribly close to her. "You bloody knew! You dirty bitch."

"No, I didn't know. Please. I don't understand now."

The Irish terrorist suddenly lunged forward, propelling himself out of the blinding white floodlights. He ripped off his mask. She saw a dirty, reddish-blond beard; black holes for eyes. She saw the close-up, gaping mouth of a Russian SKS assault rifle . . .

Tears involuntarily flooded Caitlin's eyes. She tried to tell the terrorist not to fire, to stop, please stop. Her senses were overwhelmed with all kinds of horrifying impressions. She wondered if this was the way it was going to be, one burst of crazy clarity and then you're dead: that solitary, heightened moment the last thing you take with you.

There were shrill police sirens and ambulances and gunfire outside; the air was pierced with the maddening chaos of these noises.

Through her tears she watched the door of the apartment burst open. Somebody she'd never seen before stood poised with a drawn pistol—

A deafening volley of automatic gunfire flared out of the gun aimed into Caitlin's face. It made a rrrrrurrr sound, like a horrifying, mundane dentist's drill. *Oh, no! Oh God no . . .*

Caitlin tried to twist and turn away. That one, urgent, paramount thought stuck in her mind – *get away now! Get away! Get away! Get away!*

Only she couldn't possibly move as fast as the sudden automatic rifle-fire. She didn't move an inch off her chair.

Then Caitlin Dillon simply fell away from it.

Carroll

"Get out of my way! *Get out of the way, you bastards!*"

Carroll screamed wildly at three Belfast men standing

210

squarely in his path. The Irish hoods were stubbornly posted between him and the tenement house stairway. They were viciously waving Gaelic football bats in the dimly lit hallway.

"Why dontcha make us move, mate? Come on now. Make us move. See if you can?"

The tracking beeper was singing desperately, actually vibrating in his jacket pocket. Caitlin had to be upstairs. She was somewhere right in this building.

Police sirens, emergency Army sirens were shrieking everywhere. Steady sniper gunfire was still raining and ricocheting down on the Falls Road. *Move! Now! Move!*

Carroll suddenly leapt between the three surprised Irish youths. They wisely side-stepped the charging, bull-shouldered American. Carroll crashed two and three steps at a time up a twisty flight of dusty, darkened stairs. *Please God no!*

He was fighting against furious rage, and an even worse fear building inside him. He kept the machine gun clipped off automatic fire. There were too many civilians swarming inside the tenement house.

Apartment doors kept opening, then rapidly slamming shut. Carroll felt their wind in his face. There were dangerously hostile looks and abusive screams in every direction as he charged upward.

As Carroll finally reached the top landing, the fourth floor of the dismal building, he saw the dingy yellow door of an apartment thrown open.

His brain was clenched unbelievably tight, filled to exploding with a searing, unnatural heat. Suddenly he knew what he was going to find there. Carroll knew it. He just knew it.

He could see inside the grubby doorway already. Then he could see her lying there, still in her overcoat. Her gaily striped muffler was off casually to one side. She lay thrown up against a fallen wooden chair where she had apparently been questioned.

The IRA henchmen were gone, up to the roof, up over other roofs, gone, escaped somewhere.

"Oh God no." Carroll choked back a horrible sob, a desperate, hopeless prayer. He experienced that awful, hollow bitterness of death all over again. He felt a terrible hurt, from some infinite store of pain.

Very slowly then, Caitlin rolled over. She rolled just a few inches. Then Caitlin struggled to sit up and Carroll ran forward. . . . Her face was a blank, dazed stare. Nothing was recognizable in her eyes at all. . . . But she was alive.

Carroll gently held Caitlin. He cradled her like an injured child in his arms, against his broad chest.

Then she suddenly drew her face away from him; she stared at something that obviously terrified her across the room.

Carroll followed the line of her eyes to an inert shape that lay on the other side of the barren room. The body seemed to be that of a young man, except you couldn't really tell. Half the head had been blown away. The dark-ish hair was matted with blood. The figure was shrouded with the dark blue uniform of a Belfast policeman.

"Who is he?" Carroll asked.

Caitlin slowly shook her head. "I don't know. I only know that if it hadn't been for him coming when he did, I'd be dead. He came through that doorway. He started shooting at them."

Carroll couldn't take his eyes away from the murdered Irish policeman. A hero, Carroll thought. A hero with no name or face anymore. *Police work in all its glory.*

Caitlin was sobbing quietly, almost without any sound.

"Shhh, now, shhh," Carroll whispered softly.

Then Caitlin couldn't help herself anymore. Her sobbing became uncontrollable. She cried into Arch Carroll's chest. She held him with all her remaining strength, which wasn't much right then.

They were still enfolded that way, tightly holding one another, when the teams of British Special Branch men and Irish police arrived. Once again, Green Band was nowhere to be found.

21

Kenny Sherwood

By the evening of December 12, the letters, all stuffed inside eight-by-eleven manila envelopes, had finally arrived. Over three thousand bulky letters had been mailed to every region across the United States.

The letters had come to the strangest, the most unlikely places. To Sedona, Arizona; to Dohren, Alabama; Totowa, New Jersey; Buena Vista, California; Iowa City, Iowa; Stowe, Vermont; Cambridge, Massachusetts; Boulder, Colorado.

Kenny Sherwood in Erie, Pennsylvania, turned out to be one of *the chosen few*.

Sherwood was home from work that day, because if he went to the mill, he'd just say something dumb and get his ass either royally chewed out, or fired. For nine years he'd been a machine operator with Hammond Tool and Dye.

He made almost twenty-four thousand now, thirty-five hundred of which went for shrink sessions with a psychologist in Pittsburgh, little goateed fellow who treated him for his recurrent war dreams.

There was a neatly typed cover letter inside the envelope; it looked government official, a littly scary even.

Dear Mr. Sherwood,
During the years 1968 to 1972, you served your country proudly as a Specialist in the U.S. Army. You were a POW from January 1970 to June of 1972. You received two purple hearts in Viet Nam.

213

Please consider the enclosed, a token of our appreciation for your services, a chance for *your country to serve you.*

Kenny Sherwood cautiously slid a peculiar piece of parchment paper out of the envelope. Now what the hell was this?

There was some kind of chained woman, holding a globe of the world at the top of the parchment paper.

Further down, the certificate clearly said *General Motors common stock.*

The legend went on: "This certifies Kenneth H. Sherwood is the owner of five thousand shares." Tied around the parchment paper was a shiny green ribbon, a kind of green band.

PART TWO

Black Market

22

Hudson

Colonel David Hudson woke with a headache in his room in the Washington-Jefferson Hotel. It was lightly snowing outside, the satiny whiteness evenly blanketing West 51st Street.

Hudson pinched his wristwatch off the wobbling nightstand. It was just past two. He sat upright and he yielded to an uncharacteristic moment of panic. His throat was dry, his hands clammy. His whole body felt fevered.

It wasn't Green Band troubling him this time.

Green Band was hurtling along without an apparent hitch. Even at its psychological core, Green Band was moving beautifully, creating uncertainty in all the places where Hudson wanted to create it.

It wasn't the time he'd spent in a North Vietnamese prison camp, either. The memories of the shrieking, taunting Lizard Man had stayed out of his dreams that night at least.

None of these things bothered David Hudson right now. It was something else. . . . Something completely unexpected and unplanned.

It was Billie Bogan . . .

Like the poet, Louise.

He was angry with himself, disappointed that he'd let the Englishwoman affect him. It was unlike him; it was so undisciplined and out of character for Hudson to permit such a distraction before his mission was complete. Yet somehow he felt he could handle it, that he could keep everything in acceptable perspective . . .

Or was he fooling himself? Was she going to be the reason he finally ruined everything? The one serious slip-up, his fatal flaw? Would he allow himself to blow Green Band because of Billie Bogan? This woman he barely knew, this expensive escort.

He needed to see her at least once more, he decided. *Tonight*, if he could. The most vivid images of Billie suddenly drifted past his eyes inside the darkened West Side hotel room.

Hudson felt himself aroused. He threw on an old mufti shirt and trousers and went down to the Washington-Jefferson lobby, where he prowled around nervously, watched by a suspicious clerk at the desk. He finally called the Vintage service, not wanting to use the phone in his own room again.

"I'd like to see Billie Bogan. Tonight if it's possible. Would that be possible? This is David. Number 323."

There was a pause as he was put on hold; three or four minutes, which seemed even longer.

"Billie's not on her beeper, love. She doesn't seem to be available right now." The answer finally came back. "You could meet one of our other escorts. They're all very beautiful. They're former and part-time models and actresses, David."

David Hudson hung up the public telephone. He felt disappointed, unsatisfied and empty in a cold, gnawing way. . . . Maybe he *couldn't* handle this right now. Maybe he shouldn't ever try to see Billie Bogan again.

The idea of blowing Green Band over some English whore – it almost made him laugh. It would indeed be ludicrously funny – if it all ended like that somehow.

Only David Hudson knew that was quite impossible. The final Green Band plan was designed to be flawless. It was so good, *it could work without him from here on.*

Deception, David Hudson remembered. *The very beginnings of Green Band. Deception and illusion that had started as far back as Viet Nam.*

La Hoc Noh Prison; July, 1971

Captain David Hudson's tortured, one-hundred-and-fifteen-pound frame slumped forward like that of a bar room drunk. The fragile shell of his body threatened to shatter into pieces, to finally collapse in exhaustion or perhaps death. David Hudson's mind silently screamed for him to give up this useless fight.

What remained of his body was wracked by excruciating pain, intense suffering that would have been unthinkable before the last eleven months of North Vietnamese prison camps. He was unsuccessfully trying to put his mind somewhere else now. He ached to be outside the seething bamboo hut, somewhere safe and relatively sane in his past, even as far back as his Kansas boyhood.

He'd been trained to resist interrogation and enemy brainwashing. *Sisyphus*, the program was called at Fort Bragg, North Carolina.

He remembered that now. *Sisyphus* had supposedly prepared him for enemy interrogation – or so the Army instructors had told him.

You must put your mind in another place altogether.

It had sounded so simple, so coldly, attractively logical as a concept. Now it all seemed highly unlikely and absurd, infuriating in its stupidity and typical American arrogance. *Sisyphus* had been yet another cruel fraud invented by the U.S. Army . . .

The Lizard Man, the obdurate North Vietnamese commandant of La Hoc Noh, mechanically raised a white stone game marker.

He decisively put one of David Hudson's black stones in check.

There was a hard *clack* of the playing piece against the highly polished teak board.

The North Vietnamese prison guards, all dressed in muddy black pajamas, tipped homemade rice wine from long-necked green bottles. They snorted out ridiculing laughter at this obvious mismatch of competitors.

The prison camp commandant was frighteningly swift, completely sure of his game moves. He was on a different skill level, David Hudson understood.

According to the strict rules of Go, the game should have been played with a sizable handicap called *okigo*. *Should have been.* . . . But strict adherence to rules meant nothing here because this was a place beyond all decency, all logic, all understanding.

"Yow play!" the Lizard Man once again screeched. "Yow play now!"

He seemed to want his victory right now: the cruel bloodletting – the slow death for the loser in the festering jungle swamps just beyond the prison camp.

The guards were physical extensions of their leader's personality. They too became impatient now, grumbling and growling for faster action, like spectators at a cock fight who aren't getting the fix of swift, bloody action they need.

Clack!

David Hudson finally made an obviously ridiculous, almost an arbitrary move on the Go game board. He smiled crookedly at the commandant, as if he'd suddenly turned the game in his favor.

"*You* play!" Hudson snapped. He knew the smile on his face was hopelessly spacey, but he savored the small moment of triumph.

The Lizard Man was momentarily confused, clearly so.

Then he howled shrill, birdlike laughter.

The Vietnamese soldiers howled high-pitched laughter as well. They inched even closer to the two players as the commandant made a surprisingly conservative move with one of his white stones.

Disappointment immediately etched itself across the soldiers' faces. Here was uncertainty for the first time. David Hudson was amazed at the commandant's sudden hesitation.

"*Yow!*" Lizard Man screamed. "Fast play! Yow play riii now!"

"Fuck you, asshole. . . . Watch this one."

A faint smile, hollow and incomprehensible, slipped across David Hudson's blistered white lips.

Once again, he made a bizarre, a seemingly pointless and foolish game move.

"You play!" he said in a barely audible whisper. "You play *fast*, too."

The Lizard Man squinted, and studied the exquisite, highly reflective teak board more closely. He carefully gazed into Captain Hudson's bloodshot eyes, then looked down again at the Go board.

The North Vietnamese guards crushed in closer still.

This was getting better, much more dramatic, finally. A real game was starting to develop.

The soldiers began to whisper conspiratorially among themselves. They were like the professional gamblers, the unsavory flotsam always crowded into the fantan parlors of Saigon.

Something interesting and very curious was happening in the game of Go now. Even the wily camp commandant was confused, troubled for the moment by his American opponent, by his seemingly unfathomable moves.

For the first time, one of the prison camp guards offered a side bet on the American officer. The commandant threw the soldier the most bitter glance.

Suddenly then, smoothly and so coolly, as if he was performing an ordinary movement such as lighting a cigarette, Captain David Hudson removed the revolver from one of the Vietnamese soldiers' loosely dangling holsters.

Hudson swiveled back to the straight ahead position, directly facing the hated Lizard Man.

Once again, the faint half-crazed smile crossed David Hudson's blistered lips. "Fucker. Miserable shit fucker."

A heartbeat later, the revolver loudly thundered.

It was like an Army field cannon in the tiny bamboo room. White smoke blossomed everywhere around the game table.

Unbelievably, the prison camp commandant's small

head flew straight back. Bone cracked hard against the wooden wall's main support post. The commandant's military hat sailed away saucer style across the smoking hut.

A dark hole gushed like slashed fruit in the Vietnamese officer's forehead. The Lizard Man's mouth dropped open to show broken, ugly yellow teeth. A lathering, pale white tongue flopped out.

David Hudson reflexively fired the service revolver a second time.

He fired a third time.

He felt like a weary, wildly confused child – playing with a toy gun. *Bang, bang, bang.*

He thrust the point of the revolver directly in the frozen wide eyes of the guard who had provided the weapon. The man's face shattered like delicate pottery. Skull, flesh, bone flew apart.

Another Viet Cong guard was shot in the throat, directly in what had been his Adam's apple.

The two remaining guards had dropped their near-empty liquor bottles; they were frantically struggling to get out holstered pistols.

The next three deafening gunshots tore through one man's chest, pierced the other's stomach, then his heart. The foul-smelling, boiling jungle hut was suddenly a bloody, smoking abattoir.

Then David Hudson was very shakily running outside the command hut. He limped badly on legs that felt like they couldn't actually be his. He stumbled, scrambled forward on the unfamiliar, unsteady supports. His legs were acting like wooden stilts.

Every object he saw now seemed part of a blurred, impossible dream. Everywhere he looked, there was harsh unreality of the highest possible disorder. A late-afternoon sun flared orange and bright red over the dense wall of jungle green. Screeching monkeys skittered away from the place of the many gunshots. Insects buzzed angrily between the trees.

The humidity, stifling, choking, filled David Hudson's

lungs. He thought he would surely drown in the moist weight of this awful air.

Machine gun fire suddenly erupted from a bamboo guard post overhead, a control post which subtly blended into the dark green of the jungle.

David Hudson awkwardly weaved back and forth across the exposed exercise yard. Prisoners cheered from their locked cells, their bamboo animal cages.

He ducked into the thick jungle that kept threatening to swallow up the prison camp, and served as a natural barrier to escape for all the prisoners. David Hudson lunged forward. He tripped ahead anyway.

He had no choice now.

Nowhere else to go but into the terrifying jungle.

Death in the jungle.

He was breathless already, clumsily crashing against trees, against thick, tangled jungle brush. He kept running, faster than he thought possible. Dizziness grabbed and clawed at him. Whirling bright, then rolling colors came. Shivering cold flashes. Diarrhea. Vomit that wouldn't stop flowing from his mouth, seemingly from his every pore.

He kept running, zigzagging forward, vomiting bile like it was fuel exhaust. As the jungle foliage got incredibly thicker, the trail became darker than he thought possible – almost complete blackness less than three hundred yards from the Vietnamese camp.

He ran forward anyway. A half mile, a mile – he had no idea of either time or space now.

A cold paralyzing thought struck at him and suddenly held David Hudson tight as the final grip of death. *They weren't even chasing him. . . . They weren't even giving chase back into the jungle.*

Hudson continued running – falling, picking himself up, falling, picking up, falling, picking himself up.

Then it was so impossibly dark there was suddenly nothing left in the world. Hudson kept running all the same. Falling, picking himself up. Falling, picking up. Falling, falling, falling . . .

A song from the Doors played in his head. "Horse Latitudes" . . . then nothing at all . . .

Captain Hudson woke with a nightmarish jolt. A silent scream never quite made it out of his tight, dry larynx.

Long grass was stuck to one side of his face. Sticky, gummy tears had formed in his half-closed eyes. Fat black flies had attached themselves to his lips and nostrils. Hundreds of black flies were plastered all over his body.

Trying to right himself, he nearly laughed out loud. It was exactly as he'd always believed this putrid affair called life to be: resolutely unfair, pointless in the end, and in the beginning, and in the middle, too. Anyone with any reason could see the absurd eternal pattern. *David Hudson fell away into the unrelenting darkness once again.* "Horse Latitudes" played again. Why that fucking song now?

Strangely for him, the incessant fighting, the mind-numbing combat, the death and suffering in Viet Nam, had worked for a time against the bitter truth of his life. It had distracted Hudson from his natural cynicism, the overwhelming pessimism, his natural self-destructiveness.

Just before his capture, he'd been secretly dreading going back to the States, trying to mentally fit himself into civilian life somehow, even into the droning sub-existence of the peacetime Army. . . . He knew a lot of others who felt as he did. A lot of his men felt that way . . .

He woke again. Wildly confused. Unnaturally alert. He had to concentrate everything, every trace of energy he had now. He wrestled with himself to stay awake, to hold onto a thin, sane lifeline this time. Tormenting waves, disconnected images and thoughts kept coming. Ghosts just beyond his full comprehension. Raging rivers of shadowy, half-formed images, words, hellish fantasy shapes. Almost a psychedelic experience. As if he'd been smoking the strongest Thai sticks. Shooting skag. . . . There was no sense of real time or spatial

224

relationships out here. He was on a sensory depriva-
tion overload. He had this shifting, disturbing sense of
place.

His brain tightened like a clasped, clenched fist, and he
began to gag.

His entire body squeezed and relaxed, squeezed and
painfully released.

This was so horrible, *too horrible*, too much for anyone
to take much longer. What happened to him then? What
did it feel like when you cracked wide open? . . . The
severe gagging stopped as soon as he wasn't thinking
about it.

Captain David Hudson began to scream. He was
swimming toward some kind of release. Eternity was
rushing forward – leaping at him in the form of a sea
of leeches, screeching, clawing monkeys, indistinct,
shadowy, jungle insects and reptiles. He screamed for
hours and hours without end. The hallucinations were so
powerfully real they became reality, his only reality.

Then the prison camp guards came!

So suddenly.

They were there! On him! Everywhere!

They'd finally come to take him back. Busy hands were
scrabbling, poking, reaching all over his body . . .

Hot hands were probing, continually poking him.
Blood roared in the funnels of Hudson's ears. The vicious
leeches were crawling all over him, too. Sharp little leach
stings. Strong hands were suddenly lifting him.

Then whispering, almost choral voices. There were no
distinct, recognizable words.

"Leave me alone! Leave me alone!" David Hudson was
pinioned down and helpless. *"Please leave me alone!"*

Something very large and jet black, a huge flapping
bird grabbed onto his face. It smelled like burning
rubber, even worse than that. It began to crawl all over
his face.

"Get it off me! Get it off me! Please get it off me!"

A shaft of light suddenly opened. Gleaming, almost
beautiful light shone in his deep dark tunnel of terror.

A scream came that seemed very far away. . . . *No!* . . . It was *his own* scream.

Impossible.

Impossible.

This was so impossible.

Army corpsmen were staring down . . .

Army corpsmen were staring down . . .

Army corpsmen were staring down.

Ours.

Our corpsmen!

"Breathe deeply, Captain Hudson. Just breathe now. Just breathe. Breathe. There, that's good. That's very good. . . . That's excellent, Captain Hudson.

"It's pure oxygen, Captain. Oxygen! Don't think right now. Breathe. Breathe. Breathe deeply."

White cloth straps were holding him very tightly, painfully so. Blue and red plastic tubes ran in and out of his nose. More tubes were connected to his arms and legs. Colored wires, rubber plugs were attached to his chest, and from there to an icy blue machine.

"Captain Hudson. Captain Hudson, can you hear me? Can you understand me?"

"You're in the Womack Hospital at Fort Bragg, Captain. You're going to be all right. Just fine. Captain, can you understand me? You're in the Womack Hospital?"

"Oh please help me."

He was sobbing uncontrollably for the first time since he'd been a little boy. What was happening? Oh, please, what was this? What was real and what wasn't?

"Captain, you're in the Fort Bragg Center. You're in the JFK Special Forces Center. Captain Hudson? Captain? . . . Just breathe the oxygen! Captain, that's an order. Breathe in . . . breathe out . . . that's *very* good. Very, very good. *That's excellent*, Captain."

Lying on his back, staring silently up at vague forms and swimming shapes, David Hudson thought that maybe he knew this man. How was that?

226

Familiar voice? Familiar drooping blond walrus moustache. Did he know him? Was the man actually there? Hudson reached forward to touch, but couldn't move because of the cloth straps.

"Captain Hudson, you're in the Fort Bragg Center for Special Forces. This was a stress and tolerance test. Do you remember now?

"Captain Hudson, this has been a drug-induced test. You haven't left this room inside the hospital. You were flashing back to Viet Nam."

Nothing real?

None of this happened? . . .

No – there had been a Viet Cong prison camp!

Hallucinations? . . .

There had been a Lizard Man!

Oh, please, make this all stop now.

"Captain Hudson, you revealed nothing about your mission. You passed your tolerance *test*. Flying colors, chum. You were really great. Congratulations."

Mission?

A test?

Sure thing. Just a little pop quiz. Okay.

"You're beginning to understand illusion, Captain. You refused to be interrogated under drugs. . . . You're learning to be illusion's master. You're learning the fine art of deception, Captain Hudson. The art of our deadliest enemies . . ."

"Horse Latitudes" was playing somewhere in the hospital. . . . *In the Special Forces Center*. Deception.

"Breathe that good air, Captain Hudson. Just breathe in easily. Pure, pure oxygen. You passed, Captain. You're the best so far. You're the best we've tested."

Stress and tolerance tests.

The Womack Hospital at Fort Bragg.

Deception.

He was learning to be illusion's master.

Deception.

You passed, Captain Hudson. Flying colors, chum.

Of course – I'm the best you have!

I've always been the best – at everything.
That's why I'm here, isn't it?
That's why I was chosen for this training.
Hallucination.
Deception.
Important to understand.
The key!
The solution, the answer to everything about the future was deception!

"Breathe that pure oxygen, Captain Hudson."

Monday; December 13;
No. 13 Wall

23

The Carroll Family

Arch Carroll was only barely awake, barely functioning.

Familiar home surroundings coalesced . . . Books on the mantle – Carroll loved nonfiction, and also mysteries: *The Brethren, Fatal Vision, The Pope of Greenwich Village, The Fate of the Earth.* . . . An oil painting of his father, done by Mary Katherine, hung on one wall.

And there were children.

Lots and lots of small children.

They were eyeing him suspiciously, waiting for him to speak his mind, to say something characteristically flip and amazing.

Carroll slowly sipped fresh-brewed coffee from a cracked *Revenge of the Jedi* mug. "Sunrise Semester" flickered on the portable TV with the sound off. The horizontal line lazily flipped out of synch with the rest of the room.

The Carroll clan was together for a rare family conference. Coffee, cocoa, and Arch Carroll's world-famous-pop-up-toaster French toast comprised the menu. It wasn't quite 6:00 on the morning of December 13. Green Band felt somehow dead and buried in his mind.

"Mmff . . . mmff . . . Lizzie mmff . . . Lizzie was a son of a bitch, Dad. While you were gone away."

Mickey Kevin reported this important news as he chewed gooey, heavily syruped wads of toast. His mouth flapped open in a rubbery, half-smiling circle.

229

"I think I told you about that kind of gutter talk."

"Mmff, mmff. *You* use gutter talk."

"Yeah, maybe *my* dad didn't kick my rear end enough. I won't make that same mistake, okay?"

"Besides, I wasn't a son of a bitch. He was." Lizzie suddenly glared up from the soggy remains on her plate.

"Lizard! You're not too big to get an Ivory soap sandwich, either. Big bar, right fresh out of the wrapper."

The most angelic smile lit up Lizzie's face. "An Ivory soap sandwich, *Daddy? . . .* Better than Eggo, *still-a-little-frozen* french toast!" She *leveled* her father with a deadpan, brutal evaluation of his not entirely home-cooked breakfast offerings.

They all began to laugh, then. Clancy and Mary nearly fell off their chairs giggling. Mickey Kevin did topple off, like a drunken carnival kewpie doll.

Carroll finally gave up. He broke into a sleepy smile. He winked over at Mary K., who was letting him run the familiar, four-ring circus this morning.

He had been *trying* to tell them about his almost tragic trip to Europe. He'd been trying to be a reasonably good dad for the four of them. . . . He fuzzily remembered how his own father had done the same sort of thing: telling sanitized stories about the 91st Precinct, right in that very same breakfast nook on Sunday mornings.

Finally, after putting it off at least thirty minutes, Arch Carroll came to the really difficult part of his story; the punchline so to speak; the *core* of his tale of adventure and foreign intrigue in England and Ireland . . .

He was going to try and make this all sound very casual now. . . . No big deal, right? *So begin.*

"Over in Europe, I was working with someone. . . . They had these special teams of police with financial people. Our best people. We worked in London, then in Belfast together. She was nearly killed there, in fact. Over in Ireland. Her name's Caitlin. Her name is Caitlin Dillon."

Silence. The big chill comes to the Carroll house.

Keep going. Don't stop now.

230

"Sometime, I'd like you guys to all meet her. She's originally, uh, she's from out in Ohio. She's pretty funny, actually. Very nice. For a girl. Ha ha."

Absolute, stone-cold silence . . .

Finally, a very tiny, muffled reply from Lizzie. "No thank you."

Carroll's eyes slowly, ever so slowly, passed from face to small stony face.

Mickey, who looked all soft and vulnerable in his Yankee pinstripe pj's with slipper socks, was amazingly close to tears.

Clancy, in an oversized robe that made him look like ET in the fantasy movie's beer-drinking scene, was silent and more stoic. His small body was rigid with control.

They were angry, and unbelievably hurt – *all at the same time*. They knew *exactly* what was happening here.

"Hey, come on, lighten up, okay?" Carroll tried to make it seem a little funny. Bill Murray on "Saturday Night Live," which he did pretty well, despite the lack of any facial resemblance.

"I *talked* to a woman who I *happen* to work with. Just *talked*. Hello, blah, blah, blah, goodbye."

They wouldn't say a word to him. They stared at Carroll as if he had just said he was going to leave them. They made him feel so horribly bad – so hollow and hopeless about everything, literally everything in his or their life.

Come on, it's been three goddamn years.

I'm closing up inside. I'm actually dying.

"Come on, kids." Mary Katherine finally spoke up from her purposely low-key spot at the kitchen table. "Be a little fair, huh. Doesn't your father get to have some friends, too?"

Silence.

No, he doesn't.

Not women friends.

Lizzie finally started to cry. She tried to muffle her sobs, choking back the breathless gasps with both little hands.

231

Then they were all crying, except Mickey Kevin, who kept staring murderously at his father.

It was Carroll's worst moment with them since the night Nora had actually died on some high and mighty, antiseptic white floor in New York Hospital. His chest was beginning to heave now, too; his heart felt as if it was being cruelly, brutally ripped in half.

They weren't ready for someone else – *maybe he wasn't ready, either.*

For the next several minutes, nothing he could say could make it any better. Nothing could make any of the kids laugh. Nothing could make them loosen up at all.

They all hated Caitlin. They weren't going to give her a chance. Period. End of nondiscussion.

They were fiercely determined to hate anyone who wasn't their dead mother.

24

No. 13 Wall

Two hours later in Manhattan, Carroll's head, most of his body, was throbbing with dull pain. He felt that he needed a stiff shot of Murphy's Irish whiskey. He also felt like going back to the role of Crusader Rabbit, *running away* into the convenient, strangely comfortable fantasy of the ragman. For the first time, *maybe*, he thought he was beginning to understand the past three years of his life.

Later that day, he would vaguely remember weaving a mostly aimless path inside No. 13 Wall Street at around nine o'clock. The fluorescent lights were too bright; the glaring overhead lamps were harsh, tearing at his eyes.

It was all wrong, the place felt wrong. There was too much gloom and doom, palpable frustration was evident everywhere Carroll walked. The police investigators, the Wall Street researchers bent over mountainous documents or hunched in paralysis in front of computer screens – they were like people who have been trapped indoors too long, men and women who haven't seen the light of day for weeks. Even his own people, the usually unflappable Caruso included, had the quirky, tense mannerisms of heavy smokers suddenly deprived.

Around 9:30, Arch Carroll set to work again inside his monastic office.

The broken windowpane hadn't been replaced and the sheet of brown paper he'd stuck in the space hung limply now, like a beat-up old blind in an abandoned tenement. He kept the ceiling lights purposely bright, glaringly

233

unpleasant. The door was shut tight, so the radiator heat would build up.

An illusion of warmth, he thought.

Carroll himself was dressed appropriately for the overheated weather inside: a Boston Celtics T-shirt that had the look of something left over from a banquet of moths, Levis, Crusader Rabbit's very own workboots. *He* was going to be comfortable at least.

He also had a bottle of Murphy's Irish whiskey on the desk. What would Walter Trentkamp say? Oh, to hell with Walter and his imposing virtues, his old world cop mores.

For a few minutes there, slowly sipping the Irish, Arch Carroll thought about his job, jobs in general, the overwhelming job of life.

This particular job had been an important part of *his* life for almost nine years now. He hadn't exactly planned it like that, but life tended to go its own idiosyncratic way. After the Army tour, Carroll had finished up at Michigan State Law. He'd also married Nora. Right about the same time, both his father and Walter Trentkamp had come along – to convince him to do some *legal* work for the DIA. So it was that Carroll had originally become an agent – a combination of financial pressures, plus his long policeman heritage, and the coaxing of Trentkamp and his father.

It was weird, completely unfathomable, the ways of life. Society chose to overpay Wall Street salesmen, various marketing experts, obfuscating corporation lawyers, investment bankers. At the same time, society grossly underpaid the teachers of its children, its police, even its political leaders. Some kind of crazy society.

Well, they seriously underpaid him to work at protecting them from harm's way. But he was going to protect them anyway – as well as he possibly could.

The nagging question was whether his best was going to be good enough. He'd had six good men, plus himself, on the streets since the night of December 4. So far they'd come up with almost nothing. How the hell could that be possible?

He wandered around the cramped room for a while, like a man without any particular sense of direction. Then he went to his desk and sat down, waiting for the day's first suspects to appear.

Green Band – why did he have the feeling just then that there was something important on the top of his mind, an obvious insight that had evaded him until now? It was infuriating and elusive, like soap that gets away from your hand in the bathtub. Like a forgotten name.

Was it something to do with Green Band's inside information? A spy at No. 13?

But the half-formed thought, whatever it was, had already vanished.

Transcripts

From a transcript taken in Room 312; No. 13 Wall Street; Monday, December 13.

Present: Arch Carroll; Anthony Ferrano; Michael Caruso.

CARROLL: Hello, Mr. Ferrano, I'm Mr. Carroll, antiterrorist division, State Department. This is my associate, Mr. Caruso. Mr. Ferrano, to get right to the point, not to waste any of your time, or mine, I need some information . . .

FERRANO: Figured that out already.

CARROLL: Uh huh. Well, I read your earlier transcript. I just read over the conversation you had with Sergeant Caruso. I'm a little surprised you haven't heard *anything* about the bombings on Wall Street.

FERRANO: Why's that? Why should I have?

CARROLL: Well, for one thing, you being a heavy gun and explosives dealer, Mr. Ferrano. Doesn't it strike you as odd, uh, peculiar, you wouldn't have heard something? There must be rumors floating around on the street. I'm sorry, would you like a sip of whiskey?

FERRANO: I want whiskey, I've got money in my pocket. Listen, I told you, I told somebody, *him*, I don't deal guns. I don't know what you're talking that shit for. I own Playland Arcade Games, Inc., on Tenth Avenue and 49th Street. You got that straight now?

CARROLL: Okay, that's *bullshit*. Who do you think you're talking to? Some punk off the street? Just some street *punk* here?

FERRANO: Hey, all right, fuck you. I want my lawyer in here now! . . . Hey, you understand English, pal? *Lawyer! Now!* . . . Hey! Hey! . . . Ohhh . . . oh, *shit!*

(Loud scuffling, fighting sounds. Furniture crashing; man groaning.)

CARROLL (Breathing heavily): Mr. Ferrano, I think . . . I feel it's important you understand something. Listen carefully to what I'm saying. Watch my lips . . . Ferrano, you've just entered the Twilight Zone. You *don't* have the right to remain silent in the Twilight Zone. All your constitutional rights have been temporarily cancelled. You have *no lawyer*. All right? We set to continue our discussion, fuckhead?

FERRANO: Shit, man. My tooth's broken. Gimme a break for . . . awhh, *shit*, man.

CARROLL: I'm trying to give you every break in the world. Don't you understand anything yet? What this is here? What's happening? . . . *Somebody* stole money from *the man*. Some very important people are severely pissed off. Big, big people. Why don't you imagine that this is Viet Nam and you're the Viet Cong? Would that help you?

FERRANO: Wait a minute! I didn't do anything!

CARROLL: No? You sell pump-action shotguns, revolvers to fourteen, fifteen-year-old kids. Black, P.R., Chinese kids in gangs. I'm not gonna say any more than that. . . . Your lawyer is a Mr. Joseph Rao of 24 Park Avenue. Mr. Rao doesn't want any part of this . . . I think you better tell me everything you've heard on the street.

FERRANO: Look. I'll tell you what I know. I can't tell you what I don't know.

CARROLL: That I can buy.

236

FERRANO: All right, I *heard* there was some heavy artillery available. In the city. This was about, beginning, I guess, maybe middle of November. Yeah, five weeks ago.

CARROLL: How heavy are we talking about?

FERRANO: Like M-60s. Like M-79 rocket launchers. Soviet RPD light machine guns. SKS automatics. That kinda stuff. *Heavy!* I mean what the fuck they gonna do with that kind of munitions? That's basic ground assault equipment. Like in Nam. What you'd use, take over a country. That's all I heard . . . I'm telling the truth, Carroll . . . Hey that's all *anybody* knows on the street. . . . Awhh, c'mon, don'tcha believe me? . . . Hey! Seriously?

CARROLL: Tell me what you know about François Monserrat . . .

FERRANO: He ain't Italian.

CARROLL: Mr. Ferrano, thank you so much for your help. Now get out of my office, please. Mr. Caruso will show you to the nearest rathole out.

From a transcript taken in Room 312; No. 13 Wall Street. Present; Arch Carroll; Muhammed Saalam.

CARROLL: Hello there, Mr. Saalam. Haven't seen you since you had Percy Ellis killed on 103rd Street. Very nice djellaba. Sip of Irish whiskey?

SAALAM: Liquor is against my religious beliefs.

CARROLL: This is Irish whiskey. It's blessed. Well, we'll get right down to official police business then. . . . Tell me, uh, are you a hunter, Mr. Saalam?

SAALAM (Laughs): No, not really. A hunter? . . . Actually, if you stop to think about it, I'm a *huntee*. Ever since I fought for you whites in Southeast Asia. My name is Sah-*lahm* by the way.

CARROLL: Sah-*lahm*. I'm sorry. . . . No, you see, I thought you must be a hunter. Something like that. You see, we found all of these hunting guns, these *hunting* bombs in your apartment up in Yonkers, M-23 squirrel-hunting guns. Opossum-hunting sniper rifles, the ones

237

with star nightscopes. Chipmunk-hunting fragmenta-
tion grenades. B-40 duck-hunting rockets.

SAALAM: You bust into my place?

CARROLL: Had to. What do you know about a Mister
François Monserrat?

SAALAM: You had a warrant from a judge?

CARROLL: Well, we couldn't get an official bench
warrant. We did talk to a judge off the record. He said,
don't get caught. We took it from there.

SAALAM: No search warrant or nothing?

CARROLL: You know, this is really shocking. Didn't
anybody read the June 16, 1982, *Time* magazine? Story on
me? Little squared-off red box thing? Doesn't anybody understand who I am? *I'm* a terrorist! Just like you
guys . . . I don't play by international Red Cross of
Switzerland agreements. Mr. Saalam, you sold some
M-23 squirrel-hunting guns, also some quail-hunting
sniper rifles to a couple of fellas. About six weeks ago.
Who . . . are . . . they? . . .

(Long pause) ". . . Uh, oh. Uh, oh . . . Mr. Saalam,
please let me explain something else to you. Explain this
as clearly as I can. . . . *You're* a bright, U.S. college-
educated terrorist. You went to Howard University for a
year; you did a little time in Attica. You're one of the Mark
Rudd-Eldridge Cleaver-Kathy Boudin school. . . . Me, on
the other hand, I'm a terrorist of the PLO-Red Brigade –
Blow-away-anything-that-moves school. . . . Now then.
You sold a full case of stolen M-23s on or about November
first. That's a *fact* we both know about. You say – "Yes,
I did" or I'll break your right hand. Just say "Yes, I
did" . . .

SAALAM: Yeah, I did.

CARROLL: Good. Thank you for your forthrightness.
Now, *who* did you sell the M-23s to? Wait. Before you
answer. Remember that I'm the PLO. Don't say anything you'd be afraid to say to a PLO investigator in
Beirut.

SAALAM: I don't know who they are.

CARROLL: Oh, *Jesus* Christ.

SAALAM: No, wait a minute. *They* knew who I was. They knew everything about me. I never saw nobody, I swear it. I felt like they had set me up.

CARROLL: I love former inmate sincerity. Unfortunately, I happen to believe you. . . . Because that's what your current roommate, Mr. Rashad, said, too. Please get the hell out of here now. . . . Oh, by the way, Mr. Saalam. We had to rent your apartment up in Yonkers. We rented it to a very nice Welfare lady, with these three little kids.

SAALAM: You did what?

CARROLL: We rented the apartment you were selling guns out of. We rented it to a nice lady with a batch of kids. Skoal, brother.

Caitlin

"It's all so incredibly methodical. That's what is mystifying. They keep evading all contact with this huge international police dragnet. *How?*"

Caitlin Dillon lit up a cigarette and drew in millions of carcinogens slowly.

She and eighty-three-year-old Anton Birnbaum, both red-eyed and exhausted, sat together on stiff leather Harvard chairs in Birnbaum's lower Wall Street office. Caitlin was a good six inches taller than the birdlike, deceptively frail Financier. Earlier in her career, when she had worked for Birnbaum, he wouldn't walk anywhere on Wall Street with her for that very reason. "Vanity is a living legend," she'd kidded him once she found out the truth.

Now, Anton Birnbaum rubbed the small of his back as he talked. "*Something* so very methodical, so carefully orchestrated. . . . *Something* absolutely systematic is happening throughout Western Europe right now."

Caitlin watched Birnbaum's face with its corrugated lines, which shifted and moved like the box of a concertina as he spoke. She waited patiently for more to come. It usually did with Anton, who thought much faster than he could now speak.

"There is a book. . . . *The Real War*, it's called. The book's central thesis – that Germany, Japan, have found an eminently reasonable road to further world conquest. Through *commerce*. That's the real war. As a country, we're losing that war spectacularly, don't you think, Caitlin?"

The former chairman of the venerable investment house Birnbaum, Levitt was something of a prig, Caitlin knew. He could be savagely impatient with people he didn't like or respect, but he was also undeniably brilliant. Anton Birnbaum had been advisor to presidents, to kings, to multinational corporations such as Fiat, Proctor & Gamble, Ford Motor. He had controlled the fate of untold billions of dollars. Anton Birnbaum had also been one of Caitlin's staunchest backers ever since she'd first left the Wharton Business School. Only as she'd come to intimately know Birnbaum, had Caitlin begun to understand why.

Caitlin Dillon was a *challenging* mystery which Birnbaum still hadn't completely solved. She was a natural businesswoman, perhaps the most gifted Anton Birnbaum had met. Caitlin had the intelligence, the necessary discipline, and the kind of instincts Birnbaum rarely saw anymore. And yet, she seemed to have little interest in actually making money.

She was a confounding mystery in other ways, as well. She had been brought up in a small Ohio town, yet she exhibited the most cosmopolitan tastes and opinions. She spoke German and French fluently. She kept surprising Birnbaum with new talents whenever they spent time together.

Of course, her father had been teaching her about the Stock Market since she had expressed an interest in high school. But there was more to it than early coaching. Caitlin Dillon obviously wanted to be a force on Wall Street. Anton Birnbaum was certain that Caitlin wanted to be a legend one day herself. He steadfastly refused to

240

ever say it out loud, to even hint it to his male peers, but the Financier's *protégé* was *a woman*.

"What do you think is happening in Western Europe? We're having an impossible time piecing it together, Anton. Some very important data is missing. One absolutely essential thread of logic that might explain who they are." Caitlin wandered around the old man's office as she talked.

She stopped with her back to the window, and looked at the framed photographs on the walls. There was Anton snapped in the company of the very powerful and famous. Statesmen, controversial industrialists, people from the entertainment industry . . . there was Konrad Adenaeur and Harold Macmillan and Anwar Sadat. There was Henry Ford and J. Paul Getty. John Kennedy and Richard Nixon and Ronald Reagan.

Anton Birnbaum scratched the bridge of his blotched and mottled nose as he contemplated his choice of the next few words. He was reminded once again that Caitlin was one of the few people on Wall Street he could really talk to. Complex explanations of his theories and insights were unnecessary when speaking with her.

"The Europeans simply don't trust us," he finally began again, hunching forward in his seat. "Which is precisely why they don't talk to us anymore. They believe we have different attitudes, different priorities toward the Middle East, also toward the Soviet bloc. They're certain we're too casual about the dangers of a nuclear war. They don't feel we understand Marxist-Leninist ideology."

Anton Birnbaum stared very directly into Caitlin's deep brown eyes. His own eyes were watering hopelessly behind thick, bottle-glass lenses. He reminded Caitlin of a character in *Wind in the Willows*, Mr. Mole.

"I sound like an alarmist, no? But I feel the intrinsic truth of what I'm saying. Almost *prima facie*, I feel it. There will be a crash now. I believe there will be a serious crash, possibly another Black Friday. Very, very soon."

Caitlin had to sit back in the stiff leather club chair. She

241

heard the cushion let out a deep sigh. Perhaps the sigh was partly her own.

Another Black Friday, her mind raced. *A Stock Market crash! Her own worst fears had been confirmed by the man she most respected on the Street. Her father's jeremiads twenty years before had finally come home to roost.*

Complete collapse; the entire economic system falling. Impossible ideas were formulating inside her brain.

She stared at Birnbaum, and saw that he was watching her with an expression of vague sorrow. His face was lit by an antique brass lamp which turned the lines on his skin into deep dark bands, little gulleys of flesh.

Complete collapse, the phrase continued to ring.

It meant the end of an entire way of life.

And after the failure of an economic system, who would survive? Who would finally crawl out into the rubble and be able to go on? If she had the answer to that, maybe she'd also have the answer to the mystery of Green Band.

Anton Birnbaum spoke again. "As I said, I think we could be in the middle of a war. *The money wars.* The great Third World War we have so long feared – it may already be upon us."

25

No. 13 Wall – The Crisis Room

"Goddamn it! Look at this! Look at this now!" The speaker was Walter Trentkamp, and his voice was harsh with disbelief. "Gentlemen, it's happening everywhere!"

Philip Berger, Director of the CIA, Trentkamp, and General Frederick House were tightly gathered around the computer terminals when Caitlin and Carroll arrived. Several display screens were working simultaneously, rapidly flashing words as well as color graphics.

Berger glanced up as Caitlin Dillon and Carroll hurried across the Crisis Room floor. He frowned.

"Emergency reports have been coming in for about fifteen, twenty minutes, " he said to the others. "Since three-thirty our time. They've definitely got something hopping. Something's happening *all over the world* this time."

La Compagnie des Agents, Paris

At one o'clock Paris time on December 13, La Compagnie des Agents was sudenly closed by official order of the President of France.

All stock trading was immediately halted on the Bourse.

Bourse officials reluctantly admitted that the Market's CAC index had fallen *over 3 percent in a single morning*.

The afternoon newspapers in Paris carried the most shocking headlines in four decades:

MARKET CLOSE TO PANIC!
BOURSE CRASH!
PARIS MARKET IN SHAMBLES.
FINANCIAL DISASTER!

For once, the tabloids were actually being written with some understatement, however.

Emergency government meetings were immediately called in the Palais des Elysées, rue de Faubourg Centre. But no one had a vague clue what to do next about the unparalleled panic situation in Europe.

The Frankfurt Stock Exchange

The Frankfurt Stock Exchange was in complete chaos, meanwhile, but still managed to stay open for the entire session.

The Commerzbank Index had fallen under a thousand for the first time since back in 1982.

The largest losers for the immensely tragic day included Westdeutsche Landsbank, Bayer, Volkswagen, and Philip Holzmann.

As yet, none of the economists in West Germany understood *why* prices were dropping; or how far they might plummet in the very near future.

The Toronto Exchange

The Toronto Stock Exchange was one of the very worst hit anywhere in the world.

The exchange's composite index of 300 stocks *fell 155 points to under 2000.*

Trading volumes set new records, until the major Canadian Exchange was officially closed at 1:00 P.M.

The Tokyo Exchange

In Tokyo, the Nikkei-Dow Jones index was extremely shaky all day, finally closing at 9200. This was a full 2½ percent decline in a single day.

Hardest hit were all companies trading heavily with the Middle East. These included Mitsui Petrochemical, Sumitomo Chemical, Oki Electric.

Almost on cue, Japanese student riots broke out in major cities all over the islands.

Johannesburg

Heavy European and American deposits made the Johannesburg Stock Exchange the only apparent *winner* anywhere around the world. Bullion was suddenly trading at $1,000 an ounce. The rand instantly appreciated to $1.50.

Hundreds of millions of dollars were made in South Africa. Suspicions rose, but still no satisfactory answers came.

The London Stock Exchange

London dramatically shut down at 12:00 noon, three and a half hours shy of regular closing.

The *Financial Times* Index of 750 companies had fallen nearly 90 points; it was down almost 200 since the initial Green Band bombings in New York.

The scene on Threadneedle Street, near the Bank of England, was nearly as bleak and without hope as bombed-out Wall Street in New York.

No. 13 Wall

With its forty-button, telephone-computer consoles, the Crisis Room at No. 13 Wall was beginning to resemble the *Starship Enterprise* more than the traditional Chippendale feel and look of the Street. Nonetheless, the thirty or so police, Army, and financial experts in the room had absolutely no idea what they were supposed to accomplish next.

The Western economic system seemed to be crashing to a disastrous halt, right before their eyes. Not one of them had a reasonable clue why.

And still there was only maddening silence from Green Band.

Moscow

Major General Radomir Raskov very nervously peered over half-moon reading spectacles. He studied the august group seated at a long, highly polished, mahogany conference table inside the Moscow KGB offices, specifically, the offices of the S. Dictorate.

All of the Politburo officials who had been at Zavidavo were also at the emergency meeting. They were joined now by Mikhail Slepovik, Director of Soviet Security, and a very *kulturny* gentleman, Popo Tvardevsky, Undersecretary of the Communist Party, some said the future Premier.

Premier Yori Belov slapped shut the thin black folder set before him.

He looked at the others, and scowled menacingly. "I find it utterly, *utterly* incomprehensible that we have no more knowledge than this. During this crisis! During this world-threatening emergency situation!"

Premier Belov's gray eyes were piercing, absolutely forbidding to encounter for more than a brief glance. *"Not five months ago,* I sat in this very room and I *listened* to a plan, 'The Red Tuesday Plan.' In this highly detailed proposal, it was *clearly, emphatically* stated that it was in the best interests of Soviet Russia to sabotage and disable Wall Street, in effect the entire Western economic system.

"This plan, as you may all recall, was thoroughly analyzed and finally approved by the parties here in this room. It was an immaculate plan and a daring one, but there was every possibility it would succeed."

Premier Belov paused. A nerve in his jaw twitched.

Something stormy crossed his eyes. "*Now, that very thing has happened!* And all of you expect me to believe that we have no complicity, no knowledge whatsoever of any of the causes."

Premier Belov slammed his heavy palm down hard on the gleaming wooden table.

His next words were spoken in a gravelly voice, almost a whisper. Several of his listeners had to lean forward to hear every word.

"The entire world is hurtling toward chaos, perhaps even its destruction. . . . Now someone please tell me – what is Green Band? What is Green Band's precise relationship to the Red Tuesday Plot? For there *is some relationship*. . . . Who is running Green Band? . . . And *why?*"

26

Carroll and Caitlin

The infernal noise Arch Carroll heard inside his head was the sound of financial markets and empires collapsing all over the world. It was a brutal, grinding noise that felt like a buzzsaw working right up against his skullbone.

He and Caitlin sat on an old floral couch in Carroll's Manhattan apartment, facing down over the 79th Street Boat Basin. A Beethoven concerto played soothingly on the tape deck. River winds occasionally buckled the dark living room windows.

Once again, they were waiting for Green Band. There was nothing to do but wait for morning.

"I think I have to turn in." Caitlin finally spoke in an already half-asleep whisper. She hunched herself forward and lightly kissed Carroll's forehead. "Get a few hours, anyway."

Carroll raised his wristwatch to his face; his eyes seemed unbelievably heavy. "What a party pooper. No sense of adventure. It's only two-thirty."

Caitlin's head tilted to one side. Her brown eyes were already softly filling with sleep. "People from Ohio go to bed at nine-thirty, ten o'clock. The Lima Holiday Inn restaurant is filled at five-thirty. Closed down by eight."

"Yeah, but you're a sophisticated New Yorker now. We party until two or three on weekdays here."

Caitlin kissed Carroll again and the idle talking stopped. He was frankly amazed at how comfortable he was with her. Watching someone you thought you cared about almost being killed seemed to accelerate the courting process.

248

"Is anything the matter? You look, I don't know, a little sad? Tell me . . ." Her eyes were digging for more, more to understand who Carroll really was.

"It's probably my dumb, Irish-Catholic conscience. Guilt about not doing my duty properly. Taking myself too seriously, as usual."

"Are you telling the truth? About being all right? Sometimes I can't tell with you." She nestled gently against Carroll's shoulder. She was no longer untouchable.

"I'm not quite ready for bed yet. That's all. I'm overtired I guess. I'll be in soon. You go ahead."

Caitlin leaned in closer and kissed Carroll very softly again. She always smelled so wholesome and nice, he couldn't help thinking. She had the softest lips he could imagine kissing.

"Do you want me to stay with you?" She whispered one more time.

Carroll shook his head decidedly.

Caitlin finally left the living room, sleepily huddled in the cocoon of a blanket.

Carroll almost immediately stood up from the couch. He started to pace back and forth past the darkly reflective parlor windows. His body was feeling all wrong: *wired; incandescent.*

Next, Arch Carroll began to peek into several dusty, littered desk drawers.

He looked inside an old antique blanket chest he'd bought years back in central Pennsylvania. His mind was wandering into very odd places, weird time zones . . .

He wondered if Caitlin liked kids much . . .

Carroll thought for a few minutes about the possibility of getting hurt by Caitlin. How she might just move on after Green Band and the investigation was finally over. Her romantic interlude with a real-life policeman.

He then considered what he felt to be a somewhat lesser possibility; that he might somehow hurt her.

She'd already told him things about her two previous

249

love affairs. One guy had been a highly successful New York investment lawyer who was so busy making his second, or was it his third, million he hadn't bothered to notice that Caitlin wasn't just an extraordinarily pretty face, an asset in certain demanding social situations. . . . The second old flame had been a professional tennis player, "with an ego as big as Forest Hills Stadium," as Caitlin had described him. Number two had somehow expected her to be his housemate, his sexy Playboy bunny, and his mom. Caitlin had finally said no to all three roles.

Jesus, he was so incredibly wired. So uptight tonight.

Finally, he did it though. The worst thing possible under the particular set of circumstances – the absolute worst thing he could have done . . .

On the anniversary.

Nora's death three years before.

December 14.

First, Carroll gathered together a handful of old photographs. He found most of the photos in a cluttered, bottom shelf inside a glass-enclosed book cabinet.

Next, he pulled a tattered wicker chair up close beside one of the tall windows facing onto the lights of Riverside Drive and the river.

Carroll stared down at the West Side Highway, the peacefully quiet Boat Basin. He was letting the present go all fuzzy and blurred.

Then he stood up again.

He dealt three particular record albums off the uneven stacks on either side of the stereo. One album was *52nd Street*, Billy Joel self-consciously holding a trumpet on the cover. The second album was mainstream country and western, *I Believe In Love* by somebody called Don Williams. The third was Barbra Streisand and Barry Gibbs' *Guilty*.

Carroll switched on the stereo and the big floor speakers immediately hummed. He felt the power surge through the soles of his bare feet. He turned the volume way down.

He'd never been a big Barbra Streisand fan, but there were two particular songs he wanted to hear on this album: "Woman in Love," and "Promises." Out in the world, a moving van rumbled along Riverside Drive. He was feeling slightly ridiculous, but not quite enough to stop this right now.

He still kept an old framed picture of Nora, hidden away face down in the bottom of the bookcase.

He slid it out now. He carefully propped the photo on the arm of the couch.

For a long, pensive moment, he stared at Nora sitting there in a hospital-issue wheelchair. Anniversary of her death. Pain still sharp and fresh as yesterday, it seemed.

He could remember *exactly* when the snapshot had been taken. After they'd operated. After the surgeons had failed to remove her malignant tumor.

In the wheelchair photo, Nora was wearing a simple yellow-flowered sundress, a knitted blue cardigan sweater. She had on a pair of crazy high-topped sneakers which became her trademark as an invalid.

Nora was smiling radiantly in the picture. Not once to his knowledge had she completely broken down during the illness, not once had she felt sorry for herself. She'd been thirty-one years old when they'd found the tumor. She'd had to watch her blond hair fall out from the chemotherapy treatments; then she'd had to adapt to life in the inflexible iron clutches of her wheelchair. Nora had *somehow* accepted that she wasn't going to see her children grow up, or anything else the two of them had laughed and dreamed about, and always taken for granted.

Why couldn't he finally accept her death?

Why couldn't he ever accept the way life was apparently supposed to be?

Arch Carroll stopped and listened more closely to Barbra Streisand singing.

The song "Promises" made him remember the stretch when he'd visited Nora every night, night after night at

251

New York Hospital. After the hospital visits, Carroll would eat at Galahanty's Bar up the hill on First Avenue. A very tired burger, soggy home fries, draft beer that tasted the way swamp gas smells. Probably the beginning of his drinking problems.

The two Streisand songs had been local favorites on Galahanty's jukebox.

They always made him think of Nora – all alone back at that scary, skyscraper hospital.

Sitting in the bar, he always wanted to go back – at ten, eleven o'clock – to talk with her just a little bit more; to sleep with her; to hold Nora tight against the gathering night inside her New York hospital room. To squeeze every possible goddamn moment out of the time they had left together . . .

The worst, the very truest line for him in "Promises" finally came. . . .

Tears slowly rolled down his cheeks. The pain inside was like a rock solid column that extended from the center of his chest all the way up into his forehead. The sadness, the inconsolable grief was for Nora, though, not for himself: the *unfairness* of what had happened to her.

Carroll began to hold himself fiercely tight, squeezing hard with both arms. He was remembering more than he wanted to about the time around Nora's death. He felt like he was going to blow apart one of these times. Real tough guy cop, right?

When would this cold, hollow feeling please stop? The past three years had been unbearable. When would it please fucking stop?

He always had this same insane urge – *to break glass. Just to punch out glass.*

Blindly, irrationally, punch out glass.

Caitlin, meanwhile, stood immobile, perfectly silent in the darkened apartment hallway. She couldn't catch hold of her breath, couldn't even swallow right then. She had wandered back from the bedroom when she'd heard noises. Faint strains of music . . .

252

She'd found Carroll like this. The old photographs. So sad to watch.

She finally walked back to the bedroom. She huddled deep down into the body-warm covers and sheets.

Lying there alone, Caitlin bit down hard on her lower lip. She understood and felt so much more about Carroll – clearly, in an instant. Maybe she understood more than she wanted to.

She stared through shadows walking the bedroom ceiling; she thought about her own life since she'd come to New York. Somehow, she'd known she would never completely fit out in Lima, Ohio. There were so many other experiences she needed to try. There was her longstanding need to involve herself in the financial arena. Maybe to vindicate her father, maybe just to make him proud again. So she'd gone to the Wharton Business School; then to New York, and a job with Anton Birnbaum on Wall Street. Next it was Washington and the public sector: her enforcement job with the SEC. *She'd become a success*; everybody acknowledged that.

Only recently, for the first time in many years, she wasn't sure if success was what she wanted; if she'd even done the right thing leaving the Midwest. Right at the moment, Caitlin wasn't completely sure about anything.

. . . Except maybe one thing. She was in love with Carroll. She was certain she was falling deeply in love.

She wanted to hold him right now, only she was afraid to go and ask. Caitlin was afraid to intrude. She closed her eyes and she felt a great sense of solitude assail her: would she always be a trespasser in Carroll's life?

She didn't know exactly how long she'd been alone in the big silent bedroom over the river. The bed felt so empty without Carroll.

The telephone on the bedstand began to ring.

It was 3:30 in the morning.

He didn't pick up outside. Where was Carroll now?

She waited, four, five rings, and he still didn't pick up.

Caitlin finally grabbed for the receiver.

A high-pitched, a very excited voice was on the phone

line. A man was talking, before she had a chance to say a word.

"Arch, sorry to wake you. This is Walter Trentkamp. I'm down at No. 13 right now. The Stock Exchange in Sydney just opened. There's a massive panic! You'd better come now. *It's all going to crash!*"

Tuesday; December 14;
the Stock Market

27

Hudson

While Caitlin and Carroll were hurrying downtown, David Hudson hadn't been able to sleep very well in his room at the Washington-Jefferson Hotel. At 3:20 A.M. he found himself riding aboard the strangely crowded Eighth Avenue subway.

The rattling, gray metal cars were filled with staggering, vacant-eyed drunks. There were clusters of 42nd Street prostitutes. Here and there a late night Irish bartender or transit worker sat in wary silence.

In order to avoid the unpleasant sweet-sour liquor smells, Hudson had stationed himself in the open bridge between two of the jouncing cars. Sometimes when he couldn't sleep, David Hudson would ride the mesmerizing subways for hours like this – nothing on his mind but the passing stations and the speed. It was a little like walking a night patrol in Viet Nam.

He'd worked late at the Vets' garage. It was down to the agonizing final details now, always the last details to get exactly right.

It all happened so quickly, so completely unexpectedly on the train . . .

As the subway relentlessly raced north, the heavy metal door between the cars suddenly opened. Four black men in their middle twenties shuffled into the swaying space between the cars.

"Mind movin' on, my man!" One of the four sniffled and showed off a row of dull gold caps.

Hudson said nothing. The train was just braking into the 59th Street station, a maze of connecting, blue-tinted platforms which were flashing by on either side.

"I *said* – move on, my man!"

Colonel David Hudson's feet shifted slightly on the throbbing steel threshold plates. He slipped into the combat stance almost automatically, without a conscious thought.

The train bucked and squealed loudly to a stop and the one with the gold caps started to move.

The rest was like a familiar, memorized dream for David Hudson. Almost without any conscious command, his clenched left fist shot forward.

It was followed immediately by a martial arts kick.

The lightning blows were like lethal hardwood clubs. One accurately smashed into the group leader's temple; the second crunched his cheek like wallboard. He reeled backward and fell, unconscious before he hit the metal floor.

The second man pulled a knife. Hudson struck before he considered how he might use it. Blood seemed to explode, redness gushed over the attacker's right eyebrow.

"You! Hey, *you! Stop right there.*"

David Hudson heard shouts as the synchronized line of subway doors slammed open. Two TA policemen in black leather jackets, a man and a woman, were running his way. They were coming fast, a dark blur hurtling down the crowded late-night platform.

The police officers' nightsticks were out. The heavy wood stanchions were flying, pumping up and down as they ran.

Colonel David Hudson burst from the gaping train doors before they could reach him.

"You! Stop! Stop!" The transit cops were suddenly screaming sharp commands from the rear.

David Hudson felt incomprehensible terror as he

256

pushed and stumbled along the jammed subway platform. His chest and thighs started to burn. The Lizard Man was flashing back. *The lessons of the Lizard Man . . .*

For it to all end like this was so absurd. So impossible to imagine or foresee. He had a "sample" bond inside his jacket, and they'd search him for certain.

How could it possibly end this way? How could Green Band end *here*? In a mundane New York City subway station?

David Hudson could see all his careful planning, all the detailed pieces of Green Band swept into disarray by nothing more significant than a stroke of bad luck. It was the kind of random whim of chance you could never take into account when planning something in such detail.

Hudson ran alongside colorful advertising billboards. Long-running plays, Perdue chickens, current movie hits, they went swirling past in a technicolor blur.

The stone floor was slick with rainwater drained down from the street. The smell of urine was overpowering in the endless, fetid tunnel.

For it all to end like this was unthinkable.

"Stop! Stop, you!"

Not a single person dared move toward him, to help the trailing TA police team. Hudson looked too determined, too potentially dangerous to grapple with. He was a flying, one-armed madman!

His legs were pumping furiously high and his face was fearsome in its intense concentration.

He sideswiped a weaving drunk, and didn't really feel the insubstantial body bounce off.

It was too absurd for the plan to end here! Wasn't it too absurd?

An explosion suddenly echoed through the long stone tunnel behind him. People all over the station began to scream. A teen-aged Puerto Rican girl crouched low, palms flat against the wet concrete. An elderly man held his feathered fedora down with both hands.

The TA cops had actually fired warning shots.

257

They were shooting inside the crowded, late-night subway station. It was so insane for it to end like this.

Dark stone stairs were off to his right! Stairs to what, though?

Colonel Hudson could see the street looming above, a patch of purplish-gray sky like a spread umbrella.

Hudson ran three steps at a time.

Up, he screamed at himself.

Outside!

Out of this careless, stupid trap he'd stumbled into.

Hudson sprinted blindly down West 60th Street.

Hudson ran across the empty street against the red light. He was trailing rags of his own breath.

He continued on down 60th Street, past Columbus, slipping into a maze of high-rise beige and gray apartment buildings.

His heart pounding, he finally stopped in a darkened doorway. His breath hung in the air. Blood roared in his veins.

Seconds later, the two TA cops spun around the same corner of the gray brick apartment building. He hadn't lost them, after all.

He slid his gun from his coat, Hudson trained it on the male first.

His finger curled round the trigger. . . . *Heart shots would be necessary here*. He inhaled deeply two or three times.

The two cops didn't see him yet. He watched as they searched among dark building shadows.

"Where the hell did he go?" the guy asked, breathing hard, wheezing like a much older man.

Colonel Hudson continued to watch from the building's doorway. . . . They only had to start walking toward him and they were dead. Both of them . . .

"You wanna call this off?" the patrolman asked. "I don't see him."

The female cop shrugged and she pulled off her duty cap.

David Hudson held his breath. Don't come any closer, he thought. Not another step closer.

258

Don't come toward me. . . . Please, don't.

The two cops continued to stare at each other. Then the woman laughed and her shrill voice carried in Hudson's direction. "Yeah. He's probably miles away. That creep could *run*."

Hudson blinked. He listened as their footsteps slowly faded, becoming nothing at all.

A quick, cruel pain exploded inside Hudson's chest. His legs were quivering, so that he finally had to sit on the frozen curb.

If he'd had to shoot those two TA cops? . . . But he hadn't.

He stuck the gun back inside his jacket.

He didn't need any kind of disaster now. He didn't need to be running pell-mell through subways pursued by New York City transit cops.

Everything was coming down now. He was certain of it. The high and mighty United States was going to come crashing down to reality now. Colonel David Hudson thought it was a fate well deserved.

28

The World Trade Center

"What's happening, Arch, *I think*, is a disorderly, almost a riotous Market condition. Everybody desperately wants to sell. Except there's a corresponding lack of buyers," Caitlin said.

"What *exactly* does that mean?" Carroll asked. "What happens now?"

"It means the bottom line price of stocks and bonds *has* to plummet dramatically. . . . The crash that's apparently coming could last a few hours, days, or drag on for years."

"Years?"

"Back in sixty-three, on the day Kennedy was assassinated, the Market collapsed and was shut down early. The next day it recovered. But it wasn't until after World War II that the Market recovered from the crash of 1929. There's *never* been a situation to match this one against, though. This panic is happening all over the world. All at the same time."

Carroll and Caitlin Dillon were hurrying across the immense marble lobby of the World Trade Center.

It was here, on the ground floor and mezzanine, that the fiduciary nerve center of the banks and trust companies had been established after the bombings on Wall Street.

The escalator stairs to the mezzanine were frozen to a stop. An impromptu sign over a red arrow said FINANCIAL SECTION, and pointed straight up.

Carroll and Caitlin started to jog up the oddly motionless metal stairs. It was just past 4:00 A.M.

"This looks a little more organized than Number thirteen. Not much though," Carroll observed.

Red and blue intercom wires were strung up everywhere, hung like Christmas decorations over the escalators and fire exit stairways. Open radio channels connecting uptown offices with the Financial Center squawked and chattered endlessly.

Even at that time in the morning, the hum and buzz of electronic noise was unrelenting.

Out a row of high-vaulted windows, Carroll and Caitlin could see a black Bell Army helicopter landing. Limos and other official cars were discharging somber-looking men carrying business briefcases.

A crash coming this morning?

Another Black Friday?

"What happened? What's causing the worldwide panic?" Carroll wanted to know as he and Caitlin entered a cavernous marble hallway with no visible way out.

Caitlin rubbed her arms warm as she walked. The glass doors to the outside were constantly opening, and the building was cold as a meat freezer.

"None of the usual safeguards in the systems are working. Not enough failsafe devices were ever built in for a situation like this. Academic economists have been warning the New York Stock Exchange for years. Every MBA candidate in the country knows that something like this could conceivably happen."

Carroll finally pushed open heavy pine doors into a huge, disturbingly frantic business conference room: a miniature Stock Exchange almost. Brokers on complex NYTECH telephone consoles, analysts with IBM desk top computers, were talking all at once.

The room was absolutely jammed with frenetic, shadowy figures, many of whom were shouting into phone receivers which they managed to cradle, in a practiced defiance of gravity, between jaw and shoulder. Carroll had the impression of madness, a bedlam: what this place reminded him of, give or take some modern accoutrements, was a print he'd once seen of a Massachusetts insane asylum in the late 1800s.

Unconditional orders were being issued to *sell*, at the very best price possible. Jobs and business relationships were being routinely threatened over the long distance telephones.

Jay Fairchild, tall, jowly, bald as an infant, lumbered forward out of a clique of gray suits to meet Caitlin and Carroll. Fairchild was an Undersecretary of the Treasury, a man who'd come to rely regularly on Caitlin's judgments, her usually astute, almost uncanny hunches about the market.

"Jay, what the hell has happened tonight? Who started it? *Where* did it start?" It was Caitlin's turn to appear confused for a change.

The Undersecretary of the Treasury's eyes had all the animation right then of glass beads. There was a standing joke that all undersecretaries were illegitimate children of past congressmen and presidents. They definitely had a rare, collective ability to look completely out of place.

"Just about *every* nightmare scenario you or I have ever imagined has come true tonight," Jay Fairchild finally said. His voice held a tiny, whistling sibilance, like a crack of wind sneaking inside the building.

"At the end of the day yesterday, out in Chicago, metal skyrocketed way up. A ton of futures, coffee, sugar, flopped badly. Bank of America and First National began calling in their loans."

Caitlin couldn't hold back her anger at that news. "Those unbelievable shits! Morons. The commodity people out of Chicago won't listen to anybody, Arch. There have been all sorts of speculative excesses on the options market long before this. For years and years. That's one more reason we were ripe for this panic."

"None of that is the *real* problem right now, though," Jay Fairchild said. "The crash is being precipitated by the goddamn banks! . . . The banks are almost completely responsible. Let's wander back to the lobby. You'll see what I mean. It's worse than it looks up here. It's quite sad, really."

"I imagine Black Friday was, too." Caitlin nodded her head and followed the Undersecretary with Carroll.

*   *   *

FBI agents and particularly hardnosed-looking New York City police officers were conscientiously screening the credentials of everyone trying to get into the conference room on the ground floor level. Carroll knew the FBI guys, so they walked right in.

Once inside, the thundering noise and activity was easily double what Carroll and Caitlin had witnessed and heard upstairs.

It was still only 4:30 A.M., but a nightmarish fear had taken firm hold – you could see it on every face inside the overcrowded room.

The business investigators who squeezed into the conference hall included some of the more sophisticated new breed of bankers. In the not-so-distant past, most banks had wanted to be viewed as impregnable places for their depositors' money, secure fortresses of capital. So bankers tended to be characterized by physical and emotional restraint, by almost compulsive neatness, by conservatism in both their behavior and thinking.

That was hardly the case with the men and women packed into this room. These were glossy, well-tailored globe-trotters, most of them as comfortable in Geneva, in Paris, in Beirut, as they were at home in New York. The spiritual leader of this cosmopolitan group was Walter Wriston, the now retired head of Citicorp. In Caitlin's opinion, Wriston had been little more than a glorified traveling salesman, but some thought him a genius.

"There's another factor contributing to the current disaster," Jay Fairchild said. "The very real possibility of a *worldwide crash*, rather than an isolated one in the U.S. This time, the whole bloody world really could go up. It's been that volatile a situation, potentially, for at least the last four years."

Everyone they passed in the formal conference room appeared hopelessly grave, and, once again, battle-weary, to Carroll. The scene was something like a general alarm on a Navy warship.

Caitlin said, "Seven days of brokerage transactions are now unresolved. The banks are competing, they're

263

actually competing to see who can take the most clear-cut, absolutely amoral advantage of the chaos!" Her face was flushed and there was an anger in her voice Carroll hadn't heard before.

Carroll didn't technically understand some of what was being said, but he grasped enough. When you misappropriate people's money, *a lot of small investors' money given to you on trust*, he figured you were a common criminal.

Call him naive and old-fashioned, but that was how he felt.

"It sounds to me like *nobody's* protecting the ordinary investor right now."

Jay Fairchild nodded. "*Nobody is*. The big banks are all busy maneuvering for the oil billions. They couldn't give a damn about the poor bastard out there with a hundred shares of Polaroid or AT and T."

"Arch, Arab oil money is the name of the game. Arab money is almost always conservatively managed. Since last Friday they've been trying to move out of the U.S. Treasury Bills. Into gold. Into other precious metals. The banks are all shamelessly scrambling for the huge Arab fees. They're like rats on a ship, bailing out of the dollar – rushed into sterling, the yen, the Swiss franc, all the more stable currencies . . . Chase, Manufacturers, Bank of America, they're *making* small fortunes right now." Caitlin's lips were tight and her jaw clenched as she spoke.

"Do the two of you really know what you're talking about?" Carroll finally asked in desperation.

Caitlin and Jay Fairchild looked at one another. They answered in unison. "Right now, no. *Nobody* knows *exactly* what this is about. But what we've just told you is generally true."

The three of them stood by helplessly watching the potential Stock Market crash gain a frightening momentum of its own.

Reports from London, Paris, Bonn, and Geneva came rushing in. The news was as depressing as that of a natural calamity, like the death toll left behind by a vicious earthquake.

Men in white shirtsleeves and loosened neckties took turns calling out the more substantial Telex quotes for the benefit of beleaguered clerks who reported them into a massive central computer.

Phibro Solomon	bought at	12½	Down 22.
General Electric	bought at	35	Down 31.
IBM	bought at	80½	Down 40.

By 11:30 on the morning of December 14, most U.S. banks, including every savings and loan, had been closed. The Chicago, Philadelphia, Boston, Pacific and Midwest exchanges had all been officially shut down.

The emotional panic for investors was in full force; it was virtually unstoppable in every city, every small town across the United States.

At noon, an elderly man made his way toward the hub of action at the front of the World Trade Center Crisis Room.

Many of the young brokers and bankers didn't recognize Anton Birnbaum. Those who did regarded him with sharp, uneasy glances. It wasn't every day that one encountered a Wall Street legend.

Birnbaum actually looked more like an ancient New York City pawnbroker than one of the world's acknowledged financial geniuses, a man with a reputation that had been unblemished over all his years in business.

President Justin Kearney had arrived by helicopter from Washington less than thirty minutes before. He was conferring with Philip Berger from the CIA. Both of them recognized Anton Birnbaum as the old man approached. The President warmly greeted the Financier, speaking with great deference and obviously sincere respect.

"It's awfully good to see you again, Anton. Especially right now." The President spoke formally, as he might to a visiting foreign dignitary he respected but didn't know well enough to be totally direct with. Kearney's whole manner was more than a little uncertain lately: for more than a week now both the American and foreign press had been lashing his administration for its failure to deal with the economic crisis. It had had the same effect on Kearney as a shameful public flogging.

Kearney and Anton Birnbaum eventually disappeared inside a small private office, the door of which was guarded by beefy protectors from the Secret Service.

"It's good to be *seen* out in the world, Mr. President. I don't get out so much anymore. Mr. President, if I might be allowed to speak first, I have an idea, a plan you might wish to consider . . .

"I have just gotten off the phone with two gentlemen you've possibly never heard of. It's worth repeating both conversations. One man is from Milwaukee, a Mr. Clyde Miller. The other man resides in Nashville, Tennessee – Mr. Louis Lavine."

Anton Birnbaum said all this in a slow, very deliberate style which made each word seem vitally important.

"Mr. Miller is a CEO for a large Milwaukee brewing company. Mr. Lavine is currently Treasurer for the State of Tennessee. . . . I have just convinced Mr. Miller to buy five hundred thousand shares of General Motors stock, which is right now at forty-seven. He will buy the General Motors stock, and keep buying it until the price goes back to sixty-seven. He is prepared to invest up to two hundred million dollars.

"I've asked Mr. Louis Lavine in Tennessee to buy NCR stock which is now at nineteen, and continue to buy it until the price moves up to thirty. He's prepared to commit up to seventy-five million dollars for the purchase." Anton Birnbaum then went on to explain to the President why the plan he'd conceived could actually work.

"I only hope that the courage of these two gentlemen will actually turn the direction of this catastrophe. I pray it will restore some necessary *optimism*. Mr. President, I have a belief that it will . . .

"Once the market sniffs a demand for these two bellwether issues, smart money will undoubtedly start moving. The risks arbitragers, who can spot an uptrend

266

in an avalanche and who command billions in ready cash, will begin testing the waters.

"I have advised a select few of my associates, who have responsibility for mutual and pension funds around the country, that a dramatic break in the crisis situation is now imminent. I have strongly suggested that they look for opportunities to begin bargain hunting, before they lose out on a very fast and favorable profit spiral. A spiral back close to where the market began this morning."

The news of Anton Birnbaum's recovery plan traveled with appropriate dispatch through the main Trade Center conference room. Emotional arguments over whether the daring strategy was right, or disastrous, raged immediately.

"Clyde Miller has just bankrupted his own corporation." One of the harsher detractors laughed with derision at the news.

Two other middle-aged bankers argued their way into a fist fight. Creaking haymakers were thrown and somehow managed to connect with some authority. A loop of bankers and stock analysts surrounded the breathless, wheezing pugilists and at least a couple of side bets were laid. The fight ended with both bankers leaning against each other in fatigue, as if they were each trying to shore up the other's dignity. In a small way, they symbolized the shambles of the system that had worked in spite of itself for so long.

As the winter morning passed into steely gray afternoon, however, it was obvious that the dramatic Birnbaum plan was either too late or too little. There was no significant change in the attitude and therefore the momentum of the declining market.

The largest single-day losses ever had already been recorded on the world's stock markets.

On October 29, 1929, losses had been fourteen billion.

On December 14, the single day's recorded losses around the world exceeded two hundred billion.

29

The Press

At seven that night, Carroll and Caitlin Dillon watched a truly chilling evening news report with over a hundred of the principals who were actually making the headlines inside the World Trade Center. TV camera teams, top free-lance national magazine and newspaper photographers, network radio reporters carrying lightweight tape recorders on their shoulders, were swarming all over the man on the street in New York City.

A TV news interviewer stopped people entering St. Patrick's Cathedral on Fifth Avenue.

"How do you personally react to today's financial tragedy? What they're now calling a Black Market."

"It makes me very frightened. Very sad. Nothing in this society of ours seems secure anymore. I had a few dollars. Safe. In IBM, in AT and T, the blue-chippers only. Now I have virtually nothing. I'm seventy-three years old. What am I going to do?"

A TV interview crew from Eyewitness News was set up to intercept pedestrians near Lincoln Center on Columbus Avenue.

"Excuse me, sir. What's your response to the latest reports, the critical situations on Wall Street?"

"My response! I'll tell you what. There's nothing you can believe in anymore. After Watergate, you couldn't believe in the President of the United States. After Viet Nam, you couldn't believe in our military's moral stance. You can't believe in Church leaders anymore. Now? Now you can't even believe in the almighty dollar . . ."

268

TV news teams roamed 42nd Street near Grand Central Station.

"You're a police officer. You've undoubtedly seen this city in other times of great stress . . . blackouts, racial riots. . . . How do you compare this situation right now?"

"This is about the hairiest I've seen it in New York. Not violent. Not yet, anyways. It's just, people are like, they're like walking zombies. Everybody I talk to, totally blitzed. It's like somebody changed all the rules of our life."

TV camera crews were a constant fixture all over Wall Street and the World Trade Center area. The TV newsman Curt Jackson had actually been living in a construction company trailer on Wall Street since the original Friday night bombings. He promised his audience he wouldn't leave until the crime, the Green Band mystery, was solved.

"You're a native New Yorker, sir?" Curt Jackson asked an older gentleman in his familiar, highly authoritative voice.

"That's right, Curt. I'm a New Yorker, thirty-eight years."

"What comment do you want to make about the terrible panic, the tragedy in the Market today?"

"A comment for you? Well . . . you see this gold chain I wear? You see this beautiful gold watch I wear? That's where I keep my emergency money . . . always ready to travel. Always right here with me at all times. . . . Any more trouble like this, it's *adios* New York City. You oughta buy a gold watch for yourself. Just in case we don't do so good tomorrow."

Walter Trentkamp

Around ten-thirty, Caitlin and Carroll ran into Walter Trentkamp. They had been walking the long, broad hallways inside the Trade Center, still waiting for definitive news from around the world. The two of them were

269

holding hands when they came upon the avuncular FBI head.

Walter didn't say anything, but he smiled a lot. His brown eyes fairly sparkled with delight, or surprise, or both.

"You see," he finally spoke to Caitlin and Carroll, "something decent can come out of anything. Damn, this is the first good thing I've seen or heard in a week."

With that, and a special wink toward Caitlin, Trentkamp continued on his way down the corridor.

Suddenly he turned, and called out to Carroll. "Hey, I thought I told you to keep me posted on what was going on!"

Then Walter Trentkamp disappeared around the next corner.

The World Trade Center

Late that night, Caitlin swallowed warm sips of diet soda and sat entranced before a forty-inch television screen just off the main crisis room. The monitor's reception was crisp and terrific, the antennas for the major national networks all being up on the Trade Center roof.

"This is it," she whispered to Carroll. "The exchange in Hong Kong will be the first important one to open around the world. Sydney and Tokyo are both staying closed until noon, we hear. Yesterday, the Hang Seng Index fell 80 points. This will really tell the story."

Caitlin and Carroll were sitting within a tightly clustered nest of Wall Street bankers, frayed men and women who were like spectators burned out by watching some unlikely sport event that stretched day after day. A closed-circuit TV broadcast was being beamed by satellite transmission from Asia to New York. The blackest gallows humor had gained control of the waiting room – as it often does in the worst disasters and emergencies.

On the flickering color TV screen, they all watched

270

cameramen and news reporters – live – recording history from behind Hong Kong police lines. Farther down the crowded, rowdy street, tens of thousands of Hong Kong residents were loudly chanting, waving hand-printed political placards. Meanwhile, single lines of dark-suited stockbrokers were beginning to solemnly march into the exchange itself.

"The brokers look like pallbearers," Carroll whispered to Caitlin. He very lightly stroked her arm. She took his hand in hers.

"It isn't exactly a cheery sight, is it? It certainly *does* look like a state funeral."

"Yeah. And whose funeral?" Carroll asked.

A foreign correspondent for one of the major American networks eventually stepped up to a TV camera planted on the mobbed cacophonous Hong Kong street. The newsman wore a rumpled seersucker suit and spoke with an affected, clipped British accent.

"Never before have we seen such a graphic demonstration of the polarization between Third World and Western hopes and dreams. Here in Hong Kong I believe we are seeing a mini-drama of the imminent future of the world. It is now the day after stock prices tumbled precipitously everywhere. . . . The bond market is in shambles; the French and Arabs are liquidating their holdings at literally the rate of billions a day. . . . And in Hong Kong this morning, many people are deeply concerned, even sad faced. . . . But *the majority*, surprisingly large numbers, mostly university and street gang youths, but also the unemployed – are shouting anti-U.S. slogans, even praying for a shattering Stock Market crash. These people are clearly rooting for a full-scale world economic crash. They're expecting the worst, and they're gleeful about the expected disastrous outcome. . . . *The long awaited fall of the West*."

Suddenly everything changed!
Unbelievably.
Beautifully, and all around the world.

271

Almost as if it had all been prearranged, too.
Carefully, carefully orchestrated financial panic.

Not forty minutes after the Hong Kong Exchange opened, stock prices on the Hang Seng began to stabilize; then stock prices started to actually rise – to surge powerfully upward on the index.

To the keen disappointment of many of the jeering university students and workers mobbing the streets outside – a dizzying spiral of nearly seventy-five points followed in the next hour alone.

The exchange in Sydney opened in very much the same manner. Grim and hopelessly exhausted brokers at first; highly organized labor and student rallies against capitalism, against the United States in particular – then a burst of excited buying. A dramatic index spiral up.

The same scenario followed at the late opening exchange in Tokyo.

In Malaysia an hour later.

Everywhere.

Carefully orchestrated chaos.

The manipulator's manipulation – but to what end?

At 8:30 A.M. New York time, looking as though he'd recently been liberated from the dustiest carrel in the New York Public Library, Anton Birnbaum peered inside the World Trade Center emergency meeting area. This time, however, a boisterous entourage surged forward and escorted the Financier to the front of the pandemonious room.

President Justin Kearney appeared relaxed, almost jovial as he met the aging financial mastermind. Vice-president Thomas Elliot was standing beside him, still looking controlled and restrained. The Vice-president actually appeared to be the coolest of the Washington leaders, a surprising and resourceful man, a mystery man in many ways. Birnbaum himself seemed quietly astonished by the general hubbub, the strange celebration before nine in the morning. He was equally astonished by the way the market, like some whimsical thing.

subject not to the rules of money but rather the patterns of the wind, had come back so strongly.

"Mr. Birnbaum. Good morning."

"Yes. Good morning, Mr. President, Mr. Vice-president. And I hear it *is* a pretty good morning."

"By God, you did it."

"By God. Or in spite of Him, Mr. President."

"This is amazing. It's quite moving, actually. See? . . . Real tears." Caitlin stood hanging lightly onto Carroll's arm. She finally dabbed at her eyes, and was hardly alone in the gesture.

They were at the heart of the frenzied celebration inside the World Trade Center. Off to one side of the room, President Kearney was emotionally clutching his Chief of Staff. The secretaries of Treasury, State and Defense were positively boyish with their loud whoops, their echoing hand clapping. The gray-suited Chairman of the Federal Reserve had danced briefly with the cantankerous Chairman of the Joint Chiefs.

"I don't believe I've ever seen bankers so joyous before," Caitlin said.

"They still dance like bankers though." Carroll smiled at the odd but genuinely affecting scene of relief. "No threats to Michael Jackson here."

He couldn't help feeling elation in the midst of this crazy, almost riotous room, though. It wasn't as if they'd actually found Green Band, but it was something, a sliver of merriment at the heart of all the recent grimness, the frustration trailing back for days.

Caitlin lightly nuzzled the side of his face with her mouth. "I'm already getting worried again. I only hope . . ."

"What do you hope?" Carroll gently held Caitlin's arm. He felt unbelievably close to her. They had already shared more charged moments than some people do in a lifetime.

"I hope that it continues like this, and doesn't come crashing down."

273

Carroll was silent, studying the oddly uplifting scene being performed in front of him. Somebody had found a phonograph and the sound of Scottish bagpipers could be heard playing over the general din. Somebody extremely resourceful was dragging in a couple of cases of champagne. There was something just a little forced in the celebration – but what the hell? These were people who'd been about to fall off the edge of their world and, slippery though it might be, they'd found some kind of temporary footing.

Still . . .

Still . . .

Even as Carroll eventually sipped champagne, something inside kept him from getting too hopeful. *This is all premature, and therefore dangerous*, he was thinking as the party heightened in intensity. The policeman inside Carroll never stopped working, never stopped probing, figuring out all the possible angles. Damnit, police work *was* in his blood.

Where is Green Band? Is Green Band watching all this right now?

What were they thinking? Where are they taking us next? What kind of party are they having today?

Who's telling them everything we do, before we do it?

Wednesday; December 15;
the Vets

30

Anton Birnbaum

There was no more valuable time to waste. Clearly, there was no time at all. Every passing hour was vitally important now. Anton Birnbaum's hyperactive mind was automatically clicking on and off, trying out hundreds of different circuit paths like an expensive, if slightly dated, computer.

Birnbaum had begun to make urgent phone calls from his eleven-room apartment on Riverside Drive near Columbia. He had definite hunches now – strong suspicions after talking to Caitlin Dillon and her policeman friend Carroll.

At junctures in his life, Birnbaum had been thought of as the consummate international businessman, at times as the world's preeminent economist. Certainly he was an intense student of life, intrigued by the vicissitudes of human behavior. His curiosity was boundless even at his age.

Never a day passed that Anton Birnbaum didn't read for a minimum of six or seven hours. Because of that lifelong habit, the Financier knew he was still several steps faster than the other people in his business, especially the lazy boys on Wall Street nowadays.

What was the operative connection between Green Band, the bombings on December 4, and the dangerous economic events of the past two days?

Why had nothing conclusive been discovered about the Green Band group yet?

Why were the Green Band *provocateurs* consistently a step or two ahead of those conducting the police investigation? How could that be happening again and again?

Like nature itself, Anton Birnbaum abhorred a vacuum and that was precisely what Green Band had masterfully created. A huge empty space in which even logical questions had no apparent answers.

Months back, he had heard rumors, more than rumors, of a Russian-sponsored plot to dramatically disrupt the Stock Market. . . . His closest and most reliable contacts at the CIA had been worried about the activities of the wretched François Monserrat. Was Monserrat connected with the Green Band plot somehow? And what about certain members of the government here in America? The CIA's Philip Berger? He was a character Birnbaum had never found it in himself to believe, or trust. . . . Or Vice-president Thomas Elliot? He was a chilly one as well, at least he played everything extremely close to the vest.

A lot of possibilities. *Too many*. Almost as if *that* was part of the plan: all the contiguous possibilities.

As the tiny, ancient man made his inquisitional phone calls that morning – to Switzerland, England, France, South Africa, to both West and East Germany – he felt like someone with an important name right on the tip of his tongue – the lurking secret of Green Band was about to come tumbling forth. . . . The thinnest connecting link was still missing.

Anton Birnbaum wrote down the most suspicious items.

Philip Berger . . .

Thomas More Elliot . . .

François Monserrat . . . Tripoli meetings.

The Red Tuesday Crash . . .

Somewhere among these clues, these names and indisputable facts, was the beginning of the answer they were searching for. He was certain of that, at least.

276

If he could just find a satisfactory connecting link. . . . If he could figure the logical *motive* for the steady progression of events thus far. . . . It had to be here somewhere.

Anton Birnbaum worked at his desk, sketchily making notes, picking up the telephone, answering every highly confidential call himself. He worked feverishly, like a man who feels his time is runnng out.

No. 13 Wall

Carroll had decided to start at the beginning, square one again, and thoroughly check and recheck every early lead, every hunch he'd ever had about Green Band. The task would take countless hours, he knew. It would require an intense search through the computers, even allowing for the fact that he had high-speed data at his disposal. *Ah, police work.*

He asked for clearance from both the CIA and the FBI to make a search of their computer files. Neither organization gave him too much trouble, although Phil Berger imposed certain limitations on Carroll's access, for the usual reasons of public security.

Nearly eleven hours later, Carroll stood before the dozen or so computer screens inside the Emergency Room at No. 13 Wall. Carroll stared at the screens and his eyes ached from the dull green glow.

He glanced at Caitlin, who sat with her slender fingers raised over a computer keyboard, ready to type out a password for further access to the FBI's files. There was no skill she didn't seem to have in abundance.

When the display screen answered, she rapidly typed again, this time requesting a readout of active and nonactive Viet Nam veterans who, for whatever reason, had been under police surveillance during the past two years – a time frame she and Carroll had agreed on.

She added the subcategory: *Explosive experts. New York and vicinity. Possible subversive leanings.*

There was a long pause, a spooky electronic pause, then

the machine began its requested readout of American soldiers.

Carroll had been down this particular route of investigation, only not with the Crisis Room equipment and Caitlin's help. American terrorist-related groups were out there, but none were considered very powerful or well-organized. Phil Berger of the CIA had been investigating American paramilitary groups himself. He had waved Carroll off that trail once before.

"Can you print out a list of the real hard cases?" Carroll asked Caitlin.

"This is a computer. It can do anything if you ask nicely."

The printer obligingly kicked back into life. Paper slid through it as the dot matrix clacked back and forward. A total count showed no more than ninety names of current soldiers and veterans with extensive explosives experience in Viet Nam; men who the FBI considered important enough to keep track of. Carroll ripped the scroll of paper from the printer and took it to a desk, spreading the thing out.

Adamski, Stanley. Corporal. Three years VA Hospital, Prescott, Arizona. Member of left-wing oriented veterans group called the Rams, ostensibly a biker's club.

Carroll wondered how much of this was standard FBI paranoia?

The list was filled with dizzying cross-references, he soon discovered. One name was connected to another, creating a mazelike effect. You could spend months working on all the permutations.

Keresty, John. Sergeant. Munitions expert. Discharged VA Hospital, Scranton, Pa., 1974. Occupation: custodian, plastics corp. Member of the American Socialist Party. Ridgewood, New Jersey. SEE: Rhinehart, Jay T.; Jones, James; Winston files.

The lists went on and on for pages.

Carroll massaged his eyelids. He went for two coffees, returned to the work desk and even more sprawling computer sheets.

He said, "Any one of these men, or two or three of them, working in tandem, *could* have helped blow up the financial district."

Caitlin gazed over his shoulder at the printout list. "So where do we start?"

Carroll shook his head. He was filled with doubts again. They would have to investigate, maybe even visit every name on the lists. They didn't have time.

Scully, Richard P. Sergeant. Plastique expert. Hospitalized Manhattan 1974 for alcoholism. Extreme right-wing sympathizer. Occupation: cabdriver. New York City.

Downey, Marc. Military assassin. Hospitalized 1971–73: Occupation: bartender. Worcester, Mass.

Carroll gazed at the burgeoning list again. He had another idea. An Army *officer*, maybe? A disaffected officer with a grudge, or a cause? Somebody exceptionally smart, nursing a grievance, year after year.

Carroll laid his hands on the warm computer console. He wished he could coax all the secrets out of it, all the electronic links of which it was capable. He stared at the already lengthy printout again. "An officer," Carroll said. "Try that."

Caitlin went back to the keyboard to request more information. He watched her fingers move expertly over the keys. She was requesting information on *known or suspected subversives, who had been officers in Viet Nam.* Under the general rubric of "subversive" were included all kinds of people.

The screen began to issue more names. Colonels. Captains. Majors. Some were listed in these official records as schizophrenics. Others were supposedly burnt out on drugs. Others still had become evangelists, panhandlers, small-time bank and liquor store robbers. Carroll received a printout of these names as well. There were twenty-nine of the hard-core category in and around New York City.

The screen flickered again.

Names of the various officers on the FBI list now shimmered forth. Carroll once again ran his eye over them.

Bradshaw, Michael. Captain. Discharged VA Hospital Dallas, Texas, 1971. Occupation: Real estate salesman, Hempstead, Long Island. Post Traumatic Stress Disorder victim.

Babbershill, Terrance. Major. Discharged dishonorably 1969. Known Viet Cong sympathizer. Occupation: English-language tutor for various Vietnamese families. Brooklyn, New York.

Carroll blinked and tried to focus. His eyes were beginning to water. He needed to feel the fresh cold night air on his face. He didn't move: he continued to run his eyes up and down the screen.

Rydeholm, Ralph. Colonel.

O'Donnell, Joseph. Colonel.

Schweitzer, Peter. Lieutenant Colonel.

Shaw, Robert. Captain.

Craig, Kyle. Colonel.

Boudreau, Dan. Captain.

Kaplan, Lin. Captain.

Weinshanker, Greg. Captain.

Dwyer, James. Colonel.

Beauregard, Bo. Captain.

Arnold, Tim. Captain.

Morrissey, Jack. Colonel.

Too many names, Carroll thought.

Too many casualties in a war of total waste.

"Can you get me cross-references, Caitlin? Associations and connections between any of these men? The officers. The real hard asses out of Viet Nam?"

"I'll try." Caitlin tapped a few keys. Nothing happened this time.

She stared at the screen thoughtfully, then tapped another brief message.

Nothing happened.

She tapped out another message still.

Nothing happened.

"Is something wrong?" Carroll asked.

"This is the best I can get, Arch. Damn it."

The unfortunate message that shone in front of them read:

Further data: see files

"See files?" he asked. "These *are* the files."

"They apparently have more information in FBI files that *aren't* on the computer, Arch. They're down in Washington. Only in Washington. Why is that?"

Vets 24

At ten o'clock on the evening of December 15, Sergeant Harry Stemkowsky was thinking that he was actually solvent. He was financially comfortable, probably for the first time in his entire adult life.

He'd just bought a new Ford Bronco, also a luxurious beaver coat at Alexander's for Mary. Life was suddenly getting decent for them, for the first time in their four married years together.

But Harry Stemkowsky couldn't bring himself to comfortably believe in any of it. This was all like Santa Claus, and trips to Disneyworld – that kind of transient shit.

Who could identify with the sudden net worth of $1,152,000?

Harry Stemkowsky felt a little like one of those loonietunes who won the New York State Lottery, then nervously kept their little jobs as janitors or U.S. postal employees. It was a matter of too much, too fast. He kept getting the uneasy feeling that somebody was going to take it all away again.

At twenty past ten that evening, Stemkowsky carefully nosed his Vets cab out of the street noise and blazing yellow lights of Midtown Manhattan in the East 60s. He'd finished his regular ten-hour shift, all according to the Vets' master plan, Colonel Hudson's prescribed step-by-step plan for their ultimate success. The Checker cab bumped and rattled onto the 57th Street entrance to the bridge.

A few minutes later, the Checker cab turned onto a busy avenue in Jackson Heights, then edged onto 85th Street, where Harry Stemkowsky lived with his wife, Mary.

He absently licked his lips as he drove down 85th. He could just about taste the French stew Mary had said she was fixing when he'd left this morning.

The sudden expectation of beef, shallots, those little, light puffed potatoes she usually made, was exhilarating. Maybe he and Mary should retire to the south of France after this was over, he began to think. They'd be filthy rich enough for sure. They could eat four-star French food until they got absolutely sick of it. Maybe move on to Italy. Maybe Greece after that. Greece was supposed to be cheap. Hey. Who cared if it was cheap or not?

Harry Stemkowsky began to accelerate down the last flat stretch toward home.

"Jesus Christ, buddy!" Stemkowsky suddenly shouted out loud and pounded his brakes.

A tall, balding guy, with an incredibly pained look, had run right out in front of the cab. The guy was frantically waving both arms over his head; he was screaming something Stemkowsky couldn't make out with the windows up.

Harry Stemkowsky recognized the look from Viet Nam though, from dreaded clean- up patrols into villages after devastating Phantom air strafes. His heart had already dropped through the floorboards of the cab. Something horrible and unexpected had happened here – something awful had happened in Stemkowsky's own neighborhood.

The terrified man was up against the cab window now. Still screaming at the top of his voice. "Help me, please! Help! Please help!"

Stemkowsky finally got the window rolled down. He had his radio mike in hand, ready to call for whatever kind of emergency help was needed.

"What the hell happened? What happened, mister?"

Suddenly, a small black Beretta was shoved hard, crunching like a nightstick against Harry Stemkowsky's temple. *"This* is the matter! Don't move. Put back that mike."

A second man appeared now, suddenly emerging out

of the smoky side street darkness. He yanked open the creaking passenger side door.

"Just turn the cab right around, Sergeant Stemkowsky. We're not going home quite yet."

An indefinite time later – Hours? Maybe it was days? There was no possible way to accurately gauge because all time had collapsed under him – Harry Stemkowsky felt hands angrily ripping under his armpits, lifting him rudely.

The hands propped him hard onto a badly creaking wooden chair again. They'd injected him twice so far with drugs, probably Pentothal.

A man's face, a blur of soft pink, seemed to float down and stop close to Stemkowsky's face. The man was uncomfortably close. Harry Stemkowsky was aware of faintly minty breath and musky cologne.

Then his mind went into complete shock! Sergeant Harry Stemkowsky's watery eyes began to blink rapidly; he tried to look away from this *particular closeup face* . . .

Harry Stemkowsky couldn't believe who this was.

His eyes kept trying to lock into focus.

This face, he'd seen it before, recently, always distilled by a network TV screen or a newspaper –

No, he was confused: the injected drug had fucked his brain over –

What was going on here? This person couldn't be –

The face smiled horribly and said, "Yes, I'm François Monserrat. You know me under another name. This is an extraordinary shock, I know."

Harry Stemkowsky shut his eyes a moment. This was all a bad dream; make it go away.

Stemkowsky opened his eyes: he violently shook his head.

Suddenly, Harry Stemkowsky's head ached unbelievably. His eyeballs felt indescribably heavy, as if they were hanging on elastic bands. He simply could not believe it. So incredibly near the top. The ultimate traitor . . .

When Stemkowsky finally spoke, he was close to being incoherent; incomprehensible words squirmed through

283

his gummy, swollen lips. His tongue seemed at least twice its normal size.

"Ga fuh-fuh-fuck yrrself. Fuh-fuck yrrself."

"Oh, please. Your time for being morally indignant is long past. . . . All right, then . . . look at what we have here. Look at this."

Concentrate, Stemkowsky fiercely reminded himself. *Focus. Concentrate.*

Monserrat's hands were holding out a brown paper shopping bag. Up close to Stemkowsky's face.

Monserrat was taking something out. "A blue cooking pot. Familiar?" Once again, that horrible smile.

Harry Stemkowsky screamed! He fought insanely against his bonds, forcing them to rip into his skin.

Up close to Stemkowsky's eyes, a fork dipped slowly into the depths of the pot. The fork speared a dripping chunk of beef bourgignon that oozed brown gravy.

Stemkowsky screamed once again. He screamed and screamed.

"It seems you guessed my secret. You should also know by now how deadly serious this interrogation is. How important this is to me." Monserrat turned to his lieutenants.

"Bring in the unfortunate cook."

Harry Stemkowsky recognized his wife Mary, but only slightly. She was such a pitiful caricature of her former self. Her face was badly bruised, purplish and raw in extended areas. Her bloated mouth opened crookedly as she saw Harry. Some of her front teeth were missing; her swollen gums were pulpy and bloody.

"Puh-puh-pleez?" Stemkowsky struggled; he lifted the chair legs right off the floor with his tremendous arm strength. "*She doe kno.*"

"I know that. Mary doesn't know how you came to possess stolen Stock Market bonds in Beirut, then in Tel Aviv. *You* know, though."

"Pleez. Doh-doh-don hur' her . . ."

"I don't want to hurt her. So you tell me what you know, Sergeant. Everything that you know. You tell me right now. How did you get the stolen Stock Market bonds?"

Once again, that horrible smile from Monserrat.

It took another excessively cruel and gruesome fifteen minutes to get the information, to find out *some*, not all, of what Sergeant Harry Stemkowsky knew . . .

Information about the stolen bonds and Wall Street securities; about the bombings on December 4. Not where Colonel Hudson was right now. Not even precisely who the Vets leader was. But a start, a beginning at least. And a beginning was better than what Monserrat had been accustomed to recently.

François Monserrat stared down at crippled Harry Stemkowsky and his wife. From Stemkowsky's perspective the terrorist leader seemed to be looking right through them, as though they were both totally insubstantial. The look on Monserrat's face was almost inhumanly frightening, sickening.

"You see now? None of your pain, none of poor Mary's suffering was necessary. It could have been five minutes of talking together at most. Now, how's this for just rewards?"

A compact black Beretta appeared, paused so that the Stemkowskys could see what was coming, then fired twice.

The very last thing U.S. Army Sergeant Harry Stemkowsky ever thought . . . he and Mary never got to enjoy their money. Over a million dollars, which they'd earned. It wasn't fair. Life wasn't ever fair, was it? That same question always left hanging, always unanswered in the end.

Carroll

That night, Arch Carroll traveled home to Riverdale in the Bronx. As he slumped up from the floodlit clapboard garage, the ground around him seemed to be spinning.

He climbed creaky front porch steps. Twinges of guilt

struck painfully hard. He'd been neglecting the kids for too long this time.

The nightlight was on, but nothing much else downstairs. There was the soft electric buzz of kitchen appliances. Carroll took off his shoes, and tiptoed quietly upstairs.

He stopped and peeked inside the front bedroom where Elizabeth, a.k.a. Lizzie, bunked with Mickey Kevin. Their tiny baby figures were delicately sprawled across twin beds.

He remembered buying the beds years before, at Klein's on 14th Street. *Just look at the little creepolas. Not a problem, not a care in the world. Life as it ought to be.*

An ancient Buster Brown clock from Carroll's own childhood glowed and clicked softly on the far wall. It was next to posters of Def Leppard and the Police. Strange world to grow up in for a little kid.

Strange world for the big kids, too.

"Hi, you guys." He whispered, too low to be heard. "Your old dad's home from the salt mines."

"Everybody's just fine, Archer," Mary K. suddenly spoke. She'd snuck up from behind, and scared the living shit out of him.

"They understand all the problems you're having. We've been watching the news."

Mary K. gave her big brother a hug. She'd been seventeen the year both their parents had died in Florida. Carroll had brought her up after that. He and Nora had always been around to talk to her about her boyfriends – about Mary Katherine wanting to be a serious painter, even if she couldn't make any decent money at it. They'd been there when she needed them, and now it was the other way around.

"Maybe they understand okay about my work. How about the other thing? Caitlin?" Carroll's head turned slowly toward his sister.

Mary K. took his arm and draped it over her housecoat and shoulder. She was such a softie, such a sweet, gentle and good lady. It was time she found someone terrific as she was, Carroll often thought. Probably she wasn't helping her cause, living with him and the kids, either.

"They trust your parental judgment. Within reasonable bounds, of course."

"That's news."

"Oh, you're the Word and the Light to them, and you know it. If you say they'll like Caitlin, they instinctively believe it – because you said it, Arch."

"Well, they didn't show it the other morning. I *think* they'll like her. She's a terrific person."

"I'm sure she is. You have good instincts about people. You always knew which of my beaus was worth a second look. You're a sucker for people who are full of life, full of love for other people. That's what Caitlin's like, isn't she?"

Arch Carroll looked down at his baby sister, and gently shook his head. Finally he grinned. Mary K. was so smart. She had an artist's sensibility, but she was so practical. A curious combination, and irresistible in his opinion.

Carroll stretched his arms. The wound, that souvenir of a morning in France, still ached. "One day soon, I'm going to take a week off. I swear it. I've got to get back in touch with the kids."

"What about your friend, Caitlin? Could *she* take a week off too?"

Carroll said nothing. He wasn't sure if that was such a good idea. He went off to bed, where he lay exhausted, but unable to fall over the edge into sleep. The No. 13 Wall computer screens were still running through his mind, perplexing images. If there was any one avenue he could follow on the trail of Green Band, it would lead inevitably to Washington, and deeper into the restricted files of the FBI.

Arch Carroll snored quietly, slept dreamlessly, and when his bedside alarm went off it was just before dawn and dark still.

Thursday; December 16; Washington, D.C.

31

Carroll

Washington, D.C., Carroll had always thought, was the ultimate Hitchcock movie location: so elegant, so quietly lovely and distinguished, yet sleeping with paranoia in all its twisting, changing forms.

At nine A.M. he squirmed from a faded blue Metro cab with a badly dented fender. His face was immediately slapped with raw cold and drizzle on Washington's 10th Street. Carroll hiked his jacket collar up. He squinted through a thick, soupy, morning haze, which obscured the concrete box that was the J. Edgar Hoover Building.

Once inside the Hoover memorial, he found the procedure at the escort desk mechanical and unnecessarily slow. It irritated Carroll in the worst bureaucratic way. The Bureau's famous procedures, the inefficiency they created, played like a mocking skit appropriate for "Saturday Night Live."

After several minutes of serious and pompous phone checks, he was granted a coded blue tag with the FBI's official insignia. He slid the plastic card into a metal entry gate, and passed inside the hallowed halls.

An attractive woman agent, a researcher for FBI Data Analysis, was waiting outside the elevator on the fifth floor. She wore a man-tailored suit; her chestnut hair was wound back in a tight, formal chignon.

"Hello, I'm Arch Carroll."

"I'm Samantha Hawes. People *don't* call me Sam. Nice to meet you. Why don't you come this way, please." She started to walk away, pleasant but efficient. "I've already collected as much material as I can for you to look at. When you told me what you were fishing for, I put in some hours of overtime. My material comes from the Pentagon and from our own classified files. Everything I could collect this quickly on your lists of names. It wasn't easy, I must say. Some of it I transcribed from material already on computer file. The rest – as you can smell – is contained in some really musty documents."

Samantha Hawes finally delivered Carroll to a library-style carrel beside a silent row of gray metal copiers. The desk was completely covered with thick stacks of reports.

Carroll's heart nearly stalled as he gazed at the mountainous stacks. Each report looked like any other. How was he supposed to find something unusual in this great, yawning heap of history?

He walked around the table, sizing up his task. Hidden among all these folders were connections between men – the tracks, the spoor they laid down; the events they lived through during and after Viet Nam. Somewhere, surely, tracks would crisscross, correspondences would have been made, relationships established.

"I have more. Do you want to see them now? Or is this enough to hold you for awhile?" Samantha Hawes asked.

"Oh, I think this will do me pretty well. I didn't know we collected *this much* dirt on everybody down here."

Agent Hawes grinned. "You should see your file."

"Did you?"

"I'll be back over there, working in the stacks. You just holler if you need any more light reading, Mr. Carroll."

The FBI agent started to turn away, then she suddenly turned back. Samantha Hawes *seemed* to be a very contemporary Southern woman, very pretty, very confident, genteel and proper Southern from her looks, anyway. In days of old, Carroll couldn't help thinking, she would already have been a young mother of two or three tucked away in Alexandria. She would have definitely been a Sam, too.

"There *is* something else." Her face was suddenly quite serious and concerned. "I don't know exactly what this all means. Maybe it's just me. But when I went through these files yesterday evening . . . I had the distinct feeling that some of them had been tampered with . . ."

A small, very unpleasant warning rang in Arch Carroll's head. "Who would tamper with them?"

Samantha Hawes shook her head. "Any number of people have access to them. I don't know the answer."

"What do you mean when you say they've been tampered with, Samantha?"

The agent looked straight at Carroll. "I mean, that I think documents are *missing* from certain files."

Carroll reached out and lightly grasped her wrist. He was excited by this information because it meant that certain files, in some ways, were already different from the rest. They stood out.

Someone else had looked at them.

Someone had possibly pilfered documents from them. Why? Which files?

He saw a strange look crossing her face, as if she were asking herself about the precise nature of this unorthodox man who'd been admitted into FBI headquarters.

"Can you remember *which* files, Samantha?"

"Of course I can." She moved toward the work table and began sifting. She picked out five thick files, dropping them in front of Carroll, saying, "This one . . . and this . . . this . . . this one . . . this one."

He gazed quickly at the names on the files.

Scully, Richard.
Demunn, Michael.
Freedman, Harold Lee.
Melindez, Pauly.
Hudson, David.

"Why these five?" he asked.

"They served together in Viet Nam, according to their documents. That's one good reason."

arroll sat down. He still expected to come away from Washington empty-handed. He expected that the faint sense of anticipation he felt now would turn out to be nothing more than a false alarm. Five men on the FBI computer list of "subversives" – a term he knew was next to meaningless, at least the way the FBI used it.

He checked his own printouts, and his heart suddenly clutched.

Scully and Demunn had been explosives experts.

And David Hudson had been a colonel, who, according to the brief note on the printout, had been active in the organization of veterans groups and veterans rights after Viet Nam.

Five men who had served together in the war.

Five men who were on both his list, and the FBI's.

He slipped off his jacket, then the tie he'd worn especially for his big trip to Washington. He began to read about Colonel David Hudson.

32

Colonel David Hudson

When he had finished reading, Arch Carroll tilted his creaking chair back. He softly shook his head.

The ledger on U.S. Army Colonel David Hudson lay flopped open before him. Hudson's thick 211 file, his entire life in the U.S. military, was spread out on the desk.

Suddenly, the Green Band investigation was more hopelessly complex and confusing than it had ever been.

Colonel David Hudson was the final enigma.

David Hudson's military career had begun with high promise at West Point, where he was an honor graduate in 1966. He'd been a four-year member, and finally captain, of the tennis team. He was also a popular cadet according to all the available reports – a modern-day version of the All-American boy.

It got even better, or worse, from there. David Hudson had subsequently *volunteered* for Special Forces "Q" courses, followed by a special Ranger training. On a first impression at least, the Army couldn't have asked for a more diligent or professional young soldier.

Colonel David Hudson: All-American Boy.

Every succeeding report Carroll read was highlighted and underscored with phrases like "one of our very best"; "the kind of young officer who should make us all proud"; "a model soldier in every way. Unbridled, absolutely infectious enthusiasm"; "definitely one of our future leaders"; "the kind of material we can build the modern Army around."

In Viet Nam, Captain Hudson had been awarded the

292

Medal of Honor and the Distinguished Service Cross during his first tour. He had been captured and transported into North Viet Nam for interrogation. He'd spent seven months as a P.O.W. Apparently, Hudson had almost died in the prison camp. . . . He had then *volunteered for a second tour*, and performed with "conspicuous gallantry and intrepidity" on several occasions.

Then, three months before the evacuation of Saigon, he'd been savagely wounded by a Viet Cong grenade blast and subsequently lost his right arm. Hudson reacted with characteristic bravura.

A hospital report read: "Colonel David Hudson has been a godsend, helping other patients, never seeming to feel sorry for himself. . . . In every way, a thoroughly idealistic young man."

Following Viet Nam though, quite suddenly after his return to the United States, Colonel David Hudson's career, his entire life, seemed to become disturbingly unhinged. According to the files, the change was bewildering to his friends and family.

"It was almost as if a different man had returned from the war." His father was interviewed and quoted several times. "The fire, that wonderful, contagious enthusiasm was burned out of David's eyes. His eyes were those of a very old man."

Colonel David Hudson: enigma, almost phantom after coming home from the Viet Nam War.

First at Fort Sam Houston in Texas, then at Fort Still in Oklahoma; at Fort Polk, Hudson was quietly disciplined for "activities detrimental to the Army." . . . Another report indicated that he was transferred twice within three months, for what seemed on the surface to be petty insubordinations. . . . His marriage to Betsy Hinson, his hometown sweetheart, ended abruptly in 1973. Betsy Hinson said, "I don't even know David anymore. I don't know this man who I'm supposed to be married to. David's become a stranger to everyone he knows."

Hudson, in the postwar years, had become almost obsessive about his participation in a handful of Viet

Nam veterans' organizations. As an organizer and spokesman at rallies around the country, Hudson had met and been photographed with liberal motion picture stars, with sympathetic big business leaders, with recognizable national politicians.

At one point during the morning, Arch Carroll meticulously laid out Xerox copies of every available photo of David Hudson.

He rearranged the pictures until he liked the pattern of his collage. One photo was stained with coffee or cola. *The stain looked recent. Samantha Hawes? Someone else? Or was he just getting squirrely?*

In the photographs, at least, Colonel David Hudson looked like the classic, idealized military man of past decades. With his Jimmy Stewart wholesomeness, he looked the way American soldiers had been pictured in the years *before* Viet Nam. He had short blond hair in almost all the war photographs, a tightly set somewhat heroic jaw, a pinched, slightly uncomfortable smile, that was disarming, anyway. Colonel David Hudson was clearly very sure of himself and what he was doing. He was obviously proud, fiercely proud, to be an American soldier.

Carroll got up from the mess of official papers and wandered around the research library room. Okay – what did he have here?

A leader, a natural soldier, who somewhere along the way had fucked up royally. Or maybe Hudson had been royally fucked?

There were probably hundreds, maybe even thousands of men like David Hudson across the country. Some of them went berserk and had to be removed to the "screaming floors" in VA hospitals. Others sat quietly in dingy, lonely rooms and ticked slowly, like time bombs.

Colonel David Hudson? . . . Was he Green Band?

Samantha Hawes reappeared with a pot of coffee, deli sandwiches and assorted salads on a tray.

"Getting into it, I see."

"Yes, it's something, all right. Odd, and absolutely mesmerizing. Hard to figure though."

Carroll rubbed the palms of his hands in circles over his red-rimmed eyes. "Thanks for the food, especially the coffee. The whole file is extraordinary. Colonel Hudson especially. He's a very complex, very strange man. He was so perfect. The perfect soldier. Then what? What happened to him after he returned to the States?"

Samantha Hawes sat down at the FBI researcher's desk beside Carroll. She took a healthy bite of an overstuffed sandwich.

"As I said, there are some really peculiar gaps in his military records. In all of their records. Believe me, I look at enough of them to know."

"What sort of peculiar gaps? What *should* be in there that isn't?"

"Well. There were no written reports on his special training at Fort Bragg, for example. There was nothing on his 'Q,' or his Ranger training. There was almost nothing on his time as a P.O.W. Those should all be in there. Marked highly confidential if need be, but definitely there in the file."

"What *else* is missing? Would there be photostated copies or originals anywhere else?"

"There should definitely be more psychological profiles. More reports after he lost his arm in Viet Nam. There's very little on that. He was tortured by the Viet Cong. He apparently still has flashbacks. All the back-up data on his P.O.W. experience is conveniently missing. I've never seen a 211 file without a complete psych workup, either."

Carroll selected a second, thick roast beef sandwich half. "Maybe Hudson took them out himself?"

"I don't know how he could get in here, but it makes as much sense as anything else I read yesterday."

"Like? Please keep going, Samantha."

"Like the way they made him a cipher right after Viet Nam. He had *very* high level intelligence clearance in Southeast Asia. He was a *heavy* commander in Viet Nam. Why would they give him such a nothing post back in the States? The arm? Then why not write it up that way?"

"Maybe that's why he ultimately quit the service," Carroll suggested. "The second-rate assignments once he got back home."

"Maybe. Probably, I guess. But why did they do it to him in the first place? . . . They were *grooming* David Hudson before he came home. Believe me, they had serious plans for him. You can see tracks to glory all over those files. In the early years, anyway. Hudson was a real star."

Carroll jotted down a few notes to himself. "What would a more predictable assignment have been? Once he was back in the States? If he was still on the fast track?"

"At the very least, he should have gotten the Pentagon. According to his records, he was on an *extremely* fast track. Until the disciplinary problems, anyway. He got all these bush-league assignments *before* he did anything to deserve them."

"It doesn't make sense. Not yet, anyway. Maybe they'll know something at the Pentagon. That's my next stop."

Samantha Hawes put out her hand to shake. "My sincere condolences. The Pentagon makes this admittedly austere place seem like a hippie commune."

"I've heard they're a party group." Carroll smiled back at Agent Hawes. She was smart and he liked her.

"Listen," she said. "There is something else you should know. One other person definitely went through the 211 files. At least one other person in the past two weeks. On *December fifth*, actually."

Carroll stopped packing up and stared at Samantha Hawes. "Who?" he asked.

"On the fifth of December, certain 211 files were ordered over to the White House. *Vice-president Elliot wanted to see them. He kept the files for over six hours.* Listen, Carroll. You come back here if you need any more help. Officially or otherwise. . . . Promise?"

"I promise," Carroll said, and absolutely meant it.

The Carroll Family

The young Carroll boy had his marching orders, really strict orders, too.

Six-year-old Mickey Kevin Carroll had been allowed to walk the three blocks home from CYO basketball practice since the second month of the school year. He had very precise orders for the walk, which his Aunt Mary K. actually made him *write out* inside his salt-and-pepper composition note pad. *Mickey's orders were:*

Look both ways at Churchill Avenue.

Look both ways at Grand Street.

Don't talk to strangers for any reason at all.

Don't stop at the Fieldstone store before supper.

If you do, it's instant death by torture.

Mickey Kevin was pondering the confusing mechanics of the basketball lay up as he covered the long double block between Riverdale Avenue and Churchill Street. Brother Alexander Joseph had made it *look* kind of easy – the lay up. Except when Mickey tried it himself, there were just too many things to remember to do, all practically at the same time. Somehow your leg, and your same arm, had to come up; then you had to throw the ball perfectly into the high, high hoop. All at the same time.

As he rehearsed the confusing sport's primary action, Mickey Kevin gradually became aware of footsteps growing loudly behind him.

He finally turned and saw a man. The man was walking his way. Walking pretty fast.

Mickey Kevin's body tightened. TV movies and stuff like that made you scared when you were alone by yourself. Somebody was always out to get the little kid, or the baby-sitter all alone at home. It was a pretty creepy world. Some of the people out there were unbelievably creepy.

The man walking behind him looked pretty normal, Mickey guessed, but he decided to hurry it up a little, anyway.

Without looking too obvious, he started to take longer steps, faster steps. He walked the way he always did when he was trying to keep up with his dad.

There weren't any cars or anything at the corner of Grand Street. Mickey stopped according to his rules anyway. He looked both ways.

He looked back then – and the man was really close. Really, really close.

Mickey Kevin *ran* across Grand Street, and Aunt Mary K. would have killed him on the spot. His heart was pounding a little now. Really thumping out loud. Right down into his shoes, he could feel his heartbeat.

Then Mickey Kevin did the really, really dumb thing. He knew it the second he did it. The instant!

He suddenly cut through the empty lot at the Riverdale Day School.

There were all these tricky bushes and stuff back there. Everybody left empty beer cans and broken wine and liquor bottles. Mary K. had forgotten to put that on the list: *don't cut through the Riverdale Day School lot*. It was too obvious for words.

Mickey pushed the prickly bushes out of his way, and he *thought* he heard the man coming through the lot behind him. *Crashing* through the lot.

He wasn't completely sure. He'd have to stop walking, to listen close enough to tell. He decided to just keep running, to run like hell.

Full speed ahead running now. As fast as he could run with all the dark, thorny bushes, the hidden rocks and roots trying to trip him up.

Mickey Kevin stumbled forward, his feet seeming to catch in dirt holes. He glided over slippery leaves.

He nicked a rock and almost went over, head first. He was panting now, his breath was too loud in his own ears, his footsteps were echoing like gunshots.

The back of his house suddenly appeared: the glowing, amber porch lights, the familiar gray outline against the much darker blackness of the night.

He had never been so glad to see home.

Fingers touched the side of his cheek and Mickey loudly yelled out. "Hey!"

A stupid tree branch!

He almost had a heart attack. Mickey then ran like a midget halfback bound for seven across the last icy patch of back lawn.

Halfway there, his metal lunchbox popped open. It just about exploded as an orange, rolled-up papers, a thermos tumbled out.

Mickey Kevin dropped the lunchbox.

He crashed up the back steps and got his hand on the cold metal stormdoor.

And then . . .

Then Mickey Kevin turned. He *had* to look back.

His chest was pounding nonstop now. Ka-chunk, ka-chunk, like a huge machine was inside there. Making ice or something equally noisy to hear. He *had* to look back.

Nobody was there!

Nobody was following him at all.

Oh brother! Oh boy, oh boy.

Nobody was behind him.

Nobody!

It was completely quiet in the backyard. Nothing moved. His lunchbox lay overturned in the middle of the snow. It glowed a little in the dark.

Mickey squinted real hard.

He was feeling pretty stupid now. He'd made it all up; he was almost sure of it. . . . Except he still wasn't going to go back and pick up his fallen lunchbox. Maybe in the morning. Maybe in the spring some time.

What a little baby! Afraid of the dark! He finally disappeared inside the house.

Mary K. was dicing vegetables with a big knife on the butcher block in the kitchen. The TV was turned on to Mary Tyler Moore.

"How was practice, Mickey Mouse? You look beat up. Wash, huh. Dinner's almost ready. I *said* – how was your basketball practice, fella?"

"Oh, uh . . . I don't know how to do a stupid lay up. It was okay."

Then Mickey Kevin smoothly disappeared, slid like a shadow into the downstairs bathroom.

He didn't wash his hands and face inside, though. He left the overhead light switched off.

Mickey Kevin very slowly lifted a handful of lace bathroom curtain. He stared out into the dark, very creepola backyard, squinting his eyes tightly again.

He still couldn't see anybody.

The stupid cat, their stupid cat Mortimer, was playing with his lunchbox. There was nobody else. Nobody had really chased him, he was suddenly sure. He couldn't see anybody . . .

He couldn't see the real-life bogeyman watching the Carroll house from the darkened back lot. Mickey Kevin couldn't see the fearsome Sten machine gun pistol. Or the man holding it, fingering it so expertly.

Pentagon Interview

It was just after five o'clock when a black Army colonel named Duriel Williamson emphatically strode into a windowless office hidden away inside the thirty-four-acre Pentagon complex.

Arch Carroll was already waiting in the Spartan, bureaucratic green room.

So was a Captain Pete Hawkins, who had formally escorted Carroll from the visitor's pickup desk, back through the dizzying grid of tightly interlocking Pentagon corridors.

Colonel Williamson was outfitted in the full dress uniform of the U.S. Special Forces – including a blood-red beret, cocked jauntily. Colonel Williamson's hair was short and bristling, a salt-and-pepper crew which looked appropriately stern. His voice was starched as well, but showed heavy hints of irony.

Everything about Duriel Williamson said: *no bullshit permitted here. State your business, mister.*

Captain Hawkins made the introductions in a polite if strictly formal military fashion. Hawkins was clearly a career bureaucrat, a survivor.

"Mr. Arch Carroll from the Defense Intelligence Agency, on special assignment by order of the President . . . Colonel Duriel Williamson from Special Forces. Colonel Williamson is stationed at Fort Bragg, North Carolina. Colonel Williamson was David Hudson's immediate superior during both phases of his Special Forces training. Colonel, Mr. Carroll is here to ask you some questions."

The Special Forces officer put out his hand to Arch Carroll. He smiled amicably, and most of the preliminary nervousness and formalities dissolved. "Glad to meet you, Mr. Carroll. May I sit down?"

"Please, Colonel," Carroll said. Both men sat, followed by Captain Hawkins, who would remain in the room for the interview, a matter of protocol.

"What is it you need to know about David?"

Carroll's eyes widened and rose from a short, written list of questions he'd prepared for the interview. "The two of you were on a first-name basis?" he asked Colonel Williamson.

"Yes, I knew David Hudson fairly well. I should amend that, to be as accurate as possible. I spent some time with David Hudson. Not at or because of the Special Forces school. This was after the war. I bumped into him a few times. At different veterans' affairs, mostly. We were both active. We had a couple of beers together, a couple of times."

"Tell me about it Colonel Williamson. What was Hudson like? What was he like to have a beer with?"

Carroll controlled his eagerness to ask more probing questions. His mind was still clouded from the long morning at the FBI, but he knew better than to pressure a Special Forces Colonel.

"David Hudson was stiff at first. Though he tried like

301

the devil not to be. Then he was just fine. He knew a lot about a lot of things. He was a thoughtful man, extremely bright."

"Colonel Hudson's Army career seemed to disintegrate after Viet Nam. Do you have any guess why?"

Duriel Williamson shrugged his shoulders. He appeared mildly puzzled over the question. "That's something that's always troubled me. All I can say is that David Hudson was a *very* outspoken man."

"Meaning, Colonel?" Carroll continued to probe carefully.

"Meaning he was capable of making important enemies inside the Army. . . . He was also extremely disappointed. *Bitter,* I guess is the better word."

Bitter, Carroll thought. Exactly how bitter? Carroll studied the Army colonel in silence.

"The treatment our men got after Viet Nam made David Hudson a very angry person. I think it disillusioned him more than most of us. He considered it a national disgrace. He blamed President Nixon at first. He wrote personal letters to the President, also to the Chief of Staff."

"Just letters? Was that the extent of his protests for the veterans?" I need somebody, Carroll thought, with the kind of bitterness that would go well beyond letters. Hell, anybody could sit down and write a crank letter —

"Actually, no. He was involved in several of the more vocal protests."

"Colonel, any answers you can elaborate on would be helpful. I've got all night to listen."

"He called attention to Washington's long string of broken promises to our veterans. All the betrayals. *'The disposable GI'* was a phrase he liked to use. . . . Let me tell you, Mr. Carroll, *that* kind of high-profile activity can earn you a fast assignment to Timbuktu or to some Podunk reserve unit someplace. That would put him in the Pentagon computers too. Hudson was very active with radical veterans."

"What about his training at the Special Forces school? At Fort Bragg?" Carroll then asked. "Colonel, these answers of yours, as I said, *please* try to be thorough."

"Some of this was quite a while ago. It didn't seem so important at the time. I'll try."

For almost an hour, Colonel Williamson was painstakingly thorough. He elaborately described a brilliant young Army officer, with seemingly boundless energy, with small-town American enthusiasm and talent – a model soldier. Many of the epithets Carroll had read earlier in the 211 files, he heard again from Colonel Williamson.

"What I remember most, though," Williamson said, "what stands out to this day about Hudson is the time at Fort Bragg. We were instructed to push and drive him. Push him to his physical and emotional limits. We redlined David Hudson at Bragg."

"More than other officers who were assigned to the Bragg program?"

"Oh, absolutely. Absolutely. Without any doubt we pushed him more. No punches were pulled. His POW experience was *used* to pump up his hatred for 'our enemies.' Hudson was programmed to seek revenge, *to hate*. In my opinion, he was a time bomb."

"Who instructed you to do that, Colonel? Who told you to push Captain Hudson? Somebody obviously must have singled him out for special attention."

Colonel Williamson paused in his answers. His dark eyes didn't leave Carroll's eyes, but there was a perceptible change in his broad, severe face. Carroll couldn't quite read the change at first.

"I suppose you're right. At this point, uh, after all these years. . . . I'm not sure I can tell you *who* though. . . . Isn't that funny? I remember we were unusually tough on him. Also that Hudson was pretty much up to it. He definitely had character to spare. Great stamina. The heart of a teen-ager."

"But his training wasn't typical, not the regular course? His was different somehow?"

"Yes. David Hudson's training at Fort Bragg was

beyond the established norm, which was demanding in itself."

"Give me *some* idea, Colonel. *Put me* at the training camp. Can you make it come alive for me? What was the actual training like?"

"All right, I don't think you can imagine it, unless you actually went through it. . . . Up at two-thirty in the morning. Physical abuse. Drug-induced nightmares. Interrogation by the best in the Army. Pushed like a dirt farm tractor until you dropped at eight. Up again at two-thirty – I mean pushed, *drained*. Each day was one hundred percent harder than the last. Physically and emotionally, psychologically. . . . The men chosen to go to Bragg were all considered top rank. Hudson had West Point *and* extensive combat behind him. He'd been a successful commander in Nam. . . . Uh, Captain Hudson was also a military assassin in Viet Nam. He was very heavy. With a good rep."

Carroll, hearing the word "assassin," felt that he had taken still another step into the endless Green Band maze. The further he moved, the more confused and lost he became. The All-American soldier had an even darker side: assassin. He brought Hudson's clean-cut photographs back to mind: the sunshine face of determination, the bristling crewcut hair, the honesty in those eyes.

"Meaning what, Colonel? What does a good rep mean in that context? As a military assassin."

"It means he wasn't a thrill killer – which most of the top hitters were. . . . A very real problem is what to do with some of *those* guys, once they *leave* the Army. If the generals had decided to take out Ho Chi Minh, something very big, very delicate, Hudson most likely would have been considered. I'm telling you, Carroll, he was one of our fair-haired boys."

"You seem a little awed by Hudson yourself."

Williamson absently smiled; he finally chuckled softly into his chest full of medals.

"I don't know about awe. Awe isn't the right word. Definitely respect, though."

"Why, Colonel?"

"He was one of the best soldiers I've ever trained. He had physical endurance and all the technical skills. He had strength and tremendous smarts. A martial arts background. He also had something else, human dignity."

"So what went wrong? What happened to Hudson after the war? Why did he finally leave the service in 1976?"

Colonel Williamson rubbed his hard-boned, clean-shaven jaw. "As I said, the one potential problem was his attitude. He could be extremely judgmental. . . . He also thought he had answers to some controversial Army problems. Some career officers might not have appreciated Hudson's judgment of them and their actions. The other thing was the loss of his arm. David Hudson had big, big plans for himself. How many one-armed generals are you aware of?"

Arch Carroll paused and thought before he spoke again. For all the apparent cooperation, he had a sneaking feeling that Colonel Williamson was still holding something back. It was the Army way, he remembered from extensive past dealings with the Pentagon. Everything had to be a huge "need to know" secret, shared only inside the sacred fraternity of Army blood brothers, shared with the other *warriors* only.

"Colonel Williamson, I've got to ask the new few questions with the authority of the Commander in Chief. That means I need complete answers."

"That's what you've been getting, Mr. Carroll."

"Colonel Williamson, did you know the *official purpose* of David Hudson's Special Forces training at Fort Bragg? Why was he at the JFK school? If that information was in any of your orders, if you heard it anywhere on the base, *I need to know it, Colonel.*"

Colonel Duriel Williamson stared back hard at Arch Carroll, then at Captain Hawkins.

When he spoke, his voice was softer but seemed an octave deeper than it had been.

"Nothing was ever *written down* in any of the orders. . . .

As I said, I don't remember who actually issued our daily orders. I do know *why* he was supposed to be there though . . ."

"Go on. Please, Colonel Williamson."

"It was something we were told at the very first briefing on David Hudson. *Verbally* told. This first briefing sounded like total CIA bullshit by the way. Until we actually *met* Hudson. . . . You see . . .

"They told us Captain David Hudson had been specially chosen to be our version of the Third World superterrorist. David Hudson had been selected, and he was being *trained to be our version of the terrorist Juan Carlos.*"

Arch Carroll's stomach had suddenly dropped; his forehead felt flushed. Very tense now, he leaned forward in his chair.

"That's why he was at the Bragg school? Why he was pushed ahead, beyond all the others?"

"That's what we helped teach him to be. . . . And Mr. Carroll, Captain Hudson was scarily good at it. He *is* still scarily good, I'm sure. From potentially planning a terrorist raid – even a cold-blooded mass murder if it was necessary, *David Hudson was on a level with Carlos. He's on a level with that madman Monserrat!* . . . The U.S. Army trained Hudson to be the best in the world . . . and in my opinion, he was. Maybe *that's* why they couldn't keep him content in the peacetime Army."

Carroll didn't speak – because right at that moment, he couldn't. The realization that the United States Army had secretly trained its own Carlos, and that he had now quite possibly *turned* – it was unbelievable. Colonel Williamson's words rang in his ears: *From potentially planning a terrorist raid . . . even a cold-blooded mass murder if it was necessary.*

"Colonel Williamson. In your opinion, could David Hudson have been involved with Green Band? Could he have technically masterminded an operation like that?"

"I don't doubt it, Mr. Carroll. He has all the technical skills."

Williamson paused, sighed. "One more fact about Colonel David Hudson, though. When I knew him, at least, and I think I knew the man fairly well, he loved the United States very much. He loved America. Make no mistake, David Hudson was a patriot."

When Arch Carroll departed from the vast, nearly empty Pentagon parking area at a little past ten that night, his mind was rapidly turning over all kinds of possibilities. *Finally, something had connected. Something made sense in Green Band.*

As he drove, weary and stonefaced to the Washington Hotel in town, he tried to review the long day. His eyes were rimmed with bright red and they burned. But he felt legitimately close to something for the first time since Green Band had begun.

Colonel David Hudson was trained to be our version of Carlos. . . . our version of Monserrat.

David Hudson was a patriot . . .

Was David Hudson also a traitor? Perhaps the most significant traitor since Benedict Arnold?

A plain blue sedan unobtrusively followed Arch Carroll as he drove through the suburban fringes of Washington. Both cars slipped and curled around icy George Washington Parkway.

Carroll then turned onto Constitution Avenue at a sedate thirty-five miles per hour. So did the plain blue sedan.

A team of eight professionals then alternated through the night both in and outside of Georgetown's Washington Hotel. They watched to see if Arch Carroll went out again, if he met anyone else at the hotel, if he tried to reach Colonel Duriel Williamson or Samantha Hawes of the FBI again.

Both Carroll's room and telephone were expertly bugged.

There was a single incoming call, which was recorded by the surveillance team.

"Hello. This is Carroll speaking."

"Archer, it's Walter. I just spoke with Mike Caruso. He said you were in Washington."

"It's as weird as ever down here, Walter. Maybe even a little weirder right now."

"Mike told me about your latest theory. I think it's a good one. One thing bothers me a lot. I wonder why Phil Berger of the CIA warned you off the track of Viet veterans earlier?"

"I wondered about that, too. Maybe he thought he had it covered. At any rate, I'm definitely touching exposed nerves down here."

"Well, be careful about that. Philip Berger isn't someone to fool with, or to underestimate either. And Archer –"

"Yeah, I know Walter, I'll try to keep you involved."

"If you don't, you could wind up all alone on this. And I mean *all alone*. I'm serious, Archer. Be careful as hell in Washington."

Carroll made one call home to Riverdale and a second to Caitlin Dillon of the SEC in Manhattan. He made a late call to the FBI researcher, Samantha Hawes, at her home in Arlington. Then Arch Carroll slept.

The surveillance team didn't.

33

President Justin Kearney

That evening, very late in Washington, President Justin Kearney was feeling completely debilitated and old, decades older than his forty-two years. The sheen of sweat covering his neck was slickly cold and made him feel ill. It was past 1:30, and the White House was quiet, deceptively still along the second floor.

As he walked the corridors of power, the President of the United States held a confidential document under his arm. The sheaf of papers was pressed tightly against his right side by his elbow, but seemed to burn through the material of his suit and shirt, to scald his skin.

Nearly every president, as well as a few *chosen* first-time senators and key congressmen, had learned an important U.S. history lesson when they arrived in the capital city of Washington. Justin Kearney had learned his within the first month of his Presidency. The history lesson was that within the broadcast scope of American power and its immense wealth, the politician was little more than an appendage to the system. A concession to form, a necessary inconvenience in many ways.

The politician – senator, congressperson, judge, even the President – was grudgingly tolerated, but each was expendable.

The presidents before Justin Kearney – Reagan, Nixon, Ford, Carter, Kennedy, Johnson – had all learned the invaluable lesson in one way or another.

Even the seemingly powerful and secure Secretary of State Kissinger had eventually learned his lesson . . .

There was a higher order working inside, working above and beyond the United States government. There had been a higher order for decades. It made all the sense in the world, actually; it made sense of almost everything that had happened over the past forty years: the Kennedys, Viet Nam, Watergate, Koreagate, the "Star Wars" plan.

They were waiting for President Kearney in the dramatic and imposing National Security Council briefing room. Twelve of them had been inside there for some time, working right through the night.

They appeared to be an ordinary enough committee, all in white shirtsleeves and loosened ties. They stood en masse as the President of the United States entered. They rose out of respect for the office, for the lofty traditions, for what *they themselves* had rigorously maintained about the office.

The forty-first President of the United States then took his accustomed seat at the head of the highly polished oak wood table. Pens and lined yellow writing pads had been set neatly at his place.

"Did you read the position papers through, Mr. President?" one of the twelve committeemen quietly asked Justin Kearney.

"Yes, I read it in my office just now," the President solemnly answered. His strongly handsome face was pale, drained of its natural color.

The President then laid the substantial packet of confidential papers he'd been carrying on the table. The booklet was approximately 160 typewritten pages. It had never been copied, and never would be. It looked somewhat like an investment offering book or perhaps a condominium plan.

On the dark blue cover something had been printed in regal-looking gold letters.

Green Band. Extremely Confidential and Classified.

The title page was dated May 16.

Nearly seven months before the actual bombing attack on Wall Street.

PART THREE

Arch Carroll

Friday; December 17;
Washington, D.C.

34

General Lucas Thompson: 0700 Hours

Friday in Washington, D.C., dawned with rain clouds rolling across a nearly colorless horizon. A spitting wind blew wintry gusts in from Maryland. The temperature was dropping hourly. From 7:00 A.M. on, Arch Carroll waited impatiently in the front seat of a rented sedan parked in the Washington suburb of McLean.

The dark car blended neatly with a wall of even darker fir trees overhanging Fort Myers Road.

Detective work, Carroll thought as he stared off into nothingness. *First you wait. Always the waiting.*

Carroll passed the early time eating breakfast out of a deceptively warm cardboard box from Dunkin' Donuts. The actual doughnuts weren't nearly as hot as the box itself. They also had no taste he could discern. The coffee he sipped was room temperature, a little less satisfying than the doughnuts.

Carroll read some Tracy Kidder, *The Soul of a New Machine*, and that was quite good, at least. Several times he found himself thinking about Colonel David Hudson.

The classic All-American Boy? West Point honor student . . .

Then Viet Nam assassin? America's Juan Carlos? America's jackal? America's François Monserrat?

He wanted to meet David Hudson now. He wanted to encounter him one-on-one, face-to-face. Maybe inside the cramped interrogation room at No. 13 Wall, Carroll's

313

own turf. *Tell me, Colonel Hudson, what do you know about the Green Band firebombings? What about the stolen Wall Street securities? Tell me why you left the Army, Colonel Hudson?*

He wondered how far he'd get with somebody like Colonel David Hudson, a U.S. saboteur trained to resist interrogation. It would be a battle, and one Carroll wasn't sure he'd win.

About 7:30, a second-floor light finally blinked on inside the white colonial across the roadway. A second light followed moments later. Bedroom and bathroom, probably. Showtime at General Thompson's was about to begin.

Moments later, a light went on downstairs. Kitchen? The porch light blinked out.

Just past 8:00, which Carroll thought a respectable hour, he trudged up the flagstone front walk and rang a bell which made a chimey sound like old department store bells.

A tall, distinguished man of about sixty appeared in the pristine white doorway. He wore plaid trousers, house slippers, a powder blue cardigan sweater. His head, shaped like a torpedo, was topped with white-gray stubble.

General Lucas Thompson, former Commander-in-Chief of the United States Evacuation Forces in Viet Nam, still had a craggy, commanding presence. He still appeared capable of taking on the most difficult combat duty demands. There was something hard and alert in his gray eyes, like small electric lightbulbs burning there.

"General Thompson, I'm Arch Carroll with the DIA. Sorry to bother you so early in the morning. I'm here about the Green Band investigation."

General Thompson looked appropriately suspicious: his eyes became slats of loose flesh. "What about it, sir? I'm up, but as you say, it's still quite early in the morning."

"I would have called last night, to say I was coming, General. It was late when I left the Pentagon. I thought

314

that might have been a worse breach of etiquette than just coming out here this morning."

The look of consternation and puzzlement faded on General Thompson's face. It was as if the mention of the word "Pentagon" had reassured him; a look of pleasant recognition spread across his features.

"Of course. Arch Carroll. I've read about you."

"General Thompson, I have just a few questions. It's about your command in Southeast Asia. It shouldn't take more than, say, twenty minutes."

"That means an hour," Lucas Thompson said with a sniffling laugh. He swung open the front door anyway. "That's fine. I have the time. Time is plentiful these days, Mr. Carroll." He spoke in the tone of a retired soldier stricken by writer's block halfway through his memoirs. Vaguely frustrated, a little bored, abandoned not only by his muse but by his sense of purpose.

General Thompson led the way inside, through a formal 1930s dining room, into an even more imposing library chamber. There was a white-birch fireplace screened by a brass curtain with heavy brass andirons. Tall oak bookshelves stood erect on every wall; a double bay window looked onto a backyard with a covered pool and yellow-and-lime-striped cabana.

General Thompson sat in a comfortable wing chair.

"Out of sight in Washington, pretty much out of mind. Since my retirement, I've had very few *official* visitors down here. Other than my two granddaughters, who fortunately live up the lane, and who adore their grandmother's baked goods and double fudge."

General Thompson shook his head and smiled warmly. He was easing into the interview more than Carroll had expected or hoped.

In Viet Nam, Carroll had heard that General Thompson was an extremely rigid disciplinarian. Now, in his retirement, Lucas Thompson seemed like just another grandfather, patiently waiting for the next smiling Kodak snapshot to be taken.

"I'm searching – groping, is the word I think I want –

315

for some useful information about a Colonel David Hudson. Hudson was on your command team in Saigon, right?"

General Lucas Thompson nodded in the manner of a practiced good listener. "Yes, Captain Hudson served on my team for about fifteen months. If my recollection is holding up better than the rest of me."

"Your recollection and my records match exactly," Carroll said. "What can you tell me about Hudson?"

"Well, I'm not sure where you want me to start. It's fairly complex. David Hudson was an extremely disciplined and effective soldier. Also a very charismatic leader, once he got his command over there . . .

"When I first met him, he was ramrodding a, I believe it was a demolition team. He'd also been trained to sanction human targets. He sanctioned trash, Carroll. War profiteers, a couple of high-level infiltrators. Traitors."

"Why was he chosen to be a military assassin?"

"Oh, I think I have the answer for that one. He was chosen because he didn't like to kill. Because he *wasn't* a psycho. I think Hudson's philosophy was that once you undertook to fight in a just war, you *fought*. You balls-out fought with everything you had. I happen to believe that philosophy myself."

During the next thirty minutes, General Lucas Thompson elaborated on his association with David Hudson. It was an overall laudatory review, an A-plus for Hudson – high marks for conduct, combat team leadership, especially high marks for courage and charisma, that latter a nebulous quality the modern Army seemed to take into account the way a Civil War battalion, say, would have given a man a commendation for his musket aim.

Arch Carroll kept getting the very uncomfortable feeling that he was chasing after a goddamned American war hero. Once again, it didn't make complete sense.

Carroll leaned way forward in the red leather easy chair he'd taken in the retired officer's library. General Thompson was beginning to repeat himself slightly.

He seemed to be slipping into a genial story-telling mode.

It might have been sad, ordinarily. In a way, it reminded Carroll of his own father, retiring from the New York police force to Sarasota. Dead of heart failure, or maybe it was boredom, within nine months.

Except that Carroll didn't believe General Lucas Thompson's act for a minute right now . . .

Carroll had checked carefully – and General Thompson *had* been receiving official visitors out in McLean; high-ranking VIPs from the Pentagon, even regular visitors from the White House. General Lucas Thompson was *still* an influential advisor to the National Security Council.

"There are a couple of things that still bother me, General."

"Shoot away, then."

"Just for openers . . . why can't anyone tell me where Colonel Hudson is now? . . . *Second* point. Why can't anyone explain the mysterious circumstances under which he left the Army in the mid '70s? *Third* point, General Thompson, why did somebody rifle through his war records at the Pentagon and the FBI before I could see them?"

"Mr. Carroll, judging from the *tone* of your voice, I think maybe you're getting a little out of order," General Thompson said in a voice that remained low, perfectly in control.

"Yeah, well, I do that sometimes. *Fourth point.* The last thing that bothers me. Really frosts me . . . *Why was I followed from the Pentagon last night, General?* . . . Why was I followed out here to McLean General? On *whose* orders? What *the hell* is going on here in Washington?"

General Lucas Thompson's shiny, clean-shaven cheeks, his crinkle-cut neck blossomed bright red. "Mr. Carroll, I think you'd better leave right now. I believe that would be the best for all concerned."

"You know, I think you're probably right. I think I'd be wasting my time here. . . . General Thompson, I think *you*

317

know a whole lot more about Colonel Hudson, though. That's what I think."

General Lucas Thompson smiled, just a faint condescending twist of his upper lip. "That's the unappreciated beauty of our country, Mr. Carroll. It's free. You can think whatever you like. . . . I'll show you to the front door."

35

Hudson; 1100

On the morning of December 17 in New York, Colonel David Hudson was feeling more self-conscious about his affliction than he had in many years. Nervously clutching Billie Bogan with his good arm, he steered her in a protective manner through an onrushing tide of people on Fifth Avenue. He didn't want to think about the resumption of Green Band, not for a few more hours anyway.

David Hudson's self-consciousness was particularly unnecessary that morning. The two of them, paired together, were undeniably striking. They looked as if they'd been painted with thick, very bold strokes – while everyone else had been lightly drawn by pencil or pen.

Billie Bogan watched David from the corner of her eye; so very serious charting their appointed path through the crowd. She felt an odd but growing fascination. That he was obviously taken with her made the attraction she felt much more irresistible. She allowed herself to be pulled forward . . .

Toward whatever was looming up ahead.

Where *were* they headed anyway?

"Are you a Christmas lover?" Billie asked, as they moved ahead through the cold flat knife of the winter day around them.

"Oh, it depends on the Christmas. This Christmas, I have a strange passion for the season . . . I want to drink in the sights: the evergreen trees and the holiday wreaths, the glimmering store windows, Santa Clauses, churches, choral music."

"You do seem to go all the way on things," she lightly teased Hudson.

"Or not at all. Just look at *this* insanity! This wonderful monstrosity!" He suddenly whooped and grinned broadly. It was quite unlike his usual self, at least the part she'd seen.

They'd finally come up close to the glittering, extravagantly overdecorated Rockefeller Center tree. A crowd, lovers mostly, from college aged to quite elderly, was clustered over the top of the skating rink and attached restaurant. A small boys' choir, innocent in cassock and surplice, sang the loveliest carols down below.

Colonel David Hudson's brain had finally slowed; he was relaxed and relatively comfortable right now. An exceedingly rare treat. To be savored. He occasionally felt a stab of guilt about his mission, about possibly losing concentration, but he knew the release of tension could be valuable, too.

"Do you miss your family, your home? Being away from England during the holidays?" he asked.

He and Billie caught one another's eyes, and held on for a long few seconds. As it had been with the two of them from the start, they seemed almost alone now. In spite of the shoving masses crowding the square.

"I miss certain incidents from the past. . . . Some charming things about my sister, my mother. I don't miss home too much, no. Life in the Midlands. Birmingham is one of those places from which all the young people, all the reasonably bright ones, want to get away . . .

"If you remain in Birmingham, you work for British Steel, or perhaps the new exhibition center. Once you marry, you stay home with your brood. Watch the new morning BBC. You get fat, your thinking petrifies. After a few years, no one can imagine that any of the women were ever pretty slips of young girls. Almost no one over forty looks like they were *ever young*."

"So you escaped? London? Paris?"

"I went to London when I turned eighteen. I was very crude, unpolished, in the way that I looked, the way I

320

thought about the world. I wanted to be an actress, a fashion model, anything that would keep me from ever going back to Birmingham. *Ever.*"

Billie smiled, and she was so charmingly self-effacing. "I made a few minor misjudgments in London," she said with a mocking laugh.

"And then?"

"After, I guess it was five years there, I decided to either come to New York, or Paris. That's me up to the present. I'm hopeful I can do well as a model. I'm putting together a book for press advertising – that's magazines and newspapers. I know that I'm attractive – physically attractive, at least."

She had delivered most of the autobiographical speech very shyly, with her eyes downcast, glancing anywhere but into David Hudson's eyes. Color had crept up from her neck, finally covering her entire face.

"I've made a few tiny misjudgments myself. Just a few." Hudson laughed then. So many stored-up emotions were being released inside him now. It had been so long since he'd allowed himself this.

Billie began to laugh again. "Oh, to hell with the past," she said, her eyes a little sad however, ironic, slightly pinched at the corners. They both ran out of words at exactly the same time. The moment seemed especially poignant for some reason, confused, with far too many emotional crosscurrents.

Billie finally turned to face Hudson again. She spoke very softly, feathers of her warm breath lightly touching his ear.

"Please kiss me, David. That might not sound like anything so very dramatic.. . . . Except that I don't think I've said it to anyone, and meant it, since I was about sixteen or seventeen years old."

Hudson and Billie Bogan, her slender body loose and pliant, his strong, almost at military attention, kissed in the deep shadows of the grand Christmas tree at Rockefeller Center. Holiday music sweetly played around them: "Adeste Fidelis," "Silent Night," "Joy to the World."

For that moment, at least, Colonel David Hudson conveniently forgot his *other* plans for the world.

Not *joy*, exactly. No, something else that was badly needed, though.

Justice for mankind.

Revenge for a very special few.

36

No. 13 Wall; 1300

Caitlin Dillon hurriedly entered the crowded formal conference room inside No. 13 Wall. She passed repairmen plastering over cracks in cement. Three cleaning women hauled buckets at the end of the hallway, clanking as they moved. Caitlin paused at the buzzing entrance to the conference room and raised one hand to her hair. She was thinking right then how much she missed Carroll, who was expected back from Washington at any moment. He'd called, but his voice had been strained, almost as if he'd been afraid to tell her anything over the telephone.

She stepped into the meeting room, passing through a phalanx of policemen and Army personnel. The word had already spread up and down the hallways – *there had been some sort of significant break in the Green Band investigation. Only this morning, finally, a break.*

Walter Trentkamp of the FBI stood in dramatic silence before the restless audience. He was obviously tense. Streaks of light sweat highlighted his face and the collar of his shirt was damp. Caitlin hadn't seen the FBI Bureau chief this anxious before.

Trentkamp cleared his throat. The scene reminded Caitlin of highlevel press conferences held in Washington, emergency meetings called on short notice. Walter Trentkamp looked as distinguished as any senator on the hill.

"You have no doubt heard the rumor that a significant development has occurred in the Green Band case. . . . It was uncovered through the tireless effort of Captain Francis Nicolo and Sergeant Rizzo in NYPD Ballistics."

Nicolo, Waxy Frank, appeared in the crowd alongside Joe Rizzo. Both men were beaming, taking an imperceptible bow.

"These men have been working tirelessly since the bombing on December fouth. Finally, all their labors have paid a big dividend."

There were a couple of appreciative mumbles in the room and a half-hearted attempt at applause. Nicolo and Rizzo shuffled their feet like schoolboys at an honors presentation.

"Sergeant?" Trentkamp said. "Come up here please."

Rizzo awkwardly stepped forward, hoisting a Styrofoam chart up on a metal stand. On the chart a police artist had sketched the major buildings of the financial district in black and white. The structures which had been bombed were colored traffic-signal red. Each of the bombed-out buildings also had a bold violet ring drawn around it. Caitlin noticed that the purple rings were at widely different levels on the fourteen buildings.

Rizzo began, "The buildings marked with red were all hit around six-thirty on December fourth. The bombs were definitely detonated by remote signals. The signal might have been operated from as far away as eight to ten miles."

Rizzo paused, blew his nose unselfconsciously in a big white handkerchief, then went on: "The violet rings on the buildings were drawn to indicate where the explosions actually took place. The plastique packages were actually placed. *Here, here, here,* et cetera.

"As you can see, the plastique was planted on *different* floors in all fourteen buildings. The second floor at Twenty-two Broad. Fifteenth floor at Manufacturers Hanover. And so on. You can all see that plainly." Rizzo looked around at the faces in the room as if he were challenging someone to disagree.

"There's no special pattern to this. At least, that's what

324

we've thought up to now. Last night though, we found a connection we'd missed . . .

"Look here! Each of the circled floors actually contains one of that building's messenger drop-off and pick-up rooms. Either a drop-off *or* a package mail station. What threw us off this approach was the fact that messenger drop-off stations and the mail room in these buildings isn't always the same. Not even on the same floor. Some of the Wall Street buildings have drop-off stations on *every* floor. You all see what I'm driving at?"

Sergeant Joe Rizzo paused for effect.

Rizzo said, "Gentlemen, the actual bombs were all hand-delivered. Probably by a *regular commercial messenger*, who would go unnoticed."

Rizzo once again looked around the suddenly quiet room. "There are more than two hundred messenger services in and around Wall Street. Jimmy Split, Speedo, Fireball, Bullet, to name a few. You've probably seen most of them yourselves. We're going to contact *every single one of those services*. Chances are at least one of them was contacted by our friends Green Band. Perhaps several were used to deliver the plastique on December fourth!"

Rizzo paused again. "What this means is that some goofball messenger is going to help break this thing open! Tonight we hit the streets. Tonight we run this thing down to earth!"

Caitlin felt the tremendous energy that coursed through the meeting room as the men began to disperse. They had come suddenly alive, after days of pounding on unyielding walls, days of pursuing an investigation that had been going absolutely nowhere. She was almost swept aside as eager policemen and detectives crushed toward the door.

A Wall Street messenger service.

A slight shiver suddenly traveled through her.

Messenger service? . . .

Caitlin turned and left the meeting room; she started back in the direction of her own office. She had just remembered something, except she wasn't sure now if her memory was playing tricks on her.

Caitlin started to run down the corridor inside No. 13.

Carroll; 2300

Carroll was certain he had been followed back from Washington. A dark car had tracked his Checker taxicab from Kennedy Airport all the way back into the Financial District.

When he stepped out of the taxi at No. 13 Wall, the tracking car went skirting past. He couldn't see faces inside, only shapes, two or three men huddled together. *Why were they following him? Who had sent them? Who was tracking the tracker?*

He disappeared inside No. 13 and went straight to Caitlin's office on the second floor. He hurried because he was filled with the strongest need to see her, to talk to somebody he could trust right now.

She rose from behind her desk, where she'd been studying a printout of the names of U.S. veterans the computer had supplied before. She stepped out to hug him, and Carroll didn't seem to want to let her go. They pressed tightly into one another's bodies. They kissed with a startling urgency neither of them had acknowledged before.

Caitlin finally disentangled herself. "How was Washington?" She was smiling, obviously relieved to see him.

"Interesting. More than just interesting," Carroll said.

He told her about the FBI's files on David Hudson, about his eventual visit with General Lucas Thompson.

Caitlin brought him up to the moment on the developments explained by Sergeant Rizzo. She indicated the computer printout she'd been studying when he had arrived.

"Maybe this is coincidence, Arch. Maybe it doesn't mean a thing. But on this FBI list of veterans there's an

326

explosives expert whose occupation is cabdriver and *messenger*. The home address is New York City."

"Which name?" Carroll asked. He was already scanning the lengthy list.

"A man called Michael Demunn . . . who just happened to serve under Colonel David Hudson in Viet Nam."

"Does it say which messenger service?" Carroll looked up from the printout.

Caitlin shook her head. "It shouldn't be too difficult to find out. Let's see."

Carroll waited while Caitlin made a quick couple of telephone calls. He slid his investigation notebook out of his coat and impatiently flipped through those familiar pages that had chronicled Green Band's false starts and stops from the beginning.

There were several different organizational headings now: *Interviews. Physical Evidence. Suspects. Miscellaneous.*

David Hudson . . . the mastermind of all this chaos?

West Point. 1966. Special Forces. Rangers.

Golden Boy? The All-American Boy?

Fort Bragg. JFK Training School. Severe stress testing. Experimentation with drugs. Preparing Hudson for what?

Special terrorist training. By whose orders? Where did that particular chain of command end?

Carroll finally shut the notebook in frustration. He absently studied Caitlin, the delicate curve of her spine as she stood with her back to him. The way she was poised – on one foot with the phone cord twisted around her waist.

What do I know, that I don't know I know? Carroll's thoughts went back to Green Band.

What could I know? What have I seen that's crucial?

Washington, D.C? General Lucas Thompson? A genial white-haired liar. Somebody following me now.

Following me for what reason? On whose orders?

He watched Caitlin put the telephone receiver down.

"Vets Cabs and Messengers," she said with a sudden grin. "They have a garage near here in the Village."

Carroll stood up. "Call Philip Berger. Then could you

call Walter Trentkamp? Tell them to get their men organized, to meet me at . . ."

Caitlin interrupted, "There's more, Arch."

She paused for just a beat.

"David Hudson works there, too. He's been there for over a year. I think we've finally found Colonel Hudson. We've found Green Band."

Saturday; December 18;
Colonel David Hudson

37

The Vets; 0030

Just past midnight on December 18, Colonel David
Hudson emotionally addressed the assembly of twenty-
four Vets gathered inside the Jane Street garage.

"This has been a long and particularly hard mission for
all of you," he said. "I know that. But at each important
stage you've done everything that has been asked of you.
. . . I feel very humble standing here before you."

Hudson paused and looked over the upturned faces
that watched him motionlessly. "As we approach the
final stages of Green Band, I want to stress one thing. I
don't want anyone to take needless risks. Is that understood? Take no chances. Our ultimate goal from here on
is zero KIA."

Again, Hudson paused. When he finally spoke, there
was an uncharacteristic edge of emotion in his voice.

"This will be our last mission together. Thank you once
again. I salute you all."

Combat Patrols; 0035

From that moment, Green Band was designed to be a
thoroughly disciplined, Army- style *field maneuver*. Every
possible detail had been scrutinized again and again.

The grease-stained garage doors at Vets Cabs and

Messengers rolled open with a heavy metallic roar. Diffuse amber headlights suddenly pierced the darkness.

Vets 5, Harold Freedman, ran outside the Vets building. He looked east and west on Jane Street, then Freedman began to bark orders like the Army drill sergeant he'd once been.

It was just past 12:30 A.M.

If anyone in the West Village neighborhood saw the three Army transport trucks emerge from the garage, they paid little attention, in the tired and true tradition of New Yorkers.

The trucks finally hurtled up Tenth Avenue.

Colonel David Hudson crouched forward attentively in the passenger seat of the lead troop truck. He was in constant walkie-talkie contact with the two other troop transports. . . . This was a disciplined Army field maneuver in every respect.

They were carefully moving into full combat again. None of them had realized how much they missed it. Even Hudson himself had forgotten the intense clarity that came before a major battle. There was nothing else like this anywhere in life; nothing to compare with full combat.

"Contact. This is Vets One. You are to follow us straight down Tenth Avenue to the Holland Tunnel entrance. We'll be maintaining *strict* military speed limits inside the city. So sit back. Just relax for the ride. Over."

Two hours passed before the lead transport truck pulled to a shuddering stop at a military guardpost less than sixty yards off Route 34 in New Jersey. Over the wooden sentry box the sign said FORT MONMOUTH, UNITED STATES ARMY POST.

The Army private on duty had been very close to falling asleep. His eyes were glazed behind horn-rimmed glasses and his movements comically wooden as he approached the lead transport truck.

"Identification, sir." The private cleared his throat. He spoke in a high-pitched whine, and didn't look much

330

more than eighteen years old to Hudson. Shades of Viet Nam, of brutal wars fought by innocent boys for thousands and thousands of years.

David Hudson silently handed across two plastic ID cards. The cards identified him as Colonel Roger McAfee of the 68th Street Armory, Manhattan. The inspection that followed was pro forma. The regular duty guard speech was given by the Fort Monmouth sentry.

"You may proceed, sir. Please obey all posted parking and traffic regulations while you are a visitor at Fort Monmouth. Are those transport vehicles behind with you, sir?"

"Yes, we're going on bivouac. We're here to pick up supplies. Small arms and ammunition for our weekend in the country. Two helicopters have been requisitioned. They'll have the details inside. I'm to see Captain Harney."

"You can all proceed then, sir."

The youthful Army base sentry finally stepped aside. He crisply waved the small Army Reserve convoy onward.

"Contact. This is Vets One." As soon as they passed the gate, Colonel Hudson spoke into the PRC transmitter. "We're now less than twelve hours until the termination of the operation code-named Green Band. Everyone is to use extreme, *repeat* extreme caution. We're almost home, gentlemen. We're almost home at last. Over and out."

Carroll; 0130

Inconspicuous and drab, the Vets garage on Jane Street wasn't the kind of place to draw unwarranted attention. It sat in the middle of a West Village block, its large metal doors rusted and grease stained and bleak.

At both ends of the block, the desolate street had silently been cordoned off. NYPD patrol cars were positioned everywhere around the garage. Carroll counted seventeen of them.

331

Beneath the darkened edifice of a Shell gas station, he could see unmarked FBI cars and as many as thirty heavily armed agents. Each of them watched the front of the garage with the kind of serious-faced intensity that represents professionalism within the Bureau.

The police and the FBI agents carried MI-6s, M-16 automatic assault rifles, 12-gauge riot shotguns, .357 Magnums. It was as frightening an attack force and arsenal as Carroll had ever seen.

Carroll leaned against his own car, studying the metal doors, the crooked, bleached sign that read VETS CABS AND MESSENGERS. He tapped his fingers nervously on the car hood.

Something was wrong here. Something was wrong again.

Arch Carroll peered hard in the direction of the Shell station. The FBI guys stood perfectly still, waiting for the signal that would bring them rushing into action.

At his side was Walter Trentkamp. Carroll had kept Walter informed. Now Trentkamp was inside the dangerous maze with him.

Carroll took out his Browning. He turned the heavy weapon over in the palm of his hand and thought it was strange how some voice inside his head was telling him to be careful. *Careful,* he thought. He hadn't been careful before – so why start now? Carroll thought he *knew* why.

"Archer." Walter nudged him. A black limousine was suddenly threading its way down the grim, quiet street.

Police Commissioner Michael Kane solemnly climbed out. The Commissioner, whose street experience was limited, and who was more politician than cop, had a gleaming blue bullhorn in one hand. He held it as if he'd never touched such a thing before.

"Oh Jesus Christ, no . . ." Carroll muttered.

Commissioner Kane's voice echoed down the deserted West Village street. "Attention . . . this is Commissioner of Police Kane. . . . You have one minute to emerge from the Vets garage. You have sixty seconds before we open fire."

Carroll's eyes roamed over the red brick garage. His

body was tense, his neck and forehead damp. He slowly raised his pistol to the firing position.

The Vets garage remained quiet.

Something definitely wasn't right about this.

"Twenty-five seconds . . . come out of the garage . . ."

Walter Trentkamp leaned close and forced a whisper. One of the things Carroll appreciated was that Walter was still basically a street cop. He still needed to be in on the action himself. "Suppose this is all bullshit? Suppose we've got the wrong men, the wrong messenger service? Something's not right here, Arch."

Carroll still said nothing. He was watching, and thinking.

"Twenty seconds . . ."

"C'mon Walter . . . come with me."

Carroll suddenly stepped forward. Walter Trentkamp somewhat reluctantly followed him toward the garage doors. The Police Commissioner had stopped counting down.

Then the FBI agents and city cops were everywhere, pushing through the jagged edges of the broken doors and into the darkened building itself.

Somebody turned on a light revealing a somewhat ordinary, gloomy and cavernous garage.

Carroll, Browning in hand, froze. His eyes blinked several times. He could smell oil and grease, all the harsh odors left behind by sick and aging automobiles. Slick puddles of oil covered the concrete floor. There were professional mechanics' tools lying around in disarray.

But nothing else was left in the Vets garage.

There were no vehicles of any kind on the basement floor.

There were no people, no Viet Nam veterans. Colonel David Hudson was nowhere to be seen.

Nothing was left of whatever had been here before.

Carroll and Trentkamp wandered around the garage, their guns still clutched in their fists. They entered each small side room in a careful police crouch. They finally climbed narrow, twisting stairs to the top floor.

And then they both saw it . . . the message left for them.

It was taped to the grease-stained wall and it mocked them, mocked them all. It laughed at all the helpless police investigators – a shrill funhouse cackle, the screeching caw of jungle birds.

A green ribbon had been tied in a perfect bow, and it hung on a barren wall like something left over from a glittering Christmas package.

Yeah, Arch Carroll thought.

Have a merry one.

Green Band had disappeared from the garage on Jane Street – as always, one frustrating jump ahead of him.

One cold, calculating jump . . . *moving toward what?*

Caitlin Dillon; 2230

Caitlin Dillon carried a leather portfolio overflowing with her notes as she walked down the darkened hallway of an Upper West Side apartment building. The door to 12B was halfway open.

Anton Birnbaum was standing there waiting. Caitlin wondered why he had called her so late at night. What did Anton want from her now?

He let her in and they walked together to his library, a room crammed to its high ceiling with old books and periodicals.

"Thank you for coming right away," he said. He seemed incredibly relieved to see Caitlin. "Coffee? Tea? I've been living on the unhealthy stuff lately." He gestured to a tarnished espresso pot near the glowing fireplace.

Caitlin declined. She sat down on an antique sofa and lit a Du Maurier as the old Financier poured himself a demitasse from the pot on the hearth.

His hands were trembling slightly. This whole room, in its papery disarray, indicated that Anton Birnbaum had been burning the midnight oil with a fevered vengeance.

"Let me begin all the way back in Dallas, Caitlin." Birnbaum, his small face looking like a burned-out moon, finally sat down alongside her. "The tragic assassination of President John Kennedy . . . it's a good place to start, I think. In terms of the fantastic versus the expected reality. The assassination was probably orchestrated, as we all know."

Caitlin crushed her cigarette. Her throat was suddenly dry. Anton Birnbaum was agitated as well.

"Next comes Watergate, 1973. I think, I firmly believe that Watergate was *permitted* to escalate. Its flames were purposely fanned . . . in order to remove Richard M. Nixon from office. That, my dear, is history. American history." Birnbaum's cup gently rattled in the saucer. "Both these events were clearly *orchestrated*. Both events were devised by a cabal cleverly working both inside and outside the United States government. This elitist group is a remnant, Caitlin, a cell of the old OSS, our own World War II intelligence network.

"I have heard them called the Wise Men. I've also heard them called the Committee of Twelve. They *exist*. Permit me to continue before you comment.

"In 1945, the men who ran the OSS realized that the cloak of responsibility they had assumed in wartime was coming to an end. They were faced suddenly with giving their enormous power back to the same politicians who had almost managed to obliterate the human race a few years before. . . . They had no desire to do so, Caitlin. None at all. In many ways, one can almost justify their actions."

Birnbaum sipped his coffee. He made a sour face. "A high-ranking clique of these OSS men surrendered only *some* of their wartime powers to President Truman. They remained working behind the scenes in Washington. They began to maneuver a long series of political puppets. These men, and their protégés, the *current* Committee of Twelve, have gone so far as to select the presidential candidates for political parties. For *both* parties, Caitlin, in the *same* election."

335

Caitlin stared at the old man. She could manage little beyond a stare. The Wise Men? The Committee of Twelve? A secret cabal with unlimited powers? She already knew a great deal about real and imagined government conspiracies. They had always seemed woven firmly into the tapestry of American history. Unconfirmable rumors; uncomfortable realities. Uncomfortable whispers in high places. "Who are these men, Anton?"

"My dear, they are not exactly faces familiar from *Newsweek* or *Time* magazine. But that's beside the point right now. What I am trying to tell you is that I have *no doubt* this group is somehow involved in the Green Band incident. Somehow, Caitlin, they encouraged or caused the December fourth attack on Wall Street. They're behind whatever is happening right now."

Caitlin didn't have the appropriate words to respond to what Birnbaum was saying. With any other person, she might have dismissed this whole thing; with Birnbaum she knew he wouldn't have told her any of this if he wasn't certain himself. Anton Birnbaum double- and triple-checked all his information, no matter the source.

The Financier stared at Caitlin and there was an unusually weary glaze over his eyes. She looked slightly European smoking the Du Maurier, not completely like herself.

"This veterans' group—" Birnbaum started again.

"You've heard of them already?" Caitlin was surprised. An alarm sounded somewhere inside her brain.

Birnbaum smiled. A slender fissure opened across his small face. "My dear, information has always been the wellspring of my success. Of course I have heard of the veterans' group. I have my sources inside Number 13.

"But what I don't know yet is whether the Committee of Twelve manipulated these poor misfits, or whether the veterans are actually paid operatives. . . . I do believe I know why the dangerous mission was undertaken. . . . I think it can be traced directly to a dangerous, Soviet-run provocateur called François Monserrat. A cold-blooded mass-murderer. A killing machine that has to be destroyed."

"But what is Monserrat's connection with the Committee of Twelve, Anton? What's going to happen now? Can you tell me that?"

Anton Birnbaum smiled, but the smile was strangely tight. "I believe that I can, my dear. Are you sure you don't want some coffee or tea? I think you should have something warm against the cold."

Sunday; December 19;
Vets Cabs and Messengers

38

Hudson; 0930

Early on Sunday morning Colonel David Hudson patrolled the dimly lit corridors of the sprawling Queens VA Hospital. *The home of the brave*, he thought bitterly.

The Queens VA was situated at Linden Boulevard and 179th Street. It was a dismal, red-brick complex that purposely called no attention to itself. Eleven years before, David Hudson had been an outpatient there, one of tens of thousands who had been subjected to VA hospitals after the Viet Nam War.

A hollowness, like that at the heart of an empty gymnasium, caused his footsteps to echo as he plunged deeper and deeper into the hospital complex.

There were buzzing voices, but no people he could see. Ghosts, he thought. Straining voices from another dimension of reality. Voices of cruel pain and madness.

He turned a corner – and suddenly he encountered a gruesome row of veterans. They were pathetically emaciated wraiths mostly, but a few were obscenely overweight. The odor in the still, dead air was overpowering: part industrial disinfectant, part urine, part human feces. A synthetic Christmas tree blinked spastically at the heart of the claustrophobic room.

At least half of the patients seemed to have tiny metal radios pressed like cold packs to their heads. A black hussar in a torn, pinstriped johnny was discoing around an amputee fitfully sleeping in his wheelchair. Hudson saw broken, gnarled bodies harnessed into steel and leather braces. *"Metals of honor"* the hospital aides used to say when Hudson had been there.

He felt such rage now, such hatred for everything American, everything he'd once loved about his country.

There were still no hospital personnel in sight. There wasn't a single corpsman, not a nurse or nurse's aide in any of the halls.

David Hudson kept walking – faster – almost hearing a soft military drum roll in his head.

He went down a bright *yellow* hallway, a falsely cheery one.

He remembered all of the surroundings with vibrant clarity now. Almost uncontrollable rage swept through his body.

In the fall of 1973, he'd been admitted into the VA, ostensibly for psychiatric evaluation and tests. A smug, Ivy League doctor had talked to him twice about his affliction, his unfortunate loss of an arm. The Army doctor was equally interested in Hudson's POW experience. Had he killed a Viet Cong camp commandant while making his escape? Yes, Hudson assured him, in fact the escape was what had first brought him to the attention of Army Intelligence. They had tested him in Viet Nam; then they sent him back to Fort Bragg for further training. . . . The interviews lasted no more than fifty minutes each time. Hudson had then filled out endless Veterans Administration questionnaires and numbered forms. He was assigned a VA caseworker, an obese man with a birthmark on his cheek, whom he never saw again after their first half-hour interview.

At the end of the yellow hallway were glass double doors to the outside. Through the hospital doors, Hudson could see fenced-in back lawns. The fences were not intended to keep the veterans in, he knew. They'd been built to keep the people outside from seeing what was inside: *the terrifying, awful disgrace of America's veterans.*

David Hudson hit the glass door squarely with his

right shoulder. He was instantly plunged outside into sharp winter cold, into the dark clinging dampness.

Directly behind the main hospital building was a steep frost-covered lawn which ended in threadbare scrub pines. Hudson moved across it quickly. Concentrate, he instructed himself. Don't think about anything but the present. Nothing but what's happening right now.

Two men stepped suddenly from behind a row of thickly snow-laden firs.

Monserrat; 0940

One man had the impressive, very formal appearance of a United Nations diplomat. The other was a common-looking street thug with a tough, expressionless face.

"You might have chosen the Oak Bar at the Plaza just as easily. Certainly that would have been more convenient," the impressive-looking man spoke first. "Colonel Hudson, I presume? . . . I am François Monserrat."

The distinguished man's English was slightly accented. He might have been French? . . . Swiss? . . . *Monserrat. Carlos's replacement.*

David Hudson smiled without any real mirth. He showed slightly parted teeth. Every one of his senses was coming alive now. "The next time we meet, it can be your turn to choose locations. Under the clock in the Biltmore Hotel? The observation deck of the Empire State Building? Whatever site pleases you," he offered.

"I'll remember that. You have a proposition for me to consider, Colonel? The remainder of the securities from Green Band? *A substantial amount*, I take it."

Hudson's eyes remained hooded, showing almost no emotion, not a hint of the seething rage inside.

"Yes, I would say substantial. *Over four billion dollars.* That's enough to cause an unprecedented international incident. Whatever you wish."

"And what do you want from us, dare I ask? What is your final reward out of this, Colonel?"

340

"Less than you might think. The deposit of one hundred fifty million in a secure, numbered account. Your assurance that the GRU won't pursue my men afterward. The end of Green Band, as far as you're concerned."

"That's all? I can't accept that."

"No, I suppose it isn't all. I have something else in mind. . . . You see, I want you to destroy the pathetic American way of life. I want you to end the American century a little early. We both intensely hate the American system – at least what it's become. We both want to set it on fire, to purify the world. We've been trained to accomplish that."

The European terrorist briefly stared into Colonel Hudson's eyes. Hudson's apocalyptic words hung in the chilled air. Finally, François Monserrat smiled. He understood Hudson perfectly now. His smile was chilling, quite hideous.

"You're planning to complete this transaction soon I take it? The final exchange?"

Hudson looked at his wristwatch as if to check the time. He knew precisely what time it was. He was only going through the expected motions. "It's nine-thirty now. In six hours, gentlemen."

Monserrat hesitated, an uncharacteristic flicker of indecision and doubt, but only a second's pause.

"Six hours is acceptable. We will be ready by then. Is that all?"

Colonel David Hudson seemed to have a sudden insight as he stood huddled with the two men. His head cocked slowly, at an odd angle. A smile finally appeared, full of charm, his old West Point charisma.

"There is another matter. One more serious problem we have to discuss."

"And what might that be, Colonel Hudson?"

"I realize that no one is supposed to know who you are. That's the primary reason I wanted you here. Why I insisted on it, if you were to get the bulk of these bonds. You see me, and I see you. . . . Except for one thing . . ."

341

"Except what?"

"Next time, I want to see the *real* François Monserrat. If he doesn't come in person, there will be no final exchange."

Having said that, Colonel David Hudson curtly turned away. Hudson walked briskly back toward the VA hospital and disappeared inside.

His revenge, his fifteen-year odyssey was almost complete now. The final, telling moment was coming for each and every one of them.

Deceit! As it had never been seen before. Not since the Viet Nam War, anyway . . .

They had taught him so very, very well to destroy. . . . *Whatever he wished to destroy* . . .

Vice-president Elliot; 0820

In a fashionable and expensive part of New York City, Vice-president Thomas More Elliot was alone and troubled that morning. He walked at a quickening pace along the rim of the East River, directly behind the United Nations complex.

There was the customary parade of bundled-up joggers plodding along the concrete promenade. A spinsterish woman looked like she might be contemplating suicide. A slender young model blissfully walked her dog.

There were apparently no bodyguards for the Vice-president of the United States, no crewcut Secret Service men were anywhere in sight. There was nothing and nobody to protect Thomas Elliot from recognition and possibly from harm.

The walk alone was something the Vice-president did infrequently, but it was something he needed to do now. It was a fundamental human need: simply to be alone. Thomas Elliot needed to be able to think, to be able to see a complex and challenging plan in its entirety.

The Vice-president finally let his mind settle on the

real reason why he desperately needed to be off by himself . . .

He paused and stared into the sluggish wintry gray river. Smoke drifted lazily upward on the other bank. He thought about his childhood then, as if those comforting recollections might put everything in perspective. The casual rise of smoke reminded him of those autumnal bonfires on the grounds of his family home in Connecticut – how could that small boy, whose face he saw in memory, have come all this way? All the way to this present, seminal moment in American history?

Vice-president Elliot placed his gloved hands in the deep pockets of his overcoat. Green Band was almost at an end. Out there, someplace in this vast city, the terrorist François Monserrat, the New York police, Colonel David Hudson and his men were rushing toward their personal rendezvous with destiny. Meanwhile, other powerful forces were slotting quietly into place.

He frowned. A barge crawled over the oily surface of the river. Dirty washing hung on a rope and smoke rose upward from a blunt funnel. The Vice-president thought he saw a shapeless figure move aboard the barge.

Colonel David Hudson had his moment of destiny to come . . .

As he did, the Vice-president of this country.

In a very short time, when the considerable dust had cleared on the brief reign of Justin Kearney – a disillusioned man who hadn't been able to come to terms with the strict limitations of his power, a man who would resign his office in the wake of an economic crisis, who would probably be exiled to some rustic estate and live out the remainder of his days writing heavily censored memoirs – when all the dust had cleared, Thomas More Elliot, like Lyndon Baines Johnson twenty-odd years before, like Gerald Ford a little more than a decade ago, would step up to the presidency of the United States.

Everything depended on the final act of Green Band.

39

Detective Ernie "Cowboy" Tubbs,
Detective Maury Klein; 1450

The Vets cabs appeared suddenly. They paraded single file out of an abandoned warehouse garage in downtown Manhattan. The cabs were assimilated into normal traffic flow until they branched onto Division and Catherine streets leading toward the East River and FDR Drive.

Each of the Checker cabs had been equipped with PRC-77 transmitter-receivers, known in Viet Nam as *monsters*. The PRC units automatically scrambled and unscrambled all transmissions. There was no practical way the New York police could intercept messages traveling back and forth between the cabs.

There were six cabs, which could carry fourteen heavily armed Vets: an assault platoon with rifleman-snipers, M-60 gas-operated machine-gunners, a thumper man with an M-79 grenade launcher, a communications operator.

The most spectacular touch in the commando raid was that the ground attack force had air support. Two Cobra Assault copters would be backing the Vets if any combat action started on the street.

David Hudson, who scouted and studied the street from the lead cab, was beginning to feel an unexpected sense of release. It was almost over. Finally, dignity. Finally, revenge.

He experienced some of his old combat sensations from Viet Nam, only this time with a difference.

A big, important difference.

This time, they were going to be allowed to win.

A New York police detective, Ernie "Cowboy" Tubbs,

who had been dragged unceremoniously out of bed to join the manhunt, saw one of the cabs go past on Division Street. Then he saw two more Vets cabs.

He turned to his partner, Detective Maury Klein, a short man in a black tent of a raincoat. Tubbs said, "Christ, that's them. That's Green Band. Bingo, Maury."

Detective Klein, who was addicted to Rolaids *and* Pepto-Bismol, peered sorrowfully through the windshield. His stomach was already killing him. "Jee-sus Christ, Ernie! Half those bastards are supposed to be Special Forces."

Ernie "Cowboy" Tubbs shrugged and swung their late model Dodge out behind the line of yellow cabs. Only a single car separated them from the rearguard Vets cab. *"We've spotted Green Band!"* Tubbs rasped into the hand-mike on his dashboard.

Maury Klein uneasily cradled an American-180 submachine-gun in both arms. The assault gun looked terribly out of place inside the Dodge, middle-class family car. The American-180 fired thirty rounds per second. It was almost never used in city fighting for that reason.

"This sucks, man. *Sucks!* Bar on 125th Street, I tangled with *one* Green Beret Special Forces dude. That was enough for me, *forever*." Maury Klein continued to complain. The notion of mixing it up with ex-Special Forces veterans seemed like one of the worst ideas he'd ever had in his police-force life. Maury Klein was a vet, too, class of '53, Korea.

At Henry Street there were only a few working traffic lights. There was almost no other traffic. An eerie, dockside feeling pervaded the steamy gray area of lower Manhattan.

"Looks like they're going to the FDR Drive for sure. . . . Entrance is down here somewhere. Right around Houston."

"North or south?" Ernie Tubbs yelled to his partner and gave a quick glance.

"I think both ways. South for sure. We'll see it here any . . . *there!* That's it."

Just then, Tubbs spotted the dilapidated ramp to the south lanes of the drive himself.

The Vets cabs were approaching fast from both directions. The first cabs were already rattling up the crumbling stone and metal rampways.

Tubbs flicked on his hand mike again. "Contact! All Panther units. They're getting on the FDR! They're heading due south! Over."

Suddenly the rear Vets cab veered sharply. It tried to cut Tubbs's car off.

"Son of a bitch!"

Tubbs swerved left with skillful, near-perfect timing. The unmarked police sedan continued to shoot up the half-blocked entranceway that didn't look wide enough anymore.

"Jesus Christ, Ernie! Watch the walls!"

The Vets cab meanwhile had finished its tailspin. It was blocking off every police car except one, Tubbs's, which had somehow slipped by. "Son of a bitch! Son of a bitch!" Detective Tubbs yelled as he fought the unmarked car's steering wheel for control.

"All units, all units! They set a roadblock on the FDR! Repeat. There's a roadblock on the FDR! Over."

Meanwhile, the single police sedan was screeching into teeming traffic filling all three narrow, twisting lanes of the FDR south. A truck slammed to a jolting stop behind. Horns blared from every possible direction.

The police car was hemmed in tight by two of the Vets cabs. The black barrels of M-16s were jammed out both windows of the cab to their left.

Ernie Tubbs couldn't breathe. He was bottled in at fifty-five miles an hour. One of the M-16s fired a round.

The warning shot flared over the police sedan roof like night tracers in a combat battle zone.

A Vet in military khakis and black greasepaint screamed over at Tubbs. His voice was muffled under the traffic whistle, but Tubbs could hear every word.

"Get off at the next stop! Get the fuck off this road! . . .

Everybody but the driver hands up! *I said hands up!* Hands up!"

Closing on the next exit, Tubbs spun his wheel hard right toward the guardrail. The unmarked police sedan shot at a seventy-degree angle toward the off ramp.

It bumped hard over loose plates, sending off sparks. The patrol car went up on two wheels. It threatened to turn over. After a moment when gravity seemed an indecisive force, the car finally bounced back onto all four wheels. It shimmied down the off ramp, then stopped dead on the bordering city street.

"We lost them! Over." Ernie Tubbs screamed into his radio transmitter. "We lost them on the FDR!"

Detective Maury Klein finally whispered out loud inside the police sedan, "Thank fucking God."

Carroll; 1500

As soon as he heard the news that Green Band had been spotted, Carroll spun down several steep flights of stairs inside No. 13. He took the rubber-edged steps two and three at a time. He was racing outside, hoping to find a police helicopter waiting.

Everything was happening at once on the street. Crashing footsteps of other running men. Police squad car engines starting. Tires screeching up and down Wall Street and Broad and Water.

Carroll was carting an M-16 rifle, which felt weird bouncing against his body. *Flashback time* – he was an Army infantry soldier again. . . . Except for one thing: this was downtown Manhattan and not Viet Nam.

His sports coat flew open as he ran, revealing the Browning holster as well as a heavy bulletproof vest. His heart was pounding at a volume consistent with the chaotic street noise.

A radio squad car he passed relayed the latest information on Green Band's whereabouts.

"They're moving at about thirty-five miles per hour. Six vehicles. They're all regular Checker cabs. All are heavily armed. They're proceeding *east.*" *It's a set-up for something else,* Carroll suddenly thought.

What though? What were the Vets going to do now? What was Colonel David Hudson's plan? How was he going to escape the tightening dragnet?

A silver and black Bell helicopter was waiting in a Kinney parking lot. A few weeks earlier, the parking lot would have been filled with the luxury cars of inveterate Wall Street workaholics. A rate sign said $14.50 plus NYC tax for twelve hours. The police helicopter was whirring like an outsized moth. It was ready to fly.

"M-16 and a Bell chopper." Arch Carroll winced as he swung his body inside the hot, cramped helicopter cockpit. "Christ, this brings back memories. Hi, I'm Carroll," he said to the police pilot seated inside.

"Luther Parrish," the pilot grunted. He was NYPD, a heavyset black man with a leather flak jacket and clear yellow goggle glasses. "You ex-Viet Nam? You look like it. Feel like it." Parrish snapped a thick wad of gum as he talked.

"Class of 1970." Arch Carroll finally smiled. He purposely played it a little combat cool, like you would boarding a copter in Nam. The truth was, he hated choppers. He hated *seeing* the goddamn things. Carroll didn't like the idea of being suspended in air with nothing to rely on but slender blades that furiously slashed the air.

"How 'bout that! Class of '70, too. Well, here we go again, sports fans. I take it you don't much like airplane rides?"

Before Carroll had a chance to answer in the extreme negative, the Bell copter jumped straight up from the parking lot cement. The ascent left Carroll's small intestine somewhere behind. The chopper pierced the smoky city morning, hugging the dusky walls of nearby buildings. The pilot cleverly avoided swift winds sweeping off the river.

Then the copter swung out wide toward the East River. A second helicopter, another Bell, joined in from due south.

"No, I'm not real crazy about helicopters. No offense, Luther."

Adrenaline flowed wildly, it raged like a flooding river through Carroll's body. Down below, he could see traffic streaming on the FDR highway.

The police pilot eventually spoke up over the rotors' noise. "Beautiful morning, man. You can see Long Island, Connecticut, almost see Paris, France."

"Beautiful morning to get shot in the fucking heart."

The black pilot snorted out a laugh. "You been to Viet Nam all right. Let's see, we've got two, three armed patrol helicopters on them right now. Pick up more help once we find out which borough they're goin' to. I think we'll be fine."

"I hope you're right, Luther."

"You see them down there? Little toy taxicabs. See? See right there?"

"Yeah, with little toy M-16s, toy rocket launchers," Carroll said to the black pilot.

"You talk *just* like ex-infantry. Ironic-type shit. Makin' me all misty-eyed."

"*Still* infantry from the look of things. Except I'm afraid *we're* fighting the Green Berets today."

The black pilot turned to Carroll with a knowing look. "They're *bad* dudes all right. *Definitely* Special Forces." He nodded as if to a secret beat. He almost seemed proud of the Vets' bravado. Their urban street fighting style had hit a chord.

A thousand feet below, the FDR Drive was a delicate ribbon of silver and shiny jet black. The Vets cabs looked intensely yellow, almost tawdry down there. As the line-up of cabs crossed the Brooklyn Bridge, both Bell helicopters swung high and wide to avoid being seen. The copters actually briefly disappeared into low-flying clouds.

Carroll's shirt was already soaked through. Everything seemed to be happening at a distance. The world was slightly fuzzed and unreal. *They were going to solve Green Band after all.*

On the Brooklyn side of the bridge, he could see that traffic was heavy but moving. The steady whoosh of cars, an occasional bleating horn, traveled all the way up to the helicopter cockpit.

"They're getting off at the Navy Yard exit! This is Carroll to control. The Vets convoy is exiting at the Navy Yard! They're proceeding northeast into Brooklyn!" Carroll screeched into the microphone.

Brooklyn Navy Yard; 1513

At that same instant, a deafening explosion jarred the underbelly of the police helicopter with a jolt that seemed to rattle right through Carroll's bones. His head cracked hard against the metal roof and sharp bolts of pain stabbed behind his eyes.

Then a second jarring blast struck the reverberating cockpit.

Splinters of glass flew in all directions. Star fractures cobwebbed across the windshield. Everywhere, metal was ringing with gun shots. Glaring red flashes were angrily ribboning the sky.

"Ohhh, goddamn, I'm hit. I'm hit," the police pilot moaned as he slumped forward.

Meanwhile a machine-gun loudly chattered off to Carroll's left. Arch Carroll caught a brief glimpse of floating, blinking red lamps *on the right* and the hulking shapes of two choppers he hadn't seen before.

Christ! Two Cobras were attacking them.

Suddenly the sky was filled with bright, jarring yellow orbs of light, with roaring fire and billowing black smoke. *The companion police helicopter had disintegrated before Carroll's disbelieving eyes.*

Where the chopper had hovered just seconds before, there was nothing except for leaping gold and orange flames. Nothing was left except this eerie, fading after-image in the sky.

Carroll could see that Luther Parrish had been hit

350

badly. Puddles of blood were collecting from a wound somewhere on the left side of his head. The electric circuits in the helicopter cockpit seemed to be completely useless.

Heavy machine-gun fire suddenly welled up from below. The pilot temporarily revived, moaning, grabbed both his legs. The helicopter had begun to fall, to somersault and plummet helplessly. Parrish didn't notice.

Carroll reflexively fired his M-16 at one of the attacking Cobras. The red light winked derisively – then the copter calmy disappeared from sight.

Carroll froze. He was pressed extremely hard into his helicopter seat. Blood was rushing, swirling through his head. The police helicopter had suddenly flipped completely upside down.

Then the helicopter was in a dead fall, sailing and spinning into the gauzy gray nothingness of the Brooklyn Navy Yard below.

A flat black rooftop with a water tower mounted on it suddenly loomed enormously, coming as fast as another airplane at the copter's windshield. The flailing helicopter skimmed over an expanse of shadowy factory buildings a block long, at least. It missed a smoking industrial chimney by inches. The copter's tail was clipped off by a high brick retaining wall.

A deserted grid of avenues and streets appeared through the windshield as the helicopter cleared the last building. Cars were parked in long, uneven lines up both sides.

Carroll reflexively grabbed at the controls. He knew what everything was, from too many trips in Viet Nam, though not how to really use any of it. His body was trembling. Deep, jolting spasms flew up his spine.

He was beyond any compartment of fear he'd previously known. Beyond anything he'd felt in combat or police action. He was in a new realm of sensation – a clear, hard place where he seemed acutely conscious of everything going on around him.

351

This was the moment of impending death, he thought without real comprehension.

The helicopter's belly cleanly sheared the rooftops off a half a dozen parked cars. Carroll covered his face. He shielded the wounded police pilot as best he could with his body.

The helicopter struck the street on a side angle. It skidded, bounded violently. The copter's belly issued a grinding shriek, and Carroll could feel his blood turn to ice.

Sparks, plumes of intense red flames, flew in every possible direction. Whole sides of parked automobiles, headlights and bumpers were effortlessly cut away. A red fire hydrant popped out of the cement like a bathtub plug.

The police helicopter, skidding on its side, finally slowed. It plowed to a tearing, screaming, crunching halt up against two crushed compact cars.

A man in a factory security uniform was running crazily, zigzagging down the deserted street toward the unbelievable accident.

"Hey, hey! That's my car! That's my *car!*"

Carroll was cradling the badly wounded pilot, "Grab hold. You just hold me," he whispered, hoping the man wasn't already dead. "Just hold me, Luther."

Then he was limping away from the burning helicopter wreckage. He was half-dragging, half-carrying the hulking NYPD pilot in his arms.

His eyes nervously searched the skies for the attacking Vets' Cobras, but there was nothing there now.

Nothing at all.

The choppers might as well have been the vehicles of some unlikely nightmare. It was like being in Viet Nam again. It was exactly like combat duty in Nam.

Except that the helicopter crash had happened right here on the streets of Brooklyn.

And now Archer Carroll was out of the grand chase after Green Band. He had lost them one final time. Green Band had escaped again.

Colonel Hudson; 1525

The Vets cabs proceeded northeast, then almost due east across Brooklyn. They were moving inexorably toward François Monserrat. They were headed toward the appointed end of Green Band. Everything was precisely on schedule.

Erect and alert behind the wheel, David Hudson was experiencing a moment of unusual anxiety. It had something to do with being this close to the end. They were less than seven minutes from the rendezvous point with Monserrat.

David Hudson tried to concentrate as if he were entering a combat zone. Nothing could distract him from Green Band now.

Nothing could look even mildly suspicious either . . .

François Monserrat's soldiers could be watching the streets from neighborhood rooftops and darkened apartment windows. If they spotted the unexpected attack force, the final massive exchange of Wall Street securities wouldn't happen. Green Band would fail in the end.

Like an advance scout in Nam, Hudson checked and rechecked the squat, cheerless brick buildings as he drove closer to the agreed-upon meeting place. Hudson noted everything. A knot of black youths was easing out of Turner's Grill. Their voices carried – low, guttural sounds in syncopated street rhythms.

Hudson drove slowly on. He found a parking spot further down the slope-shouldered Bedford-Stuyvesant side street.

He parked and climbed out of the car. Very nonchalantly, he continued to look around the quiet neighborhood chosen for the meeting. He finally popped open the cab's dented and scarred trunk. The Wall Street securities were there in ordinary looking, gray vinyl suitcases.

Hudson hoisted up the bags, and he began to trudge as rapidly as he could toward a red brick factory at the next street corner.

He was almost certain he was being watched. François Monserrat was nearby. All his senses and instincts corroborated that single message.

This was the moment of reckoning, then. All of Hudson's Special Forces training to be matched against Monserrat's years of experience, his years of meticulous deceit.

Hudson shouldered open the heavy wood front door of a building which housed shabby apartments and a small Italian-American shoe factory, *The Gino Company of Milano.*

He pushed into a dark hallway, where trapped cooking smells immediately assaulted him. The musty scent of old winter clothes hung in the air. The meeting place seemed appropriately isolated, almost too mundane.

"Don't turn around, Colonel."

Three men had suddenly appeared in the dim corridor with long-nosed Magnums and Berettas drawn.

"Move right up against the wall. That's good. Right there. That will be fine, Colonel Hudson."

The leader had a cultivated Spanish accent, more than likely Cuban. François Monserrat ran the Caribbean, and most of the terrorist activities in South America, Hudson remembered. At the rate he was going, one day Monserrat was going to run the entire Third World.

"I'm not armed," Hudson quietly said.

"We have to search you anyway."

One of the men positioned himself less than three feet away from Colonel David Hudson. He pointed his gun at an imaginary spot between Hudson's eyes. It was a popular gunman's trick, one Hudson himself had been taught at Fort Bragg. *At close range, shoot out the eyes.*

354

The second man patted him down, quickly and professionally.

The third man searched the gray suitcases, slashing them with a knife, looking for false siding, a bottom that wasn't actually a bottom.

"Upstairs!" the terrorist who held the gun finally commanded Hudson. He spoke like a military officer, Hudson noted.

They began to climb a steep and creaking flight of stairs, then another flight. Were they leading him to Monserrat? Finally, the enigmatic Monserrat himself? Or would there be more deception?

"This is your floor, Colonel. That blue door straight ahead. You can just walk inside. You're most definitely expected."

"Point of information? I have a question for you, for all of you. Curiosity on my part." David Hudson spoke without turning to face his escort group.

An impatient grunt came from behind . . .

The Lizard Man. Past interrogations. Special Army training. Hudson's mind continued to churn at a furious rate.

All to prepare him for this very moment? For this and no other?

"Do they ever tell you what's *really* happening? Has anyone bothered to tell you the *truth* about this operation? Do you know what this meeting really is? Do you know why?"

David Hudson was introducing some element of doubt into all their minds, petty doubts and confusion, paranoid unease he could use later, if he needed to.

Deception.

Always deception.

"Don't bother to knock, Colonel." The man in charge calmly spoke once again. "Just go right in; you're expected. Everything you try to do is expected, Colonel."

A slice of dull, yellow light emanated from within as David Hudson peered inside the fourth-floor tenement room.

David Hudson paused at the doorway's edge.

He was about to confront the mysterious and dangerous Monserrat. He was about to conclude Green Band's appointed business, to end his long mission.

The Viet Cong's Lizard Man had taught Hudson an essential lesson in Viet Nam: *it was to play games in which your opponent wasn't given the rules.* This was the principle behind all successful guerrilla warfare, Hudson believed.

Colonel David Hudson versus Monserrat.

Now it began.

Carroll: 1540

"All blue and white units! We've picked them up again. . . . We've got our friends Green Band!"

NYPD cruiser radios echoed brassily above the noise of whining police and hospital emergency sirens at the helicopter crash site near the Brooklyn Navy Yard.

"They're moving into a residential neighborhood. Bedford-Stuyvesant. It's right in the heart of the fucking ghetto. They're traveling on Halsey Street in Bed-Stuy, now. Over."

Arch Carroll sagged heavily against the open front door of one of the half-dozen police cruisers that had arrived after the helicopter accident. Crime-scene technicians were already swarming onto the fire-lit street.

He wasn't sure if he'd heard the radio report right? . . . *Green Band appeared; Green Band disappeared. Which was it now?*

Carroll tried to clear the gauze from his head as he listened to the minute by minute updates squawking over nearby police cruiser radios.

He couldn't feel any recognizable emotion. His regular system of response to stimuli had come to a halt. He was beyond pain as he'd known it before.

The police helicopter pilot had been carried on a litter into a waiting EMS ambulance. KIA, Carroll was almost certain.

"Carroll? You're Arch Carroll, aren't you? Do you want to go with me? I'm heading to Halsey Street. It's about ten minutes from here." A police captain, a plump, white-haired man Carroll knew from a saner niche in his life, came up alongside him.

Carroll knew he appeared badly dazed and confused. In fact, he felt far worse than that, but he finally nodded. *Yes, he definitely wanted to witness the end. He had to be there.* Colonel David Hudson – Monserrat – Archer Carroll – they all had to be there, didn't they? Why was that? Why had everything led to this point – like veins of glass back toward the impact point in a shatter.

A moment or so later, he was uncomfortably hunched forward in a police patrol car, feeling like he might be sick. Hammers of fear were regularly tripping off inside his head.

The police cruiser lurched into motion. The flashing light began to revolve, cherry red. The siren of the speeding car warbled above the rooftops of Brooklyn.

Colonel David Hudson; 1540

This was the master terrorist Monserrat.

This was François Monserrat.

David Hudson could not believe what his eyes told him was true.

Monserrat? . . . Or was this more incredible misdirection? Another trick? The highest manifestation of deception?

Smoke sifted through his mind, obscuring his vision, scrambling his full understanding. And there was renewed tension: an electric tingling in his fingertips, his arm, his legs.

He watched the mysterious, dark-suited figure come forward toward him. He noted the two gunmen who waited in shadows against the far wall.

"Colonel Hudson." The handshake was quick, surprisingly firm. "I'm François Monserrat. The real one this time." A thin smile played at the corners of the terrorist's

357

mouth. It was the most confident and assured look David Hudson had ever witnessed.

Monserrat's smile almost immediately dimmed. "Let's get to business. I believe we can complete our transaction quickly. Look at what he's brought, Marcel. *Rapidement!*"

Another person in a dark suit stepped inside the room at Monserrat's command. The man was perhaps sixty, and had the pallid complexion, the weak eyesight of someone who spends much of life looking through the lenses of microscopes and magnifying glasses. He bent low to examine the securities Colonel David Hudson had brought with him.

Hudson watched closely as he rubbed the individual trading bonds carefully, lightly testing their texture between his thumb and forefinger.

He smelled selected bonds, testing for fresh ink, for any unusually pungent odors, anything that would suggest too recent printing. He worked extremely fast.

Each minute nevertheless passed with excruciating slowness.

"For the most part, the bonds are authentic," he finally looked up and spoke to Monserrat.

"Any problems at all?"

"I have a slight question about the Morgan Guaranty, perhaps about the smaller Lehman Brothers lot. I think there are possibly some counterfeit papers in those stacks. As you know, there are *always* some counterfeits," he added. "Everything else is quite in order."

François Monserrat nodded curtly. Even Monserrat seemed uneasy now. The terrorist picked up the plain black telephone on the table. Monserrat dialed a telephone company business office, gave a four-digit number, then spoke to what was clearly an overseas operator. Seconds later, the terrorist was speaking directly to someone obviously known at a bank in Geneva, Switzerland.

"My account is Number 411FA. Make the agreed-upon deposit into the account . . ." Less than four minutes later, Monserrat hung up.

Moments afterward, the phone rang and Colonel

Hudson received a confirmation that the money had indeed been successfully transferred in Europe. *Over two hundred million dollars* had gone out of the Soviet accounts into special accounts opened by the Vets in London, Paris, Amsterdam, and Madrid. Vets 28, Thomas O'Neil, the Customs Chief of Shannon Airport, had come through once again. The Green Band plan *was* perfect.

"Colonel, I believe our business is concluded. You seem to have won each round. This time, anyway." Monserrat executed a coldy deferential bow.

As Colonel David Hudson stood up from the table, he felt that a terrible weight had finally been lifted. He was free of an obsession he'd carried for almost fifteen years.

At that exact moment, *he was silently counting down to zero.*

Green Band was almost at an end.

Almost, but not quite.

Just one more twist, one final surprise element.

Deception at its best.

A game in which Hudson alone knew the rules. An amazing game called Green Band.

Less than forty seconds remained. . . . Two pistols were drawn in the room . . .

Concentrate. David Hudson eased himself toward a controlled calmness.

Talk to them. Keep talking to Monserrat.

"I have one question before I leave. May I? May I ask one troubling question?"

Monserrat nodded. "What harm? You may *ask* anything. Then perhaps *I* have a question."

Colonel Hudson watched Monserrat's eyes as he spoke. He saw nothing there – no effect, no emotion. The two of them were close in so many ways. *Killing machines.*

"How long have you been with the Russians? How long have you been one of their moles?"

"I was *always* with the Russians, Colonel. I *am* a Russian. My parents were stationed in middle America. They were among the literally hundreds of agents who came here in the late 1940s.

"I was taught to infiltrate myself – to *be* American. There are many others like me. *Many* others. They're all over the U.S. right now. *Waiting*, Colonel. We want to destroy the United States financially, and in every other way."

Fourteen seconds. Twelve seconds. Ten seconds. Colonel David Hudson kept counting in his head, kept talking in a monotone to François Monserrat. His heartbeat remained low. He was still in complete control.

"Harry Stemkowsky . . . Do you remember a man named Stemkowsky? A poor crippled sergeant? One of my men?"

"One of the casualties of war. Your war, Colonel, not ours. He wouldn't betray you under any circumstances."

As he reached *three* in his countdown, Colonel David Hudson took two fast, unexpected steps to his left. Both Russian terrorists awkwardly swung up their pistols to fire. They were too late.

Hudson tucked his chin down hard against his chest. He dove headfirst through a pane-glass window, crashing into the factory section of the building.

At that precise moment, the entire building shook from the first savage round of M-60s, which completely pulverized the tenement's fourth floor.

Flash fires broke out simultaneously in three separate areas of the factory. Bright orange and crimson flames danced, straining to reach the stained yellow ceiling. Huge panes of glass buckled, then leaped from their casements and crashed to the cement below. Everywhere, the old struts and supports of the building were beginning to sag, warped by the rising heat, the hungry reaches of the lapping flames.

M-16 rifles coughed and rattled everywhere.

The Vets attack force was under way.

David Hudson waited in a low combat crouch behind heavy factory machines. The thick smoke from the fire was an advantage and his enemy at the same time. The billowing smoke and flames made it impossible for Monserrat and his people to locate Hudson, but it also made him vulnerable, exposed to sudden attack from any side.

At that instant, Colonel Hudson heard the sound he'd been waiting for. The whirring of the helicopter rotors was unmistakably loud and clear.

The Cobra had arrived on the rooftop. Exactly as they'd planned it. *Everything was perfect, right to the final escape.*

Colonel David Hudson finally allowed himself a trace of a smile. Just a trace.

Carroll; 1556

"Get the fuck out of my way! Move it! Move it! *Move, move, move!*"

A roaring, absolutely unbelievable firefight had erupted. Arch Carroll saw rows of flat rooftops shooting flames as he roughly pushed and elbowed his way through the crowd already gathered on Brooklyn's Halsey Street to watch the action. Ghouls, he thought. The worst kind of ambulance chasers.

He winced in tremendous pain. His left arm was numb and something was wrong with his lower spine: when he ran like this the contact of his heels with the pavement sent jarring shudders climbing up his backbone.

None of the neighborhood people – leather-jacketed teen-agers, sullen young women, very small, grinning children – seemed to realize that this violent spectacle was for real. They were shrieking with what almost sounded like joy to Carroll.

"Get back! Damnit, get back!" Carroll yelled hoarsely as he ran forward in a practiced combat crouch. "Get inside with those kids! Get back inside your houses!"

Expectant, wide-eyed faces were crowded into every available apartment window. Further down Halsey Street, hundreds of neighborhood people filed outside into the cold, rainy afternoon. They were peering toward the explosions, enthralled by the blazing fire, the sudden jolting volleys of M-16 rifle and pistol shots.

Carroll continued to run in his clumsy battle crouch, moving in closer to the exploding, gunshot riddled building.

A police bullhorn suddenly boomed out to his extreme left. It thundered over the cacophony of gunblasts and piercing human shouts.

"You there! You, running! Stop right there!"

Carroll ignored all the voices. He kept charging forward. His steps weaved as he struggled with pains that attacked his body from every direction.

As he reached the fiery building, an even more familiar and terrifying sound seized his mind.

The same Army Cobra was hovering over the factory roof. *The same helicopter that had shot him down was back. Green Band was definitely here.*

His body low to the ground, Arch Carroll vaulted the building's stone steps. He took the stairs three at a time and with each leap thought he could hear the rattle of his own skeleton, loose bones flying under his flesh.

A heavyset man suddenly burst out of the open doorway in front of Carroll. The man looked Spanish or maybe Cuban. He was holding an 870 riot gun across his barrel chest.

Carroll's gun was set on rapid-repeat. A full round of .30-calliber bullets flickered into the unfortunate terrorist's face and throat. He reeled back inside the doorway and then Carroll couldn't see him any more.

The smoke, forcing itself out of the broken first-floor windows, took root deep in Carroll's lungs. He kept running.

Then Carroll was climbing over the body of the dying gunman sprawled inside the doorway. The man gazed upward with the astonished eyes of an animal under the butcher's knife.

Instinctively, Carroll hugged the hallway wall. Cheek tight against cold, peeling plaster, he gasped for breath.

His head seemed to be spinning at an unbelievable speed.

An Army Cobra helicopter? How did they manage a Cobra?

Getting an Army Cobra just wasn't possible. . . . Green Band was waiting upstairs, and that didn't seem possible, either.

Colonel David Hudson; 1558

A heavy, grated iron door opened slowly onto the tenement rooftop. Columns of smoke, scattered by the wind, temporarily blurred David Hudson's vision. The doorway was less than forty yards from the waiting Cobra helicopter.

Colonel Hudson walked cautiously at first, then he began to trot like a victorious athlete toward the waiting Cobra. He'd done it. They had all done their jobs almost perfectly. The Green Band mission was finally over. The sudden exhilaration of victory was unbelievable to savor.

Hudson never saw the second figure on the roof until the skillful assailant was on top of him. His heart squeezed up into his throat. He'd been careless. For once, just once, he'd forgotten to check, to double-check every possibility.

"You can stop right there, Colonel."

Face and shoulders still obscured in shadow, a figure cautiously appeared from behind the water tower. One hand, which held a Beretta revolver, preceded the rest of the body. Then a face came into the light.

A face came into the light.

François Monserrat stood fully exposed before Colonel David Hudson.

Monserrat smiled – a final smile of triumph.

"My congratulations, Colonel. You nearly accomplished the perfect crime."

Carroll; 1559

Carroll was unsure which way to head once he was inside the burning tenement building. He choked on a thick gust of smoke, and thought he was going to be violently sick. His lungs chafed as if they'd been rubbed down by sandpaper.

Crackling reports of M-16s, booming incendiary bombs rang against his eardrums. He could still make out the sharp repeating sound of the rotors of the Cobra helicopter that had *landed on the rooftop. Monserrat and Colonel Hudson were inside the building. . . . Get up there,* his mind commanded an aching and weary body.

Carroll coughed and gasped as he climbed sets of steep winding stairs. All around him, flames curled at shadows, throwing off violently flickering light and heat. The shooting pain in his legs was unbearable. Something felt wrong, cracked at the base of his spine.

At the head of the stairs, there was a heavy metal door blocking his way. It stuck at first – then Carroll put his shoulder into it hard. He shouldered the stubborn door a second time.

The metal door finally swung open with a loud shriek. The rooftop was revealed. Carroll's eyes widened involuntarily.

The crimson taillights of a U.S. military helicopter shone and sparkled impressively in the haze of smoke. Colorful, slashing streaks were thrown across the dark asphalt of the roof toward Carroll.

The Army Cobra was being readied for takeoff. The rotors were spinning out loud thunder and sparks. It was a familiar war zone scene.

Somewhere in the smoke shrouding the rooftop, Carroll suddenly heard voices. The voices were strident and angry.

They originated from off to his left, beyond a high brick retaining wall. Fear raised the hammers of Carroll's heart. Fear because he was finally beginning to understand.

"You see, you must see that governments of the past are no longer viable. The currently elected governments are mere illusions. They are ghosts of a sentimentalized reality. You must understand *that* at least. There *are* no more democracies." The first voice was filled with the unbearable tension of the moment.

The second voice was harsh, erupting like another gunshot in the air.

The wind muffled the exact words. Whatever the second person had to say was whipped away by the roar of the chopper and the wind that was shuffling the smoky clouds.

Carroll pressed his body closer to the crumbling brick wall. He slowly edged toward the voices. The conversation became clearer now. Each word pierced the noise and swirling smoke. His heart physically ached from the relentless pressure.

"I love this country," one of the two shouted clearly above the wind. "I hate what it did to the veterans after the war. I hate what some of our leaders did. But I love this country."

At that moment, Carroll finally saw them both. Just as he thought he was beginning to understand, he realized that he understood nothing.

Colonel David Hudson. The same man who was pictured in all the FBI library and Pentagon photographs . . . handsome, tall, strikingly blond . . . "the consummate military commander," according to his classified records. America's carefully programmed Juan Carlos.

And the other . . .

Dear God, the other.

Arch Carroll felt something precious and vital subside deep inside him. It wasn't really a physical thing. It wasn't a bone, or a pain in the heart, a collapse of muscle. It was much worse than that. Suddenly, he remembered the first time he'd experienced the horror of death – his father's death in Florida. He remembered his exact feeling on the night Nora had died in New York Hospital.

His mouth was dry and his head a cave of sad, hopeless chaos. His emotions were wilder than the horrifying guerrilla war raging everywhere around him. He was without speech and numb. All he could do was stare straight ahead. His legs shivered and buckled at the knees.

Nothing could have possibly prepared him for this awful moment. All his years as a policeman hadn't prepared him.

The man Colonel David Hudson had addressed as Monserrat was Walter Trentkamp. . . . Except the clenched, shadowy face Carroll saw on this man was almost a stranger's. The face was shockingly ruthless and uncaring.

Carroll's world wheeled violently and turned completely on its side. Whatever sense of reality he had left, shattered in that instant. He closed his eyes. He raked one hand over his smoke-blackened face. He could feel burning tears pushing, pressing against his lids.

His mind's eye seemed to flood with exploding white light. *Uncle fucking Walter*. It was the worst hurt, the worst conceivable betrayal of his life. How could this have happened? How?

He thought about everything Trentkamp had been privy to in the past. He reviewed his own long investigation of Green Band, how Trentkamp knew every detail he'd learned at each maddening turn.

Had Trentkamp dispatched him on the early wild goose chases? *Why?* Well, he knew the simplest answer to that. So he could watch, and control Carroll. So he could carefully control the DIA's terrorist group. *Talk to me on this one, Archer. Let me know what you find out. Will you promise me that?* In a way, François Monserrat had enlisted Carroll to help him find Colonel David Hudson and the Vets.

Talk to me, Archer . . .

Promise me, Archer!

Walter Trentkamp had sat in on the highest level meetings inside the White House, always observing and studying. What incredible self-confidence and gall. How many years had this been going on? How many fucking years? . . . François Monserrat! The most ruthless of the world's terrorists was none other than Walter Trentkamp. It was impossible for him to conceive of. Yet it was true. This obscenity before his eyes was as real as anything could be.

The rage inside Carroll seemed to clutch and rip at the back of his throat, tearing at his flesh. He'd been used. Just like the Vets, he'd been horribly used. He'd been shamelessly violated one more time. Contradictions attacked his mind from every imaginable angle.

Carroll carefully moved forward toward Trentkamp and Colonel David Hudson. The shaking rage inside him heightened. He was fighting against the blind, overwhelming urge to wildly fire his Browning. He wanted to pull the trigger. Right now, he ached to *fire* on these two men. He couldn't; he couldn't shoot. Somehow, he was more than a trained killer. *And what are you, please tell me, mister?* Somehow he was more than these other two bastards.

Carroll finally stepped out from behind the shadowy retaining wall. He spoke in a powerful whisper that carried with the wind.

"Hello, Walter. I wanted to keep my promise. I did promise to talk to you about everything I found out."

Trentkamp's face registered brief surprise, then the terrorist once again seemed supremely confident, almost indifferent to Carroll's presence. He was Monserrat now, not Walter Trentkamp at all.

"It was never anything personal," he spoke, then shrugged at Carroll. "You were my *listok*. That's a Russian word. You were my *solution* to a problem. Nothing more than that. My mission is total Soviet domination in this century. We have an interesting face-off," Trentkamp went on speaking. "The world's premier terrorists. America's very own terrorist hunter. All of us in check for the moment. A powerful snapshot in history, no?"

Archer Carroll raised his Browning to eye level. Colonel David Hudson . . . François Monserrat . . . himself. It seemed that none of them could really win. Carroll wasn't even sure what "win" meant right now. *And what are you, please tell me, mister?*

"How do you live a life made of nothing but lies?" He

367

edged closer to Hudson and Trentkamp. "Nothing but fucking deceit and lies."

"I don't believe in the same truths as you. It follows that I don't believe in the same lies. Don't you realize that *you're* living with lies, too. Your own people have deceived you again and again. . . . Everyone has lied to you, Archer. Your government is the greatest lie of all."

Colonel David Hudson; 1605

Nothing but his instincts counted from here on, from this moment. Colonel David Hudson rigidly held that thought only.

Nothing but his reflexes counted now.

Hudson had a flashing image of the prison camp in North Viet Nam. Crucial lessons he had learned there. Lessons that could mean his survival right now.

Deception, Hudson remembered. Sometimes you even had to deceive yourself . . .

Monserrat was much like the Lizard Man, he thought. *Monserrat was the same as the Lizard Man. The same kind of enemy.*

Instincts.

Reflexes.

Monserrat seemed to be concentrating on Carroll . . . "*Everyone has lied to you, Archer. Your government is the greatest lie of all.*"

A silent scream rose from Hudson's throat. At that moment, David Hudson's arm chopped upward in a short, powerful arc.

The bone in Monserrat's elbow shattered with a sickening crunch. The Beretta dropped. A harsh, ugly growl escaped from his twisted mouth – his teeth were bared like an animal's.

A needle-thin knife seemed to appear from nowhere in Colonel David Hudson's hand. A deep pocket in his trousers flopped open in the wind.

Assassin.

François Monserrat took a surprisingly fast, an agile, step away from Hudson and the knife. Monserrat was better than the Lizard Man had been.

Monserrat was very good, *still* very good. A true master, an artist of death.

David Hudson followed as if he were Monserrat's shadow. The sleek, flashing stiletto lanced forward, an extension of his arm. Everything was *instincts, reflexes for survival. Two perfect machines against one another.*

François Monserrat's hands rose and shielded his face, expertly shielded his upper body. His arm was slashed. It seemed nothing at all.

He was moving into a practiced martial arts crouch, almost dancing. He was going to fight back, to suddenly explode at his enemy.

Colonel Hudson screamed as he feinted one move, a second move, *then* he struck. . . . Seemed to strike? . . . Feinted? . . . The silver knife blade shivered forward with apparent accuracy and great fierceness . . .

The surgical knife blade drove several inches into its target area. The long, piercing needle disappeared into the flesh and bone of Monserrat's rib cage. Monserrat merely sighed and kept coming.

The knife blade was twisted, then immediately pulled away, unplugged it seemed. In one continuous motion the stiletto was thrust forward again. This time it split the center of Monserrat's throat. Blood gushed everywhere, all at once.

The terrorist's legs suddenly went limp. He began to violently convulse. His face no longer seemed smug – no longer confident and in control. Monserrat was clearly surprised, in brutal shock as he fell forward toward the asphalt roof.

Carroll hadn't known whom to shoot. He'd carefully watched, waiting for the victor. He trained his Browning on Colonel Hudson now. His finger tightened, turned to stone around the trigger.

Suddenly he heard the distant *click* of yet another automatic weapon!

369

The disturbing, terrifying sound came from directly behind him in the thickening smoke.

Carroll started to whirl around, to turn completely on past instincts, policeman's reflexes, three generations' worth.

His mind was suspended by pain and the moment's bewildering chaos. He needed all of the madness to stop for a moment.

He saw men he thought he recognized. Four men in tattered khaki green were closing around him on the Brooklyn rooftop. Their M-21s were pointed at him. Four M-21 rifles.

They looked like soldiers Carroll had fought with years before in Viet Nam. *They were Vets*, he realized. *This was Green Band.*

Here was everything he'd wanted to know – only now Carroll didn't want to know any of it.

The outrage continued.

The outrage.

Walter Trentkamp's throat had been savagely slashed. His trench coat had spread open like an umbrella in the wind. The tall, imposing figure had slid down until he sat limply on the ground. His chest was bloodied, redness was seeping down into his trousers. His hard gray-green eyes were already glazed and sightless. *Christ! Christ!*

Carroll tried to grab hold of something. He suddenly began to shout at the top of his voice. "Who are you, Hudson? *What the hell do you want?* Who sent you to Wall Street?"

Outrage!

Something hard crashed, the most brutal force exploded against the top of Carroll's head.

His skull was crushed so easily. He staggered, he almost fell, but he stayed upright somehow. The insane, Bronx streetfighter inside him wouldn't go down. *Goddamn! Them!*

Arch Carroll saw streaks of blood red merging. He felt as if he must be going blind. The pain and chaos, the

370

sudden light show was powerful, unbearable inside his skull.

"Who are you, Hudson?" One final, maddening question formed on his lips. He had no idea whether he spoke the words or not.

He took another lunging step toward Colonel Hudson, toward the fallen body of François Monserrat – of Walter Trentkamp.

The metal base of the revolver fell on his skull again, with tremendous force. It struck the same tender spot, harder even than the first time.

A terrible, *mashing* noise echoed inside Carroll's brain. Fire lit on the left side of his chest.

He was falling then, collapsing against his will, toward the dark cement. Carroll heard himself moaning. He had the lonely thought that he was choking on his own blood. So sad, so wrong.

The revolver crashed down hard another time.

He spun around and saw Colonel David Hudson rigidly standing there. Carroll desperately tried to speak. Shit, he couldn't. He had so many questions about Hudson. He fought the onrushing unconsciousness with all the strength he had left. *Not much. Not enough!* He tried to run toward Hudson. Then Archer Carroll sailed into the most awful, hopeless tunnel of darkness and desolation.

It wasn't over yet.

41

Anton Birnbaum; 1607

With a shaking hand, Anton Birnbaum poured miserly portions of aged Sandeman port for himself and for Caitlin Dillon.

Suddenly, he felt at least a thousand years old. He had a piercing headache from his recent sleeplessness and hyperactive mental activity. Now, in the thin daylight that streaked his apartment, he went to the window and peered into the streets of his beloved New York. *What in hell was happening out there?*

Caitlin Dillon, whose head also reeled from the hours of intense concentration without sleep, took a cigarette from her purse and started to light it. Then she changed her mind. Her throat was raw and there was a heavy pressure behind her eyes. What she needed, she knew, was a long sleep. Both she and Birnbaum were waiting for final news of Green Band, news from Carroll. Caitlin now understood what it was like to be a policeman's wife. She didn't know how those women could bear it.

"We know *some* of what we need to know," Birnbaum said. "Two years ago, in Tripoli, François Monserrat met with important leaders from the Third World. In particular, he met key leaders from the Middle Eastern, oil-producing countries. The heads of these nations' military forces were in attendance there as well." Anton Birnbaum walked away from the apartment window.

'I'm convinced that they planned a cunning new way to disrupt the economic system of the West. Their plan called for the cartel to ultimately gain control of *the entire American Stock Market.*"

"They already had enough economic leverage to definitely influence the Market," Caitlin said quietly. Her head pounded mercilessly. Some small sadist with a jackhammer was working way back in the recesses of her skull, digging for God only knew what. She thought about Carroll, who was out there right this moment in pursuit of Green Band. Why hadn't they heard anything?

"That spring, our newly elected President learned of the frightening Tripoli plot. More important, the Committee of Twelve must have heard about 'Red Tuesday.' Only they moved much faster than President Kearney could in Washington."

The old man's eyes became as cold as fire going suddenly out. "Caitlin, I believe they created Green Band to counter the 'Red Tuesday' plot. Effectively, the Committee of Twelve has *stolen* the Arab's billions away. Green Band is the very finest of *trompe l'oeils*, the best.

"Now, they're selling them back their own funds. This has been *an economic world war*. The first of its kind – unless we include the 1970s oil embargo."

Caitlin thought that if it had been anyone other than Anton Birnbaum making these accusations, outlining these hypotheses. . . . But *it was* Birnbaum. And he was serious about everything he was proposing. . . . Why hadn't she heard from Carroll yet?

"How does Hudson fit in? What's his part in this, Anton?" Caitlin asked.

"Ah, the enigmatic Mr. Hudson." Birnbaum allowed a tight smile to cross his face. "I've given great thought to Colonel Hudson. Either he's in the pay of the Committee of Twelve . . . or they're ruthlessly *using* Hudson and his veterans group. It wouldn't be the first time, would it? It wouldn't be the first time these men were used by those who wield great power in this country. Either way, we'll know in a few hours. We'll know the truth soon, won't we?"

As he arrived at the designated address, Colonel David Hudson felt exactly the way he'd always known he would – *if they had won in Viet Nam*. The adrenaline, the magical excitement of victory, was pumping, rushing furiously through his body.

This would certainly be the most unusual safe house he'd ever used, Hudson thought as he reached York Avenue on Manhattan's fashionable East Side. He finally entered an elegant glass-and-grillwork doorway just beyond the corner at 90th Street.

Billie Bogan's apartment was located on the river side of the starkly modern building, a building which apparently had paper-thin ceilings and walls, because Hudson could hear a piano playing as he approached the doorway on the fifteenth floor.

The lovely music surprised him. He hadn't even known that Billie played.

David Hudson hesitated before pushing the doorbell. *Warning alarms*, his usual alert signals were going off again. It was all perfectly natural. One didn't stop being a military terrorist and saboteur overnight.

Billie answered the door seconds after the first ring. She was wearing a pink T-shirt that said *winter* across her chest. She had on tight black French jeans, no shoes or socks. She looked stunning and exotic, even now.

"David."

Her brilliant blue eyes passed from the slightest puzzlement to undisguised pleasure as she saw who it was at the door. She wore no makeup; she didn't need it.

She reached out and pulled Hudson in toward her. She held him tightly in the doorway. David Hudson ached to have his arm back – to hold her in both arms just this once.

"Was that you playing the piano?" he asked.

Billie pecked at his cheek and gave him an extra hug. "Of course it was me. . . . You know, I think the piano is the reason I ultimately escaped from Birmingham. As I found out about Mozart, Brahms, Beethoven, I was convinced there had to be more than the dreary dullness I was used to. Come inside. I'm so happy to see you. It's so *good* to see you." She kissed him again.

David Hudson smiled more willingly than he had in a long time. "I'm happy to see you. I feel like I'm home at last," he said.

Once inside, they talked. They held one another. They stared into one another's eyes for a long time. Hudson told Billie about his past, talking with the speed of a man who has observed vows of silence for too many years. It all came tumbling out – West Point, the horrors of Viet Nam, his early, abortive career in the Army.

David Hudson told her everything, except about the past year, which he was tempted to tell her as well. How his brilliant revenge had become his sweet victory. A material reward – millions of dollars for himself and the other Vets. He wished he could share it with her, share everything right now.

Under the tent of a brightly striped wool blanket, with the windows thrown half open, they made love once and then again. Hudson was still learning to feel, and the vigorous lovemaking helped enormously. She brought him closer and closer to climax . . . right to the delicious edge. He just couldn't make it over. Then the most debilitating wave of exhaustion swept over David Hudson.

He felt shaky. Then he was sliding headlong toward a tranquil dream state. The warning alarms still hadn't completely stopped. The warning alarms almost seemed a natural part of him, now.

One moment he was softly stroking Billie's thick blond hair, touching the elegant oval of her face. The next, he was apparently falling into sleep. His eyes gently closed shut.

Billie lay awake in the large brass bed, watching the ember glow on a filtered American cigarette. She sighed quietly, blowing smoke between lightly touching teeth.

375

Sometimes she surprised even herself with her ability to effortlessly create a lie, *in perfect context*, consistent with a whole world of other lies. . . . Deception.

Her being able to play Chopin, and fitting that so naturally into the Birmingham, England, framework, was an inspiration. But then again, wasn't that precisely why she was here with the great Colonel David Hudson?

She rose silently from the double bed, tossing off rumpled designer sheets. She was certain it would be a miracle to wake Colonel Hudson with a cannon.

She returned to the bedroom with something close to that: a Beretta with a blunt-nosed silencer attached.

She knew better than to hesitate for even a fraction of a second. She swung both of her arms up stiffly. She moved to fire the revolver into his lightly pulsing temple, just below the blond hairline. *Then*, she hesitated.

The sleeping body went rigid and suddenly jumped forward. Colonel David Hudson's eyes blinked open and he fired through the bedsheets. He fired again and again and again.

Warning signals were shrieking in his head. Sirens of terrible pain screamed out at David Hudson.

Deception – *forever*, deception.

Horrifying deception everywhere he turned. Even *here*.

The Committee of Twelve, the American Wise Men – there was no way they could have let him live once Green Band had ended. They had easily recruited him after the disappointments of Viet Nam, the disappointment in knowing his early promise in the Army could never be realized. He'd been their *agent provocateur* for crises around the world. They had been so attractively intelligent, every bit as smart, as precise as he was. They'd sent the girl, of course, his *escort*. They'd known about Vintage, about all his habits. They'd *used* him so well.

Finally, Colonel David Hudson understood Green Band himself.

42

Carroll; 1625

Carroll slowly opened his eyes and painfully pushed himself into a sitting position. All around him were startling crashing sounds, police and U.S. Army personnel, blinding bright lights, flashing, running shapes. There was more chaos and confusion than before on the rooftop.

Faces peered down at him. New York cops, a physician? There were others he couldn't place right now. The images registered sporadically.

"What happened?" Carroll finally asked. "How long have.... *What happened to the body that was up here? A body was over there!*"

The body of Walter Trentkamp had been near the water tower – except there wasn't any body there now ...

A uniformed New York cop knelt down alongside him. Carroll had never seen the man before. "What other body are you talking about?"

Arch Carroll rotated his head so he could see all the way around the rooftop. "There was a body there, over near the Cobra. Walter Trentkamp of the FBI was killed right over there."

The policeman shook his head. "I was one of the first up here on the roof. There wasn't any other body. You know, you've got a small watermelon growing up on top of your head. You *sure* you're all right?"

Carroll clumsily pushed himself to his feet, then he nearly fell back to the suddenly spinning cement. "Oh, yeah, I'm fine. Tip-top shape."

Arch Carroll's eyes were watering badly. His body wasn't his own. Using bricks in the wall for handholds,

377

he started down the metal stairs winding away from the roof.

Somebody had taken Walter Trentkamp's body away.

The cop called after him, "Hey, buddy, you ought to get yourself treated! Have somebody look at your head. There wasn't any body up here."

Carroll hardly heard the policeman's last words.

Suddenly he had a different priority in mind: *he wanted to go home.* He needed to go home right away.

Carroll thought about his kids and about Caitlin.

He thought about Caitlin's meeting with Anton Birnbaum and wondered what might have transpired there. He was worried about the people he loved. . . . *There wasn't any body up here on the roof. . . . Sure thing – this was all a dream, a horrible nightmare.*

He had no clue how he managed the first wild minutes of the drive to Riverdale. Maybe it was practice – all those half-drunken nights of his recent past. Maybe God *did* look after babies and drunks. But there was a time coming when God might abdicate his responsibilities, all his watchfulness . . .

And what then?

The Carrolls; 1730

The familiar lights of the old house in Riverdale were glittering brightly. As he drove up his street, Carroll remembered a time when his father and mother would have been there, a time when everything had seemed so much saner in America . . . when Trentkamp was Uncle Walter for God's sake.

Walter Trentkamp had been his father's friend for all those incredible years. Had his father ever begun to guess anything? Had his father ever sensed the horrifying betrayal coming from Trentkamp? We had all been so naive about foreign governments back then. About our own government as it was turning out. Americans thought of democracy as the world's one superior political system. We felt that we

378

understood the parameters of our government's power. We understood *nothing*, Carroll now saw.

Trentkamp and the KGB had been so brilliant at fooling everyone around him. Walter Trentkamp had been so confident, he hadn't hesitated at using Carroll himself. What better conduit for information? Walter's hubris was startling, but his modus was consistent at least. As Carroll thought back now, he remembered that Walter had spent time in Europe after World War II. He recalled "fact-finding" trips to South America, to Mexico, to Southeast Asia while Carroll had been serving there himself. It was no wonder they had never been able to identify Monserrat. *They hadn't been looking in the right places.*

No one had thought to look right there in New York or Washington. No one had begun to suspect the living legend, Walter Trentkamp. And Trentkamp had obviously *known* that they wouldn't. His confidence was galling. He had no fear or respect for American Intelligence, and he had been absolutely right not to. His ruse, the classic misdirection, had been perfect – the life-work of a master spy, this past decade's Donald McLean or Kim Philby.

Suddenly, Arch Carroll's eyes were watering again – only now it was because he was so glad to see his kids. They all jumped up and ran to him as he stumbled inside the house. Then the Carroll family was hugging and kissing. They were squeezing their father as tightly as they could.

"We have to get out of here," Carroll whispered to Mary Katherine as the two of them got to hold one another. "We have to move out of the house now. . . . Help me dress them. Try to explain as little as you can. I have to call Caitlin."

Mary Katherine nodded. She didn't even seem that surprised at the news. "You go call Caitlin now. I'll outfit the troops."

Two hours later, the Carrolls, the family of six plus Caitlin Dillon, quietly checked into the Durham Hotel on West 87th Street in Manhattan.

Carroll's initial plan was to stay there for a night, maybe a few nights, until they could decide how to work with Anton Birnbaum, how to work with the New York police, whoever they could trust right now. Life was sudddenly full of treacherous false bottoms. Carroll didn't want another one to suddenly fall out. He wouldn't let it happen.

Once they were alone together in the West Side hotel, Caitlin and Carroll fell into an embrace. They shared a long, tender kiss which neither of them wanted to end. Caitlin pushed against Archer Carroll with a fierce, undisguised need. There was no more reason to hide anything, to hold back her feelings.

"I love you so much." She locked her eyes into Carroll's strong gaze.

"I love you, Caitlin. I was afraid today. I thought . . . that I might never see you again."

They made love in the hotel room, and it was all passion, definitely not Lima, Ohio. When they did it a second time, Caitlin and Carroll gently held hands – almost as if they might never do this beautiful thing again.

"I hated it when you were out there after them," Caitlin finally whispered as she lay beside Carroll. Her breath was like feathers on his cheekbone. "I've never felt so alone and afraid. I don't want to feel that way again."

Carroll brushed individual strands of hair away from her face. She was so unbelievably precious to him. "I told Walter Trentkamp that I planned to quit once Green Band was over. I haven't changed my mind."

Caitlin stared deeply into his eyes. "There's a catch, though."

"Yes, there's one catch. Green Band isn't over yet."

There was so much terrifying evidence to be considered and carefully studied. There were classified files from the FBI and Pentagon; there were also taped statements from Birnbaum's highly placed contacts in Washington and Europe . . .

. . . They just had to get to the right people with what they knew, with the truth.

Who were the right people, though? Whom could they definitely trust now? The New York Times? The Washington Post? "Sixty Minutes?" The New York police? The CIA?

The Committee of Twelve seemed to be everywhere. Were they connected with the police, the CIA? Did they somehow control the newspapers and TV?

Whom could they go to with the truth?

Whom could they trust now?

The feeling of helplessness was unbelievably shitty.

The paranoia was so strong. And so very real.

During the first brutalizing hours in the hotel, Carroll and Caitlin read every major newspaper report. Twice that afternoon, Carroll took cabs to the large out-of-town newspaper stand in Times Square. He and Caitlin read and reread everything written about Green Band. They desperately searched for a faint shadow of what they knew to be the truth.

There was none that they could find. *Nothing* had been reported about secret intragovernment groups. *Nothing* had been reported about a terror plan called "Red Tuesday." Or about the whereabouts of Walter Trentkamp. Had the body been spirited away by the Twelve? . . . Nothing was said about Colonel David Hudson's Special Forces training at Fort Bragg, North Carolina. In the news, Colonel Hudson was described as a "Jackal-like *provocateur*," the renegade mastermind of Green Band. Hudson was depicted as an obsessed man still looking for some justice, some personal meaning, years after Viet Nam . . .

It all sounded so plausible and right, if you didn't know any better.

The Durham Hotel; 0600

Early the morning of December 21, Caitlin and Carroll had some visitors at the hotel. The visitors were Anton

381

Birnbaum and Samantha Hawes, the FBI researcher who had helped Carroll in Washington. They met in another room on the same floor as the Carroll suite.

The best and the worst part of the Green Band investigation had begun. The tension and pressure were even more relentless than before. Carroll's stomach had been doing an uncomfortable dance of panic for the past twenty-four hours.

A working picture of Green Band was finally emerging. If not a complete portrait, it was at least an outline, a foreshadowing of the truth. The story was certainly different from anything reported in the newspapers or on TV.

"The Twelve, the American Wise Men, are descended from our own OSS, America's intelligence team during World War II," Anton Birnbaum said in a voice that seemed to grow weaker each day. "The route is serpentine, but it can be followed. . . . The existence of the Twelve goes back to the elder Dulles, his reluctance to surrender his wartime intelligence machine over to the politicians in 1940s Washington. When the OSS was transformed into the CIA, the Twelve began to meet *outside* official circles. They were still probably the most powerful men in Washington. At first they gave counsel, then they took things into their own able hands. . . . The original OSS was probably the best American intelligence unit ever.

"The Twelve still smugly believe they are the elite. They're *convinced* they are doing the country a grand service, guiding us through the Cuban Missile threat, the time of the assassinations, Watergate, now Green Band. Every year, each decade, they become more and more powerful."

Birnbaum was looking pale and brittle. At the outset of the morning, he'd told Caitlin that he was fearful of a heart attack or stroke if he continued at this pace. "The Red Tuesday plot could have incited another Market crash, the worst since 1929. Green Band worked to stop that, at least. Of course the Committee members also managed to profit from the results. The companies they control have already made hundreds of millions of dollars."

Samantha Hawes spoke after Birnbaum. She had information about Colonel Hudson. She'd managed to retrieve some of the missing Vets files during the past few days.

"David Hudson was approached by at least one Committee member when he was still in the Army, while he was at Fort Bragg after Viet Nam," she told the others. "General Lucas Thompson, his old commander, approached Hudson first. General Thompson knew everything about Hudson's POW experiences. He knew about Hudson's training at Fort Bragg, too. Army Intelligence had prepared Hudson to be their Juan Carlos. They backed off when Hudson lost his arm. Well, *the Committee* had plenty of uses for Colonel Hudson and his special skills. . . . Another interesting note – Philip Berger of the CIA ran Hudson's original commando training at Fort Bragg. Several Committee members have spoken at veteran affairs over the past few years. The connections are there, the manipulation is feasible. The Committee needed a paramilitary group, and they used David Hudson."

Carroll had read the missing FBI and Pentagon files which Samantha Hawes had brought with her. "Hudson was given a lot of help with Green Band, probably more than he needed. The help came in the form of Wall Street information, and precise tips about what we were doing inside Number 13. That's why he was able to play so many cat-and-mouse games. He also had Pentagon files on all the potential candidates for Vets. As it turned out, Hudson chose men who'd served with him in Viet Nam. The Committee promised him millions as a reward once Green Band was ended."

"Yes, only half the Vets are dead now," Birnbaum spoke up. "The rest are missing. Colonel Hudson is missing. Where is David Hudson now, I wonder?"

Caitlin had been unusually quiet for most of the

session. She had retrieved the necessary financial backup information. She was still angry. She felt *used* by this grandiose *Committee* which believed it was above the government, above laws.

"We're beginning to make progress," Caitlin finally spoke in a quiet, businesslike manner. "But we are still faced with an overwhelming problem. Who do we trust beyond the people right here in this room? Do we take our information to the newspapers? Do we go to the Director of the FBI, Samantha? Who can we tell this story to?"

There was silence in the hotel room. They were all beginning to understand the frightening power that was in the grasp of a select few. They were beginning to understand the real political system. The question remaining was so simple, yet so impossibly complex – *who could they trust with the truth?*

The cover-up was almost as clever and masterful as the Green Band plot itself. The cover-up was brilliantly executed.

For another twenty-four hours on December 22, the Carrolls managed to live in cramped quarters in the West Side hotel. So far, they had no other choice to consider. *Whom could they trust?*

Late at night, Carroll and Caitlin stayed in the smaller of the two bedrooms. They lay in each other's arms, passing the long, eerie hours exploring each other's bodies. They were realistic enough to know that something nightmarish might still happen – that they might never be together like this again.

"Hudson said something up on the rooftop in Brooklyn," Carroll whispered as he stroked Caitlin's hair. "He said that he loved his country. You know, I still feel that way myself. I almost feel closer to Hudson than to any of the others."

Caitlin nodded in the tingling darkness.

Her eyes were stinging when she finally whispered to Carroll, "I feel so *angry* at whoever was deceiving all of us, at the ones who've lied and misled us *all these years*. We've lived with so many awful lies."

When Caitlin and Carroll made love again that night, it was more tender than it had ever been. They fell asleep holding each other, like children allowed to sleep together during a storm.

At 6:00 o'clock on December 23, Caitlin found that she couldn't sleep anymore. She finally pushed herself up in bed.

When she switched on a tiny portable radio, Caitlin heard absolutely the last thing she wanted to hear in all the world. Caitlin heard the news that finally broke her heart.

"*. . . advisor to several U.S. Presidents, Anton Birnbaum, was killed on Riverside Drive near his home in Manhattan early today. The elderly, still-active statesman was struck in late-night traffic by an unidentified hit-and-run driver . . . Anton Birnbaum was eighty-three years old at the time of his death.*"

Caitlin shook Carroll's shoulder until he mumbled in his sleep and finally blinked awake. In a voice that was trembling, racked by sobs, she began to tell him what had happened.

"Oh, Arch, they killed him. The Committee killed Anton this morning. *They killed him as if he was nothing.* What's happening now? What's going to happen? Oh, poor Anton."

Carroll shivered as he got up from bed. He dressed, then hurried down to Broadway, where he bought the *Daily News, The New York Times*, the *New York Post*.

All the front-page stories about Anton Birnbaum contained respectful eulogies. They also contained substantial, what Carroll could only take to be purposeful, lies. At best, the newspapers revealed a frighteningly small fragment of the truth.

At the news kiosk, Carroll read the articles with cold, trembling fingers. It was as if nothing real had ever happened. There was no high-placed traitor in the FBI. There was no Monserrat, no mention of the whereabouts of Colonel David Hudson.

That same awful morning, trudging back to the hotel from Broadway, Carroll saw the two men following him.

There was no way anyone connected with Green Band could live.

43

The Carroll Family; 2330

Escape. It was the only possibility that remained.

On the night of December 23, Arch Carroll, Caitlin Dillon, the four Carroll children, and Mary Katherine tightly locked hands. They walked rapidly down Columbus Avenue. There had to be some way for three adults and four small children to escape a surveillance team. So far, Carroll had found none. But the New York crowds would provide temporary safety.

Columbus Avenue was still buzzing with holiday music and a festive bustle at night. The energetic crowd – every other person holding a bright Christmas bundle, a tree, a special Lincoln Center program – parted reluctantly for the hurrying family.

It wasn't like any Christmas that Carroll had ever known before – it was as if a terrible, unfathomable darkness lurked in the shadows between the bright lights and the fir trees. Caitlin, Mary K., the kids – how could he shield them when he felt that some unknown, professional gunman lingered in every doorway?

"Can we please stop running, Daddy? Please?" A tiny voice trailed after Carroll, echoing thinly inside the symphony of the New York City street noise. The bizarre cacophony of Christmas sounds wouldn't stop, wouldn't let up for a moment of relief. Why did he think it would?

Four-year-old Lizzie was dragging herself along on the hem of his sports coat. "Please, Daddy. Just for a minute? Please?" Up ahead of them, Caitlin and Mary Katherine had the three other children in tow. They were bravely hurrying the children forward.

387

Carroll finally stopped and stooped to wrap his arms around his little girl. He whispered soothingly against Lizzie's chilled, red-rimmed ear. "Please, baby, please be good. Just a little longer, sweetheart."

Carroll immediately straightened again. It was so infinitely sad – what he was almost certain was going to happen next. It was so unfair, so tragic. He had reached the most hollow place of his existence, a terrible numbness hung around his heart.

He gazed due north, then down the bright lights of Columbus Avenue. His weary eyes brushed over colorful signs that said Sedutto's, Dianne's, Pershings, La Cantina.

Columbus Avenue had changed dramatically since he'd last been above 72nd Street. The area had once been crowded with Spanish food stores as well as transient hotels, and oriental rug dealers. Now it was a trendy, self-conscious version of Greenwich Village.

Carroll reflexively glanced over his shoulder again. The same persistent pair of men was still following. Now, though, there were more than two of them. There were as many as five men following the Carroll family.

And they were much closer – no more than half a city block away. He could actually see lines of sweat running down their faces. He thought he sensed their powerful frustration, the difficulty of their mission.

Where in the name of God do we go from here? Somebody help us, he thought to himself.

The back of Carroll's neck was soaking wet, even in the chill air. His skin, his dark brown hair, was plastered against his shirt collar.

He was so listless and hopelessly tired. He felt he could lay down on a parked car, sleep right there in the middle of crowded Columbus Avenue.

The passersby looked so preoccupied, so self-interested and city cool. Would any of them help?

Carroll's mind was silently screaming, pleading for some form of reason to finally prevail.

388

This is happening, he thought. Whether I choose to believe it or not, this is happening.

Escape was the only reality he could allow.

He had one idea, a kind of desperate prayer, which he didn't think could work. His mind was close to bursting. There was nothing left but rage, the constant, maddening stab of fear. He could see the same emotion pressed onto Caitlin's face. As for Mary Katherine, her face looked blank. All its usual ruddy color was gone.

He reached out suddenly for Caitlin. He tightly held her narrow shoulders. "Listen to me. Listen closely." He whispered something *hopeful*, something so innocent it started tears in her soft brown eyes. "I love you so much, Caitlin. Everything *has* to be all right."

"Oh, Arch, why now? Why now?"

Then Carroll gently pushed her away. He sent Caitlin and his sister and the tangle of children in the opposite direction. *Up* 72nd Street. Away, far away from him.

"I'm going down Columbus! Take them! Take them away, please! Caitlin! Take them now!"

"Daaa-ddy! . . . Daa-ddy!"

The final thing Carroll heard was his babies' cries as he raced away.

As he put his head down hard, chin into his heaving chest.

As he started to run as fast as he could along the clogged sidewalk.

Suddenly, powerful arms grabbed him, wrenched him to a spinning stop. A hand clamped down hard, twisting into his face. Searing pain ripped through Carroll's eyes.

His mind was racing: *they were attacking him in the middle of New York City, in one of the most crowded, residential areas of the city. They had come for him in full view of a hundred witnesses . . .*

They didn't even care about witnesses anymore.

"Get the hell off me! Get off me, you pieces of shit!" Carroll's shouts rose like fighting kites above the honking horns, above the city's deafening street rumble. "Somebody, please help!"

They were giving him a needle! Some kind of long, terrifying needle pierced through his trousers into his leg.

They were giving it to him right out here in the open. Right on West 70th Street in New York City.

"Somebody help! Somebody fucking help!"

There were obviously no secrets anymore. There was no bullshit pretense that this was a police bust, that they were New York detectives.

"Get off! . . . no needle . . . nooooo!"

Arch Carroll roared his last words savagely. He screamed and he fought back. He clawed at them with his remaining strength. He broke a jaw with a short, powerful punch. His elbow smashed hard into a forehead. A bone snapped loudly. His?

Everything was unreal. Everything was impossible to comprehend, or slow down even a fraction. Carroll was being dragged into a dark blue sedan. *He was being held upside down!*

He looked back as they pulled him off Columbus Avenue, out of the staring crowds.

As he was hanging upside down, he saw the second car arrive!

He saw Caitlin and his sister and the kids being snatched away.

"*Not the kids!* You goddamned bastards! Not my kids, not my kids! . . . No, *please*, not my kids!"

No one connected with Green Band could live. The Committee, the American Wise Men, couldn't allow that.

44

Vice-president Thomas More Elliot

Thomas More Elliot's palms were unpleasantly dry and cold. He suppressed a nervous tic which was starting to pulse in his throat. He finally stepped out of the dark blue stretch limousine and into the chill Virginia winter air. Dead trees hung against the gray skyline and in the distance there were the gunshots of bird hunters.

He turned and walked up the fieldstone steps that led to the large double doors of an imposing, thirty-room country house. He paused at the top of the steps and sucked air deeply into his lungs.

Inside, the cavernous front hall was badly overheated. He felt a trickle of sweat run along his collar with the stealth of an insect. His footsteps echoed on marble as he crossed to a great curving flight of stairs that led upward to the floors above. It was not a house that Thomas More Elliot enjoyed. Its very size, but more, its recent history made him uncomfortable.

When he reached the landing he came to a door ornately carved out of walnut. It shone so deeply from years of meticulous care that he could see his own indistinct reflection in the wood.

He opened the door and entered the room beyond.

A group of men sat around a long, polished oak table. They were dressed mostly in dark business suits. Some of them, including General Lucas Thompson, were retired military and naval commanders. Some actively ran large multinational corporations. Others were influential bankers, landowners, proprietors of TV stations and highly respected newspapers.

391

The man at the top of the table, a retired admiral whose bald head shone in the room like a bone, waved one hand at the Vice-president. "Sit down, Thomas. Sit. Please."

The Vice-president sat down.

The Admiral smiled and it wasn't an expression of mirth. There was an immediate silence in the room.

"A year ago," the Admiral said, "we met in this very room. Our mood that day was one of some agitation . . ."

There was a polite ripple of laughter. Self-satisfied laughter spread around the formal library table.

"We debated, I'm sure we all remember, the complex problem posed by the so-called Red Tuesday plan, the plan hatched – if that's the word – by the oil-producing nations in Tripoli. . . . There were rather heated arguments that day."

The Admiral smiled. Thomas Elliot thought he resembled a rather smug school principal on award day at a private academy.

"On that day we reached a decision – unanimous finally – to create what we called Green Band. I believe the name was something I suggested myself, a name with both financial and military connotations."

A bird appeared against the casement window of the room, a bleak little sparrow that briefly looked in, then hopped off into the late afternoon light.

The Admiral continued in sanctimonious tones, "We are here today to confirm that the paramilitary operation called Green Band was a success. We created *temporary* panic in the economic system. A panic we were able to control. We took hundreds of millions of dollars back from the oil-producing cartel.

"We brilliantly usurped the terrorist plan known as Red Tuesday. The world will find Jimmy Hoffa before they locate the body of François Monserrat. . . . And with the destruction of Green Band, the inevitable death of our volatile associate, Colonel Hudson, the file should be closed on this unfortunate episode in our history. . . . We are making *every* effort to make certain that it is."

Thomas Elliot shifted his body in his chair. The

atmosphere in the large room was changing subtly. The men were beginning to loosen up, to move toward as celebratory an atmosphere as they might ever aspire to – which meant muted, quiet and, most of all, tasteful.

The Admiral said, "In approximately two weeks, Justin Kearney will dramatically resign his presidency. . . . He will be remembered chiefly as a scapegoat for the economic near-tragedy. . . . More importantly, though – " and here all eyes in the room turned toward Thomas More Elliot – "Thomas Elliot will ascend to that office . . ."

There was an outbreak of mild applause. Elliot looked around at the eleven men in the room. His own presence brought the number to an even dozen.

The twelve men who effectively ran America, the Twelve American Wise Men.

"Later," said the Admiral, "there will be champagne and cigars. For the moment, Thomas, our dry congratulations to you. . . . And I think to everyone in this room . . ."

The Admiral looked reflective for a moment.

"In a few weeks, for the first time, one of us will occupy the highest office in the land. And that means our control is tighter, more sure than ever before . . ." The Admiral looked down at the white hair on the back of his hands. "Which means we will no longer need to contend with a President who doesn't think the way we do . . . someone who imagines his power is independent of what we bestow."

Thomas More Elliot stared off into the gray light that lay against the window. He blinked his pale eyes twice.

He licked his lips, which had become suddenly dry. He opened his mouth and his throat felt parched. He reached for the water pitcher on the table and poured himself a glass.

He realized that he was about to say something that would not contribute to the general mood of contentment within the room. But that couldn't be helped. He didn't like the prospect, but somebody had to deliver the news.

He adjusted the cuffs of his shirt and said, "I have heard from our people in New York City."

Eleven heads swiveled toward him.

"A man called Archer Carroll is in police custody there."

A silent pause came to the Virginia conference room with all the suddenness of a stilled pulse.

"It is my information that he is talking. . . . That he's telling his story to anyone who will listen. . . . And that certain media representatives are paying very close attention."

The silence was a long, unhappy thing.

Thomas More Elliot sipped his tepid water.

"What does he know?" the Admiral asked eventually.

"Everything," the Vice-president said.

45

The NYPD

New York Police Sergeant Joe Macchio and Patrolman Jeanne McGuiness were rolling out of the wooded 72nd Street transverse through Central Park when they spotted a scene they wished they hadn't spotted, especially not so close to the end of their 4:00 to 12:00 o'clock night shift.

"This is Car One-three-eight. Please give me *immediate assistance* at Seventy-second Street and Central Park West!" Patrolman Jeanne McGuiness, a tall skinny woman with an impassive face, was already speaking into the patrol car radio. The red police bubble on top of their cruiser had begun to revolve slowly.

Up ahead on 72nd Street, traveling at maybe fifty or fifty-five miles per hour, was a dark blue Lincoln. That *wasn't* the problem.

The problem was some suicidal or homicidal maniac trying to wiggle out of the shattered back-seat window of the Lincoln. He had his torso halfway out. The only thing holding him inside were two other men. They looked as if they were trying to land an ocean-sized fish in the speeding vehicle.

"Look! Look there! The second car behind!" Patrolman McGuiness pointed straight ahead. Inside the second car, children, a host of screaming kids, seemed to be fighting and struggling *to get out.*

"Godfuckingdamnit!" Joe Macchio growled even louder. He had been dreaming of Christmas Day and something of the peaceful spirit had created a glow inside him. Now all that was instantly gone.

Sergeant Macchio and Patrolman McGuiness left their police cruiser with revolvers drawn. They cautiously approached the two sedans, now stopped against the southwest corner of 72nd. Other police blue and whites, sirens screaming, were already racing up 72nd from the direction of Broadway.

"We're Federal agents." A man in a dark business suit burst out of the lead sedan. He was confidently holding out a portfolio wallet and an offical-looking badge.

"I don't care if you're the Commander-in-Chief of the United States Army," Sergeant Macchio croaked in his most convincing street-cop voice. "What the hell's going on here? Who the hell's this guy? Why are all these kids screaming like somebody's being murdered?"

A second dark-suited man stepped out of the trailing sedan. "I'm Michael Kenyon of the CIA, officer." He said it calmly, but authoritatively. "I think I can explain this whole thing."

Carroll was still half in, half out of the back window of the lead sedan. He was groggy, almost out on his feet. He hollered at the two New York City police officers. "Hey! Please!" His speech was slurred. "My kids. . . . They're in danger . . . I'm a Federal officer . . ."

Sergeant Joe Macchio couldn't help himself – he finally started to laugh. "Not that I think this is funny, pal. *You're* a Federal officer?"

Ten minutes later, the situation wasn't any closer to being solved. Several more police blue and whites had arrived. So had cars from the New York FBI and more from the CIA. There was a buzzing cluster of police officials on 72nd Street.

Two EMS ambulances had pulled up, but Caitlin and Mary Katherine wouldn't let them take Carroll to Roosevelt Hospital, *or any place else without them.*

Caitlin was yelling at the New York policeman, telling them that she and Carroll were part of the Green Band investigation team. She had proof in her pocketbook.

The CIA agents had lots of impressive proof that they were who they said they were. The arguing continued on the corner of 72nd Street, getting more heated with every passing moment. It began to draw a curious New York sidewalk crowd.

Mickey Kevin Carroll finally sidled up to Sergeant Joe Macchio, who had walked off to try to think the whole crazy thing out.

"Can I see your hat?" Mickey Kevin asked. "My dad's a policeman. He doesn't get to wear a hat."

Joe Macchio looked down at the small boy, and finally offered a tired smile. "And which one *is* your dad?" he asked. "Is your dad here now?"

"*That's* my dad." Mickey Kevin pointed at the man peacefully slumped, seemingly sleeping on an EMS litter-cot, looking like Crusader Rabbit one final time.

"He's a policeman, son?"

"Yes, sir."

Well, that settled it for Sergeant Macchio – because the alleged CIA agents were claiming that the other man *definitely wasn't* a police officer. "That's what I needed to know, son. That's what I needed to know for *starters*, anyway."

NYPD Sergeant Macchio stooped down and handed Mickey Kevin Carroll his hat. Then he hastily walked in the direction of the disturbance that had closed down 72nd Street, not to mention the downtown lanes of Central Park West, and the park transverse.

"Tell you what we're gonna do, eh!" Sergeant Macchio clapped his hands for a little old-fashioned order and attention. "We're gonna sort this all out *down at the station house!*"

At that news, the entire Carroll family started to do a very odd thing, at least Sergeant Macchio and the rest of the New York cops thought it was peculiar. The kids started to balls-out cheer and clap for the NYPD.

The New York cops weren't used to that. A couple of the older patrolmen even started to blush. They'd almost never been treated like the arriving cavalry before, like the good guys in the white hats.

"All right, *all right* now! Everybody pile into the

397

wagons. Let's get this show on the road. See who's been naughty and nice, eh?"

Photographs of the scene were snapped by somebody from *The New York Times*, also by a free-lance photojournalist who lived across 72nd Street in the Dakota. A shot of Mickey Kevin wearing Sergeant Macchio's hat was featured in *Newsweek* magazine.

Eventually, the *Newsweek* shot of Mickey Kevin appeared framed on the Carroll's Riverdale house mantel. . . . Lizzie, Mary III, and Clancy all loudly complained about favoritism. Arch told them to shut their yaps, they were all family, weren't they?

They truly were family.

46

A direct line to the President of the United States signaled through at 0600 on the morning of March 7. Clustered inside the Oval Office were most of the members of the National Security Council. Not one of the high-ranking officials could believe what was happening now.

A prerecorded message came over the telephone wire.

"The White House is scheduled to be firebombed this morning, in a matter of a few minutes. . . . This decision is irrevocable. This decision is nonnegotiable.

"You are to evacuate the White House immediately. Evacuate the White House right now."

Inside the telephone kiosk less than a mile from the White House, Colonel David Hudson pushed down the recording machine's stop button. He stuffed the compact recorder into the pocket of his Army fatigue jacket. David Hudson was actually smiling. For the briefest moment, Hudson laughed out loud.

All of Washington waited, but the White House was never struck that morning. Instead, the home of General Lucas Thompson was firebombed. So was the home of Vice-president Elliot, the homes of Admiral Thomas Penny, of Philip Berger, of Lawrence Guthrie . . . twelve homes in all.

David Hudson finally climbed into a nondescript, light green touring van. He drove west out of the serene and strikingly lovely capital city. For a moment, at least, no more nightmare voices screeched inside his head. His

arm had stopped aching – the arm that was no longer there.

Finally, an end to deception.

1985 – New York – London – Los Angeles

BLACK MARKET

HIDE AND SEEK

For Carole Anne, Isabelle Anne, and Mary Ellen:
the mothers of invention

HIDE AND SEEK

I

I LAY WITHOUT MOVING in the low, narrow crawl space under the front porch of our home near West Point. My face was pressed tightly against the brutally cold, frozen ground littered with dry leaves and scratchy brambles. I knew I was going to die soon, and so was my baby girl. The words from a song, Crosby, Stills, and Nash — *"Our house is a very, very, very fine house"* — played in my mind.

"Don't cry . . . oh please don't cry," I whispered into my baby's ear.

There was *no way out* — no escape from here, at least not carrying the baby. I was smart, and I'd thought of every possible escape route. *None of them would work.*

Phillip was going to kill us when he found our hiding place. I couldn't let him. I just didn't know how I could stop it. I kept my hand lightly over Jennie's mouth. "You musn't make a sound, sweetheart. I love you. You musn't make a sound."

I could hear Phillip raging above us inside the house. *Our house.* He was rampaging from floor to floor, ransacking rooms, overturning furniture. Angry. Relentless. Absolutely crazy.

Worse than he'd ever been. It was cocaine this time, but really it was life that Phillip couldn't handle very well.

"Come out, come out, wherever you are, Maggie . . . come out, Maggie and Jennie . . . *it's only Daddy*. Daddy's going to find you anyway," Phillip screamed over and over until he was hoarse. "Come out, come out, Maggie . . . game's over.

"Maggie, *I command you* to come out wherever the hell you're hiding, you disobedient little bitch."

I lay shivering under the old sagging porch. My teeth were chattering again. *This couldn't be happening. It was unthinkable.* I gently held my little girl, who had wet her pants. "You musn't cry, Jennie. Please don't cry. Don't cry. You're such a good little girl. I love you so much."

Jennie nodded, and stared into my eyes. I wished that this were a nightmare. That it would go away. But it wasn't a bad dream. This was as real as my mother's fatal heart attack when I was thirteen years old and the only one home. This was even worse.

I could hear my husband, *my husband,* stomping up and down the stairs of the house. He was still screaming . . . hadn't stopped screaming for over an hour. Pounding his fist against the walls. *Captain Phillip Bradford. Math instructor at the Academy. Officer and gentleman.* That was what everyone believed, what they wanted to believe, what I had believed myself.

The hour stretched to two hours.

Then to three hours in the pitch-black, freezing-cold crawl space — in this living hell.

Mercifully, Jennie had finally fallen asleep. I held her to my chest, tried to keep her warm. I wanted to sleep myself, give up the fight, but I knew I musn't do that. It was very early in the morning. One of Phillip's witching hours — maybe three A.M.? Maybe four?

I heard the front door slam like a clap of thunder in the night. Loud footsteps exploded on the porch just over my head.

4

Jennie woke up. "*Shhh*," I whispered. "*Shhh.*"

"Maggie! I know you're here. *I know it!* I'm not a stupid man. There's nowhere to run to."

"*Daddy . . . Daddy!*" Jennie cried out, the way she had so many times in the safety of her crib.

A flashlight suddenly shone under the porch. Bright, terrifying light blinded me. A thousand sharp splinters in my eyes.

"*Peekaboo! There you are!* There's Jennie and Maggie. There's my two girls," Phillip shouted in triumph. His voice was so hoarse and raw, it was nearly unrecognizable. I could almost make myself believe that this insane man *wasn't* my husband. How could he be?

Two deafening shots came from his gun. He fired right at us. He meant to kill either Jennie or me, maybe both of us.

I had a surprise for Phillip, just this one time.

Peekaboo yourself!

I fired back.

II

SOMETIMES, I feel as though I'm wearing a horrifying scarlet letter — only the letter is *M*, for *Murderess*. I know this feeling will never completely go away and it seems so unfair. It *is* unfair. It's inhuman and indecent.

The memories are jagged and chaotic, but at the end so vivid and horrifying that they are etched into my brain. They will be with me forever.

I'll tell you all of it, sparing no one, especially myself. I know that you want to hear. I know this is a "big news story." I know what it is to be "news." *Do you have any idea?* Can you imagine yourself as a piece of news, as cold black type that everybody reads, and makes judgments about?

Area newspapers from Newburgh, Cornwall, Middletown called the first shooting the worst "family tragedy" in the history of West Point. To me, at the time, it seemed as though it had happened to someone else. Not to Jennie and me, or even to Phillip, as much as he may have deserved it.

Yet a dozen years later, after time and my own denial had clouded the events still further and made even my emotions hazy, a *second killing* has forced me to remember West Point in all of its horrible vividness.

I obsessively confront the questions that pound in my brain: Am I a murderer?

Did I kill not one, but two of my husbands?

I don't know anymore. *I don't know!* As crazy as that sounds, I honestly don't.

It gets terribly cold here — sometimes it seems as cold as it was that Christmas Eve when Phillip died. All I can do is sit in this prison cell, in torment, and wait for the trial to begin.

I decided to write it all down. I'm writing it for myself — but I'm also writing it for you. I'll tell you everything.

When you've read it, *you* decide. That's how our system works, right? A jury of my peers.

And, oh yes, I trust you. I'm a trusting person. That's probably why I'm here, in all of this terrible trouble.

BOOK ONE

STAR-CROSSED

1

More snow. Another Christmas season. Almost a year after Phillip's death — or as some would have it, *his murder.*

I sat back in the yellow cab as it bounced and plowed through the slush-filled New York streets. I was trying to put my mind in a calm place, but it wouldn't be still for me. I had promised myself I wouldn't be afraid — but I was *very* afraid.

Outside the streaked, wet taxi window, even the Salvation Army Santa Clauses looked miserable. Nobody sane or sensible was out walking today; those who were would not take their hands from their pockets to make a donation. The traffic cops looked like abandoned snowmen. The pigeons had disappeared from every windowsill and rooftop.

I glanced at my own reflection in the cab's window. Very long, blond hair, mostly with a mind of its own, but my best physical attribute, I thought. Freckles that no amount of makeup would ever cover. Nose a little out of proportion. Brown eyes that had, I knew, regained at least some of their half-forgotten sparkle. A small mouth, thickish lips — made, as Phillip joked in the happy days, for fellatio.

11

The thought of him made me shudder. The idea of sex still makes me afraid, and much worse.

It had been a year since the terrible shooting at West Point. My recovery was slow, both physically and mentally, and it wasn't complete. My leg still hurt, and my brain didn't function with the clarity I'd once taken pride in. I found myself frightened by small noises. I saw threats in nighttime streets when none existed. Previously in pretty good control of my feelings, I had lost that control. I would cry for no reason, grow angry at a neighbor's kindness, be suspicious of friends and afraid of strangers. There were times when I hated myself!

There had been an investigation, of course, but no trial. If Jennie hadn't been so badly beaten, if it had been only me with bloodied hair and a damaged leg, I might have been sent to prison that first time. But the fact that my three-year-old was injured too made our claim of self-defense more convincing.

No prosecutor wanted to take on the case, and the military academy was only too happy to have it hushed up.

Officers, it was a well-known fact, *did not attack their wives and daughters. Wives and daughters really didn't exist at the Point. We were decorative.*

So I took flight, and traveled to New York City, where I rented a two-bedroom apartment. It was a second-floor walk-up in a dreary brownstone on West Seventy-fifth Street. I located a day school for Jennie. Our lives began to move at a slower pace.

But I hadn't found what I wanted most: an end to the pain, a beginning to a new life.

I was twenty-five years old. I wore the letter M. I had taken someone's life, even if it had been in self-defense.

No guts, no glory, I urged myself on. I was definitely moving on sheer guts that day. I was chasing a dream I'd held on to and cherished for more than a dozen years.

Perhaps today that new life would start. But was I doing the right thing? Was I ready for this? Or was I about to make a horribly embarrassing mistake?

I tightly held a briefcase in my lap, filled with songs I had written during the past year. Songs — the music and the words — were my way of exposing my pain and expressing my hopes for the future.

Actually, I'd been writing songs since I was ten or eleven. Mostly in my head, but sometimes on paper. The songs were the one thing that everybody seemed to like about me, the one thing I did well.

Were they any good? I thought maybe they were, but Jennie and a squirrel named Smooch were the only ones who had heard them, and, eager for praise as I was, I knew enough not to trust the opinion of a four-year-old, or a squirrel.

Soon, though, there would be another listener. I was on my way to audition the songs for Barry Kahn, *the* Barry Kahn, the singer-composer who had electrified America a decade ago and now was one of the most important record producers in the world.

Barry Kahn wanted to hear my songs.

Or so he said.

2

I WAS PETRIFIED.

And then it got much worse.

"You're late," he said. Those were his very first words to me. "I work on a very tight schedule."

"It was the snow," I said. "It took forever to find a cab, and then it kept skidding. I guess I was nervous and asked the driver to go faster, only he went slower, and —"

Jesus, I thought. *You sound like a dumb parakeet. Pull yourself together, Polly. Right now!*

He was unmoved. Seemed like a real bastard. "You should have left earlier. My days are full. I plan ahead. So should you. Would you like coffee?"

The question, the sudden politeness, took me by surprise. "Yes, please."

He rang for his secretary. "Cream and sugar?" I nodded. His secretary appeared. "Coffee for Ms. Bradford, Lynn. The works. Danish?" I shook my head. "Nothing for me," he instructed, his voice filled with the huskiness that made his singing so distinctive.

He dismissed Lynn with a wave, then sat at his desk with his

14

eyes closed, as though he had all eternity. I wondered: *Who the hell is this guy?*

He was in his early forties, I guessed, with a receding hair-line and brown hair, a long nose, thin mouth, and a slight per-petual stubble on his chin. A homely face (the fans who think he's "sexy" are attracted by his soul, not his looks), but its lines suggested struggle and its repose peace. At our first meeting he was dressed casually, in gray flannel slacks and a blue shirt, open at the neck, obviously expensive but worn with lack of care. Barry Kahn *looked* rather sweet and harmless.

Single, I deduced, and living alone. I wasn't interested in him that way, but I noticed anyway. I'm good with details. I always notice things, especially about people.

Lynn returned with coffee in a china cup, and I took it from her, splashing it on my wrist. Not very relaxed. Indeed, kind of an ass. That's how I felt at the time anyway.

Petrified! As in wood — that never, ever moves.

Barry stood to offer assistance, but I waved him away. "I'm fine." I'm in control. I'm cool. Pay no attention to the scarlet *M*.

Barry sat back down. "You're quite a letter writer," he said. I *guess* it was a compliment.

In the hospital, as my recuperation progressed and I began composing song after song, I had planned to write only one letter to him, telling him that I admired him and hoped I could audition for him someday. But the one letter gave rise to an-other, and by April, I was writing him nearly every week, let-ters from deep inside my heart, to a person I had never met. *Hooo boy!*

Weird, I know, but that's what I'd done. I sure couldn't take the letters back now.

He didn't answer any of them, and I wasn't even sure he read them. I only knew they were never sent back unopened. But I continued to write the letters. Actually, the letters kept me going. Talking to somebody, even if the person didn't talk back.

In a way, I think writing the letters helped me recover. I

gradually got stronger, began to believe that one day I would be all right again. I knew Jennie would be okay, or at least as okay as you can be if, at age three, you've witnessed horrible mayhem in your own house.

My sisters traveled from upstate New York, and took turns watching her. The hospital let Jennie visit as often as they could bring her. She was fascinated by my wheelchair and the electric bed. And she could thrill me whenever she hugged me and pleaded, "Sing me a song, Mommy. No. Make up a new song, and sing it."

I sang to Jennie often. I sang for both of us. I wrote a new song a day.

Then, an amazing thing happened. A miracle. A letter arrived for me at West Point Hospital.

Dear Maggie, the letter said.
Okay, okay, you win. I've no idea why I'm answering you, but I guess I'm an easy mark even though I don't like to think so and if you tell anybody else, that'll be it for us forever.

In fact, your letters moved me. I get lots of mail, most of which my secretary throws away without showing it to me. And the letters she does give me I throw away.

But you — you're different. You remind me that there are real people out there, not just sycophants wanting to get into my studio. I feel I've actually come to know you a little bit, and that says a whole lot about what you've written so far.

I was impressed with some of the lyrics you sent me. Amateur stuff — you need a songwriting education — but powerful all the same because they say something. None of this means that (a) the education will do you any good; or (b) you can write music for a living, but okay, okay. I'll give you the half hour of my time you asked for "to find out once and for all if I've got a talent for songwriting or not."

*When you get out of the hospital, call Lynn Needham,
my secretary, to set up an appointment. But in the meantime, please don't write me any more letters. You've taken up
enough of my time already. Don't write to me — write more
songs!*

3

HE SIGNED THE LETTER "Barry," and now here I was and he was looking at me, and I felt hopelessly out of place, one of those "sycophants" he had grumbled about. I definitely hadn't overdressed — that wasn't my style. I had on a white peasant's blouse, pink camisole, a long black skirt, flat shoes.

But at least I was here. I was going for it.

I was trying so hard not to have any negative thoughts . . . but things like this, really good things, never happen to people like me. They just *don't*.

"Do you sing your songs, or do you just write them?" he asked.

"I sing them too, at least I hope you'll call it singing." *Stop apologizing, Maggie. You don't have to apologize for anything.*

"Ever performed professionally?"

"I did some backup singing in clubs around West Point, Newburgh. But my husband didn't like it when I did."

"He didn't like much, did he?"

"He thought I was exposing myself. Couldn't stand other men looking at me." *So I shot him — three times.*

"But you'd be willing to try it now? Sing in public? You could do that?"

18

My heart raced at the thought. "Yes, I could." It seemed the right thing to say.

"Good answer." He gestured toward a beautiful, shining black Steinway at the far end of his office. "But your first test's in private. Did you bring anything?"

I picked up my briefcase. "Lots. Do you want to hear ballads? Blues?"

He winced. "No, Maggie. Just one. This is an audition, not a gig."

One song? I thought. My heart sank.

I had no idea which song to pick. *One* song? I had brought at least two dozen, and now I stood rattled and confused, as though I were standing naked in front of him.

Put it in gear. He's human. He just doesn't act like it. You've sung these songs a thousand times before.

"Go on," he said, looking at his watch. "*Please*, Maggie."

I sucked in a deep breath and sat down at the piano. I'm fairly tall, self-conscious about it, so I prefer to sit. From the seat I could see the silent chaos of Broadway through his window.

Petrified wood.

Okay, I thought. *You're here. You're actually auditioning for Barry Kahn. Now, knock his socks off. You . . . can . . . do . . . it.*

"This is a song called 'Woman in the Moon.' It's about a . . . a woman who works nights cleaning buildings in a small town. How she always sees the moon from a certain window while she works. What she dreams about all night in the offices she cleans."

I looked over at Barry Kahn. *Jesus, I was in his office. I was the Woman in the Moon.* He was sitting back, feet on the bottom drawer of his desk, fingers steepled together, eyes closed. He didn't say a word.

Musically, "Woman in the Moon" was like Barry's own "Light of Our Times." I began to play, to sing in a soft, uncertain voice that suddenly seemed dreary and ordinary to me. As I sang, I sensed I was losing him.

19

I finished. Silence. I finally dared to look at him. He hadn't changed position, hadn't moved. Finally he said, "Thank you."

I waited. Nothing more came from Barry Kahn.

I put the music back in the briefcase. "Any criticism?" I asked, dreading his answer, but wanting to hear something more than "thank you."

He shrugged. "How can I criticize my own child? It's my music," he said, "not yours. My voice, imitated by yours. I'm not interested."

I could feel a deep blush redden my face. I felt so humiliated, but also angry. "I thought maybe you'd be pleased. I wrote it in honor of you." I wanted to run out of the room, but I forced myself to stay.

"Fine. Okay, I'm honored. But I thought you were here to play *your* songs. If I want echoes, I'll sing in a subway tunnel. Are all your songs like mine?"

No, goddamn you. They're not like anybody else's songs! "You mean do I have something more original?"

"Originality's what I'm looking for. Originality's a start."

I began leafing through my sheet music. My fingers felt numb and unsure. A full marching band was stomping around inside my head. "Would you listen to one more?"

He stood up. He was shaking his head, trying to stop me from going on. "Really, Maggie. I don't think —"

"I do have one. Many. My own, not yours." I had promised myself I wouldn't be embarrassed.

He sighed, having already given up on me. "Since you're here . . . *one* more song. One song, Maggie."

I plucked out "Cornflower Blue." It was a little like an old Carole King hit. Maybe not original enough. *Too precious. Too clever. More bullshit.* The noise inside my brain had become a loud roar like the sound of an approaching subway train. I felt as though I were about to be run over.

I stuffed "Cornflower" back in the briefcase and chose another song — "Loss of Grace." Yes. This was a better choice. I had written it recently, since I had come to New York.

One song.

I could feel Barry Kahn's eyes on me, feel his growing impatience. The room felt hot. I didn't look at him. Just at the music for "Loss of Grace."

The song was about my marriage to Phillip. It was deeply personal. The initial ecstasy, the love I'd felt, or thought that I did. Then the mounting terror. The horror of that first fall from grace . . . and never being able to stop falling.

One song.

I turned to the piano, took one deep breath, and began to play.

I sang very softly at first, then with mounting passion as the song gripped me and I remembered exactly what had inspired it. *Phillip, Jennie, myself, our house near West Point.*

I could sense something new in the room as I sang, a kinship and understanding I had longed for in my letters, a bond between me and the man sitting silently at the other side of the room.

I finished, and waited for what seemed like forever for him to say something. Finally, I turned around. His eyes were closed. He looked as though he had a headache. Barry Kahn opened his eyes.

"You shouldn't rhyme 'time' with 'mine,' " he said. "It's a false rhyme, and while you might get away with it in a country song it's distracting when you're trying something serious."

I began to cry. I couldn't help it. It was the last thing in the universe I wanted to do. I was furious at myself.

"Hey," he said, but I had already jammed the song into my briefcase and was heading for the door. I almost started to run. *I wouldn't run though.*

"Hey," he repeated. "Stop crying. Hold on a minute."

I turned to him. "I'm sorry I took up so much of your

21

precious, valuable time. But if all you can talk about is one lousy rhyme, when I've just sung my heart out, then there's no way we can work together. And don't worry. I won't bother you again."

I rushed out the door, past an astonished Lynn Needham, and took the fancy Deco elevator to the lobby. *Screw him. Screw Barry Kahn.*

I was tough enough to deal with this — I had to be. I had a little girl to take care of, not to mention myself to look out for. That was why I had written to half a dozen music companies besides Barry Kahn's from West Point Hospital. Tomorrow I would see one of the others. And then another. And another after that if I needed to.

Somebody was going to like my music, my songs. They were too good, too *true,* for somebody not to listen, and to feel something.

It's your loss, Barry Kahn, Mr. Big Shot. Mr. My-Time-Is-So-Precious!

You missed out on Maggie Bradford!

4

DID YOU EVER want to say, even to shout out loud, *Hey, I'm smart. I'm an okay person. I have some talent.*

I shouted those very words in Times Square. No problem. Nobody even noticed. I fit right in with the rest of the loony-birds there.

I wandered for a couple of hours, oblivious to the falling snow, then went to pick up Jennie at her school on West Seventy-third. I felt like absolute crap and hoped I didn't look it. *Sheesh, what a day.*

"Let's celebrate," I said. "Tomorrow starts the Christmas holiday. Give your favorite mom a big hug, and we'll go to some fancy New York restaurant. Just the two of us. Where do you want to eat? Lutèce? Windows On The World? Rumpelmayer's?"

Jennie carefully thought the offer over, wrinkling her forehead and pulling on her chin, as she always does when she has to make an important decision. "How 'bout McDonald's. Then we can go see a flick."

"Quarter Pounders it is!" I laughed, and took her small hand. "My sweet bunny rabbit, you're what's important. And you like my songs."

23

"I *love* your songs, Mommy."

The two of us began to babble at each other — just like always. We were "best friends," "girlfriends," "the original motormouths," "soul sisters," "the odd couple." We would "never be alone, because we would always have each other."

"How was your day, Sweetie? Boy, you've got to be tough to make it in New York. Fortunately, we're tough."

"School was fun. I made another new friend named Julie Goodyear. She's *real* funny. Mrs. Crolius said I'm *smart*."

"You are smart. You're also pretty, and you're a very nice person. You're awfully *short* though."

"I'm going to be bigger than you, don't you think so?"

"Yes, I think so. I think you'll be around seven foot or so." On and on and on like that.

The motormouths.

Best friends.

We were both doing pretty well actually; getting used to New York — kind of; getting over Phillip as well as we could.

To hell with Barry Kahn.

You blew it, Mr. Big Shot!

It was as dark as Phillip's heart by the time Jennie and I got home. All my feelings of defiance had evaporated, and I looked at the front of our run-down brownstone with complete dismay.

Shit, shit, shit. I guess we'll have to live here a while longer. Like maybe the rest of our lives.

I opened the front door, and it yawned as it always did. Typical New York reaction.

Damn, damn, damn! The lights had gone out in the hall and on the first-floor landing.

All I could see was a pattern of light edging its way through the first-floor window from the lamppost in front of the house.

"Spooky," Jennie whispered. "Scary and spooky."

"No," I said. "This isn't spooky. This is fun in the Big Apple." I took her hand and we started up the "fun" stairs.

24

I stopped moving. My body tensed, and I tucked Jennie behind me to protect her.

Somebody was sitting in the shadows on the landing. The person was silent, unmoving. It was somebody tall and well built.

This wasn't good. This *was* scary and spooky.

I moved toward the figure cautiously. "Hello. Who is it? Hello up there," I called out, thinking of the horror stories I had heard about New York — and about the horrors I had recently endured in West Point.

The person seemed to be wearing something on his head. A strange top hat? *Something* weird as hell.

Phillip! I thought the unthinkable. I knew better, but the flashback came anyway.

Phillip loved to frighten me, jumping out from behind a bush, from behind a closet door, knowing he could scare me and thinking it funny when he did. Once, on Halloween, he wore an Indian headdress and came at me with a tomahawk. It was the worst of the scares. At the end, of course, it was I who had jumped out at him, had leaped at him with the gun in my hand, firing . . . firing . . .

But Phillip was dead, I told myself, and there were no such things as ghosts, not even in New York.

I inched closer. Still, the figure did not move. I neared the landing. "Hello!" I called again. "This *isn't* funny. Please talk to me. Just say hi."

The sound of our stealthy footsteps on the stairs reminded me of Phillip's steps, the way he *stalked* around the house.

Becoming a little hysterical, consumed by ancient fear, I forced myself to reach the landing.

Behind me, Jennie whispered, picking up my fear. "Who is it, Mommy?"

Not twice, I thought. *You won't hurt us twice. No damn way!*

I lunged at the threatening figure, striking out at it with my heavy case. I hit the bastard hard.

He toppled unresistingly, and I realized what I had done. "Oh my God! I can't believe it!" I started to laugh, relief not entirely wiping out the dread. "Hooo boy."

Jennie hurried up the final stairs, laughing with me. "Phillip" was a mammoth basket of what had to be a few hundred dollars' worth of long-stemmed roses.

I opened the note that came with them.

TO MAGGIE BRADFORD.

HERE'S TO THE FIRST DAY OF YOUR RETURN TO GRACE. IF YOU REALLY WANT THE JOB, YOU'RE CRAZY, BUT YOU'RE HIRED. YOU MADE MY 'PRECIOUS TIME' PASS LIKE IT WAS NOTHING TODAY. TRUST ME ON THAT.

BARRY

A kind of funny story, in retrospect anyway. A happy ending for sure. But as I write it now, the question comes again, and it's not so funny anymore. Not to me.

When I'm in trouble, is my first impulse always to kill?

Have I murdered, not once, but twice?

A lot of people think so. One of them happens to be a prosecuting attorney for the southern district of New York.

First, there was Phillip Bradford.

And then — *there was Will.*

26

5

San Diego, California, July 1967

Will Shepherd, age six, was dreaming of Indians. Fierce and remorseless, they came at him in waves, their horses neighing and rearing, their arrows as long as spears, pointed at his heart. He loved the excitement, loved the movie in his head, loved the danger.

He heard a splash!

It didn't make any sense. Will opened his eyes, shut them almost immediately, then drifted back to sleep.

Cowboys and Indians again.

No splashes. Not in his movie anyway.

Will woke again at quarter to eight, dressed quietly so as not to disturb his still-sleeping brother, Palmer, and hurried down through the quiet house.

In the kitchen he fetched an armful of Welch's grape jelly, peanut butter, milk, and half a loaf of bread. Breakfast for one. *Who needed a mother? Who needed anybody?*

Will saw his face and uncombed blond hair looking back at him from the side of the shiny toaster. He had to admit it, he

27

thought. *He missed his mother a lot. He missed her terribly. He missed her making peanut butter and jellies.*

He knew that she had gone to live in Los Angeles. He didn't have to suffer through the terrible fights she had with his father anymore, but at this moment he would have preferred the fights to the silence. Sometimes he and Palmer missed their mom so bad it made them cry at the stupidest times. But usually he *hated* her. Usually, but not today.

The splash in the swimming pool?

Suddenly Will remembered. He collected his dish and glass and put them in the sink, then ran out the screen door into sweet, dappled sunshine and the call of sparrows.

He came tearing around the corner of the blue-trimmed white clapboard house, and ran to the edge of the pool. He stopped so suddenly he nearly fell over his own sneakered feet.

And he screamed and screamed, screamed so shrilly he woke his little brother, whose face appeared at the window above him.

Will screamed so bitterly that neighbors came rushing to his rescue. They held him, and tried to shield him from what he had already seen, and would never forget.

What the six-year-old boy saw floating on the shimmering water of the pool was his father in his red-plaid bathrobe and beige trousers. On one foot was a yellow slipper; the other foam slipper was drifting as free as a lily pad.

His father's eyes were open, and staring right at him. *Your fault*, they seemed to tell him. *Bad boy. This is your fault, Will.*

You know what you did!

You know what you did!

At 5:52 A.M. Anthony Shepherd had purposefully walked outside his house and drowned himself in the family pool.

And whatever part of Will Shepherd that was worth saving seemed to drown with his father.

*　　　*　　　*

28

A few days after their father's suicide, Will and Palmer spent their final California afternoon choosing from among all of their clothes and toys. Just enough to fill two suitcases each. *No more than that.*

Their mother had refused to take them to live with her. Nobody told Will or Palmer why. *The stupid cunt,* Will thought, using bad words his father had used when he fought with her. The brothers had spent the days after the suicide with their nanny, who would not take them either, and now they were told they were going to England to people who would. They were to begin a new life with their aunts, Eleanor and Vannie, whom they had never met, but who had made the *two-suitcase rule.*

In loud, chaotic, swarming Los Angeles International Airport, the two look-alike blond boys sat stone-faced and bewildered, awaiting their flight with Dr. Engles, one of their father's few friends. Dr. Engles was telling them about London, and the stupid Queen and the stupid changing of the guard at Buckingham Palace, just like in the poems his mother had read Will before she went away. But Will barely heard what stupid Dr. Engles was saying. He was remembering his father floating in the pool, staring up at him from some dead place.

"*Ladies and gentlemen,*" Will did hear, "*we are now ready to board Pan American flight four-eleven to New York and London.*"

Dr. Engles held out a hand to take Will's. "Well?" Suddenly, Will bit it savagely, as hard as he could, drawing blood.

"Damn it," Dr. Engles said, cuffing him with his free hand. "You little shit! You little monster."

Will opened his mouth. His front teeth were red. "I don't want to go to England," he howled. "Can't we stay here?"

Please, Daddy.

Please, Mommy.

Please, somebody help me.

I didn't mean to kill my daddy. I didn't mean to do it.

Daddy, please stop looking at me like that. Please, Daddy.

29

6

WILL WOULD NEVER forget his first few hours in England. He and his brother might as well have traveled to the moon.

Aunt Eleanor met them at the landing gate. She was a fat, fussy, powder-white-faced woman who was, Will guessed, more scared of him than he was of her. He disliked her instantly. *She can't hurt me,* he decided. *No one will ever hurt me again, but especially not her.*

She explained that Aunt Vannie had stayed home to cook a special dinner for the boys. *It'll taste like crud,* Will decided. *England is the worst place ever.*

On the way from Heathrow Airport, Aunt Eleanor never stopped talking, and the boys had little chance to observe their surroundings. Whenever they looked away from her, she would jab a finger and remind them to pay attention. Will seriously thought of biting the finger off.

"A great many people who work in London live outside the centre. Close to an Underground stop. We live in Fulham, for example, and we have ever since your mother moved out to make her fortune in America. And I suppose she did, didn't she, marrying your father? She'll inherit all his money, you know, with nothing for you except as she chooses to give it, and goodness knows nothing for us, though we never expected anything from her. Not *her*."

No. Never expect anything from my mother. Will knew Aunt Eleanor taught history in primary school, and that explained why she droned on, but her smell was of sweat, and who was she to be talking about his mother? He could tell Palmer didn't like her either. He was pretending to be asleep, the little faker.

At last the cab pulled up in front of a three-story house, red brick with tiny windows and six steps leading up to the front door.

"Here we are," announced Aunt Eleanor cheerfully, but Will thought about the trees and space and sunshine in San Diego and his chest grew tight.

There were similar houses crowding in on each other on both sides of the street, and the one tree he could see was bent and beaten by the rain, and it had no leaves. Palmer took one suitcase, Aunt Eleanor another, and Will carried his own two up the steps, straining with the effort.

Before they reached it, the front door was flung open, and a woman appeared wearing tight black trousers and a black turtlenecked sweater.

Will gave a little, muffled cry. He felt his heart pound and his face suddenly grow hot.

The woman was young, with ash-brown hair falling halfway down her back. Her eyes were blue and her skin was pale. *It's my mother,* he thought.

Only of course, she wasn't.

She was his Aunt Vannie, his mother's younger sister, but she reminded him achingly of the woman who once, long ago, it seemed, held him, cuddled him, told him she loved him, and then went away. And he was filled with a curious mixture of dread and delight. He wanted at once to fling himself into her arms, and to run away screaming down the street.

"Take off your shoes before you come in," Vannie said. "We don't want dirt trodden all over the house, do we?"

The house. *England*. His new home. His new life. His very own horror story. It was just beginning.

7

THE LEGEND BEGAN early, and it never really varied.

Will is an extremely intelligent and very clever boy, but he seems to be an incorrigible master of the Charming, Audacious, Very Big Lie! So wrote the headmaster of the Fulham Road primary school in the spring of 1970.

If he worked harder, his marks would be much improved, but he seems interested only in sports, where he excels, and in picking fights with his classmates, where he is the acknowledged champion. I personally wonder if he is even aware of the elemental aspects of social behavior or, for that matter, the elemental difference between reality and fantasy.

Will understood the difference — but he had made his choice about which he preferred.

On weekends, Will often took solitary walks around his neighborhood. One day, when he was eleven, he heard shouts coming from a stadium about a mile from his aunts' home. Intrigued, he went to investigate. He paid a week's pocket money to get in.

There, in front of him, was a perfectly dazzling sight: twenty-two men, divided in uniform but united in purpose,

33

were playing what they called "football" in England, but what Will knew as soccer. Only on TV had he seen the game played this way.

He had played the game well at school, but felt it had been haphazard, just a bunch of boys kicking the ball around any way they could.

Here, there was symmetry, geometry, coordination in attack, a beauty as inevitable as the waves of the ocean. One man, controlling the ball with his feet, moved forward; another raced to his side; a third began a run down the wing, received the ball from the second man without breaking stride, and veered toward the center of the field, pursued by an opponent who dived at the attacker's feet and managed to push the ball to one of his teammates.

And then, suddenly, everything reversed, like the tide going out. Defenders became attackers, attackers defenders, a whirling mass; Will was reminded of a kaleidoscope his father had given him when he was five.

And the noise! Each time there was a reversal, each time one team threatened the goalkeeper, the crowd roared, as though they shared the breath coming out of the athletes' mouths, and when eventually a goal was scored, the roaring rose to such a pitch Will thought his ears would burst and his heart explode.

That night his mother came to him in his dream, and while he watched in horror, she kissed his father's open dead eyes, and laughed at Will. Her teeth were red, dripping blood.

You know what you did, Will.

It's all your fault.

One morning, several days later, he found a lost dog on the streets of Fulham. The dog was male, a tan-and-brown runaway. Finally, he had a pal in shitty old England.

"C'mon, dog. C'mon with me," he said and patted the side of his thigh several times. "C'mon, Lassie."

Will wandered into a municipal park and the lonely mutt followed like his shadow. He didn't know why he was feeling angry, but he was. The feeling came over him a lot actually, ever since he'd left California. Ever since his father had killed himself. His father's suicide was a really bad deal for Will. He still felt responsible, but even worse, he'd convinced himself that was how he himself would end up.

He sat down by a small pond. The dog was still with him. His new buddy.

Will finally shook his head at the mutt. "Big mistake, staying with me," he said. "Bad luck follows me around. I'm not kidding."

The dog gave a whimper, and put out its paw.

But Will was getting angrier about lots of things. His father, his aunts, Palmer. He felt as though he had a tight belt around his chest. His head was tingling. He was seeing mists of light red.

Will reached down into the cold, shallow water and pulled out a fist-sized stone. Without a hint of warning, he whacked the dog on the side of the head. He struck the dog a second time, and it fell over moaning. One sad, brown eye looked up at him. He kept hitting the dog until it was dead.

He didn't know why he'd done it. He liked the dog. At any rate, Will found that he wasn't angry anymore. He felt okay. Actually, he didn't feel much of anything.

He had even made a little self-discovery; there was a distinctly good part in him, but also a bad part.

There were two Wills, weren't there?

8

WILL KNEW from the start that he had greatness in him, and that he wasn't really impressed by it. But others sure were.

Will Shepherd was the youngest ever to play for the Fulham School's first eleven. When he was just eleven, he persuaded the coach to let him train with the team; he was immediately selected and, oblivious to the jeers of his teammates, who were older than Will by five or six years, he became the team's leading scorer. Their top striker!

When he was twelve, Fulham won the London school league championship, and did not lose again until after Will left the school. As a fourteen-year-old he scored nine goals in a game his team won 12–0.

Will was wispy and long-legged for his age, but surprisingly well balanced. He was extraordinarily fast — he ran, his coach said, "as an arrow flies." He ran like southern California halfbacks and wide receivers in American-style football.

Will practiced every day, every spare hour, until the ball seemed almost an extension of his foot, or at the very least a satellite body attached by an invisible wire. He sometimes practiced as much as sixteen hours on a Saturday or Sunday. The field was his home, not that shitty place where his aunts and Palmer lived.

Local newspaper reporters made him a schoolboy legend around London. They always commented on his reckless style, highly personal and unusual, which they attributed to his being American-born.

But that wasn't the reason at all. What none of them understood was that Will secretly worked on, and perfected, *his individualistic style.* He had. Will decided it was essential to be different, to be noticed, *to stand out,* rather than to be viewed as a loner. Will understood precisely what the game meant in his life: English-style football meant not being lonely and afraid; this new kind of football meant not thinking about his sodding mother and father ever again.

Football was his only weapon. It was going to save him. It had to.

9

Spring 1985

For a year and a half, Barry Kahn worked my piano-playing fingers to the bone. We started with lyrics, and the theories behind them: Bob Dylan's theory, Joni Mitchell's theory, Rodgers & Hart's theory, Johnny Mercer's theory. Barry's *basic* theory was that hard work conquers mediocrity.

He made me write and rewrite, forcing me deeper and deeper into my past until there were days when I wanted to beg him not to push me so hard, to let me rest. But I *didn't* ask for a bit of mercy. I secretly wanted to be pushed even more.

He was remorseless, and so was I. "You're denying," he'd say. "You're hiding in cheap rhymes and phony sentiment." Or: "You're not feeling anything. I know it because I can't feel it. And if I'm left cold, just think what an audience will do. They'll crucify you, Maggie."

"*What* audience?" I asked him.

"You don't *see* an audience? You don't feel an audience that *has to* hear your songs? If you really don't, then get out of here. Don't waste my time."

So on I went until at last we were both satisfied, and I was

38

able to turn to the art of composing. Here too he was strict and unyielding, but music came more easily to me than words. I felt comfortable with it. One day he said I could turn it on and off like water from a faucet. I think he was a little jealous. I kind of liked that — competing with him, being on his level.

Last came the singing, and Barry was a true master of this. He taught me phrasing, accenting, diction. How to sing in front of an audience, how to use a mike in a recording studio. I had, he told me, a natural voice, unlike any other singer's, but it was in this area that it was hardest to judge. "The public alone will decide," he said. "Who could have imagined Bob Dylan's voice capturing an audience's heart — until it did? *Your* voice is edgy, openhearted. Lots of sudden shifts of mood intonation to fit your lyrics. You can sound caring, cold, bored, maternal, loving. I love your voice!"

He did? Finally, a compliment. I memorized it, word for word.

I practiced in the nearby Power Station recording studio, not only performing my songs but acting as a gofer, going on endless sandwich-and-coffee errands. I wore a long black overcoat down to my boots; I wore it *everywhere*. I was "tall blondie with the coat, can you get us sandwiches?" I was "sure, no problem. What do you like?"

I resented being treated like that, figured Barry would never do it to a man, but he insisted it was an important part of the job, and if I didn't like it I could go elsewhere.

There was, I knew, no "elsewhere."

There was Jennie, of course. The "motormouths" were alive and well.

There was Lynn Needham, who had turned into a real pal, an occasional sitter, my official New York tour guide, my shoulder to lean on.

There was our West Side walk-up, the den of iniquity, which had only one really cool feature — a turn-of-the-century bathtub built right in the kitchen. I *loved* taking hot bub-blebaths in the kitchen!

There were occasional dates, but nothing even close to any-thing serious. I began to remember what I'd felt like before Phillip — too tall, too gawky, a little tongue-tied, inadequate for all the wrong reasons, not big enough breasts, too many bad hair days. But really, what it all came down to, was that I was afraid to get involved again. I didn't want to have to tell anyone what had happened with Phillip — no, *to Phillip*. I had this *huge* scarlet M on my chest, and I didn't think it would ever come off, wash off, *whatever*.

Nope, there was no "elsewhere."

10

SO, I WAS the coffee-and-sandwiches person, but do you know what — it was so much better than my life had been. It really sucked sometimes, I *hated* those despicable runs to the Famous deli, hated being "blondie with the coat," but I also loved it. It was writing, composing, learning. I was part of something that on occasion could be very beautiful and moving.

One morning at the "music factory," my buddy Lynn Needham peeked into my cubicle/storage bin. "You better drop everything, except maybe that hot coffee. Mr. Wonderful calls."

Barry tried to reserve some time for me at the end of most days, so this was an unusual summons. I hightailed it to his office. His time was still precious.

"I've got good news, and unfortunately, bad news," Barry said as I entered the room where I had once auditioned to be his gofer.

I could feel my pulse racing a little. *Tell me what's happened! Don't drag it out.*

"I sent one of your songs to California," he continued. " 'Loss of Grace.' The revision you showed me last week. Someone likes it out there. Wants to record it."

41

Impulsively, I ran and hugged him. I don't think I'd ever done that before. I know I hadn't.

He smiled and gently pushed me away. He looked me squarely in the eye. "Now for the bad news. That 'someone' wants to sing it herself."

It was *my* song. "Tell her no," I said. Suddenly, I was crest-fallen. "*No.* Barry, please."

"Don't you want to know who that someone is? I *had* to agree she could sing it. That was the deal breaker."

I had a nightmarish vision of some third-rater, some other up-and-comer getting my song all wrong. "Of course I want to know who she is. But if she messes up, I'll murder her!" Bad choice of words, I know.

"I think she'll get it right." He grinned like the sweet person he could be sometimes. "It's Barbra Streisand. She wants to re-cord 'Loss Of Grace.' And she wants you out there with her."

I hugged Barry again. I crushed him and kissed him on both cheeks. Good-bye to shlepping for coffee and pastrami sandwiches — hello to Hollywood!

11

I BOOKED a flight to Los Angeles for Jennie and me. We deserved it; we'd earned it. Once we got out there, I found myself driving a rented Saab Turbo up to the Beverly Hills Hotel. It seemed as though we were a million miles from West Point.

"It's pink!" Jennie exclaimed as we curled up the hotel driveway and stopped in front. "My favorite color. It's pink *everywhere*."

"I had it painted, *just for you*," I told her. "I called ahead. I told them to *think pink*."

"Motormouths!" Jennie yelled as we sat in the impressive hotel carport.

"Forever!"

A handsome, beachboy-blond bellhop carried our beat-up overnighters as if they were Louis Vuitton. He led us to a lovely cottage tucked behind the main hotel — Bungalow Six, our own private pied-à-terre, all arranged by Barry ("so you and Jennie make exactly the right impression"). He would know about that — I sure didn't.

"This is you, ma'am. And you too, little ma'am." The bellhop smiled and swung open the door with a flourish.

I had to take a quick step backwards. Dozens of American Beauty roses were waiting inside. "*Jeez*," I whispered. The blush-red flowers were everywhere I looked.

"Are there always this many flowers?" I joked. The humor sailed over the bellhop's shaggy blond mop. *The lights are on*, I realized, *but there's nobody home at Hotel California.*

"Oh, no, ma'am. It's a gift. There's a card."

WELCOME TO TINSEL TOWN.
I THINK YOU'RE ABOUT TO HIT IT VERY BIG.
DON'T BE FOOLED BY ALL THE GLITTERY GOLD,
THOUGH . . .
OR A FEW DOZEN ROSES EITHER.
                              LOVE YA AND JENNIE TOO,
                              B.

Love ya too, Barry. But I'll never bring you another cup of coffee for as long as I live.

44

12

MAYBE YOU CAN imagine what I was feeling, or maybe nobody ever could.

This was everything I had dreamed of. All my mind-breaking work, all of Barry's merciless bullying, all the voice lessons and the rewrites. Now, here I was, my stomach tied in sailor's knots, peeking down the semidarkened corridor leading to Recording Room A in the famous Devan Sound Studios.

Famous songs are recorded here. My song could be famous too. Hooo boy.

This was it, boom or bust; that one big shot everybody says they want, but that so many of us never get, and I sure never thought I would.

I knew that different studios achieved a curious mystique, sometimes a superstitious reputation, within the tight clique of major musicians, superstar singers, and their managers. For years, Elton John would record only in an isolated chateau in the south of France. The Rolling Stones had recorded in a ticky-tacky houseboat in Jamaica to get a certain sound. A lot of country singers wanted a specific Nashville studio, and only Chet Atkins could produce their records.

Devan was like that in L.A. I held Jennie's hand. We watched in a kind of dream as a Barry Kahn/Barbra Streisand recording session unfolded before our eyes.

I didn't like it! I hated it, actually. I wanted to scream at the two of them. Barbra's voice was not the one I'd had in my head when I composed "Loss of Grace." Her style was *too* distinctive, too overpowering.

"What do you think?" I asked Jennie. She had heard me sing the song hundreds of times at home. She knew my phrasing, the big emotion shifts.

"Not as good as you," Jennie said after a moment's deliberation, "but I like this one too. It's so pretty." *Traitor. Infiltrator.*

It got prettier as they worked on it though. Each take got better. I began to hear things in my own song I never knew existed. It was my song, but it became hers too. I realized it was a nearly perfect collaboration.

I sat back and quietly ate some crow. Barry kept stopping by between takes. He was being so nice to Jennie and me, so supportive and encouraging suddenly.

After a while, I imagined Barbra Streisand was singing only for me, the way I had sung to Jennie, and I felt transported to a place where the music and all my emotions came together. I was back at West Point, but in happier times, when I used to sing to Smooch the squirrel, and only occasionally let myself dream about moments like this.

I began to feel numb all over, but *nice*-numb.

There were at least a hundred different takes before Barbra and Barry pronounced themselves satisfied, and the tension in the control room dissolved into dumb jokes and contagious laughter. I felt a powerful surge of relief, as though I had done the actual singing. I bowed my tired head.

I felt a hand touch my shoulder. I turned, and looked into the face of Barbra Streisand. She had snuck up on me.

In real life (*if this was real life*) she was striking, but not conventionally beautiful. There was kindness in her eyes, and her smile was sympathetic. I'd already seen that she could be tough, but she had a soft, sweet side as well. Don't believe everything you read in the papers — *trust me on that one.*

"I know what you must feel right now," she said. "A little bit, anyhow. I remember my Broadway debut, *my* first recording session. Butterflies and the shakes, right?"

"Just your basic out-of-body experience," I said.

She sat down next to Jennie and me. "Just remember that you earned this. All the sweat and the tears and the troubles *before* today give you a right to enjoy this tremendously. Your song would be a hit no matter who sang it. Because I did, it'll get the attention it deserves. I love your music, Maggie, and so will everyone else. Write more for me. Please?"

Then she kissed me on the cheek, and gave me a hug. "Thank you," she whispered. "Your song is so true, and the truth inside you is staggering."

For a moment I was tongue-tied, then began to regain my composure. "Shoot, I'm trying not to say anything too stupid," I whispered to her. "You can't imagine what this means to me, to Jennie and me."

"Oh yes," she said. "I can definitely imagine. The first song is the best of them all." Then she looked at Jennie. "Your mom is amazing."

Jennie smiled and nodded. "I know," she said, "but sometimes, *she* doesn't."

47

13

I USED TO DAYDREAM all the time about stuff like this happening. Everybody does. So this had to be a crazy daydream, didn't it?

I sold a lot of songs in a very short period of time. I was hotter than a ten-dollar pistol. I had the same thought every morning as I woke up in the tiny New York walk-up that I was still too insecure to give up: *None of this can be happening.*

One night, Barry took me to a very ritzy New York restaurant to celebrate "Maggie's greatest hits," as he called them. I continued to be a hot item. Stories about me had appeared in *Rolling Stone, Spin, People.* It was bizarre, unreal, not my style, but I didn't want it to stop. I felt like somebody, probably for the first time in my life.

It was twilight when we arrived at Lutèce on Fiftieth Street in Manhattan. We were seated with a certain amount of pomp and circumstance in the garden room. Barry knew the chef, the owner, the busboys.

"Is this a date?" I asked him. I was kidding — I *think* I was.

"This is my way to make up, once and for all, for our very first interview," he said and smiled. He was in a great mood. We

48

both were. We ordered champagne cocktails, then I had foie gras, salmon with sorrel sauce, a plum soufflé. *None of this can be happening.*

"I could have cooked all that," I said as we finished and ordered brandy and coffee.

"I believe that you could. You know," Barry went on, "nothing has made me any happier than watching you —"

"Come back to life?"

"Blossom," he said. "You know that it's hard for me to talk like this, but it's true. It's how I feel."

Suddenly, I was a little nervous and uncomfortable. I wondered if this really was a date. I didn't think I was ready for it yet. I was also afraid of spoiling the friendship that Barry and I had.

Barry winked at me then. He must have sensed my discomfort. "More and more, people are going to want to hear *you,* Maggie. Your words, your music, your special voice. That sultry contralto of yours. There isn't going to be any stopping you, Maggie. There are no limits to where you can go."

I started to cry. In the garden room of Lutèce. I didn't really care who saw me. I was so goddamn happy, so absolutely thrilled.

Barry used his napkin to dab at my cheeks. We both started to laugh.

"So tell me about yourself. Who the hell are you, Maggie? You're not 'blondie in the coat' anymore. That's for sure."

I had kept everything bottled up inside, but that night I let some of it out. Barry was my friend and I trusted him, which was a big step too.

"There's a small town about twenty miles above West Point. Newburgh," I began.

"Been there. No desire to go back," he said and made a façe. "The main street looks like Beirut. *That* Newburgh?"

"It used to be a beautiful city, Barry. Sits right over the Hudson River. Small town America, that's me."

"I hear some of that in your songs, Maggie. Honest, sincere, not too much cynicism. Corny, but what the hell." He grinned mischievously.

I was feeling very self-conscious. "You sure you want to hear this?"

"Stop putting yourself down. *Pleez.* You're going to be a big star now. Everything you say will be considered interesting. You were *interesting* the first day you came to my office."

I punched Barry in the arm — hard — for that one. I shut my eyes, opened them again. This was hard for me. I didn't like to talk about it, not even to Barry.

Finally, I took a deep breath, and began:

"My parents drank too much. Slight understatement there. They were both alcoholics. My father was wild, ran around. He left us when I was four. *My pop.* I developed this horrible stutter that used to embarrass me to tears. I buh-buh-beat it though. Mom died when I was in the eighth grade. My two sisters and I stayed with my Aunt Irene. I moved out when I graduated from high school. My sisters both married and moved upstate.

"Teachers all wanted me to go to college. I just couldn't see myself there. I got a job at a fancy restaurant near West Point. Met Phillip. *He loved me.* Said he did, acted like it. I *really* needed for somebody to love me. I mean — *really* needed it."

Barry frowned. "Phillip was your pop all over again, Maggie. We have a tendency to repeat our worst mistakes, don't we?"

"I guess so. He was a mathematician in the new army. Repressed. Vulnerable. Even needier than I was. Phillip turned out to be a drinker too. Just like Daddy. I wanted to save him, of course. Thought I could."

"He hit you, beat you up?" Barry said and lightly touched my cheek. It was just the right thing to do. My friend.

"I didn't know how to get out of it. Not back then. I didn't know where I could go, how I could possibly bring up Jennie. I used to escape to the attic of our house and write songs all the time. I'd sing them for Jennie. Both of us up in the attic."

"You never performed them around West Point?"

I shook my head. "Forget it! I was much too afraid for that."

"You lied to me during your job interview. You're fired."

"That's okay," I said. I touched Barry's cheek. "I can take care of myself and Jennie now. Thanks for helping me."

"I did nothing. I just watched it happen. You're an amazing person, Maggie. I hope you realize that yourself someday."

I leaned across the table and gave Barry the gentlest kiss. We were such good friends and I loved him. I could *think* that — I just couldn't say it.

"You're the best," I whispered.

"No. Only the second best. I mean that, Maggie. Remember where you heard it first."

14

JULY SECOND of my year of years, the best time in my life by about ten thousand percent. I was at the Meadowlands sports stadium outside New York City. I was there with Jennie and Barry.

I *will never* forget this. No one can take this part away.

A few minutes after eight-thirty the outrageous New York disc jockey, Bret Wolfe, came prancing out onto the Meadowlands' concert stage. He was dressed like a naughty teenager who shouldn't have been let out of the house by his parents.

The first warm-up act was scheduled to begin soon. Everybody in the audience knew that the headliners — R.S.V.P. — wouldn't make their grand appearance until at least ten, probably even later than that.

They were in for a shock though.

Bret Wolfe could barely be heard over the noise of the crowd: "*It is my distinct pleasure to introduce . . .*" The orchestra struck up a familiar melody. Glowing fluorescent flying objects flickered up toward the bland-faced quarter moon sitting over the stadium roof.

"... *My distinct pleasure to introduce to you — Ladies and Gentlemen* ... *R.S.V.P!*"

Stunned silence followed, then there was chaos in the audience that was still lazily milling into the stadium.

"I can't believe it's *them*. They shouldn't be on for hours!"

"Jesus, what's going on? What is this shit?"

From backstage, I watched as long paper streamers and electric blue fireworks rocketed high above the stage. Billowing smoke and gold lamé sparks erupted and drifted east toward New York. The R.S.V.P. lead singer, Andrew Tone, lithe and very sexy, stepped to the microphone and held it like a live snake. He ran a hand through his long, sandy-brown hair.

"We're Alive and Kicking!" He raised his fist. The band hit its trademark downbeat. R.S.V.P. began to sing the song that was currently number one just about everywhere in the world.

Next came "Champion of Myself."

Then the ballad "Loving a Woman of Character."

The audience was in an absolute frenzy. No one could understand what was happening. Tens of thousands of fans wouldn't come until nine-thirty, when, ordinarily, the local bands and warm-up groups would just be finishing.

The music finally stopped. Andrew Tone stepped to the microphone. He held up his hands for silence.

"Don't worry," he said. "We'll sing those songs over again when everybody's here. You early birds deserved a treat though. You're the *real music lovers*, right?"

Cheers. Some laughter. But the baffling mystery continued for the audience. What was R.S.V.P. doing onstage already?

"We sang those songs for a special reason. 'Alive.' 'Champion.' 'Woman.' I know they're three of our best songs. *You know* they are."

Loud applause confirmed Andrew Tone's opinion of *their* opinion.

"The thing of it is, these three songs were all written by our

53

first — and only — warm-up act tonight. And this is the best warm-up act we've ever had."

Some in the audience might have known my name. Few could have realized I was a singer. Behind Andrew Tone, a bevy of stagehands wheeled out a piano. The stagelights went off and a spotlight hit the keys.

There was a murmur in the crowd, expectant but wary. Everybody's curiosity was up.

"*She* is a real woman of character," Tone went on, speaking softly, away from the light. "It's her first live concert appearance — which is why we came out early. We wanted to introduce her. It's our way of thanking her for her songs.

"I guarantee you one thing! This is the last time the lady will be opening for anyone. So listen. Hold on to your heads. Hold on to your hearts. *THIS IS THE MIND-BLOWING, HEART-STOPPING MAGGIE BRADFORD!*"

15

I LISTENED to Andrew go on and on. *Too much,* I thought. He was raising their expectations way too high. He made it sound as though some scintillating world-class singer were coming onstage.

He wasn't talking about *me.* He couldn't be. The building pressure put a steel band around my chest. I had a contralto voice anyway, and had trouble hitting the real high notes.

I thought I wouldn't be able to play, much less sing. Not only didn't I feel like "a woman of character," I felt I had absolutely no spine.

I could barely breathe.

I made myself walk onto the massive concert stage. There was applause, sincere but scattered.

I remembered Andrew Tone's words: *"It's her first live appearance."*

I got my first full look at the slow-rising mountain of faces; the brightly colored, ragtag quilt of clothes; the streaming spotlight that made the piano look huge and frightening and self-important.

Oh, God, I can't possibly do this. There's an entire city out there watching me.

A wave of panic suddenly swept over me. I felt exactly as I did when I used to stutter and stammer in school.

I knew many of the orchestra players from recording sessions in New York. They were standing now and clapping for me too.

"Cut it out, guys," I yelled to them. "It's only *me*. Stop, stop, stop!"

"Go get 'em Maggie!" a drummer named Frankie Constantini yelled at me. "You're the best."

Somehow, I made it to the piano. I even managed to sit down without fainting, or having a major coronary.

I am considered tall at five feet eight inches, and Barry said I was "striking" that night, but I just felt gawky — the same way I'd felt as a teenager. I'd let my hair grow very long, and it cascaded down my back. At least I liked my hair. If nothing else, my hair was cool.

"I was living in West Point," I managed to say, speaking in a low voice into the gleaming silver microphone. "I was living in West Point, near the military academy there. I was a housewife and a mother named Mrs. Bradford. I loved to sit in the attic, I remember. There was a squirrel there named Smooch, and before my daughter, Jennie, was born, he was my friend. I loved to sit in the attic because there I was safe. There I wasn't afraid that my husband might come and hit me. There I began to write songs."

My mind felt as though it had exploded. Phillip was in it, as vivid as when he was alive. I could hear his footsteps on the stairs in our old house, the menace in his voice: *You can't hide from me!* My hand was trembling.

I willed my fingers to strike the piano keys. I sang with all my heart, everything inside of me:

56

I used to be a housewife
A new wife
A midwife
I used to live the good life
High in the storm king mountains.
I used to give him haircuts
Fix cold cuts
Mend shirt cuffs
My name was Mrs. Bradford
And I thought I was going to die.
Battery
He hit me!
This can't be me
This can't be me
Battery
I used to be a housewife
A new wife
A midwife
He hit me!
How can he say he loves me
When I think I'm going to die?

The applause grew louder, and then unbelievably louder. People began to stamp their feet in rhythm to the beat. The noise was like a physical presence rising out of the stadium. It carried me higher than I had ever been in my life.

It told me that all these people believed in me. They believed my story.

It was like nothing I had ever experienced, not even in dreams, and I have to confess, I never wanted it to stop.

Hooo boy, hooo boy, *hooo boy*.

16

THAT WAS THEN; and this is now.

I could never have imagined being *where I am right now*, in prison in New York.

It seems so inconceivable, so impossible. I couldn't conceive of any set of circumstances that would have gotten me here.

This week they brought a top, well-respected psychiatrist to see me, a woman named Deborah Green.

I guess I couldn't blame anyone for thinking that I might be crazy.

The husband killer. That's what I'm called in the newspapers. *The black widow of Bedford.*

I visited with Dr. Green in a small conference room beside the chapel, which made me smile at least.

I was pleased to learn that Dr. Green specialized in physical-abuse cases, rather than homicides.

She made it easy for me. She told me about herself, and why she had been chosen, and that if she wasn't right *for me*, she'd leave. She was my age, soft-spoken, unassuming.

I guess I liked her well enough. Trust? Well, that might come later.

"How's this?" I said to her. "I'll make this easy. I'll tell you everything that's on my mind. I don't see the point in the two of us having secrets."

I was facing Dr. Green, rather than lying on the cot that had been provided. She nodded, then she smiled. She was good at this, getting people to talk.

Of course, I wasn't being truthful with her — there was one important secret I wasn't telling her, or anyone else.

Ironically, it was what might have saved me.

"However you want to do this, Maggie," she said. "If you want to unload a lot of junk, go ahead."

I laughed. "It is junk, isn't it?"

Yes, I wanted to unload.

So, in those first few sessions, I told Dr. Green everything that all the newspapers and TV stations wanted to know, and couldn't get out of me for any amount of money.

I told Dr. Green what made me anxious, ashamed, and also, very angry.

Like about my father, and how he'd left my mother in 1965. Just walked out and left us as though we were some motel he'd visited going cross-country.

Like my terrible stuttering from around age four to thirteen. How it had hurt so much when kids made fun of me; how it had made me feel worthless and small; how I had beat it by myself, *with no help from anyone.*

Like writing songs in my head, to escape from the negative voices in my childhood world.

Like Phillip, who everybody thought was this nice, quiet college professor — but he wasn't, really. He had his black Corvette that he used to *back* out of the drive at about forty miles an hour; he had his gun collection; he had his *rules* to be followed at every waking moment, and probably while I was sleeping too.

I talked for about two hours at a clip, and Dr. Green rarely stopped me.

Finally, though, I was talked out during our third or fourth session.

"I do think you left something out," she finally said.

"What's that?" I asked her.

"Well, what about Will Shepherd? Remember him?"

Oh yes, *Will*.

The man I was in here for killing.

"I've been working up to Will," I said. "Will is in his own special class."

17

WILL HAD LEARNED to put on a good act in school, and to get by with it. He was already being touted as the best young football player in London. And he was very popular — with the girls anyway. He still didn't have a good friend though.

Early in the summer following his fourteenth birthday, he came down with the Asian flu. Chills and fever possessed him. He actually was afraid he might die, and go join his father.

His Aunt Vannie nursed him through the high fever. She was there for him. This was unusual, for until now, anytime Will got sick, it was Aunt Eleanor who brought him his food and comforted him. Indeed, sick or well, Vannie was a remote figure in his life. She went out almost every night, often on dates with men who squired her for a few evenings, and then disappeared to be replaced by others.

Mostly, Will and Vannie played chess, and they chatted. She was an avid player, but he learned the game rapidly, and by the end of the week they were able to play competitively. He found himself looking forward to the games with increasing excitement.

Chess enabled him to study his aunt up close. He and his

brother, Palmer, had conducted countless, sworn-secret, late-night conversations about her. They wondered about Vannie's men, about her occasional trips to Bournemouth or the South of France. And now, as she studied the board, he was able to stare at her, watch her every move.

He examined her breasts whenever her eyes were occupied with the game board. He imagined kissing them, gently sucking on the soft nipples, which taunted him under every blouse and dress she wore. He imagined biting each nipple clean off.

"You can't fool me the way you do all the others," Vannie told him during one of their tensest games. "I know that you're very clever, Will, and I know that you don't want us to know. But I know. I even know what you're thinking, dear boy."

After six days, Will woke feeling a little bad about feeling so much better. He would have to get up, he knew, and the prospect of being able to play football again delighted him. But the times with Vannie would be over.

There was a knock on his door around nine-thirty that morning. Palmer was already gone — Eleanor was taking him to the Regent's Park Zoo — and Will decided he would pretend to be sicker than he actually felt. He liked to pretend, to act, to see how good he was.

"I'm awake," he said in a weak voice like Tiny Tim's in *A Christmas Carol*. "Come in, please."

Vannie opened the door. She was wearing a gingham dress, cut tightly across her breasts. He noticed her breasts right away — *every time*.

"I'm going to make eggs," she said. "Scrambled eggs. Could you assist in the eating thereof, Master Will?"

"A little," he said, still playing Tiny Tim, acting his heart out. "Maybe a half portion."

"I don't know if I'm up to cooking *that* much." She winked. Which finally got him to smile.

Vannie called his smile scampish. He knew that she liked it. So he smiled for her. *More acting on his part.*

"Just lie there. I'll bring breakfast to you, *Master Will*."

Trembling, he watched her leave. She returned in a half hour, bearing scrambled eggs and mashed potatoes for them both, and sat on the bed next to him. Now *that* was extremely nice.

Will felt as though he hadn't eaten properly in a month, but her nearness took away his appetite for food.

"Still not hungry?" she asked, finishing her own portion. "Then how about one last game. For the championship of Fulham? You look recovered enough to play."

"You're on. For the championship."

"And what shall we play for, Vannie? What is our championship worth?"

I think I know what you want to play for. I think I know.

18

VANNIE QUICKLY cleared away the dishes, and set up the board on his bed. "The smaller pieces in front, they're called pawns," she teased. "Please move any one of them, so I can begin to thrash you."

Now he concentrated on the game. Her challenge had aroused his huge competitive spirit, and he was determined to win. He even forgot about her breasts, and the rest of her.

The game was their best so far. It was incredibly close — closer, he knew, than Vannie had expected — but at the last minute, in a move he should have foreseen, she took his rook with a knight. She leaned back in smug satisfaction.

"I'm afraid — checkmate, my darling, Mr. Competitive."

"Oh, sod it!" Will roared and struck the game board in frustration. Pieces flew on the bed and across the floor and under the night table.

"Typical loser. Typical man," Vannie said. "How do you think *your* opponents feel on the football pitch?"

They both laughed. Then they scooted around the bedroom, picking up the scattered pieces: queen under the night table;

knight somehow on top of the bureau; king underfoot on the imitation Oriental rug.

On hands and knees, they reached for the king simultaneously. Will's elbow grazed the slick cloth of Vannie's dress; he could feel the warmth of her skin underneath. She didn't pull away. Neither did Will.

Every sound, every tiny movement, suddenly became intensified in the bedroom. Electricity spiraled up his spine, and he could scarcely breathe. *She wants me. I was right. I knew it.*

Vannie stared into his eyes for a long second. She actually *stared* at him. The room was so quiet. He was conscious of the staccato pounding of his heart, and was afraid she could hear it. He wanted to hear *her* heart.

Without saying a word, Vannie's fingers gently traced Will's cheeks. Then, they trailed down over his throat, rode the lump of his Adam's apple. He gave a little moan.

She leaned forward and kissed him softly. Then she nipped his unpuckered lips with her teeth. She wrapped her arms around him, pressing him against her breasts.

Her tongue slid inside his mouth. Her tongue was *inside* him, and it was *hard*.

"Dear, sweet boy," she whispered. "You *are* something else. You're very special, Will."

Will's hands finally reached for her, tentatively at first, as though they themselves barely believed the miracle that was happening. Then more aggressively, up and down her surprisingly well muscled back, her soft face, her neck, and then, blessedly, to those wondrous breasts. *She wants me. Finally, someone does.*

"Not so fast," she whispered. "We have time, Master Will."

"I know that. I've thought about this a lot."

She smiled and her eyes opened wide with amusement. "You *have,* have you?"

His hands slid down along the outside of her legs. Vannie's dress made a sound like light static in the air.

She tugged at her own belt, then pulled him even closer. He didn't know what would happen next — what *could* happen?

He was already taller than she by half a foot, and much stronger, though she *was* strong. Her hands slipped all over him, reaching down into his pajamas. Her dress fell away to the floor. How many hands did she have? Where had she learned all this?

Will's face and neck were extremely hot — on fire; his ears were loudly ringing. His penis felt huge, and he rubbed against her bare flesh with a cry of utter joy. He wasn't sure what to do now, exactly where to go from here, but he would figure it out. He *was* smart, just as she suspected.

Naked, Vannie lay on her back on the bed. She was holding herself open with her hands. Her cheeks were red, blushing, and he loved that look, would never forget it.

"Now," she said, reaching for him. "Now would be a very good time, Will."

She wanted it to happen. She wanted him as much as he wanted her.

Will watched her face — studied her beautiful brown eyes; then her rising breasts; the luscious V of her legs and the dark hair at the center. He was so hard that he almost couldn't believe it was *he*. He felt stronger and more powerful than he ever had. Most important, he knew what to do with her. *He just knew it. Naturally.*

"Don't rush it, Will," she whispered to him. "Take your time, young Master."

"Don't worry. I don't want it to be over either."

When it was, though, when they lay together, and she gently stroked his long blond hair, she said, "You're so very beautiful. You're going to be able to have anyone that you want." She smiled warmly. "You're quite irresistible, Will."

This, Will already knew. He just wasn't sure what it meant. *To be irresistible.* Was that good, or was it very, very bad?

66

19

ALLAN "SKIPPER" THOMAS appeared to be an ordinary fellow, a tradesman perhaps, but Will understood that Thomas was the most important man he had met in his entire life.

Thomas was in his early forties now, manager of the Hammersmith Rangers, but rumor had it he trained as hard as his players, and that he offered bonuses to any on the team who could go past him one-on-one. Rumor also had it that *no bonus had ever been paid.*

He and Will were sitting like proper gentlemen in the living room of his aunts' house. Eleanor and Vannie had tactfully gone out, leaving the men to talk football, as men so love to do.

"I've watched you play, Will," Thomas said, playing everything close to the vest, as Will had expected he would.

"I'm honored to hear that, sir. I really am." *Like hell.* Every club in London had sent scouts to see him play.

"You've got natural talent, no question about it. I could make you into a fine player, over time I could."

Will watched Skipper Thomas calmly, the way Will did most everything. "I'm a fine player already, sir. You know it, or you wouldn't be here."

"You're fifteen years old. Nobody is a player at that age, just a *potential* player."

"I am," Will said.

"And modest too," Thomas laughed heartily.

"No, I'm not modest, sir. That would be false of me. But I am a goal scorer, sir. I have no particular sense of team, of anyone else on the field. I'm a loner, a striker pure and simple. I'm cut from the same cloth as Johan Cruyff, Pele, Gerd Müller. I'm the best at my age that England has ever seen. Fast as any pro, *and* stronger too. All the papers say so."

Thomas smiled broadly at the audacity of this young Turk, but most of all, because he just might be right. "The *local* papers say so, Will."

"And *The Telegraph*. And *The Sun*. Look, Mr. Skipper Thomas, why don't you just get on with it? You want me to play for you; I want to play for you. So cut through it. How much are you willing to pay, sir?"

"Come on, Will, dribble past me. If you think you can. You're the next Cruyff, isn't that right?"

Skipper Thomas and Will were the only ones who stayed on the pitch this late after practice. It was the same thing night after night, practice after practice. Thomas had never seen such maniacal desire in a player, even a young one. Will was indeed an incredible striker, a natural goal scorer.

"What'll you give me if I do? What's in it for me?"

"Twenty pounds," Skipper said and spat.

Will laughed and walked away. He was bare-chested, shaking his long blond hair. "I wouldn't fuck your wife for twenty pounds."

"All right. Fifty pounds. But you have to get right past me."

Will turned back, took the challenge. Thomas tossed him the ball; Will trapped it with his feet. Real casual-like. *Acting like a dumb, cocky little shit.*

Skipper Thomas crouched, but stayed on the balls of his feet. "Whenever you're ready, son."

He was ready now, and he wasn't anyone's son.

Will feinted left, quickly feinted right, headed directly at his coach and then, with fist toward the sky, middle finger raised in the universal gesture of contempt, glided past him as though Skipper Thomas's shoes were glued to the grass.

"Keep your money," he said and laughed at the coach. "I won't need it where I'm going."

Will played two years for the Rangers before his contract was bought by Liverpool, perennial champions of the English League's First Division, for one point five million pounds. He was already the biggest star in England. In his first year he was the League's leading scorer and was barely edged out as Footballer of the Year. He was nineteen years old.

The papers glowingly wrote about his "great inner fierceness," his "uncanny ability to actually fly across the pitch." "He can swoop like a golden eagle, then fly off to his natural aerie — the opposition's goal," the *Guardian* said.

"He is like a Blond Arrow — stretching toward the goal."

"Will Shepherd is the complete egomaniac on the field; he has the consummate scorer's mentality. He plays as though he were *alone* out there."

At nineteen, the Blond Arrow began to make the gossip columns as well. He was "fox hunting with friends in Gloucestershire," "grouse shooting on Lord Dunne's moor near Balmoral," "playing polo at Swinley Forest, in the presence of the Royal Family. The Blond Arrow cuts a dashing figure — *wherever* and with *whomever.*"

When he was twenty, Will led Liverpool to the League championship. He was arguably the biggest star in Europe. He was runner-up for FIFA's Best World Player award. "Frankly, Scarlet," he commented on the award, "I don't give a fuck what anyone thinks of my playing. *I'll* tell *you* whether I'm the best or not."

During that same time, Will had been playing international football with the U.S. team. It was his stubborn attempt to keep some connection with America. He quickly tired of being a very good player on a team of donkeys. He quit the team, and thus all international play.

The news stories rapidly became disturbing, and therefore much more interesting to the public. There were hints of alcohol abuse, of drugs, and worse. "Personal reasons" made him miss practices before games. Liverpool transferred him to an ambitious rival for two million pounds. In the off-season, Will began to drive Grand Prix race cars, an avocation forbidden by his contract. "If I live, it doesn't matter. If I die, it doesn't matter," he was quoted on the racing flap.

The Blond Arrow was all the rage — absolutely *irresistible*.

20

Irresistible.

Will drove Melanie Wellsfleet's supercharged red Ferrari sports car to her estate in Somerset. He got the new automobile up to over 115 at one point on the narrow, curvy road, and was seldom under ninety for the length of the trip.

"It's not a bloody *race car!*" Melanie laughed and shouted during one harrowing stretch of high speed and danger.

"It is now. With me at the wheel it is. Hang on, Mel. Ride of your life and all that."

The estate in Somerset was everything Will had expected — and much, much more. The grounds seemed to have been tended with tweezers; the twenty-six rooms inside Ryertton Hall were like a Tudor museum.

"My boss lives very well off my efforts," Will said to Melanie as she guided him through each of the nine bedrooms. Melanie was the thirty-one-year-old wife of Sir Charles Wellsfleet, who owned Will's football team, as well as a stable of racehorses and a well-respected publishing house. Charles Wellsfleet was sixty-nine years old.

"Charles owned this house long before you made the scene,"

Melanie laughed, and gave Will a hug. They had been carrying on their secretive affair for the past four weeks. She couldn't get enough of Will, and was sure he felt the same way about her. *He couldn't be faking that,* the former high-fashion model reassured herself during an occasional "blue" moment.

"I missed you, I want you, I need you," Melanie announced when they reached the master suite with its commanding view of a topiary garden and water terrace. "What do you *need?* What do you *want?*"

He seemed bemused by the question. He wandered around the spacious suite, searching through Melanie's dresser drawers and her huge walk-in closet. He selected several dresses, evening gowns, lingerie, stockings, shoes, and laid them all out on the bed and floor.

"May I ask what you're up to, Will?" Melanie pouted just a little. "I didn't know you had a fetish for my clothing."

"As a matter of fact, I do. Will you model for me? I've never seen you in any of these lovely getups. I'd very much like to."

Melanie smiled. She loved his imagination, his games, his need to play. He wasn't another empty-headed player like so many others she'd sampled in the past. Will had also lived up to his reputation as a sensational lover. She now thoroughly understood this "Blond Arrow" business. She was obsessed with him, and couldn't imagine any healthy woman who wouldn't be. He was *that damn good.*

She tried on Karl Lagerfeld evening dresses, a black dress by Jil Sander, sandals by Chloé. Will sat on the bed, gloriously naked, playing with himself, and watching her every move.

She already knew that he could keep himself hard for hours. If he had a problem in the sack, it was climaxing. So far, he hadn't with her. It was something to look forward to, no?

She was wearing a red gown and a lustrous pearl choker when she found that she couldn't stand it any longer. She scampered across the floor toward Will and his beautiful *arrow.*

"Please, please, *please me!*" she laughed and swooned in a theatrical fashion. "Let me fall on your sword."

Will didn't let her take off the Carolina Herrera, worth thousands of dollars. Not even her Ernesto Esposito pumps. He used the Hermès scarfs and nylons to tie Melanie to the bedposts. Then he made love to her for several hours. He helped her come so many times that he finally lost count. He didn't climax himself.

Sir Charles Wellsfleet arrived at the estate in Somerset around eleven that evening. He'd had a frightfully long day of meetings in London, and expected to find Melanie asleep in the bedroom, as usual.

His wife was wide-awake, however. Her eyes were like huge blue marbles, and she looked as though she had been sobbing for days. She was still tied to the bedposts with the scarfs and nylons, wearing nothing but the choker. Her face was puffy, but as pale as the pearls. The expensive Italian lingerie was strewn about the bed along with the shoes and the torn Herrera gown.

That summer, Will was transferred from Sir Charles's team. The press suspected everything except the truth: Will had tired of Melanie. The Blond Arrow needed to move on to a much larger stage.

21

WILL INVITED HIS BROTHER, Palmer, to his Chelsea apartment one afternoon before the new season began. Though it was expensively furnished, the living space seemed sterile, almost as if no one lived there. A Maggie Bradford record played softly, soothingly, in the background.

"I need your help," Will said, sipping the expensive brandy he had poured for them. Actually, it was his fourth or fifth brandy, and the third time he'd played the same record.

Palmer looked at his brother, surprised. *Will never seemed to need anything, from anyone.* "How could I possibly help *you*, Will?"

"I need a manager. I think you'd be perfect. I've thought about it a lot, actually."

"A manager! I thought Jacob Golding did that."

"He handles my business affairs. I mean a personal manager. Someone to look after me. Keep me out of trouble." *I'm starting to scare myself, brother. If you won't help me, then who will?*

"A bloody nursemaid, Will?" Palmer shook his head and laughed.

Will shrugged. "If that's what you want to call it. Will you do it? The pay is awfully good."

Palmer swallowed his brandy and stood up. "Not a chance, big brother."

"Why? What are you doing now that's so important?"

"As a matter of fact, I've got a good job in the marketing department of Cadbury's. But even if I were out of work, I wouldn't do it."

Will smiled. "Because you hate me?"

Palmer shook his head. His hair was blond, like his brother's, but cut short. "No. Because I hate living in your shadow. I don't hate you, Will. No one can hate you."

"You won't help then? Even if I told you that I'm desperately unhappy? That I'm running on empty? That night after night I think of killing myself?"

Palmer couldn't take his eyes off his fabulously handsome and successful brother. He sat down again. "Are you bloody serious, Will? Or are you play-acting again? Is this another of your mind *games?*"

"*Completely* fucking serious. I want to kill myself right now. Even as we speak. Do I sound like I'm playing a mind game?"

"My God," Palmer said. "I think you are serious. Or mad. Or quite possibly, both."

"I'm no good," Will said. "No damn good. Never have been. You're the only one who can help me, Palmer. We have to stick together."

Palmer stood, a strange, sad half smile on his face. "I'm sorry," he said. "I can't help you, Will. You'll have to find somebody else."

Will watched his brother leave. He refilled his snifter with brandy and drank it in a gulp. "But who is there to find?" he whispered. "Who could there possibly be to really love me?"

22

FACE THE MUSIC, Maggie. It's time to get to Will, to really talk about Will, to get it out once and for all. This is what everybody came to hear.

People ask, especially reporters, how I could have fallen in love with Will? I always want to say — *you would have too, in a millisecond. Don't kid yourself.* That wasn't the way it happened though — not for me.

But Will could be extremely charming. You have no idea! And I was *extremely* needy. I wanted to be loved more than anything else. I'd always wanted that. Doesn't everybody? Don't you?

It happened like this, more or less anyway. This is the truth, and nothing but, so help me.

I began my first European tour in London. It was tense, wild, but quite wonderful. The best of times. Jennie and I stayed at Claridge's. We went to the changing of the guard at Buckingham Palace, and saw *The Mousetrap,* Westminster Abbey, Big Ben. We were fantastic tourists together, and best friends. The two of us never shut up.

I was to give two concerts in London. And I was the honored guest at a costume ball in Mayfair, admission £1000, all receipts given to the fight against children's cancer.

The night of the charity party, I made a "grand entrance" into the living room of our hotel suite.

"Mom, no! You're *not* going out in public like that!" Jennie said, and made a face as though she'd just had a sip of warm stout.

I held a gold lamé vizard, a costume ball mask, up to my eyes. I peered into the mirror and then doubled over with laughter. Jennie was right on. I was straining the seams of my stiff antique ball gown, and my breasts were exposed farther than I'd imagined. *Sheesh.*

"Of course I'm going out like this. I think it's perfect. So would Barbara Cartland."

"Who's Barbara Cartland? Your fancy dressmaker? The costume designer for *Dracula?*"

"You don't know who Barbara Cartland is? Well, that proves you don't know anything about masquerades. You don't get a vote on this."

Jennie rolled her eyes. She buried both hands in her long hair. "But who are you supposed to *be*? Don't leave me in such *terrible suspense.*"

"A queen in the court of Louis the Fourteenth. Who else?"

Jennie giggled. She dropped down to the thick carpet and rolled over a few times.

"You look more like a stripper. *Sorry.* Sorry. Just kidding, Mom."

"You better be."

Anyway, what difference did it make how I looked? It was all a dream, wasn't it? None of this could possibly be real. It was too good, and I was way too happy.

23

THIS WAS SO *not-me*. That's why it was perfect.

The grand ball was held in the home of Lord Trevelyan, a four-storied Georgian mansion lit for the evening by enormous searchlights placed on the roofs of the opposite buildings.

When my car arrived, so did the black cab of a boisterous group impersonating the Bloomsbury literary crowd. They were dressed in knickers, suffragette blouses, and long puffed skirts, carrying dusty books and baskets of cut flowers. Jennie would have approved.

I went inside with the Bloomsbury characters to find at least two hundred guests, all outfitted in an array of costumes from all centuries and walks of life, sipping champagne (a glass was quickly served me) and chatting the night away.

Soon a trumpet sounded and the guests grew silent. Down the steps leading to the main foyer in which most of us were gathered came — Queen Elizabeth I! Her crown of rubies and sapphires glistened in the light; her dress, festooned with a thousand pearls, was as regal as its wearer. *This is a dream, right? A neat dream though.*

The "Queen" was, of course, Lady Trevelyan, our hostess.

"Supper is served," a butler announced, and we entered a magnificent dining room. We feasted on salmon, salads, cheeses, fresh fruits, and petit fours. After an hour or so, Lady Trevelyan rose and nodded to two footmen. The doors were swung open to the grand ballroom. Soon music started, a series of waltzes and fox-trots.

A man strode toward me on the dance floor. I would have turned away, but it was crowded, and there was nowhere to go.

He was dressed all in black, a hood over his head, a mask covering his face, so that only his eyes were visible. He had beautiful eyes, I couldn't help noticing. Something moved inside me. *Strange.*

"You're Maggie Bradford," he said. "Please give me your jewels or I'll be forced to steal them."

"You have the advantage," I said. "You know my name, but I don't know yours."

He bowed and raised my hand to his lips. "I'm Raffles, the infamous thief, at your service. And I'd rather steal your heart than your jewels."

I didn't look away from his eyes. "Then let me see your face. I don't let just anyone steal my heart."

I didn't know what to make of him. Lots of men had tried to seduce me since I had become *someone,* but this was a new approach. *Hi, I'd like to steal your jewels, or maybe, your heart.*

He bowed again, and with a single gesture removed his mask and hood.

Before me, without any exaggeration, stood one of the most handsome men I had ever seen. His blond hair hung down to his shoulders, and his green eyes blazed with an all-consuming light. Music came into my head. His tanned skin announced that he spent a lot of time outdoors, but his face was unlined; he was still young. His smile — and he was smiling now — revealed perfect white teeth and the skin around his jaw was smooth and taut.

"Raffles. Really? And what do they call you in the light of day?" I asked.

"Will," he said, "Will Shepherd." He took a step back to study the effect his name had.

It had *no* effect. I had never heard of him. "A nice name." I had noticed his accent. "You're American?"

"By birth. I've spent most of my life in England. I resisted *sounding* like one of them. I'm stubborn sometimes. *Most* of the time."

"And what do you do, Mr. Shepherd? Besides conduct highway robberies?"

If possible, his smile grew even brighter. "I'm afraid that I play football. Or soccer, as you would call it. You could come someday to see me play."

"I'd enjoy that. I guess I would. Although I should warn you, I'm not much of a sports fan."

"Yet I'm an unabashed fan of yours," Will said.

"I love your music," he went on. "The lyrics especially. You seem to *understand*."

Suddenly he took me by the arm. "I play your songs all the time, Maggie Bradford. I want to take you home with me tonight. I'm telling you the truth. I want to make love to you. Let's get out of here. You know you want to."

How could he say that to me? *How could he? . . . You know you want to!*

"How dare you speak to me this way," I shouted over the music.

I slapped him hard, and he stepped back, surprised. My voice must have reached the musicians, for they stopped in mid-melody. Everyone was staring at us.

I didn't care. His touch on my arm was Phillip's touch; his words were Phillip's words.

"If you had *really* listened to my songs, you'd know what I think of cheap come-ons," I said. My voice was shaking, my whole body was. "You've ruined this party for me. I don't give a

80

damn if you're the best soccer *and* football player in the world. To me you're dirt-common, filth, and if you ever *dare* speak to me again, I'll —" I was about to say — *kill you.*

He had already moved away, so I didn't finish. I watched him — we all watched him — walk across the room to the door, his head held high, long hair flowing, his steps measured, manly, but absolutely revolting to me.

I stood very still, fighting down embarrassment and rage. The music started again; people began to dance. Lady Trevelyan came up to me and gently touched the back of my hand.

"I'm sorry," I blurted, and felt close to tears. "So sorry. I didn't mean to make a scene. I'm so sorry."

"Don't even think about it," she said, her voice on the edge of laughter. "You gave Will Shepherd exactly what he deserved, and there isn't a woman in this room who isn't cheering for you right now." Finally, the hostess did laugh. "Of course, they'd all hop into bed with him given the chance. But bravo for you anyway."

BOOK TWO

CALM BEFORE
THE STORM

24

IT WAS ONE of the earliest court appointments — I don't remember which. All I know was that I was so glad to be leaving prison for any reason, even just to travel back and forth to court.

I felt that I was wearing my scarlet M, of course. I'm innocent, until proven guilty, but not in the minds of an awful lot of people, or so I've found. People who don't know me have already prejudged and condemned me.

For some, I'm guilty of murder. For others, they assume that I must have slept around, though God knows, nothing could be farther from the truth. The worst hurt of all, the deepest wound, comes from those who judge me a bad mother. If they saw me for ten minutes with my children — if they asked my kids about their mother — they'd know how wrong they are.

But I am prejudged. Women, I think, are guilty until proven innocent. And many of the worst accusers are other women. Why is that?

So I wore my scarlet M to court that summer morning. I was just glad to be outside. The pollen count must have been high, since several people we passed on the streets were sneezing, and the parked cars were blanketed with a thin, green dust.

The guards from the prison knew me, and liked me, and they tried to protect me from the inevitable crowds at the courthouse. A few of the "faithful," "Maggie's mob," had brought their angry placards. "Maggie Is a Murderer" and "Husband Killer" and "Give Maggie a CHAIR, She Looks Tired From All That Killing."

"Keep your head down, Maggie, and just follow us straight in," one of the guards told me.

I had spent so much time inside, cut off from the world, that I wanted to look — but the guard was right. I dropped my head, even though it made me *look* guilty.

The press was clever; they knew the best places to hide in wait at the courthouse. They trapped us on the way in, then they pounced.

There was the usual barrage of insensitive questions. Microphones thrust at me — *did they want me to sing?* TV cameras staring with their large, unblinking eyes.

A woman reporter with frazzled blond hair leaned in close over the restraining ropes at the side door. "Maggie! Over here, Maggie. Please?" she pleaded.

My head rose involuntarily, my eyes went to hers.

"What about Patrick?" she suddenly asked, a TV eye mercilessly staring behind her. "Did you murder him too? Did you, Maggie?"

I have never spit at a human being. I don't spit. Ever . . . but that morning I spat at that reporter. I don't know what possessed me.

The TV camera caught it — the incident, the shot, was on every TV news program, played over and over again. An uncontrollable temper. The *real* Maggie Bradford?

What about Patrick?

Did you murder a third man, Maggie?

Is anybody going to be surprised if you did?

25

"ACCOUNTANTS DON'T KNOW SHIT. So why in hell do we pay them a cent? Now *there's* some cost savings I could live with!"

Thus spoke Patrick O'Malley, standing in the bathroom of the unfurnished Tower Suite of his unfinished, unnamed, unopened hotel on Sixty-fifth Street and Park Avenue.

He was glaring at his accountant, his *C.F.O.*, Maurice Freund. Freund had heard his boss's opinion of accountants before. "But we do know costs," he said, unruffled, "and you're costing yourself an unnecessary fortune."

"Pears soap is necessary," O'Malley raged. "Porthault towels are *necessary*. A Jacuzzi in the Tower Suite bathroom is *essential*."

Freund sighed and shrugged. "The good news is that every room is booked. The bad news is that we're losing money on every booking."

"We'll refigure the damn rates. When you promise the best you deliver the best, and this hotel will *be* the best, goddamnit, or that soap goes right up your ass."

"As long as it's Pears," Freund said, grinning.

O'Malley grunted. "The construction's on schedule?"

"Yup. *Their* schedule. Eight months late at an overrun of twenty percent."

"That's still less than you estimated originally?"

"Ten percent less."

"Then take the soap and the towels from that ten percent."

"No way." Freund took O'Malley's arm and steered him out of the suite toward the makeshift elevator. "Knowing you, there'll be overruns everywhere. The rates go up."

If O'Malley had an opinion, he didn't express it. Rather, he said, "I know what to name the hotel."

Good news, Freund thought. *And about time.* "What?"

"I want to call it The Cornelia."

"The Cornelia. Splendid!" Freund knew his boss was watching his reaction closely, but his pleasure was genuine, his smile sincere. "That's good. The perfect choice, Patrick."

"I don't believe a world-class hotel's ever been named after a woman." O'Malley sounded almost shy.

"Then it's a unique name for a unique hotel. Besides, the time is right."

"She was a unique woman," O'Malley said. "That's for certain. We can finally agree on something, Maurice."

Freund took his hand and gravely shook it. The accountant actually seemed to have *felt* something. "The hotel's her testimonial. Your tribute to the one woman you loved."

26

FOR TWENTY YEARS, Cornelia and Patrick O'Malley were one of New York's most courted and undeniably popular couples. Seeming opposites — he, the gruff, self-made entrepreneur who had parlayed a string of motels into a grand hotel chain in the United States, Europe, and Asia; she, the society beauty who outraged her family, the Whitings, by falling in love with, and then marrying, a *Catholic who had not gone to Princeton* — they were actually perfectly matched. Cornelia's cool tempered his heat; Patrick's passion aroused her own; and in the richest of rich skies in which they orbited like moons, no scandal was ever attached to them. Despite innumerable temptations, he remained faithful to her, and his support gave her strength. Beneath her regal demeanor she let herself grow soft and trusting — only for him, forever for him.

Until forever was cut short by a glioblastoma that took her life in eighteen months, her spirit long before that, and he was left, at age fifty-four, with nothing except wealth, their rebellious son, Peter, and the tremendous sympathy of friends.

*   *   *

Now he was building his most magnificent hotel around the shell of an antique mansion, much as Helmsley had done with the Palace. At completion, there would be four hundred rooms, including seventy suites, some with original marble from Witherspoon House. Guests would have a pick of styles: Renaissance Italian; eighteenth-century French; ultramodern American.

And in every room in The Cornelia — O'Malley wondered why he had not settled on the name sooner as he envisioned the hotel — there would be Pears soap and Porthault towels. It was going to be a truly Grand Hotel, the way they used to build them in the best of times, before the invention of accountants.

He spent the entire day at the hotel, meeting with Freund in the morning, personally directing the centimeter-by-centimeter polishing of the marble columns in the lobby, checking the seating and lighting in the Gold Bar, and then, at noon, meeting with the chief architect, Michael Hart.

Their conversation lasted through lunch. Hart went through several crucial items, most important, the gilding of the Renaissance ornamentation of the main lobby and the filigree above the windows at the entrance on Lexington.

Alone once more, O'Malley moved into the kitchen, at last hearing the sweetly satisfying racket of hammering and drilling — the stainless steel stoves, warming ovens, and counters were finally going in after a fourteen-week wait for materials. There were already enough copper pots, O'Malley noted with pleasure, to open the largest supply store in Manhattan.

At seven-thirty, O'Malley found himself once again passing beneath the lobby's antique clock, a timepiece that had once adorned the Winter Palace of Catherine the Great.

At the center of the hotel atrium in the rear of the lobby, an original Bernini fountain, imported from Rome, had been restored to its matchless splendor. That afternoon, plumbing had finally been completed by Timothy Sullivan of the Bronx Local 41, who called O'Malley to announce that all systems were go.

"All ready for lift-off," O'Malley muttered, unlocking the knob that controlled the spigots and spray.

The water rose in gentle bends and bows. O'Malley's face shone like a child's on Christmas Day. "*Damn* but that's fine," he said aloud in the deserted garden.

But the spray had to go higher still, he considered as he studied the fountain. He turned the knob. The water remained at its level. *It would never catch the afternoon sunlight,* he thought. It was like the ejaculàtion of a ninety-year-old man.

That bastard Sullivan. All systems go my ass! I'll fix it so he never ejaculates again.

Already, Patrick O'Malley had made his first mental note for the next day.

He passed under the lobby clock again, then stopped and checked his own watch. *Eight-sixteen! The lobby clock was three minutes fast!*

He felt murder in his chest. "Slow down, Pat," he imagined Nellie's voice telling him. "Careful, careful." He didn't give a good, flying fuck about "careful." With incompetent kiss-asses all around him — and with Nellie gone — what good was living anyway?

91

27

WHEN JENNIE WAS THIRTEEN and it was almost time for her to go to high school, I bought a beautiful house on Greenbriar Road in Bedford, New York. It was time for both of us to have a real home. More important, I wanted Jennie settled into a good school.

I wanted stability, and peaceful surroundings, both for Jennie and myself. We picked out the house together. Both of us loved it, the sprawling grounds, and the town of Bedford. We finally had a home again.

I was already infamous for being extremely selective about playing concerts and being on the road. I think I had my priorities straight, and my head screwed on as well. I'd never wanted to think of myself as a star, or live like one either. I vowed not to bring up Jennie that way.

The years with Phillip had made me afraid of hoping for too much more than peacefulness and contentment in my life. *It wasn't so bad,* I kept telling myself.

There was a wonderful school for Jennie in Bedford; we were less than an hour's drive from the city; I could have complete privacy when I needed it, and socialize if I felt like it. It seemed a perfect town for us, peaceful and enduring, the right place to erase the last vestiges of a still painful history.

Jennie dubbed our house Shangri-la, la, la. Not to be spoken — to be *sung*. She had a good voice, and an even better sense of humor.

Most nights were blissfully peaceful at our house. The noises were the singing of birds, the occasional yapping of a dog, sometimes the sound of a radio as teenagers drove by. The "cruising" cars reminded me of growing up in Newburgh, which was only thirty miles to the north.

I was startled one evening in April to hear a pounding on the front door. I was expecting no one. As far as I knew, I was not in trouble with the police. Jennie was in her room doing her homework, and I hoped she was too young for a jilted boyfriend.

I had been careful to keep my whereabouts unpublicized, so the intruder was almost surely neither a fan nor a rival. Someone knocking on the wrong door? Probably.

Curious, and a little nervous, I went to the door. Through the peephole, I could see a man, his body distorted by the glass. He was in a rumpled suit but well dressed, his tie askew, his hair uncombed, his face apoplectic. I sensed he was harmless enough, and opened the door.

"Mrs. Bradford?" he said, somehow managing to sound exasperated.

"Yes. Can I help you? How did you know my name?"

"There's a BRADFORD on your mailbox. A deduction."

"There's a bell on the door. Why not use that instead of pounding?"

"There is?" He seemed genuinely surprised. "I guess I was so angry I didn't notice. Sorry about that."

His anger had evidently evaporated. There was definitely no danger in him. I invited him in. "What's this about?"

He followed me down the foyer to the living room. "If I built

93

hotels the way GM builds cars, I'd be crucified. Yet those shitkickers —"

Ah. That was the explanation. "It's your car, then?"

"A brand-new Mercedes convertible. Not a thousand miles on the useless rattletrap. And here I am, exhausted, minding my own business, happy to be off the highway, when the son of a bitch dies. I mean *dies*. No warning, not even a death rattle. The mother just says to me, 'Fuck you, Pat,' and quits. And do I have a car phone? Of course not. If I had one, I'd use it, and I like the driving time for thinking and enjoying myself in blessed peace. The only reason for a phone is in case the car has a breakdown, and is a brand-new, eighty-thousand-dollar car going to cause trouble? No way. Ha!" Suddenly he stopped and grinned. His smile reminded me of Paul Newman's — *a lot*. "So can I use your phone? I may be the only Irish Catholic who's a member of AAA and not AA."

"Sure thing," I said, hiding a smile. He was funny, and the humor was contagious, at least it was that night. "The phone's in the den. What were you doing on Greenbriar at this time of night?"

"I *live* on Greenbriar. About three miles further down. You must have passed my house a thousand times going to the village. My name's O'Malley. It's the oversized Georgian. I live in it to impress my friends."

I knew the house, or more accurately, the estate. It was one of the grandest on Greenbriar. "You said hotels. Then you must be —"

"Patrick O'Malley. I'm building one on Park Avenue. The Cornelia. Do you like the name? Say yes, and you'll be its first guest as my guest."

This time I couldn't suppress the laugh. "Yes. I might take you up on it. Would you like a drink, Mr. O'Malley?"

He bowed. "You're very, very kind and understanding. Scotch if you have it. Neat."

I showed him to the den, then went to the kitchen to fix a

drink. There really was something about this poor/rich blitzed man that struck me as funny. The look on his face was classic silent-movie comedy. He had star quality.

I didn't get a lot of visitors, besides music-business people, into my safe, comfortable, closed world. I was getting good at pretending that I liked it that way. *I didn't like it at all.*

I poured a Scotch, and went back to the den, knocking gently before entering. I stepped inside the room, then stopped and began to laugh out loud. I couldn't help myself.

Patrick O'Malley had taken off his rumpled suit jacket and hung it carefully over the back of a chair. He had removed his black cordovans and put them neatly beside the jacket.

He lay stretched out on my old, flowered sofa, and he was fast asleep.

28

I WOKE UP EARLY, but Patrick was gone by the time I went downstairs. Jen and I did a three-mile run, then a power drink, and off to school for her. I went into my den and began working, lost in the lyrics of "A Lady Hard as Love."

Around ten-thirty, I walked to the riding stables, noticing that the day had assumed the gauzy look of life shot through a telephoto lens. I felt content. Not a great feeling, but not so bad either. Something was missing from life, but I certainly had a lot, and no complaints.

A florist truck came bumping up the drive and a boy with spiked orange hair and Coke-bottle glasses came hurrying toward me, bearing an arrangement of freesias and decorative ribbons.

There was a note. *O'Malley,* I thought, pleased for some reason.

Dear Margaret Bradford,

Forgive me for not having immediately recognized your name, but the only singers I've heard of are the Clancy Brothers.

*I don't know for certain if I can face you again. Not after
last night. But I'm going to try. Give it my best.*

*Will you please have dinner with me some evening this
week? Let me try to make amends.*

*You have the most beautiful blue eyes I've ever seen, and
I will spend the time between now and our dinner listening
to Maggie Bradford records until I've memorized your
songs.*

> *The Mortified Sleeper (your neighbor),*
> *Patrick*

My eyes were chestnut brown, and I had a feeling that Patrick O'Malley knew it, and knew I knew he knew it.

Dinner? Why not? I needed to meet more people in Bedford. I left a message on his machine making a date for Thursday night.

Blue eyes — that's Sinatra, not me.

29

THURSDAY was an unexpected and unqualified *hit*. He made me laugh — a lot. He had stories weaved inside of stories, weaved into still more stories. He had a wonderfully warm smile, and a generous nature. I knew I'd made my first friend in Bedford, and it felt good.

Over the next few weeks, I saw Patrick several times. I enjoyed his odd, wry, but honest sense of humor; his unique comic timing; his oversentimental but nevertheless touching stories about growing up in an Irish family of ten; his thrill at putting up his parents in the honeymoon suite of his first grand hotel.

In deference to his globetrotting, I began to call Patrick names that amused him: Padriac, Patrice, and Patrizio. But Patrick had no silly names for me. Sometimes he called me Margaret, the first person to do that since my mother.

"My first love," Patrick told me, "was actually the sea. It's the one powerful image that I still have of Ireland, and when I was growing up there."

Patrick had a modest sailboat, and one weekday morning we took it out on the Sound. Patrick played hooky from his hotel project; I could afford one morning away from the piano, and my own rituals.

Soon, we were out on the water, and I found that I loved it too. Since it was early on a weekday, there weren't many other boats out, even though the day was in the low seventies, with clear blue skies. I could see heavy traffic as we slid away from shore, and watching the cars heading to work reminded me of how lucky I was.

"There but for the grace of God," Patrick said and saluted the commuters. "Suckers!" he shouted into the sea breeze and laughed. He wasn't being mean, just playful.

He and Jennie had obviously conspired, since he'd smuggled some of my power drink onboard, and had made me my usual breakfast. He even joined me for the special mixture of several fruit juices and vitamins.

"So are you finally over the bastard, Maggie?" he asked as we sipped juice. As usual, he was spontaneous and *himself*. I understood that he meant Phillip, who we'd talked about before, but not very much.

"Yes and no," I told Patrick the truth. I felt that I could.

"I think I know what you mean." He gave me a hug with one arm as the two of us stood staring out over the oncoming breakers.

"Sorry I don't have any good advice for you," he said. "I never shot any bastards, though several I know deserved it. Is it all right if I make this light — it's my way, you know."

I nodded. It *was* Patrick's style to be able to joke when things got particularly dark. He made me laugh constantly, and I liked it a lot.

"He *was* a bastard, and I'm sorry I married him."

Patrick waved his free arm angrily. "Awww, he just took advantage. You were very young, and not so long out of your aunt's house. He did his fine officer's act, made his lofty promises, lied to you. I know, let's sail north to West Point. We'll dig up his grave, then we'll pulverize the bones."

I shook my head, but I was smiling. "You make me laugh."

"It's my job. It's what I'm good at."

I looked at him. "What do you think I'm good at?"

He gestured with both hands. "Oh, everything. Everything that I've seen at least. You're closing yourself off a little — that's the only area for improvement that I can see."

"You're funny, and you can be very sweet."

"You think so?" he asked.

"Yes, I do. I definitely believe that. I'm sure of it."

"Well good, there's an object lesson, 'cause I'm not ten percent as sweet as you. The way you talk, the way you think, raise your beautiful girl, Jennie, what comes out in your songs. That's why your music's so popular, don't you know it?"

"I do —"

"I know — and you don't. I have a favor, a big favor."

I tensed a little.

Patrick winced. "See what he did to you, sweet Maggie? I hate it when you're afraid. That *reflex*. Your back is like a washboard."

"I'm getting better," I said.

"I know that you are. Now *don't clutch*. Here's the favor. It's the most wonderful thing I can imagine."

I *couldn't* imagine. I wasn't tense anymore — Patrick had made me comfortable — but I couldn't figure where he was heading with this.

"All right," I finally said, "I'll do anything. That's how much I trust you."

"Excellent. The best words I've heard you speak so far. Now what I'd like, Maggie, what I'd love — would you sing me one of your songs. Any song of your choosing. Right here, just the two of us, would you softly sing a beautiful song just for me?"

It was a beautiful request, and I sang for Patrick.

30

ONE NIGHT, it must have been a week or so later, I had a light dinner with Jennie. Around eight, I drove her to her friend Millie's house where she was having a sleep-over. Then, I went to Patrick's house for a second meal.

Patrick had excused his "chief cook and bottle-washer" for the evening. He said that he wanted to do the honors: roasted lobster with garlic butter, thickly sliced and crisped french fries, succulent corn on the cob. A simple, satisfying *feast*.

After dinner, we took a walk on the grounds to a grove of apple trees at the far end of his estate. There Patrick slid his arm around me and gently kissed the top of my head.

"You smell like orange blossoms. How is that?"

"More like No More Tears shampoo from Johnson and Johnson."

"Whatever. You smell wonderful." He kissed both my cheeks, then my forehead, my nose, the tip of my chin. He kissed me on the lips, and I felt his tongue touch mine.

I pulled away. We had kissed before, though I had never really felt his passion; I always drew back. Tonight was different. *He kisses absolutely beautifully,* I thought. *I just felt his heart and I like the feeling.*

I felt safe with him. The night wind whispered softly through the grove of trees. He kissed me again, and this time I could feel myself responding.

I can't shut myself off any longer. I can't spend my life afraid, even if I am.

"Let's go inside," Patrick said. "I slept at your house once. In the den, and without your permission, as you constantly remind me. Will you sleep at my house tonight?"

I turned my body into his, smiling at the two of us. For once, I was happy about one of Jennie's sleep-overs. "Not in the den, I hope."

I could feel him grow hard against me. "No," he whispered. "Come with me. Please. Trust me."

My reluctance must have been stronger than I imagined, for he had surely sensed it. *Trust him.* Oh, how I wanted to, yet as we turned toward the house I could see Phillip's face, feel the menace of him. I shuddered involuntarily. *Damn* him. We should have pulverized the bones.

"We don't have to," Patrick said, reading my fear. "I don't know everything that happened to you long ago, but we can wait. You're the first woman who's meant anything to me in a while. But I want this to be exactly right for both of us."

He *was* the most considerate and loving man. I did trust him.

"I want to," I said, conscious of how tight my throat felt, how cold my skin. "I do, Patrick. Let's go inside."

31

WE WERE UNUSUALLY QUIET as we slowly undressed in Patrick's sprawling, moonlit upstairs bedroom. In the spun-out silence the beat of my heart was electric, loudly amplified. All sorts of questions and self-doubts began circulating through my head. *I'm too tall for him. He won't like me once he really gets to know me. Do I know enough about him? Relax, Maggie. Please, just relax.*

He looked wonderful in the moonlight. Hard, working-man's stomach. Well-muscled legs. Broad chest lightly covered with silver and light-brown hair. *Sexy,* I thought, and I liked what I was feeling.

Open yourself up to him, Maggie. Don't be afraid. This time it's right.

He held me in his arms for the quietest moment, kissing my hair and my neck. He *held me* as we stood before the moonlit window and waited for me to relax. I sensed that he was willing to wait for a long, long time.

He kissed me again, and I had the feeling that we were falling toward each other. He kissed my cheeks, my forehead, my nose, then both my eyes. Soft, lingering kisses. Finally, I began to kiss him back. I kissed his cheeks, his forehead, his eyes. I continued to fall toward him, at least I had that sense.

"Dear sweet Maggie," he whispered. He *knew* that I was still a little afraid. *He always knew what I was feeling.* He was wise, intelligent, but he never showed off, never seemed impressed with himself.

"You are such a lovely and special woman. I adore you, Maggie."

It was *Patrick's* voice, *Patrick's* arms, and as he lifted me up and carried me to the massive bed, I felt a release, as though he had severed the invisible chains that had held me captive. This was such a sweet, slow dance. It was so new for me — either forgotten, or never experienced. He took his time, and then entered me gently, carefully.

From a fragile place inside me, a place forgotten, pleasure rippled through me, and I shivered. I felt a deep, warm sensation flowing, spreading, rushing out. It was a feeling that had been missing for so long. And it went on and on that night.

"Gentle Patrick," I said finally, and I didn't think I would ever stop *smiling*. I touched his face once again. He was smiling too. "You're so good for me. You're so good, period."

"It will be better and better," he said. "Trust me." Then he whispered, "*Trust us.*"

I did. Finally, I trusted someone again.

32

WILL SHEPHERD should have felt at the absolute top of the world, but somehow he didn't. He was certainly famous, and filthy rich, but he hated it. That night, he was also dangerously high. *The werewolf of London,* he thought. *Beware.*

The cocaine he'd taken as the concert began, and again immediately before the appearance of Maggie Bradford, made him feel all-powerful. And why the hell not? He was a star not only on the football field, but also among the elite attending the special performance at Albert Hall.

Will looked around, grinning, waving. Pete Townsend was there, and Sting, and Mick Jagger — *a new rock group: the Has-beens* — along with Rupert Murdoch and Margaret Thatcher, *the two people currently destroying England.*

They had come to hear Maggie Bradford soothe their tortured souls. Her ballads did that to people. Her songs were rare, a miracle actually — strong melody, lyric, and mesmerizing. No singer put so many different emotions into one song — all of her songs imitated the dizzying complexity of modern life, or so it seemed to Will.

She came onstage to loud, adoring applause, and yet she

seemed *so shy*. Tickets had been sold out for months. She sat at the piano . . . and simply began to sing.

Will had no memory of the scene at Lady Trevelyan's party, and so he looked at her with a fresh eye. There was her long, flowing blond hair. And the simple beauty of her face.

But she seemed to *glow* on this particular night. He wondered why? What was her secret? What had this woman learned that he hadn't?

Her voice wasn't large or particularly dramatic; there was no melodrama in her style. She sang with a purity that pierced his heart like a sword, and he could actually feel the pain as well as the honest beauty of her music.

She was singing about the sadness of lost dreams, about a fall from grace. Will felt she was singing about him.

Tears rolled down his cheeks. The music moved him in ways he couldn't understand, but it was as though a great light were embracing him from the stage, and then transporting him from the concert hall into a place for only the two of them. *What the hell am I thinking?* he wondered. He was tempted to laugh at himself. He felt like such a damn fool.

God how he loved the sound of her voice though. He could listen to it for the rest of his life.

He had the strange, haunting feeling that Maggie Bradford could save him from himself.

"Did you forget I was with you in there? You did, didn't you, Will? You bastard!"

Will looked at the slender, dark-haired woman who was holding on to his arm as he left the concert hall. He had forgotten about her — hadn't a clue who the hell the beautiful woman behind the dark glasses was. Ah, the werewolf strikes again!

She was stunning, but they all were. Model? Actress? Would-be-actress? Shopgirl? Where the hell had he met her? Christ, this was embarrassing — even for him it was a new low.

"So, how long have you been getting this royally fucked-up on coke? You have, haven't you? Can you play like this?"

Ahhh, Will sighed with relief. *Reporter!* Now he remembered who the hell she was. She was the *Times.* She wanted to do a piece on him. He wanted a piece of her. Fair trade.

He recovered his poise, and immediately went into one of his best Prince Charming acts. He could, he knew, fool the pants off any of them. Even a *Times* reporter.

"No, it wasn't drugs, Cynthia," he said. *Cynthia Miller! That was her name.* He was so proud of himself. "I love her songs. I really do."

"So you said on the way over. Your car is full of her tapes."

"Her music is so damn real, comes right out of her life," Will continued. "Do you like it much yourself?"

"As I told you, *on the way over,* I do like her music, indeed. I also enjoyed the concert, but maybe not as much as you did."

Will pecked her on the cheek — gently, very chastely. *"Now what shall we do?"* he asked. *Careful, Will. She's a reporter.*

Cynthia Miller smiled a sly grin. "I'd like to hear more about the Blond Arrow," she said. She was typical of most reporters, an incredible cynic, a romantic gone bad.

"Would you like to see it?" Will teased. He added a twinkling smile.

He knew that she did. All of them did — except maybe one.

Maggie Bradford! That's who he wanted, he needed — *a real person to understand and challenge him.*

107

33

THE DOORBELL RANG, and Will stopped reading the morning newspaper. He peered out the window. A showy, silver-blue Rolls-Royce was parked in his driveway. He could hear his maid greeting the newcomer, then footsteps approaching the living room.

"Mr. Shepherd, Mr. Lawrence."

At the entrance stood a smiling, sandy-haired man, perhaps ten years older than Will. Will knew who Winifred "Winnie" Lawrence was. The man was a major force behind the development of soccer in the United States, a man determined to bring the beauty and grace of this refined sport to a nation overdosed on American football mayhem. Lawrence was a lawyer, an agent, but most of all, a hustler par excellence.

Will waited in his chair until Lawrence had entered the room; then he got up slowly, uncoiling as though from a nap, and shook hands with the American. Like so many people from his country, *their* country, Lawrence skipped preamble and pretense, and got right into it. Cut to the chase.

"Tell me, Will, why do you think the Germans remain so powerful a threat to win the Cup?" Lawrence said, his smile seemingly *pasted* across his face. "Year after year, no matter their personnel, they seem to have a powerhouse team."

It was actually a question Will had often asked himself. "Discipline, I suppose," he said. "It's more their team style than any individual, and that makes them strong."

Lawrence beamed, reveling in the obvious, as Americans so often do. "It's a style I've incorporated into the American team. But we need world-class individuals as well. We need a scorer, a striker."

"I figured that's why you came here."

"Yes, that's right. I've come to persuade you to play for the United States. I will not leave your house until I do."

Will laughed at the idea, not to mention Lawrence's gall. "It'll take some doing. There's no way America can compete, with or without me. Why should I do all that training just to go out in the qualifying rounds? What am I too dim to see?"

Lawrence reached into a stuffed briefcase and withdrew a computer sheet, spreading it out on the living room table. The two men bent over it.

"Look here, Will. Suspend your disbelief for just a few moments. *Look.* CONCACAF. Zone Norte. Zone Centro. Zone del Caribe. The official schedule for the American team in the North Zone qualifiers."

"So what?"

"Don't you see? Let me help you then. The Americans don't have to beat anybody worthwhile. Not until they're into the final twenty-four."

Will laughed again. He enjoyed Lawrence's first-class act, but this was simply too much. "Maybe you haven't heard, Mr. Lawrence, *Winnie,* but the American team isn't considered anybody either. Any national team will be absolutely thrilled to play the United States. They'd think the game would be a complete walkover."

"And that's to our advantage!" Lawrence put his arm around Will's shoulder. Actually, he was rather a good salesman, the great American huckster. Very compelling in his way. "We'll have the benefit of *surprise*. What if I tell you that Wolf Obermeier has agreed to coach the American team?"

Obermeier had coached championship teams in his native Germany and in Argentina. He had the reputation of having one of the most brilliant minds in football — and the harshest tongue.

"I'd be somewhat impressed," Will granted. At least now you've gotten my attention. Tell me more, Mr. Lawrence. Maybe I need a challenge right now."

"Or a crowning achievement?" the American said, and grinned.

34

"TRY TO IMAGINE the World Series, the Super Bowl, the Kentucky Derby, and the Democratic and Republican Conventions all rolled into one great event," wrote Mickey Trevor Jr. in the popular American magazine *Sports Illustrated*.

Then you have some small idea of the power and glory of the World Cup.

Next imagine Rio de Janeiro, where soccer may be more important than sex and the samba, and the World Cup makes Mardi Gras seem like a Girl Scout jamboree.

That's where the World Cup final will be played.

And now think of the two teams matched in that final: heavy favorite Brazil, three-time previous winner of the cup, whose lineage is as impressive as the New York Yankees — and upstart, unheralded, pipsqueak America, the miracle men in the red, white, and blue, whose rise from nonentity to heroic challenger has all the elements of a classic fairy tale — only, miraculously and unbelievably, it is true.

Folks, this here is a fairy story to rank with "The Lion King"! You may not have taken much notice when America quietly won the North Zone qualifying tournament, thus reaching the World Cup finals. It might have quickened your pulse a bit when our boys made it past the qualifying round, with only a loss to Germany to mar their record. Good for us, good for my kids, who love soccer because they play it in school, you probably figured, but that's the end. It's all over. And so you turned your attention back to the pennant races, and the wonderful baseball season of Barry Bonds, still a bit puzzled as to why the rest of the world takes soccer so damn seriously, and meanwhile, our team edged past Nigeria into the last eight.

But when the U.S. beat Italy — Italy! — in the quarter-finals (the score was 3–2, and each of the American goals was scored by America's star of stars, Will Shepherd; and then edged Germany 2–11 in the semis, surely your attention returned, and by now if your temperature isn't boiling, if your heart isn't pounding, if you haven't canceled all plans for Sunday night so you can stay home to watch the final, then you're not an American, you don't like sports — or you're dead.

The American team has Will Shepherd and ten other guys who probably couldn't make the starting lineups of any of the leading clubs in the competition.

But Shepherd. Ah, Shepherd!

Soccer is a team sport, but even Wolf Obermeier, the U.S.A. coach, admits that in this case Will Shepherd is the team. "Without Will, we wouldn't have qualified," Obermeier said. "With him — well, look where we are now. Look where we are."

"Bravo! My congratulations to *Sports Illustrated!* Finally something of value, beyond their beloved swimsuit issue!"

Will finished the article and grunted with satisfaction. "Shepherd *is* the team," he said. "Has a nice ring to it. Accurate reporting for a change too. Bravo!"

"I read it while you were asleep," Victoria Lansdowne said.

The leggy British actress was sprawled luxuriously on top of the covers. Her striking, cobalt-blue eyes admired the physique of the man she had met for the first time the evening before. The Blond Arrow. Right now, the most famous athlete in the world.

Despite the air-conditioning in the Rio Hilton, the suite was hot, and neither of them had put on any clothes after a long bout of sex. They looked every bit as good as their starry reputations suggested. The sheen of sweat glistened on their beautiful bodies.

"What did you think of it? Just another puff piece?"

"I think that if you play football as well as you do certain other things, you'll beat the living doo-doo out of Brazil tomorrow."

He smiled. "Satisfied, I take it."

"Never. Not even close, sweet thing. I'm *insatiable*. Don't *you* read the papers? My 'string of lovers.'"

He looked at her full breasts, the slender, very tan legs that had spread for him so willingly, yet seemed to have a mind of their own. She reminded him of Vannie. Many of them did. Maybe that was why he was beginning to feel a touch angry at *vainglorious Victoria*.

"Want another go . . . on goal, so to speak?" Victoria had followed his gaze down and along her body. She reveled in the power she held over supposedly strong and powerful men. This one was different though. He was smarter than she'd expected him to be.

"I don't think so. Maybe your '*string*' has finally ended here," he said, returning her dazzling smile.

"What's the matter? No more arrows in our quiver? Are we fresh out of joy juice?"

Will fought down the rage, forcing himself to laugh. "There's a game tomorrow, a rather important game. Maybe you've heard? You say you read the papers, dear Vic."

"And sweet Lambkins wants to get up for that, but not for me?"

113

"Don't," he said. He'd *warned* her at least.

"Don't what?" she taunted him. "Tempt you?" She wet a finger with her tongue, and placed it between her legs. "If you can't do it, I suppose I'll have to do it myself. Now *here's* a juicy picture for the tabloids. *Victoria does herself! Will not able?*"

With a roar, Will was on her, all over her. Victoria *woofed* out air.

"Oh," she gasped. "Oh God, that hurts. That *hurts.*" Victoria Lansdowne tried to push him off, but he pinned her hands to her sides. "Please, dear Jesus, *stop!* Please, please, I'm begging you, Will! Stop it. I'm serious, stop."

But there was nothing that could stop the Blond Arrow.

35

ON THE AFTERNOON of the World Cup final the heat soared to ninety-three degrees on the sugary, white sand beaches of Copacabana and Ipanema. For a while, it was a quiet day, a national holiday in celebration of the World Cup. Rich and poor alike rested, saving their energy for the most popular sporting event in the world.

Then, suddenly, day melted into swarming, jungle-hot night. All of Rio de Janeiro seemed to pour outdoors to witness, and participate in, the national game of "futebol."

The wide avenues of the South American city became a raucous and dangerous carnival. Auto horns honked out *Bra-sil! Bra-sil!* Along the Avenida Brasil and Castello Branco, university students defiantly wrapped themselves in the national flag. All buses and taxis were decorated with bright-colored streamers. Women danced impromptu in the streets, blouses clinging to their breasts, skirts swirling like hoops.

By seven o'clock, the crowd had converged on Rio's legendary Maracana Stadium, police letting no one in without a ticket, though hundreds eluded them and entered the stadium to find what sight lines they could.

Inside, a hundred thousand frenzied Cariocas, waving multicolored banners and placards proclaiming sports victory and social revolution, let out cheers in cadence with the rhythm of ten thousand samba drums, and *twice* that many boom boxes.

At the end of a rampway, standing with the rest of his team amid the deafening noise, Will *listened*.

He could hear his own heart beat against the walls of his chest. He could hear . . .

"*Numero nueve . . . De America . . . Will . . . Shepherd!*" came from the loudspeaker.

There were drawn-out boos at the announcement, shouts of *palhaco*, "clown." But even in Rio, there were cheers for Will Shepherd. Some in the crowd treasured artistry over partisanship, and Will's achievements were art. A quartet of shirtless men ran out onto the field. Each had the numeral nine painted on his chest.

The cheers continued as Will raced onto the field, his fist held high above his flying blond curls. His head was filled with sound and images, fantasies and dreams. He could hardly breathe.

He felt The Thrill travel through every part of his body.

No one could stop him tonight.

He was going to make sports history in front of half the world. No one would ever forget him after this special night in Rio.

36

AT 8:32, THE COLOMBIAN REFEREE set the ball down on a bent tuft of grass.

Brazil versus America! Unthinkable, unpopular, impossible, and yet it was happening.

The World Cup final had begun!

Arturo Ribeiro, the mercurial nineteen-year-old Brazilian star, swept up the ball, passed it to a teammate in a play practiced for hours in the preceding months, and raced forward in a brilliant, weaving dance. The ball was sent back to him. His back to the goal, he cartwheeled and sent the ball flying toward the American net.

The fans exploded.

"*Gooool de Bra-sil!*" the PA announcer screamed. "*Gooool de Arturo Ribeiro!*"

Time elapsed: thirty-three seconds.

Less than six minutes later, Brazil scored again. Easily, effortlessly it seemed.

Cariocas danced in the stands and let loose black snakes and plucked chickens from hidden baskets. Outside the stadium, flares burst in the night sky; handguns were fired into the air; police sirens wailed on and on as though the long-awaited revolution had arrived.

One would have thought no greater rejoicing was possible. But the celebration of Brazil's second goal was muted, compared to the reaction when Ribeiro scored again in the thirty-third minute of play.

Brazil led 3–0 at half-time!

The game was looking like a rout . . . no, it *was* a full-scale massacre.

Listen to this pompous asshole, Will was thinking as he sat with his head hung low in the visitors' locker area.

"You play as if you are drugged," Wolf Obermeier said. He had already berated his other so-called players, and now he was speaking quietly to Will, whom he had drawn aside as the team left the dressing room to begin the second half. "Something is troubling you? *Are you drugged?*"

"Maybe." Will smiled at the overserious German's consternation. Truthfully, he didn't know what was wrong. He felt refreshed after last night, blurred though the memory of it was; no, it was something else holding him back. He shrugged at the German. Whatever it was, The Thrill had passed through him like a thunderbolt, and he could not recapture it. He felt sullen and slow.

"We need you to become a *madman,*" Obermeier went on. "Three goals. Absolutely impossible to make up. But I've *seen* you do the impossible. This is not the time to play the worst game of your life — you must be hero, not goat." He patted Will on the head, father to son. "Show me you are a man."

A man. Will walked onto the field in total shock. *You're in the World Cup championship, and you're playing like you're still in Fulham. These are the Brazilians. The best in the world. If you beat them, you'll be famous forever. Obermeier's right. Be a man.*

He took a deep breath and trotted toward the bench. He

118

heard the crowd roaring, but knew it wasn't for him; it was for the Brazilian team emerging from the clubhouse. He looked up into the stands — an ocean of dark faces rooting against him. Well, *fuck them!* He was the Blond Arrow! He did the impossible, *regularly.*

At first, Will's brilliance was all show on the Maracana field. Uncanny dribbling, sudden changes of direction creating paths where none existed, impossible velocity in the smallest spaces — but no support, not even a half-chance at goal.

Then, nine minutes into the second half, Will stepped in front of a bullet, a streaking pass meant for the Brazilian sweeper Ramon Palero.

The white ball dropped like a stone from Will's shoulder. Almost in the same motion, his right leg flew back, and he felt a small muscle tear in his thigh, the pain corkscrewing into his knee socket.

No matter. Will sent the ball flying toward the upper-left-hand corner of the Brazilian goal. The keeper could barely raise his arm, let alone stop the ball as it rocketed past him.

"*Gooool de America!*" Will heard the loudspeaker, and believed the words to be true. "*Gooool de Will Shepherd!*"

The Thrill exploded inside his brain. Adrenaline punched through his body, and the pain in his thigh and knee vanished. He felt all-powerful, the way he had the night before, when Victoria had taunted him. *All-powerful!*

The striker!

The goal scorer!

No one was on the playing field but *him!* The *loner!*

With only three minutes left in the game, he broke free again. He furiously pushed the ball down the left touchline, faked a pass inside but kept it himself, evading a defender who could only look after him in disbelief. His legs stopped suddenly, went forward again; stopped; *accelerated* from the dead stop.

119

Then he shot, and the ball cannoned forward, a white blur, nearly ripping the net at the back of the Brazilian goal.

"*Gooool de America . . . Gooool de Will Shepherd.*"

Time remaining: two minutes and forty-six seconds.

Still time enough.

37

THE HUGE, SPRAWLING CROWD had grown silent and still, their attention as much on the stadium clock as on the furious action on the field. Less than three minutes to play in what was suddenly a cliff-hanger.

No single player could defeat a great team. Not even Will Shepherd could accomplish such a feat.

Everyone watching believed that; yet none of them could be absolutely sure. He was such a dazzling scorer, perhaps the greatest striker ever. He was a magician, or perhaps he'd made a deal with the devil.

Will intercepted a pass to the Brazilian right wing and, like an eagle, swooped down the field at incredible speed. Everything was concentration now, moves practiced a thousand — no, a million times. He feinted left and went right at nearly ninety degrees, past a stranded defender. He could see the goalkeeper ahead of him, a patch of enemy color.

If he were God he couldn't stop me, Will thought, and saw fear in the keeper's eye. He switched the ball from his right leg to his left.

He used his elbow deftly on a defender. He curled *softly* to the right.

The ninety minutes were up. There would be a few seconds of stoppage time. Plenty of time to be immortal, to join the likes of Pele and Cruyff.

Relax. Let this stretch out. Feel it course through your body like heroin.

The Brazilian goalkeeper moved left, anticipating Will's shot, leaving the right corner of the goal free.

Not much daylight — a tiny sliver.

The referee was raising his whistle. In seconds it would blow and the game would be over.

It was a shot Will was famous for, a curve hit with the left foot that broke from left to right, and Will measured it carefully in his mind's eye. *An opening as wide as the gates of Hell!*

He was aware of so many things: the sudden, chilling silence of the stadium, the sound of his own breath, and even of the ball on the turf, the look of pure horror on the keeper's face, the futile pursuit of the Brazilian sweeper.

His father's face rose up before him. His eyes. His dead, open eyes on the surface of that swimming pool.

And with the force of a whirlwind the furies attacked, demons took possession of his instincts, his legs, his soul. *No! He wouldn't let that control him!*

With a roar and a shudder, Will drew back his left leg and kicked. He hit it smoothly, perfectly.

He wanted to laugh at all those who had ever doubted him — he wanted to scream in each and every face looking down from their precious stadium seats.

The crowd went mad. Literally insane. Strangers hugged and kissed, and a wild dance began, one hundred thousand people participating in the frenzy. From outside and in, horns and trumpets blared, and a thousand streamers flew upward toward the moon.

As soon as he had shot, Will had fallen, all strength gone, and now as he lay on the ground he strained for the sound he didn't hear: "*Gooool de America . . . Gooool de Will Shepherd.*"

He saw the players running off the field, fearful of the crazed mob of spectators streaming toward them. Puzzled, he tried to stand up. Fear swept through his body. He couldn't get to his feet.

But the game is a draw, Will thought. *There's extra time to play. No one but the players should be allowed on the field. Get those assholes off. Get them off the field!*

A stricken Wolf Obermeier reached his side and tried to help him to his feet. "Too bad," his coach said. "How do Americans put it? Tough luck."

"The game's a draw," Will said, but the look on Obermeier's face told him the truth, and at that instant all of his furies emerged, even noisier and more terrifying than the thousands of fans descending on them. *His father was in that crowd, carrying his mother. She was the dead one now. Blood gushed from her open mouth. His father held her out to Will, like a trophy.*

The Haunting.

And Will Shepherd began to scream. Finally, he understood.

Brazil had won the World Cup.

The Blond Arrow had missed the shot of his life.

He had failed.

It's all your fault.

It's always been your fault.

38

IT WAS LIKE CARNIVAL in Rio that night, and there was no more sensuous, no wilder time to be had anywhere in the world. Conga lines weaved along every street. Will had rented a red Corvette, and he drove it through the city like a madman. *The football bum, the football loser,* he thought. *The werewolf of Rio.*

"Your name is Angelita, right?" he asked the woman slouched beside him in the speeding car. She was tall and dark-haired; very slender and quite strikingly beautiful. She wanted to feel the Blond Arrow, she'd told him. She wanted the Arrow *deep inside her.*

"Yes, I am Angelita. You keep asking me, as if my name is going to change. Maybe the way you drive we'll both be called Dead On Arrival soon."

"That's cute. That's very funny," Will said, shifting the car into fourth on the wide avenue that ran alongside Copacabana. "A funny and beautiful woman can be very dangerous, no?"

She tossed her black hair back and laughed. "You're afraid I might steal your heart, right?"

"No, not at all, Angelita. I'm afraid that you *won't* steal my heart. I'm afraid that no one will. Do you follow me?"

"Not a word of it, darling."

"Perfect!"

He took her up to his hotel suite. The room was well illuminated by the twinkling lights of the city, so he didn't bother to switch on the lamp. The rhythm from drum-beating bands on the street sounded as though they were right in the room.

"Put it in me right here, right now, Will Shepherd, numero nueve. I don't want to wait one second longer," she screamed at him as they embraced.

That had been hours and hours ago. He had put it in her all right. She'd moaned, then she had tried to scream. Then she desperately tried to pull the "arrow" out of her heart.

"What have you done? Oh my God, what did you do to me?"

"I wanted to steal your heart," Will said in a whisper. "Did I?"

Now, he kept forgetting her name. Who the hell was she? Oh yes, yes, it was Angelita.

Now *Angelita* lay in the bathtub of his hotel room. He looked down at her and knew that he'd finally gone too far, even for him.

He had gone too far — slipped right over the edge.

If my fans could see me now, he thought. Here's the real Will Shepherd. This is the worthless scum I am. Beneath the handsome exterior beats a heart of darkness. Conrad, right? Will had finished *that* book in school. He'd understood it perfectly from the very first pages, until the end.

No one knew him, no one got it — *except maybe Angelita. Now, she knows, doesn't she?*

The woman's brown eyes were glazed over, looking up at him — looking *sideways* it seemed. He was her god, right? Her savior from the mean streets of Rio. She had wanted so badly to fuck with such a big star. Well, she had been fucked.

In his hand he held a glass filled with red liquid. He toasted Angelita. He saluted the woman with her own blood.

125

"I'm sorry," he whispered. "Well, I'm not, but I wish I were."

He drank from the glass, and knew he was lost. He had committed a murder. There would be a trial — he would be found guilty. Beads of perspiration formed on his forehead.

Blond Arrow — silver stiletto — vampire — what difference did it make, really.

He was going to prison for life.

39

I KNEW all about "falling from grace," but "falling in love" was something I realized I hadn't really understood before. It was happening though, gradually, beautifully, between Patrick and me. Day by day, our feelings for each other grew deeper and deeper. It was different from infatuation, which we'd experienced as well.

Let me count the ways that I was learning to love Patrick.

There was the way he reminded me, nearly every day, that I was very special, a worthwhile person. I began to believe it for the first time in my life.

There was the way Patrick set out to learn everything about the kind of music I wrote and sang, and how he came to understand and appreciate it better than most music writers for *Rolling Stone* and *Spin*.

There was the way he and Jennie could talk about anything and everything; and the way the three of us could do the same.

There was the way in which he surprised and delighted me with his stories, his wit, his insights.

In fact, during the first half year we were together, the only troubling point wasn't about us — *it was Patrick's son.* Peter was a genuine bastard — the opposite of his father. Peter tried to take over his father's company during that period, but he failed. Patrick mourned his failure with Peter, what he called, *his loss of his only son.*

Which was a good segue for me, I was thinking one afternoon in Bedford. If there could be a segue for this —

This was so hard, so very difficult for me. I was absolutely petrified. I sighed, got myself as ready as I'd ever be, and then said.

"We're going to have a baby, Patrick."

We were sitting in the living room in Bedford. I was about ready to show. Show, I figured — and therefore tell. We had used discretion and protection, but somehow I got pregnant anyway.

Even though I was an "artist" and "music person," I was traditional at heart and the pregnancy shook me to my roots. I told Jennie immediately. She said, "You love Patrick and he loves you. I love you both. I'm happy we're pregnant." That helped me a lot.

Now, Patrick's face registered a half-dozen emotions: amazement, shock, consternation, worry, doubt — but then — joy. Fabulous, unmistakable joy. The smile that I loved so much.

"When's the baby due? My God, tell me everything, Maggie."

"Five months, twelve days. Doctor Gamache didn't specify the hour."

He was smiling very broadly now. He held both my hands. "Boy or girl?"

"A boy, according to the amniocentesis. Allie? Do you like that name?"

"It's a lovely name." He shook his head in wonder. "I'm very happy about it, Maggie. I couldn't possibly be happier. Have I told you lately how much I love you?" He continued to grin.

"Yes," I whispered, "but tell me again. I never get tired of hearing it."

* * *

128

And that night, with a vividness I thought had long ago disappeared, I remembered. I remembered *him*.

Phillip returned to try and spoil everything.

He was drunk, as he often was. He could barely walk. He barged in the front door, yelling my name, and I cowered in the kitchen, not answering him, even when he was only a few feet away.

He had been so different when we'd first met in Newburgh. He'd been an officer and a gentleman, a scholar as well. He had swept me off my nineteen-year-old feet. I had been so needy, so alone. How could I have known that his role as professor frustrated him; that he'd joined the army to fight, but had been ordered to teach instead. He had to follow those orders, and was determined that I follow his.

"*When I call you, you say, 'Yes, Phillip,'* " *he pronounced with a superior smirk.*

"*Not when you're like this. No, Phillip. Not with me. Not ever.*"

The back of his hand slashed across my mouth. "Whenever I call, you say, 'Yes, Phillip,' " *he repeated.*

I said nothing. His wire-rimmed glasses were crooked on his nose. He looked like the effete snob that he was so afraid of being.

"*Maggie," he said softly, ominously.*

I didn't answer. His hand rose again, this time a fist. He wasn't powerfully built, but he outweighed me by sixty pounds.

"*Yes, Phillip, fuck you," I said. I don't swear like that, but I did then.*

"*What? What did you say, woman? What the hell did I just hear?*"

"*You heard me.*"

He stood stock-still. Then he leered. "Okay," he said, "let's fuck."

He lunged for me, swaying drunkenly. I ran up the back stairs to the attic, and slammed the door in his face.

Phillip kept guns up there. There were guns everywhere in the good soldier's house. I took one and cocked it. I pointed it at the attic door, waiting until his wild, angry face appeared.

"Take another step and I'll shoot, I will, Phillip." I was surprised at how calm I sounded, though I didn't feel calm.

He stared at me, tried to stare me down, but he didn't move. Then he began to laugh, a monstrous cackle.

"Oh, sweetheart," he said when he could control himself. "Sweetheart, sweetheart. You've won this round. But you'll live to regret it."

I was still regretting it, after all these years.

40

ON A PROMISING BLUE-SKIED MORNING, an uncharacteristically nervous and nonplussed Patrick had to rush me to the Northern Westchester Hospital in Mount Kisco, New York. He was so distraught, so unlike himself, it was charming and funny. Jennie came with us, and she was by far in the best shape, in the most control of the three of us.

As Patrick's car hurtled down narrow, pine-wooded roads, I couldn't keep dark thoughts from my mind though. *Think of the baby,* I told myself, but instead I remembered newspaper and magazine stories that had been tormenting me ever since my pregnancy became public:

"MAGGIE BRADFORD'S GREATEST LOVE SONG: Inside Story of the Not-So-Secret Hold Maggie Has Over Patrick."

How could our beautiful relationship be made to sound so shameful? Who wrote stories like these? Who wanted to read them? I had told Patrick I didn't care what anybody said, but the media could be so cruel. I felt wounded, humiliated.

Of course — at the time — I had no idea of how really savage they could be.

"Patrick, I know you're hurrying . . . but please, go a little faster if you can. Please?"

Dr. Lewis Gamache was waiting for us at the hospital.

"Hi there, Mom." He squinted from behind silver-framed bifocals. I had found him months before in the village of Chappaqua. He was a general practitioner who specialized in obstetrics, and I trusted him more than the far more famous doctors who had offered their services in New York.

"Hello, Lewis. I feel kind of shitty." I tried to smile, but felt I was going to faint.

"That's fine. It means you're almost there." He led me to a wheelchair, and I was taken inside.

Almost there, indeed! At eleven o'clock that night, two nurses in white tunics sped me down bright hospital corridors to the operating room. My body was soaked with perspiration. My hair was matted and looked almost brown. I felt clammy and cold. The pain was unbearable, twice what I remembered while having Jennie.

Dr. Gamache was waiting in the operating room. He was his usual wide-eyed and enthusiastic self.

"Hello, Maggie. What took you so long?"

"Ooohh." I shut my eyes as a contraction came again. "I was having too much fun in labor."

"Let's rock and roll," he said. I got the joke, but I didn't laugh.

At 11:19 in the morning, Dr. Gamache said, "Maggie, you've got yourself a little boy," and laid the baby beside me so I could look at him. He seemed to be yawning. *Bored already with planet Earth?* But he was such a beauty.

He received the classic rear-end slap, rather than the foot flick. I could hear his thin, barely perceptible cry.

"I don't think he's got your lungs," Dr. Gamache said. "Nurse, put the baby on the table warmer, please."

"His name is Allen," I said, and promptly passed out.

132

41

PATRICK NEARLY *FLEW* into my hospital room. He was beaming. He hurried to my bed, and we kissed. He *was* Paul Newman, and Spencer Tracy — all wrapped in one. He really was so wonderful: thoughtful, compassionate, tender, caring. Patrick wanted to marry me — he'd already *asked,* but something about "marriage," and my experience with Phillip, had made me ask him to wait. Patrick said that he understood. I hoped he did. I also hoped he would ask again — *soon.*

Something crunched in his sport jacket pocket as he hugged me. Curious, I reached inside.

"You've gone too far this time, buster," I said and smiled and rolled my eyes. "Cigars? How corny can you get?"

"I'm a corny guy." Patrick shrugged. "The cigars are for my friends. I bought Irish whiskey for the unwed father."

"Did you see Allie yet?"

"You bet. The *testicles* on him. Bigger than his feet. I'm so impressed."

I laughed. "That *would* interest you."

"I thought it might interest his mother just a little."

"To know that her son is well equipped for the world."

"Exactly right, and very well put."

Patrick reached out and held me gently against his chest. I could feel his heart beating. I loved that feeling, more and more so each day.

I can't think of a better father, I thought.

Then I said it aloud for Patrick to hear. I had never been happier in my life. I would marry Patrick soon, I knew. We were already a family though, and happier than most that I knew.

That night, I sang for little Allie for the first time.

42

THIS IS how it happened, dear readers. The third murder you've heard so many horrifying rumors about on TV and in the press. This is my confession, and it's never been printed anywhere before.

Patrick loved his work, the grand hotels he had built; I was sure that he loved Allie, Jennie, and me; and he loved the sea, loved to sail. The only trouble in his life was the continuing fights with his son, Peter, over control of his company, and particularly The Cornelia Hotel. In the process, Peter also made it clear that he despised me. Patrick and I decided we had to live with Peter's attacks. So be it.

I will never forget that day in early May. It was the first sail of the new spring: some time together for the two of us.

We were dressed early that morning, sharing hot chocolate by five. My new and absolutely wonderful live-in, Mrs. Leigh, appeared and wished us a happy day off. "Don't worry about anything here, Mrs. Bradford." With Mrs. Leigh, I didn't have to. She had brought up two beautiful children of her own, and she was already part of our family.

Patrick and I drove out to Port Washington on Long Island. *We had a whole day off to be together. What a special treat that was!*

By six-thirty, we were sauntering down the sun-spotted deck of the proud, Victorian Manhasset Bay Yacht Club. The air was cool, but the morning promised pleasure and relaxation. I stopped Patrick halfway down the walkway and gave him a hug and a kiss. I couldn't resist.

"I love you," I whispered. "Simple and uncomplicated as that might sound."

"Hard to come by," he smiled, "but so spectacular once you find it. I love you too, Maggie."

We reached the *Rebellion* a moment or two later. We would be sailing due east, Patrick told me, "into the sun, away from the earth."

"The storm last week beat the hell out of these boats, ours included," Patrick said, as he began a quick inspection. "Still water in here. Motor battery's probably dead. Antenna for the ship-to-shore broken. Shit. Remind me never to build a luxury liner. It'd be another *Titanic*."

The *Rebellion* made it out of the yacht club around quarter past seven. We were on our bright and merry way. As much as I loved spending nearly every waking moment with Allie, as much as I missed him already, I needed a morning off. I had been missing Patrick.

It was a blue-skied morning, the kind of day that automatically made me feel good. I could see Patrick relax at the helm. On the horizon, a forty-eight-foot ketch moved slowly, probably toward the Caribbean.

By noon, our boat was gliding through tiny whitecaps, miles away from the madness of New York. The hotel, Peter O'Malley, even Jennie and Allie, were forgotten. We were together on the privacy of the sea. I wondered if this was the day Patrick would ask me to marry him again.

Smoky, soot-black clouds appeared suddenly from the northwest: a storm, rushing toward us rapidly. The temperature fell at least ten degrees within five minutes.

"Oh *shit*," I said. "Plan a parade, right? Boo, hiss! I can't stand it."

Patrick looked at the clouds with anxious eyes. "I'll call the Coast Guard for a weather check. Maybe we can wait this out."

He walked toward the cabin, then stopped in midstride. "Hell, I can't call. Ship-to-shore's busted. Guess that means we head back in. Take the wheel, Maggie. Hold on tight."

"Aye, aye."

I wrestled with the steering wheel while Patrick reefed the mainsail. The pull was still too heavy at the helm. Patrick decided to change to a smaller storm jib from the sail locker. As a last resort, he'd take the jib down and motor back to Manhasset.

Then the storm hit! A chilling fog curved around the high-peaked sailboat, and rain poured down, soaking us. The wind howled. Seawater splashed across the deck like a flash flood. The frightening power and force of nature were in evidence everywhere.

My hand slipped on the wheel, and I had to fight to keep us on course. There was an exhilaration in the action, but beneath it, like a coiled snake ready to strike, fear had begun to lurk. This wasn't fun anymore.

Patrick cursed loudly, then he *really* cursed. He ran, slipping and sliding, to where a loosened sail flapped like a wet bed sheet.

He seemed to hesitate as he reached the sail, and drag his left leg. That was the impression I had, of his leg *dragging*.

He paused, as if he'd forgotten something, then fell to his knees, as though someone had hit him on the back of his head.

"Patrick!" I called out.

He tried to stand. I saw him raise his hand to his chest. Then he collapsed.

"*Patrick!*"

I rushed across the slippery deck to his side. His face was as white as the mainsail, and his breathing was irregular. He lay

137

on his side, and winced in pain as I moved him onto his back. Suddenly, I couldn't breathe. A tight fist clenched in the pit of my stomach.

I found wool blankets and a strip of greenish tarp. I covered Patrick as well as I could. I took his hand in mine. I was having trouble focusing my eyes.

"You went away," he whispered. "Please don't do it again. Let me look at you, Maggie."

I tried to keep his body quiet as waves rolled over us, soaking us.

"I'm here. And don't you go away either. Everything will be fine. You're going to be all right."

I believed it, at least part of me did, but the fear-snake inside me uncoiled, and I had to turn my face away so he wouldn't see it. Then I looked back at him.

Patrick's face had turned an ashen gray. Beads of perspiration appeared on his forehead and upper lip, though the wind was cold. *Oh please, God. Oh please,* I kept thinking. *I love him so much. Please don't do this.*

"Just in case I'm not around for last call," he said, "I want you to be happy. And make our son Allie happy, which I know you will. And make sure Jennie doesn't marry an Irishman. *Promise,*" he whispered in the voice I loved so.

"I promise," I finally whispered, fighting back the tears.

"I love you, sweet one," he said. "I love you, Maggie. You are the best."

Patrick had that familiar, wry look in his eyes, but suddenly they changed. He stared past me.

Then a strange sound rose up from deep inside his chest. He let go of my hand. He just let go of me. *Simple and uncomplicated, as our love had been.* I screamed as I stared into Patrick's eyes. *Oh, God, please don't let him die.*

I held him tightly and began to cry. I put my head on his chest, now silent and still.

Oh, please ... please, don't let this happen. Whoever's in charge, show us mercy.

Patrick couldn't hear me. He was gone. As swiftly as the storm that swirled about us had come up.

43

I MUST HAVE HELD HIM for an hour, not caring what would happen to me or to the floundering boat that bore us.

The storm had traveled due east, and the waters were calm again, though I barely noticed. A feeble sun cast streaks of amber light on lapping caps of grayish-green water.

I sat helpless beside him on the lonely, quietly rocking deck. I thought of the times we had shared together, and each time I did, I started to cry again.

Don't go away. Let me look at you.

Don't go away, Patrick. Don't go away and leave me . . . oh, Padriac, oh, Patrizio, I moaned.

Sailors from the Coast Guard found me drifting at the reddish edge of sunset. I was still cradling Patrick in my arms.

So there you have it — *that's how I killed him. That's my confession.*

BOOK THREE

WILL

44

WHEN WILL HEARD loud and persistent knocking at the door of his suite in the Rio Hilton, he shivered. He staggered from his bed, and hid himself in the bathroom.

He was barely able to navigate the few steps without falling. *Go away, whoever you are. Get the hell away from here!*

He heard the front door of the suite open and the sound of voices. A maid, and someone else.

Jesus Christ, they can't come in here — whoever it is. Not now!

"Thanks for letting me in," the voice said. "I can manage from here."

Palmer!

Who in hell invited him?

Nobody can be here — not even my brother Palmer! I'm out of control and I don't know if I can ever get it back!

Palmer Shepherd's eyes took in details of the puzzle: the closed bathroom door; the mirror laid flat on the night table bearing a razor, a rolled up hundred dollar bill, the remnants of God knows how much cocaine. An empty bottle of tequila on the

143

floor. A half-full glass of a red liquid on the other night table. Port? Cinzano?

But where was Will? Where in hell had Will gone to?

Here I am, little brother!

With the howl of a werewolf, a naked Will was on him, wrestling him to the ground, pinning his arms. Then Will was sitting on his stomach as he had when they were boys.

"You lose. I win!"

Only this time Will's eyes were scarily wild, and his body — God, his body! — was covered with blood.

Palmer stared up at his brother in disbelief and horror. "Jesus, Will, what in hell did you do to yourself?"

Will laughed loudly, manically. "Cut myself shaving."

Will sprang off him and appeared to dance across the room. He picked up the half-full glass and offered it to his brother. "Cut *her* shaving too. Blood actually goes with tequila. Taste?"

"You cut *who* shaving? What the hell happened here? What are you on?"

"Angelita. I've got her body in the bathroom. She's just a whore." Once more he held out the glass of dark red liquid. "I'm afraid I drank most of it myself. Breakfast of *champions*."

"You didn't," Palmer whispered. He rose to his feet on unsteady legs. "You couldn't have."

"Didn't *what?* Couldn't have *what?*"

"Kill her."

"Well, I don't know." Will's eyes were easily as large as silver dollars. Mad eyes. "Let's find out. Let's have a look."

Will opened the bathroom door, and shared his secret life with his brother.

"What's the verdict, little brother? Did I, or did I not? Are you going to help me this time?"

45

FOR ONCE the outrageous stories in the fan magazines were mostly accurate and true, and maybe even understated. Will knew this, and so did his brother.

Will *was* dangerous, even more dangerous than the tabloids suspected. He *had* spent six weeks in a private New York hospital, recovering from a "breakdown." There had been a "substance problem" in Rio.

He'd done much worse things than a little cocaine — but he'd gotten away with them. It had cost him — a sizable bribe every week to his beloved brother — but at least he was still free and on the loose. He wasn't in prison for the rest of his life.

Will and Palmer had decided he ought to live somewhere other than London for a while. The little bastard Palmer had insisted on it, actually. It was a part of their "deal." For some reason, Will found himself drawn to New York anyway.

He sublet an apartment on the East Side, and loved it so much he went looking for a house. He happened to read in the *Times* that Maggie Bradford had a place in Westchester. So did Winnie Lawrence. Will decided to look in Westchester first.

He was still a huge fan of Maggie's songs. Her music was

healing; he was convinced of it. He'd even talked to his hotsy-totsy Fifth Avenue shrink about the songs, especially the lyrics. The doc was also a Maggie Bradford fan, so he understood what Will was talking about — at least he thought he did.

Will fantasized about meeting Maggie one day in Westchester. He was certain it could be arranged somehow. He was clever enough to accomplish that, wasn't he?

46

THIS IS THE PART that doesn't make much sense. Maybe that's why it fascinates so many people, holds their attention over weeks and even months as the murder trial approaches. This is the real mystery — even for me it is. My time with Will Shepherd, my dark night of the soul. How could it have happened? How did it happen?

After Patrick's death, *his heart attack*, I kept to myself, with only Jennie and Allie, and stayed miles away from the media, whom I had come to dread and despise during my pregnancy. On a lushly green spring morning nearly a year after Patrick's death, I was working in the garden. Allie was playing by my side. We were interrupted by the security guard, hired to keep away unwelcome visitors — which meant, just about everybody.

"There's a Mr. Nathan Bailford here," he said. "Knows you don't want to see anyone, but says it's very important."

Nathan was a neighbor I didn't know well. I did know he was a high-powered lawyer, and that he was instrumental in keeping Peter O'Malley from interfering in the completion of

The Cornelia. What could he want? Why was he here now? Was there more trouble with Peter?

"Let Mr. Bailford come up," I reluctantly told the guard. "We have company," I told Allie. "Let's go get pretty."

The lawyer was in his late fifties, but looked about forty-five. He smiled in greeting, but his charcoal gray suit, white shirt, and a crimson-and-gold rep's tie were lawyer-serious, and not one silver-and-black curly hair was out of place.

Nathan Bailford took my outstretched hand in both his own. "You know, I've driven by I don't know how many times since the funeral. I've thought of you often, didn't know whether to barge in or leave you alone."

"I'm glad you finally decided to come." *Patrick's friend is my friend,* I thought, and tried to be hospitable.

"So, are you okay?" he asked.

"Oh, it comes and it goes," I told him. "The nights are the worst. I'm kind of having a bad decade."

Nathan Bailford didn't know how to answer. Finally, he just smiled. Good decision. I liked him for that.

"Actually, I'm here on business," he admitted, when coffee was served on the patio. "It's something — well, it just couldn't wait any longer. As you know, it's been almost a year since Patrick died. I *had* to stop by today."

He sipped his coffee and I noticed that his hand shook. He loosened his tie. "Patrick's will is finally scheduled to be read. It's been an incredible mess. Never seen anything like it. My staff and I have been preparing everything according to his explicit and typically complicated wishes. Maggie, I've got to tell you. It's going to mean a bad fight. Peter O'Malley is not a happy camper right now. Patrick was right about his son — Peter can be a real bastard. He *is* one."

I wasn't ready for this. I had given no thought to Patrick's money or his estate, and Nathan's edginess frightened me. The idea of a fight with Peter was disturbing, but the thought of the media hearing of it bothered me even more.

148

"What's that got to do with me?" I asked. "Nathan, I really can't get involved in all this."

Nathan Bailford stared into my eyes. "Patrick's left controlling interest in the corporation to you, Jennie, and Allen. He's bequeathed Peter a flat sum, a tremendous sum, of course, but twenty-seven percent of the business is yours and your children's."

I couldn't believe what I had heard. *I couldn't believe it!* "H-how much is it worth?" I asked. I *actually* stuttered.

"Over two hundred million dollars in cash, stock, and real estate holdings. Give or take a few mil. A lot, Maggie."

I felt a crazy burst of anger. "Oh, Nathan, why? I don't need twenty-seven percent or any percent. I've got money, more than I need. I don't want anything to do with it. I really don't."

All of a sudden, I found myself laughing, which made Nathan Bailford sit back in his chair.

But God, it was *funny!* It really was. I had just inherited something like two hundred million dollars, and I felt as though I had been put in prison.

HE WAS CARRYING JENNIE! How could that be? I couldn't believe what I was seeing, but I *was* seeing it. There it was. Ba-da-boom.

Will Shepherd, the soccer player who had tried to pick me up at the Trevelyans' party in London, was at my front door, carrying *my daughter!* It definitely was he. No mistaking that. I'd never forget the long blond hair and his face, and a few other things about him as well.

The guard had called from the front gate saying that Jennie had hurt herself and that a man from the neighborhood was bringing her up to the house. When I saw who it was, I was absolutely stunned.

This was insane.

I didn't ask about Jennie — she looked *too* comfortable, dressed in a sweatsuit, her legs dangling from his arms.

"Put her down! Please put Jennie down," I loudly told him.

"Where, ma'am?" Will Shepherd said in a soft, calm voice. Jennie was no more difficult for him to carry than a pillow.

"There. On the couch in the living room is great. Please, put her down!"

He looked at me with troubled eyes, which gave me pause. "Hey," he said, "she was hurt. I nearly hit her with my car. Lucky thing she jumped aside and only twisted her ankle. It happened right in front of the Lawrences'. That's where I'm staying. I was just going out. Didn't see her."

"It's kind of you to have brought her. Thank you," I managed. My voice was cold. "Now please leave. Thank you though. I mean that."

Jennie sat up on the couch where he had placed her. "You could at least offer him some coffee," she said. "Something?"

"I'm sure Mr. Shepherd's done enough for us and wants to get on about his business."

"You know who I am?" he asked. Now he looked even more puzzled. *The bastard.*

"We've met," I said. Curt, just like that.

He seemed surprised. "Really? Where? I don't go backstage, though I've heard you sing. It was at the Albert Hall. The Queen was there."

"Not at a concert. At a party." Curt.

"If so, I don't remember, and I'd remember meeting you. I'm quite certain of that."

He knelt to check Jennie's ankle. "Doesn't seem like there's anything broken," he said. "I've broken enough bones to be a decent judge of that. Still, you should probably call a doctor."

"As soon as you go, that's what I'm going to do. Thanks for the advice."

He rose slowly. "Nice to meet you, Jennie. Hope you feel better soon." He turned toward the door.

"Good-bye, Mr. Shepherd," Jennie said. Suddenly, I suspected some shenanigans on her part in this. She and her friends occasionally "stalked" rock stars, so why not a sports celebrity?

"I don't want you talking to him again," I told her when the door had closed.

She stared at me, her face red. I'd never seen her this angry. "How could you act that way? *Mother,*" she cried. "*God!*"

She leapt from the couch, gave a small cry, and collapsed. She *had* been hurt. Maybe Will Shepherd had done the right thing in helping her home. Maybe I had been wrong about him this time.

48

MY HOUSE was next door to one of the better Westchester country clubs, the Lake Club in Bedford. The members of the Lake Club paid astronomical dues and fees to ensure that the finest chefs and groundskeepers were employed there. Its carefully manicured lawns and private gardens reminded me of Gstaad, Lake Forest, Saint-Tropez, places I had visited on my concert tours of Europe.

I was at "the club" for a party in late September. It was one of my first forays back into the real world.

I had to stop to catch my breath at the top of the steep fieldstone steps that led from the driveway to the main clubhouse. The last big party I had been to was for the opening of The Cornelia, and a memory of Patrick came back so clearly that tears welled up in my eyes.

"Damn," I whispered. *Get a grip, Maggie.*

The beautiful lawn was filled with people. Dimly, I became aware of a wet bar, and a jazz combo playing quietly beside it. I said hello to a few Bedford residents, smiled at others whose names I should have known but didn't. A Broadway producer took me aside to insist that I name a price and the talent I wanted around me for a show. I told him that the offer was flattering, but really premature, and that I would call him when I was ready. I was pressured by his intensity though, and began to feel an all-too-familiar anxiety building.

The recluse of Greenbriar Road strikes again! I thought. It was too much too fast. I shouldn't have come. *Damn it, damn it!*

Soon I excused myself, and went to be alone in the gardens that branched off the Lake Club's riding ring. I felt like such a fool; a loser, outcast, freak. I remembered being that way all the time when I was younger; too tall for most boys, and a stutterer as well.

The gardens were empty, and I inhaled the fragrant air, relaxing into a kind of hazy satisfaction. This was better.

" 'The loss of grace is the saddest trip . . . but grace can be rewon, Maggie.' "

My words, whispered close behind me. I wheeled to face the man who spoke them.

Will Shepherd was standing next to me.

I actually *jumped*.

49

I TOOK A STEP BACK, but not too far. Somehow, he didn't seem quite as threatening in the colorful gardens and in broad daylight.

"I came to find out why you were so cold to me when I brought your daughter home."

My eyes rolled involuntarily. *He couldn't be that thick,* I thought. "You really don't remember, do you?"

He shook his head. Sunlight bounced off his blond curls. "What are you talking about? Please tell me," he said.

"The costume ball at the Trevelyans. You asked me to go home with you — be with you. You were very crude. Worse than crude, actually."

"I don't remem—" He stopped, and slapped his forehead. He actually blushed. "Oh my God," he said. "Oh shit. You have to forgive me. I was drunk, maybe drugged, and completely crazy."

"And disgusting," I added. "Don't forget that. Well, nice seeing you again. Good-bye."

I turned and began to walk back toward the party.

He ran to catch up with me.

"I'm not drunk now, not drugged, and I'm just a little crazy. Please talk to me for a moment. It's important. To me it is. Please? I think I can explain my behavior."

"But do I want to hear it?" I said to him.

"Fair enough. I'm sure I deserve that, though I still don't remember much of what I did."

I studied him for a few seconds. He was dressed in a rumpled white linen suit, and the color of his hair seemed gold. He was tan, and definitely handsome — I had to give him that.

"I only want to tell you one thing," he said, affecting a sincerity I couldn't believe was genuine. "You're an inspiration to me, to a lot of people. I heard you sing at the concert for the Queen, and I thought you were singing to me. I know you weren't, but that's what I felt. You touched me, so thank you. That wasn't so bad, was it?"

Despite myself, I turned toward him. I saw pain in his eyes. " 'Loss of Grace'?" I asked.

"That song more than any other, though I loved them all, well, most of them. I was going through a bad patch at the time. You reminded me that grace could be rewon."

"Yes. Well. Have you rewon it?" I asked.

His expression grew sadder. He suddenly seemed very genuine, almost human. "No, I'm afraid not. Not in this lifetime. Not after . . . my performance in Rio."

I shook my head. I was lost.

"In Rio? I'm sorry."

For the first time, he smiled. I hadn't seen him smile before, and it was something to see. "You mean you don't know?"

"I'm afraid not. I seem to remember that when we first met I told you I knew nothing about sports. Sorry, but I don't keep a little scrapbook of your clippings. We have one Michael Jordan mug from McDonald's at the house. That's about it for our sports collection."

"Well thank God about that," he said. The smile remained. Turned down, but still present.

156

We were silent for a moment. *He's shy with me,* I thought. *He doesn't know what to say next.*

Oh boy, Maggie, don't start this. You won't, of course, but don't even think about it.

"I ought to go back," I said. "My date —"

"He can wait a few more minutes, can't he? Take a walk with an old retired gent first."

I hesitated. "I was about to leave."

"Don't leave yet. Please. We were talking about you last night at dinner. Winnie Lawrence, June, and I."

"Oh?"

"They told me about Patrick O'Malley. I'm very sorry."

"Yes. It was terrible." There was nothing I wanted to add.

We walked through a tunnel of drooping pine trees, a lamp-lit watercolor undercourse. We began to talk of all sorts of unexpected things: the old Harlem River Railroad line (Will was a bug on railroads); how rural Westchester compared with rural England; a recent Jeffrey Archer novel we both had read. He was as correct with me as a schoolboy, and I felt my own shyness coming back.

I did fear I was being conned. But I figured he was trying so very hard . . . and he was sweet that day. And, I have to admit, *to be truthful,* he was gorgeous to look at.

A patch of laughter, scattered party applause, snuck through the blackthorn bushes. I looked at my wristwatch.

"I don't believe it. We've been talking for over an hour. I do have to go. It's my night to cook. Will, I'm sorry."

"I'm not. Not a bit. I'm some terrific guest of honor though. This could be my last retirement party. I'd better go back too."

As we walked back to the clubhouse, he took my arm for a second, a gentle touch on my elbow, then let it go. "I needed that," he said. "I haven't talked to anyone like this in a long, long time."

"I haven't either." I admitted. I smiled. "There — we've shared a secret."

157

"Could we see each other again? I'm really not the way you think."

I knew he would ask, and I knew my answer. "I'm afraid not. It's too soon for me."

"You're right," he said. "Besides, there are far better men for you than a retired football bloke."

I liked his self-deprecation, at the same time suspecting it might be part of his seduction routine. *It must be terrible for an athlete to retire, to be finished with a career so young. How would I feel if I had to give up singing?*

"And there are younger and more beautiful women for you," I said to him.

"I'm looking for something a little deeper than that now," he said. "And besides, you are beautiful. Don't you know that? . . . You don't, do you, Maggie?"

"I really have to go now," I said.

But I already realized he was different from what I had originally thought. He had substance, but he was very complex. Interesting.

50

MAGGIE BRADFORD was everything that her songs promised, and maybe even more, Will thought. She wasn't aware of it, but she was very attractive as well.

She was the one who could save him. He was convinced of it, and he began to be obsessed by her. He had to see her again. He listened to her songs constantly, at home, and in his car.

He planned everything carefully, beginning with a long letter asking not for a meeting, but for her understanding. Another time he wrote of his mother's desertion when he was a boy, then of his father's suicide. He told Maggie how her songs soothed and helped him, and asked only that she respond in some way.

There was no word from her, and, as was the usual case, he turned to other women. He lashed out at one of them. Nothing as bad as Rio, but scary anyway. The werewolf of New York.

But out of the blue, Maggie wrote him a letter. She told him that the first step was to face his pain, as he so obviously had. He finally called her and asked for a meeting — just once, in New York, and only for lunch.

They met at one o'clock, November 12, at the Oak Room in

the Plaza Hotel. The locale was meant to be as nonthreatening as possible. He had it all figured out. He was going to win Maggie over. He couldn't bear to lose again.

He planned to seduce her.

He planned to win.

He had no doubt that he would.

51

A MONTH AND A HALF passed before I saw Will again. He *wrote* to me several times. The letters revealed even more than talking with him had. He was deep, and also sensitive. When he finally called, I was ready to see him again. Just a lunch. Harmless enough, or so I thought.

This was lunch with Will Shepherd! Even if it was in the dark, gloomy Oak Room. I was sure a lot of women would have died for the opportunity. A few of them were actually there, it seemed, checking us out from nearby tables.

I must admit, he was nice to be with. Will was personable, articulate, warm, and he continued to be sensitive. As I look back on the meeting now, I have a terrible suspicion though: I wonder if he *rehearsed*.

"I like to talk to other people who've been in the spotlight," Will admitted. "As long as they have their heads on straight."

I grabbed at my neck. "My head okay?"

Will laughed. We both did. I knew exactly what he meant about talking with people who had experienced "star treatment." There definitely was a bonding that could happen.

"Tell me about Rio," I said to him about midway through lunch. "No, tell me some good stuff, first."

"I don't want to talk about me," Will said and waved off the question. That was unusual, and refreshing. The thing I *didn't* like about talking to most "stars" was that they loved talking about themselves. I'd have bet that Will was like that. Now I saw that I'd been wrong.

"Leave it at this," Will said. He took a sip of his wine and stared into space. "I'm changing now. I'm looking for grace re-won. Just like in your song."

"You'll find it," I said gently. He had touched me a bit. He was clearly vulnerable, and needy. I secretly liked the fact that he enjoyed my songs so much. I guess I wanted to be a part of his conversion.

"Help me, Maggie." He said the words softly.

"How? How can I possibly help you, Will?"

He looked at me so intensely I felt my cheeks burning. "Include me in your songs," he said.

I did better than that. I included him in my life. It was as though I couldn't help myself. As though the planets had conspired to do this to me.

He asked me out, hesitantly, and I found it not so much charming as riveting. He had a way of being attentive that told me I and I alone mattered. He shut out all distractions when we talked. He looked only at me, listened only to me, made me believe I was wise, and *worthy,* and special.

And so, I went out with Will Shepherd again.

It was very romantic in the beginning. It all came very slowly. It felt right.

We didn't even kiss until our fourth "date." It came naturally, at my front door, as he was saying good night. The kiss had gentleness *and* passion, and I felt myself responding almost despite myself.

162

I pushed him away, gently. "This will take time."

Will kissed me again, a longer kiss that was amazingly tender. For me, it was half pleasure, half pain. I wanted him and I was afraid of the need. I'd heard the stories about him; I was skeptical that he could change. And yet, he so desperately wanted to change.

This time Will moved away voluntarily. He opened the front door for me, and was gone.

My driveway was lit at night, and I stood there for a moment, watching him walk to his sports car. Long after it had disappeared into the darkness, I stared after him, my emotions confused, but definitely heightened.

52

WILL DROVE straight to Manhattan that night. He pushed his sports car to over a hundred on the Saw Mill River Parkway. Jesus, he was good! But he was also frustrated, and incredibly, painfully horny as a goat. He didn't know how much more of this slow-dance courting business he could take. He wasn't used to it.

Maggie was as straightforward and honest as her songs — but he was beginning to wonder if she was worth the challenge. He was having trouble, well, being so fucking nice all the time. Sometimes, he felt he couldn't possibly be good enough for her.

Cat and mouse, he thought as he crossed from Westchester into New York City. That's what it amounted to with women. He almost always caught them — some were just more trouble than others. It was another game really, a substitute for football, and *whatever* football was a substitute for.

Rebecca Post was an art dealer who had a big co-op on East Sixty-first Street overlooking the bridge. *Rebecca was such an easy little mouse to catch,* Will thought. Maybe she was too easy, but he could probably think of something to spice that up. Sure he could.

Will used his key to let himself into her luxury apartment. It certainly hadn't been hard to get his own key — he'd just asked, *once.*

The Blond Arrow tiptoed when he was inside the darkened apartment. He felt like an intruder. A digital clock in the living room *clicked* the time — twenty past one.

An intruder — he rather liked that. He thought he could get into it. He was an intruder — wasn't he? He *intruded* into the lives of a lot of women, and they seemed to welcome the diversion.

The werewolf of London, Paris, Frankfurt, Rome, Rio — and now New York. So be it.

He peered into the master bedroom and saw Rebecca. The dear girl was sleeping in the nude, spread out in a comfy, sexy pose on top of the sheets. Her long auburn hair fanned out across the pillow. Beautiful. Desirable as hell.

Will knew exactly what he wanted to do — *rape her, without saying a single, solitary word.* And then just leave her apartment.

That's what the Blond Arrow did — exactly what he felt like doing.

Same as it always was. Love was just a game — to be won, or lost.

53

WILL HAD TO FLY to Los Angeles for a couple of screen tests at the beginning of January. I found that I missed him more than I wanted to admit, or thought that I would. Sometimes, I feared that he was a sorcerer, a sleight-of-hand artist, a seduction artist like no other. Barry counseled me that Will was exactly that. "He's not that way with me," I told him. It was the truth.

Will came back on a Thursday, and took me to dinner in Bedford. I wore heels and a beaded black dress, a little glamorous for me, and was glad when he noticed. "I love the way you look," he said. Simple, but nice to hear.

He was in a wonderfully expansive mood. I enjoyed seeing him this way.

"The good news," Will told me, "is that the camera loves me. The bad is that I can't act." It was a funny line, and we both laughed.

He talked nonstop. He seemed genuinely amazed by his reception in Hollywood. I found that I was really happy for him. We laughed a lot over dinner. I felt completely relaxed around Will now. People kept pointing us out, but they were considerate enough to stay away. Maybe they thought that we were in love?

By the time dinner was over, it was snowing. Wind whipped the trees so they bowed like exotic dancers; the flakes bit into our eyes as we dashed for the car. Even as we ran, I wanted to reach out and hold him. I just did. It was how I felt.

Will drove home carefully, and walked me to the front door. I still wanted to be held so badly. He had on a very nice, subtle cologne. He'd only worn a sport coat and looked dashing. His cheeks were rosy red, and when he smiled, it was quite something.

"Good night," he said. "Thanks for going to dinner and listening to me talk way too much about the new career."

I didn't want him to go. *Sorcerer,* I thought.

"Hold on," I said. "It's a mess out. I don't want you driving in this storm." *There had already been too many accidents in my life.*

There was a strange, soft light in his eyes. His smile was soft and kind too. "It's only a few more miles. I think I can make it, Maggie."

"Please?" I said. "Just come in for a bit."

Will nodded, and followed me inside. He seemed reluctant to stay.

He said he had to make a quick phone call — that he was supposed to have a drink with the Lawrences and had to let them know he wouldn't be coming.

When he returned, we settled down in the living room. I'd checked on Jennie and Allie, and they were sleeping soundly. Unless someone set off a cannon in their bedrooms, they'd both be dead to the world until morning. Then I'd need the cannon to get Jennie up and ready for school.

I am a single woman, thirty-eight years old, I told myself. *I'm in control of this situation. I can handle it. I'm not doing anything wrong. I enjoy this person I'm with very, very much. Of course, he has cast a spell over me!*

"I never would have imagined *this* happening," I told Will as

167

we sat and watched the snow fall. "The two of us like this. Snowflake watching."

"Truthfully, neither did I. I didn't think you'd give me a chance to prove that I'd finally come to my senses, become a grown-up, that I could change for the better. How am I doing? Do you see any improvement?"

"You're doing just fine. Don't push it," I said, and we both laughed.

I put my head on his shoulder and enjoyed the moment. I liked feeling his back and shoulder muscles. I really would never have imagined myself with Will, but I was so comfortable now. I even allowed myself to admit that he was an incredible hunk. I loved the clean, fresh smell of him. His hair was thick and amazing. I wondered what he liked about me.

He turned his head, and kissed me. "Not *too* grown-up," he whispered. His kiss made me a little dizzy.

It was my decision, my choice. I took Will's hand, and led the way to a guest bedroom near the pool. I was conscious of his fingers curled around mine. I'd straightened up the guest room earlier in the day. Fresh linen. Aired the space out. *Just in case.*

I guess I wanted this to happen. No, I knew that I did. *And that night, it did.*

Cut to train going through very picturesque mountainside tunnel.

Again, and again, and again.

54

SPECIAL MEMORIES — *so confusing now. Like photographs that don't really tell the whole truth, like photographs that can lie.*

The blue-and-white-striped Land Rover flew up the imposing rock face at the famed resort hotel in Las Veides. Will and I had three unbelievable days to ourselves. Just the two of us.

Our Mexican driver rounded a curve so fast that the Rover nearly skidded off the narrow road; a fall would have hurtled us a thousand feet down to Acapulco Bay. I held Will tightly, wanting to be as close as I could. I was into all the tiniest details: how I fit up against him, the contours of his body, every little scar and its origin; how fast his light blond beard grew. I wanted to know everything there was to know about his life, not the exaggerated stories in the tabloids.

"How about a swim, Maggie?" he asked when we got to our room. He sounded shy, and I liked the sound of his voice. "Let's throw on our suits and explore the deep blue sea."

Will and I were gently rocking back and forth, hugging each other under a revolving teak ceiling fan in our suite.

"Maybe a little later," I murmured. "We're alone right now,

and I think I want to enjoy this. I'm sure I do. Can we . . . just . . . do nothing?"

He laughed. "Okay, no deep blue sea. How about no suits, and an exploration of the intimate, private pool that management has so thoughtfully provided?"

"That sounds better. I like that idea a lot."

We kissed softly, for a long, long time, the way we often did. I had the thought: *Am I losing myself, or am I finding something I've lost along the way?*

Will slid the glass doors that opened onto a spectacular terrazzo. We continued to undress until we stood in front of the small pool that glittered with hundreds of sun diamonds and stars. Yellowbirds and colorful parrots chattered in the surrounding brazilwood trees. This was paradise, wasn't it? Or so it seemed at the time.

Through a curtain of royal palms and bougainvillea, I could see the red roofs of other cottages, but not the other private swimming pools. I liked that touch. *No one could see us either.*

With a tiny whoop, I jumped into the pool, pulling Will after me. We weren't being silly — just playful, like a couple of children.

He grabbed my arm, drew me to him. He was already hard. I slid my hands down his slender, muscular body and stroked his thighs. He was always so warm and tender with me; he was nothing like what I had expected.

We kissed again — soft and long.

Will raised me from the tile floor of the pool, and turned me so I could brace myself against the pool's edge. He slowly, slowly entered me. I closed my eyes, becoming aware of new sensations, relishing the warm sun on my face, and an even greater heat building inside.

I had never been with anyone like Will. He made me feel so special. I have to say that, because it's the truth.

170

55

THERE IS a powerful, powerful image that never fits for me, that will always be a mystery, a beautiful and sad and troubling mystery.

After Will and I returned from our quick trip to Mexico, we spent a long weekend doing everything the kids wanted to do. Doing *some* of the things Jennie and Allie wanted to do anyway. They were so excited, and Will was wonderful with them.

We went to New York for one day, and we played out-of-towners — the Trade Center, the Statue of Liberty, the museum mile, even the Hard Rock Cafe. But then, we spent an even more special day on the grounds around the house — as a family, seeing if that's what we all wanted.

I watched Jennie and Allie with Will, and I could tell they adored him. I was almost certain he liked being around the kids, that he ached to bring up children just right, the way it ought to be done, not the way it had happened to him. He had told me as much.

I remember seeing him with Allie that afternoon at the house. The extraordinary picture sticks with me, one that will always play on my mind.

It was an Indian summer kind of day, brilliantly sunny, in the high fifties. The two of them were riding on one of our tamer horses, a sweet mare Jennie had named Fleas. Will and Allie rode across a wide field of tall grass that looked sea-green in the light.

They had their winter jackets on, but open, acting *very manly*, both of them strikingly blond. They were laughing uproariously as Fleas loped on, seemingly in very slow motion.

Will held Allie tightly and very securely in his arms, and he was beaming with joy. I knew the happiness was real, and I loved what I saw. I loved the look on their faces.

Jennie came and stood beside me. "Aren't they just beautiful?" she said. "They look like a real dad and his boy. Oh, I love it now, Mom. I feel so good inside, so right."

"Me too," I said and hugged Jennie.

56

WILL TOLD ME everything; we told each other everything, until *I believed that we had no secrets.* One night he shared a terrifying story of his father beating his mother, then of his mother's words to him: "*Only Mommy loves you. Only Mommy does.*"

Listening to Will talk, I'd never felt closer to him. Maybe I'd never felt close to anyone. Certainly, I'd never had so much pain revealed to me.

"But she left me anyway," he said. There was a faraway look in his eyes. "So she didn't really love me, you know, Maggie."

He could be so sweet, and at those times, I imagined the way he must have been as a boy. I could picture Will as a boy, as a beautiful, blue-eyed boy.

"You think it was your fault she went away?"

"Yes. But I'm getting better about it. I'm almost there. I couldn't have done this without you, Maggie. You, Jennie, Allie, just being around all of you has made all the difference."

I reached to hold Will's hand. His pain, his *love* for me, seemed so clear. It was very touching. I could identify with his sad family history, and *maybe,* I was trying to help convert my own angry father through Will.

"I'm not going to leave you," I whispered to Will. "Not ever."

"Marry me, Maggie. Don't give up on me. Promise."

In the morning, I told him I would marry him to prove it.

57

CAT AND MOUSE: *the glorious game of love.*

A wanna-be model, Cam Matthias, took Will in her mouth and rolled her long tongue slowly over and around, eliciting a groan and a tightening of his hands in her flowing red hair.

God, he was such a fabulous, untamed animal, Cam thought. *He might actually be the most exciting man on earth. Someone had to be, right?*

"Oh," Will said. "Jesus, Cam. That feels wonderful. *You* feel wonderful."

They had been going at it for hours. He was insatiable, and made her feel the same way. When she knew, or thought, he was about to come, she released him and lay on her back, placing his cock between her breasts, and once more increasing the pressure until she thought he could stand it no longer. He kept going though, on and on, like some kinky version of the Energizer bunny. The image made her howl with laughter. They both howled.

Next, she knelt in front of the wall. She reached behind and spread the cheeks of her perfect bum.

"Take your time, as if you wouldn't anyway," she said.

It was the night before Will Shepherd's wedding.

58

AT ONE O'CLOCK, three hours before "the wedding of the decade," two dozen policemen in their finest navy blue uniforms and dress-white gloves took up their positions at the main and service entrances of the Bradford home, as well as down along Greenbriar Road. Their first assignment: clear Greenbriar of the people from New York, Yonkers, and as far away as Tennessee and Texas, who had come to catch a glimpse of Will and me on our wedding day.

They would all be disappointed, I was afraid. Neither of us was interested in any publicity on the day of days, or even after, for that matter.

By three o'clock, Greenbriar Road had been officially closed to the public by the Bedford police. The entire street was off-limits to everyone except those bearing the silver-engraved cards from Cartier that simply stated: *Wedding Guest*.

I had carefully selected one of the out-of-view rear bedrooms as a dressing room, as well as for getting my head together before the madness started in earnest.

Jennie (who treated my wedding as the greatest day in *her* life), the dress designer Oscar Echavarria, and two of his young associates were fussing over me that afternoon. Allie was content to stay close to our nursemaid, Mrs. Leigh, and watch the excitement. I wore a beautiful gown of creamy satin. Both the veil and train were of understated Belgian lace. A single strand of pearls encircled my throat. I couldn't have been any happier. I *felt* beautiful inside and out. Not only was Will healed, but so was I.

"Elegant. Lovely. Perfection." Echavarria pronounced approval, eyeing me as though he were Leonardo and I the Mona Lisa. I found it hard to keep from laughing at his forgivable grandiosity.

"You look cool, Mom," was Jennie's assessment.

"Give me a few minutes alone," I finally said. "I just need a little time to take it all in."

"Sure," Jennie said matter-of-factly.

"*C'est ça,* everyone out," said Echavarria, clapping his hands like a ballet master.

They left, but I held Jennie aside. "Thanks for putting up with me these past few weeks," I told her. "Now go get pretty. Only not too much prettier than the bride, okay?"

"Don't worry about that. That couldn't happen even if I wanted it to, which I don't."

"I love you," I whispered.

"I love you even more, Mom."

"Couldn't."

"I do. Get it? I *do*."

The wedding list read like a who's who. Will's manager and friend, Winnie Lawrence, would be there, of course. Nathan Bailford, Barry, my friends from Bedford, my sisters and their families from upstate, musicians and singers, soccer world people. And reporters and photographers from all the metropolitan papers, the local TV stations, the networks, *People, Time* — I swear, there almost seemed more strangers than friends.

One of the final cars to arrive, I found out later, was a gleaming burgundy Maserati. Behind the wheel sat Peter O'Malley. Somehow, Peter had gotten an invitation.

The door to the back bedroom suddenly swung open without so much as a knock. *Now who could —*

"*Will*, you're not supposed to be —"

"— Getting married so young?" Will smiled. He looked gorgeous in a black Brioni tuxedo, but he also looked refined. "True, but with a woman as beautiful as you, I couldn't resist. Do you know how much I missed you last night? I could probably show you."

He took a step toward me. "Out. Don't you dare." I started to laugh. He could always make me laugh. "Out. I mean it."

He continued on undaunted, and took me in his arms. His hand gently touched my breast. Nothing too provocative — and thus *very* provocative.

"Ummmm," he said. "You *are* an eyeful. A handful too."

"Will!"

"Yes I am."

"I love you so much. Now, *go*."

"Enough, enough. I respect your wishes. I shall honor and obey, from this moment on."

Obediently, he left the room, humming "Always." I smiled and thought it was the perfect prelude.

59

A YOUNG PIANIST from Juilliard sent the first notes of "The Wedding March" crescendoing across the picture-book back lawn. The music, *everything,* sent a shiver up my spine. I loved my wedding day even more than I thought I would.

Latecomers were hurried to their seats. Pesky radio and TV station helicopters whirled through the blue skies overhead, while television cameras never seemed to stop shooting. What seemed like a thousand photographers snapped photographs of the guests and the groom.

I finally appeared.

The bouquet of white calla lilies that I carried trembled in my arm.

I was used to large crowds, but I felt a little nervous here. I spotted my few remaining relatives from upstate, smiling tentatively. Jennie, my bridesmaid, stood solemnly near the altar. Mrs. Leigh sat in the front row, holding Allie, who wriggled in her arms. Will's aunts were there, Eleanor and Vannie, one matronly, the other strikingly attractive.

I did a double take! Will was standing next to them instead

179

of at the altar . . . no, it wasn't Will, but Palmer. A smudged carbon copy.

I was escorted down the flower-strewn grass aisle by Barry. He looked somewhat rumpled in his tuxedo, his flower already drooping from his lapel.

"You're so beautiful. You actually have a glow," he whispered as he let go of my arm and turned to find his seat in the front row.

I lifted my eyes to the white altar trimmed with pink and white roses. It was a bit too much, but it was beautiful. Will stood beside his best man, Winnie Lawrence. He was smiling at me.

Never, for a single second, had I thought of turning back.

"I now pronounce you husband and wife," the minister said. Will lifted my veil and gently kissed me. I could feel him through the tux. He always felt so good to me. The guests applauded. Camera flashes popped like yellow daisies all over the cascading lawn. Helicopters fluttered overhead. What an unforgettable scene!

Stiff, comically correct Day Dean waiters burst from the rear of the main house, with silver trays bearing glasses of champagne. Others circulated iced shellfish and caviar, canapés of crabmeat, tea sandwiches, cheeses, fruits, pâtés. A great orchestra led by Harry Connick Jr. began to play from a highly polished pinewood platform installed at the entryway to an enormous yellow-and-white-striped tent, which would later serve as the ballroom.

Maybe not the wedding of the decade — but quite the blowout, I had to admit. I smiled, felt incredibly warm and fulfilled inside, and started to get into it.

A huge, striped tent shaded half an acre of lawn between the main house and the duck pond. Inside, bands of children ran between the dining tables covered with pale yellow linen cloths, and graced with wicker centerpieces filled with bachelor's buttons, baby's breath, and yellow rosebuds.

The music ranged from Strauss waltzes to Carly Simon to Patsy Cline. After a formal, sumptuous sit-down dinner, and just before dessert, Barry got up and sang his "Light of My Life" to a standing ovation from the guests, Will, and me.

Then my friend Harry Connick spoke, his voice cutting through the continuing murmur of the crowd: "The bride will now cut the cake. Maggie, get your butt up here. C'mon, shy girl. Time to be the center of attention again."

Waiters arrived bearing three gargantuan wedding cakes. On each stood a marzipan man in a soccer outfit and a marzipan woman leaning against a piano. Will and I mashed cake into each other's mouths, photos of our messy bites eventually making the covers of *People* and *Paris Match,* and all sorts of other ridiculous magazines.

After dinner the tables were quickly removed. The band began to play. Will and I danced the first waltz (to "Starglow," one of my songs), then the other guests joined us.

I was dancing with Barry when a man cut in, and two-stepped me away. "Are we finally happy now?" Peter O'Malley said. His speech was thick, whiskey-slurred, and he was as gray-faced as Patrick had been in death. Physically, he was a caricature of Patrick: recognizable features, but small beads for eyes, and fifty pounds heavier than his father had been.

"Let go of me," I said. "Please, Peter." He was holding my arms so tightly I could feel his nails digging into my flesh.

He was actually like a madman. "You cheap slut. Think how much you hurt *me.* You had my father, now you've got his house, his money, his death on your hands, a handsome new husband."

I tried to pull away from the drunken man, but I couldn't. He wouldn't let me. "What do you mean, 'his death on my hands'?" I finally said as quietly as I could.

181

He shouted in my face. "You know fucking well what I mean!"

"You think I killed him?"

"I think his death was convenient for you. Let's leave it at that. Let everyone draw their own conclusions. I know I have, and I'm not alone."

"He died of a heart attack, Peter. Please leave. You're drunk."

"A heart attack induced by who? What did you do to him, Maggie? *Fuck his heart out?*"

I pulled my right arm from his grasp and hit Peter as hard as I could. An open-hand slap. A wake-up call.

His dark eyes blazed in thin slits. "Quite the little bitch, aren't you?" He suddenly let go of my arm. "You're nothing but a whore! Then you're probably used to *this!*"

Red wine from a crystal goblet sprayed my face, blinding me momentarily. "And Shepherd's nothing but a stud. The whole world knows it." I heard Will's roar of rage, but I didn't see him throw himself at Peter, knocking him to the ground. He punched Peter again and again. Will was all over my tormentor.

Winnie Lawrence finally pulled him off, separated the two interlocking bodies like a referee.

"Maggie! Oh Christ, poor Maggie!" Will cried. "Are you all right?"

Peter was struggling to his feet. His face was coated with blood, one eye already half-closed. "You took my father's money. His hotels. Everything! He was my father, *and you killed him,*" he yelled.

Two security men finally led him from the tent. Peter went unprotestingly, too weak to fight back. I could already imagine tomorrow's news headlines. *Damn.*

Will took me in his arms, and gently wiped my face with his handkerchief. "Oh, Maggie, I'm so sorry," he whispered. "Forget about Peter O'Malley. We have a life that's just beginning. I love you," he whispered.

"I love you, Will."

I really did.

182

60

"WILL? Is it you? The old married man? The reformed ex-bachelor?"

" 'Tis indeed, Winnie. What's the good news from the Left Coast? Do I have an acting career or not?"

"You're not going to believe this, but Michael Caputo said yes. He loves *your ass*, and your mind. He thinks you're a natural."

The Thrill. It returned in an exhilarating rush for Will. He sprang from his chair with a loud whoop, though there was no one home to hear it.

"Tell me everything," he said.

"Well, for starters, it's the lead in *Primrose*. That's right, *the lead*. The character's named North Downing, but despite that it's an okay script. More important, it'll be a huge hit at the box office."

Primrose was the country's number one best-seller, a hundred plus weeks on the *Times* list, a saga of passionate love set in the early part of the century. Michael Lenox Caputo was the director who had bought it for a small fortune; he was producing it himself. As Selznick did with *Gone with the Wind,* he had

183

instituted a very noisy, nationwide search for an unknown to play the lead, this time a male. Box-office draw was guaranteed by the novel's phenomenal popularity and also its female star, Suzanne Purcell, a tempestuous actress whose on-screen fire was reportedly matched in her private life.

"Good going. Jesus," Will said. "I didn't think we had a chance. Maybe I am an actor, after all."

"It was *you*. You look hot on film, and you can *act*. Caputo saw it instantly. Even the novel's asshole author likes you."

"Still, if you hadn't pushed me, I'd never have had the nerve to screen-test for the great Caputo. When does the damn thing shoot? Where? I'm stir-crazy anyway."

"Australia. And it starts soon, very soon."

"Australia? For an American epic? What's that all about?"

"It's winter in Australia when it's summer here," Winnie said, as though that explained anything.

"So what?" Will asked.

"So . . . welcome to Hollywood!"

61

THE CAST of *Primrose* had been assembled, all except for Suzanne Purcell, who was not to appear in the first scene and would make her own entrance, in her own style, on her own time schedule. She was, after all, *the star.* It was 5:30 A.M. on the gentle, rolling plains of Perth.

This was the start of principal photography: scene one, take one; cameraman, Nestor Keresty; director, Michael Lenox Caputo. Everyone had huge hopes for the film. Maybe four hundred million, worldwide. The novel was *still* number one.

Will, Caputo, and several technicians were huddled inside the poorly heated trailer that served Will as a dressing room. They were all waiting for the temperamental genius Nestor Keresty to settle on his lighting — the proper play of fill, and front and back lights, to capture the feeling of early morning in a Texas farmyard. High art, indeed.

In the film's first scene, North Downing was to deliver a baby mare, by lamplight, inside a dilapidated barn. The scene had hooked book readers, apparently by the millions. North Downing was the "last American cowboy," but a sensitive lover and husband as well.

185

"I want you to make me a promise," Will said, drawing Caputo aside. "This is a serious fucking promise, Michael. I'll hold you to it."

The director frowned. He had been asked to promise weird things by actors, and this boy was a neophyte. Still, he was a very large and powerful neophyte, who reportedly had quite a temper. "Shoot. Anything at all, Will."

"I want you to make me grunt and sweat bullets out there today. When I carry that baby horse, I want it to look *hard,* as though I'm in as much physical pain as the mare was. I want you to turn me into an *actor.*"

Caputo smiled, and tried not to laugh. He bit his lip, *hard.* No one had ever asked him anything like this before. "So you don't think good looks are enough?"

"No. Not even close. Christ, Tom Cruise *looks* good."

"That's all the audience will care about, Will. Trust me. Style *is* reality these days."

"I don't give a damn about the audience, never have. I was the best there is in football. Now I want to be the best there is on the screen. I will be too. Count on it."

Michael Caputo stared at Will, stunned by his preposterous, naive request. *He's like a boy,* Caputo thought, but all he said was "I'll try my best."

"That's all I ask. I'll do the rest. You're going to eat that condescending smile you gave me a minute ago."

"I'll be happy to do it," Caputo said, then he smiled again. Actually, he liked Will Shepherd, and wanted to see him do well.

The very first scene called for North Downing to deliver the foal, then carry it across the barnyard to his young wife, Ellie. This morning, they would shoot only the birthing sequence and North's walk across the farmyard. Later, they would film the actual presentation to Ellie.

It took them twenty-two takes. Will was awkward at first,

186

despite numerous rehearsals, concentrating more on Caputo's instructions than on the subtle emotion necessary for the potentially mawkish scene.

Caputo drove him mercilessly, trying to pull out real feeling, and Will found himself sweating so much he had to have new makeup after every take. They got it right on take twenty-one; they got it perfectly.

"One more time," Caputo said. "For insurance."

Will stood behind the horse, delivered the foal with a grunt of pleasure, and, smiling, picked it up lovingly in his arms. Staggering, he left the barn, made his way across an icy patch, and entered a door in a facade meant to simulate the front of the Downing house.

Will stopped. He started to smile, then to laugh out loud. *Jesus, this was rich. This was the best.*

There was a woman standing at the back of the facade, just out of range of the cameras. When Will entered, carrying the foal, she ripped open her blouse, exposing her breasts to him.

He nearly dropped the foal. There was incredible amusement and invitation in her eyes.

Maggie, he thought. *She'll never forgive me. Screw this woman, and you're screwing yourself. She'll ruin your life.*

But he couldn't stop looking at her. She was beautiful. Breathtaking, actually. And he had seen enough of the world's famous beauties to know.

"Welcome," said Suzanne Purcell, "to *Primrose*."

62

I COULD STAY with Will in Australia for only a week. Barry kept pleading with me to finish the new album, and eventually I had to agree to come back to work.

As my car pulled up to 1311 Broadway, I thought back to a storm-blown morning years before. *Look how far you've come,* I told myself, and I had to smile. *A singing star. Happily married. Occasionally a sex junkie. Not bad. And not the same unsure and frightened Maggie who came to Barry for a job, any job.*

Today, Barry popped out of his office to greet me. He brought *me* coffee. "Come across the street with me to the studio. I've been working on several arrangements for 'Just Some Songs.' Wait till you hear them."

"Barry, I've got two new songs. From Australia."

"The arrangements first, then I'll listen. You look great, Maggie. Still glowing. Marriage is obviously agreeing with you."

"I'm happy, Barry. Really happy," I told him. Of course, Barry would never admit that he might have been wrong about Will, or anything else, for that matter.

Once in the studio, it was business as usual between the two of us. Nothing had changed; we loved our work and the chance to be together. The tough challenge was to make each album — each *song* in each album — different and better. We didn't always succeed, but we always tried like hell.

The work went extremely well that day. I was pleased with Barry's arrangements (I almost always was, though I was far more critical than I had been when we first met); he loved one of my songs and liked the other. The album was going to be a very good one.

It was midafternoon by the time we knocked off, and I decided to do some shopping. A reward. A splurge. Then home to the kids. I was cooking tonight. Then we planned to watch *Forrest Gump,* on video. We'd seen it only six times already. Maybe I'd make Bubba's Shrimp for dinner. That would give Jennie a laugh.

I found a little doodad I wanted at Bergdorf Goodman and left the store a little after three-thirty. Fifth Avenue was filled with taxis, buses, the usual pedestrian parade. I didn't see my car and driver right away.

Then, *trouble.*

A TV camera suddenly surfaced like a submarine scope out of the street crowd. Two young bearded apes from Fox News jockeyed up to me. Bad-looking guys. Real neanderthals from the look of them.

"Maggie. Maggie Bradford," one of them shouted. Instinctively, I moved away, desperately searching for my car.

"Maggie. Over here, Maggie. Is it true you and Will were having difficulties in Australia? Is that why you came home?"

I could hear the whirr of a camera. Pedestrians stopped to look at us. *Oh, damn these TV people,* I thought. *Get a life. Let me live mine.*

"No." I was curt with them.

"We hear he's gotten real close to Suzanne Purcell. That's the buzz. Know anything about that?"

My stomach spasmed. "No." Will and I knew there would be rumors about him and Suzanne. If there weren't, the studio would probably start them.

"So you didn't see this photograph?"

"No. No comment. Bye now. Nice sharing vicious rumors with you."

I couldn't push through the crowd and get away from them. *Where was the car, for God's sake?*

"The photograph, Maggie." A pushy, little bald man from Channel Five was shoving a microphone in my face. "It was in all the papers. Will and Suzanne Purcell. *Very* cozy. You didn't see it?"

I shoved him aside, pushing him back into the cameraman. I saw my car finally, and I ran and shut myself inside.

It wasn't until we were gliding through the green woods near home that I began to relax. *The nerve of those insensitive bastards!* It wasn't the first time I had clashed with a reporter. It had happened in Rome and once in Los Angeles. *What happened to privacy?* I asked myself. *Who do they think they are?*

I wished Will were home right now. In the car with me.

Oh, Will, forget about being a big movie star. Let's just disappear and be nobodies for the rest of our lives.

Will and Suzanne. The picture. Could it possibly be true? No, I didn't believe it. Wouldn't believe it. I felt that I knew Will by now. I was sure that I did. The picture was just more paparazzi crap. It wasn't the first, wouldn't be the last.

In the car, I dismissed the thought. But it came back to me when I went to bed that night. It kept me awake through the witching hours, two and three in the morning.

Will and Suzanne Purcell.

No!

Damn the paparazzi anyway.

63

THERE WERE NO PAPARAZZI for this particular moment.

SCENE: Ellie's bathroom. Beautiful morning light everywhere. Ellie is soaking in a tin tub, covered with thick suds, occasionally brushing them aside so she can look at her stomach. North enters, looking concerned.

CUT TO: Ellie's reaction. She looks at her husband with shame. North kneels next to the tub. He's not like most men. He understands the way his wife thinks.

NORTH: Why have you been avoiding me, Ellie? Ever since our baby, you won't let me come near you. This isn't the way we wanted it.

ELLIE: 'Cause I'm not pretty now. That's why. (She begins to cry.) I'm never going to be pretty again. That baby ruined my body. It's made me an old woman.

NORTH: Nineteen isn't old. You're as pretty as ever. You're my beautiful wife. (He starts to brush away the mounds of suds.) You're *Ellie,* and that will never change.

191

ELLIE: Don't! Please . . . oh North, please.

NORTH: Hush. (He swipes away the suds, revealing her breasts.) See, you're very pretty. You're so pretty, I almost can't stand it.

ELLIE: I'm swollen, like a suckling pig. I ache and I *feel* old, even if I'm not.

NORTH (Picking up a washcloth and tenderly caressing her body with it, his hand hidden by the suds as it goes beneath her breasts): Not here, you're not. Or here . . . Or especially *here*.

CUT TO: Ellie's reaction. She is obviously excited by his touch. She smiles, and the smile is beautiful. Ellie is as beautiful as North says she is.

NORTH (Continuing to caress): My beauty. My Ellie.

ELLIE (Breathing hard): Am I still? Am I?

NORTH: Yes, you are. You always will be. I told you that, and it will never change. Even when you do become an old woman.

CLOSE UP: Ellie and North kiss, more and more passionately. Suddenly the room is extremely steamy.

CAMERA: Moves down to show the bathwater moving as North's hidden hand gets more and more agitated.

"Cut!" Michael Lenox Caputo's voice knifed through the stillness of the scene. "Great take. Wrap it. I have to go masturbate now!"

Neither Will nor Suzanne Purcell stopped though. The technicians kept their cameras rolling, and would soon have film of the two stars that they could sell to any of the tabloid TV shows.

Will and Suzanne seemed to notice nothing around them. She had stepped out of the tub and, naked, unashamed, was laughing and pulling at his belt. He picked her up and, mouth on hers, in a kiss no patron of *Primrose* would ever see, carried her to his trailer. Will slammed the door behind him with his foot.

The werewolf of Perth.

64

"WHAT HAPPENS NOW?" Will asked. Principal shooting on *Primrose* was finished; only editing and dubbing remained to be done.

He and Suzanne were walking together on the dusty plain. He hadn't meant to get involved, but as they say, shit happens. Suzanne was truly one of the most beautiful women in the world, and Will had always appreciated the very best.

"I go back to California, you become Mr. Maggie Bradford, just like you were."

Will blinked. The words stung. "And what we had out here?" he asked Suzanne.

"We had some fine times, didn't we? You're good, Will. One of the best."

"*One* of?" He snorted out a laugh. "You're beautiful *and* you're a comedienne."

Suzanne laughed as well. "Yes, I have a brain, Will. Oh, sweetheart. *I've had* the best! Actors, other athletes, ski bums. But you are very good. No worry there."

He could feel ancient demons. Roused from sleep, they began to claw upward, from the pit of his stomach to his brain. Jesus, he hated to lose. He couldn't bear failure.

193

"This picture will make me a star," he said, fighting to keep his voice level. "Then I won't be 'Mr. Maggie Bradford.' "

"*I* made you the star," Suzanne Purcell said. "Don't forget that. You really shouldn't let this insane business get to you anyway. It can, you know."

Destroy her, he thought. *But not now. Take it easy, Will. Go slow. You learned your lesson in Rio.*

He kept silent. They turned back toward the hotel. "One last time?" he asked.

Suzanne grinned and reached for him. "Now that's the proper spirit. Your room or mine?"

"Yours," he said. "We'll use your toys."

Suzanne Purcell had no idea how she had gotten herself into this mess. She felt as though she were having an out-of-body experience.

The moment she'd stepped into her hotel room, Will had hit her from behind. Not that she could tell what had happened at first. She'd felt a hard wallop between her shoulder blades. Then the blue shag rug seemed to be rushing up at her face. She hit the floor hard, and lost consciousness.

And she awoke *like this.*

He'd tied her with jump ropes that she used as part of her exercise routine. He'd gagged her with her own bra, and more rope.

Then he'd put her in the bathtub.

That was when it started to get bad, unbelievably bad.

He cut both her wrists and watched her blood flow into the tub and down the drain.

He just sat there and watched her bleed.

Suzanne struggled wildly against the ropes, and made strange, muffled sounds.

She had tried to scream, but the gag was too tight. Finally, she decided to plead with Will — using her eyes.

"Oh, I see," he finally spoke to her. "*Now* you want to talk things through. You probably even want to take back some of those nasty remarks you made outside? Am I right, Suzy? You see, *I have a brain too.*"

She nodded her head as best she could. She was losing a lot of blood, and she was starting to feel woozy — as if she might pass out.

"I know this isn't an authentic suicide, but it's like one. The next best thing," Will said. "It's fascinating to watch someone die. You can't imagine. Your eyes are amazing to watch right now. About a thousand thoughts coursing through your brain, right? You can't believe that you, the great Suzanne Purcell, are about to die. It's too weird, right? Your life can't just end like this, right? *It's all in your eyes, Suzanne.* Extraordinary."

Will suddenly stopped talking.

He just watched her — bleed. It was definitely like a suicide. Like his father's.

When Michael Caputo came to Suzanne's hotel the following morning, he wanted to wish her a safe trip home, and thought, maybe, he might get lucky. Suzanne didn't answer the house phone or respond to his knock.

He finally got the manager to open her door. *Drugs,* he thought. *Damn her. Why did nearly every beautiful woman have to be a head case?*

He found Suzanne naked and badly cut, unconscious but still alive. She was handcuffed to the hotel bed. It would be half a year before she could act in another movie, and her close-ups would never be the same.

Suzanne swore to Caputo, and then to the police, that it hadn't been Will. She would say no more than that. She wouldn't press charges.

Not a word to anybody.

He had scared her that badly. She believed that Will was capable of murder, of anything.

BOOK FOUR

DARK SIDE OF
THE MOON

65

I AM NOT A MURDERER.

I never murdered anyone. Or so I've begun to tell myself, over and over again.

As we entered the courthouse everyone was staring at me, and I couldn't catch my breath. I felt I must be going mad. Maybe I am.

Policemen from the prison, as well as my faithful cadre of expensive lawyers, had me surrounded, penned in, claustrophobic. I remembered how it had been in the crawl space under the house at West Point. All the horror stories seemed to be coming together.

It was pouring, and hundreds of people, mostly with black umbrellas, but a few with blue and red ones, had turned out to catch a glimpse of the so-called famous murderess.

It destroyed me to know that my children would see me like this — *in handcuffs, wearing my scarlet* M.

We marched into the courthouse and upstairs to a room where Judge Andrew Sussman was waiting. The judge was a large man, about six foot six, with a salt-and-pepper beard that he allowed to grow in wild and bushy. He was probably in his

199

mid-forties, and reminded me of a rabbi. That was a good sign; it made me think that he would be just and fair. That was all I wanted.

Justice. Fairness. The American way, right?

Judge Sussman was holding the formal murder indictment in a solemn-looking black folder. My lawyers had told me what to expect — but I couldn't get used to it.

What in the name of God was I doing here? How could this be happening to me?

I wasn't the bad person in all of this — I was the victim. How could I be on trial for murder?

The press who would be covering the murder trial were already in the courtroom. Not one, but several artists were on hand to draw versions of the way I looked today. How goddamn *artistic!*

I stood with my chief attorney, Nathan Bailford, in front of the bench. This couldn't be happening to me. None of it seemed real.

"Good morning," Judge Sussman said in a civil tone, as though I'd come about a parking ticket, or a violation of the Bedford town code on keeping the grass cut short at the curbside around my house.

"Good morning, Your Honor." I was surprised that I could speak so confidently, that I could get the words out, that I could be civil too.

Judge Sussman held up the black folder for me to see.

"Mrs. Bradford, I have here the indictment from the grand jury. You've seen it?" he asked. He talked plainly and simply, as though I were a young child, but accused of something very serious.

"Yes, I have, Your Honor."

"You've read it, and had time to discuss the indictment with Mr. Bailford or your other attorneys?" he asked next.

"We've talked about the indictment."

"You understand the charge against you? That you are accused of the murder of your husband, Will Shepherd?"

"I've read the indictment. I understand the charge against me."

He nodded, like I was a good student, or an especially good defendant. "And do you plead guilty, or not guilty, to the charge of murder?"

I looked him square in the eye. I knew it didn't matter, but I needed to do this anyway.

"I am not guilty of murder. I plead *not guilty.*"

66

NEW YORK CITY. Central Park. Will and I had been married for nearly a year.

"Maggie, can you see anything? I can't see a damn thing. Too many bloody trees in this bloody park."

Will, Jennie, and I were sitting in the fuzzy-gray darkness of a stretch limousine. Nervously, Will lit a cigarette, the match flaring blue and gold, lighting his face. He raked his fingers back through his thick curls.

How pale he is. Tired. Scared, I thought as I watched him. *This is his World Cup all over again, isn't it? He needs to prove something tonight. Well, I can understand that.*

"What are they doing at the head of this blasted, interminable line?"

"I can't see," I told him. "Clearing away pedestrians, I suspect."

"See how popular your movie's going to be," Jennie added support.

The limo was stuck, engine idling, at the Columbus Circle entrance to the park. We were fifth in a shadowed row of

Rollses, Bentleys, and Lincolns bearing dignitaries, the producer/director, and the stars.

Finally, the caravan began to move, making its way down Central Park South, then onto Seventh Avenue and across Fifty-fourth Street to the Ziegfeld Theatre, and the world premiere of *Primrose*.

With each turn of the limo, Will's anxiety increased; his hand, when I took it to comfort him, was sweaty, and as soon as he finished his cigarette he lit another. He rarely smoked, but tonight he couldn't seem to stop. He wasn't himself.

"It'll be all right," I said. "It's just pregame jitters."

"*All right?* In fifteen minutes the critics are going to watch me on the screen, thirty feet tall, nowhere to hide, saying 'Top of the Morning, Ellie. That's a wonderful name for your horse. You take care of her, girl, just as you would your very own child.'"

"It's just a story, Will. People want it to sound like that. They want to escape from real life sometimes."

"Not the New York critics. They'll see it for the abominable shit it is, see *me* for the fake I am, and — poof — there goes my short-lived acting career."

"No way," Jennie told him.

"Way," Will joked with her at least.

The caravan stopped. Suddenly there were chubby, hairy fingers rapping at the limousine's side window. I recognized a chubby hairy face and released the door lock. "Trouble," I whispered, "always comes in pairs."

"Caputo!" Will grinned as the director squeezed his wide body into the backseat.

"They're going to crucify us," Caputo said, his face mournful. "I just know it. My instincts are always right. Aren't my instincts right, Will? Comes from growing up in Brooklyn. People from Brooklyn have great instincts."

He was so comically miserable I had to laugh.

"People are expecting big things from this film," Caputo said. "As well they should for fifty mil — but Will and I both know they're getting sheep shit. *Australian* sheep shit. Not even the good stuff."

Will laughed at the director's humor, which was nearly as dark as his own.

"Where's your wife?" I asked. "She doesn't seem to have had any more luck calming you down than I've had with Will."

"Eleanor's in the car ahead of us with my saintly mother. They can't stand me when I get *meshuga* like this. They kicked me out of my own car. So I'm here. *Somebody's* got to take me to the theater."

I opened the car door, and pulled Jennie along with me.

"Where are you going?" Will asked.

"To join Eleanor, and Michael's mother. You two artistes deserve to be alone together."

67

I REJOINED WILL when we reached the Ziegfeld, and we got through the searchlights, the screaming crowds, the reporters, the studio executives, and settled ourselves into our seats of honor.

Neither Jennie nor I had ever been to a world premiere. It was actually great fun. Everyone looked so wonderfully inappropriate in their tuxes, dark suits, and party gowns — just to go see a movie.

In about fifteen minutes, the picture started and the credits rolled. WILL SHEPHERD. There his name was, as large as Suzanne Purcell's. Even before the title appeared the crowd applauded, and I heard Will grunt. I'm not sure whether it was from fear or pleasure.

Then the movie started, and I was caught up in the gorgeous shots of the American West. Nestor Keresty had seen beauty in the landscape that I had not and had made his art come alive on the screen.

Will delivered the foal, carried it to his young wife (*she looks closer to thirty than nineteen,* I noted with satisfaction), and delivered his dreaded line.

The audience was quiet. No one snickered. Will finally relaxed in the seat beside me. Jennie flashed him a thumbs-up. "See?" she whispered. "Told you so."

The movie went on for a little more than two hours. It was fast-paced, hokey, lush, romantic. I found myself enjoying it — until North came up on Ellie in the tub and began to wash her.

The way Will looked at her was the way he looked at me when we made love. It didn't look as though he were acting; it was desire in his eyes, lust. His hand disappeared under the suds, but I sensed, just by the way his arm moved, what he was really doing.

My heart clutched. Suddenly I couldn't breathe. I had to sit up very straight in my theater seat.

They've been to bed together, I thought, and a dull ache spread through my body. I remembered the rumors in the press, and Will's firm denial of them. *They were lovers off-screen, weren't they? Oh please, don't let that be true.*

I made myself look at Will then. He was watching the screen intently, his mouth half open — *reliving it!*

When the interminable love scene finished, Will leaned over and tenderly kissed my cheek. "I was acting, Maggie," he whispered. "I know what you're thinking, but you're wrong. Maybe I am an actor."

I sighed, breathed deeply, and began to feel a little better. Yes, maybe Will was an actor, after all.

68

THE GLITZY premiere party for *Primrose* was held privately upstairs at the Russian Tea Room on Fifty-seventh Street. A hundred or more people came over to shake Will's hand and tell him how superb he was. He recognized none of them, and only acknowledged their praise with an abstracted nod.

He was somewhere else, actually. *He was looking for his mother and his father. Their ghosts, he knew, would not miss an opportunity as grand as this.*

He was losing it big time, wasn't he? Yes, this was Rio all over again. It had all the makings of a disaster. He realized that he still hadn't learned how to live with defeat.

A Caputo public relations flack came running into the restaurant around eleven-thirty. Everyone looked up. This was the moment they had been waiting for.

"A hit!" he shouted, waving a copy of the *New York Times*. "A serious rave. Well, close enough."

He handed the paper, already folded to the Entertainment Section, to his boss, then stood in the crowd which had gathered around Caputo to hear the producer/director read the important review aloud.

"*Michael Lenox Caputo, that master of blockbusters, who alone among our current crop of directors can still produce an engrossing, even enthralling, entertainment, has surpassed himself with Primrose, sure to be one of this season's biggest box-office successes. . . .*"

A cheer went up from the guests, especially the studio executives. A small band hired for the party played "Hail to the Chief." Caputo read on silently as the noise continued, then, when the room was once again quiet, flung the paper aside.

"Modesty forbids me from reading more," he said. "You'll all have your copies in the morning. Meanwhile, let's have a celebratory drink! Let's have several drinks! We've earned it tonight."

Waiters served expensive champagne. The paper, which had landed on a table near the entrance, went unheeded by everyone except Will, who picked it up with a casual air, and began to read, wondering why Caputo had not gone on.

He found his own name almost immediately:

Caputo is wonderfully served by his female star, Suzanne Purcell, who radiates innocence and sensuality in equal measures and, in her love scenes, manages to be both nineteen (which in real life she is not) and a woman comfortable with her sexual appetite. Her male counterpart, however, the former sports star Will Shepherd, is patently more comfortable on a soccer pitch than the beautifully photographed plains of Texas. He treats her as though she were some luscious morsel, no more important than a slice of New York cheesecake, or maybe even Texas cheesecake. Both stars look great without their shirts, but when Mr. Shepherd is actually called upon to act, whatever emotion is generated by the raw sex disintegrates into a pout, a forced smile, or glycerine tears applied by a makeup man, but not produced by the heart. Mr. Shepherd seems not to have much of one. He should not have been so hasty about giving up his athletic career.

Will read no further. He turned toward the guests. He was feeling crazed and frantic, absolutely wild.

He looked around the room, searching desperately for Maggie. She was standing by Caputo's side, smiling at something the director said. *Well, fuck her.*

She was supposed to be my salvation, my soul mate. That's what her songs promised.

But she told me I was wonderful in the film.

She lied to me, goddamn her.

Bitch!

He hurled the paper down, and disappeared into the night. He feared that he was going mad, or maybe that he was already there. He needed to hear the cheers of the crowd, to feel that kind of absolute love, but there was nothing for him here.

Will turned onto Seventh Avenue and he started to jog. Soon he was running at almost full speed. And still there was no cheering, no love anywhere in sight.

The werewolf of New York, he thought.

209

69

WILL HAD BEEN MISSING for two days, and I felt as though my heart had stopped.

Winnie Lawrence and I looked for him frantically, checking local and New York hospitals and police stations, calling everybody at the party with whom he might have left. The kids were in a panic too.

No one had a clue as to where Will might have gone. I remembered stories he'd told me about Rio — his disappointment. Something had happened down there that had changed him.

I had read the *Times* movie review, of course, as soon as Will had left the room — read it with horror and anger as I realized what it would do to him, how it would hurt. I'd been there myself. I'd suffered through mean-spirited reviews, some deserved, some not.

Another high-profile failure. So many failures in his own eyes.

I knew about that feeling too. I wanted to be there for him. *But where was he?* How could I help if I couldn't find Will?

On the third day I called Barry again, and asked him to

come to the house. "I feel a little out of control," I told him once he arrived. "I think I should be doing something more, but I can't think what it might be."

"He'll come back," Barry said. "He has something good to come back to. Don't forget that."

"You always overestimate me, and underestimate Will. He could have killed himself, Barry. I'm really afraid for him. His father committed suicide."

"People like Will *don't*," Barry said. "He knows what he's doing."

"How can you say that? You don't know Will. You don't know how hard he takes things."

Barry shrugged. He didn't believe it. In a way, neither did I. I thought that Will would come back. He loved me, and he loved the kids. He had to come back.

"I fantasize finding him in a ditch somewhere. Just because the police haven't found him —"

"They haven't because he doesn't want to be found. I understand how terrible this is for you, but you're overreacting, Maggie. He's probably on the bender of benders. He'll come back when it's over."

Would he? I was afraid that maybe I didn't know everything about Will. I hadn't been with him in Rio. Who had? What furies drove him then? Which were driving him now? Perhaps he wasn't telling me the truth.

And how could he just disappear?

I saw a picture in my mind — Will and Allie riding Fleas across the lot in back of our house. He had to come back. It was inconceivable that he wouldn't.

70

AND EVENTUALLY, he did.

I was awakened by a familiar hand touching my cheek, then lightly stroking my hair. *Will was in the bedroom!* I knew his touch so well. My heart jumped. Terror came over me.

"*Will!*" I finally managed to whisper, my mouth dry with fear.

I pushed his hand away and twisted myself out of bed. I faced him with a fury that had grown all the time he was away, and now was at its height.

"Where have you been? Why didn't you call us? Oh God, Will. You think you can just come back like this?"

There was something in his eyes that night — something so different, so strange. It was subtle, but I picked up on it. He didn't look like himself.

He was dressed in unwrinkled black slacks and a black T-shirt. His hair was casual, the windblown look. His jaw was covered with a day or two's light growth.

He smiled at me the way I'm sure he did at every woman in his life who had been angry at him, and whose forgiveness he needed. I wanted to scream at him, lash out at him with my fists.

"I've been in London. I went to visit my aunt. She's like a second mother to me. Only she wasn't there, off on holiday with Aunt Eleanor, so I came home."

Yes. Of course. To another mother. To me.

"I'm sorry, Maggie, I shouldn't have done it, definitely should have called. You can't *imagine* how upset I was at that dreadful premiere. You have no idea what goes through my mind."

No, I didn't, I couldn't, I didn't want to, but I tried to be patient, and to understand. Maybe, I tried too hard.

71

WILL HAD BEGUN to wear two-hundred-dollar dark glasses almost all the time now — at night and inside the house. He called it his "film star phase."

He used any and every excuse to be out of the house. In truth, he was afraid to be around Maggie and the kids. Maybe he didn't love them anymore, couldn't *feel* what he wanted to, but he didn't want to hurt them either.

He didn't want to hurt them.

He drove his new Mercedes convertible into New York one obnoxiously sunny afternoon. He felt hollow, as though there were absolutely nothing inside him. He'd spoken to his brother that morning, but of course Palmer wasn't any help. Palmer didn't want to have anything to do with him anymore.

He wanted to end it all — maybe in a spectacular car crash. He pushed the Cabriolet to over a hundred on the narrow, winding Saw Mill. He was much too skillful a driver to crash though; his reflexes were perfect. Or maybe he didn't really want to die — just yet.

Why the hell should he want to die?

Primrose was fucking soaring at the box office. The absurd movie had made it to number one, and had stayed there for weeks. Even more absurd, he was being touted as the next Eastwood, or Harrison Ford. What a goddamn idiocy. Hollywood made him ill with its amateurish reading of public tastes.

In a single week, he'd gotten over a hundred loathsome scripts to read. He'd finally selected another best-seller, a powerful psychological thriller called *Windchimes*. He'd negotiated a contract for four million up front.

Principal shooting was set to start that very day with the famed British director Tony Scott. It was going to be another hit movie, everyone was sure of it. It had all the "ingredients."

Well, Will was sure it was going to be another piece of commercial garbage. He knew what was good, and what wasn't. He knew when he was fooling the world, and that it would catch up with him sooner or later.

He couldn't stand the fucking reviews — *because they were true, his critics were right. He was dog shit on a stick.*

He couldn't stand it anymore.

He couldn't bear being Will Shepherd: the barely living legend, the ex-football great, "the incredible Hunk," "Mr. Maggie Bradford."

As he entered New York City and saw the road signs for Broadway and 242d Street, Will floored it and took the convertible to over a hundred again.

Traffic was thick, and he swerved from lane to lane as other drivers angrily honked their horns.

I don't want to be Will Shepherd anymore, he was thinking as he maneuvered the car with one hand, then one finger, then *look, ma, no hands.*

I don't want to live like this.

I can't.

Was that what my father was thinking when he first went underwater?

72

HE WAS GOING UNDERWATER. *Down, down, down. The water was cool and dark. It wasn't so bad to drown.*

It was as "Will Shepherd" that he began the early evening at the Red Lion Inn in Greenwich Village. As Shepherd he consumed seven Scotches, neat; as Shepherd he was now playing out, for an audience of mostly inebriated admirers, his greatest triumph in a Manchester United uniform.

Since he was buying drinks all around, the audience was with him, hanging on every word.

"Will, Will," one of them chanted. An Englishman. A genuine fan, probably.

"The Blond Arrow!" Will shouted back, his voice thick with irony that none of them seemed to appreciate.

"The Blond Bum," another voice called out from the back of the barroom crowd.

Will stopped in the middle of his story. It was just some punk wearing black leather and black jeans, acting the macho man. He glared at the asshole, thinking *Euro-trash,* thinking *let's get it on.*

The punk made his way through the crowd. There were two

friends with him. Will saw tattoos on their arms: falcons or eagles.

"A stinking bum," the punk repeated, now facing Will as the spectators stepped back. His accent sounded German.

"A pansy," one of the friends added. "A British fag." Definitely German.

Anger, which had struggled for days to escape, now roared from Will's mouth. A string of curses exploded.

The Euro-trash punk stepped forward, beckoning to Will. "Come get me, bum," he said. "Come get me, you has-been."

Where he got the chain he held, Will couldn't imagine. It really didn't matter. He charged the German anyway.

The Blond Arrow charged blindly. He wanted a fight; any fight would do.

He got out of the Red Lion with only cuts and bruises. Nothing important. Nothing fatal.

He remembered that he was supposed to be on a movie set. *Well, fuck that. This was a better psychological thriller anyway.*

Now came a series of white explosions in the shadows of an abandoned storage warehouse just off Hudson Street. A gang was beating up on him; *he didn't know why. Could it have been something I said, mates?* He was aware only of the intense pain of their kicks — to the head, to the stomach and groin, to the ribs — of the relentless agony each hard blow produced in his brain. *Punishment,* he thought as he was falling to the pavement.

Fair and just punishment for his crimes, his sins, his entire life.

His arms and legs were pinioned. He couldn't move a muscle. His face was smashed down onto the gritty concrete of the sidewalk. His nose was leaking blood. Then his legs were lifted off the ground like meat on a hook.

And he was really pounded. He was battered, kicked, butted, until he was sure that every bone in his body had been broken. Strangely, he welcomed the physical pain. *It told him that he was alive, right?*

217

His entire world was suddenly spinning out of control. It was all bright liquid red. Will felt he was falling, pitching forward into a black hole.

He was being left to die on the New York streets, wasn't he?

It wasn't so terrible, really.

He was just following in the footsteps of his father. He'd always known it would end like this.

Will Shepherd found dead in the street.

Strange, weird — his last thought, his final image was of the dog he'd killed years ago. He had loved that dog.

73

THIS HAD TO BE a nightmare. It couldn't be anything else. I wasn't really awake, was I?

The Manhattan police came to my home around midnight. They broke the news politely, but their good manners and tact couldn't ease any of the pain. I had to sit down immediately. I thought I was going to pass out or maybe be sick. I was in a state of shock.

I finally was able to call Winnie Lawrence. He lived close by. The two of us went to St. Vincent's Hospital in New York.

I was permitted to see Will only briefly — he was sleeping, heavily sedated, his face swathed in heavy bandages. He looked horrible.

I felt as though I were in a dream. Whatever was happening, couldn't be. What had happened to the man I had married, the person I loved? *This badly beaten person couldn't be Will!*

We were approached by Detective Nicolo, the police officer who had come to Bedford with the news. I didn't want to talk to anyone, to see anyone.

"He's pretty beaten up, but it looks worse than it is," said Nicolo. "The doctors say it'll be a couple of weeks before he can get out of the hospital. I'm sorry, Mrs. Bradford. We don't know how it happened. Or who did it. No witnesses have come forward."

"He was supposed to start shooting a film yesterday," Winnie Lawrence said.

"Good luck." The detective smiled wryly. "If the part is *Rocky V*, he might be able to manage it okay."

"Jesus!" Winnie said, and headed for a pay phone.

Detective Nicolo turned to me. He looked like Al Pacino, only with a larger hooked nose. His white hair was slicked back. "Do you have any idea why he might have been attacked, Mrs. Bradford? Do you know if he was with anyone last night?"

I shook my head. "I'm sorry. I don't, detective. I'm not myself right now. Sorry, sorry." I fought back tears.

Nicolo clucked and nodded sympathetically. "He wasn't home with you last night then?"

"I expected him. He didn't show up."

What was the detective implying? Why am I protecting Will? I wondered. *Because he's my husband, and I love him.*

"It'll be hard to find the men who beat him up." Nicolo had taken out a black notebook; now he put it away. "If Mr. Shepherd can't describe them, there's not much we can do. I'll come back here as soon as he's able to talk. I'll stay in touch with you."

He shook my hand and left, telling me to call him if I had any information. An agitated Winnie joined me in the waiting room.

"They're going to replace Will," he said. "They say they can't afford to wait until he recovers from this. Whatever the hell happened to him?"

I shrugged, feeling numb and cold all over. It was neither good news nor bad. A frightening thought crossed my mind. *I didn't know who my husband was.*

"He'll be devastated about the film," Winnie said.

"I don't know, Winnie." I felt a wave of sadness, an overlay on my fatigue. "I think maybe he'll be relieved."

74

I DROVE BACK TO BEDFORD with Winnie Lawrence. Our nursemaid, Mrs. Leigh, was there with the kids. Fortunately, everyone was still sleeping when I got home.

I didn't want to explain about Will; I wasn't sure that I could explain, that I understood.

I loved Will, but maybe he'd fooled me; maybe he was a good actor when he wanted to be. I had thought I could help him, that I was helping him. My mother had made the same mistake with my father. Oh God, I didn't know what to think. I wanted to go up into the attic — and just write songs again.

I sat in the den, staring out onto the grounds. The morning sun was up and birds were chirping everywhere. But unpleasant images were flying inside my head — bad ones. I remembered a movie with Julia Roberts called *Sleeping with the Enemy*. I felt as though I were in it, or maybe this was *Gaslight*. Or maybe I *was* dreaming. Please. Let this be a dream.

I don't know who my husband is, I kept thinking. *Is that possible? Is that what's happening? What is Will doing to himself? What is he doing to all of us?*

221

Allie wandered into the den and found me there. I did my best to act as though nothing were the matter.

"I've been waiting, waiting, waiting for you to get up and come see me," I said to him. I patted my lap for him to come sit. He ran to me and jumped into my arms.

I held Allie, and kissed and hugged him. He did the same for me. He had no idea how important that was to me right now. I felt as though I might start stuttering again. My chest seemed to collapse in on me. I loved holding him like this though. We'd done it every single morning since he was born. I don't think we'd missed a day.

Suddenly Allie turned to me. He squinted as he looked up into my eyes.

"What's wrong, Mommy?" my little boy said. "What's wrong?"

Later that morning, I returned to the dreary hospital in downtown New York. I was allowed to see Will again. He was sitting up, still incredibly dazed, and sipping juice through a straw.

The part of his face not covered by bandages was purplish; his eyes were horrible thin slits, his lips puffy, as though they had been stung by a swarm of bees again and again. He looked like one of those poor men who sleep on sidewalk gratings all over New York. *My husband looked like that.*

Will reached a hand toward me when I came in. I felt my heart soften. I couldn't help it. "Maggie . . ." he whispered.

I didn't take his hand, but instead stood looking at him. I hated holding back, but I had to.

"Maggie . . . forgive me. Please forgive me."

"How can I, Will?" I finally spoke to him.

He began to cry like a little boy. Will curled himself into a tight ball, a fetal position, and he wept. He seemed so pathetic, horribly alone, and I couldn't imagine what was the matter with him.

My heart nearly broke, but I didn't reach out to comfort Will. This time, I couldn't.

75

BAD THOUGHTS had been drifting through Will's head ever since he'd come home, but while he was in the hospital as well.

It frosted him that Maggie was still a huge star, and he was a nothing. But most of all, it incensed Will that she was *happy*. Maggie, Jennie, and Allie were a self-contained unit. They didn't need him. They functioned beautifully on their own.

Bad thoughts. Constantly. Morning, noon, and especially at night.

Like the one about Allie having an accident while they were out riding horses.

Or pretty Jennie — lots to fantasize about there. Jennie was sweet on him anyway. She was like all the others, wasn't she? They wanted him, desperately, until they discovered who he really was.

Palmer was as bad as the others, maybe worse. His own brother was taking money from him to keep a few harmless secrets. Well, at least Palmer had always been up front about being a worthless bastard.

Maggie was the real problem, and he didn't know what to do about her.

Lots of bad thoughts though.
Lots of possibilities. None of them very nice.
Like?
What if I killed myself, as my father did?
What if I took it one step further?
What if, what if, what if. . . .

76

WATCH CLOSELY NOW. *Please.* Try to listen to each word, to every nuance. This is where the ride starts to get real tricky, where I began to seriously question my sanity. Just thinking about it made me feel tense and uncertain and sick to my stomach.

Am I guilty? Am I the murderer they say I am? Or am I the victim here?

"I'm going to San Francisco. I have to go, Will," I told him a few weeks after his "incident" in New York. He was still acting strange, but he was good around Jennie and Allie, so I didn't complain too much.

"What?" Will barely glanced up from the TV. He seemed to get lost in whatever he was doing lately. Sometimes he looked a thousand miles away, spaced out, when I tried to talk to him. I didn't understand what was happening. How could I? There was an invisible wall between us.

"They've asked me to do a benefit concert at Candlestick Park, and I've accepted. I need to sing again, Will. It's been too long."

225

He clicked off the TV and turned to face me. He'd been watching the game in a T-shirt and shorts, which always made me think that he was waiting to be called in from the bench. He was still amazingly fit, and looked ready to play. "Without asking if I wanted to come along?" he said.

"It's probably best if I go alone. Barry'll be there —"

"That asshole."

"— and we'll be releasing the record as soon as we can after the performance." I had no inclination either to sugarcoat my plans, or to say what I really felt, which was "at least I *tell* you when I'll be gone."

"So you *decided* to go to California, just casual-like." His face was turning red. His eyes protruded, wild. *One of these times, he's going to go off, isn't he?* I said to myself.

He turned on me in a fury. "What am I anyway? Some bloody footman in this house? Is that it, Maggie?"

"Who said you were? I don't feel that way. God. What's happening to you? Can you please explain that to me?"

"I say where you go, and don't go! Got that?" *Suddenly, I could hear Phillip. Almost the exact same tone of voice.*

But I managed to stay calm, at least on the outside. "No you don't, Will. You can decide about your life, not mine."

He rose from his chair and walked toward me. I held my ground. He stood motionless and glared at me with dark, suspicious eyes.

I didn't like this. Not the look, not the threatening body language. I had never seen him like this, and suddenly I was afraid.

His hand flashed out! There was no way I could avoid it. With a roar, he struck my cheek, strafing across the left side of my face. His backhand caught me a second time and sent me reeling backwards.

It was as though two explosions had gone off inside my head. *I couldn't believe it!* He'd never hit me before. Never raised a hand, never threatened.

"You're *not* going to San Francisco!" he screamed. "*You're not leaving me, you bitch!*"

He drew back his hand for another blow, but then he stopped and let both hands fall to his sides.

It was as though he'd had second thoughts, or come to his senses, almost as though he were another person.

"Okay," he said. "Go to San Francisco. I don't care what you do, Maggie."

I began to shake all over. I wouldn't let myself cry. Then, I began to tremble, badly. My legs felt useless. My arms too.

"I'm taking Allie and Jennie," I told him. I could barely speak, or even look at Will. "You can't stop us. Don't try."

77

BATTERY.
He hit me.
This can't be me.

The lyrics to my own song played in my head. I was staring vacantly through the jet's oblong window, my eyes climbing a mountain range of snow-white clouds. Beside me, Allie lay asleep, his furry head nudging my lap. Across the aisle, Jennie was listening to something with her airplane earphones.

Both of them were happy to be going with me. They had no idea about my trouble with Will. The concert coincided with Jennie's vacation. Allie *always* wanted to be at my side, and usually was. The three of us were so close that we'd come up with the acronym *JAM. Jennie, Allie, Maggie.* We'd never changed it to include Will.

Coming off the plane, I was aware of the usual stares and hellos from total strangers. Some tried to get my autograph, nearly trampling us with their efforts; others reached out to touch me, as though the contact would somehow grant celebrity status to them as well.

Celebrity!

If only they knew what it really meant to be famous . . . to have so many eyes always watching.

There was a fax from Will waiting for me at the Four Seasons Hotel in town:

> GOOD LUCK, MY SONGBIRD
> FORGIVE YOUR WILL HIS TRESPASSES
> PLEASE FORGIVE ME
> HURRY HOME WITH THE CHILDREN
> I LOVE YOU — *ALWAYS HAVE, ALWAYS WILL.*

> I crumpled the paper.
> *Always Will*, indeed.

78

BARRY, JENNIE, ALLIE, and I were cuddled inside a big red-and-silver Bell helicopter. Beneath us were the bright lights of Candlestick Park, the dark waters of the bay. I was dressed in my usual outfit: a loose white peasant's blouse, long skirt, flat shoes, so I wouldn't be a millimeter taller than I was.

But was I really ready for this? I wasn't sure, but I had to try it, really wanted to.

In less than an hour I would be making my first major concert appearance in almost three years. The networks had sent film crews. This was *news,* right? — *hard copy.* A live album was being recorded tonight. There had been over five hundred thousand requests for tickets; there were fewer than eighty thousand seats.

Yet we were sealed off in the helicopter, a private family: my children, my best friend. This was better than being down there, I was thinking.

"Let's not land," I said.

Barry raised an eyebrow and made a face. He put his hand over his mouth as though he were speaking into a mike. "Uh, Earth to Maggie, Earth to Peter Pan."

"I mean it. Can't we just stay up here till tomorrow?" I was feeling a little giddy.

"What'll we use for fuel?" Jennie asked.

"They can refuel us in midair. Like long-range bombers. It'll be cool."

"We'd be hungry," Allie said, always thinking of eats.

"They can pass in sandwiches with the fuel. No problem." Jennie laughed. She liked it when I talked nonsense.

"I'm hungry *now*," Allie announced. He was always the most practical member of JAM.

"We're about to land," Barry told him, "no matter what your mother says. I'll get you some food at the Park. All-beef franks, mmm-mmm good."

I suddenly felt a wave of sadness, and also unbelievable fear. Stage fright. "I don't know if I can go on," I said. "Really, Barry. No joke."

He took my hand. "Preconcert jitters. Go with the fear. Use it."

"More than that. It seems so safe here, so *right*. Down there is danger. First the fans, and then —"

"Will," he said. I had told Barry nothing about the fight, but he'd guessed something was wrong. He knew me too well.

"Life," I said.

Okay, so I'd sold close to twenty million albums; I'd won eleven Grammy Awards.

But I could still get scared, couldn't I?

My singing style was the personal confessional mode, right? I could do that now. Just go out there in front of all those people and be myself. Be very up front and personal.

The trouble was — I was starting to feel like *my old self*. I remembered the Maggie who had existed in West Point. I even remembered the little girl who broke into tears because she couldn't stop stuttering when she had to answer questions in school.

I knew exactly what my performance was supposed to be — edgy, but also heartfelt. My songs were supposed to be succinct and catchy on the surface — infected with all kinds of influences: rock, Broadway, classical, French art song — but under the surface, complex and psychologically true.

I knew all this as I walked out on that big stage in San Francisco, as I looked down on all those expectant faces.

So why was I afraid? No, absolutely petrified? Why was I scared that I wouldn't be able to sing at all?

I sat down at the piano, and I started to mouth lyrics against the stiff, chilly breeze off the bay.

I almost got through the first song —

Then I went to pieces.

With all those strangers watching — but also my children, with Jennie and Allie right there in the stage wings.

BATTERY, I sang.

HE HIT ME

THIS CAN'T BE ME

I started to stammer, then to stutter again — something I hadn't done in so many years, something I'd fought so hard to overcome.

I couldn't sing anymore. I couldn't go on.

I finally turned and *talked* to the huge crowd — "I'm having a little trouble up here. *Whew.* I'm sorry. I'm in trouble."

I was beginning to have heart palpitations. I felt faint and thought I might fall off the piano bench.

Then Jennie and Barry and Allie were there for me. So were a couple of the musicians. They helped me offstage. I could barely walk.

"Poor Mommy," Allie kept saying. "Poor Mommy. Mommy got sick."

79

WILL HAD ALWAYS been a night creature. Now, more than ever he needed to get out and around. *The werewolf of Bedford.*

He whipped his black BMW coupe approximately five hundred yards down Greenbriar Road. He turned from one tree-lined, shadowy driveway — his own — into the next.

The main entrance to the Lake Club was marked by ten-foot-high fieldstone pillars. An uneven fence of like stone ran the length of the property, and Will drove past the entrance to a designated spot near the fence.

He parked and got out. The fence swung open; a path led to the rear of the clubhouse and a service door that would be virtually invisible to anyone who wasn't looking for it.

Inside the club, there was a tangible stillness in the air that signified privacy and privilege. It reminded Will of the silence of cathedrals and European banks. He maneuvered his way past deserted billiard and smoking rooms to yet another door, on which he knocked, paused, and knocked again.

The door was opened from inside. Will blinked at the sudden bright light assailing his eyes. Then he took in the mahogany paneling, the long oak bar, the Tiffany lamps, and the Renaissance paintings that hung on the walls of the room.

The group of men clustered at the bar had watched his entrance. They said hello once they saw it was he, and that Will belonged there.

Peter O'Malley was one of them. Strangely, he and Will had become friendly at the club. They had Maggie in common, didn't they? Maggie had brought them together, and they frequently talked about her. Peter dreamed of bringing Maggie down.

That evening, they were both attending a late-night get-together at the country club. The meeting was strictly unofficial.

Once, or sometimes twice a month, after the club closed, a few members brought in special entertainment. It was a way for the high-powered men to let off steam and have some social, and certainly politically unacceptable, fun. God knows, they couldn't seem to get it at home with "the wives."

The room was lit by the gold and red flames from an ample fieldstone fireplace. *The fires of Hell,* Will called it. *A sample of what's to come for the lot of us.*

Standing in front of the fireplace in a more or less orderly row, stood six girls. They were all young beauties. Their bare skin and long hair gleamed in the burnishing firelight.

The eldest looked twenty at the most, the youngest might have been sixteen. Each was wearing a black sleeping mask. The girls were never permitted to see the members, or even the location of the club.

The exclusive Lake Club of Bedford Hills, Will thought to himself. *It was a facade, like everything else.*

Later that night, Will picked out one of the young girls. She was tall and blond and reminded him of Jennie.

80

I THINK I KNEW in my heart, for some time, that the
marriage was over between Will and me. It was a matter of
timing now. What would be best for the children, then for
me, and finally for Will. I didn't want to hurt him, just leave
him.

Will was there to greet us when we got home. He was also
his old self. Our arrival revived him. He became almost giddy
with joy. He seemed genuinely concerned about what had happened to me in San Francisco, my minibreakdown. He said he
understood "the jitters" very well, and I believed Will did.

He promised me there would be no more anger, no more
fights, no more disappearances. His fear of desertion had made
him desperate. He was in touch with his feelings once again.

I listened to Will and everything he had to say. I heard the
words. I had already made my decision though. Will had
shown me, however briefly, a side of him that I couldn't possibly be around, or deal with.

An uneasy calm descended on the house in Bedford.

It was calm sometimes too with Phillip, I thought.

*   *   *

I was getting everything in order, talking to Nathan Bailford and taking care of the legal aspects as best I could. I just needed another day or so, then I would talk to Will. In the meantime, I saw a very good psychiatrist in nearby Tarrytown. I was, as the papers would later say, "*under a doctor's care,*" whatever that is supposed to convey.

Something came up unexpectedly. I received a call to come to Jennie's school. They said it was important. The Bedford Hills Academy's administration building was a small, neat Victorian-style house that looked like a thriving country inn. As I hurried inside, students and office staff recognized me and tried not to stare. I waved to the kids I knew, and even to some I didn't recognize.

I ran up the stairs, stopping long enough in a bathroom to comb my hair, put on lipstick, check to make sure that my head was on straight.

I was going to meet Dr. Henry Follett, Dean of the Academy, and I wanted to look no different from other mothers with children at the school. For some reason, I was already more upset than the occasion probably required.

Dr. Follett's office was small but pleasant, with a picture window looking out over the campus, and school memorabilia everywhere — pennants, championship banners, photographs of Follett with students or local officials.

He was a likable man in his fifties, compact and natty, and I guessed he had a sense of humor, though his expression was serious and his smile was professional. Still, his eyes were kind. And he had a nice handshake.

I didn't know why he had summoned me. I was busy at home, distracted with Will, but I had come to the school right away. My stomach, my back, my neck were all in knots.

"It's about Jennie," he said, as soon as I was seated in front of his large, cluttered desk.

"Yes. I figured as much. Is she in some kind of trouble?" I

asked. I was trying not to show what I was feeling inside. I had to be strong here — for Jennie. I could do that.

"I'm not sure, Mrs. Bradford. Maybe you can tell me."

I hadn't noticed anything too unusual about Jennie. She *was* a teenager though. "She seems fine. Rebellious at times, argumentative, mimics Butthead and Beavis around the house to drive me crazy."

"Acting the same at home though? Not sick lately? Not depressed or unhappy?"

I shook my head, and continued to feel both confused and worried. What was he getting at? I saw Jennie every day. Of course she had her own life and her own friends. I operated on the principle that the best thing a mother can do for her teenage daughter is to give her a reasonable amount of space to grow up in. That, plus love.

"Certainly not sick," I said. "What's going on, Dr. Follett? Please tell me why you called."

He drummed his fingers on his desk. "This semester, Jennie has skipped seventeen days of school."

Bombshell! I felt suddenly cold all over. "Skipped seventeen days?"

"Cut her classes. Didn't show up at all."

"My God! I had no idea. I almost don't believe it, but of course I do. It isn't like Jennie."

"No, it isn't like Jennie," he agreed.

He handed me some papers from his desk. A report card and several illness notes. "Is that your signature?"

I looked at the notes and the report card. My hands were shaking. "My name, not my handwriting." *Another bombshell.*

"Jennie's?"

"I'm not sure. Could be." My head was spinning too. This was the last thing I'd expected. Jennie had never been in trouble.

"We think she was trying to forge your signature," Dr. Follett said, bringing me back from my reverie.

237

"Jennie wouldn't do something like that." I winced. Obviously, she had.

"Are you sure? If it's not your signature, and it's not Jennie's forgery, then whose could it be?"

My brain whirled. "I really haven't a clue." Suddenly, I was angry at Jennie though. We had always trusted each other. I'd made time for Jennie no matter what else was going on.

"Mr. Shepherd?" the dean asked.

"No. He's her stepfather. He'd simply sign. And this isn't his signature either."

"Look at the latest report card," he said. "Have you seen this?"

I looked. B's and C's. I wanted to cry. Jennie had always been an A student. Maybe I hadn't been paying enough attention because of that?

"Mrs. Bradford, Jennie is one of the best students at Bedford Hills Academy. Then suddenly, just this semester, she gets very bad marks. For her anyway. That sometimes happens in the senior year, when a kid's been accepted at college and feels she deserves a break. But Jennie's a sophomore. Just the time her grades should be highest."

"I know. *Jennie* knows," I said. I didn't understand what could have happened. This had come out of the blue. I didn't think she had picked up on Will and me, but maybe she had. Kids can tell.

Dr. Follett stood up from his desk, and extended his hand. "We all love Jennie here at the Academy. Faculty and her classmates both. If you find out anything, please call me. It wouldn't be betraying her secrets. This isn't the first time something like this has happened to a student, and we're pretty good at fixing things."

I shook his hand, then I headed out — to try and find Jennie. She had skipped classes again today.

First though, I sat in the school's visitor parking lot and tried to stop my body from trembling. My world seemed to be falling apart again.

81

JENNIE ARRIVED HOME around three-thirty, her knapsack full of books, looking innocent of any wrongdoing. I asked her to take a ride with me.

I drove to the Pound Ridge Reservation, a nature preserve in the heart of Westchester. At around four, the two of us hiked up a hill toward an antique fire tower, from the top of which you could see Long Island Sound, and even the New York City skyline far to the south.

Jennie, of course, wanted to know what was going on. I asked her to wait. All in good time, my sweet darling.

We walked silently — I didn't know where to start — and stopped, breathless, when we reached the crest. I was feeling maternal, angry, hurt, optimistic — just as in the songs I wrote. *True songs out of life, right?*

"I've been to see Dean Follett," I finally told her. *The first shoe drops!*

Jennie had been looking at me. Now, she turned her head away. Not a word.

"He says your grades are falling. He also says you've been skipping school." *The second shoe.*

239

"School's boring and I hate it." Jennie's tone was surly and defiant. Not like her at all. It was Jennie at her absolute worst, and not something I saw very often.

"You didn't used to think so," I said to her.

"I do now. There's nothing worth learning. The teachers there aren't very bright, you know."

"So you don't go anymore. That's interesting, Jen. Quite a revelation. What do you do with your days?"

"Nothing much. But nothing is better than my classes."

"You're not home."

"How would you know that for sure? You're shut up in your study most of the day."

Now she was being completely unfair, but I kept my cool. "I'd know, and *you* know I would. I love you, Jennie, and if you're in any kind of trouble —"

"Nobody gives a damn about anybody else. Don't fake it. Don't condescend to me now."

Even without touching her, I could sense an awful tenseness in her body, the effort she had to make to speak at all. When had this happened? How had it happened? Why?

"I love you," I said, my voice unsteady. "You're the most precious thing in my life. It's always been that way."

Her composure finally broke. So did mine. "Don't say that," she suddenly wailed. "Don't say you love me, Mom. I don't deserve it."

I could barely speak. I was holding back great, racking sobs. "Why? I *do* love you. Why shouldn't I tell you what's true?"

"Because you *couldn't*. You don't know who I am, and it takes something like this to get your attention. *Failing grades!* I mean — *who cares?*"

I finally bowed my head, and I started to cry. I thought that I could handle anything, but not this.

Suddenly, Jennie flung herself at me, burying her face in my neck. I could feel her hot tears, her body's warmth.

"I can't tell you," she sobbed. "I'm not even sure that I know.

I'm fifteen and it's all a little nuts. So what's new?" she finally choked out a laugh.

"My God, Mom," Jennie said to me then. "You're shaking all over."

We sat on the ground and held each other for a long, long time. A breeze came up, and I wrapped my sweater around her. *My baby,* I thought. *My friend for so many years. My sweet Jennie.*

But I could think of no way to comfort her, and make it better for either of us. I blamed myself, of course. I'd tried so hard to be supermom, but it wasn't enough. It never is.

82

I SPENT a blessed hour the next morning, which was unseasonably warm, working in the garden behind the swimming pool. The time alone, the feel of sunlight on the back of my neck, the physical exertion — all were exactly what the doctor ordered. I began to regroup.

I needed time to think things through in a straight line. The worsening situation with Will. Jennie's problems at school. My own bad experience in San Francisco. It was a lot to take at one time; I was afraid that I wasn't handling it very well.

There was an explosion in the woods beyond the pool.

I stopped digging, stopped thinking, stopped breathing, and listened with total concentration. And dread.

A second explosion came from behind a thick wall of evergreens. The trees masked my view.

Gunshots? Oh my God.

I was on my feet, running at full speed toward the thick pocket of trees. A scream was stuck in my throat.

Oh God, dear God . . . what's happened?

What's happened now?

I plunged into the woods, heading for the sound of the

shots. My heart was pounding and there was a sharp pain in my chest.

Instinct drove me; I didn't even think of calling for help. Whom would I call to anyway?

Gunshots? Near our house? How could that be?

My ankles were stabbed by rocks and thistles. There were no more shots, just a frightening, desolate silence. Finally, I came to a clearing. I stopped running.

Will was standing there. Will was holding a rifle in the crook of his arm.

He turned at the sound of my footsteps. He looked at me as though I didn't belong there.

"What are you doing?" I managed to speak.

"Target practice," he said. He motioned to a row of beer and soda cans set up on a log. "Care to give it a go, Maggie?"

He flashed his best North Downing smile. "I'm getting quite good. I'm a natural it seems. Great hand-to-eye."

Phillip had a gun too. I had used it to kill him. I remembered dark blood pouring from his mouth, saw his look of horror, heard his grunt of surprise as the fatal bullet struck him.

"Get rid of it!" I screamed. "I don't want it anywhere near my house. Get rid of that gun!"

Will looked at me coldly, but then he grinned. "*Our* house. But it's your call, Maggie. If it disturbs you, it's gone. If you don't trust yourself around guns, I understand."

83

THIS WAS THE DAY. *I just couldn't have known it. I wouldn't have expected it. This was the day.*

Having been unable to sleep, I slipped out of the house at dawn. I was wearing a terrycloth robe and my rattiest sneakers. My long hair was in knots. Hopeless.

I figured the air would be good for me, give me a fresh start. I hoped no one would see me like this. No paparazzi sneaking shots through the fence.

I walked to the partly crumbled fieldstone wall that divided my property from the grounds of the Lake Club. My sneakers stamped defiantly through damp leaves and creepers. Chattering blue jays and robins darted among the high trees over my head.

"Oh, shut the heck up," I grumped at the birds.

I was startled to hear another kind of sound in the woods. A human voice.

"Who's there?" I called ahead. "*Hello?*"

J. C. Frazier appeared. He was coming out of a meadow that belonged to the Lake Club, where he worked as head grounds-keeper. J.C. was always outside, so we met from time to time. I

244

knew that he was seeing Mrs. Leigh, and she thought he was a good man. *Yes, and they are hard to find,* I was tempted to tell her.

"Mornin', Mrs. Bradford. You the one responsible for this fine weather?" he asked. Not a care in the world, and why should he? His grounds were in perfect order.

"I thought *you* were in charge of the weather, J.C."

"No way, ma'am. I'm charged with the grounds only. I believe *you* have the upper atmosphere. And a real good job you've made of it today. Blue skies everywhere I can see."

We stopped to talk over a mossy stone wall. J.C. probably knew more secrets about the residents of Bedford than anyone around, but his discretion was as much responsible for his keeping his job as was his skill, so our talk was of seasonal flowers and the approaching summer. Harmless small talk, but it hit the spot, and took my mind off my problems, if only for a little while.

I remembered something I'd been meaning to ask somebody at the club, or maybe something I'd been afraid to bring up before.

"Sometimes at night I've noticed lights on in the club. I'd say around one or two in the morning."

J.C. thought about what I'd said, then shook his head. "That's not possible. No, I'm afraid not, Mrs. Bradford."

"I've seen the lights. I'm positive that I have."

"No, ma'am. I don't think so. Couldn't be. The club closes at eleven. Always. That's the golden rule."

I thought of arguing with him further, but gave up. If J.C. didn't want to talk, he wouldn't talk.

He tipped his ballcap, a blue one that read "N.Y. Giants." "Got to get back, plenty of work to do. You have a pleasant day, Mrs. Bradford."

I watched J.C. make his way back toward the large estate house of the club.

Strange, I thought. *Why wouldn't he know about the lights? Or why would he lie to me?*

245

I finally went back to the house determined to talk to Will that morning. It had to be done, however painful for both of us. This seemed like as good a day as any.

Jennie and Allie were toasting Pop-Tarts in the kitchen. They were both dressed. Jennie looked *ready for school,* which pleased me.

"Is Will up?" I asked, trying to make it sound as though it were a big deal, nothing special.

"You just missed him, Mom," Jennie said. "He had to go to the city on business. Said he'd be back around four."

I groaned. Will was almost never out of the house this early. Just my luck.

This was the day.

84

WILL DIDN'T COME HOME at four that afternoon.

He still hadn't arrived at seven-thirty when we sat down for dinner.

Or at ten, when we went upstairs to get ready for bed. He never called to say he'd be late, or maybe that he wouldn't be coming home at all.

I lay in bed with the lights off, but my eyes wide open. I was blaming myself, and I knew I shouldn't do that. Will had been so incredibly romantic and sensitive in the beginning of our relationship, and then he had just switched it off. Completely.

I wondered if he was having an affair now, or maybe more than one. I guess I shouldn't have cared about that, but I did.

I don't know how I finally got to sleep, only that I did.

"Damn! Damn it to hell!" I heard.

Will's curses woke me. *He was inside the bedroom. He was home.*

I could see him standing near the door, examining his toe. He'd stubbed it in the darkness. *Well, good. Serves him right.*

The bedroom door was half-open and light from the hallway silhouetted his body. His face remained in shadow.

247

He turned to look at me, but I pretended to be asleep. I held my breath. Then he crept out of the room.

He pulled the door awkwardly behind him. The door slammed shut. More of his stupid head games? *Damn him.*

I looked at the luminous face of the bedside clock: 12:45.

Where had he been tonight? Maybe I should get up and talk with him now, while the kids were asleep.

I got up, walked to the window, and looked outside. I saw Will. What was he doing? Where was he going down there?

I put on my robe and left the bedroom. The hallway was dark. On his way out, Will had turned off the night light we kept on for Allie.

I hurried downstairs.

The lights were off in the living room and den. There was no sound, no movement.

Something seemed wrong to me! Why were the lights off?

What was he up to?

The downstairs rooms were dark and quiet too. There was no one in the kitchen, or in Mrs. Leigh's room. Fridays were her night off, I remembered.

I went back to the foot of the stairs and peered up. *Nothing to see. Was Will back inside the house?*

I started to climb the stairs again.

Halfway up, I saw something standing against the wall. My heart almost stopped. My legs nearly went out from under me.

It was the rifle! I'd finally found it. *In the middle of the stairway, where Will had left it!*

My head was filled with loud noise. Chaos and confusion. None of this made sense to me.

What was going on?

Was Will upstairs again? What was he planning to do with the rifle? Where had it come from?

I started to run up the stairs. I reached the top step and stopped. At the far end of the corridor a line of light showed from beneath a door.

It was Jennie's door. The light hadn't been on just a few minutes before.

I was suddenly terrifed that Will was in there. *He's taking the children*, I thought.

I ran to get the rifle, then I hurried back. At least I had the gun now, not Will.

Had he planned to murder us all? Disturbed men did things like that. It wouldn't be the first time, would it?

I had a flashback. Phillip!

I ran down the corridor and yanked open Jennie's door. The rifle was ready, at least I thought it was. *I really didn't know very much about guns. Next to nothing, actually.*

What I saw inside the bedroom drove me absolutely out of my mind.

85

THIS IS THE DAY! Oh, Jesus God, Will!

Don't shoot him. Don't do it. Maggie, don't! a voice inside my head screamed at a deafening level.

Jennie was on the bed, wearing short, white pajamas. Her long, bare legs were exposed. Her eyes were closed; she seemed to be breathing normally. There was a glass of milk on the night table, half-finished.

I took in every tiny detail, understanding nothing yet.

This was so bad. This was so bad.

Will stood at the foot of her bed. He was dressed in khakis and a sport shirt. What he'd worn for his business meeting in New York? He looked too casual for business. *What was Will doing in Jennie's bedroom?*

"Maggie!" he said, as cool as could be. His film star persona. "I thought you were asleep. Were you trying to fool me?"

My heart was pounding so hard and fast it was difficult for me to breathe. "What are you doing in here?" I gasped out the words. "*What is going on?*"

Jennie suddenly sat up, and rubbed her eyes. She looked

frightened. "Mom? Will? What's the matter? What's happening? Is that a gun? *Mom?*"

Will smiled at the horrifying scene. It was the most scary and evil expression I had ever seen. I didn't know the person I was looking at. *What was he doing in Jennie's bedroom? I thought that I knew.*

"Jennie and I were just getting ready for some fun," he said. "Care to join us in bed? *Ménage à trois?*"

Ménage à trois? I was too scared and stunned to speak. For a moment my body was paralyzed. My pulse was racing crazily. I felt my mind implode. *Will and Jennie? Oh, my God, no!*

I raised the gun and aimed it at Will. I didn't care about the consequences.

I couldn't pull the trigger though. I couldn't do it. I couldn't.

"Get out of this house, and don't you ever come back," I said in a steady voice.

Will pushed past me and with his great speed rushed down the corridor. I could tell by the sound that he took the steps two at a time. He was laughing in a loud, braying voice, the kind you heard in horror movies.

I went after him, hampered by the unwieldy gun. I didn't want to shoot him, just make sure he was gone — forever. *Gone from all of our lives.*

He went out the front door, and I ran after him. I could see little at first except the outline of overhanging trees, but I heard his footsteps retreating toward the back of the house.

I pitched forward. Hit my knee. Caught myself with one hand.

Suddenly I couldn't hear steps anymore!

I pushed myself up. I listened intently, as I have never listened before.

I was frightened. I thought I might be going into shock. I felt cold all over. I was *freezing* cold. *I couldn't forget seeing Will in Jennie's bedroom. The look in her eyes.*

251

It was too quiet. I couldn't hear Will, or see him either. What was he doing out here?

The moon had disappeared behind a cover of clouds. It was nearly pitch dark. I couldn't stay outside. I knew I should get back in the house.

Perhaps he had tricked me. Gone back to Jennie. I didn't know what to do.

I stood uncertainly, squinting my eyes and looking around, trying to penetrate the darkness. I remembered hiding in the crawl space beneath the house near West Point. My nightmare had completed a full circle.

Silence.

Darkness.

The cold. I was shaking all over again.

"You stupid, prying bitch! You betrayed me."

With a roar, Will attacked from behind. His strong hands struggled to grasp my throat. I fought free from the stranglehold. He struck my face, a glancing but jolting blow. It brought me to my knees. I fought to get up. Couldn't. Not even close.

Will swung his leg. With a powerful kick, he broke my rib, maybe several ribs. The pain was sharp, and unimaginable. The shock, the terror of that moment, was beyond belief.

I fell toward the hard, cold ground.

The rifle went off with a roar louder than any of my screams, louder than a clap of thunder. I rolled onto my stomach, then everything went black and I fell unconscious into the cold, wet leaves.

86

I DON'T KNOW.

I don't know.

I honestly don't know what happened on that fateful night of December 17. Did I shoot Will? Did I lure him outside and then blow him away? They say I did. Am I guilty of murder? Two murders? And if two murders, why not three?

Are they right when they call me a killer? The black widow of Bedford?

Maybe I've finally gone crazy. It feels that way. It feels so awful, so unfair. But life isn't always fair.

I woke in my own bed with my face buried in my pillow and an agonizing pain throbbing across my left side. I felt as though I'd been beaten with a work shovel. Everything was crashing loudly inside my head.

In my mind I tumbled and tumbled but couldn't stop the images of violence and horror from coming at me.

Who had fired the rifle?

Jennie, I thought. *I've got to get to Jennie. And Allie.* I was conscious of a great buzzing noise. At first I thought it was in my head, but then realized it came from outside.

Why were there voices outside my house? What in the world was going on?

My eyelids felt unnaturally heavy. Pain, like a razor cut, was behind them. Another kind of pain, particularly sharp, knifed into my ribs.

I forced my eyes open, then quickly closed them. The light was too bright. *Who had turned the lamp on?*

I heard footsteps on the stairs. Will!

I tried to sit up but couldn't. *A flaming yellow bolt crossed my vision like heat lightning, like a bold graphic on MTV.*

Again I opened my eyes.

I could barely see the heavyset black man in a dark suit, white shirt, and tie. He was standing by the side of the bed, looking down at me. He seemed seven feet tall. His horn-rimmed glasses appeared too small for his giant head.

He was *staring* at me. An odd look on his face. *What was he doing in my bedroom? Or was I in a hospital? This felt more like a hospital actually.*

"You're Maggie Bradford?"

I tried to nod, tried to understand what could possibly be going on, *wherever I was.* Maybe I was having a flashback.

"We found you outside, carried you up here," the man said. He passed some sort of badge before my face. A gold and blue insignia.

"I'm Emmett Harmon, Chief of the Bedford Police." His solemn voice boomed inside my head. *The Chief of the Bedford Police?*

Oh, dear God. What's happened? Jennie? Allie?

"What are you doing here? Please, where are my children?" I whispered. My throat was raw and ached when I talked.

"Maggie Bradford, you're under arrest for the murder of your husband, Will Shepherd. You have the right to remain silent."

BOOK FIVE

TRIAL AND ERROR

87

"MS. NORMA BREEN?"

"Yes. Who is this I'm speaking to?"

"My name's Barry Kahn."

"You don't say. My, my. The *singer* Barry Kahn?"

"The same."

"I think you're terrific! Your songs are anyway. What can I help you with?"

"It's not for me that I'm calling. We need your help."

"We?"

"Nathan Bailford and I."

"Nathan! How the hell is Nathan?"

"Up to his ears in the Maggie Bradford defense."

"Yes. I'd heard he took it on. Tough duty."

"We'd like to hire you for our team. Nathan says you're the best investigator he knows."

"I'm very good, but what difference does it make? Isn't this case pretty open and shut? That's what I hear."

"We don't think so, not at all. Nathan thinks it's anything but open and shut."

"You could have fooled me. The media has her drilling the son of a bitch, blowing his head off."

"There's more to it than that, believe me there is. You interested in finding out what?"

"He was shtupping someone else?"

"We'll never know. Probably. But Maggie wouldn't kill him for that."

"Abuse?"

"Far as I know, he hit her once. No, I'm sorry, *twice*. She wouldn't kill him for that either. She's a good person. Just like in her songs."

"Then why'd she do it?"

"That's what we're hiring you to find out, Ms. Breen. We're not entirely sure that she did."

"You need a defense, or you want the facts?"

"We need a defense."

"Ah. My thanks for your honesty. I like that in a famous singer."

"But we're sure the facts will lead to the defense. Maggie's not a killer."

"Only of husbands, it seems. Didn't she shoot hubby number one? I *do* believe I read that in the funny pages."

"That's never been proved. She was never tried for it. She was originally charged with second-degree murder, but it didn't stick."

"And her live-in? Patrick O'Malley?"

"An accident. O'Malley had a heart attack."

"I thought she confessed to the murder."

"The police claim what they have is a confession. Maggie was confused and disoriented when they brought her in. You can understand that."

"The press are already trying her. She's sure losing in their court. The first one with a handgun, the next on a boat, this one with a rifle."

"Look. If you don't want to take this on —"

"Oh, I didn't say that."

"Then you'll join us?"

"For you, Barry Kahn —"

There was a pause. "God bless you, Ms. Breen," Barry said.

"Call me Norma."

She could hear his sigh of relief, imagined the strain he was under. And she admired his loyalty to his friend, even if she was the "black widow" of Bedford, and almost surely guilty as sin.

88

MOST PEOPLE still didn't know the issues separating the Serbs and the Croats, but the murder trial of Maggie Bradford was being watched everywhere around the world. Reporters and television crews arrived not only from across the United States, but also from Europe, South America, Asia, and probably from the moon. The crush of the press was as great, Norma Breen thought, as at a presidential inaugural — only the desperation for the "inside" story was far more lunatic.

Christ, it's a goddamn murder trial, she thought. *Whatever the outcome, it won't change the world. So what if she killed a husband or two? Most of them deserve it!*

She pointed her dusty yellow Camaro down Clarke Street in Bedford Village and slowly drove past the buzzing courthouse for the second time that morning.

A procession of black umbrellas, vinyl raincoats, Boston Chicken and Dunkin' Donuts take-out bags stretched along the main street, past Hamilton Drugs, Willie's Newspapers, and the new public library. The slow parade turned onto Charles Street and continued five more blocks.

What a mess! What a freaking disaster area! Tourist buses

were parked down Millar and Grant streets: bright yellow school buses and Greyhounds with names like PITTSFIELD and CATAWBA on their foreheads. It was early December, and snow already hung in the air.

"*Maggie and Will: Bittersweet Love Tragedy.*" That was *today's* headline; similar phrases floated out to Norma from her car radio, including "*Three Strikes. She's Out!*"

Cute! Norma liked that one. Finally, a little sense of humor about this fiasco, which happened to be her *job* for now.

The chief defense investigator hated publicity, didn't care about the fame, or even getting rich. It interfered with her work, all those reporters scurrying after her. Still, she knew what she was in for. Maggie Bradford was a star. One segment of the public had decided she was guilty; the other, innocent as a lamb. And Norma?

Dammit, I still don't know what to think. Maggie isn't sure herself. What she told the police was damn close to a confession. The evidence is impressive.

Her yellow pass, pasted conspicuously on her windshield, enabled her to spin the Chevrolet into the blacktopped courthouse parking area. The lot was already packed with similarly stickered state and local police cars, and private cars belonging to the attorneys and their aides from both sides.

Judge Andrew Sussman's blue Mercedes was in his private stall beside the courthouse back door. Nearby stood Nathan Bailford's silver Porsche, looking like a car a college boy might drive to pick up pretty girls on weekends.

And it was Bailford who came up to her as she hefted her slightly overweight body out of her car.

Bailford gestured toward the crowd outside the lot. "And today's only for jury selection. Imagine the scene when the real trial starts."

"How's your client holding up?" Norma asked. She had visited the accused woman several times in the past weeks, finding her surprisingly down-to-earth, although remote, neither helpful nor hindering. "*Confused,*" she was told. *Clinically depressed,* Norma described her.

"The same. Hasn't really changed since the night of the killing. All lows, no highs." He looked at her anxiously. "Anything new on your end?"

"Nothing yet. Lot of balls in the air though. Sometimes I feel like the *court* juggler. Ha, ha."

Norma didn't tell the lawyer that there were aspects to the killing that troubled her a great deal. There was nothing really specific yet, just things that didn't hang together, or hold up to close scrutiny.

What did seem clear was this: If Maggie shot her first husband, she was forced to do it. If she shot Will Shepherd, she was also forced to. By what or by whom was unclear.

The real trouble was that there *were* two killings. One might be explained — temporary insanity, self-defense, long-term abuse. But *two?*

She would go back to the murder site that afternoon, looking for more information, looking for some trail to follow.

There was something she hadn't found, something crucial. There had to be.

Dammit. Something was definitely wrong.

In Palm Springs, a California hazy, grapefruit-pink desert sun slid over the rocky stubble topping the mountains. The early rays came shimmering down onto the swimming pool and the surrounding red tile terrace.

Peter O'Malley laid aside his copy of yesterday's *New York Times.* He removed his new mirrored Ray-Ban sunglasses, put them on a wrought-iron drink stand, and stared at the sparkling blue sheet of pool water.

His mind was sparkling too. On the surface itself, superimposed over the reflection of the stucco pool house, he could almost *see* the face of Maggie Bradford. Just as he had seen it on television last night. Pale, shadows under the eyes. She looked like a damn zombie, out of it, and his heart leapt at her plight.

Serves her fucking well right!

Later that night he'd heard her singing voice, the sound that literally *destroyed* him, blaring from his car radio. Her songs were all over the radio, of course. *The caged songbird,* the deejay called her.

Well, that voice wouldn't be around much longer. Not on the radio (who would play the songs of a convicted murderess?), not in the boardroom of his father's company either.

He put his dark glasses back on, picked up the pen and legal pad he had brought with him to the pool, and began the letter that he believed would guarantee the process of sending Maggie Bradford to her doom.

What goes around, comes around, sweetheart. Now you get yours. Trust me on that. Your "affair" with the O'Malleys isn't quite over with yet.

89

EVERYBODY who came into close contact with Dan Nizhinski, the Westchester County district attorney, had the same reaction: he was too good to be true, he was perfect for his part.

First, there were his looks. He was six foot one, with corn-blond hair prematurely thinning on top but long on the sides. His face was somewhat weatherbeaten, making it look older than its thirty-six years, but the lines around his light blue, sparkling eyes gave them a mischievousness that made women jurors light up and men jurors consider him their friend.

Second was his courtroom manner. Standing ruler-straight, he seemed to take the jurors into his confidence, yet distanced himself enough so that they regarded him with awe. "I'm telling you the truth," he seemed to be saying. "Trust me. Astonishing as the revelations are, the facts support them."

Right now, though, at ease, cordovaned feet resting on top of his desk, he was addressing his assistants about the upcoming trial.

"The facts aren't in doubt," he said for what must have been the tenth time. "She just about admitted she shot him, handed over the murder weapon to the police, has cooperated more with them, I gather, than with her own attorneys. Such behavior is not uncommon in murder cases.

"But" — and here he paused for dramatic effect — "but this woman has enough money to buy the best legal and investigative resources available. Nathan Bailford himself will do the actual cross-examination; he's had more experience in murder trials than he has in corporate ones. It's how he made his reputation. And they've hired Norma Breen as their investigator. If there's something exculpatory to find, she'll find it — only there's nothing, damn it. *Nothing!*"

Another pause, this one to control his emotions. "The defense they'll offer, the only possible defense, is self-defense. That Maggie Bradford was defending herself against Will Shepherd, that if she hadn't killed him, he'd have killed her.

"Well, I say that's bullshit, and when we're finished with her, so will the jury. It's a defense that makes me sick. We're talking about *Maggie Bradford!* She couldn't have gone to the police? She was *afraid* of him? Well, it might have worked in the shooting of her first husband, but it sure as hell *ain't* gonna work here. She's a superstar. Any court in the world would have *guaranteed* her protection if she'd asked for it. A battered wife? My ass."

A third pause, a sip of coffee. The three others in his office knew his judicial beliefs, were inured to his melodramas. They also understood just how good he was at his job — and just how much this particular trial meant to his career.

"Two husbands, two deaths. That's putting a charley horse in the long arm of coincidence, as S. J. Perelman once said. But then, *then,* there's the death of a *third* man in the life of Maggie Bradford. A man she supposedly loved most of all.

"Patrick O'Malley, her live-in lover, died of a heart attack on his boat. Well, *was* it a heart attack? So the autopsy said. *But,* we don't know what brought it on."

Nizhinski continued speaking in his very controlled voice.

"Maggie Bradford is a killer. Cold-blooded, basically heartless, and until this last time, clever as the devil himself.

"But we've got her now. Guilty as charged? I've never been so convinced of anything in my life!"

Nizhinski finished, and he looked around at his assistants. "Any questions, cubs, or are you too dazzled to speak? Anyone see any way we can lose this one? I sure can't."

90

I'M NO EXPERT on prisons, and don't want to be, but if the Bedford Hills Correctional Facility for Women is "one of the most luxurious," then I pity the women incarcerated elsewhere. This stinks big time, especially when you're innocent; but even if you're not, this can't be the way to proper rehabilitation. I am absolutely certain that it isn't.

I have no cellmate — because I'm a "star." I exercise, and eat the bad food, alone. I've made a friend, another woman accused of killing her husband. The grim irony isn't lost on either of us.

I'm surrounded by drug addicts, small-time thieves, gang members, arsonists, a few murderers. Jennie visits a few times each week, and I can't wait to see her. Allie's been told I'm away, and to mind Mrs. Leigh. I miss them so much I can't write about it.

When I think about my sweet girl, my darling boy, I can *feel* my heart ripping — I'm forced to double over with pain. I don't feel sorry for myself; I just can't live without the two of them. I can't let myself go to pieces, for their sake.

*　　　*　　　*

I finished the last entry before the lights went out. It sounds like a long whine, and I'm not like that. Not even locked up in this prison. It is now six hours before the trial begins.

What will ultimately happen? What will the verdict be? I have no idea. None, zero, not a clue. When I hear the evidence, will I be any closer to the truth? Finally know how it all happened? Who will tell me what lies hidden in my heart?

Will *you* be closer to the truth? I've told you everything so far. What do you feel? *Are you sure?* Am I telling the truth — or am I just another celebrity liar?

Are you really sure about me?

When really bad trouble comes, do I simply shoot my way out? Is killing my only weapon? Do I have a tendency to get myself involved with monsters?

Am I a monster myself?

91

HERE WE GO!

"You ready, Mrs. Bradford? Everything's going to be fine. Let's go now. We're going to get you inside the courtroom as fast as humanly possible. We need your help with that. Keep your head down. Keep walking."

"I'll do my best, Bill."

"I know you will."

More perks. They sent a specially trained guard up from New York City for me. A pro at this. His job is to oversee the *other* guards who'll protect me from the press.

He'll lead me inside, sit near me while the trial's going on, then get me back to prison as quickly and easily as he can. Bill Seibert's his name. A nice man, actually. Nice manners and an even disposition.

I felt him push me gently from behind, and I tripped slightly as I got out of the van. *A great start, huh?* I could already see the headlines: *MAGGIE TRIPPED UP ON FIRST DAY!*

I walked into the blinding TV lights, closely packed human bodies, and a barrage of embarrassing questions: Did I do it? How did I feel? Was I able to write in prison? What were the inmates like? Did I sing any of my songs for them? *Give me a break!*

The level of stupidity and "high sleaze" was beyond anything I could imagine. I felt as though I might be sick. My legs were unsteady as I tried to walk. The handcuffs I wore made me feel guilty.

"Just follow me," Seibert said. "Don't stop for anything. Don't say anything to anybody, Mrs. Bradford."

I did just what he said.

He was the pro.

State troopers in cowboy hats could barely hold back the crowd. There were a few boos, but cheers too. The scene made me absolutely dizzy. The last time I had been in such a crush was in San Francisco — not exactly something I wanted to remember now.

Hands grabbed at me from across the police barricades. *Don't touch me. Please leave me alone! I don't belong to any of you.* The thought of a stranger's hand on me made me want to scream out loud. I held it in, held everything inside.

Blessedly, most of the loud, unruly crowd was shut out by a great oak door.

Suddenly, I was inside the high-ceilinged courthouse foyer. Court clerks, extra — mostly elderly — policemen, and minor village dignitaries stared at me now as though I were an alien from outer space. There were the usual black-and-white photos on the white plaster walls leading up a marble staircase; state, local, and American flags hung limply on gilded poles. It was so unbelievably weird.

Barry and Nathan hurried to me, Nathan shaking my hand, Barry kissing me on the cheek. They followed me inside the crowded courtroom. Everything seemed so unreal. Barry and Nathan seemed unreal to me too.

I actually felt physically sick. I thought I was going to throw up. The terrifying excitement seemed to have entered the room

270

like deadly gas. Every face turned toward me as if on cue. Ordinary people. Famous writers in the gallery.

This was so horrible, so bad.

I struggled to keep my head up, *to look innocent.* I sat beside Nathan at the defendant's table; Barry took a seat reserved for him in the front row of spectators.

I held on to the defense table with both hands for support. I was trembling. I felt cold and so very alone.

I looked around for Jennie and Allie. Only Jennie was there, of course. I knew that. We waved at each other, and Jennie started to cry. *So strange and weird and wrong.*

"Hear ye! Hear ye! All people having business with Part Forty-four in this court, give attention and ye shall be heard. The Honorable Judge Andrew Sussman presiding."

It was the court clerk's big moment onstage. Every eye in the crowded room was on him. *Good. That meant they were finally off me.*

The trial was beginning.

My murder trial.

92

STRANGE *as a five-legged station wagon!* Norma Breen said to herself. *Nuts! Crazy! It doesn't add up. There's a piece missing here somewhere.*

Why had one gunshot, fired as Maggie Bradford was falling, been enough to kill that sorry bastard husband of hers? But it had, hadn't it. Not much question about that.

She was looking for the hundredth, or maybe the thousandth time at the police photographs of the murder site, taken just after Will's body had been discovered.

The body was lying facedown.

Bad luck, Will . . .

Or did you plan to have some bad luck? Did you shoot yourself, you sorry fuck? Is that your game?

He had been running away; that much was obvious from the footprints. Maggie had chased him and they had struggled. She had shot him in the head. He had fallen.

End of story, end of Will Shepherd.

Beginning of this current knotty mystery.

Norma felt a tingle travel up her spine. *Something didn't mesh. Something just wasn't tracking for her. What the hell was it?*

What was the missing piece of this goddamned five-and-dime jigsaw puzzle?

She would have to run some more experiments. Call in some favors too. Keep all those balls in the air. She would find something to set Maggie Bradford free.

To kill again?

93

IRONY OF IRONIES. I thought so anyway. *The prosecutor loved my music* — at least he used to.

I had met Dan Nizhinski once at a party at Nathan Bailford's house. He was there with his wife, an ordinary-looking woman who wore huge, oval-rimmed glasses and no makeup. I remember wondering why so attractive a man would marry this woman, but when we got a chance to talk, I liked her a lot. The Nizhinskis told me they were both fans. Hoopty-doo!

Well, I didn't like Dan Nizhinski now. He was tall and looked very scary, and the way he addressed the jury was like a beloved teacher speaking before a class of his best students.

"He's good," I whispered to Nathan.

"So are we," he answered, but his confidence did not spill over onto me.

The jury was made up of a corporate secretary in her early twenties; a high school principal; two housewives; three retirees, one of whom was an ex-army colonel; a freelance writer; two self-employed businessmen; a clerk in a Ford dealership; and an actor, "currently unemployed."

Six men, six women. Different backgrounds. With the power of God, they would somehow set me free. Or so I hoped.

My biggest fan, Dan Nizhinski, was talking about me again. Not exactly singing my praises though.

"You will hear evidence that the defendant, Maggie Bradford, did plan, over a period of several weeks, the murder of her husband, Will Shepherd.

"You will hear that this calculated murder was accomplished in a particularly cold-blooded fashion, as Will Shepherd ran for his life, as he tried to escape.

"You will discover that Will Shepherd was no ideal husband, but whatever his sins were, they were not enough to justify murder.

"And you will be presented with such a body of overwhelming evidence that there will be no doubt in *any* of your minds, as there is none in mine, that Maggie Bradford is guilty of murder in the first degree and should be punished to the full extent of the law."

Dan Nizhinski headed for his chair at the prosecutor's table, then stopped and returned to the jury, as though what he were about to say had just occurred to him, though I'd bet he had rehearsed the movement, and the speech, many times.

"One further thing. I forgot one thing. The murderess we are dealing with here is not an ordinary woman —"

"Objection! Your Honor," Nathan Bailford stood up and bellowed. "The district attorney has put a label on my client. She's not a 'murderess.'"

"Sustained."

"— Her name is Maggie Bradford, and it is a household name. She is not the woman you see on television; television presents *images,* not truth. She is not as sweet as her voice, as alluring as her melodies, as compassionate as her lyrics.

"You must divorce the public Maggie Bradford, the singer

275

and the songwriter, the star, from the real Maggie Bradford, the woman who sits before you charged with a hideous crime.

"Don't be fooled by images, taken in by fame, deluded because this woman writes so convincingly of good. The real Maggie Bradford had access to a gun. The real Maggie Bradford knew well how to pull the trigger. The real Maggie Bradford thought nothing of taking another's life. Why? Because she could *do anything*. She was a *star*.

"Well, when a star falls it blazes as it hits the atmosphere and is then extinguished. To Maggie Bradford, you, ladies and gentlemen of the jury, are her atmosphere, and because you stand for justice, *embody* justice, she will never shine again . . . she *must* never shine again."

94

NATHAN BAILFORD rose and, with passion to match the prosecutor's, outlined the defense. Throughout both speeches, I imagined that the lawyers were talking about somebody else — the disconnectedness I'd felt ever since I'd been accused of shooting Will had returned.

"The district attorney has painted a picture of a cold-blooded killer," Nathan said in a gruff, dusty whisper. "It's a scary picture, and perhaps, when it comes to killers, an accurate one. But it's not a true picture of Maggie Bradford, as you'll see when you hear from her friends, from her close colleagues, and from her."

I sat up in my seat. Quickly, I scribbled a note to Barry: *We agreed that I wouldn't testify. I will not!*

He wrote back: *Fine. Then tell us why you shot Will!!!*

And I: *No. I can't do that either.*

I had told them again and again — I wouldn't testify. I couldn't. I had my reasons for remaining silent, even if it kept me in prison for the rest of my life.

95

"MR. SHEPHERD?"

"Speaking."

"Mr. Shepherd, my name is Norma Breen, and I'm calling you from New York. You probably don't know who I am —"

"Oh, but I do. You're investigating my brother's murder. The lurid tales make the front pages here too. How can I help you?"

"I found a note from you in his possession. A simple note, actually. An odd one to keep. It said, 'Fuck you, Will.' Can you tell me what that was in reference to? And why your brother might have chosen to keep it?"

There was a brief silence. "Yes, I believe I can. He wanted me to join him in a business venture. I was in the States at the time, and he asked me over to his house. I said no."

"And that's the language you used? With your brother?"

"It was the only language he understood. We weren't very close. My brother was a crazy bastard, I'm afraid. My brother wasn't my favorite person, I might add."

Norma had known the brothers weren't close. Still — "Please tell me why. I imagine this must be difficult for you."

Palmer Shepherd laughed over the telephone. "How much time do you have? It's a long story."

"Lots of time, if you think it'd help."

"I don't see how it bears on the murder trial. By now, you must know what kind of man he was. But I could fly over to see you. Actually, I have a lot of sympathy for Maggie Bradford. You can't begin to imagine how much."

"That's kind of you. I'll certainly ask you to if I think it's necessary."

"Good. My offer is genuine. Maggie might have killed him. I'm surprised no one else did first though."

"Can you imagine why she might have done it?"

"I didn't know anything about their marriage. I stayed away on purpose. But Will was the Devil, Miss Breen. Will was *a bad man*. Frankly, whoever did it, did the world a service. I believe that with all my heart."

96

THE TRIAL moved ahead — *very slowly.* Day after exhausting day, week by week.

After testimony was finished on the exhausting twentieth day, Barry and Nathan came to visit me in prison. I almost didn't agree to see them.

I knew they wanted to press me again for an explanation, an alibi — something that I couldn't give them. I knew they were worried that the trial wasn't going our way.

"Tell me what you know about Palmer," Barry said once we were together in a small conference room used for just such meetings.

I was somewhat puzzled. It seemed a strange way to begin our conversation. Palmer Shepherd?

"What about him? He's Will's brother, of course. They weren't close. I only met him twice. He offered his condolences — *at the wedding.*"

"Was he close to his aunts, do you know?"

"Not as close as Will was."

The words came out fast and must have had a ring to them. Barry looked at me sharply, then his eyes became sad and distant.

"You *know* about Vannie and Will?" he said. "So why didn't you tell us? Why did we have to find out from Will's brother?"

Long-suppressed anger rose. I had to let some of it out. "I don't know anything. I might have suspected something. Barry, what are you trying to do to me?"

He looked at me unwaveringly. "Tell me the truth, Maggie. Was she ever in your house? Was Vannie ever there?"

"Only at our wedding." I remembered the image vividly. "She was very attractive — his mother's younger sister. You were there, Barry. You saw her. Will never got over his mother."

"I guess not! Did he ever bring any other strange women home?" Nathan asked.

"Never. Why would I allow that? That doesn't make any sense, Nathan."

"Let me ask again," Nathan said at last. "Will didn't try anything *funny* in the house? You have to trust us, Maggie. You mustn't keep secrets from us. Not at this point in the trial. We have to know what the prosecution does."

I hesitated, just for an instant. I tensed. I didn't like where this was going.

"No," I said. "I don't have anything to tell you. Why would I hold something back?"

Barry pounced. "You're lying right now. Dammit, Maggie. You're breaking my heart."

"I swear to you —" I whispered. I *was* lying, of course. I *never* lie — but I had to now.

"Who was it?" Barry nearly shouted at me. I'd never seen him this angry before. Veins pulsed all over his forehead and neck.

"*Please! . . . Barry, no!*"

His face suddenly went pale. His eyes closed, then slowly opened again. "Of course," he said and I could see tears in his eyes.

He looked toward me with such tenderness and pity that I was sure *both* our hearts would break.

281

"Oh my God, of course," he said. "Will was after Jennie, wasn't he?"

I stood and called for the guard. "Take me back to my cell. Take me back right now!"

I went away with the guard. I wouldn't say another word to either Barry or my lawyer. I couldn't, I wouldn't, drag Jennie into this.

97

"THE PROSECUTION calls Peter O'Malley."

I blanched as I heard the words spoken in open court. Actually, I was getting used to the feeling of constant anxiety and fear. We were twenty-nine days into testimony, most of it very bad for me.

Over strenuous defense objections, Judge Sussman had allowed Nizhinski to introduce evidence about the death of Phillip Bradford. Now the district attorney planned to get in as much as he could *about Patrick's death.*

It would be difficult. He could do no more than *imply* that I had been responsible. But that's what Peter wanted, I knew. To imply, to insinuate, to hurt me in any way that he could.

In a very strange move, the court had been cleared of spectators for the testimony. Peter had agreed to talk, but his lawyer had convinced the judge to allow Peter privacy.

I didn't understand. Why should Peter be protected? But very soon, I understood everything. Peter's testimony took forever in real time — there must have been a hundred objections from my lawyers — but the bottom line *would have sounded something like this.*

"Mr. O'Malley, are you a member of an establishment called the Lake Club?"

"I am."

"The club is located in Bedford Hills? Just off Greenbriar Road?"

"It is."

"What is its membership?"

"About five hundred people."

"And the activities are those of most country clubs — golf, tennis, swimming, dinners, and dancing in the evening?"

"That's right."

"Yet the Lake Club provides something more, does it not?"

"For some members, yes."

"Something not available to the full membership, but only to a special few."

"Correct."

"Are you one of those few?"

"I was."

"Who else is among the group?"

"Prominent people, on the whole."

"What does the club provide for them?"

"A meeting place, mostly. There are discussions of financial issues, matters of government."

"And after the discussions are over?"

"There's — entertainment. Not always, but on occasion."

"I see. Can you describe this entertainment?"

"Sexual entertainment for the most part."

"Can you be more specific?"

"Girls, and sometimes young men, are provided."

"Prostitutes?"

"I wouldn't exactly call them prostitutes."

"They're there for the members' 'entertainment,' and they get paid for their services?"

"Yes."

"A rose by any other name . . . tell me, Mr. O'Malley. Do you reside in Bedford Hills?"

"No. Manhattan and the West Coast."

"Yet you are a member of the Lake Club?"

"Yes."

"You've also participated in these late-night parties?"

"Yes."

"Why is that, Mr. O'Malley?"

"My father, Patrick O'Malley, was a big deal at the club. I was granted membership when he died."

"Did he participate in the after-hours entertainments?"

"Yes."

"That is, he slept with young girls."

"Yes."

"Did Patrick O'Malley have a relationship with Maggie Bradford?"

"For many months. Maybe it was a couple of years."

"And do you have a half-brother?"

"Yes. They all lived together."

"Would you say that Patrick O'Malley and Maggie Bradford were in love?"

"So my father told me."

"Yet he did not drop his membership in the club?"

"No."

"Nor stop sleeping with young girls?"

"I don't know about that."

"Was Mrs. Bradford aware of these 'entertainments' and your father's part in them?"

"Yes."

"How do you know?"

"She had pictures of my father and at least two of the girls."

"She had *pictures?*"

"I found them in her bedroom. Their bedroom. After my father died. I helped collect his papers."

"They were graphic pictures?"

"Very. My father and two girls."

"We don't need the details. Not at this time. Mrs. Bradford had possession of the pictures?"

"Yes."

"What did she think of them?"

"I don't know. She never told me."

"What did *you* think of them?"

"It's always a shock when a son sees his father *in flagrante*."

"Of course. But you weren't *surprised*."

"No."

"Now tell me, Mr. O'Malley, how did your father die?"

"I don't know."

"You don't know? How is that possible."

"He died on a boat. The cause was supposedly a heart attack."

" 'Supposedly'? He was alone on the boat?"

"No. Mrs. Bradford was with him."

"And they were alone together."

"Yes. The Coast Guard found the boat. Mrs. Bradford told them how he died."

"Did they believe her?"

"Evidently."

"Tell me, Mr. O'Malley, did you know Will Shepherd?"

"Yes."

"Would you say you were friends?"

"Social friends."

"You had business dealings with him?"

"Yes. Business and social."

"Ah. Social. Was Will Shepherd a member of the Lake Club?"

"Yes."

"Of the club within the club?"

"Yes."

"Then he partook of the 'entertainment'?"

"Definitely."

"Did Maggie Bradford know?"

Peter O'Malley paused, twisted in his seat, then he looked straight at me. "Yes, she did. That's probably why she murdered him."

As I said, there were a hundred objections during the testimony, but that was how I remembered it, and I'm sure how the jury did as well. I was losing . . . everything that I had ever loved or cared about.

98

NORMA BREEN came to visit me that night just after the dinner hour. She had become one of my favorite people to see. We were both around the same age, both from blue-collar backgrounds, and we understood each other.

"Maggie, I hate to tell you this. I don't like your songs," she started in that night. It was Norma's quaint way of saying "hi."

"Bitch," I said, but I smiled at her. She made me laugh when nobody else could; she was my buddy.

"No, you're the bitch. You won't help me do my job — which is, ironically, to help you get out of this zoo."

I was still smiling. We both were, though the subject was deadly serious. You can only be deadly serious for so long, for so many hours, days, months in a row.

"I hate to tell you," I told her, "I don't like the way you do *your* job."

"Too tough for you, huh? Too edgy?"

I put my hand across the table on top of hers. She was single, available, but probably because of the extra twenty pounds she carried, a lot of men were overlooking her. Their mistake. *Big* mistake.

"What's on your mind today, sweetie?" I asked her. There was always something with her.

"I want to try to talk you out of your martyr thing. I hate Mother Teresa anyway. Stop being a martyr, Maggie."

"I *am* a martyr. That's what I had to do to be loved in our family, when I was a kid. I can't help myself."

Norma flipped over my hand, and she clasped it hard. "I love you, Maggie. I've learned to, in a very short time for me. A lot of people love you. You're unfuckingbelievably lovable."

I snorted out a laugh — my darkest humor was bubbling up. "Yes, everybody loves me but my husbands."

"Maybe you picked a couple of losers, so you could play martyr? Like you said, maybe you can't help yourself, Maggie. Only *you can, you can help yourself.*"

I sighed deeply. I thought that I knew where Norma was going. I was tired of hearing it from Barry and Nathan, but suddenly hearing it from Norma, from another woman, it sounded a little different.

"I can't though," I finally said. "Nice try, but I just can't do it. I can't put Jennie up there."

"You can," Norma insisted, and suddenly she began to gush tears. She'd never done that before; never completely let down her guard. Then we were both sobbing, holding hands, and crying our eyes out like a couple of old ninnies.

"I talked to Jennie, Maggie. She says the two of you have to talk. She said to tell you this was a 'continuation' of Pound Ridge, and that *you owed her.*"

99

FOR THE LAST TIME, Norma Breen went to Maggie's house in Bedford Hills. She was convinced she'd missed something; that everybody had. What in God's name was it though?

Mildred Leigh met her at the door and offered her a cup of coffee. Allie was playing in the living room, and Norma was grateful for the chance to talk. She hadn't interviewed Mrs. Leigh at any length; maybe this time she could get some useful information.

"I know you've been over and over this, but tell me about the day of the murder," Norma said. "Were you in the house?"

"Until about six-thirty, then I left. It was my night off." She blushed. "And I had a date with Mr. Frazier. Didn't come back till the next morning, and then only to find the police and the press and Maggie accused of something she would never do."

She seems pleased with herself, Norma thought. *Makes sense. Her fifteen minutes of fame.* "Did anything unusual happen before you left?" she asked. "Anything you can think of might help Maggie. Say whatever comes into your head."

"It was a day like any other. No, nothing was very different. Nothing I can remember. Just like I told the police."

"The two of them didn't argue? Nothing like that?"

"They barely saw each other. Mr. Shepherd was in town, in New York for most of the day. I didn't hear any fighting."

"Describe what they did. Anything that you think of, Mrs. Leigh."

"Well, Maggie, she was in her study. Writing her songs, I guess. She would come out to talk with the children during her breaks. She and Allie love to play."

"And Mr. Shepherd?"

"He got back from the city at some time. Don't know when. Later that night, I saw him by the club. He was heading on back to the house."

Norma was momentarily confused. "You were at the club, Mrs. Leigh? Why were you there?"

"J.C., he has a house there, on the grounds. Opposite side of the main building from the parking lot."

"Do you know what Mr. Shepherd was doing there that night?"

"No, ma'am. Just saw him walk past J.C.'s."

"What time was this?"

"Around ten, ten-thirty. Something like that."

"You only saw him briefly?"

"Yes, ma'am. J.C. and I, we had better things to do than watch Mr. Will Shepherd."

"I'm sure."

What was Will doing by the club that night? It didn't track with what Maggie had told her.

"But he wasn't there for one of the parties? The ones that took place late?" Norma asked.

Mrs. Leigh glanced at her conspiratorially. "J.C. tell you? You know about those carryings-on?"

"Sure do. Did you happen to notice how Mr. Shepherd was dressed that night?"

"It was dark, ma'am. Only thing I know for sure, he was carrying his rifle back from the club."

Norma could feel the small hairs rise on the back of her arms. "His rifle? Are you sure?"

"They shoot skeet there. At the shooting range down past the golf course. He often did that."

"But not on the day he was killed."

Mrs. Leigh sighed. "I told you. He was in New York most of the day. Left real early for him."

"You told the police all of this?" Norma asked.

Mrs. Leigh nodded. "Everything that I'm telling you now."

"About Mr. Shepherd and the rifle?"

"Of course."

They finished their coffee. "Thank you, Mrs. Leigh," Norma said. "You've been very helpful."

"Happy to oblige. You see that little boy in there? He's a sweetheart, and he loves his mommy. We all want her to come home. We miss Maggie so bad."

"So do I. Is there a phone I can use?"

"In the den. I'll show you."

"I can find it," Norma said. She had to stop herself from running.

100

"BARRY, I'm up at Maggie's house. I'm onto something. At least I hope so. *No,* I actually think I have something real going."

Norma had closed the den door behind her, but she nevertheless whispered into the phone.

"I'm listening," Barry said.

"You know that celebrated rifle in question?" Norma said. "Mrs. Leigh saw Will carrying it the night of the shooting. He was out by the country club, which more and more seems to be figuring into this brutal mess."

"Why would he have had the rifle at the Lake Club?"

"First question I asked myself." Norma's voice rose in her excitement. "That's why he *went* to the club. *To fetch it.* It's where he must have kept it when Maggie told him to get rid of it. She said she looked everywhere around the house, but she could never find it. *It was at the club.*"

There was a long pause. Finally Barry said, "Now why would he want to do that? Did he stage his own suicide, Norma? Is that it? Did he frame Maggie?"

Norma felt a sudden surge of frustration and bewilderment.

"Goddamnit, I don't know yet," she said. "Not a clue. That part doesn't make any sense to me.

"But I'll tell you what I *do* know," Norma spoke again. "The Bedford police knew Will went to fetch the rifle, and they kept it to themselves. Something's rotten in the state of Bedford, and I'm going to find out what, and who, and why."

"Sic 'em, Norma."

"*Grrrr.*"

101

I LOOKED at Jennie as she entered the visiting room and I wanted to cry. I wouldn't let myself. I needed to be strong now, for both of us. I needed to listen to Jennie.

I couldn't take my eyes off her though. I'd always loved her, much more than I cared about myself. People said we were a lot alike, only I saw Jennie as having few, if any, of my faults and weaknesses. We did look like each other. Jennie was tall now, almost five nine. Her blond hair was as long as mine. We had the same eyes.

I love you, I thought as she sat across the table from me. I hated the table being there, separating us now. I needed to hug Jennie, and to be hugged back. Never more than right at that moment, right now.

Suddenly, she cracked a smile. It was pure Jennie. "I have a message from Norma. She says she has proof that Mother Teresa is total bullshit. That she's actually a Vegas act, in it for the money."

I laughed out loud at the joke.

"Norma's trying to help you, Mom," Jennie leaned across the table and said in her most mature voice.

"I think I know that, Jen. How are you?"

Jennie rolled her eyes. "Believe it or not, I'm good. I'm not great, but I'm okay." She blew me two kisses. "Those are from Allie. Actually, he sent you a hundred kisses."

"Does he still remember who I am?"

She rolled her eyes again. "We make him watch videos of your concerts so that he doesn't forget. We read him your letters, show him your pictures. I'm here to talk about something else. We're going to talk, Mom dear."

"I understand," I said to Jennie. "I respect your wishes."

"Good, that's a neat start. Now, I think you have to ask me questions, *because* you have certain ideas in your head, but I'm not sure what they are. So we'll employ the Socratic method."

I smiled. "I'm not even going to ask you about your grades."

"Tops in my class. Stay on track. Stay with me here."

This was the hardest yet, the worst thing I'd been through. *Yes, I had certain ideas in my head. No, I wasn't ready to talk about them. Maybe I would never be ready.*

"I guess we could start with the night of the . . . of Will's death," I said.

"That's a very good place to begin — *at the end*."

"I saw Will up in your room. What was he doing there, Jennie?"

"He came to say good night."

There was an innocence in Jennie's words that made me stare. "That's all? Jennie, you can't lie, either to protect Will, or even my feelings. Are we agreed about that?"

"Sure. Those are the game rules. We're agreed. Now, let's play."

"You tell me the truth, and I'll do the same. Anything you want to know. About Will's death."

Jennie's eyes stayed on mine. "I do have questions."

"First me, then you, okay?"

She nodded. "Yep. That's fine with me."

I didn't know exactly where to go next with my questions. I picked an obvious place.

"Did Will come to your room to say good night often?"

"He did sometimes. He'd bring me warm milk. He said that his aunt used to bring him tea, when he was a boy in England."

The mention of Will's aunt startled me, though Jennie couldn't have known why. I took a deep breath. I didn't know if I could go on with this. Prison wasn't the place I wanted to have this kind of talk with Jennie.

She reached for my hand. "Can I try to make this easier . . . for both of us?"

"If you think you can," I whispered. I didn't have much of a voice left. I felt hollowed out, empty. Out of it. Unreal.

"Will was very complicated. You already know that. I think he, I think part of him, actually wanted to be a good father. He would come up to my room and talk sometimes, just talk. I think he wanted to prove he could be there *and just talk.* He told me a lot about when he was growing up. He was a good listener. Sometimes."

"Yes, he could be," I remembered.

"I had a wicked crush on him, Mom. I thought he was so beautiful, like a god, like Ralph Fiennes or Mel Gibson on steroids. I used to think about him *all the time.*"

"But nothing ever happened?"

"I know he told you that he did, *that we did* — I was there, I heard it — but nothing ever happened, Mom. You don't have to protect me. Please believe me, *nothing happened.*"

I put both my hands up to Jennie's face. I wanted to be even closer, but that was the best we could do in this horrifying place.

"Let me be your witness, Mom. Please, please, let me do that for you? I *need* to help you, just this once. I think I can. Nothing happened between Will and me. You don't have to protect me."

102

NORMA BREEN was in one of her usual bitching, grousing moods when she arrived at the Lake Club. *The missing goddamn pieces to the puzzle! They're around here somewhere,* she kept telling herself, hoping that it might come true if she said it enough.

She had come to the club, specifically, to see J. C. Frazier. J.C. was in his late forties, his face weathered by the outdoors, his body trim and well muscled.

Well, he's a looker, Norma Breen thought as she sat with him on the porch of the main building at the Lake Club. *Now, let's hope he's a goddamn talker.*

Norma eased into things, convincing J.C. to verify what she already knew: that there were late-night "parties" at the club; and that Will Shepherd had been an invited guest on several occasions.

"Would there be a list of names anywhere?" she asked. "Of the party boys?"

The groundskeeper shrugged his broad shoulders. "If there is, I've never seen one. I sure doubt it."

"Then tell me some of the names. People you've seen here after hours. C'mon, J.C."

J.C. shook his head. "Couldn't do that. If anyone found out I had told, I'd lose my job. I'm not even supposed to *know* about it."

"But you told me about Mr. Shepherd."

"I'm trying to help you. I just can't help as much as you might like."

"Dammit, this is a *murder* investigation. What you know might save Mrs. Bradford's life!"

J.C. shifted uneasily in his chair. "I realize that. That's why I'm talking to you. Only don't make me tell you the names. That, I can't do."

Norma glared at him. It didn't seem to make any difference though. "Then at least show me where. Let me take a peek for myself."

"Oh, Ms. Breen, if I did that —"

"If you don't I'll have you subpoenaed and you can testify about it in open court." *Grrrr, take that!*

He winced. "The entrance, then. Only if anybody asks me, I'll say you found it yourself."

"It's a deal." Norma smiled. "Now show me."

103

THE TWO OF THEM followed a winding path all the way around to the far side of the clubhouse. There was a heavy wooden door there that looked like it would only be used by the maintenance staff. J. C. Frazier had a key.

"This is it, huh?" Norma asked. It was cold and dark on that side of the building. *Like the black hearts of the lousy bastards who come here to get their kicks.*

Inside, Norma found it was comparable to the rest of the exclusive club. She and J.C. walked back through a deserted billiard room. There seemed to be a gauzy haze hanging in the air.

They entered a surprisingly elegant barroom with mahoghany paneling everywhere. Norma knew that this was the place. The club within a club. *The rich boy's playroom.*

"This is where they met, right? It's where they had their sex parties?"

"Yes ma'am," J.C. muttered. He seemed serious and withdrawn.

Norma could almost picture "the boys club." Their expensive clothes, the best whiskeys, their high-and-mighty demeanor, their prostitutes. She wasn't sure about it, but she sensed that *this room* might be central to Maggie's defense. She believed there was even the possibility that one of the club members had killed Will Shepherd.

Had Will finally fucked the wrong wife? Or screwed one of these powerful men in a business deal? Done something else to get himself murdered? Norma thought it was very possible that he had.

"Pour yourself a drink, J.C.," she said to the groundskeeper of the Lake Club, "then plop your butt down. We have to talk. We're *going* to talk."

He shook his head. "I can't do that."

Norma pointed her hand at the much taller and larger man. "Listen, you, and listen good. Maggie Bradford might yet be convicted of murder, but not because you held the truth back. You talk to me, now, or you'll lose your job for sure, and you'll lose a whole lot more than that. That's a promise I'll keep."

J. C. Frazier walked to the bar and he poured himself a shot of Maker's Mark.

"Good choice," Norma said. "Make that *two* shots, one for me. Then you can tell me exactly who was part of this club within a club. I want *the names.* I want every name that you know."

J. C. Frazier poured Norma Breen a drink, then they both sat at the wood-paneled bar. Finally, J.C. began to talk. He even cried.

When he was through, Norma couldn't believe what she had heard. *She could not believe it. Jesus, capital H, Christmas!*

Everything just changed, Norma thought. *My God, the whole world just moved. The enemy blinked. Gotcha, you lousy bastards. Gotcha.*

104

HOW GROWN UP *she is, how composed, and close to being a woman,* I thought as Jennie walked to the stand to begin her testimony in court. Her face seemed to glow; her long blond hair was shining. Jennie looked so confident and serene. I wished I could say the same for myself.

Nathan led her through her story with extreme care. How Will came to see her on that fatal night. How he was standing at the foot of the bed, "leering" at her, when I came in.

" 'Jennie and I were just about to have some fun. Care to join us in bed? Ménage à trois!' That's what he told my mother. I don't know why he said it, *but he did,*" she told the jury. There was no way they couldn't believe her.

And as Jennie repeated Will's words, I felt the same paralyzing rage that had overcome me then. *I'm glad he's dead,* I thought. *It's horrifying, but I am glad.*

Nathan took less than forty minutes with her. That was our agreement, and he had practically signed it in blood. He finished, and then he sat down next to me. He took my hand and I squeezed his. "Thank you, Nathan," I whispered to him, "for being so patient with me."

"Thank you for trusting me," Nathan whispered back.

The jury's faces remained impassive, but I could see that the women at least were touched by Jennie.

I had not killed in self-defense, I had killed defending my daughter. Now they knew. Jennie had done what she'd meant to do.

Unfortunately, now came the bad part. Dan Nizhinski slowly approached the witness stand. *A killer whale,* I thought, *about to eat a minnow. He's doing this to get famous. That's all this is to him: instant fame and celebrity status.*

"Miss Bradford — Jennie," he began softly, almost apologetically.

"Please don't call me by my first name." Jennie met his stare and did not waver. "You don't know me, Mr. Nizhinski."

The prosecutor sighed. Score one for Jennie.

"You have a good friend by the name of Millie Steele?" he asked after the briefest pause. It was hard to knock Nizhinski off his game.

Jennie seemed surprised by the question. "Yes, I do," she said.

"She's your *best* friend, isn't she?" the prosecutor continued. He was being unusually nice.

Jennie hesitated, then she finally nodded. I could see her mind working, trying to figure out where he was heading with the questions.

"You'll have to answer the question verbally, Miss Bradford," Judge Sussman spoke from the bench. "Is Millie Steele your best friend?"

Nathan Bailford slowly rose from the defense table. "Objection, Your Honor. I don't see what Miss Bradford's relationship to Miss Steele has to do with this case. Need I remind everyone, Miss Bradford is only fifteen years old. This trial, especially this testimony, is an unbelievably painful experience for her, and it should be kept as brief as possible."

"Your Honor," Nizhinski responded, "the jury will soon see

303

exactly where this line of questioning is leading. It's an important point, I promise you."

"Proceed," Sussman said. "I'll hold you to your promise though. Tread very lightly."

Nizhinski moved closer to Jennie, and I flinched. I didn't like that one bit. I could tell Jennie didn't either.

"You talk to Millie Steele a lot? At school? Sometimes after school?"

"Yes, sir. *Before* school too," Jennie said and she smiled. So did everyone on the jury.

I could see she was still puzzled though. *Where was he leading her? Watch out!* I wanted to call to her.

"Would you ever lie to your friend? *Have* you ever lied to her, that you can remember?"

"No. Millie and I don't lie to each other."

"Then listen to this, Jennie. On the thirteenth of October, your best friend Millie Steele made the following statement at the Bedford Hills police station —" He paused, and opened the thick binder he had carried with him to the witness stand. The binder was intimidating in itself, thick, with a black leather cover.

" 'Jennie was in love with her stepfather. She told me time and time again she wanted — she wanted — well, she wanted to go to bed with him, and would try anything to seduce him.' "

Nizhinski closed the folder gently. "Did you tell Millie Steele that you were in love with Will Shepherd?"

What's he doing to her? I thought as my stomach clenched. *Yes, she had a crush on Will.*

"Yes, but —" Jennie tried to answer the question he'd asked.

"Just answer yes or no, please. *Were* you in love with your stepfather?"

He's torturing her! He should be stopped right now. "Nathan?" I whispered.

"Wait, Maggie. Listen."

"I had a crush on Will. Yes, sir."

"Did you ever try to seduce him?"

"Not really."

"That's not answering my question, Miss Bradford. Yes or no: Did you try to seduce him?"

"Yes. In a way I guess."

"Did you go to bed with him?"

"No! You're such a *bad person!* No!" Jennie told the prosecutor. "No!"

No! Thank God! Now let her go.

"Then *where* did you make love with him? Millie Steele says that you did!"

"We never made love!"

"Forgive me, but that's difficult to believe. You're an attractive young woman, Jennie. Will Shepherd was susceptible to attractive young women. We've heard that again and again in this courtroom. Are you telling me that even though you threw yourself at him, he refused? His reputation says otherwise!"

Jennie finally began to cry. Her sobs were the only sounds in the courtroom. She was a young girl again.

"Nathan, please," I whispered again.

Nizhinski, relentless, moved even closer to Jennie.

"In fact, isn't it true that you and he had been lovers for months? That the defense contention your mother killed him to protect you is therefore nonsense. That your mother killed him for *revenge?*"

"I *didn't* throw myself at him! He *never* touched me! He never did anything *indecent,* like you're doing now."

Nizhinski took a step back and stared at her. "Do you know what perjury is?"

She nodded.

"Answer yes or no, please. The court stenographer can't record a nod."

"Yes." Her voice was faint.

"Do you know what the penalty is for perjury?"

"Not exactly. Will you unjustly put me in prison — like you did to my mother?"

"The penalty for perjury *can* mean jail, but there's no injustice here, Miss Bradford. Your mother killed Will Shepherd because she *thought* the two of you were having an affair."

Nathan was on his feet beside me. "Objection! *Objection!*"

"No further questions," Dan Nizhinski said and walked away from Jennie.

The courtroom erupted all around us. It took minutes before the banging of Judge Sussman's gavel caught anyone's attention.

Jennie was led from the witness box. She was crying. I reached my arms out to her, but I couldn't touch her.

"It's all right, Mom," she said. "Nobody can hurt us. Nobody can hurt us anymore."

I only wished that were true.

105

NORMA BREEN chewed on Rolaids, tasty, orange-flavored ones, as she sat in court and listened to the closing arguments. She had a secret, an absolute mindblower, and she had to bite her tongue to keep from blurting it out.

Maybe we can throw out this bullshit trial, Norma thought as she sat in the back row of spectators. *Or maybe, despite all the evidence, Maggie will be acquitted. Maybe the jury will see that she had to kill — and let her off on a technicality. Or at least give her the lightest sentence permissible under the law, the least punitive verdict. And maybe Mel Gibson will call me for a date while I'm sitting here on my oversized rump. You never know, right?*

Norma had decided that her best strategy was to wait for the verdict. And now, as she listened to Nathan Bailford's rebuttal, a spark of hope glimmered in her heart. *This is a good woman. Spare her. It's only right. Do the right thing, huh.*

In his redirect, Nathan had interpreted the facts so succinctly that Norma was left feeling that Maggie was the victim, Will the killer.

Still, the defense lawyer couldn't *change* the fact that Will was dead, Maggie alive. And he couldn't solve the other important question — if Maggie hadn't, then who *had* killed Will?

The prosecutor got up and immediately dismissed Nathan's case as a smokescreen. Murder was murder. That's what it was; there was no other name for it. Murder with a single motive: revenge. And because Maggie had picked up the gun, brought it knowingly into her daughter's room, it was *premeditated* murder, and deserved the maximum penalty: a life sentence.

Yet with it all, Norma considered, *something is terribly wrong about this trial.*

She was still uncomfortable. It was the gut feeling she'd had from the very start. *Maggie did not kill Will Shepherd.* She was convinced of that. *Will had committed suicide, hadn't he? According to Maggie, and even Palmer, he'd been threatening to do it for years. This was his final, terrible revenge against Maggie.*

Maybe if they had put Maggie on the stand, a reason would have emerged. Norma had reluctantly agreed with Barry and Nathan that such a strategy was a mistake. Maggie could only verify her statement to the police — that she didn't know for sure what happened, that she *might* have killed him — but it was a close call, and now Norma was second-guessing everything about the defense effort. *Everything.*

Ah well, it was too late for second guessing. Nathan Bailford finished his closing statement and wearily sat down.

The forty-six-day drama was finally over.

It was next to impossible to read the jurors' faces.

Yet Norma could guess: Maggie Bradford was going to be convicted of murder.

And then, she thought to herself, *the real fireworks can begin.*

106

"NEVER IN DOUBT. It wasn't even close, sports fans. To the victors! To us!"

Dan Nizhinski sat back in his chair, took a big sip of pilsner, and beamed at his three associates.

"To the victors!" the group chanted.

"What was it?" he asked, as if he didn't know the answer, "the all-time record for fastest verdict in a major murder case?"

"Not to suck-ass too much, but you did a great job, Dan," Moira Lowenstein, his youngest associate, said. "You got the jury to waive their emotions and look hard at what actually happened. No mean feat. You got them to realize that if they let her go, they subverted the whole system of justice."

"I couldn't have done it without you all," Nizhinski said, insincerely, leaving them with the impression he could have succeeded just as well with anyone else.

"What's next for you, boss?" Bob Stevens, Nizhinski's closest associate, helped himself to his fourth beer in less than an hour.

Nizhinski grinned. He was still performing, couldn't turn it off. "To tell you the truth, I haven't made up my mind. The exposure during the trial won't hurt. I have to admit that, I guess."

"And the state could use some cleaning up," Moira added. Peter Eisenstadt, the third associate — the quiet one — glared at her. *Yeah, and guess who wants to go to Albany on your shirttails, boss?*

"I'll decide in due course," Nizhinski said. They all knew he would run for something big. "For now, let's enjoy the moment." He raised his beer can. "To a great victory."

"To victory," his colleagues echoed, and they all drank, laughed, congratulated one another.

Then the phone rang.

Dan Nizhinski picked it up himself. "Nizhinski."

"Kahn," the caller said. "Barry Kahn." Something in his voice chilled the prosecutor. "Norma Breen and I are coming right over to your office. She's discovered something that might interest you."

107

GUILTY.
Guilty.

The word rang in my head like a religious chant. No, it was more like a dirge. *Guilty. I'll go mad in prison. I'm already half-mad.*

Norma and Barry came to see me as soon as I was transported back here from court today. They were full of smiles and secrets. Don't worry, they told me. They would start appeal proceedings immediately in a higher court. Everything was going to be all right.

How could it be? A life in jail isn't "all right." Trust me on that.

I know there are appeals, and that my fate won't be decided for months, probably years. Still, the chances for reversal are small, no matter what anybody says. My chances are terrifyingly bad.

So why was Norma hopeful and cheerful? Why did Barry press me so hard to remember exactly what happened the night I shot Will when I've gone over it, and gone over it? Simple answer: They wanted to try and take my mind off what had just happened.

Guilty.

The Scarlet M still emblazoned on my chest.

I guess I never really expected this. I'd hoped that in the end I would go free. It just didn't happen that way.

Guilty.

108

THAT NIGHT in my cell, I stayed up until two, maybe three in the morning. I lay with my eyes closed, trying futilely to recapture lost images of my life on the outside. Allie. Jennie. Concerts I'd had. Finally, exhaustion overcame frustration. I fell asleep.

I didn't dream. It was as though I had fallen away into nothingness. The long, long fall from grace continues. A bottomless pit.

I awakened to a shock.

A gray parade of police officials was standing outside the cell, led by Warden Serra herself.

I glanced at my clock.

It was quarter past six in the morning.

I didn't get it, didn't understand.

I blinked, blinked, blinked.

Warden Serra and the others were still there.

Why were they here? What had happened?

Was I going to be moved to another prison?

Was I actually awake, seeing what I thought I saw?

I doubted it. This wouldn't be the first time I'd confused a dream and reality in here.

Warden Serra?

All these other people?

"Aren't you a little early?" I finally asked. My eyes were slowly adjusting to the harsh light of the corridor.

"Please get dressed, Mrs. Bradford," Maureen Serra said. "We've received a call from the courthouse. Something's come up. You're wanted in Judge Sussman's chambers immediately."

109

I FELT COLD and was shaking all over as three guards led me through the empty courthouse. I didn't understand what could be happening. Neither did anyone from the prison.

What was going on now? What could this be?

There were four people in the judge's chambers when I arrived. Judge Sussman sat behind a large mahogany desk. To his right sat Nathan Bailford, looking somber, but successful, as always.

Barry, sitting forward on a leather couch on the left side of the room, winked at me, but he didn't smile.

Only Norma Breen, dressed in a green tweed skirt and bulky brown sweater and sitting next to Barry on the couch, seemed relaxed. "Hi, Maggie," she said; she was the only one to actually speak to me.

"Hello, Norma. Everybody," I whispered. It all seemed surreal, as though I were dreaming. What in God's name was happening now?

There was an empty chair next to Sussman's, and he motioned toward it. In a daze, I did as I was told.

Sitting, I could look at the faces of the others — the same

view that Judge Sussman had, as though I had gone from defendant to part of the judicial team. I liked that a lot.

Papers were shuffled. Briefcases snapped open. Coffee container lids removed.

The briefcases, the papers, the store-bought coffee reminded me that these people were different from me, that they led different lives from outside a prison.

Still, no one spoke to me, not even Nathan Bailford.

They were waiting for someone to arrive. Dan Nizhinski? Somebody else? Who?

I wished that someone would tell me why I was here, then maybe I could stop quivering. My mind was racing badly.

"Mrs. Bradford," Judge Sussman finally spoke to me. "Ms. Breen has discovered some remarkable information," he announced. "We're only waiting for the district attorney — ah, here he is. Dan, welcome."

Nizhinski strode into the room like a matador into a bullring, stance erect, expression fierce, afraid of no one. I thought of Norma's line on Nizhinski: *a putz of the first order,* she called him.

He looked straight at Nathan Bailford. "What's this meeting about? If you think you can get the verdict overturned because of some technicality —"

"It's hardly a technicality," Judge Sussman interrupted the prosecutor. "Tell him your story, Ms. Breen. Please, have a seat, Dan. I think you'll need one in a minute."

Norma rose slowly. She glanced at me, then directly at Dan Nizhinski, who had stopped pacing and was watching her warily, not quite the same confident matador he had been a moment ago.

When Norma spoke, it was in an assured and commanding voice. This was her time in the spotlight.

"During the trial, Maggie, you may remember Mr. Nizhinski took testimony from Peter O'Malley. He spoke about 'private parties' late in the night at the Lake Club, where, I believe, you have been a dinner guest from time to time. You had dinner at the club proper, of course."

I nodded, still having no idea where Norma was heading. "It's kind of where I met Will, actually. I couldn't join if I wanted to. There are no women members."

"I'm sorry," Nizhinski spoke up impatiently. "What does any of this have to do with Mrs. Bradford's trial? She shot her husband. The jury's said so. It's over, Ms. Breen."

"It has everything to do with it," Norma said. "The new evidence — *who* attended private stag parties at the club, and who their guests were — suggests that *lots* of people might have had a motive to harm Will Shepherd. We have evidence that Mr. Shepherd was very *indiscreet* about the existence of these parties, as he was indiscreet about much of his life. There could even have been a nasty cover-up during the trial, shielding members, hiding a motive any of them could have for killing Will Shepherd."

"Then that evidence should have been presented at the trial. It's too late now. The verdict's been rendered." Nizhinski was as cocksure as ever.

I could see the tension in everyone. My own throat was dry. My stomach was a clenched fist. Only Norma seemed calm. Now turned prosecutor herself, she was relentless.

"It's my opinion — and I should add that it's also the opinion of the attorney general of the state of New York — that Maggie Bradford may have been the victim of an elaborate and very vicious cover-up. A cover-up known to, indeed perhaps instigated by, the Bedford chief of police."

"I *object* to this!" Dan Nizhinski shouted.

"Let her finish," Judge Sussman said. He seemed to be enjoying this almost as much as Norma was.

"Important people, leaders of industry, banking, and the media have been protected from police investigation — possibly from prosecution on criminal charges here in Bedford," Norma went on.

317

She exchanged a glance with the district attorney. "Please don't look quite so ill yet, Mr. Nizhinski. *It gets much worse.*"

She was a performer now, a star. No audience has ever listened more intently.

"You're right, Mr. Nizhinski. All this would have nothing to do with the trial of Maggie Bradford except for one important thing: *Maggie's defense counsel,* the man who knew what I'm telling you, and should have acted upon it in Mrs. Bradford's defense, couldn't possibly have done so.

"Because the defense counsel himself is a member of the secret club. *Nathan Bailford is a member!*"

110

ONE LOOK at Nathan's twisted, ashen face and I understood that Norma was right. The look alone was proof of his guilt. My attorney — my *friend* — was up on his feet. He was spluttering with outrage, but I saw the lies behind his words; I saw the humiliation in his eyes, the betrayal, the selfishness and evil of what he had done.

"Judge Sussman," Nathan said. "These are the most salacious lies, drug-induced dreams or fantasies I've ever heard. I can't believe we're here listening to this."

"No, they're *not lies*," Norma shot back at him. "I have witnesses. The groundskeeper at the Lake Club, and two of the porters. I also have a sworn statement from *a member of the club within a club*. One of your pals."

She pointed at him, and he staggered back, as though there were bullets in Norma's fingers. "May God, no, may Maggie Bradford and her poor children forgive you. I sure as hell can't. You've disgraced yourself, and your already disgraceful profession. You've nearly helped convict an innocent woman. My God, Nathan. I hope they put you in jail for a hundred years. Will you do that, Judge Sussman?"

319

I sat very still, tightly gripping the armrest of my chair. My cheeks were hot, and waves of light-headedness came and went.

Hold on, I kept saying to myself. *Be calm now. This is really happening. This isn't a dream. You aren't back in your prison cell. You're right here. This is real.*

Then suddenly I was in Norma's and Barry's arms. I was shaking like crazy. We were all crying. Norma must have read my mind. "It's *really* happening, Maggie," she said. "We were still talking with the attorney general late last night, or we could have let you know."

We embraced for a long time. I can't begin to describe how it was with me, but I've never experienced anything close to the relief I felt that day. I was completely out of it, euphoric, but I knew what had just happened. I knew. I knew.

"Obviously I'll have to declare a mistrial," Sussman said to Nizhinski, his voice cutting into my consciousness, "but you may want to retry. Nothing here obviates the fact that Will Shepherd was killed and the detectives say Mrs. Bradford has admitted shooting him. We'll have to give her time to hire a new lawyer and prepare her defense. She might even want to change her strategy. Can you tell me what you plan to do?"

Nizhinski was actually speechless for several seconds. "This is all — well, it's a shock," he finally managed to say. "I don't know what I'll decide. I need some time to regroup, Your Honor."

"When you do, call me," Sussman said.

Barry spoke to the judge. "I'm not a lawyer, so I don't know the right legal words, but do you think Mrs. Bradford could be allowed to go home?"

Sussman turned and looked at me. "*She is released on her own recognizance,*" he said.

111

LIKE THE YOGI BERRA SAYING — it was déja vù all over again. But it had to be done this way. This was our justice system, in all its glory.

Months had passed. The *second* trial was about to begin, and if anything, it would probably be more disheartening than the first. The State still believed that I was guilty of murder, and because they insisted on trying me again, so did a lot of people.

I continued to wear the scarlet *M*. I felt as though great chunks of my life were being chiseled out of me. *Probably, because they were.* And I was hurt.

I arrived at the courtroom with Jennie, Barry, and Norma. Barry and Norma were an odd couple now, but sweet and wonderful to watch. Amazingly, they weren't too grumpy around each other.

Once we were inside the courtroom, I walked on steady legs to a familiar seat at the defense table. My new lawyer was Jason Wade, from Boston. He was an expert in murder defenses, very no-nonsense, and I liked him. Most important of all, he wasn't Nathan Bailford, who was now a permanent fixture in my bad dreams.

Weird, weird, so very weird.

"Maggie looks so great!" I heard one of the spectators say. *Maggie!* As if we were old best friends.

"You do. You look fantastic," Jennie whispered against my ear. It was like old times between us, only better. Jennie was one of those rare people you could stay up with all night, just talking. *I had* — only the night before. Even Allie had stayed up with us past ten. JAM was back together again.

The trial took eleven weeks. *Our tax money at work!* The same people gave much of the same testimony, though the cross-examination had a different slant, headed in a different direction.

The courtroom became increasingly hot as the summer wore on, but I didn't mind the heat, didn't mind the repetitiousness of the questioning, didn't even mind the notoriety and the consant sleaze of the press.

I wanted to be found innocent. But more than anything, I wanted to be freed from the purgatory I had lived in for so long.

I *wasn't* guilty. I was sure of that.

I *was* innocent.

I would have given everything I had just to hear those words uttered *once*.

112

I LEANED FORWARD to hear each and every word inside the jam-packed courtroom. Suddenly, I couldn't force enough air into my lungs. I felt as though a dry cloth were blocking my throat. Claustrophobia was striking again.

The faces in the courtroom were becoming blurry and ill-defined. Blood pounded in my brain like small hammers. The back of my neck was sopping wet.

The twelve jury members were slowly filing into the right side of the room.

Again.

They had reached a verdict.

Again.

I could not get my breath as the folded piece of paper was handed to Judge Sussman. He read the verdict to himself, then passed it back to the jury foreman. The procedure was necessary, I suppose, but cruel.

"Publish the verdict," Judge Sussman instructed.

"We love you, Mom," Jennie, sitting behind me, whispered. Norma slid her arm around my shoulder. Barry stroked my hair from the row of seats behind. My family, my friends, I couldn't leave them again, but that was a distinct possibility now. That morning, *USA Today* had the odds of acquittal at *even*. People were actually betting on the outcome in Vegas and London.

My mouth seemed to be filled with cotton. I was numb all over. I was sitting in that courtroom, and yet somehow I wasn't there at all.

The foreman began to speak. His voice was high-pitched, and yet surprisingly distant, as though there were a screen between him and the rest of the courtroom. There wasn't another sound.

"We find the defendant, Maggie Bradford, *not guilty*."

Not guilty.

Not guilty.

I had to close my eyes. I felt so tired and weak, and strangely, not completely relieved for some reason. I was only vaguely aware of cheers in the courtroom. People were congratulating me — Jason Wade and Norma, Jennie and Barry. Faces loomed before me like enormous balloons. The sound was as blurred as the images. Everything seemed incredibly odd and queer.

"Oh, Maggie, you did it! You won!"

How could this simple moment be so confusing to me? I was rushed from the tumultuous courtroom, enfolded in a safe cocoon of lawyers and friends and my precious family. Surrounding us were the press and fans. *Faces* were pushing microphones at me, screaming questions, begging for an autograph, even now.

Jason Wade would have to deal with them. My lawyer could answer their questions. Sign their autographs too.

I was actually *pushed,* like someone on wheels, through the cavernous foyer, then much too fast down the steps of the courthouse, and into a waiting car. Not a limo, just a regular car. I had insisted on that.

I jumped at what sounded like a gunshot. Pain pierced my heart. *The automobile door had slammed shut!*

324

Then the "regular" car started to slowly move through the press of people who had been waiting outside for a glimpse of me, win or lose. The car floated behind an escort of police cruisers, sirens crying, revolving red roof lights casting shadows on the faces of the onlookers.

I remembered the MP car in West Point. Its light was revolving too, only there were no onlookers, and it was so cold. I remembered so many scenes leading up to this moment.

I watched out the car window. People forming the tremendous crowd clogging Broadway and Clarke Street seemed to be clapping and cheering, shouting out my name. I couldn't relate to any of it.

I held Jennie and Allie tightly, never wanting to let go of them. *They held me back.* We were JAM again: Jennie, Allie, Maggie.

"I love you so much, Mom," Jennie whispered and kissed me on the cheek. "You're my heroine in shining armor."

"And you're mine," I told her.

"Mommy," Allie said, and hugged my side. "My mommy."

"Allie." I kissed the top of his head. "My Allie and my Jennie."

113

"MAGGIE! Maggie Bradford!" the crowd of idiots shouted *at her car.*

The murderer clapped and cheered too, pretending delight at the scene. He was concealed in the crowd choking the Bedford Village crossroads. Well concealed.

The murderer watched as Maggie's car passed by, then finally disappeared around a street corner.

Then the murderer disappeared as well.

BOOK SIX

HIDE AND SEEK – AGAIN

114

FIFTH AVENUE. Eastertime. New York City. Delightful! Absolutely the place to be, no?

The world's most beautiful women were on parade. Primping, prancing, shopping their little hearts out.

And every one of them eminently fuckable, Will thought. *Every one could be mine for the wooing. Some things never change. They just get better and better.*

He strolled among them, in no particular hurry, early for his appointment. He was dressed in khaki slacks and blue blazer. His dyed-black hair was cut short and meticulously combed.

The Black Arrow, he thought and smiled thinly.

Some of the women definitely looked at him — *as well they might,* he thought. He hadn't lost much as far as appearances went. If anything, he looked even better nowadays. Dark and mysterious, right? Just the way so many women liked their fantasy lovers.

At Fifty-ninth Street, he turned east toward Park, then north to Sixty-second Street, where he disappeared into a yellowish-brown Deco building on the corner. He bought mints at the lobby's newspaper store, and checked his appearance in the mirror.

Carefully cut dyed-black beard, blue eyes (the contact lenses were a good touch; an excellent touch), perfect tie from Liberty of London, the natty blazer. Just the right look for today's important meeting.

Then Will took the elevator to the twelfth floor and found the office he was looking for: *Marshall and Marshall, Attorneys.*

He pushed open the dark oak door. Immediately, he was treated to a wall of windows and a view of the teeming avenue below. Impressive and overstated, in the American way.

The company's receptionist was Irish-American from her look, a smiling, auburn-haired, alabaster girl, blooming nicely in her mid-twenties. She was first class, expensive. Like the firm that employed her. *Nice decorative touch,* Will thought.

He casually rested the Mark Cross folio on her desk.

"Good afternoon, sir. May I help you?" she asked. She was more than pleasant, he noticed. Not offended by his folio invading her space. Or maybe, like a good Irish person, she just didn't show it.

Will smiled, low-key but seductive, his charm intact. "I'm here to see Mr. Arthur Marshall. It's about an inheritance. He's expecting me, I believe."

"Yes, sir." The girl tried not to stare at the very good-looking Englishman standing before her. "Whom should I say is calling?"

"Palmer Shepherd," said Will.

115

I LOOKED AROUND the warm, familiar living room of our house and I couldn't help beaming, almost giggling out loud. *Hooo boy!*

This was the best. This was the most important thing now. The party!

A dozen of Allie's boy and girl friends from kindergarten had come to the house for his fifth birthday. No one had declined, and that meant a lot to me, and more important, of course, to Allie.

It was a strictly old-fashioned party, which Jennie and I had meticulously planned. Games and silly hats, a birthday cake for the birthday boy, a present for every child, and lots of presents for Allie the Wonder Boy.

It was going perfectly. Barry and Norma had stopped by to help. So far, we'd had tons of laughter and fun, one minor collision, not a single tear had been shed.

Allie finally came up to me. He beckoned for me to come down to his level, his size, his turf.

I knelt so that we were face to face. As he almost always did, Allie twirled my hair around his fingers.

"Know what?" he said, and his eyes had the most wonderful twinkle. "Well, do you?"

"What? You tell me. The cake is too big for you to eat all by yourself? Okay then, share it with your friends."

Allie laughed. He got all my jokes. I got his too.

"No, I just want to tell you the *very* best thing, Mommy. The *very* best thing is that you're here."

It was the happiest party, the best moment, and suddenly I was crying, and I was feeling so good that I could be there at my son's party.

"I knew somebody was going to cry soon," I told Allie.

He hugged me, and gave me kisses to make it better. But I was already better.

116

HAVING WATCHED my good mood at the birthday party, Barry the Manipulator took the occasion to try and lure me into the city, and up to his studio. I surprised him: I told him I'd come. I was ready for a little manipulation.

When I got to New York, Barry was hyper and excited, the way he usually got when he'd just written a good song, or completed an especially good business deal.

"You're scaring me. You're *too* happy," I told him, but I was laughing. Everything seemed good to me now. I was so buoyant, and free. God, was I free!

"I have a scheme," he said to me as we sat down beside his piano. "I've been scheming on your behalf."

My good mood was a match for his. And more. "Thanks, but no thanks."

Barry completely ignored me. "There's a *great* concert happening up in Rhinebeck, New York, in July."

"Barry, I read the papers. I'm not a hermit. Bedford is less than thirty miles from Manhattan. The answer is, regretfully, no. But thank you just the same."

"It's two days of fun in the sun. I know the promoters and

333

they're first-class people. They've booked seventeen acts. *Eighteen* is their magic number."

"I'd love to, but I can't. Do you happen to remember what happened to me out in San Francisco?"

Barry went right on talking. "Tell you who they've got already. Bonnie Raitt, k.d. lang, Liz Phair, Emmylou Harris."

I nodded. Started to laugh. Bit my lip. "Gee, all women. Why did you happen to start with the women?"

"You know, I never even thought of that. You're right though, I did."

"I don't think I can, Barry. I appreciate the offer, if that's what this is."

Barry wasn't in the mood to show any mercy. That was good though. It meant I didn't look as though I needed any.

"Use it, or lose it," he said. "Unless, of course, you've already lost it."

"No, I sang in the shower today. I was pretty great. I've still got it. Better than ever, actually. Passion, edge, maturity, effervescence."

Barry played the lead-in to "Loss of Grace" on his piano. I had to admit, a shiver went up my spine.

"I'll *think* about it," I told him. "But I honestly don't believe that I c-cc-can ss-ss-sing in public."

I winked at him. It was good that I could laugh about the stutter, about San Francisco.

Barry nodded, and then he smiled. "I'll take that as a yes."

He continued to play "Loss of Grace," and, as he did, I started to sing again.

And I had to admit, like everything else in this second life of mine, it felt so good, so right.

I didn't stutter, or stammer. I sang. And if I do say so myself, sang kind of beautifully. With passion, and with a real edge.

"Your timing is off, your phrasing is a mess," Barry shook his head and said. "Welcome home, Maggie."

117

MAGGIE STILL LOVED to walk the streets of New York with the other commoners. She was such a woman of the people, wasn't she? Maybe that was why so many of them identified with her, loved her songs, loved her.

She wore a kerchief and dark glasses, but every so often someone recognized her anyway. She was always so goddamned gracious. Sign an autograph. Move on with that shy little smile of hers. *Ingratiating bitch.*

Will walked several blocks behind her. No one bothered him for autographs anymore. He didn't exist, did he? The Invisible Man. Deceased and buried, right?

He followed her out of New York and up the Saw Mill early that evening. This was all very familiar to him, the road to Bedford. And ruin.

What wasn't so familiar was the bizarre path his life had taken. How do you top off a life that's been incredibly full, and is suddenly falling apart badly? Where does one go from the top?

How clever he had been up until this point, Will thought. That fatal night, he'd shot Palmer and hadn't felt a thing, no remorse about Palmer. That was the only way to stop the extortion money his greedy brother had been grubbing since Rio.

He had dressed his brother in his clothes. Then he placed the body on the grounds of the estate. He had gone inside and caused a ruckus. He'd lured Maggie outside, jumped her, beat her up, and fired the shot that practically blew Palmer's face apart. Then he'd disappeared. And just *watched* the rest.

Unfortunately, his new life had turned out to be another kind of hell. Sometimes he believed that he might be a devil, and he was living in hell.

Rio was the turning point, he knew. Killing that first girl. Crime and punishment had followed him after that night.

Up the road, he saw Maggie turn into her driveway. He hated that she could be happy without him. Strange as it seemed, he had tried to love her. He'd wanted her to save him from himself.

He knew the turning point with Maggie too. He was sure about that. It was the first time he'd failed with her in bed. It was while he was *Mr. Maggie Bradford*. He had thought about killing her nearly every day since then.

She'd failed him, and now she and her little family had to pay the awful price. *Crime and punishment.*

Will went for dinner at a little bar and grill in town. An old fave for the locals.

He thought it was quite something that he could sit there eating a greasy burger and fries, and that no one recognized him anymore.

Well, why the hell should they? He was ancient history, if he'd ever been history at all.

The Black Arrow. That's what he was now.

He wore a navy blue ballcap without an insignia, a gray sweatshirt, and khakis. He fit in okay with the bar crowd watching the Knicks lose badly to Indiana.

Nothing special about him, really. Other than that he was

stark raving mad, of course. Probably not the only madman sitting at the crowded horseshoe bar either. Not the only guy here who was a little homicidal toward his wife.

"The Knicks suck," the young brick seated next to him passed along the sum total of his acquired wisdom.

"Burgers here suck too," Will said, and the other man laughed.

Soul brothers, are we? Will wanted to continue the conversation in earnest. *Think so? Want to come with me to my ex-wife's house? I'm going to kill the bitch and her two kids. You in? You with me on this?*

"Patrick Ewing *really* sucks," the other man contributed another choice nugget.

Will nodded sympathetically, and figured it was time to get out of the bar. Truth be known, he didn't know the Knicks from the Yankees from the New York Jets.

It was dark outside. He could see that through the bar's front window.

"Well, time to head on home to the missus," he told his new mate, then stood up at the bar.

Sure you don't want to tag along, pal? This is going to be a big night in Bedford. I can promise you that.

118

IT WASN'T MUCH of a problem for him to get onto the estate grounds undetected. Will parked in one of the Lake Club lots, then crossed over through pine woods and a narrow meadow.

No sweat so far. Just the way he'd figured it.

Walking in the field of high grass made him remember something. He'd ridden on horseback there with Allie, when he was only a baby. He'd done it to impress Maggie. He *knew* it would touch her down below her belt. He knew a woman's soft spots, knew the buttons to hit. He had carefully pushed all of Maggie's, every single one, one by one.

He had been inside the house on a trial run the week before, so he'd already figured how this would go. The cellar door under the original wing was open, as it always was.

He didn't use his flashlight until he was safely inside. The cellar was a creepy place. The house had been built on bare ground, and the original boulders were still down there. There was a wooden stairway up from where the freezer was to the kitchen.

Will used the stairs and was in the house by a little past

11:40. It was a school night and everyone had gone to bed. *JAM! Jennie, Allie, and Maggie . . . Notice, no Will.*

Maggie was still a country girl at heart — early to bed, early to rise. The quiet house reminded him of a damn morgue, which seemed appropriate enough.

In a way, Maggie had given him the idea for tonight. Probably for good reasons, she noticed every news story about a husband who ran amok and killed one or more family members.

That was pretty much what Will planned to do tonight. Kill all of them, right there in the house. Then disappear for good. The murders would never be solved, and that struck him as just the right touch.

He had a Smith and Wesson, sixteen shots, plus a nasty hunting knife. That was more than enough firepower. If need be, he could do the job with his bare hands. There was merit to that approach too, the personal touch.

"Families really suck," Will mumbled as he walked up the thickly carpeted stairs to the second floor.

There wasn't a sound to be heard up there. *Maybe this is a trap,* he thought, *but he knew it couldn't be.*

This train was leaving the station. There was no way to stop it now. No way on heaven or earth to stop this from happening.

He was breathing real quietly, every breath even, and exactly the same.

He was feeling confident, real good about this. No guilt. No feelings at all.

It was the right thing to do.

Ever so slowly, he opened the bedroom door.

He could see everything in soft, yellow moonlight streaming from the window.

No surprises here. No surprises anywhere tonight.

"Hello, little buddy," Will said to Allie.

119

WHAT THE HELL was that? What was that?

We had all gone to bed early, and I'd fallen asleep almost immediately.

I had been dreaming about singing at a huge outdoor concert — and then completely losing it onstage. No need to call Dr. Freud in to explain that one.

I awoke and I thought I heard a noise upstairs.

Was Jennie just going to bed?

I sat up, looked at the luminous figures on the radio clock: 11:45. I didn't think Jennie would be up so late.

Then I heard another sound. Strange. *Well, one of the kids was definitely up.*

Then a louder noise, as though a bed were being moved around.

And finally, what sounded to me like a muffled scream or yell. Was I hearing things?

I got up quickly and hurried across the bedroom to the door.

I listened there for half a second.

Nothing more.

Then another muffled sound, this one farther away it seemed. I couldn't tell exactly where. Allie? Was Allie up for some reason?

I hurried outside into the upstairs hallway. The light was out, and I switched it back on.

No one was there. Not Jennie. Not Allie.

False alarm? Probably so. Things in the country always seemed to go bump in the night. Creaky floorboards, loose shutters, branches against a window.

I decided to check on the kids anyway. Maybe somebody was sick, or maybe one of them was having a nightmare. Goodness knows, they'd been through enough.

I gently opened Jennie's bedroom door, the first one, next to mine.

Jennie was gone!

I ran as fast as I could down the hallway to the front left bedroom, which had a choice view of our horse pastures.

I yanked open the bedroom door.

Allie was gone too!

120

THERE'S AN EXPLANATION *for this. Has to be.*

But I was frightened as could be.

I ran down the stairway loudly calling out their names, "Jennie! Allie! Where are you two? Where are you?"

There's a simple explanation.

No one was in the front hall, or the living room either.

But I could see a light coming from the den. Okay, the kids were in the den.

"Jennie? . . . Allie? . . . Is something the matter?"

I ran toward the den, clipping a pile of books on the edge of an old hallway table. The books fell loudly to the floor.

I turned the corner into the den, and I stopped. Everything stopped. All time, all forward progress, all sense of fairness and goodness in the universe.

Stopped.

Will was standing there with the kids.

I stared at the black hair and beard, but I knew it was definitely Will.

He had a gun, and he had Jennie and Allie, and the gun was loosely pointed at them.

"Hello, Maggie. Long time, huh?" Cool as could be. Psychopathic as they come. "Good to see ya."

"Are you two all right?" I asked the kids.

"We're okay, Mom," Jennie said. "We're okay. We're fine."

"They're okay," Will said. "What's the big problem? Haven't you heard of visitation rights?"

I walked further into the room. My heart wouldn't stop pounding.

Will was there. Will was alive.

"I hate you!" I said. I couldn't stop myself from saying it.

"Hate you too, darlin'. Hate you *more*. That's why I'm here," Will said and smiled. "Been hating you and hating you, for a long, long time."

I stopped myself and stared at him. I tried to be calm. "Why did you dare come here, Will? After all that's happened."

"Oh, lots of neat reasons. First of all, just to see the confusion in your eyes, the fear. I love that look. Makes me feel good all over."

"That's because you're a coward." I told him what I really thought.

"No doubt. I think you're right. *That's* exactly why I'm here. I'm afraid to go on living the way I am. That's it."

"You wouldn't hurt them. Why would you hurt them?" I asked him.

Will shrugged. "Because they're yours. Because you fucked me up even worse than I was. I could *function* before you. Now, Maggie — *shut up*. I mean it — *shut the hell up*." He pointed the gun at Allie. My little boy was trying not to cry but he was starting to shake. There was nothing I could do.

No one spoke, and Will smiled at the silence. He nodded his approval. Controlling son of a bitch.

"Okay now, here's what we're going to do," he finally said. "You all lie on the floor. Facedown. Keep very still. Everybody on the floor. Let's play a game, Allie."

"*Says who?*" Jennie suddenly turned and shouted at him.

343

"What, so you can kill us all a lot easier? That's what you're here for, isn't it? You punk! You piece of crap."

"Jennie," I tried to quiet her. Then I realized what she was doing, at least I thought I did, hoped I did, *prayed I did*.

"We're not doing anything you say!" I yelled at Will, just as Jennie had. "We all hate your guts!"

"We hate you!" Jennie screamed at him.

"We hate you!" yelled Allie in his tiny voice.

Jennie suddenly flew into Will's side, and I reached for the gun. I pulled on his wrist as hard as I could. *Both hands! The strength of a madwoman!*

At the same time, I brought up my knee — as hard as I could — into Will's groin.

Will *woofed* out air. He groaned. The gun actually came free, and I had it.

I had the gun in my hand. Now what? *Now what?*

I backed away from Will as quickly as I could. A lot of fast steps in a hurry.

So did Jennie and Allie.

"C'mon, c'mon. Get out of here now. Jennie, call the police. Call nine-one-one. Hurry. Please. Go!" I told the two of them.

Will looked at me and seemed confused, as if this wasn't in his playbook. Then he smiled again, the smile I remembered so well, the one that had always been so effective for him. Killer smile, right.

"Isn't this something," he said with a heavy sigh. "Not exactly the way I planned it. *But.* A good scorer, *a striker,* has to improvise. I know you never wanted to follow soccer, Maggie, but for a great striker, there's no team, there's no win or lose, there's nothing but the goal."

"Will," I said to him, "now *you shut up.*"

"Do you know what my goal was tonight, Maggie? Do you really get it?"

"Yes, I do. To kill us. *Jennie,* please go. Allie, go! I mean it. *Now!* Call the police, Jennie."

"Mom," Jennie said, and she was talking *very softly,* very slowly, "you come with us. Back out of the door with the gun. Come with us."

"Do you know the rest of my goal, Maggie?" Will continued to speak to me. "I think I have this figured out."

I thought I did too. I thought I understood him real well.

"To kill us, and then to kill yourself," I said.

Will slowly clapped his hands together. Applause from the great man.

"Mom, please come with us," Jennie begged. "Please."

Then Will started to walk right toward me.

"Can you do it, Maggie?" he said. His eyes were pinned onto mine now.

"I can do what I have to do," I said.

"Mom, please."

"Can you really do it, Maggie? Can you *start* this nightmare all over again? Or would you rather die? Can you pull the trigger?"

Will kept walking.

The *striker.*

Advancing on goal, just as he'd said. No team concept. Just Will — the loner. The ultimate loser.

There was no good answer to his question. There was no easy way out of this.

But maybe there was a way. *Maybe there was.*

Will kept walking toward me. He held eye contact. Then he smiled again.

I fired!

"Mom! Mom!"

He grabbed his leg, and *nearly* went over, *nearly* went down.

"Oooohh!" he moaned. "Jesus Christ, Maggie. You're quite the tiger, quite the defender."

Will started to move forward again. It was as though he hadn't even been hit.

The striker.

The attacker.

The best in the world at this.

Unstoppable once he started toward his goal.

To murder me and the kids, right here in our house.

Will took a knife from his shirt. Big knife, hunting knife. He raised it toward me. He *lunged*.

I fired a second time.

NIGHT SONGS

121

SOUTHERN CONNECTICUT in early November. Four and a half months after the shooting. Will and I were finally off the front pages of most newspapers and magazines.

There was just one more story to tell.

It was a bright and crisp fall afternoon — high school football weather. Only to me, peering out the tinted Plexiglas windows of my car, it seemed a gloomy day, a day meant for unfinished business.

Norma had come along with me, but I drove. I needed to be in control. I thought that I was. We'd see about that soon enough.

I was trying to be brave, to survive this final test.

I hadn't done anything wrong — *not ever.* I'd just protected what was important, my family. Sure, I had made mistakes, but who doesn't. With Will, I'd been a victim for his obsessions. He had lied so brilliantly, right from the start of our relationship.

Norma and I talked everything through again during the drive from Bedford. Finally, I pulled up at the Institute for Living, a Federal-style building in the outskirts of New Haven that looked like a cross between a college administration building and a prison. It was neither, nothing so benign. It was a mental hospital, supposedly one of the best.

Norma and I hurried across a poplar- and maple-lined parking area, then into the vestibule, where we approached a receptionist dressed in nurse's white.

"We're here to see Mr. Shepherd," I told her, and if she recognized me she didn't show it. I appreciated that.

"I'll have someone take you to his room," is all she said. An aide eventually materialized to escort us.

Outside Will's room, I stopped. "Can you wait here?" I said to Norma. "I think I want to see him alone."

"You're sure, Maggie? You don't have to punish yourself, honey."

"I'm sure. I'm not afraid of him anymore." *Not too much anyway.*

"Good for you then. I'll be the short, dumpy broad waiting outside. Maybe some guy in here is nuts enough to fall for me."

The aide unlocked the door and I entered. *I entered.* It was a plain enough room: clean, a made bed, desk, desk chair, easy chair, and standing lamp its only furniture. There was a bookcase built into the far wall holding a few new paperbacks, obviously unread, and a small sink for washing. It reminded me of prison, only it was nicer.

Will was standing by the window. There was no sign that he *ever* sat down. He was looking at me, looking *through* me, I guess I should say.

I'm not afraid anymore. I can do this. Whatever is necessary, I told myself.

If it was possible, Will was even more handsome than when I had first met him in London. His hair was its natural blond, long and full. It caught the afternoon sun through the heavily screened window.

"Hello, Will."

Nothing.

His face was clean shaven and pale pink; his body seemed to

have the same lithe grace, even standing still, that it always had.

"It's Maggie, Will."

He looks like a grown-up little boy, I thought, remembering Will at the very first Lake Club party, at our wedding, confessing his sorrow and pain, *and all his lies.*

I had loved him — because he could make himself seem so lovable. He was a very good actor after all. He had fooled so many people — half the world. He had worked hard to fool me.

He made a strange sound, a high-pitched wail that reverberated in the hospital room. The second shot I'd fired at the estate had struck his head, caromed off bone, but done severe damage anyway.

"Mmahhlah . . . mmahhlah," he said to me. He seemed *insistent;* but I didn't understand.

What was he trying to say?

Was it Maggie? Mother? Was it Mama? What was it?

I sat in a hard wooden chair directly across from him. I forced myself to look at his face.

I'm sorry I did this to you, Will. But I'm not guilty about it. I sleep at night — I sleep just fine. You did this to yourself.

I thought of the murder he'd committed in Bedford Hills; of his terrifying betrayal of me; of what he had done to Jennie and Allie, and what he'd planned to do to us all.

But I couldn't hate him. Not now. Not the way he was.

"Will, can you hear me? Do you understand what I'm saying?"

The dead stare didn't change. He couldn't understand, could he? He had gone to his own world forever.

It's so sad, I thought, as I watched him that afternoon at the hospital. *You're still young. You look so young, so full of promise. But you won't hurt me ever again. You won't hurt my children. I'm not scared of you, Will.*

351

A little past five o'clock, the aide returned. He was jangling his keys so I'd hear him come up on us. "Visiting hours are over."

"Thank you. I'll just be another minute. Please?"

I stood and walked to the window where Will was still standing. A cloak of solemn gray had already replaced the sunlight outside.

I turned to Will. "I feel so sorry for you," I said, "but I can't forgive you either."

I wanted him to say something. A final few words to remember him by. To explain why he had wanted to kill me. Why he had hurt us. Who was Will Shepherd, really? Did anyone know?

"Okay. Good-bye, Will. I'm sorry for you."

I gathered myself together, and started to leave the room. *I turned my back on Will.* I wasn't afraid of him anymore.

122

SUDDENLY, Will screamed with a tremendous force that echoed through the hospital. I whirled around toward him.

He shrieked again, his body rocking violently.

Aides came running down the hallway. A burly male nurse appeared with a plastic-sheathed needle clasped in his fist. I sensed that this had happened before.

"*Mmahhlah!*" Will screamed.

I thought that he might be having a stroke. Certainly this was some kind of fit.

"Mmahhlah. Mmahhlah," he continued to shout. His face and neck were bright red. His veins stood out against his skin.

I stared at Will in horror. *Maggie? Mother? What in God's name was he trying to tell me?*

In his eyes, there wasn't the slightest comprehension or recognition. He was pushed down firmly onto the bed, and I *felt* his legs shrivel.

The Blond Arrow, shriveling.

I had to get out of there. I nearly ran from the room. There was nothing I could do for him anymore. Norma was waiting for me at the end of the corridor.

"Maggie! My God! What was that? What the hell happened in there? You okay?"

I put my arms around her and held Norma tightly, as though to blot out those screams. Finally, the two of us walked out of the building and onto the black-topped parking area, the trees now ghostly silhouettes.

Halfway across the parking lot I turned. I felt as though someone had just stepped out of a grave.

I had the powerful intuition that something was chasing after me. *Mmahhlah . . . Mmahhlah* was coming fast, right behind me.

Those lifeless, haunting eyes . . .

But there was no one looking out from Will's hospital window. There was no one when I looked back.

123

IN HIS BARREN, insular hospital room Will screamed and screamed. Screamed and screamed. Until his throat was raw and felt as though it had splinters in it. *Still, he continued to scream.*

As the night-shift aides tried to feed him his dinner, changed him, and put him to bed, he continued to scream. His strength, his stamina, were amazing to all of them. He was still young, and very athletic, and so powerfully strong.

"Mmahhlah! Mmahhlah! Mmahhlah!" He cried over and over.

"Mmahhlah! Mmahhlah! Mmahhlah!

"MMAHHLAH!"

He had *seen* Maggie today. He'd been *aware* of everything. He'd wanted to speak to her, but he couldn't. He couldn't. *Mmahhlah* was all he could get out.

Why didn't she understand him? Why didn't anyone?

"Mmahhlah."

I'm alive!

I'm alive!

Please don't leave me like this!

I'm trapped inside this body. Can't you see that? Won't you help me?

"Mmahhlah!

"Mmahhlah!"

I'm alive!

I was halfway home to Bedford when it hit me, and I understood what Will had been trying to say to me at the hospital.

It took my breath away.

But I never went to see him again.

I never will.